The Vampyre

The Vampyre

and other British stories of the Romantic era

Second edition, revised and enlarged

Edited by Henry M. Wallace

Universitas Press
Montreal

Universitas Press
Montreal

www.universitaspress.com

First published in October 2023

Library and Archives Canada Cataloguing in Publication

Title: The vampyre and other British stories of the Romantic era / edited by Henry M. Wallace.
Other titles: Vampire and other British stories of the Romantic era
Names: Wallace, Henry M., 1970- editor.
Description: Second edition, revised and enlarged.
Identifiers: Canadiana 20230497675 | ISBN 9781988963679 (softcover) | ISBN 9781988963662 (hardcover)
Subjects: LCSH: Short stories, English. | LCSH: English prose literature—19th century.
Classification: LCC PR1302 .V36 2023 | DDC 823/.010807—dc23

FOR CRISTINA

TABLE OF CONTENTS

Introduction ... ix
Chronology of Events ... xix

Henry Kirke White
    Charles Wanely (1802) ... 1
Amelia Opie
    The Black Velvet Pelisse (1806) ... 6
Samuel Taylor Coleridge
    Story of Maria Schöning (1809) ... 21
Maria Edgeworth
    The Dun (1809) ... 37
James Hogg
    Duncan Campbell (1811) ... 61
Mary Leadbeater and Elizabeth Shackleton
    The Scotch Ploughman (1814) ... 81
Amelia Opie
    The Welcome Home; or, The Ball (1818) ... 90
John William Polidori
    The Vampyre (1819) ... 115
Leigh Hunt
    A Tale for a Chimney Corner (1819) ... 135
John Galt
    The Buried Alive (1821) ... 145
Margaret Gardiner, Countess Blessington
    The Auction (1822) ... 149
William Harrison Ainsworth
    The Wanderings of an Immortal (1822) ... 158
Mary Russell Mitford
    Cousin Mary (1823) ... 168
Amelia Opie
    A New Tale of Temper (1823) ... 175
Walter Scott
    Wandering Willie's Tale (1824) ... 190
Mary Russell Mitford
    Jack Hatch (1825) ... 209

Walter Scott
    The Two Drovers (1827)   217
Mary Russell Mitford
    The Village Schoolmistress (1827)   243
Anna Brownell Jameson
    Halloran the Pedlar (1827)   254
Walter Scott
    The Tapestried Chamber (1828)   275
Anna Maria Hall
    Master Ben (1829)   290
William Mudford
    The Iron Shroud (1830)   301
John Banim
    The Church-Yard Watch (1831)   315
Letitia Elizabeth Landon
    Experiments; or, The Lover from Ennui (1832)   326

Introduction

The Romantic era in British fiction is a tale of two writing modes. Some authors tried to make Romanticism—or, rather, their own version of it—work in prose fiction, often with mixed results. Others rejected it outright and decided instead to find a way to communicate through fiction their views on the manners of the gentry and the lives of the lower classes. An oversimplification, but one that can help illustrate not only the choices that fiction writers of the period believed they could make but also the fiction that the readership of the period was quickly learning to expect, would be to say that the writing modes mentioned above orbited around two different luminaries: Walter Scott and Jane Austen. It is safe to say that Romanticism had a mixed fate in prose fiction, in Britain and elsewhere. It was instrumental in the rise of the historical novel, in a revival of the Gothic, and in making folk beliefs acceptable as subjects of high literature; but it also generated a powerful reaction which ultimately gave rise to realism.

The period between 1800 and 1832, from which the stories in this volume have been selected, is especially associated with the great English Romantic poets, as well as with their aesthetic creeds, which, for many fiction writers, translated into a predilection for leaps of fantasy, larger-than-life characters and uncanny situations (some inherited from the popular 18th-century "romance" form). This is also consistent with one of the two important trends in the production of short fiction at the time. Authors like John William Polidori, John Galt, William Harrison Ainsworth, William Mudford and Walter Scott (all included here) incorporated Gothic elements into their own take on Romanticism, in which Byronic heroes become vampires; in which characters become victims in an exoticised and orientalised Greece or southern Italy or become immortal and condemned to eternal peregrination; in which characters are buried alive or forced to face ghosts or the undead.

The success or failure of Romanticism in literature was also largely a matter of genre. It thrived in poetry, better suited to embrace that sort of "tyranny of art over life, which in some sense is the essence of the romantic movement" (Berlin xi). The unbounded will, the rebellious spirit and the antisocial behaviour of Romantic characters were better suited for epic poems than for novels (and short stories), which were then learning to tell the adventures (or, respectively, one adventure) of the soul by readapting to the classical unities of time, place, and action. The same tyranny of art over life, as Berlin would have it, can explain why Romanticism brought little that was new or worthy in drama (despite the early successes of the Sturm und Drang in Germany). In fiction, Romanticism brought a revival of the Gothic (but the Gothic would prove to have a life of its own); from its interest in folklore, it brought art tales (*Kunstmärchen*) and the supernatural (but the excesses down this road were from the beginning much criticised as bad literature); and the historical novel (especially if it had medieval knights and damsels for characters; if set in more recent periods, it was often praised for its realism). Sometimes, the fact of trying or refusing to try to make Romanticism work in fiction must have been connected to the authors' own perception of their work in another genre. It is significant, for example, that, after their sojourn in the Villa Diodati near Lake Geneva, Byron and Shelley never finished their stories; only the novices Mary Shelley and Polidori did. Or that James Hogg, who felt both embraced and marginalised by the literary establishment (see especially the analysis by Alker and Nelson) tried both to make Romanticism work (in poetry and prose fiction) and to find other writing modes. In his short stories, he moves freely between romanticism and realism, incorporating folk beliefs (ghosts, brownies, etc.) and reconstructing moments in the history of Scotland; and, on the other hand, narrating the lives of the lowly with the help of satire and metafictional commentary.

Two types of explanations have been offered for what appears as a kind of inconsistency or at least extravagant multifariousness within literary Romanticism: one that sees the differences as synchronic (by speaking, for example, of the existence of regional variants, such as Scottish Romanticism, within which folk beliefs were ineluctable); and one in which the changes appear diachronically and suggest the emergence of a more "moderate" writing mode in the second part of the period. In Britain, at least, and in fiction in general, the synchronic view seems more accurate. The fact that Romanticism in general was not concerned with ways of seeing and communicating a reality that existed outside artistic imagination (although this traditional view should be taken today with a grain of salt) meant that it appeared fairly soon to many practitioners as somewhat unsuitable for novels and short stories. It also explains why Romanticism generated very early two kinds of reaction among fiction writers: some authors sought to *redeem* Romanticism, other chose to *reject* it. Novelists and short-story writers who were looking

Introduction

for the "redemption" (Kelly 164) of Romantic fiction did so by attempting to render it more "factual," by confining their plots via the rule of the three unities, and by choosing "real" historical events and "authentic" folk beliefs as their subjects.

Historical fiction was undoubtedly the most successful attempt at "redeeming" Romantic fiction, both in the sense that it found the largest audience and inasmuch as it was seen as a departure from Romanticism. Indeed, Georg Lukács thought he had found in Walter Scott "a renunciation of Romanticism, a conquest of Romanticism" (33). It is more fair to say that if it did, in fact, contribute to a departure from a Romantic mode in fiction, the historical novel itself could not have been possible without Romanticism. Historical short fiction, too, abounded in the periodicals of the time, especially in the 1820s and 1830s. Towards the mid-1810s, British short fiction had become more and more of a *rara avis* in the already existing periodicals, but a new wave of publications (inluding the Christmas annuals, which suddenly became very fashionable in the early 1820s) brought about by the success of *Blackwood's* (founded in 1817) saw a true "rise" of short stories immediately afterwards.

For all its faults, *Blackwood's* was a true saviour of British short fiction. The magazine founded by William Blackwood in Edinburgh became the arena in which greater or lesser authors were trying to redeem Romanticism in fiction by fusing it with gothic themes and settings; or with folkloric supernatural beliefs. It was also the arena where the gothic and the supernatural folk subjects themselves were being redeemed, without the involvement of Romanticism. A great output of supernatural or frightening tales (often labeled "horrid") were being published in *Blackwood's* and other periodicals. Edgar Allan Poe quite famously parodied the "*Blackwood's* Article" in 1838 only to find inspiration in several of the periodical's tales when he was putting together his theory of the "well-made" short story. Even before Poe, many such productions were being criticised for being "quite puerile," as Leigh Hunt puts it in the introduction to his "A Tale for a Chimney Corner." Walter Scott, who did write supernatural tales also criticised them—especially the ones written in Germany during the first two decades of the 19th century, "in which the most wild and unbounded license is given to an irregular fancy, and all species of combination, however ludicrous, or however shocking, are attempted and executed without scruple" (Scott 72).

There was, in other words, an effort to redeem even the very effort to redeem Romanticism in fiction. This can be recognised, for instance, in Scott's "The Tapestried Chamber," in which the ghost is clearly only a metaphor for that part of the past of any family (or nation) that we would rather see locked in a dungeon or in an old chamber, impossible to modernise (the unredeemable past). Or in a story like John Banim's "The Church-Yard Watch," which teeters on the edge of supernaturalism and psychological realism; in James Hogg's "Duncan Campbell," in which the belief in ghosts is just a nod to the folk beliefs of the author's native region; in Galt's and Mudford's stories ("The Buried Alive" and "The Iron Shroud"), which include nothing supernatural, but rather the semblance and the imminence of death, respectively. Many of the stories included in the present volume can be said to "work" as Romantic fiction: Polidori's "The Vampyre" and W. H. Ainsworth's "The Wanderings of an Immortal" manage to negotiate the exploits of Byronic heroes who travel the world and try to submit it to their will. Others, like Mudford's "The Iron Shroud," despite avoiding the supernatural, embrace other Romantic features which the "redeemers" of the time were trying to leave aside.

"The Iron Shroud" is first and foremost a Gothic tale in all its colourful xenophobia. It tells a story that, in purely stereotypical Gothic emplotment, could only happen somewhere in Southern Europe, with all its "heathen" ways (Catholicism, perceived Muslim influences, etc.). It exhibits some of the worst features of the romantic Gothic tales: it is set in Italy; the events take place during the Italian Renaissance, with its special flavour of boundless peril, when citizens of the same town could belong to warring camps and the latest mechanical invention could be used for a more sophisticated method of torture; where supposed Eastern or Muslim influences and the emergence of the Counter-Reformation were turning the country into the most dangerous place for an Englishman. It manages to avoid the sensationalistic tropes of other similar stories (something Mary Shelley's stories of the 1820s and 1830s, for example, do not): there is no ill-fated love story; no dagger-yielding spies; no secrets badly kept; no evil twins; no old legends that somehow turn out to be true; no long-standing family feud "solved" by revenge after a couple of decades.

The baggage that Romanticism (especially in its unredeemed embodiment) seemed to drag into the realm of fiction filled some authors with such dismay that they decided to reject it openly. This is why another trend in the British fiction of the early 19th century is a reaction against exotic locales, remote time periods, and fantastic or outlandish plot elements. This trend, epitomised in the novels by Jane Austen, is manifest in some of the stories included in this volume, by authors such as Maria Edgeworth, Amelia Opie, Mary Russell Mitford, Anna Maria Hall, and Anna Brownell Jameson.

Introduction

"Nothing is so tiresome," wrote Mitford in the introduction to her short-story collection *Our Village*, "as to be whirled half over Europe at the chariot-wheels of a hero, to go sleep at Vienna, and awaken at Madrid; it produces a real fatigue, a weariness of spirit. On the other hand, nothing is so delightful as to sit down in a country village in one of Miss Austen's delicious novels, quite sure before we leave it to become intimate with every spot and every person it contains" (I, 1-2). Maria Edgeworth and Amelia Opie led the way of this new trend in the early 19th century, by choosing to set their short stories in one single village, or a single neighbourhood in London (two, if the intention was to show "how the other half lived"), and by limiting the plot to a single major event unfolding in a limited period of time. With their characters often inspired by real villagers, these authors created a school of "domestic realism" (a label that became associated with them in part because many were women), to which they often added social commentary, interwoven with sentimentalism and irony, two strands inherited from 18th-century fiction. Some simply followed two basic models: "Nature and Miss Austen," as Mitford once put it (see L'Estrange II, 198).

It may be surprising, however, to discover how prepared the critics and the readership of the time really were to welcome this realist school, despite the relative absence of actual, influential models. Here is the anonymous reviewer in James Mill's *Literary Journal* (August 1806) discussing Amelia Opie's *Simple Tales*, from which one story, "The Black Velvet Pelisse," has been selected here:

> Before these tales came into our hands, we accidentally heard a lady in conversation criticising them. They were, in her opinion, very common place things. They contained nothing sublime, nothing striking, nothing wonderful, but consisted of every day transactions which every one knew and every body might write. She gave Mrs. Opie no credit for invention, and concluded that she would make a very bad romance writer. We instantly recollected Partridge's remarks on Garrick [in Fielding's *Tom Jones*], and could not but consider the lady's observations as an unintentional eulogium on the composition whose value she endeavoured to depreciate. The consequence was that we began the perusal of the *Simple Tales* with some degree of partiality in their favour. . . . The *Simple Tales*, it must be owned, contain little that is wonderful, and for the most part, detail only such transactions as might very naturally have occurred. . . . Mrs. Opie agrees with us that simple tales ought to be simple, and that it is much better to afford a correct picture of the real manners of life than to fill volumes with extravagance and absurdity. (159)

The last words, with their radical attitude against romantic excesses, are not very far in terminology from the condemnation uttered by Hannah, the character in one of Tom Stoppard's plays, looking for a definition of Romanticism: "A mind in chaos suspected of genius. In a setting of cheap thrills and false emotion" (Stoppard 39). The authors of the so-called "domestic realist" school were indeed very careful about which kind of emotions they were addressing. As Maria Edgeworth puts it in "The Dun" (written as early as 1802): "Let those forbear to follow . . . whose fine feelings can be moved only by romantic elegant scenes of distress, whose delicate sensibility shrinks from the revolting sight of real misery. Here are no pictures for romance, no stage effect to be seen, no poetic language to be heard; nothing to charm the imagination,— every thing to disgust the senses." The realism proposed by Opie, Edgeworth, and Mitford strongly appealed to Irish and Scottish authors, such Anna Maria Hall, the Banim brothers, or Andrew Picken who, in the "Introduction" to *The Dominie's Legacy* (1830) announced that "these narratives, instead of being about princes, and dukes, and lords, and other great people, and high affairs, as they should, no doubt, be, for the pleasing of the world—are nothing else but the stories of obscure persons whom nobody ever heard of, and a simple picture of joys and griefs in ordinary and lower life" (I, xviii-xix). His were "productions [of an author] who pretends to labour with little else but truth and nature [unlike an author] who works romantic figures and incidents on the coloured tapestry of his own imagination" (I, xix).

Despite all these manifestations of rejection, and despite the fact that so many of the stories published in periodicals and in short-story collections or cycles can more easily be linked to the "domestic realist" school, the fact that early-19th-century tales containing supernatural aspects were usually preferred in anthologies published in the 19th and the 20th centuries explains why the short fiction of the time "nevertheless became a genre associated with ghosts and goblins, and with bygone narrative modes" (Killick 154), a representation which persists to this day. It is simply not true that, as Wendell V. Harris believed in 1979, early 19th-century short fiction was unable "to deal with ordinary life," that "Ghost stories, humorous stories, oriental tales, legends, anecdotes, and even didactic stories could be successful. But there was immense difficulty in finding a way to focus on a series of apparently ordinary events in such a way as to make the story worth the telling" (105). Just like, in other parts of Europe, Romanticism was making room to realism, British authors of short fiction

Introduction

reacted quite early to at least some of the aspects of the Romantic movement that did not seem suitable to their genre. One reaction that really stands out due to its programmatic tone is Opie's story "The Welcome Home," with its antithesis between "the land of the plain" (realism) and "the land of the rock and the mounntain" (Romanticism).

The beginnings of Mitford's career show that she was interested in becoming a "true" Romantic poet and playwright (others, like Opie, even managed to do it) following in the footsteps of her heroes Wordsworth and Coleridge. However, she later found a different model in Jane Austen (a former acquaintance of her parents), better suited for her prose fiction. Writing about the people in her village was, of course, a more "reasonable" choice for an old maid who did not travel. However, Anna Brownell Jameson, who was well travelled, decided to satirise romantic attitudes in her *Diary of an Ennuyée*, before switching to realistic stories about people of rural Ireland. Letitia Elizabeth Landon, who also travelled, went further and satirised both Byronic adventures in a sort of Orient-in-Italy similar to the setting of many Romantic epic poems; as well as the customs of the "simple gentlefolk," thereby warning about the dangers of simply "redeeming" Romanticism in gentle comedies of manners.

When the century began, the Napoleonic Wars were in full swing. Britain and its empire appeared to be in danger. Soon after the victory of Waterloo, Britain as a beacon of liberty suffered the great defeat of Peterloo. It was perhaps a time of chaos, which nonetheless means that it was a period like any other period, as Dickens insisted the best and worst of times are. And embracing an entire period with all its artistic and intellectual trends will certainly give a more accurate representation of the way both the authors and the readers saw the literary field at any particular time: what the readers expected to consume and the authors to produce; what choices the authors felt entitled to make, and what content the readers expected to acquire. Of course, the Romantic era in British literature did not begin in 1800, nor did it end in 1832; however, the late 18th century was not particularly romantic in the realm of short fiction, and 1832 seemed like a good place to stop, not just because of the Reform Act, but because 1833 is already the year of the publication of the first sketches by Boz. The chronological order of the stories collected here is meant to show that "domestic realism" as well as the attempts to either embrace or "redeem" Romanticism coexisted.

Note on the second edition

The second edition (revised and enlarged) of this anthology was born soon after the publication of the first. In 2019, the volume did not include a chronology of events, which, I had just discovered, can be a very difficult undertaking. The present edition has a 30-page chronology, in which the events of each year are divided into three categories: "Britain and the World," "Literature and the Arts," and "Short Stories and Short-Story Collections." The last of the three is the least developed here simply because I have decided to let the selected stories themselves speak about the evolution of the genre in the 32 years covered by this anthology. There are, on the other hand, so many historical and literary-historical events because I wanted the reader to have an idea about the chaos of the era in which the authors selected here lived and about the competition they were facing from the other genres. The most important addition, of course, is that of the seven new stories (the first edition included seventeen, all of which have been preserved). First, there is Henry Kirke White's "Charles Wanely" from 1802, which is probably a better opening than Amelia Opie's 1806 quasi-realistic story (which opened the first edition of this anthology), not only because it belongs to the very first years of the period, but especially because it is so clearly romantic (it even preserves a bit of pre-Romantic innocence). From the first "mode" I had described in the 2019 introduction, that of fiction either working well within Romanticism or aiming to redeem it, I selected Coleridge's "Story of Maria Schöning," Hunt's "A Tale for the Chimney Corner," and Scott's "Wandering Willie's Tale." The first two have notable similarities: they are reworkings of old accounts the authors had read; they are both set in Germany (seen by both authors as the birthplace of Romanticism); and they are organised as essays in which gothic elements are both rejected and redeemed in order to illustrate the madness of the world (for Coleridge) or the very possibility of that redemption (for Hunt). There is no supernatural element in Coleridge's story, however: the monstrous emanates from a society that has lost its humanity.

Two stories by Scott have been added to this second edition, each belonging to a different mode: "Wandering Willie's Tale" (which is an attempt to redeem Romanticism in fiction by blending Scottish supernatural folklore, folk humour, and literary regionalism) and "The Two Drovers" (a realistic/naturalistic tale in which Scott even managed to make use of his knowledge of the

Introduction

courtroom). The two stories deserve to be discussed together not just because they are both Scott's, but because they both belong to a category that I avoided in the first edition: that of the short story that is part of the body of a novel or any other longer fictional work (framed stories, composite novel, etc.). I credit a recent essay (Daniel Cook's "Scott's Wandering Tales") with the suggestion (which I have embraced here) that incorporating such stories within a novel means ultimately providing them with a medium, not unlike that of the periodical. (I am still not entirely convinced, because I believe what Scott and others were doing was enriching their own novels with these tales, even when they were manifestly unrelated to the plot of the novel.) However, another reason for selecting Scott's two stories is the fact that they are among the most popular and the most discussed British short stories of the Romantic era.

The last two stories that have been added are among the most realistic ones: "The Auction" by the Countess of Blessington and "Jack Hatch" by Mary Russell Mitford: a sketch of fashionable London and one of village life. Thus, if the first edition may have seemed dominated by one author (Amelia Opie, who was present with three stories), the second edition includes three authors with three stories each: Opie, Scott, and Mitford. Of the twenty-four stories selected in the present volume, twelve each were written by male and female authors. Finally, the first edition included 215 footnotes, while the second edition has 398.

Works cited

Alker, Sharon, and Holly Faith Nelson. "Hogg and Working-class Writing." *The Edinburgh Companion to James Hogg*. Eds. Ian Duncan and Douglas S. Mack. Edinburgh: Edinburgh University Press, 2012. 55-63.

Berlin, Isaiah. *The Roots of Romanticism*. Ed. Henry Hardy. Princeton, NJ: Princeton University Press, 1999.

Cook, Daniel. "Scott's Wandering Tales." *European Romantic Review* 34: 1 (2023), 47-65.

Harris, Wendell V. *British Short Fiction in the Nineteenth Century. A Literary and Bibliographic Guide*. Detroit: Wayne State University Press, 1979.

Kelly, Gary. "The Limits of Genre and the Institution of Literature: Romanticism between Fact and Fiction." *Romantic Revolutions: Criticism and Theory*. Eds. Kenneth R. Johnson, Gilbert Chaitin, Karen Hanson and Herbert Marks. Bloomington: Indiana University Press, 1990. 158-175.

Killick, Tim. *British Short Fiction in the Early Nineteenth Century: The Rise of the Tale*. Aldershot: Ashgate, 2008.

L'Estrange, A. G., Ed. *The Life of Mary Russell Mitford . . . in a Selection from Her Letters to Her Friends*. I-III. London: Richard Bentley, 1870.

Lukács, Gyorgy. *The Historical Novel*. Trans. by Hannah and Stanley Mitchell. Introduction by Fredric Jameson. Lincoln and London: University of Nebraska Press, 1983.

Mitford, Mary Russell. *Our Village*. Volume I. London: G. and W. B. Whitaker, 1824.

Picken, Andrew. *The Dominie's Legacy*. Vol. I-III. London: William Kidd, 1830.

"[Review of *Simple Tales. By Mrs. Opie. In Four Volumes*]." *Literary Journal; Review of Domestic and Foreign Literature*. Second Series. Vol. II: 2 (August 1806). 159-167.

Scott, Walter. "On the Supernatural in Fictitious Compositions; and Particularly on the Works of Ernest Theodore William Hoffmann." *Foreign Quarterly Review* I: 1 (July 1827), 60-98.

Stoppard, Tom. *Arcadia*. London: Faber and Faber. 2009 (1993).

CHRONOLOGY OF EVENTS

1801
BRITAIN AND THE WORLD

The United Kingdom of Great Britain and Ireland becomes official on 1 January (100 Irish MPs are added to the House of Commons, 4 bishops and 28 peers to the House of Lords) ~ William Pitt (prime minister since 1783) resigns and is replaced by Henry Addington (-1804) ~ The London Stock Exchange is built ~ The first official British Census estimates the population of Great Britain at 10.5 million (8.33 million in England, 1.6 in Scotland, 0.54 in Wales) ~ A similar census in France finds a population of 29 million ~ Much of Italy comes under French control through the Treaty of Lunéville between France and Austria, which puts an end to the War of the Second Coalition; Spain cedes Louisiana to France ~ British troops sent to Egypt defeat the French and capture Alexandria and Cairo; the Rosetta Stone, found by the French in 1799, is part of the spoils of war and is carried to England ~ The Earl of Elgin obtains permission from Ottoman authorities to remove the Parthenon Marbles and transport them to London ~ In the first naval Battle of Copenhagen, Nelson defeats the Danish fleet ~ Thomas Jefferson becomes the third United States President; the US begins the First Barbary War against Tripoli (-1805) ~ Russian emperor Paul I is assassinated and replaced with his son Alexander I (-1825) ~ Elizabeth Hamilton publishes *Letters on the Elementary Principles of Education* ~ Helen Maria Williams publishes *Sketches of the State of Manners and Opinions in the French Republic*.

LITERATURE & THE ARTS

The first version of Jacques-Louis David's *Napoleon Crossing the Alps* is exhibited at the Louvre ~ In Vienna, Beethoven completes *The Moonlight Sonata*; Haydn's *The Seasons* are first performed ~ In France, Chateaubriand publishes *Atala*; the Marquis de Sade is arrested and will spend the last 13 years of his life in confinement ~ In Germany, August and Friedrich Schlegel publish the first instalment of their *Characteristics and Critiques* ~ JMW Turner exhibits *Dutch Boats in a Gale* ~ At Sadler's Wells, Joseph Grimaldi stars in *The Great Devil* by Dibdin the Younger ~ George Ellis publishes an expanded version (3 vols.) of his 1790 anthology *Specimens of the Early English Poets* ~ In January, William Wordsworth publishes, under his name, the second edition (dated 1800) of his and Coleridge's *Lyrical Ballads*, in two volumes and including a new preface ~ Robert Southey publishes *Thalaba the Destroyer* (rev. ed. in 1809) ~ James Hogg publishes *Scottish Pastorals, Poems, Songs, etc., Mostly Written in the Dialect of the South* ~ Matthew Gregory Lewis publishes *Tales of Wonder* (some ballads are contributed by Walter Scott and others) ~ Thomas Moore publishes *The Poetical Works of the Late Thomas Little, Esq.* ~ John Thelwall publishes *Poems Chiefly Written in Retirement* (which includes his melodrama "The Fairy of the Lake"); and (as John Beaufort) his only novel, *The Daughter of Adoption: A Tale of Modern Times* ~ Maria Edgeworth publishes *Belinda* ~ Amelia Opie publishes *The Father and Daughter*.

SHORT STORIES AND SHORT STORY COLLECTIONS
Anonymous. *The Moral Legacy; or, Simple Narratives*. London: William Miller, 1801.
Joseph Moser. "The Turban, a Turkish Tale" and "The Adventures of Frank Fidget." *Tales and Romances, of Ancient and Modern Times*. 5 vols. London: T. Hurst, 1801. III, 189-229; IV, 227-292.
Mary Pilkington (?). "The Turnpike Gate. A Tale." *Lady's Monthly Magazine* 7 (July 1801), 13-18.

1802
BRITAIN AND THE WORLD
The Treaty of Amiens ends hostilities between the United Kingdom and France; many British writers and painters travel to Paris and admire the art brought by Napoleon from Italy to the Louvre ~ In France, Napoleon becomes First Consul for life; he establishes the Légion d'honneur and offers amnesty to most émigrés ~ Napoleon also reinstates slavery in the French colonies; in Haiti, French troops gain only minor victories, but capture the revolutionary leader Toussaint Louverture ~ Matthew Flinders aboard the *Investigator* begins the circumnavigation of Australia ~ In London, a special Parliament committee recognises the merits of Edward Jenner's smallpox vaccination ~ In Germany, G.F. Grotefend initiates the decipherment of the cuneiforms ~ Humphry Davy becomes Professor of Chemistry at the Royal Institution (Coleridge attends his lectures) ~ William Wilberforce founds the Society for the Suppression of Vice ~ Malcolm Laing publishes *History of Scotland* ~ Paley publishes *Natural Theology* ~ William Cobbett begins editing *Cobbett's Political Register* (-1836), written mostly by himself ~ Sarah Trimmer begins editing *The Guardian of Education* (-1806) ~ *Rees's Cyclopaedia* begins publication (-1819) ~ Mary Hays publishes the 6 volumes of *Female Biography; or, Memoirs of Illustrious and Celebrated Women* (dated 1803).

LITERATURE & THE ARTS
In Germany, Louis Spohr composes his first violin concerto ~ Thomas Girtin exhibits *Eidometropolis*, a large panorama of London (now lost) ~ In France, Chateaubriand publishes *René* and Mme de Staël, *Delphine* ~ In Italy, Ugo Foscolo publishes *The Last Letters of Jacopo Ortis* (English translation in 1817) ~ Novalis's unfinished novels, *Heinrich von Ofterdingen* and *The Novices of Sais* are published posthumously ~ In Scotland, the first "Burns supper," on the anniversary of Robert Burns's birthday, takes place in Alloway ~ Sydney Smith, Francis Jeffrey, Henry Brougham, and Francis Horner found *The Edinburgh Review* (-1829) ~ Charles Lamb publishes *John Woodvil, a Tragedy* ~ Thomas Holcroft's afterpiece *A Tale of Mystery* is the first play advertised in England as a "melodrama" ~ Joseph Ritson publishes his edition of *Ancient Engleish Metrical Romanceës* ~ The first edition, in two volumes, of *Minstrelsy of the Scottish Border*, ed. by Walter Scott (2nd ed., in 3 vols., in 1803) ~ Wordsworth publishes a third edition of *Lyrical Ballads*, with an expanded preface ~ In *The Morning Post* appear several poems by Coleridge (including "Dejection: An Ode") and

The Romantic Era

Robert Southey's ballad "The Inchcape Rock" ~ Amelia Opie publishes *Poems* ~ Walter Savage Landor publishes *Poetry, by the Author of Gebir*.

SHORT STORIES AND SHORT STORY COLLECTIONS
George Brewer. "[The Story of Moredius]." *The European Magazine* 42 (July-August 1802). No. 18 in "Essays after the Manner of Goldsmith."

Henry Kirke White. "Melancholy Hours, No. II [Charles Wanely]" and "Fanny Mortimer." *The Monthly Mirror* (June 1802), 385-388; 392-393.

1803
BRITAIN AND THE WORLD
The United Kingdom declares war against France ~ Napoleon's forces march into Germany and occupy Hanover; the French "Grande Armée" prepares for an invasion of Great Britain ~ The Louisiana Purchase is completed in Paris: France sells more than 2 million square kilometres to the United States ~ The French are defeated and surrender at Vertières, being forced to leave Haiti ~ Despite scarcity of evidence, Edward Despard and six accomplices are hanged for plotting to assassinate King George III and inciting a revolution ~ A new rebellion in Ireland proclaims a "Provisional Government," but its leader, Robert Emmet, is captured and hanged ~ Arthur Wellesley's (the future Duke of Wellington's) decisive victory at Assaye against the Maratha Empire, and General Lake's conquest of Delhi lead to the expansion of the Bengal Presidency, the largest territory of the British India Company ~ William Cobbett begins editing *Cobbett's Parliamentary Debates* (which will become *Hansard's Parliamentary Debates* in 1818) ~ Thomas Malthus publishes the second edition ("very much enlarged") of *An Essay on the Principle of Population*, which he urges to be considered "as a new work."

LITERATURE & THE ARTS
In Vienna, the premiere of Beethoven's *Piano Concerto No. 3* and of the *Symphony No. 2*, in the newly built Theater and der Wien; Beethoven's *Kreutzer Sonata* also premieres at the Augarten Theatre in Vienna ~ Napoleon banishes Mme de Staël from France ~ James Barry completes his *Self-Portrait as Timanthes* ~ John Crome and Robert Ladbrooke found the Norwich School of Painters ~ Dorothy Wordsworth writes "Recollections of a Tour Made in Scotland" (first published in 1894) ~ Charles Dibdin publishes his four-volume autobiography, *The Professional Life of Mr. Dibdin* ~ William Hayley publishes two volumes of *The Life and Posthumous Writings of William Cowper* (vol. 3 in 1804) ~ Arthur Aikin begins editing *The Annual Review, and History of Literature* (1808) ~ James Mill begins editing the weekly *Literary Journal* (-1806) ~ M.G. Lewis's gothic drama *The Captive* is performed at the Covent Garden, but the author withdraws it because "spectators went into hysterics" ~ One of the better remembered plays from this year is James Kenney's farce *Raising the Wind* ~ Robert Southey and Joseph Cottle publish their edition of *The Works of Thomas Chatterton* ~ Coleridge publishes a new edition of his *Poems* ~ Thomas Campbell publishes *Poems* (with a new edition

of "The Pleasures of Hope") ~ Erasmus Darwin's poem *The Temple of Nature* appears posthumously ~ Robert Southey publishes his translation of *Amadis of Gaul* in 4 volumes ~ Jane Porter publishes *Thaddeus of Warsaw* ~ Sydney Owenson publishes her first novel, *St Clair; or, The Heiress of Desmond*.

SHORT STORIES AND SHORT STORY COLLECTIONS
Charles Fothergill. *The Wanderer: or, A Collection of Original Tales and Essays, Founded upon Facts; Illustrating the Virtues and Vices of the Present Age*. 2 vols. London: Wynne and Scholey, 1803.

Sarah Scudgell Wilkinson. "The Pilgrim." *The Subterranean Passage; or, Gothic Cell. A Romance*. London: Ann Lemoine, s.a., 30-36.

1804
BRITAIN AND THE WORLD
Addington resigns and Pitt becomes prime minister again (-1806) ~ The Lewis and Clark Expedition begins in western Illinois, with the aim of exploring the Louisiana Purchase ~ Alexander Hamilton, the U.S. Secretary of the Treasury, is killed in a duel with Aaron Burr, the U.S. Vice-President ~ The end of the First Republic in France: Napoleon is proclaimed (then crowned) emperor; the French civil code (known as the Code Napoléon) is introduced ~ In response to Napoleon's decision, Holy Roman Emperor Francis II proclaims himself Emperor of Austria as Francis I; the title will survive until 1918 ~ Spain declares war against the United Kingdom and allies itself with France ~ The Serbian Revolution against the Ottoman Empire begins (-1817) ~ The Russo-Persian War begins (-1813); Russia occupies the Caucasus ~ Haiti becomes independent and Jean-Jacques Dessalines its emperor; the French on the island are massacred ~ In Wales, the first locomotive to run on rails (built by Richard Trevithick) carries iron on a distance of 10 miles ~ Wilberforce and others create the British and Foreign Bible Society ~ German pharmacist Friedrich Sertürner isolates morphine from opium.

LITERATURE & THE ARTS
Ingres paints *Bonaparte, First Consul*, commissioned by Napoleon as a gift to the city of Liège ~ In Weimar, Friedrich Schiller's *Wilhelm Tell* is performed for the first time ~ In Saxony, E.A.F. Klingemann publishes *The Nightwatches of Bonaventura* (first English translation in 2014) ~ JMW Turner opens his own gallery ~ Joanna Baillie publishes *Miscellaneous Plays* ~ William Blake begins writing *Milton* (-1810) and *Jerusalem* (-1820) ~ James Grahame publishes anonymously his poem *The Sabbath* ~ Maria Edgeworth publishes *The Modern Griselda* (dated 1805) ~ Anna Maria Porter publishes *The Lake of Killarney*.

SHORT STORIES AND SHORT STORY COLLECTIONS
Maria Edgeworth. *Popular Tales*. 3 vols. London: J. Johnson, 1804.

Mrs. [Ives] Hurry [Margaret Hurry]. *The Faithful Contrast; or, Virtue and Vice accurately delineated, in a series of Moral and Instructive Tales*. London: J. Harris, Successor to E. Newbery, 1804.

The Romantic Era

1805
BRITAIN AND THE WORLD

The Treaty of Saint Petersburg leads to the formation of the Third Coalition; Austria, Russia, and the United Kingdom wage the War of the Third Coalition against France and Spain until 1806; Prussia remains neutral ~ Major-General Sir Arthur Wellesley is recalled from India and commands a brigade in the unsuccessful Hanover Expedition ~ Napoleon is crowned King of Italy with the Iron Crown of the Lombards ~ British and Russian forces occupy the Kingdom of Naples ~ Napoleon invades the Austrian Empire, captures 60,000 Austrian troops in the Ulm campaign, then defeats the Russo-Austrian army in the Battle of Austerlitz; French troops enter Vienna ~ The Peace of Pressburg has Austria give up territories that are either attached to Napoleon's Kingdom of Italy or to France's German allies (Bavaria, Baden, and Württemberg) ~ Admiral Nelson attacks and defeats the French and Spanish navies in the Battle of Trafalgar; Nelson is killed and his body is carried to England ~ The expedition of Lewis and Clark reaches the Pacific ~ Thomas Jefferson is US President for a second term; US Marines defeat the Pasha of Tripoli in the Battle of Derma ~ Mungo Park begins his second expedition along the Niger (he disappears and is presumed drowned the following year) ~ Muhammad Ali becomes ruler of Egypt (-1848) ~ Young Simón Bolívar ends his Grand Tour in Rome, where he swears to end the Spanish rule in the Americas.

LITERATURE & THE ARTS

The British Institution for Promoting the Fine Arts is founded ~ In Vienna, first public performances of Beethoven's *Symphony no. 3 (Eroica)* and the opera *Fidelio* (the latter, in front of French officers of the occupation army); he publishes the *Waldstein Sonata (No. 21)* ~ In Germany, Achim von Arnim and Clemens Brentano publish their collection of folk poems and songs *Das Knaben Wunderhorn* (two more vols. in 1808) ~ The first part of Jan Potocki's *The Manuscript Found in Saragossa* is published in St. Petersburg ~ Richard Payne Knight publishes *An Analytic Inquiry into the Principles of Taste* ~ *The Eclectic Review*, a London monthly dedicated to book reviews, begins publication (-1868) ~ Thomas Holcroft edits *The Theatrical Recorder* (-1806) and publishes his last novel, *Memoirs of Bryan Perdue* ~ William Hazlitt's first work, *An Essay on the Principles of Human Action*, appears anonymously ~ Elizabeth Inchbald's last play, *To Marry, or Not to Marry*, is performed at the Covent Garden ~ Walter Scott publishes *The Lay of the Last Minstrel* ~ George Ellis publishes his edition of *Specimens of Early English Metrical Romances* ~ Robert Southey publishes *Madoc* and *Metrical Tales, and Other Poems* ~ Wordsworth finishes a second version of *The Prelude* ~ Mary Tighe's *Psyche; or, The Legend of Love* is published ~ Amelia Opie publishes *Adeline Mowbray* (early January) ~ William Godwin publishes *Fleetwood: or The New Man of Feeling* ~ Charlotte Dacre (as Rosa Matilda) publishes her first Gothic novel, *Confessions of the Nun of St Omer, A Tale* ~ Sydney Owenson publishes *The Novice of Saint Dominick*.

Chronology of Events

SHORT STORIES AND SHORT STORY COLLECTIONS
Barbara Finch. "Myrtle-Wood. A Tale." *Sonnets, and other Poems: to which are added Tales in Prose*. London: Blacks and Parry, 1805. 57-113.

Joseph Moser. "The New Year's Gift. A Tale" and "The Seven Rings of Jarchus. An Indian Fable." *The European Magazine* 47 (January and March), 15-22, 194-201.

1806
BRITAIN AND THE WORLD

William Pitt the Younger dies; William Grenville replaces him as Prime Minister (-1807); he forms the Ministry of All Talents ~ Following the Battle of Blaauwberg, Britain occupies Cape Town and establishes the Cape Colony ~ The British victory of San Domingo against the French fleet confirms British naval supremacy in the western hemisphere ~ France organises a major embargo against the United Kingdom, known as the Continental Blockade ~ British troops occupy Buenos Aires but the city is recovered by a force of volunteers ~ Napoleon creates the Kingdom of Holland (-1810) with his brother Louis as king; sixteen German states secede from the Holy Roman Empire and form the Confederation of the Rhine (client states of the French Empire); Francis II declares the Holy Roman Empire dissolved, while he continues as emperor of Austria ~ Prussia sends France an ultimatum, requesting the evacuation of Germany; the beginning of the Fourth Coalition (United Kingdom, Prussia, Russia, Sweden) against France ~ The French Grande Armée begins its campaign against Prussia; Napoleon and Davout defeat the Prussians at Jena and Auerstedt; Napoleon enters Berlin ~ The French army enters Prussian-occupied Poland and Napoleon arrives in Warsaw ~ A French army led by Masséna invades the Kingdom of Naples and instals Joseph Bonaparte as king ~ In the US, the Pike Expedition begins exploring (-1807) the south and west of the Louisiana Purchase ~ A Russo-Turkish War begins (-1812).

LITERATURE & THE ARTS

Beethoven's *Violin Concerto in D major* is first performed in Vienna ~ In Germany, Ernst Moritz Arndt publishes the first part of the anti-Napoleonian *Geist der Zeit* ~ At the Covent Garden, Joseph Grimaldi registers his greatest success in Thomas Dibdin's pantomime *Harlequin and Mother Goose* ~ Philip Astley opens the Olympic Pavilion in the Strand ~ Elizabeth Inchbald begins publication of her critical anthology in 25 volumes *The British Theatre; or, A Collection of Plays* (-1809) ~ Byron's debut with *Fugitive Pieces* is privately printed ~ Walter Scott publishes *Ballads and Lyrical Pieces* ~ Robert Bloomfield publishes *Wild Flowers; or, Pastoral and Local Poetry* ~ Thomas Moore publishes *Epistles, Odes, and Other Poems* (he challenges Francis Jeffrey to a duel because of the latter's critique in *The Edinburgh Review* but they are reconciled) ~ Anne Grant publishes her *Letters from the Mountains* ~ James Montgomery publishes *The Wanderer of Switzerland* ~ Maria Edgeworth publishes *Leonora* ~ Charlotte Dacre publishes *Zofloya; or, The Moor: A Romance of the Fifteenth Century* ~ Sydney Owenson (later, Lady Morgan) publishes *The Wild Irish Girl: A National Tale*.

The Romantic Era

SHORT STORIES AND SHORT STORY COLLECTIONS
Amelia Opie. *Simple Tales*. 4 vols. (London: Longman, Hurst, Rees, and Orme), 1806.
Sarah Wilkinson. *The Spectre; or, The Ruins of Belfont Priory*. London: A. Kemmish, 1806.

1807

BRITAIN AND THE WORLD

Tory cabinet led by William Cavendish, Duke of Portland (-1809) ~ William Wilberforce publishes *A Letter on the Abolition of the Slave Trade*; the Abolition of the Slave Trade Act is passed (it does not affect the slave trade in the colonies, which will be abolished in 1833) ~ US Congress passes an act prohibiting the importation of slaves ~ British troops occupy Montevideo (which they hold for seven months) ~ Denmark allies itself with France; Britain unleashes the Bombardment of Copenhagen and the entire Danish fleet surrenders ~ Napoleon defeats the Russians in the Battles of Eylau and Friedland ~ In the Treaty of Tilsit, Napoleon first signs an alliance with Russia; then a peace agreement with Prussia; three new entities are created: the Kingdom of Westphalia (ruled by Jérôme Bonaparte until 1813), the Duchy of Warsaw, and the Free City of Danzig ~ Franco-Persian Alliance (-1809) following the Treaty of Finckenstein ~ As Portugal refuses to assent to the French-imposed Continental Blockade of Britain, France signs a secret agreement with Spain for the partition of Portugal; the two allies invade and occupy Portugal; the royal court flees to Brazil; one year later, Rio de Janeiro becomes capital of the Kingdom of Portugal ~ Janissaries depose sultan Selim III and place his cousin Mustafa IV on the throne ~ Gas lighting is introduced in Pall Mall ~ Fulton's *Clermont* sails on the Hudson ~ In Germany, Hegel publishes *The Phenomenology of the Spirit* ~ Fichte delivers his first of his *Addresses to the German Nation* (-1808) ~ Alexander von Humboldt publishes *Essay on the Geography of Plants* ~ Thomas Hope publishes *Household Furniture and Interior Decoration*.

LITERATURE & THE ARTS

The Elgin Marbles are exhibited in London and admired by British artists ~ In France, Madame de Staël publishes *Corinne, ou l'Italie* (English translation the same year) ~ In Germany, two major hymns by Hölderlin ("Pathmos" and "Der Rhein") appear in the *Musenalmanach für das Jahr 1808* ~ In the United States, Washington Irving and James Kirke Paulding create the satirical periodical *Salmagundi* (-1808) ~ William Hazlitt's *A Reply to the Essay on Population, by the Rev. T.R. Malthus* appears first in Cobbett's *Weekly Register*, then in volume form ~ Sydney Smith publishes the first of his satirical series later known as *Peter Plymley's Letters* ~ Robert Southey publishes *Letters from England: by Don Manuel Alvarez Espriella* and his anthology *Specimens of the Later English Poets: with Preliminary Notices* (3 vols.) ~ George Burnett publishes his edition of *Specimens of English Prose-Writers, from the Earliest Time to the Close of the Seventeenth Century* ~ Leigh Hunt publishes his anthology of *Classic*

Tales ~ Charles and Mary Lamb publish *Tales from Shakespear* ~ Thomas and Henrietta Bowdler publish the expurgated *Family Shakespeare* (new, complete edition, in 1818) ~ Wordsworth publishes *Poems, in Two Volumes* ~ Byron publishes *Poems on Various Occasions* and *Hours of Idleness* (both Wordsworth's and Byron's poems are attacked in *The Edinburgh Review*) ~ James Hogg publishes *The Mountain Bard* ~ Charlotte Smith's *Beachy Head: with Other Poems* appears posthumously ~ George Crabbe publishes *Poems* ~ *The Remains of Henry Kirke White* are published, edited by Robert Southey ~ Charlotte Dacre publishes *The Libertine* ~ Anna Maria Porter publishes *The Hungarian Brothers* ~ Charles Robert Maturin (as Dennis Jasper Murphy) publishes *Fatal Revenge; or, The Family of Montorio*.

SHORT STORIES AND SHORT STORY COLLECTIONS

Elizabeth Hamilton. "The Story of the Tame Pigeon." *La Belle Assemblée* 2: 13 (January 1806), 26-30.

Mrs. [Margaret] [Ives] Hurry [formerly Miss Mitchell]. *Moral Tales, for Young People*. London: Longman, Hurst, Rees, and Orme, 1807.

1808

BRITAIN AND THE WORLD

France turns against its Spanish allies and occupies the major Spanish cities; citizens of Madrid rebel against the army of occupation; hundreds are executed ~ Joseph Bonaparte abdicates his throne in Naples in favour of Murat and becomes King of Spain ~ Spanish militias defeat French troops in several engagements; the United Kingdom sends an expeditionary force led by Sir Arthur Wellesley; beginning of the Peninsular War (-1814); the French are chased out of Portugal (they agree to evacuate by signing the Convention of Cintra) ~ Napoleon intervenes personally in Spain, regaining the major cities and entering Madrid towards the end of the year ~ Because the Pope opposes the France's blockade against Britain, Napoleon occupies Rome ~ Russia fights Sweden in the Finnish War (-1809), at the end of which it will annex Finland ~ Sierra Leone becomes a British colony ~ In Canada, Simon Fraser explores the country west of the Rockies and descends the river that now bears his name ~ Mustafa IV is deposed in a coup; Mahmud II becomes sultan of the Ottoman Empire (-1839) ~ John Dalton publishes *New System of Chemical Philosophy* ~ James Mill publishes *Commerce Defended*.

LITERATURE & THE ARTS

A major concert at the Theater an der Wien includes the first performances of Beethoven's 5th and 6th Symphonies, the Piano Concerto no 4, and the Choral Fantasy ~ At the Paris Salon, Antoine-Jean Gros exhibits *Napoleon on the Battlefield of Eylau*; Anne-Louis Girodet exhibits *The Burial of Atala* ~ In Germany, Goethe publishes what is now known as *Faust, Part One* ~ At the Court Theatre in Weimar, the premiere of Heinrich von Kleist's comedy *The Broken Jug* ~ A fire destroys the Covent Garden theatre and several contiguous buildings, killing 22 people ~ At the Royal Institution, Coleridge gives his Lectures

The Romantic Era

on the Principles of Poetry ~ *The Examiner* begins publication (-1881), with Leigh Hunt as its editor (-1821) ~ Charles Lamb publishes his anthology of *Specimens of English Dramatic Poets, Who Lived about the Time of Shakspeare* ~ R.H. Cromek publishes *Reliques of Robert Burns* ~ Byron publishes *Poems Original and Translated* ~ Amelia Opie publishes *The Warrior's Return, and Other Poems* ~ First instalment of Thomas Moore's *Irish Melodies* (10 vols. and a supplement until 1834); Moore also publishes *Corruption and Intolerance: Two Poems with Notes* ~ Felicia Hemans publishes *Poems* (by subscription, in Liverpool); as well as the epic poem *England and Spain; or, Valour and Patriotism* ~ Moore's *Corruption and Intolerance: Two Poems with Notes Addressed to an Englishman by an Irishman* appears anonymously ~ Walter Scott publishes *Marmion: A Tale of Flodden Field* ~ Maria Edgeworth publishes *The Match Girl. A Novel* ~ Sydney Owenson publishes *Woman; or, Ida of Athens* ~ Hannah More's novel *Coelebs in Search of a Wife* appears anonymously ~ Elizabeth Hamilton publishes *The Cottagers of Glenburnie.*

SHORT STORIES AND SHORT STORY COLLECTIONS

Anthony Frederick Holstein. *Sir Owen Glendowr, and Other Tales*. 3 vols. London: Lane, Newman, and Co., 1808.

Charles and Mary Lamb. *Mrs. Leicester's School*. London: M. J. Godwin, 1808 [dated 1809].

Mary Linwood. *Leicestershire Tales*. 4 vols. London: For the author, 1808.

William Mudford. "The Evils of Suspicion; a Narrative." *The Universal Magazine*. New Series. IX (June 1808), 474-476.

1809
BRITAIN AND THE WORLD

Portland resigns and Spencer Perceval becomes Prime Minister (-1812) ~ In the Peninsular War, the French defeat the British at Corunna and gain control of northern Spain; Arthur Wellesley chases the French out of Portugal at Grijó and wins the inconclusive Battle of Talavera, after which he is created Viscount Wellington ~ British troops invade the Netherlands in the disastrous Walcheren Campaign; Castlereagh, the war secretary, and George Canning, the foreign secretary, have a row over the Dutch expedition and they fight a duel in which Canning is wounded ~ With the Treaty of the Dardanelles, the United Kingdom and the Ottoman Empire become allies ~ Austria declares war on France, which signals the beginning of the War of the Fifth Coalition; Andreas Hofer, Austrian folk hero, also begins his guerrilla war against French and Bavarian occupation; Napoleon's victory in the Battle of Wagram effectively puts an end to the war ~ France occupies the Papal States and pope Pius VII is arrested ~ Sweden loses Finland to Russia; after a coup, Gustav IV Adolf abdicates and is replaced by his uncle, king of Sweden as Charles XIII, who accepts a liberal constitution ~ James Madison is sworn in as the fourth US President ~ Wordsworth publishes the pamphlet *Concerning ... the Convention of Cintra* (first published in two instalments in *The Courier* in Dec. 1808 and Jan. 1809) ~ In Paris, Lamarck publishes his theory of evolution as *Philosophie zoologique* ~ Wilhelm von Humboldt founds the University of Berlin.

Chronology of Events

LITERATURE & THE ARTS

In Germany, Goethe publishes *Elective Affinities* and August Wilhelm Schlegel begins publication (-1811) of the *Lectures on Dramatic Art and Literature* (English translation in 1815) ~ In the United States, Washington Irving publishes *A History of New-York to the End of the Dutch Dynasty* ~ The Covent Garden reopens but immediately closes when faced to the O.P. (Old Price) Riots: the audience protests for weeks against new prices for tickets; the Drury Lane theatre is destroyed by fire ~ *The Quarterly Review* begins publication (-1967), under William Gifford's editorship (-1824) ~ Coleridge begins writing his periodical *The Friend* (-1810) ~ Byron publishes *English Bards and Scotch Reviewers* ~ Thomas Campbell publishes *Gertrude of Wyoming; a Pennsylvanian Tale; and Other Poems* ~ Thomas Moore publishes *The Sceptic: A Philosophical Satire* ~ William Combe serialises the poem *The Tour of Doctor Syntax, in Search of the Picturesque* (in volume in 1812) ~ Maria Edgeworth publishes *Ennui* (as vol. I of *Tales of Fashionable Life*).

SHORT STORIES AND SHORT STORY COLLECTIONS

Samuel Taylor Coleridge. "[Story of Maria Schoning]." *The Friend* 13 (16 November 1809), 193-208.

Maria Edgeworth. *Tales of Fashionable Life*. 3 vols. London: J. Johnson, 1809 [vol. 4-6 in 1812].

James Hogg. "The Long Pack. A Tale. By the Ettrick Shepherd." *The Universal Magazine of Knowledge and Pleasure* 12: 69 (August 1809), 95-101.

1810

BRITAIN AND THE WORLD

George III has a final relapse of his mental disorder after the death of his favourite daughter, Princess Amelia, and is recognised as insane by physicians ~ British troops seize Mauritius from the French and the Spice Islands from the Dutch ~ Napoleon's marriage to Josephine is annulled and he marries Marie-Louise of Austria ~ The French army withdraws from Portugal ~ French Marshall Bernadotte is elected successor to the throne of Sweden ~ The Netherlands is incorporated into the French Empire ~ Venezuela proclaims its independence; beginning of the Venezuelan War of Independence (-1823) ~ May Revolution in Buenos Aires and beginning of the Argentine War of Independence (-1818) ~ Colombian declaration of independence and the First Republic of New Granada (-1816) ~ Miguel Hidalgo's insurgency triggers the Mexican War of Independence (-1821) ~ Simon Bolivar is in London, arguing in favour of Venezuelan independence ~ Cobbett is imprisoned for 2 years and fined 1,000 pounds; Leigh Hunt and his brother are acquitted of seditious libel for the same protest against flogging in the military ~ Alexander von Humboldt publishes *Views of the Cordilleras* (translated in 1814 by Helen Maria Williams) ~ Wordsworth's *Guide to the Lakes* appears in a first version as an anonymous preface to Joseph Wilkinson's *Select Views in Cumberland, Westmoreland and Lancashire* (2nd ed. in 1820, 5th in 1835).

The Romantic Era

LITERATURE & THE ARTS

In Spain, Francisco Goya begins *The Disasters of War*, a series of 82 prints (-1820) ~ At the Berlin Academy, Caspar David Friedrich exhibits *The Monk by the Sea* and *The Abbey in the Oakwood* ~ In Berlin, Heinrich von Kleist publishes the novella *Michael Kohlhaas*; his play *Katie of Heilbronn* has its premiere in Vienna ~ James Hogg begins writing his periodical *The Spy* (-1811) ~ The first volume of Southey's *History of Brazil* (-1819) is published ~ Lucy Aikin publishes *Epistles on Women, Exemplifying their Character and Condition in Various Ages and Nations* ~ In the April issue of *The Monthly Mirror*, Leigh Hunt publishes "Memoir of Mr James Henry Leigh Hunt, Written by Himself;" he begins editing *The Reflector: A Quarterly Magazine* (-1811) ~ Anna Letitia Barbauld publishes her anthology of the works of *The British Novelists* (50 vols.) ~ Joanna Baillie's *Family Legend* is first performed in Edinburgh ~ Isaac Pocock's most successful musical farce, *Hit or Miss!* Is produced at the Lyceum ~ Walter Scott publishes *The Lady of the Lake; a Poem* ~ Scott's edition of *The Poetical Works of Anna Seward* is published in 3 vols. (Seward had died in 1809) ~ Southey publishes *The Curse of Kehama* ~ George Crabbe's *The Borough: a Poem, in Twenty-Four Letters* appears in two editions (the second one, revised) ~ Samuel Rogers publishes *The Voyage of Columbus. A Poem* ~ Thomas Love Peacock publishes *The Genius of the Thames: A Lyrical Poem, in Two Parts* ~ Maria Edgeworth publishes *The Wife; or, A Model for Women. A Tale* ~ Jane Porter publishes her historical novel *The Scottish Chiefs* (5 vols.) ~ P.B. Shelley publishes *Zastrozzi, a Romance* and *St Irvyne; or, The Rosicrucian: a Romance* (the latter, dated 1811).

SHORT STORIES AND SHORT STORY COLLECTIONS

Maria Edgeworth. *Tales of Real Life*. 3 vols. London: Henry Colburn, 1810.

James Hogg. "The Danger of Changing Occupations,—verified in the Life of a Berwickshire Farmer." *The Spy* 3-4 (15 and 22 September 1810). Expanded as "The Renowned Adventures of Basil Lee." *Winter Evening Tales* I, 1-99.

James Hogg. "Dreadful Narrative of the Death of Major MacPherson." *The Spy* 13 (24 November). Reprinted as "Dreadful Story of Macpherson" in *Winter Evening Tales* I, 190-194.

James Hogg. "Amusing Story of Two Highlanders." *The Spy* 17 (22 December). Reprinted as "Story of Two Highlanders" in *Winter Evening Tales* I, 194-197.

James Hogg. "Story of the Ghost of Lochmaben." *The Spy* 18 (29 December 1810). Revised as "Country Dreams and Apparitions. No III: The Wife of Lochmaben" in *Winter Evening Tales* II, 223-231.

1811

BRITAIN AND THE WORLD

Under the terms of the Regency Act, the Prince of Wales becomes Prince Regent ~ A census reveals a population of 12.5 million (9.5 million in England, 1.8 in Scotland, 0.6 in Wales, and 0.64 in the Army and the Navy) ~ First Luddite uprisings occur in Nottinghamshire ~ More than 1,900 British sailors are killed in the North Sea in the

Chronology of Events

Christmas Gale of 1811 ~ Wellington prevents a French incursion into Portugal at Fuentes de Oñoro; the Battle of Albuera, the bloodiest of the Peninsular War, is indecisive ~ A British force invades and occupies Java, a Dutch colony ~ Mexican insurgents are defeated by Spanish troops in the Battle of Calderon Bridge; Miguel Hidalgo is executed ~ Uruguayan patriots defeat the Spanish in the Battle of Las Piedras ~ The Venezuelan Declaration of Independence is adopted ~ British explorer David Thomson claims present-day Washington State for the United Kingdom ~ While on his Grand Tour, Charles Robert Cockerell excavates the Temple of Apollo at Bassae, in Greece, and persuades the British Museum to purchase (in 1815) what will become known as the Bassae Frieze ~ The return match between the British boxing champion Tom Cribb and the American Tom Molineaux (a former slave) draws a crowd of 15,000 ~ In Lyme Regis, Mary Anning unearths the first complete ichthyosaur fossil ~ In Vienna, Friedrich Schlegel lectures *On Recent History*.

LITERATURE & THE ARTS

First performance of Beethoven's Piano Concerto no 5, in Leipzig ~ At the Royal Academy, where he is Professor of Perspective, JMW Turner begins his lectures (-1828) ~ In Germany, La Motte Fouqué publishes his novella *Undine* (English translation in 1818) ~ Goethe publishes the first volume of *Dichtung und Wahrheit*; first English translation in 1824 (-1833) ~ Jonathan Scott publishes his translation of *The Arabian Nights Entertainments* (6 vols.) ~ At the London Philosophical Society, Coleridge begins a series of Lectures on Shakespeare and Milton in Illustration of the Principles of Poetry (-1812) ~ P.B. Shelley publishes *The Necessity of Atheism*; he and his friend (and possible co-author) T.J. Hogg are expelled from University College, Oxford; Shelley also publishes *Poetical Essay on the Existing State of Things* ~ Walter Scott publishes *The Vision of Don Roderick; a Poem* ~ A collection of Mary Tighe's poetry (*Psyche, with Other Poems*) is published posthumously ~ Mary Russell Mitford publishes *Christina, the Maid of the South Seas; a Poem* ~ Jane Austen publishes *Sense and Sensibility* ("By a Lady") ~ Mary Brunton publishes *Self-Control: A Novel* ~ Sydney Owenson publishes *The Missionary: An Indian Tale*.

SHORT STORIES AND SHORT STORY COLLECTIONS

James Hogg. "The Country Laird." *The Spy* 24-26 (9, 16, 23 February 1811). Expanded as "The Wool-gatherer" in *The Brownie of Bodsbeck* (1818), II, 87-228.

James Hogg. "Dangerous Consequences of the Love of Fame." *The Spy* 35 (27 April). Reprinted with changes as "Adam Bell" in *Winter Evening Tales* I, 99-104.

James Hogg. "History of the Life of Duncan Campbell." *The Spy* 49 & 51 (3 & 17 August). Reprinted as "Duncan Campbell" in *Winter Evening Tales* I, 105-129.

Walter Scott. "The Inferno of Altisidora." *Edinburgh Annual Register for 1809*. Vol. Second—Part Second. Edinburgh: James Ballantyne, 1811. 582-591.

The Romantic Era

1812
BRITAIN AND THE WORLD

Prime minister Spencer Perceval is assassinated by John Bellingham, a Liverpool merchant; Robert Jenkinson, 2nd Earl of Liverpool becomes prime minister (-1827) ~ Byron delivers his maiden speech in the House of Lords, against the Frame Work Bill; the bill passes and Luddites are subject to capital punishment for breaking machines ~ War of 1812 begins; at Queenston Heights, a British force drives back an American invasion of Canada ~ Wellington defeats the French in the Battle of Salamanca; British forces re-enter Madrid ~ First liberal constitution in Spain ~ France signs alliance treaties with Prussia and Austria against Russia; Britain mediates a peace treaty between Russia and Turkey allowing Russia to prepare for French invasion; five weeks later, Napoleon invades Russia ~ Napoleon wins a pyrrhic victory at Borodino and enters Moscow; Russians set the city on fire; Napoleon decides to retreat and his army is destroyed on the way back ~ An earthquake destroys Caracas; US sends international aid for the first time ~ William Jones publishes *The Scourge: or Monthly Expositor of Imposture and Folly*; one of its frontispieces is George Cruikshank's "The Prince of Whales or the Fisherman at Anchor" ~ Leigh Hunt attacks the Regent in *The Examiner* ("The Prince on St Patrick's Day"); he and his brother John (editor of *The Examiner*) are fined £500 and sentenced to 2 years in prison.

LITERATURE & THE ARTS

At the Royal Academy, Turner exhibits *Snow Storm: Hannibal and his Army Crossing the Alps* ~ Jacques-Louis David's portrait *The Emperor Napoleon in His Study at the Tuileries* is first shown at Hamilton Palace ~ *The Charging Chasseur* by Théodore Géricault is exhibited at the Paris Salon ~ In Berlin, the Brothers Grimm begin publication (-1857) of the fairy tales (first English translation in 1823-1826) ~ In Zurich, Johann David Wyss publishes *The Swiss Family Robinson* (first English translation in 1816) ~ Hazlitt delivers lectures on philosophy at the Russell Institution; he begins working for *The Morning Chronicle* (first as parliamentary reporter, then as theatre critic) ~ Pierce Egan publishes *Boxiana*, his collection of sports articles ~ The Drury Lane theatre (destroyed by fire in 1809) reopens with a production of *Hamlet* preceded by Byron's "Address, Spoken at the Opening of Drury-lane Theatre;" James and Horace Smith publish the book of parodies *Rejected Addresses*, imagining other poets' submissions for an opening address ~ Coleridge's play *Remorse* (a reworking of the 1797 *Osorio*) is finally performed (successfully) at Drury Lane ~ Walter Savage Landor publishes his play *Count Julian* ~ John Nichols publishes the first 4 out of 9 volumes of *Literary Anecdotes of the Eighteenth Century* (-1815) ~ Coleridge lectures on European Drama at Willis's Rooms and on the Belles Lettres at the Surrey Institution; parts of his lectures are used by Southey in a collaborative book of essays, *Omniana; or, Horae otiosiores*, published in November ~ Byron publishes the first two cantos of *Childe Harold's Pilgrimage* ~ Samuel Rogers publishes *Poems* ~ George Crabbe publishes *Tales in Verse* ~ A.L. Barbauld publishes *Eighteen Hundred and Eleven, a Poem* ~ T.L. Peacock publishes *The Philosophy of Melancholy: A Poem in Four Parts* ~ Felicia Hemans publishes *The Domestic Affections and Other Poems* ~ Amelia Opie publishes *Temper, or Domestic Scenes; A Tale* ~ Maria Edgeworth publishes *The Absentee* (vol. 5-6 of *Tales of Fashionable Life*) ~ Jane West publishes *The Loyalists.*

SHORT STORIES AND SHORT STORY COLLECTIONS
James Hogg. "The History of Rose Selby." *The Scots Magazine* 74: 3 (March 1812), 179-183. Signed "by the Ettrick Shepherd."

1813
BRITAIN AND THE WORLD
Wellington wins the Battle of Vitoria against the French, effectively ending the Peninsular War; Napoleon relinquishes the crown of Spain back to Ferdinand VII ~ As the Russian army advances, French troops evacuate Berlin; the War of the Sixth Coalition begins with Russia and Prussia allied against France ~ Napoleon defeats the allies at Lutzen and Bautzen; after Austria joins the coalition, France suffers several defeats, culminating in the Battle of Leipzig ~ The Confederation of the Rhine is dissolved; Dutch independence; the Low Countries become a monarchy ~ Peace treaty between Russian and Persia; Russia gains Georgia, Dagestan, and Azerbaijan ~ Simon Bolivar defeats the Spanish and proclaims the Second Republic in Venezuela ~ James Madison begins his second terms as US president ~ Swiss explorer Johann Ludwig Burckhardt, who had discovered Petra the previous year, finds the Great Temple of Ramesses II ~ Robert Owen publishes *A New View of Society* ~ Southey publishes *The Life of Nelson* ~ John Hobhouse publishes *Journey through Albania.*

LITERATURE & THE ARTS
In Venice, the first performances of the operas *Tancredi* and *L'Italiana in Algeri* bring fame to the young Italian composer Gioachino Rossini ~ Beethoven's *Symphony No 7* is premiered in Vienna ~ Madame de Staël's *De l'Allemagne* (ready for print in 1810 but with all copies confiscated by Napoleon's censors) as well as the English translation *Of Germany* are both published in London ~ James Northcote publishes *The Life of Sir Joshua Reynolds* (2 vols.) ~ Walter Scott declines laureateship, which is accepted by Southey ~ Coleridge's tragedy *Remorse* (a reworking of *Osorio*, rejected in 1797) is successfully produced at the Drury Lane (20 nights) and also published later the same year ~ Walter Scott publishes *Rokeby; A Poem* and *The Bridal of Triermain* (in 3 cantos) ~ Byron publishes *The Giaour* and *The Bride of Abydos* ~ Shelley publishes *Queen Mab; A Philosophical Poem: with Notes* ~ James Hogg publishes *The Queen's Wake: A Legendary Poem* ~ Thomas Moore publishes the volume of satirical verse *Intercepted Letters; or, The Twopenny Post-Bag* ~ Thomas Love Peacock publishes *Sir Hornbook; or, Childe Launcelot's Expedition: A Grammatico-Allegorical Ballad* (dated 1814) ~ Mary Russell Mitford publishes in New York a series of *Narrative Poems on the Female Character* ~ Publication of *Tales of the Dead*, translated by Sarah Elizabeth Utterson from German

The Romantic Era

authors via a French intermediary (the 1812 collection *Fantasmagoriana*) ~ Jane Austen publishes *Pride and Prejudice* ~ Amelia Opie publishes the 3 vols. of *Tales of Real Life* (2 novels and 2 novellas) ~ Maria Edgeworth's novel *The Ballad Singer* is published ~ Frances Holcroft publishes *The Wife and the Lover*.

SHORT STORIES AND SHORT STORY COLLECTIONS

Amelia Opie. *Tales of Real Life*. 3 vols. London: Longman, Hurst, Rees, Orme, and Brown, 1813.

[Sarah Elizabeth Utterson]. "The Storm." *Tales of the Dead. Principally Translated from the French*. London: White, Cochrane, and co., 1813. 178-192.

1814
BRITAIN AND THE WORLD

First permanent gas lighting on the streets of London ~ Anglo-Dutch treaty: Britain retains the Cape Colony and what will become British Guiana, but returns other Dutch possessions ~ Treaty of Kiel: Denmark loses Norway, which is forced into a union with Sweden ~ While Wellington advances north of the Pyrenees, Russian and Prussian armies enter France and, after several engagements, occupy Paris; Napoleon abdicates and sent into exile on the Isle of Elba; Louis XVIII becomes King of France ~ The French are also pushed out of Italy ~ The Congress of Vienna begins ~ British troops win the Battle of Bladensburg, occupy Washington and set important buildings on fire; another British expeditionary force is defeated in the Battle of Plattsburgh and retreats into Canada; a turning point is the failure by the British to capture Baltimore; the two sides sign the peace treaty restoring status quo ante ~ Beginning of the Anglo-Nepalese War (-1816).

LITERATURE & THE ARTS

In Madrid, Goya paints *The Third of May 1808* ~ The Elephant of the Bastille is installed in Paris (-1846) ~ In Vienna, Beethoven's *Symphony No 8* is premiered ~ In Germany, E.T.A. Hoffmann publishes *Fantasy-Pieces in the Manner of Callot* (3 vols.), including the novella "The Golden Pot" (a 4th vol. in 1815); Theodor Körner's last poems appear posthumously as *Leyer und Schwerdt*; and Adelbert von Chamisso publishes the novella *Peter Schlemihl* ~ In the United States, Francis Scott Key writes and publishes "The Defense of Fort M'Henry" ~ Edmund Kean delivers his first performances on the stage of the Drury Lane theatre ~ *The New Monthly Magazine* (-1884) begins publication ~ Coleridge publishes "On the Principles of Genial Criticism" in *Felix Farley's Bristol Journal* ~ Byron publishes *The Corsair* ~ Byron's *Lara* and Samuel Rogers's *Jacqueline* are published anonymously in a single volume ~ Coleridge publishes *The Feast of the Poets, with Notes, and Other Pieces in Verse* ~ Wordsworth publishes *The Excursion: Being a Portion of The Recluse, a Poem* ~ Peacock publishes *Sir Proteus. A Satirical Ballad* ~ Southey publishes the epic poem *Roderick, the Last of the Goths* ~ Jane Austen publishes *Mansfield Park* ~ Maria Edgeworth's novel *Patronage* is published ~ Fanny Burney publishes her fourth and last novel, *The Wanderer: or, Female Difficulties* ~ Mary Brunton publishes *Discipline* ~ Jane West publishes *Alicia de Lacy; an Historical Romance* ~ Sydney Owenson (Lady Morgan) publishes *O'Donnel: A National Tale* ~ Walter Scott publishes his first novel, *Waverley; or, 'Tis Sixty Years Since* ~ A huge bestseller in the English-speaking world is the Christian missionary tale *The History of Little Henry and His Bearer* by Mary Sherwood.

SHORT STORIES AND SHORT STORY COLLECTIONS
Mary Leadbeater and Elizabeth Carleton Shackleton. *Tales for Cottagers*. Dublin, James Cumming, 1814.
Regina Maria Roche. *London Tales; or, Reflective Portraits*. 2 vols. London: John Booth, 1814.

1815
BRITAIN AND THE WORLD
The first Corn Law is passed, preventing the importation of cheap grains ~ Napoleon escapes from his exile and begins the Hundred Days Campaign of 100 days, which ends on the battlefield of Waterloo, where he is defeated by an Anglo-Prussian army led by Wellington and Blücher ~ Napoleon is transferred to the island of Saint Helena; Louis XVIII is restored again to the throne of France (-1824) ~ The Congress of Vienna ends; the German Confederation is created (with Frankfurt as capital); Congress Poland is formed in personal union with the Russian Empire ~ The Netherlands becomes officially a kingdom (it includes present-day Belgium) ~ The Ionian Islands become a British protectorate ~ Austria regains control of much of Italy; beginning of Risorgimento ~ Andrew Jackson defeats the British in the Battle of New Orleans (both sides unaware of the peace treaty that had ended the War of 1812) ~ George Stephenson gives the first ever locomotive (designed in 1814) the name of "Blücher" (he will name a second one "Wellington" in 1816) ~ Mount Tambora erupts in Indonesia ~ Helen Maria Williams publishes *A Narrative of the Events which Have Taken Place in France* ~ The first volume of Alexander Humboldt's *Personal Narrative of Travels to the Equinoctial Regions of the New Continent* (written in French with Aimé Bonpland) is published in Paris (12 vols. until 1831); the English translation by Helen Maria Williams appears the same year and continues simultaneously.

LITERATURE & THE ARTS
In Germany, E.T.A. Hoffmann publishes the first volume of his novel *The Devil's Elixirs* (2nd vol. in 1816) ~ The *North American Review*, the first literary magazine in the US, is founded in Boston as a bimonthly (a quarterly after 1820) ~ In France, Béranger is instantly famous after his first volume of poetry, *Chansons morales et autres* (dated 1816) ~ The Arzamas literary society is founded in Saint Petersburg (-1818) ~ Leigh Hunt is released from prison and publishes *The Descent of Liberty, a Mask* ~ James Sheridan Knowles's successful tragedy *Caius Gracchus*

The Romantic Era

premieres in Belfast (in London in 1823) ~ Wordsworth publishes *Poems by William Wordsworth* (in 2 vols., with new poems and a new preface) as well as *The White Doe of Rylstone* (in 7 cantos) ~ Byron publishes *Hebrew Melodies* (both as a book of poetry and as a book of lyrics set to Jewish tunes collected by Isaac Nathan) ~ Southey publishes *Minor Poems* ~ William Drennan collects his poems and essays in *Fugitive Pieces, in Verse and Prose* ~ Walter Scott publishes *The Lord of the Isles*, in 6 cantos, *The Field of Waterloo; A Poem*, as well as the novel *Guy Mannering; or, The Astrologer* ~ Jane Austen publishes *Emma* (dated 1816) ~ Thomas Love Peacock's novella *Headlong Hall* appears anonymously (dated 1816) ~ Christian Isobel Johnstone publishes *Clan-Albin: A National Tale* (4 vols.) anonymously.

SHORT STORIES AND SHORT STORY COLLECTIONS

Lucy Peacock. "Emma Seaforth; or, The Talent Applied." *Friendly Labours, or, Tales and Dramas for the Amusement and Instruction of Youth*. 2 vols. Brentford: P. Norbury, 1815. I, 92-139. [Written in the 1780s, but never before published.]

1816
BRITAIN AND THE WORLD

The Year without a Summer caused by the Tambora eruption ~ Spa Fields riots; followers of deceased revolutionary Thomas Spence are quelled are arrested ~ Giovanni Belzoni removes the Ancient Egyptian statue of "Younger Memnon" on behalf of the British (it will arrive in England in 1818 and it will prompt Shelley to write "Ozymandias") ~ The Kingdom of the Two Sicilies is formed ~ Austria creates the Kingdom of Illyria (based on Napoleon's Illyrian Provinces) as its own crown land ~ Argentina and the United Provinces of South America declare independence ~ The French frigate *Medusa* is wrecked on the coast of Senegal ~ The last journey of James Kingston Tuckey (he dies in the Congo) sparks interest for the "scientific exploration" of Africa ~ Cobbett begins publishing a two-penny version of the *Political Register* ~ Nikolay Karamzin begins the publication of *The History of the Russian State* (-1826) ~ Coleridge publishes *The Statesman's Manual*.

LITERATURE & THE ARTS

Percy and Mary Shelley travel to France, then Switzerland, where they meet Byron and Polidori ~ In Spain, Goya publishes a series of prints known as *La Tauromaquia* ~ In Essex, John Constable paints *Wivenhoe Park* ~ First performance of Rossini's opera *Il barbiere di Siviglia*, in Rome ~ Benjamin Constant's novel *Adolphe* is published first in London, then in Paris (with an English translation the same year) ~ In Germany, E.T.A. Hoffmann publishes *The Night Pieces*, a volume of short stories including "The Sandman" (a second volume in 1817); his short story "The Nutcracker and the Mouse King" appears in a collection published in Berlin ~ In Mexico, José Joaquín Fernández de Lizardi publishes the first volume of *The Mangy Parrot* (-1831), the first Latin American novel ~ Leigh Hunt publishes "Young Poets" in *The Examiner* ~ Wordsworth publishes *Letter to a Friend of Robert Burns* ~ Walter Scott publishes *Paul's Letters to His Kinsfolk* (travel impressions through France and Belgium, in the wake of Waterloo) ~ Thomas Holcroft's unfinished *Memoirs* are completed and published by William Hazlitt ~ Charles Robert Maturin's play *Bertram; or, The Castle of St Aldobrand* opens at Drury Lane ~ William Charles Macready makes his debut on a London stage ~ This year, Byron publishes first a volume containing 2 narrative poems: *The Siege of Corinth* and *Parisina*; then, the third canto of *Childe Harold's Pilgrimage*; finally, *The Prisoner of Chillon and Other Poems* ~ Coleridge publishes *Christabel; Kubla Khan, a Vision; The Pains of Sleep* ~ Shelley publishes *Alastor; or, The Spirit of Solitude: and Other Poems* ~ John Keats publishes "On First Looking into Chapman's Homer" in *The Examiner* of 1 December ~ Southey publishes *The Poet's Pilgrimage to Waterloo* ~ Leigh Hunt publishes *The Story of Rimini, a Poem* ~ Felicia Hemans (as "A Lady") publishes *The Restoration of the Works of Art to Italy: A Poem* ~ J.H. Reynolds publishes *The Naiad: a Tale, with Other Poems* ~ Walter Scott publishes *The Antiquary* and the first four volumes of the series "Tales of My Landlord," containing *The Black Dwarf* and *The Tale of Old Mortality* ~ Amelia Opie publishes *Valentine's Eve* ~ Lady Caroline Lamb publishes her first novel, *Glenarvon*.

SHORT STORIES AND SHORT STORY COLLECTIONS
Walter Scott. "The Fortunes of Martin Waldeck." *The Antiquary*. 3 vols. Edinburgh: Archibald Constable; London: Longman, Hurst, Rees, Orme, and Brown, 1816. II, 58-84.
Jane Taylor. "Lucy's Wishes." *The Youth's Magazine: or, Evangelical Miscellany* (November 1816), 368-374.

1817
BRITAIN AND THE WORLD
Habeas corpus suspended for a year (March 1817-March 1818) for fear of insurrection ~ The Blanketeers' March, protesting the suspension, is violently dispersed ~ Third Anglo-Maratha War begins (-1819) ~ James Monroe is sworn in as the fifth US president ~ P.B. Shelley publishes *A Proposal for Putting Reform to Vote throughout the Kingdom* (anonymously) and *An Address to the People on the Death of the Princess Charlotte* (signed "The Hermit of Marlow") ~ Coleridge publishes *A Lay Sermon, Addressed to the Higher and Middle Classes, on the Existing Distresses and Discontents* ~ Sir Thomas Stamford Raffles publishes *The History of Java* ~ James Mill publishes *The History of British India* ~ Sydney Owenson (now Lady Morgan) publishes *France* ~ David Ricardo publishes *On the Principles of Political Economy and Taxation* ~ Hegel publishes the first edition of the *Encyclopaedia of the Philosophical Sciences* ~ The Lyceum, the Drury Lane and the Covent Garden introduce gas lighting on stage.

LITERATURE & THE ARTS
In Rome, Antonio Canova completes *The Three Graces* ~ In France, Stendhal publishes *Histoire de la Peinture en Italie* as well as *Rome, Naples et Florence en 1817* ~ In Austria, Franz Grillparzer registers his first success

The Romantic Era

with the tragedy *The Ancestress* ~ William Hone is acquitted in three separate trials, having been accused of blasphemous and seditious libel ~ *Blackwood's Edinburgh Magazine* founded (-1980) ~ *The Literary Gazette*, edited by William Jerdan, begins publication (-1862) ~ The radical satirical journal *The Black Dwarf* is founded (-1824) ~ Mary Shelley publishes *History of a Six Weeks' Tour through a Part of France, Switzerland, Germany and Holland* (anonymously) ~ *The Round Table: a Collection of Essays on Literature, Men, and Manners*, co-authored by Hazlitt (40 essays) and Leigh Hunt (12) is published in 2 vols. ~ Hazlitt publishes *Characters of Shakespear's Plays* ~ Nathan Drake publishes *Shakespeare and His Times* ~ The first instalment of "On the Cockney School of Poetry" (mostly by John Gibson Lockhart) appears in *Blackwood's*, attacking Leigh Hunt (7 more will appear until 1825, targeting Hunt, Keats, Hazlitt, and others) ~ Coleridge publishes *Biographia Literaria; or Biographical Sketches of My Literary Life* and *Sibylline Leaves: A Collection of Poems* ~ An unauthorised edition of Southey's dramatic poem *Wat Tyler* (written in 1794, at the height of his Jacobin youth) causes embarrassment to the author, who is now Poet Laureate (since 1813) ~ Coleridge's last play, *Zapolya*, is published ~ Byron publishes *Manfred, a Dramatic Poem* and *The Lament of Tasso* ~ John Hookham Frere publishes the first two parts of mock-heroic poem *Prospectus and Specimen of an Intended National Work* (-1818; subsequently known as *The Monks and the Giants*) ~ John Keats publishes *Poems* (reviewed by Leigh Hunt in two instalments in *The Examiner*) ~ P.B. Shelley publishes "Hymn to Intellectual Beauty" in *The Examiner* and *Laon and Cythna: or, The Revolution of the Golden City* (revised after complaints from readers and republished in 1818 as *The Revolt of Islam; a Poem*) ~ Thomas Moore publishes the poem *Lalla-Rookh: An Oriental Romance* ~ Felicia Hemans publishes *Modern Greece, A Poem* (anonymously) ~ Peacock publishes the satirical novel *Melincourt* ~ Maria Edgeworth publishes *Harrington, a Tale; and Ormond, a Tale* (3 vols.) ~ William Godwin publishes *Mandeville, a Tale of the Seventeenth Century in England* ~ Jane Austen's *Northanger Abbey; and Persuasion* (4 vols.) appear posthumously (dated 1818) ~ Frances Holcroft publishes *Fortitude and Frailty* ~ Walter Scott publishes *Rob Roy* (dated 1818).

SHORT STORIES AND SHORT STORY COLLECTIONS
James Hogg. "Tales and Anecdotes of the Pastoral Life." *Blackwood's Magazine* 1: 1 (April 1817), 22-25; 1:2 (May 1817), 143-147; 1:3 (June 1817), 247-250. Reprinted as chapters III-V of "The Shepherd's Calendar" in *Winter Evening Tales* II, 180-204.

Walter Scott. "[Aspirations of Christopher Corduroy]." *The Sale-Room* 1: 6 (8 February 1817), 43-45.

Walter Scott. "Alarming Increase of Depravity among Animals." *Blackwood's* 2: 7 (October 1817), 82-86.

1818
BRITAIN AND THE WORLD
Defeat of the Marathas by the British East India Company ~ Beginning of the Fifth Xhosa War in South Africa (-1819) ~ John Ross undertakes

his first journey in search of the Northwest Passage ~ Russian sailor Otto von Kotzebue returns from his first circumnavigation journey, which included the exploration of the Northwest Passage (Chamisso also travelled as the ship's botanist) ~ Congress of Aix-la-Chapelle; foreign troops withdraw from France; France becomes a member of the Holy Alliance ~ Former French Marshal Bernadotte becomes King of Sweden ~ Silvio Pellico and Giovani Berchet found the influential Milanese weekly *Il Conciliatore* (suppressed by the Austrians in 1819) ~ Chile proclaims its independence, which is ensured through the victory of Maipú ~ The Prado Museum is inaugurated in Madrid ~ Henry Hallam publishes *A View of the State of Europe during the Middle Ages*.

LITERATURE & THE ARTS

In Germany, Caspar David Friedrich produces one the best-known Romantic paintings, *Wanderer above the Sea of Fog* ~ In Heidelberg, Hegel delivers his *Lectures on Aesthetics* (transcripts were first published in 1835) ~ In Leipzig, Arthur Schopenhauer publishes *The World as Will and Representation* (dated 1819) ~ In Vienna, premiere of Grillparzer's tragedy *Sappho* (English translation 1820; Byron read it in Italian and thought it "superb and sublime") ~ The Countess of Blessington begins holding her first London salon (-1822) ~ Cobbett publishes *A Year's Residence in the United States of America* ~ Coleridge publishes "Treatise on Method" in *Encyclopaedia Metropolitana* and a 3-volume edition of *The Friend* ~ Hazlitt lectures on English poets at the Surrey Institution; then publishes both *Lectures on the English Poets* and *A View of the English Stage; or, A Series of Dramatic Criticisms* ~ First performance (10 nights) of Coleridge's play *Zapolya: A Christmas Tale* at the Surrey Theatre ~ H.H. Milman's tragedy *Fazio* is first performed at the Covent Garden ~ John Howard Payne's tragedy *Brutus; or, The Fall of Tarquin* is performed at the Drury Lane ~ Byron publishes the fourth canto of *Childe Harold's Pilgrimage* and the poem *Beppo: A Venetian Story* ~ John Keats publishes *Endymion: A Poetic Romance* (viciously criticised by John Wilson Croker in *The Quarterly Review* of April) ~ P.B. Shelley publishes "Ozymandias" in *The Examiner* (signed "Glirastes") ~ Felicia Hemans publishes *Translations from Camoens, and Other Poets, with Original Poetry* ~ Leigh Hunt publishes *Foliage; or, Poems Original and Translated* ~ Thomas Moore publishes the verse novel *The Fudge Family in Paris* ~ Peacock publishes *Rhododaphne; or, Thessalian Spell, a Poem* (7 cantos) and the short novel *Nightmare Abbey* (a Gothic parody) ~ Walter Scott publishes *The Heart of Midlothian* (as the "second series" of "Tales of My Landlord") ~ Mary Shelley publishes *Frankenstein; or, The Modern Prometheus* (anonymously) ~ Charles Robert Maturin publishes *Women; or, Pour et Contre. A Tale* (in three volumes) ~ Susan Ferrier publishes *Marriage, A Novel* ~ Sydney Owenson, Lady Morgan, publishes *Florence Macarthy: an Irish Tale*.

SHORT STORIES AND SHORT STORY COLLECTIONS

John Gamble. *Northern Irish Tales*. 2 vols. London: Longman, Hurst, Rees, Orme, and Brown, 1818.

James Hogg. *The Brownie of Bodsbeck; and Other Tales*. 2 vols. Edinburgh: William Blackwood; London: John Murray, 1818.

The Romantic Era

Amelia Opie. *New Tales.* 4 vols. London: Longman, Hurst, Rees, Orme, and Brown, 1818.

Anne and Annabella Plumptre. *Tales of Wonder, of Humour, and of Sentiment; Original and Translated.* 3 vols. London: Henry Colburn, 1818.

Daniel Keyte Sandford. "A Night in the Catacombs." *Blackwood's Magazine* 4:19 (October 1818), 19-23.

1819
BRITAIN AND THE WORLD

Peterloo Massacre in Manchester: cavalry charges into a crowd demanding parliamentary reform ~ The Six Acts follow; one of them, the Newspaper Act, raises the duties of stamps, running many papers out of business ~ The end of the third Anglo-Maratha War leaves the British East India Company in control of most of India ~ William Edward Parry leads the most successful journey through the Northwest Passage before being blocked by ice ~ German playwright August von Kotzebue is assassinated; in response, Metternich passes the reactionary Carlsbad Decrees ~Antisemitic Hep-Hep riots in Germany ~ Gran Colombia becomes independent after Bolivar's victory in the Battle of Boyacá (the new country includes present-day Colombia, Ecuador, Panama, and Venezuela) ~ Stamford Raffles founds the city of Singapore ~ First financial crisis in the US, known as the Panic of 1819 ~ Spain officially cedes Florida to the US ~ Establishment of the *Monumenta Germaniae Historica* ~ Hone publishes *The Political House that Jack Built* ~ Richard Carlisle is sent to prison for publishing Paine's *Age of Reason* and anti-government articles in his newspaper *The Republican* ~ Hazlitt publishes *Political Essays, with Sketches of Characters*.

LITERATURE & THE ARTS

Géricault's *The Raft of the Medusa* is on display at the Paris Salon (it comes to London in June 1820) ~ Ingres's *Grande Odalisque* (painted in 1814) is first shown at the Paris Salon ~ At Steyr, in Austria, Franz Schubert's *Piano Quintet* known as the "Trout" is played for the first time ~ In France, Marceline Desbordes-Valmore publishes her first volume of poetry, *Elégies, Marie et romances* ~ In Germany, E.T.A. Hoffmann publishes the first volume of *The Life and Opinions of the Tomcat Murr* (second vol. in 1821) as well as the novella *Mademoiselle de Scuderi* ~ In the United States, Washington Irving publishes the first 4 (out of 7) instalments of *The Sketch Book of Geoffrey Crayon, Gent.* (-1820); a British edition in 2 vols. appears in 1820 (two different publishers) and it includes new pieces ~ *The Literary Chronicle and Weekly Review* begins publication (-1829, when it merges with *The Athenaeum*) ~ Thomas Campbell publishes his 7-volume anthology of *Specimens of the British Poets; with Biographical and Critical Notices*; William Lisle Bowles replies to some of his statements with *The Invariable Principles of Poetry* (to which Byron will react in 1821) ~ Hazlitt answers reviews of his work in *The Quarterly Review* by publishing *A Letter to William Gifford, Esq.*; he also publishes *Lectures on the English Comic Writers* ~ Leigh Hunt begins editing *The Indicator* (-1821) ~ P.B. Shelley publishes *Rosalind and Helen: A Modern Eclogue; with Other Poems* ~ Byron publishes *Mazeppa, a Poem* and the first two cantos of *Don Juan* (anonymously); a 10-volume French translation (in prose) of his complete works begins publication in Paris (-1821) ~ Samuel Rogers publishes *Human Life: a Poem* ~ Wordsworth publishes *Peter Bell. A Tale in Verse* and *The Waggoner: a Poem. To which are added, Sonnets* ~ Felicia Hemans publishes *Tales, and Historic Scenes, in Verse* ~ George Crabbe publishes *Tales of the Hall* (2 vols.), a composite narrative in verse ~ Barry Cornwall (Bryan Procter) publishes *Dramatic Scenes and Other Poems* ~ Walter Scott publishes the third series of "Tales of My Landlord" (*The Bride of Lammermoor* and *A Legend of Montrose*) and *Ivanhoe; a Romance* (dated 1820) ~ Mary Brunton's *Emmeline. With Some Other Pieces* appears posthumously ~ John Polidori publishes *Ernestus Berchtold; or, The Modern Oedipus. A Tale* ~ Thomas Hope publishes the three volumes of *Anastasius: or, Memoirs of a Greek*.

SHORT STORIES AND SHORT STORY COLLECTIONS
Leigh Hunt. "The Beau Miser, and What Happened to Him at Brighton." *The Indicator* 4 (Wednesday 3 November 1819), 25-31.

Leigh Hunt. "A Tale for a Chimney Corner." *The Indicator* 10 (Wednesday 15 December 1819), 73-79.

John Polidori. "The Vampyre." *The New Monthly Magazine* 11:63 (1 April 1819), 195-206. Reprinted in volume: *The Vampyre; A Tale* (London: Sherwood, Neely, and Jones, 1819).

Anna Jane Vardill. "Sir Christopher Hatton in London." *The European Magazine* 76 (July 1819), 9-13.

1820
BRITAIN AND THE WORLD
George IV (Prince Regent since 1811) becomes king on the death of George III ~ The Cato Street Conspiracy to kill all cabinet members is discovered ~ Week of strikes and unrest in Scotland (the Radical War); leaders are executed or transported ~ Liberal revolution in Spain forces Ferdinand VII to accept the Constitution of 1812 ~ Liberal revolution in Portugal ~ Carbonari insurrection in Naples ~ First large group of British settlers in South Africa (known today as the 1820 Settlers) ~ Antarctica is first sighted by British sailor Edward Bransfield ~ Venus de Milo is discovered by a Greek peasant ~ James Mill publishes the essay "Government" in the supplement to *Encyclopaedia Britannica* ~ William Godwin publishes *Of Population*, a very late answer to Malthus ~ Malthus publishes *Principles of Political Economy*.

LITERATURE & THE ARTS
In France, Lamartine publishes *Méditations poétiques* ~ In Saint Petersburg, Alexander Pushkin publishes his epic poem, *Ruslan and Ludmila* ~ *The London Magazine*, edited by John Scott, begins publication (-1829) ~ Hazlitt publishes *Lectures on the Dramatic Literature of the Age of Elizabeth* (they were given in Nov-Dec 1819 at the Surrey Institution)

The Romantic Era

~ Peacock publishes the essay "The Four Ages of Poetry" in *Olliers Literary Miscellany* (P.B. Shelley answers with the essay "A Defence of Poetry," written in 1821 but published posthumously in 1840) ~ Charles Lamb publishes the first Elia essay in *The London Magazine* of August ~ Dorothy Wordsworth writes a "Journal of a Tour on the Continent" (first published in 1897) ~ James Sheridan Knowles's *Virginius* is first performed at the Covent Garden ~ P.B. Shelley publishes *The Cenci: A Tragedy in Five Acts* (dated 1819), which had also appeared anonymously in 1819 in Livorno, Italy; and *Prometheus Unbound: a Lyrical Drama in Four Acts, with Other Poems* (including "Ode to the West Wind," "Ode to Liberty" and "To a Skylark") ~ John Keats publishes *Lamia, Isabella, The Eve of St Agnes, and Other Poems* (including "Ode to a Nightingale" and "Ode on a Grecian Urn") as well as "La Belle Dame Sans Merci" in *The Indicator* of 10 May ~ Wordsworth publishes *The River Duddon, A Series of Sonnets*, and *Miscellaneous Poems* in 4 volumes ~ Felicia Hemans publishes *The Sceptic. A Poem* ~ John Clare publishes *Poems Descriptive of Rural Life and Scenery* ~ Charles Robert Maturin publishes *Melmoth the Wanderer* ~ Walter Scott publishes *The Monastery. A Romance* and *The Abbot* (both 3-volume novels) ~ John Galt serialises *The Ayrshire Legatees* in *Blackwood's* (June 1820-February 1821); the novel appears in 3 vols. in 1821.

SHORT STORIES AND SHORT STORY COLLECTIONS
James Hogg. *Winter Evening Tales, Collected among the Cottagers in the South of Scotland*. 2 vols. Edinburgh: Oliver & Boyd, 1820.
Leigh Hunt. "The Fair Revenge." *The Indicator* 14 (Wednesday 12 January 1820), 109-112.
Amelia Opie. *Tales of the Heart*. 4 vols. London: Longman, Hurst, Rees, Orme, and Brown, 1820.

1821
BRITAIN AND THE WORLD
A new census shows the population of Britain had reached 14.4 million; first census in Ireland reveals a population of 6.8 million ~ Death of Queen Caroline, the estranged wife of George IV ~ The Greek War of Independence begins ~ Mexican independence ~ The Austrian army crushes the Carbonari revolts ~ Belzoni, Egyptian Hall ~ James Monroe begins his second term as US President ~ Peruvian declaration of independence ~ The Treaty of Cordoba establishes Mexican independence ~ The Act of Independence of Central America is enacted in Guatemala ~ Napoleon dies on Saint Helena ~ Frances Wright publishes *Views of Society and Manners in America* ~ Sydney Owenson (Lady Morgan) publishes *Italy* simultaneously in Britain and France ~ *The Manchester Guardian* begins publication ~ Wilhelm von Humboldt reads his essay "On the Historian's Task" at the Prussian Academy.

LITERATURE & THE ARTS
John Constable's *The Hay Wain* is exhibited at the Royal Academy ~ In Germany, Carl Maria von Weber's opera *Der Freischütz* is first performed

~ Goethe publishes the first version of *Wilhelm Meister's Journeyman Years* (the second version in 1829) ~ Publication of an English translation of *Faustus: From the German of Goethe*, probably by Coleridge ~ In Vienna, first performance of Heinrich von Kleist's posthumous play *The Prince of Homburg* ~ In the United States, James Fenimore Cooper publishes his first successful novel, *The Spy: a Tale of the Neutral Ground* ~ John Scott (editor of the *London Magazine*) dies after a duel with Jonathan Christie (John Gibson Lockhart's literary agent) ~ William Hazlitt publishes *Table-Talk; or, Original Essays* (vol. 2 in 1822), collected from his contributions to *The London Magazine* ~ Thomas De Quincey's *Confessions of an English Opium-Eater* appears in *The London Magazine* of September and October (in volume form in 1822) ~ Byron publishes *Letter to *** [John Murray], on the Rev. W.L. Bowles' Strictures on the Life and Writings of Pope* ~ Byron also publishes *Marino Faliero, Doge of Venice. An Historical Tragedy* (an unauthorised version is performed at the Drury Lane); the composite volume *Sardanapalus, a Tragedy; The Two Foscari, a Tragedy; Cain, a Mystery*; as well as Cantos 3, 4, and 5 of *Don Juan* ~ Barry Cornwall's *Mirandola: a Tragedy* is staged at the Covent Garden ~ W.T. Moncrieff's *Tom and Jerry; or, Life in London* (at the Adelphi) is the most successful of several adaptations of Egan's book ~ P.B. Shelley publishes *Adonais. An Elegy on the Death of John Keats* (first in Pisa, then in *The Literary Chronicle* in London) ~ John Clare publishes *The Village Minstrel and Other Poems* ~ Joanna Baillie publishes *Metrical Legends of Exalted Character* ~ J.H. Reynolds publishes *The Garden of Florence and Other Poems* ~ Felicia Hemans publishes *Welsh Melodies* ~ Scott publishes the novels *Kenilworth; a Romance* and *The Pirate* (dated 1822) ~ John Galt publishes the novel *Annals of the Parish* ~ Pierce Egan publishes in instalments *Life in London*, a late example of "ramble fiction."

SHORT STORIES AND SHORT STORY COLLECTIONS
James Hogg. "Pictures of Country Life. No I-II. Old Isaac." *The Edinburgh Magazine* 9 (September & November 1821), 219-225, 443-452.

John Galt. "The Buried Alive." *Blackwood's* 10: 56 (October), 262-264.

John Howison. "The Floating Beacon." *Blackwood's* 10: 56 (October), 270-281.

William Maginn. "The Man in the Bell." *Blackwood's* 10: 57 (November), 373-375.

1822
BRITAIN AND THE WORLD
Lord Castlereagh, the Foreign Secretary, commits suicide; George Canning is appointed in his place ~ Martin's Act (named after Richard Martin) is passed to prevent the cruel treatment of cattle, horses, and sheep ~ The Royal Pavilion in Brighton is completed ~ The massacre by Turks of the inhabitants of Chios leads to increasing support for the Greek cause ~ Liberia is founded by freed slaves from the US ~ Brazil declares its independence from Portugal ~ Champollion deciphers Egyptian hieroglyphs.

The Romantic Era

LITERATURE & THE ARTS

Delacroix's *The Barque of Dante* is exhibited at the Paris Salon ~ In Berlin, Hegel begins delivering his *Lectures on the Philosophy of History* (-1830), first published in 1837 ~ In the United States and, simultaneously, in England, Irving's *Bracebridge Hall; or The Humourists, A Medley* is published ~ In Baltimore, John Neal publishes *Logan, a Family History* (anonymously) ~ In Italy, Manzoni publishes his tragedy *Adelchi* ~ In France, Charles Nodier publishes *Trilby; or, The Fairy of Argyll* ~ Victor Hugo publishes *Odes et poésies diverses* ~ In Vilnius, Adam Mickiewicz publishes the first volume of *Poems* (including "Ballads and Romances"); second volume in 1823 ~ William Maginn, James Hogg, John Wilson and J.G. Lockhart co-write the first part of the imaginary conversations titled "Noctes Ambrosianae" in *Blackwood's* for March (-1835) ~ De Quincey collects his *Confessions of an English Opium-Eater* (1821) in book form ~ Wordsworth publishes *A Description of the Scenery of the Lakes in the North of England* ~ Leigh Hunt edits the first issue of *The Liberal: Verse and Prose from the South* (-1823), containing Byron's *The Vision of Judgment* ~ Byron publishes *Werner, a Tragedy* ~ Thomas Love Beddoes publishes *The Brides' Tragedy* ~ Wordsworth publishes two volumes of poetry: *Memorials of a Tour on the Continent, 1820* and *Ecclesiastical Sketches* (later expanded and renamed *Ecclesiastical Sonnets*) ~ Samuel Rogers publishes *Italy, a Poem. Part the First* (rev. ed. in 1823; second part in 1828) ~ Thomas Moore publishes *The Loves of the Angels, a Poem* (revised in 1823 as *The Loves of the Angels, an Eastern Romance*) ~ Amelia Opie publishes the novel *Madeline, a Tale* (2 vols.) ~ Peacock publishes the short novel *Maid Marian* ~ Scott publishes *The Fortunes of Nigel*, a novel in 3 vols. ~ John Galt publishes the novels *The Provost* and *The Entail: or, The Lairds of Grippy* ~ Lady Caroline Lamb publishes the novel *Graham Hamilton*.

SHORT STORIES AND SHORT STORY COLLECTIONS

William Harrison Ainsworth. "The Imperishable One." [Signed: A.] *The European Magazine and London Review* Vol. 81 (June 1822): 510-515. Submitted as "The Wanderings of an Immortal" to *The Edinburgh Magazine*, which rejected it (February). It will appear with original title in *December Tales*.

Marguerite, Countess Blessington. *The Magic Lantern; or, Sketches of Scenes in the Metropolis*. London: Longman, Hurst, Rees, Orme, and Brown, 1822.

Marguerite, Countess Blessington. *Sketches and Fragments*. London: Longman, Hurst, Rees, Orme, and Brown, 1822.

Rebecca Edridge. *The Scrinium*. 2 vols. London: G.&W.B. Whittaker, 1822.

John Wilson. *Lights and Shadows of Scottish Life*. Edinburgh: William Blackwood; London: T. Cadell, 1822.

1823

BRITAIN AND THE WORLD

Home Secretary Robert Peel introduces the Judgement of Death Act, which makes the death penalty mandatory only for treason and murder; and the Gaols Act (inspired by the social work of Elizabeth Fry), which is the beginning of prison reform ~ In Ireland, Daniel O'Connell founds the Catholic Association ~ The King's Library is donated to the British Museum, for which expansion works begin ~ James Weddell's expedition to Antarctica reaches what is now known as the Weddell Sea ~ The first Anglo-Ashanti War begins in present-day Ghana (-1831) ~ French military intervention in Spain puts an end to the Three Liberal Years ~ Emperor Agustin I is deposed and the first Mexican Republic is proclaimed ~ Mary Anning finds a complete plesiosaur skeleton ~ US president James Monroe announces the Monroe Doctrine in a speech to Congress ~ Guizot, *Essay on the History of France* ~ John Malcolm, *A Memoir of Central India* ~ Emmanuel de Las Cases publishes *The Memorial of Saint Helena* (English translation the same year).

LITERATURE & THE ARTS

British government purchases 38 paintings (by Titian, Raphael, Rembrandt, Rubens, Velázquez, Van Dyck, Poussin, and Claude Lorrain) from the estate of John Julius Angerstein; they will form the basis of the future National Gallery ~ In the US, James Fenimore Cooper publishes *The Pioneers* ~ An anthology of German stories is published in London as *Popular Tales and Romances of the Northern Nations* (both the editor and the translators remain unidentified) ~ Charles Lamb collects and publishes the first series of *Elia* (later known as *Essays of Elia*) ~ Isaac D'Israeli publishes a second series of *Curiosities of Literature* ~ De Quincey publishes the essay "On the Knocking at the Gate in *Macbeth*" in *The London Magazine* ~ Mary Russell Mitford's *Julian: A Tragedy in Five Acts* is performed at the Covent Garden ~ Richard Brinsley Peake's *Presumption; or, the Fate of Frankenstein* is performed at the Lyceum ~ Byron publishes "Heaven and Earth, a Mystery" and "The Blues, A Literary Eclogue" in Leigh Hunt's *The Liberal*; the poem *The Age of Bronze; or Carmen Seculare et Annus Haud Mirabilis* (anonymously); *The Island, or Christian and His Comrades* (in 4 Cantos); as well as three volumes containing, respectively, Cantos 6-8, 9-11, and 12-14 of *Don Juan* ~ Letitia Elizabeth Landon publishes the series of poems "Medallion Wafers" in *The Literary Gazette* ~ Felicia Hemans publishes *The Siege of Valencia: A Dramatic Poem...with Other Poems* ~ Thomas Moore publishes *Fables for the Holy Alliance, Rhymes on the Road, &c. &c.* ~ Hazlitt publishes *Liber Amoris; or, the New Pygmalion*; and a short collection of *Characteristics, in the Manner of Rochefoucault's Maxims* ~ Walter Scott publishes the novels *Peveril of the Peak* (4 vols.), *Quentin Durward* (3 vols.) and *St Ronan's Well* (3 vols., dated 1824) ~ Mary Shelley publishes the novel *Valperga* and a corrected edition of *Frankenstein* ~ Lady Caroline Lamb publishes *Ada Reis, A Tale* ~ John Wilson publishes *The Trials of Margaret Lyndsay*.

SHORT STORIES AND SHORT STORY COLLECTIONS

William Harrison Ainsworth. *December Tales*. London: G. & W.B. Whittaker, 1823.

William Frederick Deacon. *The Inn-Keeper's Album*. London: Thomas McLean, 1823.

John Galt. "Sawney at Doncaster." *Blackwood's* 14: 8 (October), 468-470.

The Romantic Era

Mary Russell Mitford. "Cousin Mary." *The Lady's Magazine* IV (31 May), 237-240.
Amelia Opie. "A New Tale of Temper." *Friendship's Offering*. London: Lupton Relfe, 1824 [1823], 66-93.

1824
BRITAIN AND THE WORLD

The British attack Burma and take Rangoon; the war (-1826) marks the beginning of British rule in Burma ~ National Gallery opens after the purchase of John Julius Angerstein's collection ~ The Royal Society for the Prevention of Cruelty to Animals is founded ~ Louis XVIII dies and is followed by his brother Charles X as king of France ~ William Godwin publishes the first of the four volumes of his *History of the Commonwealth of England* (-1828) ~ Ranke publishes the *History of the Latin and Teutonic Peoples from 1494 to 1514*.

LITERATURE & THE ARTS

Delacroix's *The Massacre at Chios* is shown at the Paris Salon ~ Near Dresden, Caspar Friedrich completes *The Sea of Ice* ~ In Vienna, Beethoven's *Symphony No 9* is first performed ~ Schubert's lied series *Die schöne Müllerin* is published ~ Hazlitt publishes *Sketches of the Principal Picture Galleries in England* ~ In New York, Cooper publishes *The Pilot; Tale of the Sea* ~ Washington Irving's new collection, *Tales of a Traveller*, is published simultaneously in London and Philadelphia ~ First issue of *The Westminster Review* (-1914), founded by Jeremy Bentham ~ Walter Savage Landor publishes the first two volumes of his *Imaginary Conversations* (-1829) ~ Thomas Medwin publishes *Journal of the Conversations of Lord Byron* ~ Thomas Moore publishes *Memoirs of Captain Rock, the Celebrated Irish Chieftain*, a political satire about the history of Ireland ~ Byron publishes *The Deformed Transformed; a Drama*, and the last two Cantos (15-16) of *Don Juan*; three months after Byron's death, the editor John Murray and a few of the poet's friends decide to destroy the manuscript of Byron's memoirs ~ P.B. Shelley's *Posthumous Poems* (ed. Mary Shelley) are published ~ Letitia Elizabeth Landon publishes *The Improvisatrice and Other Poems* ~ James Hogg publishes *The Private Memoirs and Confessions of a Justified Sinner* ~ James Morier publishes *The Adventures of Hajji Baba, of Ispahan* (a sequel set in England appears in 1828) ~ Walter Scott publishes *Redgauntlet. A Tale of the Eighteenth Century* (3 vols.) ~ Susan Ferrier publishes the novel *The Inheritance* (3 vols.).

SHORT STORIES AND SHORT STORY COLLECTIONS

Theodore Hook. "Martha, the Gypsy." *Sayings and Doings. A Series of Sketches from Life*. 3 vols. London: Henry Colburn, 1824. III, 321-358.
Mary Russell Mitford. *Our Village*. London: G. and W. B. Whittaker, 1824.
Walter Scott. "Wandering Willie's Tale." *Redgauntlet. A Tale of the Eighteenth Century*. 3 vols. Edinburgh: Archibald Constable; London: Hurst, Robinson, and Co., 1824. I, 225-261.
Michael James Whitty. *Tales of Irish Life, Illustrative of the Manners, Customs, and Condition of the People. With Designs by George Cruikshank*. 2 vols. London: J. Robins and Co., 1824.

Chronology of Events

1825
BRITAIN AND THE WORLD

Stock market crash spreads from the Bank of England to twelve other banks (the Panic of 1825) ~ The Stockton and Darlington Railway (-1863) is the first public railway with steam locomotives ~ Harriette Wilson, a famous courtesan and one of Wellington's mistresses, publishes *The Memoirs of Harriette Wilson: Written by Herself* ~ Alexander I dies and his brother Nicholas I becomes emperor of Russia; his ascension causes the Decembrist revolt in Saint Petersburg, which is suppressed; many of its leaders are executed or departed to Siberia (they will be granted amnesty in 1856) ~ John Quincy Adams is sworn in as the sixth US president ~ Robert Owen begins experimenting with communal living in the US ~ Anna Wheeler and William Thompson publish the feminist manifesto *The Appeal of One Half the Human Race, Women* ~ Brillat-Savarin publishes *The Physiology of Taste*.

LITERATURE & THE ARTS

William Etty's *The Combat* is exhibited at the Royal Academy ~ Premiere, in Vienna, of Grillparzer's tragedy *The Fortune and Fall of King Ottokar* ~ In Saint Petersburg, Pushkin publishes the first part of his verse novel, *Eugene Onegin* (-1832) ~ In Sweden, Esaias Tegnér publishes the modern version of *Frithiof's Saga* ~ In Stuttgart, Wilhelm Hauff begins publishing his fairy tales in the annual *Märchen-Almanach* (-1827) ~ William Hazlitt publishes *The Spirit of the Age; or, Contemporary Portraits* ~ William Parry (assisted by Thomas Hodgskin) publishes *The Last Days of Lord Byron* ~ Thomas Moore publishes *Memoirs of the Life of the Right Honourable Richard Brinsley Sheridan* ~ Thomas Babington Macaulay's essay on "Milton" appears in the *Edinburgh Review* ~ Coleridge publishes *Aids to Reflection in the Formation of a Manly Character* ~ Thomas Crofton Croker publishes *Fairy Legends and Traditions of the South of Ireland* ~ Maria Jane Jewsbury publishes *Phantasmagoria; or, Sketches of Life and Literature* ~ John Poole's farce *Paul Pry* is a great success at the Haymarket Theatre ~ Felicia Hemans publishes *The Forest Sanctuary; and Other Poems* ~ Robert Southey publishes *A Tale of Paraguay* ~ Letitia Elizabeth Landon publishes *The Troubadour; Catalogue of Pictures, and Historical Sketches* (or *The Troubadour, and Other Poems*, as it appears on the half-title page) ~ Thomas Hood and J.H. Reynolds publish *Odes and Addresses to Great People* ~ Scott publishes the novels *The Betrothed* and *The Talisman* (as *Tales of the Crusaders*, in 4 vols.) ~ John Wilson's novel *The Foresters* is published ~ John and Michael Banim publishes *Tales by the O'Hara Family* (containing three novels).

SHORT STORIES AND SHORT STORY COLLECTIONS

Archibald Crawfurd. *Tales of My Grandmother.* 2 vols. Edinburgh:
    Archibald Constable and Co., 1825.
Thomas Crofton Croker. *Fairy Legends and Traditions of the South of Ireland.*
    London: John Murray, 1825.
Francis Barry Boyle St. Leger. "An Adventure among the Alps."
    Friendship's Offering. Ed. Thomas K. Hervey. London: Lupton Relfe,
    1826 [1825], 3-22.

The Romantic Era

1826
BRITAIN AND THE WORLD

University of London (later, University College London) is founded ~ Alexander Gordon Laing becomes the first European to cross the Sahara and to reach Timbuktu; he is killed soon afterwards ~ Maria II becomes queen of Portugal ~ Victory at Arachova keeps the Greek revolution alive ~ The Janissaries revolt against sultan Mahmud II, but are defeated; countless are executed, imprisoned or exiled; the corps is disbanded ~ The Akkerman Convention between Russia and Turkey recognises the autonomy of the Principality of Serbia ~ Beginning of the Russo-Persian War (-1828) ~ Dost Mohammad Khan becomes Emir of Afghanistan ~ Antonio Sucre becomes president of newly independent Bolivia.

LITERATURE & THE ARTS

Delacroix exhibits the first version of his Byron-inspired *The Combat of the Giaour and Hassan* ~ Nicéphore Niépce creates the first surviving photograph, *View from the Window at Le Gras* ~ Constable exhibits *The Cornfield* at the Royal Academy ~ William Blake's *Illustrations of the Book of Job* is published ~ In Italy, Paganini composes his *Violin Concerto No 2* ~ In the United States, James Fenimore Cooper publishes *The Last of the Mohicans; a Narrative of 1757* ~ In France, Alfred de Vigny publishes *Cinq-Mars* ~ In Stuttgart, Wilhelm Hauff publishes the historical novel *Lichtenstein* ~ In Berlin, Joseph von Eichendorff publishes *Memoirs of a Good-for-Nothing* ~ Robert Pearse Gillies publishes his translation of *German Stories* (3 vols.) ~ William Hazlitt publishes *The Plain Speaker: Opinions on Books, Men, and Things* (2 vols.) and *Notes of a Journey through France and Italy* (first serialised in *The Morning Chronicle*) ~ De Quincey begins his "Gallery of the German Prose Classics" in *Blackwood's* with a translation of Lessing's *Laokoon* ~ Anna Jameson publishes *Diary of an Ennuyée* (initially as *A Lady's Diary*) ~ John Baldwin Buskstone's first play *Luke the Labourer; or, The Lost Son* is a success at the Adelphi ~ Elizabeth Barrett publishes *An Essay on Mind with Other Poems* ~ Felicia Hemans publishes "Casabianca" in *The Monthly Magazine* ~ R.S. Hawker's poem "The Song of the Western Men" (also known as the Ballad of Trelawny) appears anonymously ~ Letitia Elizabeth Landon publishes *The Golden Violet with Its Tales of Romance and Chivalry: and Other Poems* (dated 1827) ~ Thomas Hood publishes *Whims and Oddities, in Prose and Verse* (a second series in 1827) ~ Mary Shelley publishes the novel *The Last Man* (3 vols.) ~ John Galt publishes the novella *The Omen* ~ Scott publishes *Woodstock; or The Cavalier. A Tale of the Year Sixteen Hundred and Fifty-One* (3 vols.) ~ John and Michael Banim publish *Tales by the O'Hara Family. Second Series* (containing two novels) ~ Thomas Henry Lister publishes *Granby* ~ Benjamin Disraeli publishes the first 2 volumes of *Vivian Grey* (3 more volumes in 1827).

SHORT STORIES AND SHORT STORY COLLECTIONS

Matthew Henry Barker. *Greenwich Hospital, A Series of Naval Sketches, Descriptive of the Life of a Man-of-War's Man*. London: James Robins and Co., 1826.

Chronology of Events

William Frederick Deacon. *November Nights; or, Tales for Winter Evenings.* London: Thomas MacLean, 1826.

Mary Russell Mitford. *Our Village: Sketches of Rural Character and Scenery.* Volume II. London: Geo. B. Whittaker, 1826.

Leitch Ritchie. *Head-Pieces and Tail-Pieces.* London: Charles Tilt, 1826.

1827
BRITAIN AND THE WORLD

Lord Liverpool resigns and George Canning becomes prime minister; Canning dies of tuberculosis and is succeeded by the Viscount Goderich (-1828) ~ In the Treaty of London, France, Britain, and Russia agree on an armistice between Turkey and Greece; the allied navies defeat a Turkish fleet in the Battle of Navarino ~ Nicéphore Niépce creates the first photograph ~ France breaks diplomatic relations with Algiers ~ Walter Scott begins publishing a *Life of Napoleon Buonaparte* in 9 vols. (-1828) ~ Henry Hallam publishes *The Constitutional History of England from the Accession of Henry VII to the Death of George II* ~ In Pest, Joseph von Hammer-Purgstall begins publication of his monumental *The History of the Ottoman Empire* (-1835).

LITERATURE & THE ARTS

John Simpson exhibits *The Captive Slave* at the Royal Academy ~ In Italy, Manzoni publishes the third and last volume of *The Betrothed* (dated 1826); the first two volumes had appeared in 1825 (the first, partial, English translation appears in 1828, in Pisa) ~ In France, Stendhal publishes *Armance*; Hugo, *Préface de Cromwell*; Nerval, his translation of Goethe's *Faust* (dated 1828) ~ In Hamburg, Heinrich Heine publishes *Buch der Lieder* ~ De Quincey's essay "On Murder Considered as One of the Fine Arts" appears in *Blackwood's* ~ Hazlitt's essay on "The Dandy School" appears in *The Examiner* ~ A new annual, *The Keepsake* begins publication (-1856) ~ John Clare publishes *The Shepherd's Calendar; with Village Stories, and Other Poems* ~ Wordsworth's *Poetical Works* appear in 5 vols. ~ Thomas Hood publishes *The Plea of the Midsummer Fairies... and Other Poems* ~ John Keble publishes the popular *The Christian Year; Thoughts in Verse for Sundays and Holy Days throughout the Year* ~ Catherine Gore publishes *The Lettre de Cachet; a Tale. The Reign of Terror; a Tale* ~ Thomas Moore publishes the historical novella *The Epicurean. A Tale* ~ Jane Webb (later, Loudon) publishes the science-fiction novel *The Mummy! A Tale of the Twenty-Second Century* (3 vols.) ~ Sydney Owenson, Lady Morgan, publishes *The O'Briens and the O'Flahertys; a National Tale* (4 vols.) ~ Walter Scott publishes the first series of *Chronicles of the Canongate* (2 vols.), including *The Highland Widow, The Two Drovers,* and *The Surgeon's Daughter*; also, the first series of *Tales of a Grandfather: Being Stories Taken from Scottish History* (-1830; the fourth series deals with French history).

SHORT STORIES AND SHORT STORY COLLECTIONS

Thomas Hood. *National Tales.* 2 vols. London: William H. Ainsworth, 1827.

Anne Jameson. "Halloran the Pedlar." *The Bijou; or Annual of Literature and the Art* (London: William Pickering, 1828 [1827]). 205-239.

The Romantic Era

Alexander Sutherland. *Tales of a Pilgrim*. Edinburgh: William Hunter; London: James Duncan, 1827.

1828
BRITAIN AND THE WORLD
Wellington becomes prime minister for the first time (-1830) ~ The London Zoo opens to members of the Zoological Society ~ Mary Anning discovers the first pterosaur fossil ~ The Democrat Party is founded in the US ~ Russia acquires Armenia at the end of the Russo-Persian War ~ The French military expedition in the Peloponnese in favour of Greek autonomy (the Morea Expedition) begins (-1833) ~ Frenchman René Caillié becomes the first European to enter Timbuktu and live to tell the story (1830; English translation the same year) ~ The mysterious Kaspar Hauser is found on the streets of Nuremberg ~ Miguel I overthrows his niece Maria II and proclaims himself king of Portugal; beginning of the Liberal Wars (-1834) ~ The Russo-Turkish War (-1829) is fought in the Balkans and the Caucasus ~ The Netherlands claims sovereignty over the western half of New Guinea ~ Hazlitt publishes the first two volumes of *Life of Napoleon Buonaparte* (last two volumes in 1830).

LITERATURE & THE ARTS
Noah Webster's *An American Dictionary of the English Language* is published in New York ~ Adam Mickiewicz publishes the epic poem *Konrad Wallenrod* ~ *The Athenaeum* is founded (-1921) ~ Thomas Hood edits *The Gem for 1829* (with contributions from Scott and Charles Lamb) ~ *The Spectator* (founded by R. S. Rintoul) begins publication (today the oldest weekly magazine) ~ Leigh Hunt's periodical *The Companion* appears (January-July); he publishes two editions of *Lord Byron and Some of His Contemporaries* ~ William Taylor publishes the first of 3 volumes of his *Historic Survey of German Poetry* (-1830) ~ An unauthorised edition of Lamb's *Elia: Second Series* is published in Philadelphia ~ Mary Russell Mitford's play *Rienzi* premieres at the Drury Lane ~ Coleridge's *Poetical Works* are published by William Pickering (3 vols.) ~ Felicia Hemans publishes *Records of Woman: with Other Poems* ~ Thomas Moore publishes *Odes upon Cash, Corn, Catholics, and Other Matters* ~ Robert Montgomery publishes the theological poem *The Omnipresence of the Deity* ~ Scott publishes the second series of *Chronicles of the Canongate* (consisting of *St Valentine's Day; or, The Fair Maid of Perth*), in 3 vols. ~ Edward Bulwer-Lytton publishes *Pelham; or, The Adventures of a Gentleman* (3 vols.) and *The Disowned* (dated 1829) ~ James Morier publishes *The Adventures of Hajji Baba of Ispahan in England*.

SHORT STORIES AND SHORT STORY COLLECTIONS
Thomas Crofton Croker. *Fairy Legends and Traditions of the South of Ireland.* Part II and III. London: John Murray, 1828.

George Croly. *Tales of the Great St. Bernard*. 3 vols. London: Henry Colburn, 1828.

William Hay. *Tales and Sketches, by Jacob Ruddiman*. Edinburgh: John Anderson, London: Simpkin & Marshall, 1828.

Mary Russell Mitford. *Our Village*. Vol. III. London: Geo. B. Whittaker, 1828.

Richard Thomson. *Tales of an Antiquary: Chiefly Illustrative of the Manners, Traditions, and Remarkable Localities of Ancient London*. 3 vols. London: Henry Colburn, 1828.

1829
BRITAIN AND THE WORLD

Parliament grants Catholic emancipation ~ Robert Peel creates the Metropolitan Police Service in London ~ George Shillibeer introduces the first omnibus service in his native London (he had developed it first in Paris in 1827) ~ George Stephenson's Rocket locomotive wins the Rainhill trials ~ Andrew Jackson is sworn in as the seventh US president ~ The London Protocol, signed by Russia, France, and Britain, grants autonomy (but not independence) to Greece; Turkey accepts its terms in the Treaty of Adrianople, which ends the Russo-Turkish War ~ The Swan River Colony (now Perth) is established in Western Australia ~ Coleridge publishes *On the Constitution of the Church and State* ~ Carlyle publishes "Signs of the Times" in the *Edinburgh Review* of June ~ Coleridge publishes *On the Constitution of the Church and State* (dated 1830) ~ James Mill publishes *Analysis of the Phenomena of the Human Mind* ~ Anna Wheeler delivers her speech on the "Rights of Women" (published in 1830 in the *British Co-Operator*).

LITERATURE & THE ARTS

Constable exhibits *Hadleigh Castle* at the Royal Academy ~ Rossini's opera *William Tell* premieres in Paris ~ In France, Hugo publishes *Les Orientales* and *Le dernier jour d'un condamné à mort* ~ Honoré de Balzac publishes *Les Chouans*, the first novel of the series later knowns as *La Comédie humaine*, as well as his essay *Physiologie du mariage* ~ Prosper Mérimée publishes the historical novel *Chronique du règne de Charles IX* as well as several short stories, including "Mateo Falcone" and "Tamango" ~ In the United States, Edgar Allan Poe publishes *Al Aaraaf, Tamerlane and Minor Poems* ~ Anna Brownell Jameson publishes *The Loves of the Poets* ~ Premiere of Douglas Jerrold's popular melodrama, *Black Eyed Susan; or, All in the Downs* ~ Fanny Kemble makes her stage debut as Juliet in *Romeo and Juliet* ~ Maria Jane Jewsbury publishes *Lays of Leisure Hours* ~ Letitia Elizabeth Landon publishes *The Venetian Bracelet...and Other Poems* ~ Caroline Norton publishes *The Sorrows of Rosalie: A Tale, with Other Poems* ~ James Hogg publishes *The Shepherd's Calendar* ~ T.L. Peacock publishes *The Misfortunes of Elphin* (satire of medieval romances) ~ Scott publishes the novel *Anne of Geierstein; or, The Maiden of the Mist* (3 vols.) ~ Bulwer-Lytton publishes *Devereux. A Tale* (3 vols.) ~ G.P.R. James publishes the historical novel *Richelieu, A Tale of France* ~ Frederick Marryat publishes his first novel, *The Naval Officer*.

SHORT STORIES AND SHORT STORY COLLECTIONS

Catherine Gore. *Hungarian Tales*. London: Saunders and Otley, 1829.

Anna Maria Hall. *Sketches of Irish Character*. 2 vols. London: Frederic Westley and A. H. Davies, 1829.

The Romantic Era

Leitch Ritchie. *Tales and Confessions*. London: Smith, Elder, 1829.

Walter Scott. "Donnerhugel's Narrative." *Anne of Geierstein; or, The Maiden of the Mist*. 3 vols. Edinburgh: Cadell and Co; London: Simpkin and Marshall, 1829. I, 287-314.

1830

BRITAIN AND THE WORLD

George IV dies and his brother William IV becomes king (-1837) ~ Wellington resigns over the question of parliamentary reform; Whig electoral victory and Earl Grey becomes prime minister (-1834) ~ Swing riots begin in Kent with the destruction of threshing machines and spread through the rest of England; over a thousand rioters are either imprisoned or transported (nineteen are hanged) ~ Opening of the Liverpool and Manchester Railway, first passenger railway operating with steam locomotives between two cities ~ Geographical Society of London is established ~ A new London Protocol (signed by Russia, France, and England) recognises Greek independence ~ France invades and conquers Algeria ~ July Revolution in France; Charles X abdicates; Louis Philippe becomes king (-1848) ~ In Germany, beginning of the period knowns as Vormärz (-1848) ~ Belgian Revolution begins in Brussels; France sends troops in its aid; the London Conference recognises Belgian independence ~ November uprising in Poland; the Polish-Russian War (-1831) ends with Russian victory ~ Gran Colombia separated into three independent states: Ecuador, Colombia, and Venezuela ~ Sir Charles Lyell publishes *The Principles of Geology* (2nd vol. in 1832) ~ Humphry Davy's *Consolations in Travel; or, The Last Days of a Philosopher* appears posthumously ~ Lady Morgan publishes *France in 1829-30* (2 vols.) ~ Auguste Comte begins his *Course of Positive Philosophy* (-1842) ~ François Guizot publishes *Histoire de la civilisation en France* ~ Joseph Smith publishes *The Book of Mormon*.

LITERATURE & THE ARTS

At the Royal Academy, William Etty exhibits *Candaules, King of Lydia, Shews His Wife by Stealth to Gyges* ~ First performance of Hector Berlioz's *Symphonie fantastique* at the Paris Conservatoire ~ In Warsaw, Chopin plays for the first time his composition, the *Piano Concerto No 1* ~ In France, Hugo's *Hernani* opens at the Théâtre Français (English translation the same year) ~ Stendhal publishes *Le rouge et le noir* (dated 1831) ~ Balzac's short story "Sarrasine" appears in the *Revue de Paris* ~ Alfred de Museet publishes the poems of *Contes d'Espagne et d'Italie* ~ In Russia, Pushkin publishes the tragedy *Boris Godunov* (dated 1831), first staged in 1866 ~ Leigh Hunt begins writing mostly by himself his new periodical *The Tatler* (-1832) ~ *Fraser's Magazine* begins, founded by William Maginn and Hugh Fraser (-1882) ~ Thomas Moore publishes *Letters and Journals of Lord Byron* (2 vols.) ~ William Cobbett publishes *Rural Rides* (first serialised, 1822-1826, in his *Political Register*) ~ Alfred Tennyson publishes *Poems, Chiefly Lyrical* ~ Felicia Hemans publishes *Songs of the Affections, with Other Poems* ~ Caroline Norton publishes *The Undying One, and Other Poems* ~ Maria Jane Jewsbury publishes *The Three Histories* (3 novellas) ~ John Galt publishes *The Life of Lord Byron* and the novel *Lawrie Todd; or, The Settlers in the Woods* (3 vols.) ~ William Godwin publishes the novel *Cloudesley: A Tale* (3 vols.) ~ Bulwer-Lytton publishes the novel *Paul Clifford* (3 vols.) ~ Mary Shelley publishes *The Fortunes of Perkin Warbeck, A Romance* (3 vols.) ~ Thomas Colley Grattan publishes *The Heiress of Bruges*.

SHORT STORIES AND SHORT STORY COLLECTIONS
John Yonge Akerman. *Tales of Other Days*. London: Effingham Wilson, 1830.
William Carleton. *Traits and Stories of the Irish Peasantry*. 2 vols. Dublin: William Curry, 1830.
Mary Russell Mitford. *Our Village. Vol. IV*. London: Whittaker, Treacher, & Co., 1830.
William Mudford. "The Iron Shroud." *Blackwood's* (August 1830).
Andrew Picken. *The Dominie's Legacy*. 3 vols. London: William Kidd, 1830.

1831
BRITAIN AND THE WORLD

Census: 16.5 million in Britain; 7.7 million in Ireland ~ The Reform Act passes in the House of Commons but is defeated in the House of Lords; riots in London, Nottingham, Derby, and Bristol ~ Merthyr Rising: riot of Welsh miners violently suppressed ~ Cholera arrives in Britain (over 32,000 death until 1833) ~ The new London Bridge is opened ~ During his sixth arctic exploration, James Clark Ross locates the Magnetic North Pole ~ Darwin sails from Devonport on *The Beagle* (-1836) ~ Alexis de Tocqueville visits the United States ~ Nat Turner's slave rebellion in Virginia ~ The Polish army wins a pyrrhic victory against Russia on the outskirts of Warsaw; depleted in another battle, at Ostroleka, the Polish army withdraws ~ The Belgian Constitution comes into effect; the Dutch "ten days' campaign" against secessionist Belgium is thwarted by the Franco-Belgian alliance ~ John Stuart Mill publishes "The Spirit of the Age" in *The Examiner* (January) ~ Thomas Moore publishes *The Life and Death of Lord Edward Fitzgerald* ~ Hermann, Fürst von Pückler-Muskau's *Tour in England, Ireland, and France, in the Years 1828 and 1829* appears in English translation (a prequel, *Tour in Germany, Holland and England in the Years 1826, 1827, and 1828* appears in 1832; they will be collectively known as *Tour of a German Prince*) ~ William Godwin publishes *Thoughts on Man* ~ Mary Prince publishes *The History of Mary Prince: A West Indian Slave* ~ Cobbett is tried for and acquitted of inciting the Swing Riots.

LITERATURE & THE ARTS

Delacroix exhibits *Liberty Leading the People* at the Paris Salon; Horace Vernet exhibits *Judith and Holofernes* ~ Constable exhibits *Salisbury Cathedral from the Meadows* at the Royal Academy ~ Hokusai creates *The Great Wave off Kanagawa* ~ Vincenzo Bellini's *Norma* is first produced at the Scala in Milan ~ In France, Hugo publishes *Notre-Dame de Paris*; first performance of his play *Marion de Lorme* ~ Balzac publishes *La Peau de chagrin* ~ In Saint Petersburg, Pushkin publishes *The Tales of the Late Ivan Petrovich Belkin* ~ Griboyedov's famous comedy *Woe from*

The Romantic Era

Wit (written and circulated privately in the early 1820s) is finally staged posthumously as well as published (in German translation) ~ In the United States, Poe publishes *Poems. By Edgar A. Poe* ~ *Figaro in London* is founded by Gilbert Abbott a Beckett (-1838) ~ Maria Jane Jewsbury publishes "Literary Sketches No. 1. Felicia Hemans" and "Literary Women—No. 2. Jane Austen" in *The Athenaeum* (Feb. and Aug.) ~ Arthur Hallam publishes the essay "On Some of the Characteristics of Modern Poetry, and on the Lyrical Poems of Alfred Tennyson" in *The Englishman's Magazine* ~ Catherine Gore's comedy *The School for Coquettes* is a success at the Theatre Royal, Haymarket ~ Thomas Hood publishes the poem "The Dream of Eugene Aram, the Murderer" (in *The Gem* and then in a separate volume) ~ Edward John Trelawney publishes the novel *Adventures of a Younger Son* ~ John Galt publishes the novel *Bogle Corbet* (3 vols.) ~ Peacock publishes the satirical novel *Crotchet Castle* ~ Letitia Elizabeth Landon publishes the novel *Romance and Reality* (3 vols.) ~ Susan Ferrier publishes the novel *Destiny* (3 vols.) ~ Mary Shelley publishes a revised edition of *Frankenstein* ~ Edward John Trelawny publishes the novel *Adventures of a Younger Son* ~ Bulwer-Lytton publishes the novel *Eugene Aram* (3 vols., dated 1832) ~ Scott publishes *Count Robert of Paris* and *Castle Dangerous* in the fourth series of "Tales of My Landlord" (4 vols., dated 1832).

SHORT STORIES AND SHORT STORY COLLECTIONS
John Banim. "The Church-Yard Watch." *Friendship's Offering*, 305-320.
Allan Cunningham. "The Master of Logan." *The New Monthly Magazine*, 321-336.
Anna Maria Hall. *Sketches of Irish Character. Second Series*. London: Frederick Westley and A.H. Davis, 1831.
Andrew Picken, Ed. *The Club-Book*. 3 vols. London: Cochrane and Pickersgill, 1831.

1832

BRITAIN AND THE WORLD
First Reform Act extends suffrage and abolishes rotten boroughs ~ Durham University is founded ~ Samuel Sharpe's slave rebellion is brought to a violent end in Jamaica ~ The Treaty of London creates the independent Kingdom of Greece; Otto of Bavaria is elected king (-1862) ~ In the Ottoman-Egyptian War, the Egyptian army occupies Konya and controls most of Anatolia; Russia comes to Turkey's rescue ~ Carl on Clausewitz's *On War* is published posthumously in Berlin~ Fanny Trollope publishes *The Domestic Manners of the Americans* ~ Harriet Martineau begins *Illustrations of Political Economy* (-1834) ~ Leigh Hunt publishes *Christianism; or, Belief and Unbelief Reconciled* ~ Anne Jameson publishes *Characteristics of Women, Moral, Poetical and Historical*.

LITERATURE & THE ARTS
Frédéric Chopin has his Paris debut and publishes his three *Nocturnes* ~ In Germany, Goethe's *Faust: Part Two* appears posthumously ~ In France,

Charles Nodier publishes *The Crumb Fairy* ~ George Sand publishes her first novels, *Indiana* and *Valentine* ~ Balzac publishes the novel *Louis Lambert* and the novellas *Colonel Chabert* and *Le Curé de Tours* ~ Hugo's *Le Roi s'amuse* premieres at the Théâtre-Français ~ In Saint Petersburg, the first of Pushkin's "little tragedies" to be staged is *Mozart and Salieri* ~ Nikolai Gogol publishes *Evenings on a Farm Near Dikanka* ~ Adam Mickiewicz completes his poetic drama *Forefathers' Eve* (published in his fourth volume of *Poems*) ~ In the United States, Poe publishes his first short stories in *The Philadelphia Saturday Courier* ~ Irving's *Tales of the Alhambra* appear simultaneously in London and Philadelphia ~ The weekly *Chambers's Edinburgh Journal* is founded (-1956) ~ The monthly *Tait's Edinburgh Magazine* is founded (-1861) ~ Lady Blessington begins publishing "Journal of Conversations with Lord Byron" in *The New Monthly Magazine* (-1833) ~ Anna Brownell Jameson publishes *Shakespeare's Heroines* ~ Alfred Tennyson publishes *Poems* (dated 1833) ~ John Galt publishes three novels: the political satires *The Member: An Autobiography* and its sequel *The Radical*, as well as *Stanley Buxton; or, The Schoolfellows* ~ Benjamin Disraeli publishes the novel *Contarini Fleming: a Psychological Auto-Biography* (4 vols.) ~ De Quincey publishes the historical novel *Klosterheim: or, The Masque* ~ Bulwer-Lytton publishes *Eugene Aram: A Tale* ~ Walter Scott dies and his novel *The Siege of Malta* remains unfinished.

SHORT STORIES AND SHORT STORY COLLECTIONS

John Banim. "The Soldier's Billet." *The Athenaeum* 239 (26 May 1832), 336-337.

Henry Glassford Bell. *My Old Portfolio; or Tales and Sketches*. London: Smith, Elder, and Co., 1832.

Letitia Elizabeth Landon. "Experiments; or, The Lover from Ennui." *Heath's Book of Beauty*, 222-245.

Mary Russell Mitford. *Our Village V*. London: Whittaker, Treacher, & Co.

NOTE ON THE TEXTS

Each story is accompanied by a brief introductory note on the text, mentioning the time and place of first publication and the exact source preferred for this anthology. As a rule, we have preferred a version that, as far as it is known or at least assumed with a reliable degree of certainty, the authors themselves have corrected and revised. When this is not known or the revisions do not seem to match the most genuine authorial intent, the original version has been preferred.

A lot of the English vocabulary (and, to a lesser degree, the grammar) of the early 19th century was in a period of transition. Some of the more unusual spellings and lexical preferences are explained in footnotes. When they are not (because they differ very little from what we are used to today), the reader is invited to assume that they represent choices made by the authors themselves and that they were variants in circulation at the time.

Henry Kirke White

Charles Wanely

(1802)

The author: Henry Kirke White was born on 21 March 1785 in Nottingham, where his father was a butcher. His mother, Mary Nevill, opened a school for girls in 1799, with the help of her daughters. His middle name was probably Kirk, but he preferred a more archaic spelling. He was apprenticed to a lawyer and began his clerkship in 1801. He published *Clifton Grove, A Sketch in Verse, with Other Poems* (London: Vernor and Hood, 1803). The volume was not well received, but it caught the eye of Robert Southey. The ailing White, who was suffering from tuberculosis, benefited from the help of family of friends and was able to enter St. John's College, Cambridge. He struggled there, as he was going deaf, but he proved to be a very good student (he came first in Latin but toiled with mathematics) until 19 October 1806, when he died in his college room. His posthumous fame, which lasted the better part of a century, as a poet who showed a lot of promise before his premature end, came in large part from Southey's edition of his works (published one year after White's death) as well as from the prominent place Byron granted him in his 1809 satire *English Bards and Scotch Reviewers*.

The text: The story appeared as "Melancholy Hours. [No. II.]" in *The Monthly Mirror* for June 1802 (385-388). It was signed "W." White published twelve pieces in this essay-series, most of which were nonfictional. It was collected by Robert Southey in *The Remains of Henry Kirke White, of Nottingham, late of St. John's College, Cambridge; with an Account of His Life. In Two Volumes* (London: Vernor, Hood, and Sharpe, 1807), II, 222-227. The *Remains* appeared only months after White' death. In 1813, Southey published a corrected edition (the sixth). The following version is from the ninth edition of the Henry Kirke White's *Remains* (London: Longman, Hurst, Rees, Orme, and Brown, 1821), 224-229.

1

Henry Kirke White

It is a melancholy reflection, and a reflection which often sinks heavily on my soul, that the Sons of Genius generally seem predestined to encounter the rudest storms of adversity, to struggle, unnoticed, with poverty and misfortune. The annals of the world present us with many corroborations of this remark; and, alas! who can tell how many unhappy beings, who might have shone with distinguished lustre among the stars which illumine our hemisphere, may have sunk unknown beneath the pressure of untoward circumstances; who knows how many may have shrunk, with all the exquisite sensibility of genius, from the rude and riotous discord of the world, into the peaceful slumbers of death. Among the number of those whose talents might have elevated them to the first rank of eminence, but who have been overwhelmed with the accumulated ills of poverty and misfortune, I do not hesitate to rank a young man whom I once accounted it my greatest happiness to be able to call my friend.

Charles Wanely was the only son of an humble village rector, who just lived to give him a liberal education, and then left him unprovided for and unprotected, to struggle through the world as well as he could. With a heart glowing with the enthusiasm of poetry and romance, with a sensibility most exquisite, and with an indignant pride, which swelled in his veins, and told him he was a man, my friend found himself cast upon the wide world at the age of sixteen, an adventurer, without fortune and without connection. As his independent spirit could not brook the idea of being a burden to those whom his father had taught him to consider only as allied by blood, and not by affection, he looked about him for a situation which could ensure to him, by his own exertions, an honourable competence. It was not long before such a situation offered, and Charles precipitately articled himself to an attorney, without giving himself time to consult his own inclinations, or the disposition of his master. The transition from Sophocles and Euripides, Theocritus and Ovid, to Finche and Wood, Coke and Wynne,[1] was striking and difficult; but Charles applied himself with his wonted ardour to his new study, as considering it not only his interest, but his duty so to do. It was not long, however, before he discovered that he disliked the law, that he disliked his situation, and that he despised his master. The fact was, my friend had many

---

[1] The last four names belong to authors of legal treatises.

mortifications to endure, which his haughty soul could ill brook. The attorney to whom he was articled, was one of those narrow-minded beings who consider wealth as alone entitled to respect. He had discovered that his clerk was *very* poor and *very* destitute of friends, and thence he *very* naturally concluded that he might insult him with impunity. It appears, however, that he was mistaken in his calculations. I one night remarked that my friend was unusually thoughtful. I ventured to ask him whether he had met with any thing particular to ruffle his spirits. He looked at me for some moments significantly, then, as if roused to fury by the recollection—"I have," said he vehemently, "I have, I have. He has insulted me grossly, and I will bear it no longer." He now walked up and down the room with visible emotion.—Presently he sat down.—He seemed more composed. "My friend," said he, "I have endured much from this man. I conceived it my duty to forbear, but I have forborne until forbearance is blameable, and, by the Almighty, I will never again endure what I have endured this day. But not only this man; every one thinks he may treat me with contumely, because I am poor and friendless. But I am a man, and will no longer tamely submit to be the sport of fools, and the foot-ball of caprice. In this spot of earth, though it gave me birth, I can never taste of ease. Here I must be miserable. The principal end of man is to arrive at happiness. Here I can never attain it; and here therefore I will no longer remain. My obligations to the rascal, who calls himself my master, are cancelled by his abuse of the authority I placed in his hands. I have no relations to bind me to this particular place." The tears started in his eyes as he spoke, "I have no tender ties to bid me stay, and why *do* I stay? The world is all before me. My inclination leads me to travel; I will pursue that inclination; and, perhaps, in a strange land I may find that repose which is denied to me in the place of my birth. My finances, it is true, are ill able to support the expenses of travelling: but what then—Goldsmith, my friend," with rising enthusiasm, "Goldsmith traversed Europe on foot,[2] and I am as hardy as Goldsmith. Yes, I will go, and perhaps, ere long, I may sit me down on some towering mountain, and exclaim with him, while a hundred realms lie in perspective before me,

Creation's heir, the world, the world is mine."[3]

It was in vain I entreated him to reflect maturely, ere he took so bold a step; he was deaf to my importunities, and the next morning I received a letter informing me of his departure. He was observed

[2] Oliver Goldsmith (1728?-1774) took a walking tour of Western Europe in 1755-1756 before he settled in London and began his writing career.
[3] From Goldsmith's 1764 philosophical poem "The Traveller."

about sun-rise, sitting on the stile, at the top of an eminence which commanded a prospect of the surrounding country, pensively looking towards the village. I could divine his emotions, on thus casting probably a last look on his native place. The neat white parsonage-house, with the honey-suckle mantling on its wall, I knew would receive his last glance; and the image of his father would present itself to his mind, with a melancholy pleasure, as he was thus hastening, a solitary individual, to plunge himself into the crowds of the world, deprived of that fostering hand which would otherwise have been his support and guide.

From this period Charles Wanely was never heard of at L——, and, as his few relations cared little about him, in a short time it was almost forgotten that such a being had ever been in existence.

About five years had elapsed from this period, when my occasions led me to the continent. I will confess I was not without a romantic hope, that I might again meet with my lost friend; and that often, with that idea, I scrutinised the features of the passengers. One fine moonlight night, as I was strolling down the grand Italian Strada di Toledo, at Naples,[4] I observed a crowd assembled round a man, who, with impassioned gestures, seemed to be vehemently declaiming to the multitude. It was one of the Improvisatori, who recite extempore verses in the streets of Naples, for what money they can collect from the hearers. I stopped to listen to the man's metrical romance, and had remained in the attitude of attention some time, when, happening to turn round, I beheld a person very shabbily dressed, stedfastly gazing at me. The moon shone full in his face. I thought his features were familiar to me. He was pale and emaciated, and his countenance bore marks of the deepest dejection. Yet, amidst all these changes, I thought I recognised Charles Wanely. I stood stupified with surprise. My senses nearly failed me. On recovering myself, I looked again, but he had left the spot the moment he found himself observed. I darted through the crowd, and ran every way which I thought he could have gone, but it was all to no purpose. Nobody knew him. Nobody had even seen such a person. The two following days I renewed my enquiries, and at last discovered the lodgings where a man of his description had resided. But he had left Naples the morning after his form had struck my eyes. I found he gained a subsistence by drawing rude figures in chalks, and vending them among the peasantry. I could no longer doubt it was my friend, and immediately perceived that his haughty spirit could not bear to be recognised in such degrading circumstances, by one who had known him in better days. Lamenting

[4] Via Toledo, a major thoroughfare in Naples.

the misguided notions which had thus again thrown him from me, I left Naples, now grown hateful to my sight, and embarked for England. It is now nearly twenty years since this rencounter, during which period he has not been heard of; and there can be little doubt that this unfortunate young man has found, in some remote corner of the continent, an obscure and an unlamented grave.

Thus, those talents which were formed to do honour to human nature, and to the country which gave them birth, have been nipped in the bud by the frosts of poverty and scorn, and their unhappy possessor lies in an unknown and nameless tomb, who might, under happier circumstances, have risen to the highest pinnacle of ambition and renown.

Amelia Opie

𝒯HE 𝐵LACK 𝒱ELVET 𝒫ELISSE

(1806)

The author: Amelia Opie (née Alderson) was born in Norwich, on 12 November 1769. At the age of 15, she began taking care of the family household, after the death of her mother. In the radical circles in which she and her father moved, she befriended Anna Letitia Barbauld, William Godwin and Mary Wollstonecraft. In 1798, she married painter John Opie (1761-1807). Her first notable publication was *The Father and Daughter, a Tale, in Prose: with an Epistle from The Maid of Corinth to her Lover; and Other Poetical Pieces* (London: Longman, Hurst, Rees, Orme & Brown, 1801). This was followed by *Poems* (1802). The March 1801 issue of *The Lady's Monthly Museum* opened with "Memoirs of Mrs. Opie. With a Portrait," evidence of her early fame. Her engraved portrait (by Ridley after John Opie) appeared with a biography in the *European Magazine* (May 1803). Her novel *Adeline Mowbray: or, The Mother and Daughter* (1805) was partially based on the relationship between Godwin and Wollstonecraft.

The text: First published in her collection *Simple Tales: By Mrs. Opie. In Four Volumes.* (London: Printed for Longman, Hurst, Rees, and Orme, Paternoster Row, 1806), Vol. I, 1-40. The following is from the fourth edition (1815, same pages), which has been preferred since it contains some changes operated by Opie.

Further reading: Gary Kelly, "Discharging Debts: The Moral Economy of Amelia Opie's Fiction." *The Wordsworth Circle* 11: 4 (Autumn 1980), 198-203.

Mr. Beresford was a merchant, engaged in a very extensive business, and possessed of considerable property, a great part of which was vested in a large estate in the country, on which he chiefly resided.

Beresford was what is commonly denominated *purse-proud*; and so eager to be honoured on account of his wealth, that he shunned rather than courted the society of men of rank, as he was fond of power and precedence, and did not like to associate with those who had an indisputable claim to that deference of which he himself was desirous. But he earnestly wished that his only child and heiress should marry a man of rank; and being informed that a young baronet of large estates in his neighbourhood, and who was also heir to a barony, was just returned from his travels, and intended to settle at his paternal seat, Mr. Beresford was resolved that Julia should have every possible opportunity of showing off to the best advantage before so desirable a neighbour: and he determined that his daughter, his house, and his table, should not want any charm which money could procure.

Beresford had gained his fortune by degrees; and having been educated by frugal and retired parents, his habits were almost parsimonious; and when he launched out into unwonted expenses on becoming wealthy, it was only in a partial manner. His house and his furniture had a sort of pye-bald[5] appearance;—his style of living was not consistent, like that of a man used to live like a gentleman, but opulence with a timid grasp seemed to squeeze out its indulgences from the griping fingers of habitual œconomy.— True, he could, on occasion, be splendid, both in his public and private gifts; but such bounties were efforts, and he seemed to wonder at himself whenever the exertion was over.

Julia Beresford, his daughter, accustomed from her birth to affluence, if not to luxury,—and having in every thing what is called the spirit of a gentlewoman, was often distressed and mortified at the want of consistency in her father's mode of living; but she was particularly distressed to find that, though he was always telling her what a fortune he would give her when she married, and at his death, he allowed her but a trifling sum, comparatively, for pocket-money, and required from her, with teasing minuteness, an account of the manner in which her allowance was spent; reprobating very severely her propensity to spend her money on plausible beggars and pretended invalids.

But on this point he talked in vain:—used by a benevolent and pious mother, whose loss she tenderly deplored, to impart comfort to the poor, the sick, and the afflicted, Julia endeavoured to make her residence in the country a blessing to the neighbourhood; but,

[5] Alternate spelling of "piebald," i.e., irregular, eclectic.

too often, kind words, soothing visits, and generous promises, were all that she had to bestow; and many a time did she purchase the means of relieving a distressed fellow-creature by a personal sacrifice: for though ever ready to contribute to a subscription either public or private, Beresford could not be prevailed upon to indulge his daughter by giving way to that habitual benevolence, which, when once practised, can never be left off.

But though the sums were trifling which Julia had to bestow, she had so many cheap charities in her power, such as sending broth to the neighbouring cottages, and making linen of various sorts for poor women and children, that she was deservedly popular in the neighbourhood; and though her father was reckoned as proud as he was rich, the daughter was pronounced to be a pattern of good nature, and as affable as he was the contrary.

But wherever Beresford could have an opportunity of displaying his wealth to advantage, he regarded not expense:—and to outvie[6] the neighbouring gentlemen in endeavours to attract the rich young baronet, whom all the young ladies would, he supposed, be aiming to captivate, he purchased magnificent furniture and carriages, and promised Julia a great addition to her wardrobe, whenever sir Frederic Mortimer should take up his abode at his seat.

Julia heard that the baronet was expected, with a beating heart. She had been several times in his company at a watering-place,[7] immediately on his return from abroad, and had wished to appear as charming in his eyes as he appeared in hers; but she had been disappointed.—Modest and retiring in her manner, and not showy in her person, though her features were regularly beautiful, sir Frederic Mortimer, who had only seen her in large companies, and with very striking and attractive women, had regarded her merely as an amiable girl, and had rarely thought of her again.

Julia Beresford was formed to steal upon the affections by slow degrees; to interest on acquaintance, not to strike at first sight. But the man who had opportunities of listening to the sweet tones of her voice, and of gazing on her varied countenance when emotion crimsoned her pale cheek, and lighted up the expression of her eyes, could never behold her without a degree of interest which beauty alone often fails to excite. Like most women, too, Julia derived great advantages from dress: of this she was sensible, though very often did she appear shabbily attired, from having expended on others sums destined to ornament herself; but, when

[6] To outdo a rival.

[7] Old term for a resort, especially one where visitors went to drink water from mineral springs and to socialise.

The Black Velvet Pelisse

she had done so, a physiognomist[8] would have discovered in her countenance probably an expression of self-satisfaction, more ornamental than any dress could be. But, generally, as Julia knew the value of external decoration, she wisely wished to indulge in it.

One day Julia, accompanied by her father, went to the shop of a milliner, in a large town, near which they lived; and, as winter was coming on, and her pelisse,[9] a dark and now faded purple, was nearly worn out, she was very desirous of purchasing a black velvet one, which was on sale; but her father hearing that the price of it was twelve guineas,[10] positively forbade her to wish for so expensive a piece of finery; though he owned that it was very handsome, and very becoming.

"To be sure," said Julia smiling, but casting a longing look at the pelisse, "twelve guineas might be better bestowed:" and they left the shop.

The next day Mr. Beresford went to town on business, and, in a short time after, he wrote to his daughter to say that he had met sir Frederic Mortimer in London, and that he would soon be down at his seat, to attend some pony races which Mr. Hanmer, who had a mind to show off his dowdy[11] daughter to the young baronet, intended to have on a piece of land belonging to him; and that he had heard all the ladies in the neighbourhood were to be there.

"I have received an invitation for you and myself," continued Mr. Beresford; "and therefore, as I am resolved the miss Traceys, and the other girls, shall not be better or more expensively dressed than my daughter, I enclose you bills to the amount of thirteen pounds; and I desire you to go and purchase the velvet pelisse which we so much admired; and I have sent you a hat, the most elegant which money could procure, in order that my heiress may appear as an heiress should do."

Julia's young heart beat with pleasure at this permission; for she was to adorn herself to appear before the only man whom she ever *wished* to please: and the next morning she determined to set off to make the desired purchase.

[8] Physiognomists (adherents to a pseudo-science, very popular in the 18th and 19th centuries) claimed to be able to assess someone's personality from their facial features.

[9] A woman's long, sleeveless, hooded cloak, often trimmed with fur.

[10] The guinea, discontinued in 1816, was a 21-shilling coin (or 1 pound and 1 shilling).

[11] Dowdy means dull, unattractive (especially about the clothes one wears), frumpy.

That evening, being alone, she set out to take her usual walk; and having, lost in no unpleasing reverie, strayed very near to a village about three miles from home, she recollected to have heard an affecting account of the distress of a very virtuous and industrious family in that village, owing to the poor man's being drawn for the militia, and not rich enough to procure a substitute.[12]—She therefore resolved to go on and inquire how the matter had terminated. Julia proceeded to the village, and reached it just as the very objects of her solicitude were come to the height of their distresses.

The father of the family, not being able to raise more than half the money wanted, was obliged to serve; and Julia, on seeing a crowd assembled, approached to ask what was going forward; and found she was arrived to witness a very affecting scene: for the poor man was taking his last farewell of his wife and family, who, on his departure to join the regiment, would be forced to go to the workhouse,[13] where, as they were in delicate health, it was most probable they would soon fall victims to bad food and bad air.

The poor man was universally beloved in his village; and the neighbours, seeing that a young lady inquired concerning his misfortunes with an air of interest, were all eager to give her every possible information on the subject of his distress.—"And only think, miss," said one of them, "for the want of nine pound only, as honest and hard-working a lad as ever lived, and as good a husband and father, must be forced to leave his family, and be a militia-man,—and they, poor things, go to the workhouse!"

"Nine pounds!" said Julia, "would that be sufficient to keep him at home?"

"La![14] yes, miss; for that young fellow yonder would gladly go for him for eighteen pounds!"

On hearing this, how many thoughts rapidly succeeded each other in Julia's mind!—If she paid the nine pounds, the man would be restored to his family, and they preserved perhaps from an untimely death in a workhouse!—But then she had no money but

[12] During the late 18th century and the Napoleonic Wars, lower-class Englishmen could be conscripted into the army but, in turn, they were allowed to find and pay a substitute to replace them.

[13] Workhouses provided shelter and food for the indigent in exchange for work. Living conditions in workhouses were much criticised by British authors throughout the 18th and 19th centuries.

[14] An interjection, now obsolete, used to draw attention to the following statement.

The Black Velvet Pelisse

what her father had sent to purchase the pelisse, nor was she to see him till she met him on the race-ground!—and he would be so disappointed if she was not well dressed! True, she might take the pelisse on trust; but then she was sure her father would be highly incensed at her extravagance, if she spent twelve guineas, and gave away nine pounds at the same time:—therefore she knew she must either give up doing a generous action, or give up the pelisse, that is, give up the gratification of her father's pride and her own vanity.

"No, I dare not, I cannot do it," thought Julia; "my own vanity I would willingly mortify,—but not my father's.—No—the poor man must go!"

During this mental struggle the bystanders had eagerly watched her countenance; and thinking that she was disposed to pay the sum required, they communicated their hopes to the poor people themselves; and as Julia turned her eyes towards them, the wretched couple looked at her with such an imploring look! but she was resolved:—"I am sorry, I am very sorry," said she, "that I can do nothing for you:—however, take this." So saying, she gave them all the loose money she had in her pocket, amounting to a few shillings, and then with an aching heart walked rapidly away; but as she did so, the sobs of the poor woman, as she leaned on her husband's shoulder, and the cries of the little boy, when his father, struggling with his grief, bade him a last farewell, reached her, and penetrated to her heart.

"Poor creatures!" she inwardly exclaimed; "and nine pounds would change these tears into gladness, and yet I withhold it! And is it for this that Heaven has blest me with opulence? for this, to be restrained, by the fear of being reproved for spending a paltry sum, from doing an action acceptable in the eyes of my Creator! No; I will pay the money. I will give myself the delight of serving afflicted worth, and spare myself from, perhaps, eternal self-reproach!"

She then, without waiting for further consideration, turned back again, paid the money into the poor man's hand; and giving the remaining four pounds to the woman, who, though clean, was miserably clad, desired her to lay part of it out in clothes for herself and children.

I will not attempt to describe the surprise and gratitude of the relieved sufferers, nor the overwhelming feelings which Julia experienced; who, withdrawing herself with the rapidity of lightning from their thanks, and wishing to remain unknown, ran hastily along her road home, not daring to stop, lest her joy at having done a generous deed should be checked by other considerations.

But at length exhausted, and panting for breath, she was obliged to relax in her speed; and then the image of her angry and disappointed parent appeared to her in all its terrors.

"What can I do?" she exclaimed.—"Shall I order the pelisse, though I can't pay for it, or go without it? No; I ought not to incur so great an expense without my father's leave, though I know him to be able to afford it; and to run in debt he would consider as even a greater fault than the other. Well, then,—I must submit to mortify his pride; and though I rejoice in what I have done, the joy is amply counterbalanced by the idea of giving pain to my father."

Poor Julia! her own wounded vanity came in for its share in causing her uneasiness; and the rest of that day, and the next, Julia spent in reflections and fears, which did not tend to improve her looks, and make a becoming dress unnecessary.

The next morning was the morning for the races. The sun shone bright, and every thing looked cheerful but Julia. She had scarcely spirits to dress herself. It was very cold; therefore she was forced to wear her faded purple pelisse, and now it looked shabbier than usual; and still shabbier from the contrast of a very smart new black velvet bonnet.

At length Julia had finished her toilette, saying to herself, "My father talked of Mr. Hanmer's dowdy daughter. I am sure Mr. Hanmer may return the compliment;" and then, with a heavy heart, she got into the carriage, and drove to the house of rendezvous.

Mr. Beresford was there before her; and while he contemplated with fearful admiration the elegant cloaks, and fine showy figures and faces of the miss Traceys, between whose father and himself there had long been a rivalship of wealth, he was consoled for their elegance by reflecting how much more expensive and elegant Julia's dress would be, and how well she would look, flushed, as he expected to see her, with the blush of emotion on entering a full room, and the consciousness of more than usual attraction in her appearance.

Julia at length appeared, but pale, dejected, and in her old purple pelisse!

What a mortification! His daughter, the great heiress, the worst dressed and most dowdy-looking girl in the company! Insupportable! Scarcely could he welcome her, though he had not seen her for some days; and he seized the very first opportunity of asking her if she had received the notes.

"Yes, I thank ye, sir," replied Julia.

"Then why did you not buy what I bade you? It could not be gone; for, if you did not buy it, nobody else could, I am sure."

The Black Velvet Pelisse

"I—I—I thought I could do without it—and—"

"There now, there is perverseness.—When I wished you not to have it, then you wanted it; and now—I protest if I don't believe you did it on purpose to mortify me; and there's those proud minxes, whose father is not worth half what I am, are dressed out as fine as princesses. I vow, girl, you look so shabby and ugly, I can't bear to look at you!"

What a trial for Julia! her eyes filled with tears; and at this moment sir Frederic Mortimer approached her, and hoped she had not been ill; but he thought she was paler than usual:—

"Paler!" cried her father: "why, I should not have known her, she has made such a fright of herself."

"You may say so, sir," replied the baronet politely, though he almost agreed with him; "but no other man can be of that opinion."

Julia was rather gratified by this speech; but, without waiting for an answer, sir Frederic had gone to join the miss Traceys; and as he entered into an animated conversation with them, Julia was allowed, unattended, to walk to a window in the next room, and enjoy her own melancholy reflections.

At length, to Julia's great relief, they were summoned to the race-ground; the baronet taking miss Hanmer under one arm and the elder miss Tracey under the other.—"So," cried Beresford, seizing Julia roughly by the hand, "I must lead you, I see; for who will take any notice of such a dowdy? Well, girl, I was too proud of you, and you have contrived to humble me enough."

There was a mixture a tenderness and resentment in this speech, which quite overcame Julia, and she burst into tears. "There,—now she is going to make herself worse, by spoiling her eyes.—But come, tell me what you did with the money; I insist upon knowing."

"I—I—gave it away," sobbed out Julia.

"Gave it away! Monstrous! I protest I will not speak to you again of a month." So saying, he left her, and carefully avoided to look at or speak to her again.

The races began, and were interesting to all but Julia, who, conscious of being beheld by her father with looks of mortification and resentment, and by the man of her choice with indifference, had no satisfaction to enable her to support the unpleasantness of her situation, except the consciousness that her sorrow had been the cause of happiness to others, and that the family whom she had relieved were probably at that moment naming her with praises and blessings. "Then why should I be so selfish as to repine?" thought Julia:—"perhaps no one present has such a right as I to rejoice;

13

for how poor are the gratifications of vanity to the triumphs of benevolence!"

So like a philosopher reasoned our heroine; but she felt like a woman, and, spite of herself, an expression of vexation still prevailed over the usual sweetness of her countenance.

The races at length finished, and with them she flattered herself would finish her mortifications; but in vain. The company was expected to stay to partake of a cold collation, which was to be preceded by music and dancing; and Julia was obliged to accept the unwelcome invitation.

As the ladies were most of them very young, they were supposed not to have yet forgotten the art of dancing minuets,—an art now of so little use;[15] and Mr. Hanmer begged sir Frederic would lead out his daughter to show off in a minuet. The baronet obeyed; and then offered to take out Julia for the same purpose; but she, blushing, refused to comply.

"Well, what's that for?" cried Beresford angrily, who knew that Julia was remarkable for dancing a good minuet.—"Why can't you dance when you are asked, miss Beresford?"—"Because," replied Julia in a faltering voice, "I have no gown on, and I can't dance a minuet in my—in my pelisse."

"Rot your pelisse!" exclaimed Beresford, forgetting all decency and decorum, and turned to the window to hide his angry emotions, while Julia hung her head, abashed; and the baronet led out miss Tracey, who, throwing off the cloak which she had worn before, having expected such an exhibition would take place, displayed a very fine form, set off by the most becoming gown possible.

"Charming! admirable! what a figure! what grace!" was murmured throughout the room. Mr. Beresford's proud heart throbbed almost to agony; while Julia, though ever ready to acknowledge the excellence of another, still felt the whole scene so vexatious to her, principally from the mortification of her father, that her only resource was again thinking on the family rescued from misery by her.

Reels[16] were next called for; and Julia then stood up to dance; but she had not danced five minutes, when, exhausted by the various emotions which she had undergone during the last eight-and-forty hours, her head became so giddy, that she could not proceed, and was obliged to sit down.

[15] Allusion to the fact that the minuet, though still popular in England, was no longer performed in France, its country of origin, after the 1789 Revolution, because it was associated with aristocracy and the court.

[16] Popular dances of Scottish origin.

The Black Velvet Pelisse

"I believe the deuce is in the girl," muttered Mr. Beresford; and, to increase her distress, Julia overheard him.

In a short time the dancing was discontinued, and a concert begun. Miss Hanmer played a sonata, and miss Tracey sung a bravura song with great execution. Julia was then called upon to play; but she timidly answered that she never played lessons:—[17]

"But you sing," said miss Hanmer.

"Sometimes;—but I beg to be excused singing now."

"What! you will not sing neither?" said Mr. Beresford.

"I can't sing now, indeed, sir; I am not well enough; and I tremble so much that I have not a steady note in my voice."

"So, miss," whispered Mr. Beresford, "and this is what I get in return for having squandered so much money on your education!"

The miss Traceys were then applied to, and they sung, with great applause, a difficult Italian duo, and were complimented into the bargain on their readiness to oblige.

Poor Julia!

"You see, miss Beresford, how silly and contemptible you look," whispered Beresford, "while those squalling misses run away with all the admiration."

Julia's persecutions were not yet over.—"Though you are not well enough, miss Beresford, to sing a song," said Mr. Hanmer, "which requires much exertion, surely you can sing a ballad without music, which is, I am told, your fort."

"So I have heard," cried sir Frederic. "Do, miss Beresford, oblige us."

"Do," said the miss Traceys; "and we have a claim on you."

"I own it," replied Julia in a voice scarcely audible; "but you, who are such proficients in music, must know, that, to sing a simple ballad, requires more self-possession and steadiness of tone than any other kind of singing; as all the merit depends on the clearness of utterance, and the power of sustaining the notes."

"True:—but do try."

"Indeed I cannot:" said Julia, and shrugging up their shoulders, the ladies desisted from further importunities. "I am so surprised," said one of them to the other, leaning across two or three gentlemen: "I had heard that miss Beresford was remarkably good-humoured and obliging, and she seems quite sullen and obstinate; don't you think so?"

"O dear, yes! and not obliging at all."

---

[17] "Lessons" is an obsolete term for musical compositions for a single instrument. Many piano "lessons" were later termed "sonatas." "Bravura," in the previous sentence, is a piece of music that requires great skill.

"No, indeed," cried miss Hanmer; "she seems to presume on her wealth, I think: what think you, gentlemen?"

But the gentlemen were not so hasty in their judgments—two of them only observed that miss Beresford was in no respect like herself that day.

"I don't think she is well," said the baronet.

"Perhaps she is in love," said miss Tracey, laughing at the shrewdness of her own observation.

"Perhaps so," replied sir Frederic thoughtfully.

It was sir Frederic's intention to marry, and, if possible, a young woman born in the same county as himself; for he wished her to have the same local prejudices as he had, and to have the same early attachments: consequently he inquired of his steward, before he came to reside at his seat, into the character of the ladies in the neighbourhood; but the steward could, or would, talk of no one but Julia Beresford; and of her he gave so exalted a character, that sir Frederic, who only remembered her as a pleasing modest girl, was very sorry that he had not paid her more attention.

Soon after, in the gallery of an eminent painter, he saw her picture; and though he thought it flattered, he gazed on it with pleasure, and fancied that Julia, when animated, might be quite as handsome as that was. Since that time he had frequently thought of her, and thought of her as a woman formed to make him happy; and indeed he had gone to look at her picture the day before he came down to the country, and had it strongly in his remembrance when he saw Julia herself, pale, spiritless, and ill-dressed, in Mr. Hanmer's drawing-room.

Perhaps it would be too much to say, that he felt as much chagrined as Mr. Beresford; but certain it is, that he was sensibly disappointed, and could not help yielding to the superior attraction of the lovely and elegant miss Tracey: besides, she was the object of general attention, and we know of old,

>   "that all contend
> To win her grace whom all commend."[18]

The concert being over, the company adjourned to an elegant entertainment set out in the open pavilion in the park, which commanded a most lovely view of the adjacent country.

Julia seated herself near the entrance; the baronet placed himself between the two lovely sisters; and Beresford, in order to

[18] From Milton's *Allegro* (123-124), though the first line reads "while both contend" in the original.

The Black Velvet Pelisse

be able to vent his spleen every now and then in his daughter's ear, took a chair beside her.

The collation had every delicacy to tempt the palate, and every decoration to gratify the taste; and all, except the pensive Julia, seemed to enjoy it:—when, as she was leaning from the door to speak to a lady at the head of the table, a little boy, about ten years old, peeped into the pavilion, as if anxiously looking for some one.

The child was so clean, and so neat in his dress, that a gentleman near him patted his curly head, and asked him what he wanted.

"A lady."

"But what lady? Here is one, and a pretty one too," showing the lady next him; "will not she do?"

"Oh no! she is not my lady," replied the boy.

At this moment Julia turned round, and the little boy, clapping his hands, exclaimed, "Oh! that's she! that's she!" Then, running out, he cried, "Mother! mother! Father! father! here she is! we have found her at last!" and before Julia, who suspected what was to follow, could leave her place, and get out of the pavilion, the poor man and woman whom she had relieved, and their now well clothed happy-looking family, appeared before the door of it.

"What does all this mean?" cried Mr. Hanmer. "Good people, whom do you want?"

"We come, sir," cried the man, "in search of that young lady," pointing to Julia; "as we could not go from the neighbourhood without coming to thank and bless her; for she saved me from going for a soldier, and my wife and children from a workhouse, sir, and made me and mine as comfortable as you now see us."

"Dear father! let me pass, pray do," cried Julia, trembling with emotion, and oppressed with ingenuous modesty.

"Stay where you are, girl," cried Beresford in a voice between laughing and crying.

"Well, but how came you hither?" cried Mr. Hanmer, who began to think this was a premeditate scheme of Julia's to show off before the company.

"Why, sir—shall I tell the whole story?" asked the man.

"No, no, pray go away," cried Julia, "and I'll come and speak to you."

"By no means," cried the baronet eagerly:—"the story, the story, if you please."

The man then began, and related Julia's meeting him and his family, her having relieved them, and then running away to avoid

17

their thanks, and to prevent her being followed, as it seemed, and being known.—That, resolved not to rest till they had learnt the name of their benefactress, they had described her person and her dress: "But, bless your honour," interrupted the woman, "when we said what she had done for us, we had not to ask any more, for every one said it could be nobody but miss Julia Beresford!"

Here Julia hid her face on her father's shoulder, and the company said not a word. The young ladies appeared conscience-struck; for it seemed that none in the neighbourhood (and they were of it) could do a kind action but miss Julia Beresford.

"Well, my good man, go on," cried Beresford gently.

"Well, sir; yesterday I heard that if I went to live at a market-town four miles off, I could get more work to do than I have in my own village, and employ for my little boy too; so we resolved to go and try our luck there: but we could not be easy to go away, without coming to thank and bless that good young lady; so, hearing at her house that she was come hither, we made bold to follow her; your servants told us where to find her:—ah! bless her!—thanks to her, I can afford to hire a cart for my poor sick wife and family."

"And, miss, miss," cried the little boy, pulling Julia by the arm, "only think, we shall ride in a cart, with a tall horse; and brother and I have got new shoes—only look!"

But miss was crying, and did not like to look: however, she made an effort, and looked up, but was forced to turn away her head again, overset by a "God bless you!" heartily pronounced by the poor woman, and echoed by the man.

"This is quite a scene, I protest," cried miss Tracey.

"But one in which we should all have been proud to have been actors, I trust," answered the baronet. "What say you, gentlemen and ladies?" continued he, coming forward: "though we cannot equal miss Beresford's kindness, since she sought out poverty, and it comes to us, what say you? shall we make a purse for these good people, that they may not think there is only one kind being in the neighbourhood?"

"Agreed!" cried every one; and, as sir Frederic held the *hat*, the subscription from the ladies was a liberal one; but Mr. Beresford gave *five guineas*: then Mr. Hanmer desired the overjoyed family to go to his house to get some refreshment, and the company reseated themselves.

But Mr. Beresford having quitted his seat, in order to wipe his eyes unseen at the door, the baronet had taken the vacant place by Julia.

18

The Black Velvet Pelisse

"Now, ladies and gentlemen," cried Beresford, blowing his nose, "you shall see a new sight,—a parent asking pardon of his child. Julia, my dear, I know I behaved very ill;—I know I was very cross to you,—very savage;—I know I was.—You are a good girl,—and always were, and ever will be, the pride of my life;—so let's kiss and be friends:"—and Julia, throwing herself into her father's arms, declared she should now be herself again!

"What! more scenes!" cried Mr. Hanmer. "What, are you sentimental too, Beresford?—Who should have thought it!"

"Why, I'll tell a story now," replied he:—"That girl vexed and mortified me confoundedly,—that she did.—I wished her to be smart, to do honour to you and your daughter to-day;—so I sent her twelve guineas to buy a very handsome velvet pelisse, which she took a fancy to, but which I thought too dear.—But instead of that,—here she comes in this old fright, and a fine dowdy figure she looks!—and when I reproached her, she said she had given the money away; and so I suppose it was that very money which she gave to these poor people.—Heh! was it not so, Julia?"

"It was," replied Julia; "and I dared not then be so extravagant as to get the pelisse too."

"So, Hanmer," continued Beresford, "you may sneer at me for being *sentimental*, if you please; but I am now prouder of my girl in her shabby cloak here, than if she were dressed out in silks and satins."

"And so you ought to be," cried sir Frederic. "And miss Beresford has converted this garment," lifting up the end of the pelisse, "into a robe of honour:"—so saying, he gallantly pressed it to his lips. "Come, I will give you a toast," continued he:—"Here is the health of the woman who was capable of sacrificing the gratification of her personal vanity to the claims of benevolence!"

The ladies put up their pretty lips, but drank the toast, and Beresford went to the door to wipe his eyes again; while Julia could not help owning to herself, that if she had had her moments of mortification, they were richly paid.

The collation was now resumed, and Julia partook of it with pleasure; her heart was at ease, her cheek recovered its bloom, and her eyes their lustre. Again the miss Traceys sung, and with increased brilliancy of execution.—"It was wonderful! they sung like professors,"[19] every one said; and then again was Julia requested to sing.

---

[19] In the now obsolete sense of "professionals."

19

"I can sing *now*," replied she; "and I never refuse when I *can* do so. Now I have found my father's favour, I shall find my voice too;" and then, without any more preamble, she sung a plaintive and simple ballad, in a manner the most touching and unadorned.

When she had ended, every one, except sir Frederic, loudly commended her, and he was silent; but Julia saw that his eyes glistened, and she heard him sigh, and she was very glad that he said nothing.

Again the sisters sung, and Julia too, and then the party broke up; but Mrs. Tracey invited the same party to meet at her house in the evening, to a ball and supper, and they all agreed to wait on her.

As they returned to the house, sir Frederic gave his arm to Julia, and miss Tracey walked before them.

"That is a very fine, showy, elegant girl," observed sir Frederic.

"She is indeed, and very handsome," replied Julia; "and her singing is really wonderful."

"Just so," replied sir Frederic;—"it is wonderful, but not pleasing. Her singing is like herself,—she is a bravura song,—showy and brilliant, but not *touching*—not interesting."—Julia smiled at the illustration; and the baronet continued:—"Will you be angry at my presumption, miss Beresford, if I venture to add that you too resemble your singing? If miss Tracey be a bravura song, you are a ballad,—not showy, not brilliant, but touching, interesting, and—"

"O! pray say no more," cried Julia, blushing, and hastening to join the company,—but it was a blush of pleasure; and as she rode home she amused herself with analysing all the properties of the *ballad*, and she was very well contented with the analysis.

That evening Julia, all herself again, and dressed with exquisite and becoming taste, danced, smiled, talked, and was universally admired. But was she *particularly* so? Did the man of her heart follow her with delighted attention?

"Julia," said her happy father, as they went home at night, "you will have the velvet pelisse and sir Frederic too, I expect."

Nor was he mistaken. The pelisse was hers the next day, and the baronet some months after. But Julia to this hour preserves with the utmost care the faded pelisse, which sir Frederic had pronounced to "a robe of honour."

Samuel Taylor Coleridge

Story of Maria Schöning

(1809)

The author: Samuel Taylor Coleridge was born on 21 October 1772 in the town of Ottery St Mary, Devon, where his father was the vicar and school headmaster. He studied at the prestigious Christ's Hospital (where he befriended Charles Lamb) and attended Jesus College, Cambridge from 1791 to 1794. At Cambridge, he began a long-lasting relationship with Robert Southey. In 1795, he forged another lifetime friendship, with William Wordsworth. In 1796, he published his first book of poetry, *Poems on Various Subjects*, but his enduring fame comes from the 1798 *Lyrical Ballads* (which included his poem "The Rime of the Ancient Mariner"), a collaborative effort with Wordsworth, widely seen as the starting point and the manifesto of English Romanticism. After brief studies in Germany, he lived with wife, two sons, and one daughter in the Lake District, together with the Wordsworths. He gradually separated from his wife, first by travelling, then by staying with friends, and finally by living with physicians who were trying to control his opium and laudanum addiction. In 1809 he edited a journal (*The Friend*), which he wrote almost single-handed. In 1812, he gave popular lectures on Shakespeare and Milton. In 1816-1817, he published his last important works: the unfinished poems *Christabel* and *Kubla Khan* and the half-literary-theory/half-autobiography *Biographia Literaria*. His interests were wide and he wrote on politics, theology, and society. A post-Kantian, he was working on a philosophical treatise when he died on 25 July 1834, in Highgate, London. All his children became authors, though none was as influential as their father. Henry Nelson Coleridge, his nephew and son-in-law (he had married Coleridge's daugter Sara, his cousin) became his literary executor.

The text: The story was inspired by "Nürnbergischer Justizmord" ("Judicial Murder in Nuremberg"), a chapter in the fourth volume of a series about German cities published by Jonas Ludwig von Hess at the end of the 18th century.[20] Judicial murder was a relatively recent concept, introduced in the 18th century to refer to wrongful executions. Coleridge's very personal adaptation of Hess's account appeared in *The Friend* 13 (16 November 1809) and was reprinted three years later in the volume version of Coleridge's magazine (London: Gale and Curtis, 1812), 194-208. The following is from Henry Nelson Coleridge's three-volume version of *The Friend . . . the fourth edition, with the author's last corrections* (London: William Pickering, 1844), II, 207-232. The main difference between the 1809 original and later versions is that many nouns used to be capitalised.

Further reading: Deirdre Coleman. "A Horrid Tale in 'The Friend.'" *The Wordsworth Circle* 12: 4 (Autumn 1981), 262-269.

It were a wantonness, and would demand
Severe reproof if we were men whose hearts
Could hold vain dalliance with the misery
Even of the dead; contented thence to draw
A momentary pleasure, never mark'd
By reason, barren of all future good.
But we have known that there is often found
In mournful thoughts, and always might be found
A power to virtue friendly.—WORDSWORTH, MS.[21]

I know not how I can better commence my second Landing-Place, as joining on to the section of Politics,[22] than by the following

---

[20] Hess's account was reproduced as "Maria Eleonora Schöning, ein Reichstättischer Justizmord" in *Erzählunger interessanter Geschichten, Launen, Gedichte, Anekdoten und Aufsäze für Stammbücher*. Dritter Band (Stuttgart: Friedrich Uebel, 1798), 84-113. The story had been previously told in English by G.H. Wilson in *The Eccentric Mirror: Reflecting a Faithful and Interesting Delineation of Male and Female Characters, Ancient and Modern* (London: James Cundee, 1807), II, 6-28.

[21] The lines are from Wordsworth's *The Excursion*, which would have been in manuscript in 1809, when the story appeared in *The Friend*. However, Wordsworth published the poem in 1814, but neither Coleridge nor his nephew-editor changed this note in subsequent editions.

[22] In the "new edition" of 1818, Coleridge divided the pieces of *The Friend* into two distinct sections and three miscellaneous parts ("for amusement, retrospect, and preparation") called "landing-places." The story of Maria Schoning became "Essay I" of the second landing-place.

Story of Maria Schoning

proof of the severe miseries which misgovernment may occasion in a country nominally free. In the homely ballad of the Three Graves[23] I have attempted to exemplify the effect, which one painful idea, vividly impressed on the mind under unusual circumstances, might have in producing an alienation of the understanding; and in the parts hitherto published, I have endeavoured to trace the progress to madness, step by step. But though the main incidents are facts, the detail of the circumstances is of my own invention; that is, not what I knew, but what I conceived likely to have been the case, or at least equivalent to it. In the tale that follows, I present an instance of the same causes acting upon the mind to the production of conduct as wild as that of madness, but without any positive or permanent loss of the reason or the understanding; and this in a real occurrence, real in all its parts and particulars. But in truth this tale overflows with a human interest, and needs no philosophical deduction to make it impressive. The account was published in the city in which the event took place, and in the same year I read it, when I was in Germany,[24] and the impression made on my memory was so deep, that though I relate it in my own language, and with my own feelings, and in reliance on the fidelity of my recollection, I dare vouch for the accuracy of the narration in all important particulars.

The imperial free towns of Germany are, with only two or three exceptions, enviably distinguished by the virtuous and primitive manners of the citizens, and by the parental character of their several governments.[25] As exceptions however, I must mention Aix la Chapelle, poisoned by French manners, and the concourse

---

[23] In 1818, Coleridge added "published in my Sybilline Leaves" in a parenthesis that summarized the original text of 1809. This was replaced by H.N. Coleridge with a footnote sending the reader to the first volume of his edition of his uncle's poetical works: "Poet. Work, vol. i. 219.—*Ed.*" "The Three Graves" (parts III and IV) had appeared in *The Friend* 6 (21 September 1809) and were reprinted in 1817 in *Sybilline Leaves*. Parts I and II of this poem that Coleridge was working on in the spring of 1798 appeared posthumously.

[24] Coleridge was in Germany between September 1798 and July 1799. The book where he found the account of Maria Schöning was a travelogue by Jonas Ludwig von Hess (1756-1823), the four-volume *Durchflüge durch Deutschland, die Nidederlande und Frankreich*, published in Hamburg (not in Nürnberg) from 1793 to 1797 (a three-volume sequel appeared in 1798-1800 also in Hamburg). The story of Maria Schöning is in the fourth volume, published in 1797 (97-130).

[25] A free imperial city (*Reichsstadt*) was autonomous and subordinate directly to the emperor.

23

of gamesters and sharpers; and Nüremberg,[26] the industrious and honest inhabitants of which deserve a better fate than to have their lives and properties under the guardianship of a wolfish and merciless oligarchy, proud from ignorance, and remaining ignorant through pride. It is from the small states of Germany that our writers on political economy might draw their most forcible instances of actually oppressive, and even mortal, taxation, and gain the clearest insight into the causes and circumstances of the injury. One other remark, and I proceed to the story. I well remember, that the event I am about to narrate, called forth, in several of the German periodical publications, the most passionate (and in more than one instance blasphemous) declamations concerning the incomprehensibility of the moral government of the world, and the seeming injustice and cruelty of the dispensations of Providence. But, assuredly, every one of my readers, however deeply he may sympathize with the poor sufferers, will at once answer all such declamations by the simple reflection, that no one of these awful events could possibly have taken place under a wise police and humane government, and that men have no right to complain of Providence for evils which they themselves are competent to remedy by mere common sense, joined with mere common humanity.

Maria Eleonora Schöning was the daughter of a Nüremberg wire-drawer.[27] She received her unhappy existence at the price of her mother's life, and at the age of seventeen she followed, as the sole mourner, the bier of her remaining parent. From her thirteenth year she had passed her life at her father's sick-bed, the gout having deprived him of the use of his limbs, and seen the arch of heaven only when she went to fetch food or medicines. The discharge of her filial duties occupied the whole of her time and all her thoughts. She was his only nurse, and for the last two years they lived without a servant. She prepared his scanty meal, she bathed his aching limbs, and though weak and delicate from constant confinement and the poison of melancholy thoughts, she had acquired an unusual power in her arms, from the habit of lifting her old and suffering father out of and into his bed of pain. Thus passed away her early youth in

---

[26] Aachen (or Aix-la-Chapelle) is on the border with Belgium and the Netherlands and had been occupied by French troops in 1794, becoming French territory between 1801 and 1815. Nürnberg (or Nuremberg) is in Bavaria and had been a free imperial city since 1219.

[27] Coleridge translates the German term of "Drathfabrikant" (in archaic spelling). Wire drawing is still the name of the process, except today it is mostly done with automated machinery. In G.H. Wilson's version, Maria's father is identified simply as a "mechanic."

Story of Maria Schoning

sorrow: she grew up in tears, a stranger to the amusements of youth and its more delightful schemes and imaginations. She was not, however, unhappy: she attributed, indeed, no merit to herself for her virtues, but for that reason were they the more her reward. The *peace which passeth all understanding*[28] disclosed itself in all her looks and movements. It lay on her countenance, like a steady unshadowed moonlight: and her voice, which was naturally at once sweet and subtle, came from her, like the fine flute-tones of a masterly performer, which still floating at some uncertain distance, seem to be created by the player, rather than to proceed from the instrument. If you had listened to it in one of those brief sabbaths of the soul, when the activity and discursiveness of the thoughts are suspended, and the mind quietly eddies round, instead of flowing onward—(as at late evening in the spring I have seen a bat wheel in silent circles round and round a fruit-tree in full blossom, in the midst of which, as within a close tent of the purest white, an unseen nightingale was piping its sweetest notes)—in such a mood you might have half-fancied, half-felt, that her voice had a separate being of its own—that it was a living something, the mode of existence of which was for the ear only: so deep was her resignation, so entirely had it become the unconscious habit of her nature, and in all she did or said, so perfectly were both her movements and her utterance without effort, and without the appearance of effort! Her dying father's last words, addressed to the clergyman who attended him, were his grateful testimony, that during his long and sore trial his good Maria had behaved to him like an angel;—that the most disagreeable offices and the least suited to her age and sex, had never drawn an unwilling look from her, and that whenever his eye had met hers, he had been sure to see in it either the tear of pity or the sudden smile expressive of her affection and wish to cheer him. God (said he) will reward the good girl for all her long dutifulness to me! He departed during the inward prayer, which followed these his last words. His wish will be fulfilled in eternity; but for this world the prayer of the dying man was not heard.

  Maria sat and wept by the grave, which now contained her father, her friend, the only bond by which she was linked to life. But while yet the last sound of his death-bell was murmuring away in the air, she was obliged to return with two revenue officers, who demanded entrance into the house, in order to take possession of the papers of the deceased, and from them to discover whether he had always given in his income, and paid the yearly income-tax according to his

---

[28] From *Philippians* 4: 7: "And the peace of God, which passeth all understanding, shall keep your hearts and minds through Christ Jesus."

oath, and in proportion to his property.[29] After the few documents had been looked through and collated with the registers, the officers found, or pretended to find, sufficient proofs, that the deceased had not paid his tax proportionably, which imposed on them the duty to put all the effects under lock and seal. They therefore desired the maiden to retire to an empty room, till the Ransom Office had decided on the affair. Bred up in suffering, and habituated to immediate compliance, the affrighted and weeping maiden obeyed. She hastened to the empty garret, while the revenue officers placed the lock and seal upon the other doors, and finally took away the papers to the Ransom Office.

Not before evening did the poor faint Maria, exhausted with weeping, rouse herself with the intention of going to her bed: but she found the door of her chamber sealed up, and that she must pass the night on the floor of the garret. The officers had had the humanity to place at the door the small portion of food that happened to be in the house. Thus passed several days, till the officers returned with an order that Maria Eleonora Schöning should leave the house without delay, the commission court having confiscated the whole property to the city treasury. The father before he was bed-ridden had never possessed any considerable property; but yet, by his industry, had been able not only to keep himself free from debt, but to lay up a small sum for the evil day. Three years of evil days, three whole years of sickness, had consumed the greatest part of this; yet still enough remained not only to defend his daughter from immediate want, but likewise to maintain her till she could get into some service or employment, and should have recovered her spirits sufficiently to bear up against the hardships of life. With this thought her dying

---

[29] Hess inserted a note here to explain the term. Coleridge did the same, keeping much of the original information. Here is Coleridge's version: "This tax, called the *Losung* or ransom, in Nüremberg, was at first a voluntary contribution: every one gave according to his liking or circumstances. But in the beginning of the 15th century the heavy contributions levied for the service of the Empire forced the magistrates to determine the proportions and make the payment compulsory. Every citizen must yearly take what is called his ransom oath (*Losungseid*) that the sum paid by him has been in the strict determinate proportion to his property. On the death of any citizen, the Ransom Office, or commissioners for this income or property tax, possess the right to examine his books and papers, and to compare his yearly payment as found in their registers with the property he appears to have possessed during that time. If any disproportion is detected, if the yearly declarations of the deceased should have been inaccurate in the least degree, his whole effects are confiscated, and though he should have left wife and child, the state treasury become his heir." More exactly, the term "Losung" (from the same root as the English "lot") was used in the sense of "drawing [lots]" as this tax was originally organised in the form of a lottery.

Story of Maria Schoning

father comforted himself, and his hope too proved vain.

A timid girl, whose past life had been made up of sorrow and privation, she went indeed to solicit the commissioners in her own behalf; but these were, as is mostly the case on the continent, advocates—the most hateful class, perhaps, of human society, hardened by the frequent sight of misery, and seldom superior in moral character to English pettifoggers or Old Bailey attornies.[30] She went to them, indeed, but not a word could she say for herself. Her tears and inarticulate sounds—for these her judges had no ears or eyes. Mute and confounded, like an unfledged dove fallen out from its mother's nest, Maria betook herself to her home, and found the house door too now shut upon her. Her whole wealth consisted in the clothes she wore. She had no relations to whom she could apply, for those of her mother had disdained all acquaintance with her, and her father was a Nether Saxon by birth.[31] She had no acquaintance, for all the friends of old Schöning had forsaken him in the first year of his sickness. She had no play-fellow, for who was likely to have been the companion of a nurse in the room of a sick man? Surely, since the creation never was a human being more solitary and forsaken than this innocent poor creature, that now roamed about friendless in a populous city, to the whole of whose inhabitants her filial tenderness, her patient domestic goodness, and all her soft yet difficult virtues, might well have been the model:—

> But homeless near a thousand homes she stood,
> And near a thousand tables pin'd and wanted food![32]

The night came, and Maria knew not where to find a shelter. She tottered to the church-yard of St. James' church in Nüremberg,[33] where the body of her father rested. Upon the yet grassless grave she threw herself down; and could anguish have prevailed over youth, that night she had been in heaven. The day came, and like a guilty thing, this guiltless, this good being, stole away from the crowd that began to pass through the church-yard, and hastening through the streets to the city gate, she hid herself behind a garden hedge just beyond it, and there wept away the second day of her desolation.

[30] Old Bailey is the name of the major criminal court in London.

[31] Lower Saxony (Niedersachsen) is in northwestern Germany, far from Bavaria.

[32] The lines were not identified in the original version. Henry Nelson Coleridge inserted a brief note: "Wordsworth's Female Vagrant.—*Ed.*" "Female Vagrant" is a poem from *Lyrical Ballads* (1798). In later life, Wordsworth included these lines in a longer poem entitled "Guilt and Sorrow; or, Incidents upon Salisbury Plain."

[33] St. Jakob, a medieval church in Nuremberg founded in 1209.

The evening closed in: the pang of hunger made itself felt amid the dull aching of self-wearied anguish, and drove the sufferer back again into the city. Yet what could she gain there? She had not the courage to beg, and the very thought of stealing never occurred to her innocent mind. Scarce conscious whither she was going, or why she went, she found herself once more by her father's grave, as the last relic of evening faded away in the horizon.

 I have sat for some minutes with my pen resting: I can scarce summon the courage to tell, what I scarce know whether I ought to tell. Were I composing a tale of fiction, the reader might justly suspect the purity of my own heart, and most certainly would have abundant right to resent such an incident, as an outrage wantonly offered to his imagination. As I think of the circumstance, it seems more like a distempered dream: but alas! what is guilt so detestable other than a dream of madness, that worst madness, the madness of the heart? I cannot but believe, that the dark and restless passions must first have drawn the mind in upon themselves, and, as with the confusion of imperfect sleep, have in some strange manner taken away the sense of reality, in order to render it possible for a human being to perpetrate what it is too certain that human beings have perpetrated. The church-yards in most of the German cities, and too often, I fear, in those of our own country, are not more injurious to health than to morality. Their former venerable character is no more. The religion of the place has followed its superstitions, and their darkness and loneliness tempt worse spirits to roam in them than those whose nightly wanderings appalled the believing hearts of our brave forefathers. It was close by the new-made grave of her father that the meek and spotless daughter became the victim to brutal violence, which weeping and watching and cold and hunger had rendered her utterly unable to resist. The monster left her in a trance of stupefaction, and into her right hand, which she had clenched convulsively, he had forced a half-dollar.

 It was one of the darkest nights of autumn: in the deep and dead silence the only sounds audible were the slow blunt ticking of the church clock, and now and then the sinking down of bones in the nigh charnel house. Maria, when she had in some degree recovered her senses, sate upon the grave near which—not her innocence had been sacrificed, but—that which, from the frequent admonitions and almost the dying words of her father, she had been accustomed to consider as such. Guiltless, she felt the pangs of guilt, and still continued to grasp the coin which the monster had left in her hand, with an anguish as sore as if it had been indeed the wages of voluntary prostitution. Giddy and faint from want of food, her brain becoming feverish from sleeplessness, and this unexampled

Story of Maria Schoning

concurrence of calamities, this complication and entanglement of misery in misery, she imagined that she heard her father's voice bidding her leave his sight. His last blessings had been conditional, for in his last hours he had told her, that the loss of her innocence would not let him rest quiet in his grave. His last blessings now sounded in her ears like curses, and she fled from the church-yard as if a demon had been chasing her; and hurrying along the streets, through which it is probable her accursed violator had walked with quiet and orderly step[34] to his place of rest and security, she was seized by the watchmen of the night—a welcome prey, as they receive in Nüremberg a reward from the police chest, for every woman they find in the streets after ten o'clock at night. It was midnight, and she was taken to the next watch-house.

The sitting magistrate, before whom she was carried the next morning, prefaced his first question with the most opprobrious title that ever belonged to the most hardened street-walkers, and which man born of woman should not address even to these, were it but for his own sake. The frightful name awakened the poor orphan from her dream of guilt, it brought back the consciousness of her innocence,

---

[34] Coleridge inserted here the following long note: "It must surely have been after hearing or of witnessing some similar event or scene of wretchedness, that the most eloquent of our writers (I had almost said of our poets), Jeremy Taylor, wrote the following paragraph, which at least in Longinus's sense of the word, we may place among the most sublime passages in English literature. 'He that is no fool, but can consider wisely, if he be in love with this world, we need not despair but that a witty man might reconcile him with tortures, and make him think charitably of the rack, and be brought to admire the harmony that is made by a herd of evening wolves when they miss their draught of blood in their midnight revels. The groans of a man in a fit of the stone are worse than all these; and the distractions of a troubled conscience are worse than those groans: and yet a careless merry sinner is worse than all that. But if we could from one of the battlements of heaven espy, how many men and women at this time lie fainting and dying for want of bread, how many young men are hewn down by the sword of war; how many poor orphans are now weeping over the graves of their father, by whose life they were enabled to eat; if we could but hear how many mariners and passengers are at this present in a storm, and shriek out because their keel dashes against a rock, or bulges under them; how many people there are that weep with want, and are mad with oppression, or are desperate by a too quick sense of a constant infelicity; in all reason we should be glad to be out of the noise and participation of so many evils. This is a place of sorrows and tears, of great evils and constant calamities: let us remove hence, at least in affections and preparations of mind.'" To this, Henry Nelson Coleridge added the source: "*Holy Dying*, ch. i. s. 5. with omissions.—*Ed.*" The omissions are in the first part (there are also two minor alterations). Jeremy Taylor (1613-1667) is widely seen as one of the greatest English prose writers of the 17th century.

29

but with it the sense likewise of her wrongs and of her helplessness. The cold hand of death seemed to grasp her, she fainted dead away at his feet, and was not without difficulty recovered. The magistrate was so far softened, and only so far, as to dismiss her for the present; but with a menace of sending her to the House of Correction if she were brought before him a second time. The idea of her own innocence now became uppermost in her mind; but mingling with the thought of her utter forlornness, and the image of her angry father, and doubtless still in a state of bewilderment, she formed the resolution of drowning herself in the river Pegnitz[35]—in order (for this was the shape which her fancy had taken) to throw herself at her father's feet, and to justify her innocence to him in the world of spirits. She hoped, that her father would speak for her to the Saviour, and that she should be forgiven. But as she was passing through the suburb, she was meet by a soldier's wife, who during the life-time of her father had been occasionally employed in the house as a chare-woman. This poor woman was startled at the disordered apparel, and more disordered looks of her young mistress, and questioned her with such an anxious and heart-felt tenderness, as at once brought back the poor orphan to her natural feelings and the obligations of religion. As a frightened child throws itself into the arms of its mother, and hiding its head on her breast, half tells amid sobs what has happened to it, so did she throw herself on the neck of the woman who had uttered the first words of kindness to her since her father's death, and with loud weeping she related what she had endured and what she was about to have done, told her all her affliction and her misery, the wormwood and the gall.[36] Her kind-hearted friend mingled tears with tears, pressed the poor forsaken one to her heart; comforted her with sentences out of the hymn-book; and with the most affectionate entreaties conjured her to give up her horrid purpose, for that life was short, and heaven was for ever.

    Maria had been bred up in the fear of God: she now trembled at the thought of her former purpose, and followed her friend Harlin, for that was the name of her guardian angel, to her home hard by. The moment she entered the door she sank down and lay at her full length, as if only to be motionless in a place of shelter

---

[35] The Pegnitz river flows through Nürnberg, where its banks are bordered mostly by weeping willows.

[36] Expression for bitterness and grief. The two words appear in various combinations elsewhere in the Bible, but the exact quote is from *Lamentations* 3: 19: "mine affliction and my misery, the wormwood and the gall."

Story of Maria Schoning

had been the fulness of delight. As when a withered leaf, that has been long whirled about by the gusts of autumn, is blown into a cave or hollow tree, it stops suddenly, and all at once looks the very image of quiet—such might this poor orphan appear to the eye of a meditative imagination.

A place of shelter she had attained, and a friend willing to comfort her in all that she could: but the noble-hearted Harlin was herself a daughter of calamity, one who from year to year must lie down in weariness and rise up to labour; for whom this world provides no other comfort but the sleep which enables them to forget it; no other physician but death, which takes them out of it. She was married to one of the city guards, who, like Maria's father, had been long sick and bed-ridden. Him, herself, and two little children, she had to maintain by washing and charing;[37] and sometime after Maria had been domesticated with them, Harlin told her that she herself had been once driven to a desperate thought by the cry of her hungry children, during a want of employment, and that she had been on the point of killing one of the little ones, and of then surrendering herself into the hands of justice. In this manner, she had conceived, all would be well provided for; the surviving child would be admitted, as a manner of course, into the Orphan House, and her husband into the Hospital; while she herself would have atoned for her act by a public execution, and together with the child that she had destroyed, would have passed into a state of bliss. All this she related to Maria, and those tragic thoughts left but too deep and lasting impression on her mind. Weeks after, she herself renewed the conversation, by expressing to her benefactress her inability to conceive how it was possible for one human being to take away the life of another, especially that of an innocent little child. "For that reason," replied Harlin, "because it was so innocent and so good, I wished to put it out of this wicked world. Thinkest thou then, that I would have my head cut off for the sake of a wicked child? Therefore it was little Nan, that I meant to have taken with me, who, as you see, is always so sweet and patient; little Frank has already his humours and naughty tricks, and suits better for this world." This was the answer. Maria brooded awhile over it in silence, then passionately snatched the children up in her arms, as if she would protect them against their own mother.

---

[37] Coleridge inserted the following note: "I am ignorant whether there be any classical authority for this word; but I know no other word that expresses occasional day-labour in the houses of others." *Char* or *chare* (as it appears previously in the story) comes from an Old English word meaning "a turn, a short period of time." It was used for part-time jobs and it has evolved into the contemporary word "chore."

31

For one whole year the orphan lived with the soldier's wife, and by their joint labours barely kept off absolute want. As a little boy (almost a child in size, though in his thirteenth year) once told me of himself, as he was guiding me up the Brocken, in the Hartz Forest, they had but "little of that, of which a great deal tells but for little."[38] But now came the second winter, and with it came bad times, a season of trouble for this poor and meritorious household. The wife now fell sick: too constant and too hard labour, too scanty and too innutritious food, had gradually wasted away her strength. Maria redoubled her efforts in order to provide bread, and fuel for their washing which they took in; but the task was above her powers. Besides, she was so timid and so agitated at the sight of strangers, that sometimes, with the best good-will, she was left without employment. One by one, every article of the least value which they possessed was sold off, except the bed on which the husband lay. He died just before the approach of spring; but about the same time the wife gave signs of convalescence. The physician, though almost as poor as his patients, had been kind to them: silver and gold had he none, but he occasionally brought a little wine, and often assured them that nothing was wanting to her perfect recovery, but better nourishment and a little wine every day. This, however, could not be regularly procured, and Harlin's spirits sank, and as her bodily pain left her she became more melancholy, silent, and self-involved. And now it was that Maria's mind was increasingly racked by the frightful apprehension, that her friend might be again meditating the accomplishment of her former purpose. She had grown as passionately fond of the two children as if she had borne them under her own heart; but the jeopardy in which she conceived her friend's salvation to stand—this was her predominant thought. For all the hopes and fears, which under a happier lot would have been associated with the objects of the senses, were transferred by Maria, to her notions and images of a future state.

In the beginning of March, one bitter cold evening, Maria started up and suddenly left the house. The last morsel of food had been divided betwixt the two children for their breakfast: and for the last hour or more the little boy had been crying for hunger, while his gentler sister had been hiding her face in Maria's lap, and pressing her little body against her knees, in order by that mechanic pressure to dull the aching from emptiness. The tender-hearted and visionary maiden had watched the mother's eye, and had interpreted several of her sad and steady looks according to

[38] The Brocken is the highest peak in the Harz mountain range in Saxony. Coleridge climbed it in May 1799. The boy told him, in other words, that they lacked all those things that make no real difference.

Story of Maria Schoning

her preconceived apprehensions. She had conceived all at once the strange and enthusiastic thought, that she would in some way or other offer her own soul for the salvation of the soul of her friend. The money, which had been left in her hand, flashed upon the eye of her mind, as a single unconnected image: and faint with hunger and shivering with cold, she sallied forth—in search of guilt! Awful are the dispensations of the Supreme, and in his severest judgments the hand of mercy is visible. It was a night so wild with wind and rain, or rather rain and snow mixed together, that a famished wolf would have staid in his cave, and listened to a howl more fearful than his own. Forlorn Maria! thou wast kneeling in pious simplicity at the grave of thy father, and thou becamest the prey of a monster. Innocent thou wast, and without guilt didst thou remain. Now thou goest forth of thy own accord;—but God will have pity on thee. Poor bewildered innocent! in thy spotless imagination dwelt no distinct conception of the evil which thou wentest forth to brave. To save the soul of thy friend was the dream of thy feverish brain, and thou wast again apprehended as an outcast of shameless sensuality, at the moment when thy too spiritualized fancy was busied with the glorified forms of thy friend and her little ones interceding for thee at the throne of the Redeemer!

At this moment her perturbed fancy suddenly suggested to her a new mean for the accomplishment of her purpose: and she replied to the night-watch, who with a brutal laugh bade her expect on the morrow the unmanly punishment, which to the disgrace of human nature the laws of some Protestant states[39] inflict on female vagrants, that she came to deliver herself up as an infanticide. She was instantly taken before the magistrate through as wild and pitiless a storm as ever pelted on a houseless head,—through as black and tyrannous a night as ever aided the workings of a heated brain. Here she confessed that she had been delivered of an infant by the soldier's wife, Harlin, that she deprived it of life in the presence of Harlin, and according to a plan preconcerted with her, and that Harlin had buried it somewhere in the wood, but where she knew not. During this strange tale she appeared to listen with a mixture of fear and satisfaction to the howling of the wind; and never sure could a confession of real guilt have accompanied by a more dreadfully appropriate music. At the moment of her apprehension she had formed the scheme of helping her friend out of the world in a state of innocence. When the soldier's widow was confronted with the orphan, and the latter had repeated her confession to her face, Harlin answered in these words, "For God's sake, Maria! how

[39] Here, earlier editions included a parenthesis adding "alas! even those of our country." The unmanly punishment was whipping.

have I deserved this of thee?" Then turning to the magistrate, said, "I know nothing of this." This was the sole answer which she gave, and not another word could they extort from her. The instruments of torture were brought, and Harlin was warned, that if she did not confess of her own accord, the truth would be immediately forced from her. This menace convulsed Maria Schöning with affright; her intention had been to emancipate herself and her friend from a life of unmixed suffering, without the crime of suicide in either, and with no guilt at all on the part of her friend. The thought of her friend's being put to the torture had not occurred to her. Wildly and eagerly she pressed her friend's hands, already bound in preparation for the torture;—she pressed them in agony between her own, and said to her, "Anna! confess it! Anna, dear Anna! it will then be well with all of us! all, all of us! and Frank and little Nan will be put into the Orphan House!" Maria's scheme now passed, like a flash of lightning, through the widow's mind; she acceded to it at once, kissed Maria repeatedly, and then serenely turning her face to the judge, acknowledged that she had added to the guilt by so obstinate a denial, that all her friend had said was true, save only that she had thrown the dead infant into the river, and not buried it in the wood.

They were both committed to prison, and as they both persevered in their common confession, the process was soon made out, and the condemnation followed the trial: and the sentence, by which they were both to be beheaded with the sword, was ordered to be put in force on the next day but one. On the morning of the execution, the delinquents were brought together, in order that they might be reconciled with each other, and join in common prayer for forgiveness of their common guilt.

But now Maria's thoughts took another turn. The idea that her benefactress, that so very good a woman, should be violently put out of life, and this with an infamy on her name which would cling for ever to the little orphans, overpowered her. Her own excessive desire to die scarcely prevented her from discovering the whole plan; and when Harlin was left alone with her, and she saw her friend's calm and affectionate look, her fortitude was dissolved: she burst into loud and passionate weeping, and throwing herself into her friend's arms, with convulsive sobs she entreated her forgiveness. Harlin pressed the poor agonized girl to her arms; like a tender mother, she kissed and fondled her wet cheeks, and in the most solemn and emphatic tones assured her that there was nothing to forgive. On the contrary, she was her greatest benefactress and the instrument of God's goodness to remove her at once from a miserable world, and from the temptation of committing a heavy crime. In vain. Her repeated promises, that she would answer before God for them

Story of Maria Schoning

both, could not pacify the tortured conscience of Maria, till at length the presence of the clergyman and the preparations for receiving the sacrament occasioning the widow to address her thus—"See, Maria! this is the Body and Blood of Christ, which takes away all sin! Let us partake together of this holy repast with full trust in God and joyful hope of our approaching happiness." These words of comfort, uttered with cheering tones, and accompanied with a look of inexpressible tenderness and serenity, brought back peace for a while to her troubled spirit. They communicated together, and on parting, the magnanimous woman once more embraced her young friend: then stretching her hand toward heaven, said, "Be tranquil, Maria! by to-morrow morning we are there, and all our sorrows stay here behind us."

I hasten to the scene of the execution: for I anticipate my reader's feelings in the exhaustion of my own heart. Serene and with unaltered countenance the lofty-minded Harlin heard the strokes of the death-bell, stood before the scaffold while the staff was broken over her, and at length ascended the steps, all with a steadiness and tranquillity of manner which was not more distant from fear than from defiance and bravado. Altogether different was the state of poor Maria: with shattered nerves and an agonizing conscience that incessantly accused her as the murderess of her friend, she did not walk but staggered towards the scaffold and stumbled up the steps. While Harlin, who went first, at every step turned her head round and still whispered to her, raising her eyes to heaven,—"But a few minutes, Maria! and we are there!" On the scaffold she again bade her farewell, again repeating "Dear Maria! but one minute now, and we are together with God." But when she knelt down and her neck was bared for the stroke, the unhappy girl lost all self-command, and with a loud and piercing shriek she bade them hold and not murder the innocent. "She is innocent! I have borne false witness! I alone am the murderess!" She rolled herself now at the feet of the executioner, and now at those of the clergyman, and conjured them to stop the execution, declaring that the whole story had been invented by herself; that she had never brought forth, much less destroyed, an infant; that for her friend's sake she made this discovery; that for herself she wished to die, and would die gladly, if they would take away her friend, and promise to free her soul from the dreadful agony of having murdered her friend by false witness. The executioner asked Harlin, if there were any truth in what Maria Schöning had said. The heroine answered with manifest reluctance: "Most assuredly she hath said the truth: I confessed myself guilty, because I wished to die and thought it best for both of us: and now that my hope is on the moment of its accomplishment, I cannot be supposed to declare myself innocent for the sake of saving my life;—but any wretchedness is to be endured rather than that poor creature should be hurried out of the world in a state of despair."

The outcry of the attending populace prevailed to suspend the execution: a report was sent to the assembled magistrates, and in the mean time one of the priests reproached the widow in bitter words for her former false confession. "What," she replied sternly but without anger, "what would the truth have availed? Before I perceived my friend's purpose I did deny it: my assurance was pronounced an impudent lie: I was already bound for the torture, and so bound that the sinews of my hands started, and one of their worships in the large white peruke,[40] threatened that he would have me stretched till the sun shone through me;—and that then I could cry out, Yes, when it was too late." The priest was hard-hearted or superstitious enough to continue his reproofs, to which the noble woman condescended no further answer. The other clergyman, however, was both more rational and more humane. He succeeded in silencing his. colleague, and the former half of the long hour, which the magistrates took in making speeches on the improbability of the tale instead of re-examining the culprits in person, he employed in gaining from the widow a connected account of all the circumstances, and in listening occasionally to Maria's passionate description of all her friend's goodness and magnanimity. For she had gained an influx of life and spirit from the assurance in her mind, both that she had now rescued Harlin from death and was about to expiate the guilt of her purpose by her own execution. For the latter half of the time the clergyman remained in silence, lost in thought, and momently expecting the return of the messenger. All that during the deep silence of this interval could be heard, was one exclamation of Harlin to her unhappy friend—"Oh! Maria! Maria! couldst thou but have kept up thy courage for another minute, we should have been now in heaven!" The messenger came back with an order from the magistrates—to proceed with the execution! With re-animated countenance Harlin placed her neck on the block, and her head was severed from her body amid a general shriek from the crowd. The executioner fainted after the blow, and the under hangman was ordered to take his place. He was not wanted. Maria was already gone: her body was found as cold as if she had been dead for some hours. The flower had been snapt in the storm, before the scythe of violence could come near it.

---

[40] Peruke or periwig was the wig worn by men in the 17th and 18th centuries.

Maria Edgeworth

𝒯HE 𝒟UN

(1809)

The author: Maria Edgeworth was born in Oxfordshire, on January 1, 1768, but, after her mother's death in 1773, she joined her father, Richard Lovell Edgeworth, on his estate in Ireland. She became her father's assistant, both in his business and his literary pursuits. With her father and his third wife, she published an influential pedagogical treatise, *Practical Education* (1798). Her best friend and confidante was his father's fourth wife, Frances Beaufort, who was one year younger than Maria and provided illustrations for one of her books. Her first published works were *Letters for Literary Ladies* (1795) and *The Parent's Assistant* (1796), the latter a collection of short stories about children. She achieved notoriety with her novels: *Castle Rackrent* (1800), *Belinda* (1801), *Lenora* (1806), *The Absentee* (1812), *Harrington* (1817), *Helen* (1834) and others. Always involved in issues concerning Ireland, she published a famous *Essay on Irish Bulls* (that is, on Irish quirky sayings). She continued to write well-received stories, such as her *Moral Tales* (1801) and *Tales of Fashionable Life* (1809), as well as books on education. She had a wide circle of friends and correspondents, including luminaries like Walter Scott and David Ricardo. She never married. She died at home in 1849.

The text: First published in *Tales of Fashionable Life* (London: J. Johnson, 1809), Vol. II, 331-390. The following is from this original version, rather than from the 1832 edition (London: Baldwin & Cradock), in which it later appeared (I, 295-332), supposedly corrected by Maria and her half-sisters Harriet and Honora. The sisters improved mostly the punctuation, but some of their doubtful readings make the 1832 version unreliable.

Further reading: Teresa Michals. "Commerce and Character in Maria Edgeworth." *Nineteenth-Century Literature* 49:1 (June 1994), 1-20.

> Horrible monster! hated by gods and men.
> Philips[41]

"In the higher and middle classes of society," says a celebrated writer, "it is a melancholy and distressing sight to observe, not unfrequently, a man of a noble and ingenuous disposition, once feelingly alive to a sense of honour and integrity, gradually sinking under the pressure of his circumstances, making his excuses at first with a blush of conscious shame, afraid to see the faces of his friends from whom he may have borrowed money, reduced to the meanest tricks and subterfuges to delay or avoid the payment of his just debts, till, ultimately grown familiar with falsehood, and at enmity with the world, he loses all the grace and dignity of man."[42]

Colonel Pembroke, the subject of the following story, had not, at the time his biographer first became acquainted with him, "grown familiar with falsehood;" his conscience was not entirely callous to reproach, nor was his heart insensible to compassion; but he was in a fair way to get rid of all troublesome feelings and principles. He was connected with a set of selfish young men of fashion, whose opinions stood him in stead of law, equity, and morality; to them he appealed in all doubtful cases, and his self-complacency being daily and hourly dependent upon their decisions, he had seldom either leisure or inclination to consult his own judgement. His amusements and his expenses were consequently regulated by the example of his companions, not by his own choice. To follow them in every absurd variety of the mode, either in dress or equipage,[43] was his first ambition; and all their factitious wants appeared to him objects of the first necessity. No matter how good the boots, the hat, the coat, the furniture, or the equipage might be, if they had outlived the fashion of the day, or even of the hour, they were absolutely worthless in his eyes. *Nobody* could be seen in such things—then of what use could they be to *any body*? Colonel Pembroke's finances

---

[41] From *The Splendid Shilling* (1701) by John Philips (1676-1709). The line is about a "dun," i.e., a creditor or a person hired by a creditor in order to demand payment from ("to dun") a debtor.

[42] From *An Essay on the Principle of Population* (1798; revised 1803) by Thomas Robert Malthus (1766-1834). Maria Edgeworth had not met Malthus yet, but she would soon become his friend and admirer.

[43] One's carriage and horses.

The Dun

were not exactly equal to the support of such *liberal* principles; but this was a misfortune which he had in common with several of his companions. It was no check to their spirit—they could live upon credit—credit, "that talisman, which realises every thing it imagines, and which can imagine every thing."[44] Without staying to reflect upon the immediate or remote consequences of this system, Pembroke, in his first attempts, found it easy to reduce it to practice: but, as he proceeded, he experienced some difficulties. Tradesmen's bills accumulated, and applications for payment became every day more frequent and pressing. He defended himself with much address and ingenuity, and practice perfected him in all the Fabian arts of delay.[45] "*No faith with duns*," became, as he frankly declared, a maxim of his morality. He could now, with the most plausible face, protest to a *poor devil*, upon the honour of a gentleman, that he should be paid to-morrow; when nothing was further from his intentions or his power, than to keep his word: and when *to-morrow* came, he could, with the most easy assurance, *damn the rascal* for putting a gentleman in mind of his promises. But there were persons more difficult to manage than *poor devils*. Colonel Pembroke's tailor, who had begun by being the most accommodating fellow in the world, and who had in three years run him up a bill of thirteen hundred pounds, at length began to fail in complaisance, and had the impertinence to talk of his large family, and his urgent calls for money, &c. And next, the colonel's shoe and boot maker, a man from whom he had been in the habit of taking two hundred pounds worth of shoes and boots every year, for himself and his servants, now pretended to be in distress for ready money, and refused to furnish more goods upon credit. "Ungrateful dog!" Pembroke called him; and he actually believed his creditors to be ungrateful and insolent, when they asked for their money; for men frequently learn to believe what they are in the daily

---

[44] Here, Edgeworth inserted the following footnote: "See Des Casaux, Sur le Mécanisme de Société." Alexandre Cazeau de Roumillac (1727-1796), also known as Marquis de Casaux, was an economist, born in France but naturalised British after 1759. He published *Considérations sur quelques parties du méchanisme des sociétés* (London, 1785). Edgeworth clearly adapted a sentence from the French original: "C'est le credit; c'est ce talisman prodigieux qui réalise tout ce qu'il imagine, puisque tout ce qu'il imagine a le même avantage que la réalité" (247). In the English version (*Thoughts on the Mechanism of Societies*, 1786), the translation by Parkyns Mac Mahon is less literal than Edgeworth's.

[45] The adjective "Fabian" refers both to delaying tactics and to the strategy of constantly avoiding your adversary (so called after Fabius Cunctator, the Roman consul who managed to save Rome not by defeating Hannibal in a pitched battle, but through guerrilla warfare).

habit of asserting,[46] especially if their assertions be not contradicted by their audience. He knew that his tradesmen overcharged him in every article he bought, and therefore he thought it but just to delay payment whilst it suited his convenience. "Confound them, they can very well afford to wait!" As to their pleas of urgent demands for ready money, large families, &c., he considered these merely as words of course, tradesmen's cant, which should make no more impression upon a gentleman than the whining of a beggar.

One day when Pembroke was just going out to ride with some of his gay companions, he was stopped at his own door by a pale, thin, miserable-looking boy, of eight or nine years old, who presented him with a paper, which he took for granted was a petition; he threw the child half-a-crown.[47] "There, take that," said he, "and stand out of the way of my horse's heels, I advise you, my little fellow."

The boy, however, still pressed closer; and, without picking up the half-crown, held the paper to Colonel Pembroke, who had now vaulted into his saddle.

"O no! no! That's too much, my lad—I never read petitions—I'd sooner give half-a-crown at any time than read a petition."

"But, sir, this is not a petition—indeed, sir, I am not a beggar."

"What is it then?—Heyday! a bill!—Then you're worse than a beggar—a dun!—a dun! in the public streets, at your time of life! You little rascal, why what will you come to before you are your father's age?" The boy sighed. "If," pursued the colonel, "I were to serve you right, I should give you a good horse-whipping. Do you see this whip?"

"I do, sir," said the boy; "but—"

"But what? you insolent little dun!—But what?"

"My father is dying," said the child, bursting into tears, "and we have no money to buy him bread, or any thing."

Struck by these words, Pembroke snatched the paper from the boy, and looking hastily at the total and title of the bill, read—"Twelve pounds fourteen—John White, Weaver."—"I know of no such person!—I have no dealings with weavers, child," said the colonel, laughing: "My name's Pembroke—Colonel Pembroke."

---

[46] Here, Edgeworth inserted a brief note, indicating "Rochefoucault" as her source. François de La Rochefoucauld (1613-1680) was a French writer, famous especially for his maxims, one of which (No. 122) reads as follows: "We are so much accustomed to disguise ourselves to others, that at length we disguise ourselves to ourselves."

[47] Half a crown was a coin worth 2 shillings and sixpence (1/8 of a pound).

The Dun

"Colonel Pembroke—yes, sir, the very person Mr. Close, the tailor, sent me to!"

"Close the tailor! D——n the rascal: was it he sent you to dun me? for this trick he shall not see a farthing[48] of my money this twelvemonth. You may tell him so, you little whining hypocrite!—And, hark you! the next time you come to me, take care to come with a better story—let your father and mother, and six brothers and sisters, be all lying ill of the fever—do you understand?"

He tore the bill into bits as he spoke, and showered it over the boy's head. Pembroke's companions laughed at this operation, and he facetiously called it "powdering a dun." They rode off to the Park[49] in high spirits; and the poor boy picked up the half-crown, and returned home. His home was in a lane in Moorfields,[50] about three miles distant from this gay part of the town. As the child had not eaten any thing that morning, he was feeble, and grew faint as he was crossing Covent Garden.[51] He sat down upon the corner of a stage of flowers.

"What are you doing there?" cried a surly man, pulling him up by the arm; "What business have you lounging and loitering here, breaking my best balsam?"[52]

"I did not mean to do any harm—I am not loitering, indeed, sir,—I'm only weak," said the boy, "and hungry."

"Oranges! oranges! fine China oranges!"[53] cried a woman, rolling her barrow full of fine fruit towards him. "If you've a two-pence in the world, you can't do better than take one of these fine ripe China oranges."

"I have not two-pence of my own in the world," said the boy.

"What's that I see through the hole in your waistcoat pocket?" said the woman; "is not that silver?"

"Yes, half-a-crown; which I am carrying home to my father, who is ill, and wants it more than I do."

[48] A farthing was a small coin worth a quarter of a penny.

[49] Hyde Park in London, which had become a fashionable place in the 1730s.

[50] Moorfields was a mostly open space beside the London Wall, partly inhabited by the poor. It was being developed at the time, but it soon lost its distinctiveness and most of it became part of East End.

[51] District in London, north of the Strand and west of Drury Lane, known for its theatres but also for its open-air market.

[52] An ornamental garden flower (*Impatiens balsamina*), also known as touch-me-not.

[53] Regular oranges, as opposed to the reddish Seville oranges.

"Pooh! take an orange out of it—it's only two-pence—and it will do you good—I'm sure you look as if you wanted it badly enough."

"That may be; but father wants it worse—No, I won't change my half-crown," said the boy, turning away from the tempting oranges."

The gruff gardener caught him by the hand.

"Here, I've moved the balsam a bit, and it is not broke, I see; sit ye down, child, and rest yourself, and eat this," said he, putting into his hand half a ripe orange, which he just cut.

"Thank you!—God bless you, sir!—How good it is—But," said the child, stopping after he had tasted the sweet juice, "I am sorry I have sucked so much; I might have carried it home to father, who is ill; and what a treat it would be to him!—I'll keep the rest."

"No—that you sha'n't," said the orange-woman. "But I'll tell you what you shall do—take this home to your father, which is a better one by half—I'm sure it will do him good—I never knew a ripe China orange do harm to man, woman, or child."

The boy thanked the good woman and the gardener, as only those can thank who have felt what it is to be in absolute want. When he was rested, and able to walk, he pursued his way home. His mother was watching for him at the street-door.

"Well, John, my dear, what news? Has he paid us?"

The boy shook his head.

"Then we must bear it as well as we can," said his mother, wiping the cold dew from her forehead.

"But look, mother, I have this half-crown, which the gentleman, thinking me a beggar, threw to me."

"Run with it, love, to the baker's. No—stay, you're tired—I'll go myself; and do you step up to your father, and tell him the bread is coming in a minute."

"Don't run, for you're not able, mother; don't hurry so," said the boy, calling after her, and holding up his orange: "see, I have this for father whilst you are away."

He clambered up three flights of dark, narrow, broken stairs, to the room in which his father lay. The door hung by a single hinge, and the child had scarcely strength enough to raise it out of the hollow in the decayed floor into which it had sunk. He pushed it open, with as little noise as possible, just far enough to creep in.

Let those forbear to follow him whose fine feelings can be moved only by romantic elegant scenes of distress, whose delicate sensibility shrinks from the revolting sight of real misery. Here

The Dun

are no pictures for romance, no stage effect to be seen, no poetic language to be heard; nothing to charm the imagination,—every thing to disgust the senses.

This room was so dark, that upon first going into it, after having been in broad daylight, you could scarcely distinguish any one object it contained; and no one used to breathe a pure atmosphere could probably have endured to remain many minutes in this garret. There were three beds in it: one on which the sick man lay; divided from it by a tattered rug was another, for his wife and daughter; and a third for his little boy in the farthest corner. Underneath the window was fixed a loom, at which the poor weaver had worked hard many a day and year—too hard, indeed—even till the very hour he was taken ill. His shuttle now lay idle upon his frame. A girl of about sixteen—his daughter—was sitting at the foot of his bed, finishing some plain work.[54]

"O, Anne! how your face is all flushed!" said her little brother, as she looked up when he came into the room.

"Have you brought us any money?" whispered she: "don't say *No* loud, for fear father should hear you."

The boy told her in a low voice all that had passed.

"Speak out, my dear, I'm not asleep," said his father. "So you are come back as you went?"

"No, father, not quite—there's bread coming for you."

"Give me some more water, Anne, for my mouth is quite parched."

The little boy cut his orange in an instant, and gave a piece of it to his father, telling him, at the same time, how he came by it. The sick man raised his hands to heaven, and blessed the poor woman who gave it to him.

"Oh, how I love her! and how I hate that cruel, unjust, rich man, who won't pay father for all the hard work he had done for him!" cried the child: "how I hate him!"

"God forgive him!" said the weaver. "I don't know what will become of you all, when I'm gone; and no one to befriend you, or even to work at the loom. Anne, I think if I was up," said he, raising himself, "I could still contrive to do a little good."

"Dear father, don't think of getting up; the best you can do for us is to lie still and take rest."

"Rest! I can take no rest, Anne. Rest! there's none for me in this world. And whilst I'm in it, is not it my duty to work for my wife and children? Reach me my clothes, and I'll get up."

---

[54] Needlework or sewing, as opposed to "fancy work" or embroidery.

43

It was vain to contend with him, when this notion seized him that it was his duty to work till the last. All opposition fretted and made him worse; so that his daughter and his wife, even from affection, were forced to yield, and to let him go to the loom, when his trembling hands were scarcely able to throw the shuttle.[55] He did not know how weak he was till he tried to walk. As he stepped out of bed, his wife came in with a loaf of bread in her hand: at the unexpected sight he made an exclamation of joy; sprang forward to meet her, but fell upon the floor in a swoon, before he could put one bit of the bread which she broke for him into his mouth. Want of sustenance, the having been overworked, and the constant anxiety which preyed upon his spirits, had reduced him to this deplorable state of weakness. When he recovered his senses, his wife showed him his little boy eating a large piece of bread; she also ate, and made Anne eat before him, to relieve his mind from that dread which had seized it—and not without some reason—that he should see his wife and children starve to death.

"You find, father, there's no danger for to-day," said Anne; "and to-morrow I shall be paid for my plain work, and then we shall do very well for a few days longer; and I dare say in that time Mr. Close the tailor will receive some money from some of the great many rich gentlemen who owe him so much; and you know he promised that as soon as ever he was able he would pay us."

With such hopes, and the remembrance of such promises, the poor man's spirits could not be much raised; he knew, alas! how little dependence was to be placed on them. As soon as he had eaten, and felt his strength revive, he insisted upon going to the loom; his mind was bent upon finishing a pattern, for which he was to receive five guineas in ready money: he worked and worked, then lay down and rested himself,—then worked again, and so on during the remainder of the day; and during several hours of the night he continued to throw the shuttle, whilst his little boy and his wife by turns wound spools for him.

He completed his work, and threw himself upon his bed quite exhausted, just as the neighbouring clock struck one.

At this hour Colonel Pembroke was in the midst of a gay and brilliant assembly at Mrs. York's, in a splendid saloon, illuminated with wax-lights in profusion, the floor crayoned with roses and myrtles, which the dancers' feet effaced, the walls hung with the most expensive hot-house flowers; in short, he was surrounded with luxury in all its extravagance. It is said that the peaches alone

[55] A small part of the loom, in the shape of a boat, used for passing the thread from one edge of the cloth to the other.

The Dun

at this entertainment amounted to six hundred guineas. They cost a guinea a-piece: the price of one of them, which Colonel Pembroke threw away because it was not perfectly ripe, would have supported the weaver and his whole family for a week.

There are political advocates for luxury, who assert, perhaps justly, that the extravagance of individuals increases the wealth of nations. But even upon this system, those who by false hopes excite the industrious to exertion, without paying them their just wages, commit not only the most cruel private injustice, but the most important public injury. The permanence of industry in any state must be proportioned to the certainty of its reward.

Amongst the masks at Mrs. York's were three who amused the company particularly; the festive mob followed them as they moved, and their bon-mots were applauded and repeated by all the best, that is to say, the most fashionable male and female judges of wit. The three distinguished characters were a spendthrift, a bailiff, and a dun. The spendthrift was supported with great spirit and *truth* by Colonel Pembroke, and two of his companions were *great* and *correct* in the parts of the bailiff and the dun. The happy idea of appearing in these characters this night had been suggested by the circumstances that happened in the morning. Colonel Pembroke gave himself great credit, he said, for thus "striking novelty even from difficulty;"[56] and he rejoiced that the rascal of a weaver had sent his boy to dun him, and had thus furnished him with diversion for the evening as well as the morning. We are much concerned that we cannot, for the advantage of posterity, record any of the innumerable *good things* which undoubtedly were uttered by this trio.[57] Even the newspapers of the day could speak only in general panegyric. The probability, however, is, that the colonel deserved the praises that were lavished upon his manner of supporting his character. No man was better acquainted than himself with all those anecdotes of men of fashion, which could illustrate the spendthrift system. At least fifty times he had repeated, and always with the same *glee*, the reply of a great character to a creditor, who, upon being asked when his *bond* debts were likely to be paid, answered, "On the day of judgment."

Probably the admiration, which this and similar sallies of wit have excited, must have produced a strong desire in the minds of many young men of spirit to perform similar feats; and though the

[56] Probably an allusion to a line from Alexander Pope's "Epistle IV: Of the Use of Riches": "Start even from difficulty, strike from chance."

[57] "Good things" was a general term for jests, anecdotes, bon mots, witticisms, repartees said in fashionable circles or salons.

ruin of innumerable poor creditors may be the consequence, that will not surely be deemed by a certain class of reasoners worthy of a moment's regret, or even a moment's thought. Persons of tender consciences may, perhaps, be shocked at the idea of committing injustice and cruelty by starving their creditors, but they may strengthen their minds by taking an enlarged political view of the subject.

It is obvious, that whether a hundred guineas be in the pocket of A or B, the total sum of the wealth of the nation remains the same; and whether the enjoyments of A be as 100, and those of B as 0,—or whether these enjoyments be equally divided between A and B,—is a matter of no importance to the political arithmetician, because in both cases it is obvious that the total sum of national happiness remains the same. The happiness of individuals is nothing compared with the general mass.

And if the individual B should fancy himself ill-used by our political arithmetician, and should take it into his head to observe, that though the happiness of B is nothing to the general mass, yet that it is every thing to him, the politician of course takes snuff, and replies, that his observation is foreign to the purpose—that the good of the whole society is the object in view. And if B immediately accede to this position, and only ask humbly whether the good of the whole be not made up of the good of the parts, and whether as a part he have not some right to his share of good, the dexterous logical arithmetician answers, that B is totally out of the question, because B is a negative quantity in the equation. And if obstinate B, still conceiving himself aggrieved, objects to this total annihilation of himself and his interests, and asks why the lot of extinction should not fall upon the debtor C, or even upon the calculator himself, by whatever letter of the alphabet he happens to be designated, the calculator must knit his brow, and answer—any thing he pleases—except, *I don't know*—for this is a phrase below the dignity of a philosopher. This argument is produced, not as a statement of what is really the case, but as a popular argument against political sophistry.

Colonel Pembroke, notwithstanding his success at Mrs. York's masquerade in his character of a spendthrift, could not by his utmost wit and address satisfy or silence his impertinent tailor. Mr. Close absolutely refused to give further credit without valuable consideration; and the colonel was compelled to pass his bond for the whole sum which was claimed, which was fifty pounds more

The Dun

than was strictly due, in order to compound with the tailor for the want of ready money. When the bond was fairly signed, sealed, and delivered, Mr. Close produced the poor weaver's bill.

"Colonel Pembroke," said he, "I have a trifling bill here—I am really ashamed to speak to you about such a trifle—but as we are settling all accounts—and as this White, the weaver, is so wretchedly poor, that he or some of his family are with me every day of my life dunning me to get me to speak about their little demand—"

"Who is this White?" said Mr. Pembroke.

"You recollect the elegant waistcoat pattern of which you afterwards bought up the whole piece, lest it should become common and vulgar?—this White was the weaver from whom we got it."

"Bless me! why that's two years ago: I thought that fellow was paid long ago!"

"No, indeed, I wish he had; for he has been the torment of my life this many a month—I never saw people so eager about their money."

"But why do you employ such miserable, greedy creatures? What can you expect but to be dunned every hour of your life?"

"Very true, indeed, colonel; it is what I always, on that principle, avoid as far as possibly I can: but I can't blame myself in this particular instance; for this White, at the time I employed him first, was a very decent man, and in a very good way, for one of his sort: but I suppose he has taken to drink, for he is worth not a farthing now."

"What business has a fellow of his sort to drink? He should leave that for his betters," said the Colonel Pembroke, laughing. "Drinking's too great a pleasure for a weaver. The drunken rascal's money is safer in my hands, tell him, than in his own."

The tailor's conscience twinged him a little at this instant, for he had spoken entirely at random, not having the slightest grounds for his insinuation that this poor weaver had ruined himself by drunkenness.

"Upon my word, sir," said Close, retracting, "the man may not be a drunken fellow for any thing I know positively—I purely surmised *that* might be the case, from his having fallen into such distress, which is no otherwise accountable for, to my comprehension, except we believe his own story, that he has money due to him which he cannot get paid, and that this has been his ruin."

47

Colonel Pembroke cleared his throat two or three times upon hearing this last suggestion, and actually took up the weaver's bill with some intention of paying it; but he recollected that he should want the ready money he had in his pocket for another indispensable occasion; for he was *obliged* to go to Brookes's that night;[58] so he contented his humanity by recommending it to Mr. Close to pay White and have done with him.

"If you let him have the money, you know, you can put it down to my account, or make a memorandum of it at the back of the bond. In short, settle it as you will, but let me hear no more about it. I have not leisure to think of such trifles—Good morning to you, Mr. Close."

Mr. Close was far from having any intentions of complying with the colonel's request. When the weaver's wife called upon him after his return home, he assured her that he had not seen the colour of one guinea, or one farthing, of Colonel Pembroke's money; and that it was absolutely impossible that he could pay Mr. White till he was paid himself—that it could not be expected he should advance money for any body out of his own pocket—that he begged he might not be pestered and dunned any more, for that *he really had not leisure to think of such trifles.*

For want of this trifle, of which neither the fashionable colonel nor his fashionable tailor had leisure to think, the poor weaver and his whole family were reduced to the last degree of human misery—the absolute famine. The man had exerted himself to the utmost to finish a pattern, which had been bespoken for a tradesman who promised upon the delivery of it to pay him five guineas in hand. This money he received; but four guineas of it were due to his landlord for rent of his wretched garret, and the remaining guinea was divided between the baker, to whom an old bill was due, and the apothecary, to whom they were obliged to have recourse, as the weaver was extremely ill. They had literally nothing now to depend upon but what the wife and daughter could earn by needlework; and they were known to be so miserably poor, that the *prudent* neighbours did not like to trust them with plain work, lest it should not be returned safely. Besides, in such a dirty place as they lived in, how could it be expected that they should put any work out of their hands decently clean? The woman to whom the house belonged, however, at last procured them work from Mrs. Carver, a widow lady, who she said was extremely charitable. She advised

---

[58] Actually Brooks's (but often misspelled at the time), a gentlemen's club in London, on St James's Street.

The Dun

Anne to carry home the work as soon as it was finished, and to wait to see the lady herself, who might perhaps be as charitable to her as she was to many others. Anne resolved to take this advice: but when she carried home her work to the place to which she was directed, her heart almost failed her; for she found Mrs. Carver lived in such a handsome house, that there was little chance of a poor girl being admitted by the servants farther than the hall-door or the kitchen. The lady, however, happened to be just coming out of her parlour at the moment the hall-door was opened for Anne; and she bid her come in, and show her work—approved of it—commended her industry—asked her several questions about her family—seemed to be touched with compassion by Anne's account of their distress—and after paying what she had charged for the work, put half-a-guinea into her hand,[59] and bid her call the next day, when she hoped that she should be able to do something more for her. This unexpected bounty, and the kindness of voice and look with which it was accompanied, had such an effect upon the poor girl, that if she had not caught hold of a chair to support herself she would have sunk to the ground. Mrs. Carver immediately made her sit down—"O madam! I'm well, quite well now—it was nothing—only surprise," said she, bursting into tears. "I beg your pardon for this foolishness—but it is only because I'm weaker to-day than usual, for want of eating."

"For want of eating! my poor child! How she trembles! she is weak indeed—and must not leave my house in this condition."

Mrs. Carver rang the bell, and ordered a glass of wine; but Anne was afraid to drink it, as she was not used to wine, and as she knew that it would affect her head if she drank without eating. When the lady found that she refused the wine, she did not press it, but insisted upon her eating something.

"O madam!" said the poor girl, "it is long, long, indeed, since I have eaten so heartily; and it is almost a shame for me to stay eating such dainties, when my father and mother are all the while in the way they are. But I'll run home with the half-guinea, and tell them how good you have been, and they will be so joyful and so thankful to you! My mother will come herself, I'm sure, with me to-morrow morning—she can thank you so much better than I can!"

Those only who have known the extreme of want can imagine the joy and gratitude with which the half-guinea was received by this poor family. Half-a-guinea!—Colonel Pembroke spent six half-guineas this very day in a fruit-shop, and ten times that sum at a jeweller's on seals and baubles for which he had no manner of use.

[59] The half guinea coin was worth 10 shillings and sixpence.

49

When Anne and her mother called the next morning to thank their benefactress, she was not up; but her servant gave them a parcel from his mistress: it contained a fresh supply of needlework, a gown, and some other clothes, which were directed *for Anne*. The servant said, that if she would call again about eight in the evening, his lady would probably be able to see her, and that she begged to have the work finished by that time. The work was finished, though with some difficulty, by the appointed hour; and Anne, dressed in her new clothes, was at Mrs. Carver's door just as the clock struck eight. The old lady was alone at tea; she seemed to be well pleased by Anne's punctuality; said that she had made inquiries respecting Mr. and Mrs. White, and that she heard an excellent character of them; that therefore she was disposed to do every thing she could to serve them. She added, that she "should soon part with her own maid, and that perhaps Anne might supply her place." Nothing could be more agreeable to the poor girl than this proposal: her father and mother were rejoiced at the idea of seeing her so well placed; and they now looked forward impatiently for the day when Mrs. Carver's maid was to be dismissed. In the mean time the old lady continued to employ Anne, and to make her presents, sometimes of clothes, and sometimes of money. The money she always gave to her parents; and she loved her "good old lady," as she always called her, more for putting it in her power thus to help her father and mother than for all the rest. The weaver's disease had arisen from want of sufficient food, from fatigue of body, and anxiety of mind; and he grew rapidly better, now that he was relieved from want, and inspired with hope. Mrs. Carver bespoke from him two pieces of waistcoating, which she promised to dispose of for him most advantageously, by a raffle, for which she had raised subscriptions amongst her numerous acquaintance. She expressed great indignation, when Anne told her how Mr. White had been ruined by persons who would not pay their just debts; and when she knew that the weaver was overcharged for all his working materials, because he took them upon credit, she generously offered to lend them whatever ready money might be necessary, which she said Anne might repay, at her leisure, out of her wages.

"O madam!" said Anne, "you are too good to us, indeed—too good! and if you could but see into our hearts, you would know that we are not ungrateful."

"I am sure *that* is what you never will be, my dear," said the old lady; "at least such is my opinion of you."

"Thank you, ma'am! thank you, from the bottom of my heart!—We should all have been starved, if it had not been for you.

The Dun

And it is owing to you that we are so happy now—quite different creatures from what we were."

"Quite a different creature indeed, you look, child, from what you did the first day I saw you. To-morrow my own maid goes, and you may come at ten o'clock; and I hope we shall agree very well together—you'll find me an easy mistress, and I make no doubt I shall always find you the good grateful girl you seem to be."

Anne was impatient for the moment when she was to enter into the service of her benefactress; and she lay awake half the night, considering how she should ever be able to show sufficient gratitude. As Mrs. Carver had often expressed her desire to have Anne look neat and smart, she dressed herself as well as she possibly could; and when her poor father and mother took leave of her, they could not help observing, as Mrs. Carver had done the day before, that "Anne looked quite a different creature from what she was a few weeks ago." She was, indeed, an extremely pretty girl; but we need not stop to relate all the fond praises that were bestowed upon her beauty by her partial parents. Her little brother John was not at home when she was going away; he was at a carpenter's shop in the neighbourhood mending a wheelbarrow, which belonged to that good-natured orange-woman who gave him the orange for his father. Anne called at the carpenter's shop to take leave of her brother. The woman was there waiting for her barrow—she looked earnestly at Anne when she entered, and then whispered to the boy, "Is that your sister?"—"Yes," said the boy, "and as good a sister she is as ever was born."

"May be so," said the woman; "but she is not likely to be good for much long, in the way she is going on now."

"What way—what do you mean?" said Anne, colouring violently.

"O, you understand me well enough, though you look so innocent."

"I do not understand you in the least."

"No!—Why, is not it you that I see going almost every day to that house in Chiswell-street?"[60]

"Mrs. Carver's?—Yes."

"Mrs. Carver's indeed!" cried the woman, throwing an orange-peel from her with an air of disdain—"a pretty come-off indeed! as if I did not know her name, and all about her, as well as you do."

"Do you?" said Anne; "then I am sure you know one of the best women in the world."

[60] Today in Islington, Chiswell Street was at the time in Moorfields (see note 50).

The woman looked still more earnestly than before in Anne's countenance; and then taking hold of both her hands exclaimed, "You poor young creature! what are you about? I do believe you don't know what you are about—if you do, you are the greatest cheat I ever looked in the face, long as I've lived in this cheating world."

"You frighten my sister," said the boy: "do pray tell her what you mean at once, for look how pale she turns."

"So much the better, for now I have good hope of her. Then to tell you all at once—no matter how I frighten her, it's for her good—this Mrs. Carver, as you call her, is only Mrs. Carver when she wants to pass upon such as you for a good woman."

"To *pass* for a good woman!" repeated Anne with indignation. "O, she is, she is a good woman—you do not know her as I do."

"I know her a great deal better, I tell you: if you choose not to believe me, go your ways—go to your ruin—go to your shame—go to your grave—as hundreds have gone, by the same road, before you. Your Mrs. Carver keeps two houses, and one of them is a bad house—and that's the house you'll soon go to, if you trust to her: now you know the whole truth."

The poor girl was shocked so much, that for several minutes she could neither speak nor think. As soon as she had recovered sufficient presence of mind to consider what she should do, she declared that she would that instant go home and put on her rags again, and return to the wicked Mrs. Carver all the clothes she had given her.

"But what will become of us all?—She has lent my father money—a great deal of money. How can he pay her?—O, I will pay her all—I will go into some honest service, now I am well and strong enough to do any sort of hard work, and God knows I am willing."

Full of these resolutions, Anne hurried home, intending to tell her father and mother all that had happened; but they were neither of them within. She flew to the mistress of the house, who had first recommended her to Mrs. Carver, and reproached her in the most moving terms which the agony of her mind could suggest. Her landlady listened to her with astonishment, either real or admirably well affected—declared that she knew nothing more of Mrs. Carver but that she lived in a large fine house, and that she had been very charitable to some poor people in Moorfields—that she bore the

The Dun

best of characters—and that if nothing could be said against her but by an orange-woman, there was no great reason to believe such scandal.

Anne now began to think that the whole of what she had heard might be a falsehood, or a mistake; one moment she blamed herself for so easily suspecting a person who had shown her so much kindness; but the next minute the emphatic words and warning looks of the woman recurred to her mind; and though they were but the words and looks of an orange-woman, she could not help dreading that there was some truth in them. The clock struck ten whilst she was in this uncertainty. The woman of the house urged her to go without further delay to Mrs. Carver's who would undoubtedly be displeased by any want of punctuality; but Anne wished to wait for the return of her father and mother.

"They will not be back, either of them, these three hours; for your mother is gone to the other end of the town about that old bill of Colonel Pembroke's, and your father is gone to buy some silk for weaving—he told me he should not be home before three o'clock."

Notwithstanding these remonstrances, Anne persisted in her resolution: she took off the clothes which she had received from Mrs. Carver, and put on those which she had been used to wear. Her mother was much surprised, when she came in, to see her in this condition; and no words can describe her grief, when she heard the cause of this change. She blamed herself severely for not having made inquiries concerning Mrs. Carver before she had suffered her daughter to accept of any presents from her; and she wept bitterly, when she recollected the money which this woman had lent her husband.

"She will throw him into jail, I am sure she will—we shall be worse off a thousand times than ever we were in our worst days. The work that is in the loom, by which he hoped to get so much, is all for her, and it will be left upon our hands now; and how are we to pay the woman of this house for the lodgings?—O! I see it all coming upon us at once," continued the poor woman, wringing her hands. "If that Colonel Pembroke would but let us have our own!—But there I've been all the morning hunting him out, and at last, when I did see him, he only swore, and said we were all a family of *duns*, or some such nonsense. And then he called after me from the top of his fine stairs, just to say, that he had ordered Close the tailor to pay us; and when I went to him there was no satisfaction to be

53

got from him—his shop was full of customers, and he hustled me away, giving me for answer, that when Colonel Pembroke paid him, he would pay us, and no sooner. Ah! these purse-proud tradesfolk, and these sparks of fashion,[61] what do they know of all we suffer? What do they care for us?—It is not for charity I ask any of them— only for what my own husband has justly earned, and hardly toiled for too; and this I cannot get out of their hands. If I could, we might defy this wicked woman—but now we are laid under her feet, and she will trample us to death."

In the midst of these lamentations, Anne's father came in: when he learnt the cause of them, he stood for a moment in silence; then snatched from his daughter's hand the bundle of clothes, which she had prepared to return to Mrs. Carver.

"Give them to me; I will go to this woman myself," cried he with indignation: "Anne shall never more set her foot within those doors."

"Dear father," cried Anne, stopping him as he went out of the door, "perhaps it is all a mistake: do pray inquire from somebody else before you speak to Mrs. Carver—she looks so good, she has been so kind to me, I cannot believe that she is wicked. Do pray inquire of a great many people before you knock at the door."

He promised that he would do all his daughter desired.

With most impatient anxiety they waited for his return: the time of his absence appeared insupportably long, and they formed new fears and new conjectures every instant. Every time they heard a footstep upon the stairs, they ran out to see who it was: sometimes it was the landlady—sometimes the lodgers or their visitors—at last came the person they longed to see; but the moment they beheld him, all their fears were confirmed. He was pale as death, and his lips trembled with convulsive motion. He walked directly up to his loom, and without speaking one syllable began to cut the unfinished work out of it.

"What are you about, my dear?" cried his wife. "Consider what you are about—this work of yours is the only dependence we have in the world."

"You have nothing in this world to depend upon, I tell you," cried he, continuing to cut out the web with a hurried hand—"you must not depend on me—you must not depend on my work—I shall never throw this shuttle more whilst I live—I think of me as if I was dead—to-morrow I shall be dead to you—I shall be in a

---

[61] "Spark" was a term used for young dandies.

The Dun

jail, and there must lie till carried out in my coffin. Here, take this work just as it is to our landlady—she met me on the stairs, and said she must have her rent directly—that will pay her—I'll pay all I can. As for the loom, that's only hired—the silk I bought to-day will pay the hire—I'll pay all my debts to the uttermost farthing, as far as I am able—but the ten guineas to that wicked woman I cannot pay—so I must rot in a jail. Don't cry, Anne, don't cry so, my good girl—you'll break my heart, wife, if you take on so. Why! have not we one comfort, that let us go out of this world when we may, or how we may, we shall go out of it honest, having no one's ruin to answer for, having done our duty to God and man, as far as we are able?—My child," continued he, catching Anne in his arms, "I have you safe, and I thank God for it!"

When this poor man had thus in an incoherent manner given vent to his first feelings, he became somewhat more composed, and was able to relate all that had passed between him and Mrs. Carver. The inquiries which he made before he saw her sufficiently confirmed the orange-woman's story; and when he returned the presents which Anne had unfortunately received, Mrs. Carver, with all the audacity of a woman hardened in guilt, avowed her purpose and her profession—declared that whatever ignorance and innocence Anne or her parent might now find it convenient to affect, she was "confident they had all the time perfectly understood what she was about, and that she would not be cheated at last by a parcel of swindling hypocrites." With horrid imprecations she then swore, that if Anne was kept from her she would have vengeance—and that her vengeance should know no bounds. The event showed that these were not empty threats—the very next day she sent two bailiffs to arrest Anne's father. They met him in the street, as he was going to pay the last farthing he had to the baker. The wretched man in vain endeavoured to move the ear of justice, by relating the simple truth. Mrs. Carver was rich—her victim was poor. He was committed to jail; and he entered the prison with the firm belief, that there he must drag out the remainder of his days.

One faint hope remained in his wife's heart—she imagined that if she could but prevail upon Colonel Pembroke's servants, either to obtain for her a sight of their master, or if they would carry him a letter containing an exact account of her distress, he would immediately pay the fourteen ponds which had been so long due. With this money she could obtain her husband's liberty, and she fancied all might yet be well. Her son, who could write a very legible hand, wrote the petition. "Ah, mother!" said he, "don't hope that Colonel Pembroke will read it—he will tear it to pieces, as he did one that I carried him before."

"I can but try," said she; "I cannot believe that any gentleman is so cruel, and so unjust—he must and will pay us when he knows the whole truth."

Colonel Pembroke was dressing in a hurry, to go to a great dinner at the Crown and Anchor tavern.[62] One of Pembroke's gay companions had called, and was in the room waiting for him. It was at this inauspicious time that Mrs. White arrived. Her petition the servant at first absolutely refused to take from her hands; but at last a young lad, whom the colonel had lately brought from the country, and who had either more natural feeling, or less acquired power of equivocating, than his fellows, consented to carry up the petition, when he should, as he expected, be called by his master to report the state of a favourite horse that was sick. While his master's hair was dressing, the lad was summoned; and when the health of the horse had been anxiously inquired into, the lad with country awkwardness scratched his head, and laid the petition before his master, saying—"Sir, there's a poor woman below waiting for an answer; and if so be what she says is true, as I take it to be, 'tis enough to break one's heart."

"Your heart, my lad, is not seasoned to London yet, I perceive," said Colonel Pembroke, smiling; "why your heart will be broke a thousand times over by every beggar your meet."

"No, no; I be too much of a man for that," replied the groom, wiping his eyes hastily with the back of his hand—"not such a noodle as that comes too neither—beggars are beggars, and so to be treated—but this woman, sir, is no common beggar, not she; nor is she begging any ways—only to be paid her bill—so I brought it, as I was coming up."

"Then, sir, as you are going down, you may take it down again, if you please," cried Colonel Pembroke; "and in future, sir, I recommend it to you to look after your horses, and to trust me to look after my own affairs."

The groom retreated; and his master gave the poor woman's petition, without reading it, to the hair-dresser, who was looking for a piece of paper to try the heat of his irons.

"I should be pestered with bills and petitions from morning till night, if I did not frighten these fellows out of the trick of bringing them to me," continued Colonel Pembroke, turning to his companion. "That blockhead of a groom is but just come to town;

[62] The most popular tavern in London at the time, on Arundel Street, off the Strand.

The Dun

he does not yet know how to drive away a dun—but he'll learn. They say that the American dogs did not know how to bark, till they learnt it from their civilized betters."[63]

Colonel Pembroke habitually drove away reflection, and silenced the whispers of conscience, by noisy declamation, or sallies of wit.

At the bottom of the singed paper, which the hair-dresser left on the table, the name of White was sufficiently visible. "White!" exclaimed Colonel Pembroke, "as I hope to live and breathe, these Whites have been this half-year the torment of my life." He started up, rang the bell, and gave immediate orders to his servant, that *these Whites* should never more be let in, and that no more of their bills and petitions in any form whatever should be brought to him. "I'll punish them for their insolence—I won't pay them one farthing this twelvemonth: and if the woman is not gone, pray tell her so—I bid Close the tailor pay them: if he has not, it is no fault of mine. Let me not hear a syllable more about it—I'll part with the first of you who dares to disobey me."

"The woman is gone, I believe, sir," said the footman; "it was not I let her in, and I refused to bring up the letter."

"You did right. Let me hear no more about the matter. We shall be late at the Crown and Anchor. I beg your pardon, my dear friend, for detaining you so long."

Whilst the colonel went to his jovial meeting, where he was the life and spirit of the company, the poor woman returned in despair to the prison where her husband was confined.

We forbear to describe the horrible situation to which this family were soon reduced. Beyond a certain point, the human heart cannot feel compassion.

One day, as Anne was returning from the prison, where she had been with her father, she was met by a porter, who put a letter into her hands, then turned down a narrow lane, and was out of sight before she could inquire from whom he came. When she read the letter, however, she could not be in doubt—it came from Mrs. Carver, and contained these words:—

"You can gain nothing by your present obstinacy—you are the cause of your father's lying in jail, and of your mother's being as she is, nearly starved to death. You can relieve them from misery worse than death, and place them in ease and comfort for the remainder of their days. Be assured, they do not speak sincerely to you, when

[63] After landing on Hispaniola in 1492, Christopher Columbus reported that the natives had small dogs that did not bark.

they pretend not to wish that your compliance should put an end to their present sufferings. It is you that are cruel to them—it is you that are cruel to yourself, and can blame nobody else. You might live all your days in a house as good as mine, and have a plentiful table served from one year's end to another, with all the dainties of the season, and you might be dressed as elegantly as the most elegant lady in London (which, by-the-bye, your beauty deserves), and you would have servants of your own, and a carriage of your own, and nothing to do all day long but take your pleasure. And after all, what is asked of you?—only to make a person happy, that half the town would envy you, that would make it a study to gratify you in every wish of your heart. The person alluded to you have seen, and more than once, when you have been talking to me of work in my parlour. He is a very rich and generous gentleman. If you come to Chiswell-street about six this evening, you will find all I say true—if not, you and yours must take the consequences."

Coarse as the eloquence of this letter may appear, Anne could not read it without emotion: it raised on her heart a violent contest. Virtue, with poverty and famine, were on one side—and vice, with affluence, love, and every worldly pleasure, on the other.

Those who have been bred up in the lap of luxury; whom the breath of heaven has never visited too roughly; whose minds from their earliest infancy have been guarded even with more care than their persons; who in the dangerous season of youth are surrounded by all that the solicitude of experienced friends, and all that polished society, can devise for their security; are not perhaps competent to judge of the temptations by which beauty in the lower classes of life may be assailed. They who have never seen a father in prison, or a mother perishing for want of the absolute necessaries of life—they who have never themselves known the cravings of famine cannot form an adequate idea of this poor girl's feelings, and of the temptation to which she was now exposed. She wept—she hesitated—and "the woman that deliberates is lost."[64] Perhaps those who are the most truly virtuous of her sex will be the most disposed to feel for this poor creature, who was literally half-famished before her good resolutions were conquered. At last she yielded to necessity. At the appointed hours she was in Mrs. Carver's house. This woman received her with triumph—she supplied Anne immediately with food, and then hastened to deck out her victim in the most attractive manner. The girl was quite passive in her

[64] A line from Joseph Addison's 1713 tragedy *Cato* (Act IV, Scene I).

The Dun

hands. She promised, though scarcely knowing that she uttered the words, to obey the instructions that were given to her, and she suffered herself without struggle, or apparent emotion, to be led to destruction. She appeared quite insensible—but at last she was roused from this state of stupefaction, by the voice of a person with whom she found herself alone. The stranger, who was a young and gay gentleman, pleasing both in his person and manners, attempted by every possible means to render himself agreeable to her, to raise her spirits, and calm her apprehensions. By degrees his manner changed from levity to tenderness. He represented to her that he was not a brutal wretch, who could be gratified by any triumph in which the affections of the heart have no share; and he assured her, that in any connexion which she might be prevailed upon to form with him, she should be treated with honour and delicacy.

Touched by his manner of speaking, and overpowered by the sense of her own situation, Anne could not reply one single word to all he said—but burst into an agony of tears, and sinking on her knees before him, exclaimed, "Save me! save me from myself!—Restore me to my parents, before they have reason to hate me."

The gentleman seemed to be somewhat in doubt whether this was *acting* or nature: but he raised Anne from the ground, and placed her upon a seat beside him. "Am I to understand, then, that I have been deceived, and that our present meeting is against your own consent?"

"No, I cannot say that—O how I wish that I could!—I did wrong, very wrong, to come here—but I repent—I was half-starved—I have a father in jail—I thought I could set him free with the money—but I will not pretend to be better than I am—I believe I thought that, beside relieving my father, I should live all my days without ever more knowing what distress is—and I thought I should be happy—but now I have changed my mind—I never could be happy with a bad conscience—I know—by what I have felt this last hour."

Her voice failed; and she sobbed for some moments without being able to speak. The gentleman, who now was convinced that she was quite artless and thoroughly in earnest, was struck with compassion; but his compassion was not unmixed with other feelings, and he had hopes that, by treating her with tenderness, he should in time make it her wish to live with him as his mistress. He was anxious to hear what her former way of life had been; and she related, at his request, the circumstances by which she and her parents had been reduced to such distress. His countenance presently showed how much he was interested in her story—he grew red and pale—he started from his seat, and walked up and down the room in great agitation, till at last, when she mentioned the name of Colonel Pembroke, he stopped short, and exclaimed, "I am the man—I am Colonel Pembroke—I am that unjust, unfeeling wretch! How often, in the bitterness of your hearts, you must have cursed me!"

"O, no—my father, when he was at the worst, never cursed you; and I am sure he will have reason to bless you now, if you send his daughter back again to him, such as she was when she left him."

"That shall be done," said Colonel Pembroke; "and in doing so, I make some sacrifice, and have some merit. It is time I should make some reparation for the evils I have occasioned," continued he, taking a handful of guineas from his pocket: "but first let me pay my just debts."

"My poor father!" exclaimed Anne,—"to-morrow he will be out of prison."

"I will go with you to the prison, where your father is confined—I will force myself to behold all the evils I have occasioned."

Colonel Pembroke went to the prison; and he was so much struck by the scene, that he not only relieved the misery of this family, but in two months afterwards his debts were paid, his race-horses sold, and all his expenses regulated so as to render him ever afterwards truly independent. He no longer spent his days, like many young men of fashion, either in DREADING or in DAMNING DUNS.

Edgeworthstown, 1802.

James Hogg

DUNCAN CAMPBELL

(1811)

The author: James Hogg was born in 1770 (probably in November) in Selkirkshire, in the Scottish Borders, on the family farm at Ettrickhall, in the valley of Ettrick. His father was a farmer who went bankrupt when James was 6 years old. The boy first worked as a farmhand, reading books that he borrowed. Later, while working as a shepherd, he managed to get his first poem published (in 1790). He then self-published *Scottish Pastorals* in 1801; in 1802, he met Walter Scott and assisted him with the third volume of *Minstrelsy of the Scottish Border*. Scott helped him publish *The Mountain Bard* (1807), a book of ballads. Failing as a farmer, the 40-year-old James Hogg moved to Edinburgh in 1810, where he wrote his own weekly, *The Spy*, for 52 numbers. Finally, his breakthrough came in 1813 with the poems published in *The Queen's Wake*. He helped William Blackwood start *Blackwood's Edinburgh Magazine* in 1817 and he acquired fame as the Ettrick Shepherd, in the satirical series "Noctes Ambrosianae," written mainly by John Wilson, in *Blackwood's* (he later became more and more reluctant to be associated with this persona). He published short-story collections: *The Brownie of Bodsbeck* (1818), *Winter Evening Tales* (1820), *Altrive Tales* (1832), *Tales of the Wars of Montrose* (1835); novels: *The Three Perils of Man* (1822), *The Three Perils of Woman* (1823), *The Private Memoirs and Confessions of a Justified Sinner* (1824); and the popular essays of *The Shepherd's Calendar* (1829). He married in 1820 and had seven children. He died in 1835.

The text: First published as "History of the Life of Duncan Campbell, His Difficulties, Escapes, Rencounter with a Ghost and Other Adventures," in *The Spy* 49 & 51 (3 & 17 August 1811) then reprinted as "Duncan Campbell" in Hogg's 1820 collection *Winter Evening Tales*. The following is from the second edition (Edinburgh: Oliver & Boyd; London: G. & W. B. Whittaker, 1821,

I, 105-129), in which Hogg made some revisions, as indicated by his letters to his publishers. The posthumous collection of *Tales and Sketches* of 1837, in which it also appeared (III, 136-159), has long been shown to be less than reliable.

Further reading: Sharon Alker and Holly Faith Nelson. "Hogg and Working-class Writing." *The Edinburgh Companion to James Hogg.* Eds. Ian Duncan and Douglas S. Mack. Edinburgh: Edinburgh University Press, 2012. 55-63.

Duncan Campbell came from the Highlands, when six years of age, to live with an old maiden aunt in Edinburgh, and attend the school. His mother was dead; but his father had supplied her place, by marrying his housekeeper. Duncan did not trouble himself about these matters, nor indeed about any other matters, save a black foal of his father's, and a large sagacious colley, named Oscar, which belonged to one of the shepherds. There being no other boy save Duncan about the house, Oscar and he were constant companions,—with his garter tied round Oscar's neck, and a piece of deal tied to his big bushy tail,[65] Duncan would often lead him about the green, pleased with the idea that he was conducting a horse and cart. Oscar submitted to all this with great cheerfulness, but whenever Duncan mounted to ride on him, he found means instantly to unhorse him, either by galloping, or rolling himself on the green. When Duncan threatened him, he looked submissive and licked his face and hands; when he corrected him with the whip, he cowered at his feet;—matters were soon made up. Oscar would lodge no where during the night but at the door of the room where his young friend slept, and wo be to the man or woman who ventured to enter it at untimely hours.

When Duncan left his native home he thought not of his father, nor any of the servants. He was fond of the ride, and some supposed that he even scarcely thought of the black foal; but when he saw Oscar standing looking him ruefully in the face, the tears immediately blinded both his eyes. He caught him around the neck, hugged and kissed him,—"Good-b'ye Oscar," said he blubbering;—"good-b'ye, God bless you, my dear Oscar;" Duncan mounted before a servant, and rode away—Oscar still followed at a distance, until he reached the top of the hill—he then sat down and howled;—Duncan cried till his little heart was like to burst.— "What ails you?" said the servant. "I will never see my poor honest Oscar again," said Duncan, "an' my heart canna bide it."

[65] Though "deal" has come to be a measurement unit for the volume of wood, it also means any plank of (soft)wood; here, most likely, of Scots pine.

Duncan Campbell

Duncan staid a year in Edinburgh, but he did not make great progress in learning. He did not approve highly of attending the school, and his aunt was too indulgent to compel his attendance. She grew extremely ill one day—the maids kept constantly by her, and never regarded Duncan. He was an additional charge to them, and they never loved him, but used him harshly. It was now with great difficulty that he could obtain either meat or drink. In a few days after his aunt was taken ill she died.—All was in confusion, and poor Duncan was like to perish with hunger;—he could find no person in the house; but hearing a noise in his aunt's chamber, he went in, and beheld them dressing the corpse of his kind relation;—it was enough.—Duncan was horrified beyond what mortal breast was able to endure;—he hasted down the stair, and ran along the High Street, and South Bridge, as fast as his feet could carry him, crying incessantly all the way. He would not have entered that house again, if the world had been offered him as a reward. Some people stopped him, in order to ask what was the matter; but he could only answer them by exclaiming, "O! dear! O! dear!" and, struggling till he got free, held on his course, careless whither he went, provided he got far enough from the horrid scene he had so lately witnessed. Some have supposed, and I believe Duncan has been heard to confess, that he then imagined he was running for the Highlands, but mistook the direction. However that was, he continued his course until he came to a place where two ways met, a little south of Grange Toll.[66] Here he sat down, and his frenzied passion subsided into a soft melancholy;—he cried no more, but sobbed excessively; fixed his eyes on the ground, and made some strokes in the dust with his finger.

A sight just then appeared, which somewhat cheered, or at least interested, his heavy and forlorn heart—it was a large drove of Highland cattle. They were the only creatures like acquaintances that Duncan had seen for a twelvemonth, and a tender feeling of joy, mixed with regret, thrilled his heart at the sight of their white horns and broad dew-laps. As the van passed him, he thought their looks were particularly gruff and sullen; he soon perceived the case, they were all in the hands of Englishmen;—poor exiles like himself;—going far away to be killed and eaten, and would never see the Highland hills again!

When they were all gone by, Duncan looked after them and wept anew; but his attention was suddenly called away to something

[66] Grange Toll was the southern boundary of Edinburgh. Today part of the Royal Mile, High Street (mentioned above) was the main street, leading to the intersection of North Bridge and South Bridge.

that softly touched his feet; he looked hastily about—it was a poor hungry lame dog, squatted on the ground, licking his feet, and manifesting the most extravagant joy. Gracious Heaven! it was his own beloved and faithful Oscar! starved, emaciated, and so crippled, that he was scarcely able to walk! He was now doomed to be the slave of a Yorkshire peasant, (who, it seems, had either bought or stolen him at Falkirk,)[67] the generosity and benevolence of whose feelings were as inferior to those of Oscar, as Oscar was inferior to him in strength and power. It is impossible to conceive a more tender meeting than this was; but Duncan soon observed that hunger and misery were painted in his friend's looks, which again pierced his heart with feelings unfelt before. "I have not a crumb to give you, my poor Oscar!" said he—"I have not a crumb to eat myself, but I am not so ill as you are." The peasant whistled aloud. Oscar well knew the sound, and clinging to the boy's bosom, leaned his head upon his thigh, and looked in his face, as if saying, "O Duncan, protect me from yon ruffian." The whistle was repeated accompanied by a loud and surly call. Oscar trembled, but fearing to disobey, he limped away reluctantly after his unfeeling master, who, observing him to linger and look back, imagined he wanted to effect his escape, and came running back to meet him. Oscar cowered to the earth in the most submissive and imploring manner, but the peasant laid hold of him by the ear, and uttering many imprecations, struck him with a thick staff till he lay senseless at his feet.

Every possible circumstance seemed combined to wound the feelings of poor Duncan, but this unmerited barbarity shocked him most of all. He hasted to the scene of action, weeping bitterly, and telling the man that he was a cruel brute; and that if ever he himself grew a big man he would certainly kill him. He held up his favourite's head that he might recover his breath, and the man knowing that he could do little without his dog, waited patiently to see what would be the issue. The animal recovered, and stammered away at the heels of his tyrant without daring to look behind him. Duncan stood still, but kept his eyes eagerly fixed upon Oscar, and the farther he went from him, the more strong his desire grew to follow him. He looked the other way, but all there was to him a blank,—he had no desire to stand where he was, so he followed Oscar and the drove of cattle.

The cattle were weary and went slowly, and Duncan, getting a little goad in his hand, assisted the men greatly in driving them. One of the drivers game him a penny, and another gave him twopence;

[67] Falkirk, a city in the Central Lowlands of Scotland, hosted at the time the Falkirk Tryst, the most important gathering of livestock farmers.

and the lad who had the charge of the drove, observing how active and pliable he was, and how far he had accompanied him on the way, gave him sixpence; this was a treasure to Duncan, who, being extremely hungry, bought three penny rolls as he passed through a town; one of these he ate himself, another he gave to Oscar; and the third he carried below his arm in case of farther necessity. He drove on all the day, and at night the cattle rested upon a height, which, by his description, seems to have been that between Gala Water and Middleton.[68] Duncan went off at a side, in company with Oscar, to eat his roll, and, taking shelter behind an old earthen wall, they shared their dry meal most lovingly between them. Ere it was quite finished, Duncan being fatigued, dropped into a profound slumber, out of which he did not awake until the next morning was far advanced. Englishmen, cattle, and Oscar, all were gone. Duncan found himself alone on a wild height, in what country or kingdom he knew not. He sat for some time in a callous stupor, rubbing his eyes and scratching his head, but quite irresolute what was farther necessary for him to do, until he was agreeably surprised by the arrival of Oscar, who (although he had gone at his master's call in the morning) had found means to escape and seek the retreat of his young friend and benefactor. Duncan, without reflecting on the consequences, rejoiced in the event, and thought of nothing else than furthering his escape from the ruthless tyrant who now claimed him. For this purpose he thought it would be best to leave the road, and accordingly he crossed it, in order to go over a waste moor to the westward. He had not got forty paces from the road, until he beheld the enraged Englishman running towards him without his coat, and having his staff heaved over his shoulder. Duncan's heart fainted within him, knowing it was all over with Oscar, and most likely with himself. The peasant seemed not to have observed them, as he was running, and rather looking the other way; and as Duncan quickly lost sight of him in a hollow place that lay between them, he crept into a bush of heath, and took Oscar in his bosom;—the heath was so long that it almost closed above them; the man had observed from whence the dog started in the morning, and hasted to the place, expecting to find him sleeping beyond the old earthen dike; he found the nest, but the birds were flown;—he called aloud; Oscar trembled and clung to Duncan's breast; Duncan peeped from his purple covert like a heath-cock on his native waste,[69] and again

[68] Gala Water is a river in Scotland and a tributary of the Tweed. Middleton Moor is in the Moorfoot Hills, south of Edinburgh.

[69] Heathcock is usually another name for the partridge, but in Scotland and Northern England it refers to the much larger black grouse.

beheld the ruffian coming straight towards them, with his staff still heaved, and fury in his looks;—when he came within a few yards he stood still and bellowed out: "Oscar, yho, yho!" Oscar quaked, and crept still closer to Duncan's breast; Duncan almost sunk in the earth; "D———n him," said the Englishman, "if I had a hold of him I should make both him and the little thievish rascal dear at a small price; they cannot be far gone,—I think I hear them;" he then stood listening, but at that instant a farmer came up on horseback, and having heard him call, asked him if he had lost his dog? The peasant answered in the affirmative, and added, that a blackguard boy had stolen him. The farmer said that he met a boy with a dog about a mile forward. During this dialogue, the farmer's dog came up to Duncan's den,—smelled upon him, and then upon Oscar,— cocked his tail, walked round them growling, and then behaved in a very improper and uncivil manner to Duncan, who took all patiently, uncertain whether he was yet discovered. But so intent was the fellow upon the farmer's intelligence, that he took no notice of the discovery made by the dog, but ran off without looking over his shoulder.

Duncan felt this a deliverance so great that all his other distresses vanished; and as soon as the man was out of his sight, he arose from his covert, and ran over the moor, and ere it was long, came to a shepherd's house, where he got some whey and bread for his breakfast, which he thought the best meat he had ever tasted, yet shared it with Oscar.

Though I had his history from his own mouth, yet there is a space here which it is impossible to relate with any degree of distinctness or interest. He was a vagabond boy, without any fixed habitation, and wandered about Herriot Moor, from one farm-house to another, for the space of a year; staying from one to twenty nights in each house, according as he found the people kind to him. He seldom resented any indignity offered to himself, but whoever insulted Oscar, or offered any observations on the impropriety of their friendship, lost Duncan's company the next morning. He staid several months at a place called Dewar,[70] which he said was haunted by the ghost of a piper; that piper had been murdered there many years before, in a manner somewhat mysterious, or at least unaccountable; and there was scarcely a night on which he was not supposed either to be seen or heard about the house. Duncan slept in a cow-house, and was terribly harassed by the piper; he often heard him scratching about the rafters, and sometimes he would

[70] Both Heriot (a few lines above) and Dewar are villages on the Scottish Border, south of Edinburgh.

Duncan Campbell

groan like a man dying, or a cow that was choaked in the band; but at length he saw him at his side one night, which so discomposed him, that he was obliged to leave the place, after being ill for many days. I shall give this story in Duncan's own words, which I have often heard him repeat without any variation.

"I had been driving some young cattle to the heights of Willenslee[71]—it grew late before I got home.—I was thinking, and thinking, how cruel it was to kill the poor piper! to cut out his tongue, and stab him in the back. I thought it was no wonder that his ghost took it extremely ill; when, all on a sudden, I perceived a light before me;—I thought the wand in my hand was all on fire, and threw it away, but I perceived the light glide slowly by my right foot, and burn behind me;—I was nothing afraid, and turned about to look at the light, and there I saw the piper, who was standing hard at my back, and when I turned round, he looked me in the face." "What was he like, Duncan?" "He was like a dead body! but I got a short view of him; for that moment all around me grew dark as a pit!—I tried to run, but sunk powerless to the earth, and lay in a kind of dream, I do not know how long; when I came to myself, I got up, and endeavoured to run, but fell to the ground every two steps. I was not a hundred yards from the house, and I am sure I fell upwards of a hundred times. Next day I was in a high fever; the servants made me a little bed in the kitchen, to which I was confined by illness many days, during which time I suffered the most dreadful agonies by night, always imagining the piper to be standing over me on the one side or the other. As soon as I was able to walk, I left Dewar, and for a long time durst neither sleep alone during the night, nor stay by myself in the day-time."

The superstitious ideas impressed upon Duncan's mind by this unfortunate encounter with the ghost of the piper, seem never to have been eradicated; a strong instance of the power of early impressions, and a warning how much caution is necessary in modelling the conceptions of the young and tender mind, for, of all men I ever knew, he is the most afraid of meeting with apparitions. So deeply is his imagination tainted with this startling illusion, that even the calm disquisitions of reason have proved quite inadequate to the task of dispelling it. Whenever it wears late, he is always on the look-out for these ideal beings, keeping a jealous eye upon every bush and brake, in case they should be lurking behind them, ready to fly out and surprise him every moment; and the approach of a person in the dark, or any sudden noise, always deprives him of the power of speech for some time.

[71] The farm where Hogg himself was a shepherd for two years in his youth.

After leaving Dewar, he again wandered about for a few weeks; and it appears that his youth, beauty, and peculiarly destitute situation, together with his friendship for his faithful Oscar, had interested the most part of the country people in his behalf; for he was generally treated with kindness. He knew his father's name, and the name of his house; but as none of the people he visited had ever before heard of either the one or the other, they gave themselves no trouble about the matter.

He staid nearly two years in a place called Cowhaur,[72] until a wretch, with whom he slept, struck and abused him one day. Duncan, in a rage, flew to the loft, and cut all his Sunday hat, shoes, and coat, in pieces; and, not daring to abide the consequences, decamped that night.

He wandered about for some time longer, among the farmers of Tweed and Yarrow;[73] but this life was now become exceedingly disagreeable to him. He durst not sleep by himself, and the servants did not always choose to allow a vagrant boy and his great dog to sleep with them.

It was on a rainy night, at the close of harvest, that Duncan came to my father's house. I remember all the circumstances as well as the transactions of yesterday. The whole of his clothing consisted only of a black coat, which, having been made for a full-grown man, hung fairly to his heels; the hair of his head was rough, curly, and weather-beaten; but his face was ruddy and beautiful, bespeaking a healthy body, and a sensible feeling heart. Oscar was still nearly as large as himself, and the colour of a fox, having a white stripe down his face, with a ring of the same colour around his neck, and was the most beautiful colley I have ever seen. My heart was knit to Duncan at the first sight, and I wept for joy when I saw my parents so kind to him. My mother, in particular, could scarcely do any thing else than converse with Duncan for several days. I was always of the party, and listened with wonder and admiration; but often have these adventures been repeated to me. My parents, who soon seemed to feel the same concern for him as if he had been their own son, clothed him in blue drugget,[74] and bought him a smart little Highland bonnet; in which dress he looked so charming, that I would not let them have peace until I got one of the same. Indeed, all that Duncan said or did was to me a pattern; for I loved him as my own life. At my own request, which he persuaded me to urge, I

[72] Actually Colquhar, a farmstead in the Scottish Borders, close to Dewar.

[73] The valleys of the rivers Tweed, Yarrow, and Ettrick are important geological features of Selkirkshire.

[74] A heavy, coarse woollen fabric.

was permitted to be his bed-fellow, and many a happy night and day did I spend with Duncan and Oscar.

As far as I remember, we felt no privation of any kind, and would have been completely happy, if it had not been for the fear of spirits. When the conversation chanced to turn upon the Piper of Dewar, the Maid of Plora, or the Pedlar of Thirlestane Mill,[75] often have we lain with the bed-clothes drawn over our heads till nearly suffocated. We loved the fairies and the brownies, and even felt a little partiality for the mermaids, on account of their beauty and charming songs; but we were a little jealous of the water-kelpies,[76] and always kept aloof from the frightsome pools. We hated the devil most heartily, although we were not much afraid of him; but a ghost! oh, dreadful! the names, ghost, spirit, or apparition, sounded in our ears like the knell of destruction, and our hearts sunk within us as if pierced by the cold icy shaft of death. Duncan herded my father's cows all the summer—so did I—we could not live asunder. We grew such expert fishers, that the speckled trout, with all his art, could not elude our machinations; we forced him from his watery cove, admired the beautiful shades and purple drops that were painted on his sleek sides, and forthwith added him to our number without reluctance. We assailed the habitation of the wild bee, and rifled her of all her accumulated sweets, though not without encountering the most determined resistance. My father's meadows abounded with hives; they were almost in every swath—in every hillock. When the swarm was large, they would beat us off, day after day. In all these desperate engagements, Oscar came to our assistance, and, provided that none of the enemy made a lodgement in his lower defiles, he was always the last combatant of our party on the field. I do not remember of ever being so much diverted by any scene I ever witnessed, or laughing as immoderately as I have done at seeing Oscar involved in a moving cloud of wild bees, wheeling, snapping on all sides, and shaking his ears incessantly.

The sagacity which this animal possessed is almost incredible, while his undaunted spirit and generosity would do honour to every servant of our own species to copy. Twice did he save his master's

[75] In a long note to "Kilmeny," in *The Queen's Wake* (1813), Hogg provides the story of a girl from Traquair (a small village in Peeblesshire) who was said to have been abducted by the fairies and then found in Plora Wood. The ghost of the murdered pedlar of Thirlestane Mill (near Lauder, in Berwickshire) appears in his poem "The Peddlar" from *Mountain Bard* (1807).

[76] In Scottish folklore, fairies are usually malicious. Brownies are diminutive farm and household spirits who can be very touchy and irascible. Kelpies are shape-shifting spirits who live in and near the Scottish lochs.

life: at one time when attacked by a furious bull, and at another time when he fell from behind my father, off a horse in a flooded river. Oscar had just swum across, but instantly plunged in a second time to his master's rescue. He first got hold of his bonnet, but that coming off, he quitted it, and again catching him by the coat, brought him to the side, where my father reached him. He waked Duncan at a certain hour every morning, and would frequently turn the cows of his own will, when he observed them wrong. If Duncan dropped his knife, or any other small article, he would fetch it along in his mouth; and if sent back for a lost thing, would infallibly find it. When sixteen years of age, after being unwell for several days, he died one night below his master's bed. On the evening before, when Duncan came in from the plough, he came from his hiding-place, wagged his tail, licked Duncan's hand, and returned to his deathbed. Duncan and I lamented him with unfeigned sorrow, buried him below the old rowan tree at the back of my father's garden, placing a square stone at his head, which was still standing the last time I was there. With great labour, we composed an epitaph between us, which was once carved on that stone; the metre was good, but the stone was so hard, and the engraving so faint, that the characters, like those of our early joys, are long ago defaced and extinct.

Often have I heard my mother relate with enthusiasm, the manner in which she and my father first discovered the dawnings of goodness and facility of conception in Duncan's mind, though, I confess, dearly as I loved him, these circumstances escaped my observation. It was my father's invariable custom to pray with the family every night before they retired to rest, to thank the Almighty for his kindness to them during the bygone days, and to beg his protection through the dark and silent watches of the night. I need not inform any of my readers, that that amiable (and now too much neglected and despised) duty, consisted in singing a few stanzas of a psalm, in which all the family joined their voices with my father's so that the double octaves of the various ages and sexes swelled the simple concert. He then read a chapter from the Bible, going straight on from beginning to end of the Scriptures. The prayer concluded the devotions of each evening, in which the downfall of Antichrist was always strenuously urged, the ministers of the Gospel remembered, nor was any friend or neighbour in distress forgot.

The servants of a family have, in general, liberty either to wait the evening prayers, or retire to bed as they incline, but no consideration whatever could induce Duncan to go one night to rest without the prayers, even though both wet and weary, and entreated by my parents to retire, for fear of catching cold. It seems that I had been of a more complaisant disposition; for I was never very hard to prevail with in this respect; nay, my mother used to say, that I was extremely apt to take a pain about my heart at that time of the night, and was, of course, frequently obliged to betake me to the bed before the worship commenced.

It might be owing to this that Duncan's emotions on these occasions escaped my notice. He sung a treble to the old church tunes most sweetly, for he had a melodious voice; and when my father read the chapter, if it was in any of the historical parts of Scripture, he would lean upon the table, and look him in the face, swallowing every sentence with the utmost avidity. At one time, as my father read the 45th chapter of Genesis, he wept so bitterly, that at the end my father paused, and asked what ailed him? Duncan told him that he did not know.

At another time, the year following, my father, in the course of his evening devotions, had reached the 19th chapter of the book of Judges; when he began reading it, Duncan was seated on the other side of the house, but ere it was half done, he had stolen up close to my father's elbow. "Consider of it, take advice, and speak your minds," said my father, and closed the book. "Go on, go on if you please, Sir," said Duncan—"go on, and let us hear what they said about it." My father looked sternly in Duncan's face, but seeing him abashed on account of his hasty breach of decency, without uttering a word, he again opened the Bible, and read the 20th chapter throughout, notwithstanding of its great length. Next day Duncan was walking about with the Bible below his arm, begging of every body to read it to him again and again. This incident produced a conversation between my parents, on the expenses and utility of education; the consequence of which was, that the week following, Duncan and I were sent to the parish school, and began at the same instant to the study of that most important and fundamental branch of literature, the A, B, C; but my sister Mary, who was older than I, was already an accurate and elegant reader.

This reminds me of another anecdote of Duncan, with regard to family worship, which I have often heard related, and which I myself may well remember. My father happening to be absent over night at a fair, when the usual time of worship arrived, my mother desired a lad, one of the servants, to act as chaplain for that night; the lad declined it, and slunk away to his bed. My mother testified her regret that we should all be obliged to go prayerless to our beds for that night, observing, that she did not remember the time when it had so happened before. Duncan said, he thought we might contrive to manage it amongst us, and instantly proposed to sing the psalm and pray, if Mary would read the chapter. To this my mother with some hesitation agreed, remarking, that if he prayed as he could, with a pure heart, his prayer had as good a chance of being accepted as some others that were *better worded*. Duncan could not then read, but having learned several psalms from Mary by rote, he caused her seek out the place, and sung the 23rd Psalm from end to end, with great sweetness and decency. Mary read a chapter in the New Testament, and then (my mother having a child on her knee,) we three kneeled in a row, while Duncan prayed thus:—"O Lord, be thou our God, our guide, and our guard unto death, and through death," that was a sentence my father often used in his prayer; Duncan had laid hold of it, and my mother began to think that he had often prayed previous to that time.—"O Lord, thou"—continued Duncan, but his matter was exhausted; a long pause ensued, which I at length broke, by bursting into a loud fit of laughter. Duncan rose hastily, and, without once lifting up his head, went crying to his bed; and as I continued to indulge in laughter, my mother, for my irreverend behaviour, struck me across the shoulders with the tongs; our evening devotions terminated exceedingly ill, I went crying to my bed after Duncan, even louder than he, and abusing him for his *useless prayer*, for which I had been nearly felled.

By the time that we were recalled from school to herd the cows next summer, we could both read the Bible with considerable facility, but Duncan far excelled me in perspicacity; and so fond was he of reading Bible history, that the reading of it was now our constant amusement. Often have Mary, and he, and I, lain under the same plaid by the side of the corn or meadow, and read chapter about[77] on the Bible for hours together, weeping over the failings and fall of good men, and wondering at the inconceivable might of the heroes of antiquity. Never was man so delighted as Duncan was when he came to the history of Samson, and afterwards of David and Goliath; he could not be satisfied until he had read it to every individual with whom he was acquainted, judging it to be as new and as interesting to every one as it was to himself. I have seen him standing by the girls as they were milking the cows, reading to them the feats of Samson; and, in short, harassing every man and woman about the hamlet for audience. On Sundays, my parents

[77] Scottish expression: taking turns reading one chapter each.

Duncan Campbell

accompanied us to the fields, and joined in our delightful exercise.

Time passed away, and so also did our youthful delights! but other cares and other pleasures awaited us. As we advanced in years and strength, we quitted the herding, and bore a hand in the labours of the farm. Mary, too, was often our assistant. She and Duncan were nearly of an age—he was tall, comely, and affable; and if Mary was not the prettiest girl in the parish, at least Duncan and I believed her to be so, which, with us, amounted to the same thing. We often compared the other girls in the parish with one another, as to their beauty and accomplishments, but to think of comparing any of them with Mary, was entirely out of the question. She was, indeed, the emblem of truth, simplicity, and innocence, and if there were few more beautiful, there were still fewer so good and amiable; but still as she advanced in years, she grew fonder and fonder of being near Duncan; and by the time she was nineteen, was so deeply in love, that it affected her manner, her spirits, and her health. At one time she was gay and frisky as a kitten; she would dance, sing, and laugh violently at the most trivial incidents. At other times she was silent and sad, while a languishing softness overspread her features, and added greatly to her charms. The passion was undoubtedly mutual between them; but Duncan, either from a sense of honour, or some other cause, never declared himself farther on the subject, than by the most respectful attention, and tender assiduities. Hope and fear thus alternately swayed the heart of poor Mary, and produced in her deportment that variety of affections, which could not fail of rendering the sentiments of her artless bosom legible to the eye of experience.

In this state matters stood, when an incident occurred which deranged our happiness at once, and the time arrived when the kindest and most affectionate little social band of friends, that ever panted to meet the wishes of each other, were obliged to part.

About forty years ago, the flocks of southern sheep, which have since that period inundated the Highlands, had not found their way over the Grampian mountains;[78] and the native flocks of that sequestered country were so scanty, that it was found necessary to transport small quantities of wool annually to the north, to furnish materials for clothing the inhabitants. During two months of each summer, the hill countries of the Lowlands were inundated by hundreds of women from the Highlands, who bartered small

---

[78] The most important mountain range in Scotland, situated between the Central Lowlands in the south and the Northwest Highlands in the north. It includes Ben Nevis, the highest point in the British Isles.

articles of dress, and of domestic import, for wool: these were known by the appellation of *norlan' netties*;[79] and few nights passed, during the wool season, that some of them were not lodged at my father's house. It was from two of these that Duncan learned one day who and what he was; that he was the laird of Glenellich's only son and heir, and that a large sum had been offered to any person that could discover him. My parents certainly rejoiced in Duncan's good fortune, yet they were disconsolate at parting with him; for he had long ago become as a son of their own; and I seriously believe, that from the day they first met, to that on which the two *norlan' netties* came to our house, they never once entertained the idea of parting. For my part, I wished that the netties had never been born, or that they had staid at their own home; for the thoughts of being separated from my dear friend made me sick at heart. All our feelings were, however, nothing, when compared with those of my sister Mary. From the day that the two women left our house, she was no more seen to smile; she had never yet divulged the sentiments of her heart to any one, and imagined her love for Duncan a profound secret—no,

> "She never told her love;
> But let concealment, like a worm i' the bud,
> Feed on her damask cheek;—she pined in thought;
> And, with a green and yellow melancholy,
> She sat, like patience on a monument,
> Smiling at grief."[80]

Our social glee and cheerfulness were now completely clouded; we sat down to our meals, and rose from them in silence. Of the few observations that passed, every one seemed the progeny of embarrassment and discontent, and our general remarks were strained and cold. One day at dinner, after a long and sullen pause, my father said, "I hope you do not intend to leave us very soon, Duncan?" "I am thinking of going away to-morrow, Sir," said Duncan. The knife fell from my mother's hand; she looked him steadily in the face for the space of a minute. "Duncan," said she, her voice faultering, and the tears dropping from her eyes,— "Duncan, I never durst ask you before, but I hope you will not leave us altogether?" Duncan thrust the plate from before him into the middle of the table—took up a book that lay on the window,

---

[79] A "nettie" is a wife; "norlan" means "from the north" (i.e., from the Highlands).

[80] From Shakespeare's *Twelfth Night* (Act II, Scene IV).

and looked over the pages—Mary left the room. No answer was returned, nor any further inquiry made; and our little party broke up in silence.

When we met again in the evening, we were still all sullen. My mother tried to speak of indifferent things, but it was apparent that her thoughts had no share in the words that dropped from her tongue. My father at last said, "You will soon forget us, Duncan; but there are some among us who will not so soon forget you." Mary again left the room, and silence ensued, until the family were called together for evening worship. There was one sentence in my father's prayer that night, which I think I yet remember, word for word. It may appear of little importance to those who are nowise interested, but it affected us deeply, and left not a dry cheek in the family. It runs thus: "We are an unworthy little flock, thou seest here kneeling before thee, our God; but few as we are, it is probable we shall never all kneel again together before thee in this world. We have long lived together in peace and happiness, and hoped to have lived so much longer; but since it is thy will that we part, enable us to submit to that will with firmness; and though thou scatter us to the four winds of heaven, may thy Almighty arm still be about us for good, and grant that we may all meet hereafter in another and a better world."

The next morning, after a restless night, Duncan rose early, put on his best suit, and packed up some little articles to carry with him. I lay panting and trembling, but pretended to be fast asleep. When he was ready to depart, he took his bundle below his arm, came up to the side of the bed, and listened if I was sleeping. He then stood long hesitating, looking wistfully to the door, and then to me, alternately; and I saw him three or four times wipe his eyes. At length he shook me gently by the shoulder, and asked if I was awake. I feigned to start, and answered as if half asleep. "I must bid you farewell," said he, groping to get hold of my hand. "Will you not breakfast with us, Duncan?" said I. "No," said he, "I am thinking that it is best to steal away, for it will break my heart to take leave of your parents, and"—"And who, Duncan?" said I. "And you," said he. "Indeed, but it is not best, Duncan," said I; "we will all breakfast together for the last time, and then take a formal and kind leave of each other." We did breakfast together, and as the conversation turned on former days, it became highly interesting to us all. When my father had returned thanks to Heaven for our meal, we knew what was coming, and began to look at each other. Duncan rose, and after we had all loaded him with our blessings and warmest wishes, he embraced my parents and me.—He turned about.—His eyes said plainly, there is somebody still wanting, but his heart was so full he could not speak. "What is become of Mary?" said my father;—Mary was gone.—We searched the house, the garden, and the houses of all the cottagers, but she was nowhere to be found.—Poor lovelorn forsaken Mary! She had hid herself in the ancient yew that grows in the front of the old ruin, that she might see her lover depart, without herself being seen, and might indulge in all the luxury of wo.—Poor Mary! how often have I heard her sigh, and seen her eyes red with weeping; while the smile that played on her languid features, when ought was mentioned to Duncan's recommendation, would have melted a heart of adamant.

I must pass over Duncan's journey to the north Highlands for want of room, but on the evening of the sixth day after leaving my father's house, he reached the mansion-house of Glenellich, which stands in a little beautiful woody strath, commanding a view of the Deu-Caledonian Sea,[81] and part of the Hebrides; every avenue, tree, and rock, was yet familiar to Duncan's recollection; and the feelings of his sensible heart, on approaching the abode of his father, whom he had long scarcely thought of, can only be conceived by a heart like his own. He had, without discovering himself, learned from a peasant that his father was still alive, but that he had never overcome the loss of his son, for whom he lamented every day; that his wife and daughter lorded it over him, holding his pleasure at nought, and rendered his age extremely unhappy; that they had expelled all his old farmers and vassals, and introduced the lady's vulgar presumptuous relations, who neither paid him rents, honour, nor obedience.

Old Glenellich was taking his evening walk on the road by which Duncan descended the strath to his dwelling. He was pondering on his own misfortunes, and did not even deign to lift his eyes as the young stranger approached, but seemed counting the number of marks which the horses' hoofs had made on the way. "Good e'en to you, Sir," said Duncan;—the old man started and stared him in the face, but with a look so unsteady and harassed, that he seemed incapable of distinguishing any lineament or feature of it. "Good e'en, good e'en," said he, wiping his brow with his arm, and passing by.—What there was in the voice that struck him

[81] A "strath" is a wide, relatively fertile, river valley in Scotland. The part of the Atlantic Ocean bordering Scotland to the north was sometimes called "Deu-Caledonian," in reference to the so-called Dicalydones, one of two Caledonian tribes that had inhabited Scotland in antiquity (more exactly, the northern and western parts of the country, so they were associated with Highlanders), although this division of the ancient Caledonians is today disputed.

Duncan Campbell

so forcibly it is hard to say.—Nature is powerful.—Duncan could not think of ought to detain him; and being desirous of seeing how matters went on about the house, thought it best to remain some days *incog*. He went into the fore-kitchen, conversed freely with the servants, and soon saw his stepmother and sister appear. The former had all the insolence and ignorant pride of vulgarity raised to wealth and eminence; the other seemed naturally of an amiable disposition, but was entirely ruled by her mother, who taught her to disdain her father, all his relations, and whomsoever he loved. On that same evening he came into the kitchen, where she then was chatting with Duncan, to whom she seemed attached at first sight. "Lexy, my dear," said he, "did you see my spectacles?" "Yes," said she, "I think I saw them on your nose to-day at breakfast." "Well, but I have lost them since," said he. "You may take up the next you find then, Sir," said she.—The servants laughed. "I might well have known what information I would get of you," said he, regretfully. "How can you speak in such a style to your father, my dear lady?" said Duncan.—"If I were he I would place you where you should learn better manners.—It ill becomes so pretty a young lady to address an old father thus." "He!" said she, "who minds him? He's a dotard, an old whining, complaining, superannuated being, worse than a child." "But consider his years," said Duncan; "and besides, he may have met with crosses and losses sufficient to sour the temper of a younger man.—You should at all events pity and reverence, but never despise your father." The old lady now joined them. "You have yet heard nothing, young man," said the old laird, "if you saw how my heart is sometimes wrung.—Yes, I have had losses indeed." "You losses!" said his spouse;—"No; you have never had any losses that did not in the end turn out a vast profit."—"Do you then account the loss of a loving wife and a son nothing?" said he—"But have you not got a loving wife and a daughter in their room?" returned she; "the one will not waste your fortune as a prodigal son would have done, and the other will take care of both you and that, when *you* can no longer do either— the loss of your son indeed! it was the greatest blessing you could have received!" "Unfeeling woman," said he; "but Heaven may yet restore that son to protect the gray hairs of his old father, and lay his head in an honoured grave." The old man's spirits were quite gone—he cried like a child—his lady mimicked him—and at this, his daughter and the servants raised a laugh. "Inhuman wretches," said Duncan, starting up, and pushing them aside, "thus to mock the feelings of an old man, even although he were not the lord and master of you all: but take notice—the individual among you all that dares to offer such another insult to him, I'll roast on that fire." The old man clung to him, and looked him ruefully in the face. "You impudent, beggarly vagabond!" said the lady, "do you know to whom you speak?—servants turn that wretch out of the house, and hunt him with all the dogs in the kennel." "Softly, softly, good lady," said Duncan, "take care that I do not turn you out of the house."— "Alas! good youth," said the old laird, "you little know what you are about; for mercy's sake forbear; you are brewing vengeance both for yourself and me." "Fear not," said Duncan, "I will protect you with my life." "Pray, may I ask you what is your name?" said the old man, still looking earnestly at him—"That you may," replied Duncan, "no man has so good a right to ask any thing of me as you have—I am Duncan Campbell, your own son." "M-*m-m-my* son!" exclaimed the old man, and sunk back on a seat with a convulsive moan. Duncan held him in his arms—he soon recovered, and asked many incoherent questions—looked at the two moles on his right leg—kissed him, and then wept on his bosom for joy. "O God of heaven," said he, "it is long since I could thank thee heartily for any thing; now I do thank thee indeed, for I have found my son! my dear and only son!"

Contrary to what might have been expected, Duncan's pretty only sister Alexia rejoiced most of all in his discovery. She was almost wild with joy at finding such a brother.—The old lady, her mother, was said to have wept bitterly in private, but knowing that Duncan would be her master, she behaved to him with civility and respect. Every thing was committed to his management, and he soon discovered, that besides a good clear estate, his father had personal funds to a great amount. The halls and cottages of Glenellich were filled with feasting, joy, and gladness.

It was not so at my father's house. Misfortunes seldom come singly. Scarcely had our feelings overcome the shock which they received by the loss of our beloved Duncan, when a more terrible misfortune overtook us. My father, by the monstrous ingratitude of a friend whom he trusted, lost at once the greater part of his hard-earned fortune. The blow came unexpectedly, and distracted his personal affairs to such a degree, that an arrangement seemed almost totally impracticable. He struggled on with securities for several months; but perceiving that he was drawing his real friends into danger, by their signing of bonds which he might never be able to redeem, he lost heart entirely, and yielded to the torrent. Mary's mind seemed to gain fresh energy every day. The activity and diligence which she evinced in managing the affairs of the farm,

Duncan Campbell

and even in giving advice with regard to other matters, is quite incredible;—often have I thought what a treasure that inestimable girl would have been to an industrious man whom she loved. All our efforts availed nothing; my father received letters of horning[82] on bills to a large amount, and we expected every day that he would be taken from us and dragged to a prison.

 We were all sitting in our little room one day, consulting what was best to be done—we could decide upon nothing, for our case was desperate—we were fallen into a kind of stupor, but the window being up, a sight appeared that quickly thrilled every heart with the keenest sensations of anguish. Two men came riding sharply up by the back of the old school house. "Yonder are the officers of justice now," said my mother, "what shall we do?" We hurried to the window, and all of us soon discerned that they were no other than some attorney, accompanied by a sheriff's officer. My mother entreated of my father to escape and hide himself until this first storm was over-blown, but he would in nowise consent, assuring us that he had done nothing of which he was ashamed, and that he was determined to meet every one face to face, and let them do their worst; so finding all our entreaties vain, we could do nothing but sit down and weep. At length we heard the noise of their horses at the door. "You had better take the men's horses, James," said my father, "as there is no other man at hand." "We will stay till they rap, if you please," said I. The cautious officer did not however rap, but, afraid lest his debtor should make his escape, he jumped lightly from his horse, and hasted into the house. When we heard him open the outer door, and his footsteps approaching along the entry, our hearts fainted within us—he opened the door and stepped into the room—it was Duncan! our own dearly beloved Duncan. The women uttered an involuntary scream of surprise, but my father ran and got hold of one hand, and I of the other—my mother too soon had him in her arms, but our embrace was short; for his eyes fixed on Mary, who stood trembling with joy and wonder in a corner of the room, changing her colour every moment—he snatched her up in his arms and kissed her lips, and ere ever she was aware, her arms had encircled his neck. "O my dear Mary," said he, "my heart has been ill at ease since I left you, but I durst not then tell you a word of my mind, for I little knew how I was to

---

[82] In Scots Law, "letters of horning" were a form of summons charging the debtor to pay his debt, under penalty of being "put to the horn" (i.e., declared outlaw with three blasts of a horn by the king's messenger).

find affairs in the place where I was going; but ah! you little elusive rogue, you owe me another for the one you cheated me out of then;" so saying, he pressed his lips again to her cheek, and then led her to a seat. Duncan then recounted all his adventures to us, with every circumstance of his good fortune—our hearts were uplifted almost past bearing—all our cares and sorrows were now forgotten, and we were once more the happiest little group that ever perhaps sat together. Before the cloth was laid for dinner, Mary ran out to put on her white gown, and comb her yellow hair, but was surprised at meeting with a smart young gentleman in the kitchen, with a scarlet neck on his coat, and a gold-laced hat. Mary, having never seen so fine a gentleman, made him a low courtesy, and offered to conduct him to the room: but he smiled, and told her he was the squire's servant. We had all of us forgot to ask for the gentleman that came with Duncan.

Duncan and Mary walked for two hours in the garden that evening—we did not know what passed between them, but the next day he asked her in marriage of my parents, and never will I forget the supreme happiness and gratitude that beamed in every face on that happy occasion. I need not tell my readers that my father's affairs were soon retrieved, or that I accompanied my dear Mary a bride to the Highlands, and had the satisfaction of saluting her as Mrs Campbell, and Lady of Glenellich.

Mary Leadbeater and Elizabeth Shackleton

𝒯ʜᴇ Sᴄᴏᴛᴄʜ 𝒫ʟᴏᴜɢʜᴍᴀɴ

(1814)

The authors: Mary Leadbeater (1758-1826), was born and died in Ballitore, County Kildare, Ireland, in a family of Quakers acquainted with Edmund Burke, with whom she corresponded. Leadbeater (in the picture to the right) married a small farmer in 1791 and was for a long time the postmistress of Ballitore. She first published *Poems* in 1808, followed in 1811 by *Cottage Dialogues among the Irish Peasantry*, for the London edition of which Maria Edgeworth  wrote a Preface and compiled a glossary. In 1814, together with her niece Elizabeth Shackleton (1783-1843), known as Betsy, she published *Tales for Cottagers*, and the series was continued in 1822 with *Cottage Biography, being a Collection of Lives of the Irish Peasantry*. Her last tale was *The Pedlars* (1826), published as a Kildare Place Society tract. Her best-known work remains the posthumous *Annals of Ballitore*, a collection of diaries and letters about contemporary events in Irish history from the perspective of the inhabitants of her native village.

The text: It was first published in *Tales for Cottagers, Accom[m]odated to the Present Condition of the Irish Peasantry* (Dublin: James Cumming & Co., 1814, 154-164), from which the following has been reproduced. Some of the punctuation has been corrected. The names of the two authors appear on the title page as "Mary Leadbetter and Elizabeth Shakleton."

Further reading: Helen O'Connell. *Ireland and the Fiction of Improvement*. Oxford: Oxford University Press, 2006. 73-79.

Mr. Nugent lived in a part of Ireland, where the modern improvements in farming were not understood, and where the poor were remarkably idle and ignorant. He had read in the newspapers of Scotch ploughs and Scotch ploughmen, and being desirous to cultivate his land after the best manner, he wrote to Mr. Frazer, his friend in Edinburgh, to request that he would send him these two great instruments of agriculture. Mr. Nugent hearing that Scotchmen were very eager to leave their own country, imagined that both the above-mentioned articles would arrive in a very short time, but he was disappointed. Mr. Frazer had not been negligent in making inquiries, and in going in person to seek out an expert ploughman for his friend; but some of them were unwilling to transplant their young families, others were reaping the reward of the industry with which they had cultivated their own little fields and gardens. Many adventurous young men were to be found, who were well enough inclined to travel, but they had either an old father or mother, or uncle, or aunt, whom no considerations could induce them to desert; and not a man would think of hiring himself, even for one season, to work at a distance from his family, who might starve or beg in his absence. Mr. Nugent was surprised at this account, as he knew that many of his own tenants made it their practice to go to England, or to a distant part of Ireland, during the busy season; while their wives and children went to beg, and the house was locked up during their absence.

Repeated disappointments did not discourage Mr. Frazer from continuing his inquiry, and at length the desired person was discovered. His name was Andrew Macdonald. His mother, who had been long a widow, had died a few months before, and he had not ceased grieving for the object of his tender care. His only sister was married, and Andrew's ties to his native country were loosened. Mr. Frazer was directed to furnish him with money to defray his expenses on the journey. The plough was easily procured, and both man and plough arrived safely at Mr. Nugent's. This gentleman was surprised that Andrew stood erect before him, and with a blunt civility, requested to know where he was to lodge that night. He was informed, and also told, that he should have something to eat and drink immediately. Andrew thanked his new master, but said he was neither hungry nor dry. "If you please," said he, "I will shew you the account of my expenses on the journey." "You need shew me no

The Scotch Ploughman

account," said Mr. Nugent. "I ordered Mr. Frazer to give you what money he thought proper, and I won't give you a farthing more."

"I never wronged *any one*," replied Andrew, "and if you take the trouble to look over this account, you will see that I don't want to wrong *you*."

"That is the old story over again," said Mr. Nugent, "I hear this every day of my life, and yet not a day passes but I am wronged."

"My account will shew you," replied the patient Scotchman: "If I was in my own dear country, my word would be taken, but I cannot expect this where I am not known; for which reason I have kept an exact account."

"*Your* account," said Mr. Nugent, "who cares for your accounts? I don't want a clerk, I want a good ploughman. I want a man that can make straight lines in a field, and not crooked ones on paper."

"In my country," replied Andrew, "the same hand can guide the plough and the pen. We can cultivate our fields, and calculate the expenses of cultivation. However, Sir, since you won't run your eye over my account, I shall give you the change I owe you without any more ado. But I must first look at my account to see how much it is."

Andrew then opened his box, and carefully took up the little articles which it contained; laying them on one side, till he met with his pocket-book, which was of good black leather. His master eyed him all the while with attention, and wondered that a ploughman should have all these conveniencies. Andrew opened his account, and remarked that he owed Mr. Nugent 11*s*. 7½*d*.—"Could not you say half a guinea at once?"[83] said his master. Andrew repeated, "The money, Sir, is exactly 11*s*. 7½*d*." This transaction raised Andrew's character and abilities very much in the estimation of his master, who, without considering whether his own mind would change, or whether Andrew's future conduct would merit his confidence, promised the young stranger a house and garden rent free, for the ensuing year: provided he would pay some little attention, which would not be troublesome, to the general business of the farm, in addition to his work. Andrew thanked his master, and expressed his hope that such an agreement might be advantageous to both parties. "If it is profitable to you, what need you mind whether it is so to me or not?" But Andrew well knew that the good fortune which was dependent on his master, must be of short duration if he was unsuccessful.

[83] Half a guinea would have been 10s. 6d. (10 shillings and sixpence). Mr. Nugent is obviously asking for a half-guinea coin (see note 59).

"I don't wish," said he, "to injure another by my own success, and I know very well, if this mode will not answer you, it can't long be of any benefit to me."

"Very well," retorted his master, "I perceive you are a cunning rogue, that can see before you; but they say a Scotchman can't see before him when he faces his native country." Andrew looked grave at being called a rogue; the joke on his country did not please him any better, and notwithstanding his master's fair promises, he felt no partiality for, nor confidence in a man who doubted his word one minute, offered to reward him for common honesty the next, and in almost the same breath, called him a rogue, and jested on his dear native country. If he had possessed less patience, and less good sense, the Scotchman would have packed up his box, and returned to that dear native country without farther delay; but he had accustomed himself to reason upon passing occurrences, and to endure difficulties, which determined him to give his present situation a fair trial. It was probable his master might be as good as his word, and if he should not, Andrew felt assured, that his own superior knowledge of farming, where it was so ill understood, would insure him success in the employ of another, if not for himself.

Mr. Nugent lay long in bed, his labourers took advantage of this, and never went to their work till late in the morning. Andrew had no idea of receiving payment for eight hours work, and doing only four or six, therefore he was always early in the field, and surprised his master every day by the quantity, as well as the neatness of his work. He soon perceived that the labourers disliked him on account of the comparisons made betwixt his diligence and their neglect. They even dared to censure him for his industry, and took occasion to disoblige him many ways; but he was not to be intimidated, far less corrupted. A Scotchman is naturally courageous, and conscious integrity made Andrew stand so upright amongst his enemies, that they found it impossible to frighten him, or move him from the "firm purpose of his soul."[84] Andrew had a good heart and a clear head; he saw through the faults of his new companions' good dispositions, which wanted and deserved cultivation. He loved his Creator, of course he loved his fellow creatures; and thankful for the benefits he had received from education, he thought it right to share them with others;

[84] From Book XXII of Alexander Pope's translation of the *Iliad*: "But fix'd remains the purpose of his soul."

The Scotch Ploughman

therefore, whenever he saw a hint would be well taken, he failed not to throw before them the duty they owed to their master, and the happiness they would feel at having done their duty, besides the value of a good character in the eyes of the world. He found the warm and generous Irish heart was open to advice when it was given in a gentle, kind manner, without assuming a superiority over them. Then he was always willing to instruct them in the best method of doing work; and in a manner so humble, quiet, and civil, that it was a pleasure to learn any thing from him; they found him also ready to oblige them in any thing consistent with his duty to his master, and thus his influence continually increased, as did their happiness and his own, when an accidental circumstance raised him still higher in esteem.

One morning, soon after Andrew had gone to his work, he heard a boy cry out for help in the next field. He sprung over the fence, and found that a cow which belonged to one of his fellow workmen, had fallen into a deep pit. The little boy had been left to watch that the cow should not go near this pit; he had neglected his business, and was now in the utmost affliction. He proposed to Andrew to kill the cow, haul her up with ropes, and say she had met with an accident elsewhere. Andrew paid no attention to such advice, but silently putting his hand to his forehead, considered for a few minutes what was to be done. The result was, that with all speed, he returned to the house, yoked a cart and horse, and brought a load of manure to the side of the pit. He emptied the cart, and sent the boy for another. He threw the manure by little and little into the pit, the cow still trod upon it, and was thus gradually raised to the level of the field, and walked out almost unhurt.[85] The boy's surprise and gratitude prompted him to tell his father the whole story, at the risk of a beating for his carelessness, and this good-natured and ingenious action, gained for Andrew the veneration of the little boy, the friendship of his family, and the admiration of the neighbourhood.

Andrew became a frequent visitor to the family of James Kenagh, a slater. His house was the most decent in the neighbourhood, and his wife and daughters the most industrious. Honor, the eldest, was a pretty girl, always dressed plain, though perfectly clean, and was remarkable for her good temper and kind

---

[85] Here the authors inserted the following note: "A Scotch gentleman tried this method with success in the County Kildare."

heart. Of this an instance occurred, which it may not be intrusive to introduce here. Honor hearing that her neighbour, Molly Lennon, was sick, went to visit her, and in order to entertain her, while she sat by her bedside, she talked of every pleasant circumstance which had lately occurred, for she believed Molly's complaint was chiefly on her spirits. When she mentioned the success of Mary Carty, who was nursing for Mrs. Simpson, she observed that Molly grew pale: "What ails you, Molly," inquired her young friend, who was not a little surprised at the reply, "I never hear of that woman but it makes me sick, and it is she that is the case of my sickness this minute." And then observing Honor looked astonished, she proceeded with a long story of one neighbour having overheard another neighbour, that was told by another in confidence, that a fellow servant of Mary Carty's heard her telling her mistress, that Molly Lennon had not taken proper care of the child that she had nursed for Mrs. Simpson. "Why, I tell you," continued the sick woman, "it scalds my very heart that such a thing should be said of me, and I as fond, aye, fonder of little Henry Simpson, my darling, beautiful baby, than ever I was of my own poor creatures! Did I not give him as much white bread as he could eat, when my own had hardly enough of potatoes? And more than that, she told my mistress, that I put his little elegant clothes upon my own brats. I took a pain in my stomach the minute I heard it, and it's long before I'll get the better of it; but she is making her fortune there, and going to be set up in a shop, and thought ever so much about; she that only nursed one little girl, and I that nursed two fine boys, here I am as you see me." Honor did not contradict what she knew nothing about; but while Molly was speaking, she resolved to relieve her from this distress, if it was in her power, for she was unwilling to believe that Mary Carty could be so base as to endeavour to ruin another, in order to establish herself. She soon came back to Molly with a countenance even more pleasant than usual, and had the satisfaction of telling her, that she heard a letter read from Mrs. Simpson, in which she praised Molly Lennon's care very much, and particularly mentioned the great account she had, of her affection of Master Henry, which she heard from nurse Carty. Molly sat up in her bed in amazement, and said she felt as if she had awoke from a frightful dream. Then Honor, with great modesty and gentleness, ventured to represent to her neighbour, that she might have been spared all this uneasiness, if she had considered that it is very common for a story first to be misunderstood, then to be told with exaggerations, and to be repeated again and again, by people who, without intending to tell lies, give it the colour of their own passions or humours, for which reason, Honor begged her friend would hereafter always hope for the best, till she could satisfy herself of the truth of a story at the fountain head.

The character of Honor, more than her beauty, made an impression on Andrew's heart; he never saw her but she brought his sister to his recollection, and as he listened to her singing at her wheel, he thought the Irish songs were almost as sweet as the Scotch. Indeed, he found a great similarity between the Irish language and the Erse,[86] and he was willing to persuade himself, and his new friends were very willing to be persuaded, that the Irish and Scotch had originally been one nation. He found the better he knew the people he lived amongst, the stronger claim they had upon his regard; but especially his affection for young Honor increased, and he offered her his hand. Andrew was a comely young man, and so well educated, according to the custom of his country, that he was a fit companion for a tradesman's or farmer's daughter. Honor was of this opinion, but her father and mother would not hear of their daughter marrying a ploughman. Andrew was sorely disappointed when he was desired to think no more of the girl for whom he had a most sincere affection, and he found it impossible to look towards any one else for a wife. Honor was equally steady in her attachment to him, but she submitted to her fate. Her sense of duty and his sense of honour, would not permit them to think of a clandestine marriage, but various modes of life occurred to the lover, instead of following the plough, which was the cause of his disappointment. However, he dismissed all these schemes from his mind, and resolved to adhere to that business which he understood well, and which he hoped would gradually be the means of promoting him to a situation in life more agreeable to James Kenagh. To become a steward, or to have a farm of his own was his highest aim, and this he kept constantly in his view. No discouragements were able to destroy his hopes: He would say in his own mind, "If, with all my struggle, I cannot attain either of these, I shall, notwithstanding, be the richer ploughman by my industry." By indefatigable exertions, he had rendered half an acre of ground, the richest little field on the town-land. His garden was also well cultivated, and supplied him with a constant succession of crops. All this was done before or after working hours. Andrew's leisure would have passed heavily and sorrowfully along, so far from his native land, and labouring under disappointed love, but for these occupations, and in wet or wintry evenings, he amused and improved himself reading. He had brought a small collection of books with him from Scotland,

---

[86] At the time, Scottish Gaelic was often called "Erse" ("Irish").

and he borrowed some from the country school-master. Situated as Andrew was, it is probable he might have had recourse to the alehouse or gaming-table, were it not for his love of reading. With delight and peculiar animation, he used to describe the Sundays and the winter evenings, he had spent in former times with his mother and sister. Another employment of his leisure, was planning a little benefit society; he was so much beloved and esteemed, that he accomplished it with less difficulty than he expected. Each labourer laid aside a penny a-week, and Andrew prevailed upon his master to take charge of the money, himself keeping the accounts, and relieving Mr. Nugent of any trouble, except to receive and hand out the money. This penny entitled the subscriber to receive one shilling per week in sickness, and was found to be a great advantage to them. Mr. Nugent perceiving how useful this little fund was, increased it by his own bounty, and becoming more and more interested in the concerns of his poor tenantry, his attachment to them increased, which of course was repaid by theirs to him. Thus, this young man, by his perseverance, honesty, and good sense, was the means of a material reformation in that part of the country, and both landlord and tenants, had cause to love the name of Andrew Macdonald.

The agent of a gentleman who resided in England, had long been casting a wistful eye upon the Scotchman, with whose assistance he thought he would reform the land, so as to surprise his employer. He often threw out hints to Andrew, but in vain. At length he spoke out, and offered him a bribe to leave his present master: Andrew was proof against the bribe, but proposed that the agent should speak openly to Mr. Nugent on the subject; but this the agent did not choose to do. The labourers on Mr. Nugent's land, who loved and valued Andrew too much to be willing to lose him, contrived to let their master know of the transaction, and he determined to reward the integrity of his ploughman, by letting him have ten acres of land at a moderate rent, on condition that he would continue to plough for him till he had instructed another, to be able to supply his place. Andrew taught a man on his own ground, and made him so expert, that he was soon able to resign an employment which had been such a bar to his happiness. He was now a small farmer, and about this time, his master falling sick, as he had neither son or steward to attend to his business, he left the management of it to Andrew, who had more work done under his inspection in one month, than his master ever had got accomplished in two. Yet the horses looked well, and the tools and tacklings[87] were all in good order; and what surprised Mr. Nugent still more, Andrew

---

[87] Gear, furnishings (esp. a horse's harness).

The Scotch Ploughman

brought him a clear, well written account of all the money which he had paid and received. All notes and receipts were carefully filed, and nothing was astray: For this, Andrew took no merit to himself, he had but simply performed his duty, and should have blamed himself, or another, who had done less in the like circumstances. The consequence was, that Mr. Nugent made Andrew his steward, and now being both a farmer and a steward, he renewed his proposals to Honor, and they were united with the hearty good will of her parents. Many wondered at Andrew's patience in waiting for Honor, and at his faith in hoping his situation would alter, to which Andrew replied, "Patience and a good fire would roast an ox: Patience and warm affection gained me a good wife."

Amelia Opie

𝒯HE 𝒲ELCOME 𝐻OME; OR, 𝒯HE 𝐵ALL

(1818)

The author: Only months after the publication of *Simple Tales*, John Opie, Amelia's husband, died (9 April 1807). She edited and published John's *Lectures on Painting, with a Memoir* (1809). Her next publication was in 1812: *Temper; or, Domestic Scenes: A Tale*, followed in 1813 by *Tales of Real Life*. She met Walter Scott in 1815 and published *Valentine's Eve* in 1816. In 1818 she brought out *New Tales* in 4 volumes.

The text: First published in *New Tales. By Mrs. Opie. In Four Volumes* (London: Longman, Rees, Orme, and Brown, 1818), Vol. IV, 294-363, from which the following has been taken.

"How fortunate is it for me, with my impatient spirit," said Ronald Breadalbane to General Monthermer, as they were travelling from Portsmouth to London, "that I have you with me as a companion to beguile the length of the way!"

"I can echo your words with perfect sincerity," replied the general; "as after a residence in India of sixteen years and upwards, my eagerness to reach London, and get my business transacted there, that I may hasten to my native place, is as great as yours."

"Aye!" replied the enthusiastic and national[88] Breadalbane, who was many years younger than the general: "but my native place, my Highland home, is such an enchanting spot! O Scotland, dear Scotland! land of the mountain and the vale! land of beautiful women and of brave men! land of genius and of song! land of kindness and hospitality! I bring to thee an unchanged heart, my country, and a conviction that there is nought like thee upon the habitable globe!"

[88] Obsolete term for "patriotic."

The Welcome Home; or, The Ball

Had Breadalbane been so fortunate as to have read the eulogium lately passed by a certain orator on this loved land of his birth, in his admirable speech on the education of the poor, he would, perhaps, have borrowed his language; and would have exclaimed, "What part of the world into which Scotchmen have emigrated, have they not benefited? What part where they have emigrated, have they not conferred more benefits upon than they have reaped?"[89]

General Monthermer, who loved his own country too well not to be able to make allowances for national pride in others, replied with a benevolent smile, "I fully admit the truth of what you have said of Scotland; for I have gazed enamoured on its women, listened with delight to the eloquence of its orators, have hung enraptured on its melodies, and read, with ever new transport the works of its poets and its writers. I have also had my inmost soul warmed by its hospitality; and who that has ever seen and been welcomed to the metropolis of your country, Breadalbane, but must remember it with grateful pleasure to the end of his existence, and almost pine to behold Edinburgh again!"

"Thank you, thank you, dear general," cried the warm-hearted Caledonian, grasping his hand eagerly; "then let me one day welcome you there."

"But tell me," said the general, laughing, "can you not in return say something in praise of poor Old England?"

"Oh! much, much: but you are yourself such an eulogy on your country, that I need say nothing, except that amongst the other obligations which she has conferred on the world, I rank very highly indeed that of her having produced a General Monthermer."

"You make me blush, Breadalbane," replied Monthermer, "and I know not how to show my sense of such courtesy."

"I will tell you how; come and visit me in my own dear little Highland home, and let me show you to my family and my friends. Oh! it is such a scene! I cannot think of it without tears of rapture. The rocks, the glens, the lake, Oh!—do not think me a romantic idiot, when I own that I pity every one who is not born in a mountainous country. It is so impossible, I think, for a man to be as much attached to a flat, unpicturesque home, as to one like mine. I doubt, whether one's affection for one's relations is not stronger, when one associates their image with that of fine country, and—

---

[89] Opie refers to (and paraphrases from) a very recent (8 May 1818) speech in favour of the Education of the Poor Bill, given in the House of Commons by Henry Brougham (1778-1868), who would later become an influential advocate in favour of the passing of the Reform Act and the Slavery Abolition Act.

and—Ah! I see you laugh, general, and I dare say you think that you are as impatient to see your parents and relations in the flat part of England in which they live, as I am to revisit mine and the girl of my heart, residing amidst all the prodigality of nature."

"I am sure of it," replied the general with a sigh. "Parents, alas! I have not now to welcome me," he added, passing the back of his hand across his eyes: "they are dead."

"But I hope they lived long enough to hear of your successes abroad, and of your large acquisition of fortune?"

"They did; and to profit by the latter. Ours is a decayed family; but now it will, I trust, be re-instated in its former splendour; and I have the satisfaction of knowing, that before they died, my beloved parents were restored, through my means, to some of the habitual state of their ancestors."

"Happy, happy Monthermer!"

"Yes, happy so far I am; and believe me, I feel my happiness as deeply, and that it is as great, as if I had been born on a Highland mountain, and my parents had lived upon its side. No, no; believe me, the affections are wholly independent of scenery. Were you, on your return home, to find your parents dead, your mistress false, and your friends exiled,—do you think that the scenery would give you pleasure?"

"No; at least not so much."

"Yet you must feel that it would, in order to prove that it at all heightens the present glow of the affections; and I maintain, that if I find those friends yet left to me,—well, faithful, and affectionate,—I shall be quite as happy on my barren, treeless abode, the ungraceful town of my nativity, with its bleak surrounding marshes and its flat shores, as you amidst your picturesque mountains and lofty rocks."

"I am not convinced," replied Breadalbane, "and I still bless Heaven for having made me a denizen of the mountains."

"I bless it," returned Monthermer, "for having given me affections, and preserved to me some objects, I trust, to engage and gratify them, whether it be in the land of the mountain or the plain."

At length the travellers reached London; and after having finished their business, Breadalbane set off for Scotland, and the general for his nearer and less beautiful home: but they did not part till they had promised to keep up, by letters, that acquaintance which had begun in India, and which a long voyage together in the same ship had matured into intimacy.

The Welcome Home; or, The Ball

A two days journey brought General Monthermer in sight of his native place; whose spires he saw many miles before him, rising darkly on the glowing background made by the setting sun.

"That is one advantage I have over Breadalbane," said the general to himself, while his lip quivered with strong and affectionate emotion. "As my native place is on a dead flat, I can see it so much sooner than he can his. Mistaken young man!—to be sure he has more and nearer relations to welcome him than I have; but can his heart beat more strongly at the thought of a re-union with them, than mine does this moment?"

At length the general called to the postillions to stop,[90] and draw up to a little gate by a gentle acclivity within one mile of the place of his destination: there he alighted, and desired the drivers to wait till he returned.

This gate led to the churchyard in which the remains of General Monthermer's parents were deposited; and where, till his return, he had desired that a simple stone alone should mark out the spot where they were laid. To this spot he now directed his steps, and bent over the unconscious sod in a paroxysm of filial tenderness and grief. Still they were not altogether unpleasing tears. He felt pious thankfulness subdue the murmur of regret, when he recollected that he had been permitted to cheer their declining years by bestowing on them a large portion of his affluence; and he also joyed to think that it was allowed to them to hear and to glory in the military fame of their son.

"There is one more duty to perform towards them," said he to himself: "I will raise a monument to their memory;" and then with a sigh of mingled feelings he retraced his steps towards the gate.

On his way he had nearly trodden on a toad, which crawled across his path; and with a feeling of impulsive, or rather, I hope, of principled humanity, he stooped down and removed the poor reptile off the path, that it might avoid a recurrence of the danger.

"Oh, now I'm sure 'tis he!" exclaimed a voice behind him. "It can be nobody but Mr. George Monthermer; that was so like you, sir. God bless your honour! and welcome back to Old England!"

Monthermer turned round, and saw a shabbily-dressed woman, with a mob-cap[91] flying open; and who with a torn and coloured

---

[90] Postillions rode the horses guiding a coach, especially in the absence of a coachman.

[91] A mobcap (spelled in one or two words, hyphenated or not) was a bonnet (sometimes curved forwards at the top), worn by women (especially indoors) in the late 18th and early 19th centuries.

apron was now wiping away the tears that seemed to welcome him as much as her words had done.

"I thank you, my good woman," said he, stopping and surveying her earnestly; "I thank you; but I do not recollect you, and I wonder you recollect me."

"Oh! how could I fail to know you, sir, when I saw your kindness to that nasty thing? It was so like what I have seen you do before! But no wonder you don't recollect me: times are changed with me, and with many others, you know, since your honour went away. Have you quite forgotten Lucy Simmons?"

"Lucy!—my good woman, is it you?" cried the general kindly; "you, whom I left so well settled? I wonder no one wrote me word that things did not go right with you. But come, sit down on this gravestone, and tell me what changes I am to expect. You, you know, will not want a friend now I am come."

Poor Lucy's heart was now too full for utterance immediately: but when she recovered she answered, and sometimes anticipated Monthermer's questions.

"Aye, your honour," said she, "it would have gone very hard with me when my husband died and left me without a penny, and six children to maintain, but for Miss Marian Trelawney."

"How!" exclaimed the general starting; "why I thought Mr. Trelawney spent all his personal property, and died in debt; and that his daughters, as the estates went to the male heir, have little or nothing to live upon."

"Yes, that is only too true, sir; but then, if Miss Marian had only a guinea in the world, you know, sir, she would give part of it to those who wanted it. Besides, sir, they are not so badly off neither; and Miss Marian would do very well if it was not for her sister, I fancy, who was, you know, sir, a beauty, and so her father and mother spoiled her; and so, sir, she must have her whims and her nice things still, sir: and I believe, for that reason, that she may spoil her sister as I call it. Miss Marian keeps a day-school."

"Keeps a school!" cried the general. "Marian Trelawney keep a school!"

"Yes, sir; she keeps a school in the day for gentlefolks, and for money, and twice a week in the evening she teaches poor-folks children for love, and mine amongst the rest; and that is a great help to me, sir, besides having her washing and her sister's, and a few broth now and then, and such like—But dear heart, how glad she and Miss Trelawney will be to see you!"

"Where do they live?"

The Welcome Home; or, The Ball

Lucy told him, and he started again at the humility of their abode.

"We have been expecting you, you know, sir," she continued; "and the house is ready."

"But I was not expected so soon," he replied.

"No, not for some days. Well, dear me! how different your honour will find things! There's the Aislabies that used to hold their head so high, all ruined and gone! and there's the Bensons living in a little hole of a house!"

"Indeed!" cried the general in an absent manner. "But tell me, are my brother and sister and their children at home?"

"No, sir; they went out of town a week ago to their country-house."

At this moment a shout was heard from the town.

"What noise is that?" cried the general; "it seemed like a shout!"

"Dear me, yes, and so it was! that ever I should forget to tell your honour! They are shouting for you!"

"For me!"

"Yes; one of the old members is dead, and they have put you up for a parliament-man; and every body is so glad!—so you are sure to get it!"

"Me!" faltered out the general, choked with no unpleasant feeling at this proof of his fellow-citizens' regard:—"And did my brother know of it?"

"No, sir; but I hear he is sent for; and I believe he is expected tomorrow."

"That is well," he replied. But come, I must go, the air grows chill."

"Oh dear! yes, do go," cried Lucy. "How glad the folks will be to see you drive in! I am sure they will know you directly; and then they will drag your honour into the town."

"They shall do no such thing," cried the general. "And mark me, Lucy, as you value my favour, keep my arrival secret till tomorrow."

Lucy said it would be very hard to do it, as so many would rejoice to know his honour was come; but if she must, she must.

Monthermer then slipped some money into her hand; and desiring the postillions to drive slowly to the principal inn, and to be sure not to name him to any body, he wished Lucy good-night, and with his handkerchief at his face hurried towards the town.

"And so I am to represent my native town!" thought he. "Would that my parents had lived to see this day! how pleased they would have been!"

He then hastened still more rapidly on, to escape from the poignancy of that regret.

95

"And so my brother and his family are not at home! Well then, I may go first to call on the Trelawneys." And in a few moments more he found the knocker of their door in his hand.

Instead of the powdered footmen that used to answer a knock at that door, it was now answered by a servant girl, who told him both the ladies were at home; and if he would walk into the parlour, she would let them know.—"But who shall I say is here, sir?"

"An old friend," replied Monthermer in a hoarse voice. But hoarse as it was, it was recognised by Marian Trelawney.

"Oh! it is he! it is George Monthermer!" she exclaimed: and regardless of her dress and her occupation, (for she was making pastry for the morrow,) she ran from the kitchen into the parlour. But when she saw Monthermer she could not utter one word of welcome, and she received his affectionate salute in silence and in trembling. The servant now brought candles in; and Marian found voice enough to desire the servant to tell her sister General Monthermer was there.

Miss Trelawney knew it already; but she could not think of making her appearance till she had done something to her dress, and repaired the faded roses on her cheek: and having done so, she sailed into the room with her usual dignity as a Trelawney and a beauty.

Meanwhile neither the general nor Marian had said much; for both were thinking of the altered fortunes of the latter, and of relatives and friends, dead, ruined, and dispersed since the hour when they last met; while Marian at length uttered, "You find us much altered in situation!"

"Pshaw!" cried the general in reply, closely grasping her hand as he spoke: then dropping it again, he added, "Don't talk of that,—don't talk of that: you are unchanged! you really look as young as when we parted, Marian. Countenance never grows old, mere features do."

"You are changed in manners, though not in person much," replied Marian smiling through her tears; "for you are grown a flatterer, general."

"General!—call me Monthermer if you please." And it was at this moment that Miss Trelawney entered.

The general certainly did not receive her as he did her sister. His salute was colder, and his manner more distant; and her welcome to him was one of many words.

"Dear me!" cried Marian smiling, "my sister looks so smart and so neat, I must apologize for my appearance: but really when I heard your voice, my dear friend, I forgot I had an apron on, and that my hands were covered with flour,—and only see how I have floured the sleeve of your coat!"

Monthermer looked as if he had a mind to kiss the soft small hand which now pointed to the mischief it had done. But he did not: he contented himself with kissing the flour on his sleeve, and then with a sigh he brushed it off.

"And so you are grown quite notable,[92] are you?" cried he: while Marian busied herself in untying her apron. "And you pretend to make pies and puddings, I suppose?"

"It is no pretence," said Marian cheerfully, "for I have no one to do it for me:—besides, my kind sister fancies no one's pie-crust so good as mine; therefore vanity makes me notable."

Monthermer sighed, and almost frowned; for he recollected what Lucy had said, and fancied Marian was indeed spoiling her sister, and subservient to her whims. But he resolved to think of other things; and was putting question after question to them, and they were answering them, when they were suddenly interrupted by a sound of many voices and of many feet; and in a moment they heard a violent knock at the door, which was, however, nearly drowned in shouts of "Monthermer for ever!" The servant-girl now opened the door; and "Is not General Monthermer here?" was asked by more voices than one. And no sooner was the question answered, than in rushed two or three of the principal gentlemen of the town; while the narrow hall was filled with people.

The gentlemen exclaimed, "General Monthermer, welcome to England and to us!" The general accepted and pressed their tendered hands, but only bowed in return; while Marian turned away to hide her tears, and Miss Trelawney looked her offended dignity at the intrusion.

"General," added one of the gentlemen, "your postillions, finding it was the new candidate whom they had driven, could not help betraying the secret of your arrival, and you *must* come with us and show yourself to the people."

"No, no, impossible!—not to-night," replied the general, shrinking perhaps from the word *must*; being so lately come from a country where he ruled instead of obeying. But the gentlemen persisted with such friendly violence, that the general, being conscious also of an obligation to them, at length consented to accompany them;—when, with the feeling of a true gentleman, he turned gracefully round to apologize to the ladies, for the liberty which zeal for him and his cause had occasioned his friends to take

---

[92] In the now obsolete sense of being skilled in household matters.

with them and their house. The gentlemen were forced to act on the hint he gave, and they made their excuses acceptable even to the haughty Miss Trelawney, whose "pride fell not with her fortune."[93] Monthermer then told them he would see them the next day, and departed with his friends.

It was late, very late that night ere the shouts ceased of "Monthermer for ever!" But however they might disturb the sleep of her sister, Marian was glad to be so kept awake. No one was more gratified by being the discoverer of General Monthermer's having arrived that night than Lucy Simmons; as she was now at liberty to own she had seen him, and she had longed to tell all about the toad—and all the *says I's* and *says he's*—and the promised kindnesses—and the given money. And here let me add, that the bounty of the general was not slow to gladden her widowed abode, and that he caused "the widow's heart to sing for joy."[94]

The next day General Monthermer was so engrossed with the interests of his election, that he could not call on the sisters till two o'clock, and then he found them at dinner. But Marian insisted on his coming in, though Miss Trelawney's dignity was a little offended by the intrusion.

"I had not an idea that you dined so early," said the conscious general.

"No," replied Miss Trelawney; "no one could suspect *us* of dining at so vulgar an hour; but as Marian chooses to keep school, we must keep school-mistress's hours, you know."

While she was speaking, the general looked at the dinner, and saw that before her stood a nice roasted spring chicken and young potatoes, and a pint bottle of white wine: while Marian's fare was evidently a mutton-chop and a decanter of water.

"So!" thought the general, "I suspect that Marian chooses to keep school that you (her sister) may be indulged in dainties!"

Marian saw the general look at the chicken and the wine with a peculiar expression of countenance, and she answered his thoughts as it were by saying, "My sister has delicate health, and a still more delicate appetite; and she can only eat chickens, and those kind of things: I, you know, was always robust, and could eat any thing."

"Is it forbidden me to partake of your mutton-chop?" said he, sitting down to the table; "for I am to dine late."

---

[93] From Shakespeare's *As You Like It*, in which Rosalind says, "My pride fell with my fortunes" (Act I, Scene II).

[94] From Job 29: 13: "I caused the widow's heart to sing for joy."

The Welcome Home; or, The Ball

Miss Trelawney smiled, and very graciously proffered him a share of her chicken and her wine. But the general accepted only the wine; and it was in order to have an excuse for tasting that, that he sat down.

"Do not *you* drink wine?" said he to Marian.

"No; very rarely. I do not want it; and it costs money, you know."

"This is not good wine, Miss Trelawney," cried he, tasting it: "and if you are an invalid, it is not what you ought to drink. I must insist on prescribing to you some excellent Madeira, of which I have a large cargo now in the harbour; and I will send you some of it as soon as it is unpacked: and then perhaps, for the sake of an old friend, your sister may be prevailed on to drink some."

Miss Trelawney expressed her gratitude loudly and warmly. But Marian did not speak at first; and then she only said, "No; even a present from you will not tempt me to indulge in a luxury so expensive; for I make it a principle to have as few wants and indulgences as I can."

"Well," replied Monthermer warmly, "you may go without wine on *principle* and from *choice*, if you please; but I cannot bear that you should do it from *necessity*."

Marian looked at him with grateful emotion, then rose, and left the room awhile: and Miss Trelawney took the opportunity of her absence to assure him that there was really no occasion for Marian to slave as she did, and deny herself so many things; but it was her will, and she would do it.

The general did not reply, though much tempted to do so; and he was very glad when Marian came back. When she was forced to go to her scholars, he took his leave.

At night he sent the promised wine: and though Miss Trelawney was pleased, Marian was hurt at the number of the dozens, and did not like to accept so magnificent a present from any one. "Still, if I must be obliged," she said to herself, "I had rather be so to *him* than to any one else."

That day had not only re-united the general to a brother whom he dearly loved, but had introduced him to his brother's wife and children, amongst whom was a tall girl of fifteen, who Mrs. Monthermer assured him was so well and notably brought up, that, young as she was, she was able to manage a family, and that she had found her the sweetest little nurse that ever she saw.

"So, so!" thought the general, "I see I have a house-keeper and nurse already provided for me." And he was not slow to discover,

99

that this lady, whose well-written and apparently well-felt letters to him in India had impressed him powerfully in her favour, was in reality a cold-hearted selfish woman, keeping a watchful eye over the nabob brother and uncle.

Mr. Monthermer was the direct opposite to his wife—generous, disinterested, affectionate; and instead of wishing his brother to continue single for the sake of his children, he earnestly hoped he would marry as soon as he arrived. While her husband uttered this folly (as she thought it) to herself alone, Mrs. Monthermer did not mind it: but as he at last thought proper to hold the same language to his brother, when the bustle of the election was over and General Monthermer was the returned member, she was quite astonished to see how little her husband considered his own and his children's interests.

"Well, George," said Mr. Monthermer to his brother, "now you are a general and a rich nabob, to be sure you will think of being a better thing still—and that is a *husband*?"

"If I can find a woman who will love me for myself alone, and can convince me that she does so—perhaps I may marry," replied the general.

"And pray why should you doubt it? You are a very handsome fellow yet, George, and not by any means old;—two years my junior, you know; and that I think young: four-and-forty is not old for a man:—but I do not know where to find any one worthy of you. I used to think before you went abroad that you had a secret liking for that admirable woman Marian Trelawney; and for aught I see, she is quite as good-looking as she was then, and single still."

"Yes," cried Mrs. Monthermer, "that she may easily be, and not good-looking either:—but then she is not quite so young as she was then. Dear me! how could you think the general could ever think of such a plain person as that, and now too that she is old!"

"Old!—She is some years younger than George."

"If the general must have one of the sisters, to be sure he would prefer the elder, as she has been a beauty, and has fine remains still."

"What! prefer a wreck of charms?—prefer a faded beauty to a first-rate agreeable in fine preservation? No, no, Eliza; my brother is too wise for that; and you underrate poor Marian.—Marian Trelawney, brother, is—is she not?—one of those women in whom her own sex see nothing, and ours every thing;—that is, in point of attraction I mean. She may be what they call plain; yet I scarcely ever knew a man who did not, after conversing with her half an hour,

The Welcome Home; or, The Ball

from the play of her features and her charm of manner, fancy her almost handsome."

"They must have lively imaginations then," replied Mrs. Monthermer angrily; "and I dare say the general thinks as I do: but I always thought you bewitched to the person in question."

The general for some cause or other was disinclined to talk on this subject at all:—but now he found himself called on to reply. "I remember *Miss* Trelawney," said he, "by far the most beautiful woman I ever saw. Still she had never that charm which her sister has; and which I do not presume to define." he added, "though I feel it powerfully."

"You need not trouble yourself to do it," said his brother smiling: "Homer has done it for you, when he describes the cestus of Venus,[95] without which even the Goddess of Beauty was not paramount in attraction, and with which the haughty Juno became irresistible."

General Monthermer now tried to change the subject: but his brother persisted to recommend a wife to him, and named many young ladies who might suit him. But not one of them escaped Mrs. Monthermer's censure;—one had madness in her family; another scrofula;[96] and another had a secret attachment. In short, the general saw very clearly, and wondered his brother did not, that Mrs. Monthermer would never recommend a wife to *him*.

With what pleasure did he turn from an interested, detracting woman like this, to the simple-minded and benevolent Marian Trelawney! How did he prefer to Mrs. Monthermer's welcome, even that of the proud and repellent Miss Trelawney herself!

It is not to be supposed that General Monthermer could escape the matrimonial designs of the ladies in the town of ————; nor that he should not receive many invitations and many civilities from the inhabitants both of that and the environs; and as his house was now newly painted and furnished, (the house in which his father resided,) he resolved to give a ball and supper.

Therefore, having previously consulted his brother, his cards of invitation were soon circulated, and filled with joyful expectation many a young and many an elderly woman.

[95] In Homer's *Iliad*, Aphrodite (named Venus by the Romans) wore a mysterious girdle called "zone" (or "cestus" in Latin) which conferred beauty, grace and elegance to anyone and made them irresistible. Hera (Juno in Roman mythology) wore it to seduce Zeus (Jupiter).

[96] An infection of the lymph nodes, popularly called the King's Evil, because of the long-held belief that a king's or queen's touch could cure it.

He carried a card written by himself to the sisters; and presenting it to Miss Trelawney with much respect, he hoped she and her sister would do him the honour of gracing his ball with their presence.

Miss Trelawney bowed, but did not speak, and coloured highly as if from some unpleasant feelings. Marian did the same; and then in a low voice she told him, that under their present circumstances they made it a point to decline all such invitations.

"What is it I hear?" cried the general; "and what can you mean?"

"That, fallen as we are in fortune, and I obliged to earn my own living, I do not feel that I should now be in my place at an assembly such as yours will be; and sure am I, that my appearance there would call forth many invidious remarks, to which you would be sorry to be the means of exposing us."

"And do you really think, and can I believe, that the Miss Trelawneys can ever be deemed intruders, and as out of their proper place, in any society?"

"I do;—and my sister will tell you, that having once ventured to a public ball here, since I commenced my present mode of life, she heard her dress so severely criticized, and her coming to the ball under her circumstances so severely censured, that she and her chaperone were glad to retire early; and the latter advised her never to expose herself to such illiberality, as she called it, again."

The general listened in perplexed and angry silence and surprise. At length he started up, and exclaimed, "I solemnly swear that if you, my oldest and dearest friends, cannot and may not come to my ball, I will have no ball at all." Then, suddenly rushing from the house, he went home; and before night all those who had been invited received a card to say that the ball of General Monthermer was unavoidably postponed; and he came to announce this change of plan in person to the Trelawneys: but the cause of it he would not disclose, even to his brother, who wondered and interrogated in vain. "No," said he to himself; "no feast given by me shall make them feel yet more than they now do their altered state, nor shall that noble-minded woman for a moment regret that her active virtue has excluded her from a scene which otherwise she would have rejoiced to witness. And what is the sacrifice to me? Nothing:—for how could I enjoy a pleasure purchased by one pang to Marian Trelawney?"

The Welcome Home; or, The Ball

Marian and her sister both deeply felt this marked proof of regard shown them by Monthermer; and Marian eagerly tried to persuade him to alter his determination—but in vain. He told them it was a sacrifice which friendship required of him, and make it he would.

The general spoke with vehemence; and having unconsciously, in his eagerness, crumpled up one piece of paper, the blank part of a letter which with some others was lying on the table, was about to crumple up another, when Marian laughing took it out of his hand, and begged he would do no more mischief.

"Mischief!" cried he, "what mischief have I done?"

"Not much; only you have been guilty of unnecessary waste: I can make something useful of these papers which you treat with so little ceremony." And in a short time after, by putting the direction at the bottom, and painting a little flower on the blank side, she soon cut and pinched the paper into a neat little box; and the other papers, by aid of her scissors, and the assistance of her painting brush, she soon made into tapers to light candles with.

"And pray," said the general, admiring her œconomical ingenuity, "what do you do with these things when they are done?"

"Oh," cried Miss Trelawney, "they serve as rewards to her children: and trumpery as they are, I assure you they are valued by them. They know Marian can't afford to give better presents now, and they appreciate the goodwill, and are proud of the distinction: besides, in these little boxes she teaches them to put litters,—such as ends of thread, or tape; and as they know what they are made of, it also inculcates in them a habit of not wasting any thing, as even old cards will turn to account."

"Yes," interrupted Marian, smiling; "and General Monthermer's elegant invitation, otherwise so thrown away on me, may serve a useful purpose, by making the sides of a pincushion or a needle-book."

"So, then, you teach moral principles, do you," said the general, "by means of a bit of paper?"

"I try to do it: and in addition to my other efforts, I make all my pupils learn Miss Edgeworth's inimitable tale of Waste not, Want not!"

(Had Teresa Tidy been published then, no doubt Marian Trelawney would have recommended that also to her pupils.)[97]

[97] "Waste Not, Want Not, or Two Strings to Your Bow" is a children's story first published by Maria Edgeworth in 1800 in Volume 5 of her collection *The Parent's Assistant*. *Eighteen Maxims of Neatness and Order, by Theresa Tidy* was a popular book of conduct first published in 1817 by Elizabeth Susannah Simmonds (known as Mrs Elizabeth Susannah Graham).

The general listened to his amiable friend, and admired and revered her more than ever. Insensibly, too, he fell into reverie; and remembered the hour when he, a poor lieutenant of dragoons, sighed hopelessly and in secret for Marian Trelawney, the co-heiress of the rich Mr. Trelawney. But though he had always lived with the sisters on the most intimate footing, Monthermer was not only withheld by a consciousness of poverty from disclosing his passion for Marian, but he, in common with many others, believed her attached to a gentleman her equal in fortune: and at this moment of suspense and increased despair, Monthermer's regiment was ordered to India. But Marian had *not* married,—and that gentleman married another woman. Since he returned, too, he had heard her being still single accounted for, by her having been long attached to another gentleman, who was, it was said, trying to make up his mind to marry her. This expression the general never could hear without a feeling almost insupportable to him;—as if marrying such a woman was a thing so dreadful, that it was necessary for a man to try to make up his mind to it: and he felt that if this was true, he should find it difficult to help affronting the man should he ever be in company with him.

In the meanwhile attentions and invitations to General Monthermer were not confined to the town of X. A nobleman, whose mansion in the country was at that season of the year the resort of beauty, fashion and wit, and who had daughters to dispose of, invited the general to join the festive scene. And so many persons had recommended his daughters as charming and superior women, and as likely to make excellent wives, from the education which they had received from an admirable mother, that he resolved he would put himself in the way of liking and of being liked, and see if that one image, which had so long stood sentinel over his heart, in Europe and in Asia, could be displaced by the force of youthful beauty. And as soon as his plans were fixed, he went to call on the Trelawneys.

He found Miss Trelawney alone. "General," said she, "I am very glad to have an opportunity of speaking to you when my sister is not present; as I consider you as our best friend." The general bowed, and she proceeded thus: "You must observe, general, how painful it is to me to see a descendant of such a family as ours keeping a school; while so many persons here, whom formerly we should not have noticed, are living in comparative splendour, and

The Welcome Home; or, The Ball

keeping carriages. Indeed, indeed, general, I feel it hard enough to go on foot, though born to keep my coach-and-four, without the additional pain of hearing my sister teach A B C." Here she burst into tears; and the general, who deeply felt for her altered state, expressed his sincere sympathy with her feelings.

"Now, general," she resumed, "what I think is this: Marian has great talents for drawing and painting; and as it is less degrading for a gentlewoman to be an artist than keep a school, I wish her to make drawings and paintings for sale; and with patronage, no doubt she might succeed."

"No doubt: I like the scheme much. But in what style does your sister excel?"

"Oh, general, she can take likenesses in miniature admirably. She does not succeed so well in painting women as men, I think; but the latter I am sure she would succeed in to admiration."

"What, madam!" cried the general hastily, "would you have your sister set up as a painter of gentlemen's portraits?"

"Not them only," replied Miss Trelawney; "but I will, though I know she would not like it, show you one she did many years ago from memory, which I discovered by chance, for I assure you she hides her talent in a napkin;—and it is such a likeness! She has another of the same person, which she thinks more like; therefore, knowing how highly I should value it, was willing to give me this."

"Now then, perhaps," thought the general, "I shall see the happy man whom Marian loves!" and his heart beat painfully and tumultuously, when Miss Trelawney unlocked a cabinet, and presented the miniature to him. The general started when he unclosed the case, and could scarcely believe the evidence of his eyes, for it was his own picture.

"Did Marian do this," he exclaimed, "and from *memory?*"

"Yes; not long after you went to India, I believe, but it is not many years since I discovered it; I never suspected that she had the talent. Since then she has painted me, but not like. Here it is."

The general took the picture; but he found that though Marian had flattered him, she had not flattered her sister. "She has done me more than justice," said he as he returned Miss Trelawney's picture; "but you much less." And he could not help saying to himself, "In what bright and pleasing colours must I have lived in her remembrance!"

"But see, general! here is another proof of her talents, in which I surprised her the other day, and really forced her to show me. She then went into a little back room where Marian kept her books and other things, and out of the drawer of her painting-box she took an unfinished miniature. Again the general beheld himself, but as he now was; and he stood gazing at this new proof of accurate remembrance, with a feeling of gratification which deprived him of utterance; when an exclamation of "Come, give me the pictures in a moment, here is Marian coming," roused him from his pleasing trance, and he tried to compose his feelings before she arrived.

She came in smiling with her usual calm sweetness; but her quick eye soon discovered that her sister looked rather fluttered, and the general a good deal. What could have passed between them? Could the report which she had just heard be true, that the general admired her sister? If so, she ought to rejoice. But no: it was mere gossip, and perhaps she was mistaken; and they were really as composed as she was.

At this moment two carriages passed each other before the window, and the general starting up asked "whose carriages they were, as the livery was new to him."

"Oh!" cried Miss Trelawney, "no wonder you do not know the livery, for I believe their owners wore a livery when you went away. They are the carriages of some of our *parvenus*, our new rich people, of whom we have plenty."

"Well," said Marian, "it is pleasant to see industry meet its reward; it is much to a man's credit to be the architect of his own fortune; and we ought to rejoice in his success."

"But that is not quite so easy under our circumstances," said Miss Trelawney.

"And indeed, my dear friend," said the general, "it is more painful, believe me, to witness the fall of some, than it is pleasant to behold the rise of others."

"No doubt," said Marian: "but there are some feelings one ought to strive against."

At this moment the same carriages repassed, and Miss Trelawney pettishly exclaimed, "I declare those people's carriages make twice the noise of those of other people."

"The carriages of *parvenus*, I suspect," observed Marian with a melancholy and meaning smile, "always grate more on the nerves than those of others."

"I really think so," replied her sister, unconscious of Marian's meaning; "for coaches and chariots do not seem so well hung *now*, as they were when *our* coach was built."

No one replied, and here the conversation dropped.

The Welcome Home; or, The Ball

Miss Trelawney meanwhile had resolved to be ingenuous; and in order to take advantage of the certainty she had that the general approved the new plan for Marian, she determined to propose it to her in Monthermer's presence.

Accordingly she told her, she had shown the general her own picture.

"Your own picture! Harriet," cried Marian turning pale, and then red, "how could you?—You know that"—here she looked earnestly at the countenance of both, and saw clearly that she was informed of only half the truth. "Nay, Harriet," she exclaimed in a faltering voice, "this was not fair—it was very unkind—very."

"What was unfair and unkind? to show our good friend here how well you paint, and, and—"

"No; but you showed him, I suppose, more than your own picture."

"I did."

"I did not think, sister, you would have done such a thing," said Marian, turning to the window to hide her confusion.

"How can you be so unkind," cried the general, affected and gratified by her emotion, "as to be angry with your sister for giving me so much pleasure? Little did I think that I was so well remembered by you, Marian: if I had, the thought would have gladdened many a mournful hour."

Marian now hastily ran into her own little room; and having examined the drawer of her painting-box, she saw the unfinished likeness had been meddled with; and returning, looking even paler than before, she just had power to say, "Indeed! indeed! I know not how to forgive this!" and then sunk on her chair in an agony of tears.

Though grieved to see her so distressed, Monthermer was pleased also. To have painted his likeness, and to have shown it, would have only proved her power and vanity as an artist; but to have painted it in secret, to have succeeded, and yet never have vaunted of what she had done; to have wished to conceal it from every eye, and to be agonized at having it exposed to his; this proved unquestionably, he hoped, the secret tenderness of a delicate and feeling woman, afraid, and conscious, that her secret was discovered. And while her sister hung over her, affectionately apologizing and regretting that she had distressed her, Monthermer grasped her hand, and pressed it to his lips.

Marian then suddenly rose and left the room.

"I am so sorry that my sister is thus overpowered," observed Miss Trelawney; "for I wanted to discuss the subject of her becoming a regular artist before you, as you approve the plan."

"I approve your plan! I approve your sister's having men to sit to her for their pictures? Oh! no, madam, such a scheme is too indelicate for me to approve it, I assure you. But tell me, madam, has your sister never painted any other gentleman from memory?"

"No, sir, I believe never."

"When I went abroad she was talked of for Mr. Montague, and was I thought to have—m—married him."

"Yes, so we all thought; but when he offered to her, she refused him."

"Refused him!"

"Yes, and no one knew why."

"But, madam, the world here says, that there is another gentleman who is sure not to be refused if he offers,—Mr. Ainslie."

"The world here is a very meddling world. Mr. Ainslie has offered, and was refused at once, much to my distress. But remember, general, I say this to you in confidence. It is very wrong, you know, to tell of such things. Yes, Marian certainly has always stood in her own light (as the saying is), as well as myself; but then I was ambitious, and had I believe pretensions to look high. But Marian was not ambitious; and I know not to what to attribute her dislike to marry, except she has an attachment:—and that I think I must have found out," she added with an expression of confidence in her own penetration.

Marian now re-entered the room, but evidently avoided meeting the general's eye; and sat in painful consciousness. He now told them he was going to Lord M's the next day, and should probably be away two months: and he saw Marian turn pale, while her sister said, "Lord M. has two beautiful and accomplished daughters, I think."

"He has; I have heard them much praised."

"How does your sister-in-law, general, like the idea of this visit? for, as she spares nobody, nobody spares her;—and you understand me, general...."

"I do, madam," he replied with an arch smile: "and she does not like the visit at all:—but I do; and that is enough for me."

Marian tried to laugh, but could not: and the general, saying he would call the next day before he set off, took his leave.

Before they met again, Marian, used to conquer her feelings, received him with her usual composure. Still, her look had somewhat

The Welcome Home; or, The Ball

of resignation in it, as if she had made up her mind to bear an expected evil: and long after he had taken his leave, and ceased to see her, that touching look of meek resignation haunted his fancy.

The general's attention to the Trelawneys had excited much notice, and called forth many comments in the town of X———. Still, scarcely any woman, except those who loved Marian, believed that a man whom the young, the beautiful, and the rich might be proud and happy to cultivate, would marry a woman of seven-and-thirty, of such few personal charms. And the men could scarcely think a rich Asiatic could be so rational, so self-denying, and so little of a voluptuary, as to prefer a woman like Marian Trelawney, when he could no doubt command the hand of a beautiful girl.

But they little knew General Monthermer. They little knew that his sober mind and well regulated feelings led him to seek in a wife a companion, rather than a toy; and that he was too little selfish to promise to himself any happiness in a union with one whose youth would require those gay and pleasant associations with the world, which his maturer years made him cease to relish, and which he would consequently be tempted to withhold from her.

Alas! I fear I am painting a very unnatural character for a general officer just returned a rich and prosperous bachelor from India! But I must have my own way; and paint such a man as he ought to think and feel, not perhaps as he would.

During the general's absence, the sisters received many calls—not from friendship, but curiosity in the callers; and some fancying Miss Trelawney, if not Miss Marian, had hopes of marrying their old friend, had an *amiable* gratification in assuring them (finding he had not written to either of them) that he was certainly going to be married to Lady Laura M———.

"Very likely," was Marian's calm reply; but her sister, who really had flattered herself the general seriously admired her beauty, was scarcely able to restrain her anger, as she protested she did not believe the report was true.

But at length it was so positively asserted, that even Miss Trelawney was convinced; and Mrs. Monthermer, though the general had not acquainted her husband with his prospects, called on the sisters, in order to mortify them as she hoped, if they had had any expectations, by telling them she had little doubt of the fact, for she had a great antipathy towards Marian; because, though she saw nothing in her, she found she was a general favourite with men, and particularly with her husband. But Marian's mild and open eye shrunk not from hers, and Miss Trelawney's pride kept her calm while Mrs. Monthermer talked of the dear general's happy prospects; adding, "As he *would* play the fool and marry, which certainly we could not wish at his time of life, and with his yellow skin, indicative no doubt of a liver complaint, I am glad he marries a young lady of rank, one whose alliance one can be proud of. I should have been sorry if he had married beneath him in any respect."

"So should I," replied Marian; and Mrs. Monthermer, mortified at their composure, took her leave.

A day or two after, the general returned, and his first visit was to the sisters. It was now the beginning of December; and parliament being unexpectedly called together, he was going that week to London, but he wished to visit his friends before he went.

Though Marian received Mrs. Monthermer without emotion, she was not so self-possessed when she saw the general, and she grieved to think she had lost the power of receiving him with composure; but she soon resumed her look of mild resignation. "Ha! that look again!" thought the general.

Miss Trelawney was, he saw, evidently fluttered, and full of some particular meaning: at last she said, "Well, general, out with it! tell us yourself, though I assure you we know it already."

"Know what?"

"That you are going to be married to Lady Laura M———."

Marian tried to look arch, and to smile; but she did not succeed.

"Lady Laura M——— is very charming," replied the general; "but I am not going to be married to her."

"Well, but you are going to be married to some one?"

"I have not made my proposals yet to any one," replied the general;—"I have not, upon my honour."

"Well, but . . ."

"But what? Surely, dear madam, even you, my old and very dear friend, have no right to interrogate me further."

"Right? No, General Monthermer, I don't claim any right; only as a friend, anxious for your welfare, I—"

"Well, dear madam, I know and respect your friendly anxiety; and in return I assure you again, on my honour, that when I am an accepted lover you shall be the first person informed of it, should that happy event ever take place."

"There, Harriet, are you not satisfied now?" said Marian; her own mind, she scarcely knew why, considerably lightened of its burden.

The general, whose observation did not sleep during this scene, now suddenly turned to her and said, "Marian, I know you do not mind wind and weather: and indeed why should you? you are one of the few women who may venture to walk in the wind," he added smiling. "I think a walk on the beach would do us both good. Do you not think, Miss Trelawney, Marian would be better for the walk?"

"Miss Marian will accompany you, I dare say," she replied in her most freezing manner.

"What is the matter?" cried the general, "and how have I offended?"

"Oh! do not be alarmed," said Marian laughing; "but that dear particular creature does not approve your calling me Marian, that is all."

"No? Well, I am very sorry to hear it; but I assure you, dear Miss Trelawney, I shall never presume to call you *Harriet*, and that degree of decorum must, I believe, content you."

"As to decorum, sir," said Miss Trelawney, "I rather suspect both you and my sister are going to violate it, by walking together alone. The X—— people do talk of you and us already."

"Do they? Then they shall talk still more; and after I return with Marian, if you will walk with me also, we shall puzzle them completely, and the power of gossip will, by that means, be neutralized."

Miss Trelawney could not laugh at any thing so serious as a breach of decorum; but Marian smiling took the general's arm, and hastened with him to the beach.

Their walk was long; so long, that when they returned, Miss Trelawney had waited dinner a whole hour; and poor Marian, in blushing distress, earnestly urged her sister to forgive her first fault in that way, "for you know," said she, "I never made dinner wait before."

"And I will almost venture to promise she will never do it again," said the general.

Miss Trelawney was vexed, but she was soon appeased; especially as Marian, overcome with some internal emotion, called for a glass of wine, and seemed rather faint. The general staid till she was quite recovered, and then took his leave; saying as he did so, "Remember! *only* to her!"

The next day he went to London, and did not return till the Christmas holidays; nor till the delighted Miss Trelawney had heard

111

her sister say, to the great distress of her little pupils and their parents, that she should keep school no more.

The general, before his return, had ordered invitations to be sent out to a ball and supper, which he meant to give during the recess of parliament; and he now arrived to superintend the preparations. The sisters left X—— for a few days just *before he came*, and returned the day *he* did.

The day of the ball now arrived; and as many new dresses were made up for it, as for a court presentation: for now it was well known that General Monthermer was not going to be married, and hope was again alive in the hearts of the young and the elderly.

To this ball the sisters consented to go, and brave all remarks; and their appearance at it, and their dress, did indeed excite considerable notice, and call forth rather severe animadversions; for Miss Trelawney was splendidly attired in a silver muslin, and her sister in the finest and clearest book-muslin[98] over white satin; while her fine throat was encircled by a row of orient pearls, and her fine hair fastened up with a diamond comb.

"I begin to think," whispered Mrs. Monthermer, who did the honours, and received the sisters very coldly, "I begin to think the general is not a *marrying man*:—you understand me!" and the whisper was not slow in circulating round the room, though there were few present who gave any credence to so vile an insinuation. Still, so general is the tendency to detraction, that many spread the sneer, who did not believe what it implied, and Marian found herself in a very trying situation; especially as the general, who did not dance, paid her such marked attention as could not but attract the notice of every one.

At length, at one o'clock in the morning supper was announced; and then, to the surprise of every one, and to no one more than to Mrs. Monthermer, Mr. Monthermer took the hand of Marian and led her down stairs, and to the head of the principal supper-table; while the general seated himself at the bottom of it: and when the company had all taken their seats, he filled a glass, and called on all the guests to drink to the health of the bride and bridegroom, General and Mrs. George Monthermer.

Surprise, not unmixed with consternation, now kept every one silent till the toast was repeated; and then it was drunk with an

---

[98] A type of muslin folded like a book when sold. It was the most transparent kind of muslin, worn over silk or satin, and was used for ball dresses.

The Welcome Home; or, The Ball

universal cheer from the gentlemen. Mr. Monthermer whispered his indignant wife to keep her own counsel, and no one would know she had not been in the secret, and she wisely took the hint; for by this means she avoided the disgrace of having attacked the fame of Marian or her sister, as she would seem to have been purposely imposing on those who had disseminated her base whisper.

The general had now a pride and a pleasure in declaring, that he had married the only woman whom he had ever loved, and whose image had prevented his ever marrying before; while his happy wife was not slow to own, that it was for his sake, hopeless as was her attachment, that she had refused offers which she should otherwise have been proud to accept. Monthermer had gone to Lord M's purposely to expose his constancy to the temptations which awaited him there, and had found it proof against every thing; he had then returned, sure of himself, to prove the heart of Marian, which he fancied he had read aright before he departed: and then, having drawn from Marian an exact detail of what had been said, purposely to wound her and her sister's feelings, if they were vulnerable on that subject, by his sister-in-law and others, he devised the scene of the ball and its painful surprise, as a merited and unexpected mortification to them.

Accordingly he had fixed to meet the sisters, and had met them with a special license at a very picturesque village, well known to them and him in the days of their youth, the scene of many a rural frolic; and there he received the hand of the woman whom he had loved through every change of scene, of climate, and of fortune.

Six months had now elapsed since the general parted with Ronald Breadalbane; but though he had written to him, he had never received a letter in return, and he began to fear that he was either ill or unhappy. Still he thought it right to impart to him the happy change in his situation, and to offer to visit him with his bride in the summer recess of parliament. In this letter the general assured him, that no beauty of scenery was necessary to heighten his sense of heartfelt happiness, and that if he would deign to visit the flat plains and shores of X——, he hoped he should be able to convince him, that the affections flourished as luxuriantly on the land of the plain, as on the land of the rock and the mountain.

This letter was crossed on the road by one from Breadalbane, sealed with black: it told a tale of sorrows and disappointments. "I found," said he, "the friends of my childhood dead or emigrated,

113

the girl of my heart false, and just married to another; and I fell ill in consequence of this second blow. But my parents still lived, and hung over my fevered couch; therefore I was not yet desolate; but when I recovered, their health, which had been gradually declining, and which anxiety for mine had helped to injure, soon began to decay perceptibly to my view; and they did not long survive each other. O Monthermer, how forcibly have your words ever since recurred to me! How true do I feel your observation in our last journey together!

"Yes; I now own it is only too true, that unless inhabited by objects whom one loves, the finest scenery becomes insipid and uninteresting; and I believe, therefore, that the most flat and dreary of abodes, if cheered by the looks of affection, may seem an earthly paradise.

"Dear general, Scotland is still indeed the land of the mountain and the valley, and dear to the soul and the eye of the poet and the painter; but to me it is now also the land of disappointment, of solitude and desolation, and I must quit it till I can form new ties, or forget those which exist no more."

The general could not receive this melancholy letter without feeling the tenderest sympathy for the writer; and he lost not a moment in inviting Breadalbane,—now Sir Ronald Breadalbane,— to change the scene entirely by coming to him; and he trusted that time and new ties would restore to the mourner, feelings more consonant to his years and his nature; and that the lesson of experience would teach him still more, that on the proper and complete exercise of the affections alone, the best happiness of life depends. And as the meanest scrap of gauze, of bead, or of tinsel looks beautiful and costly through the reflecting mirror of the kaleidoscope, so does the most common and dreary scene acquire attraction and value, when beheld through the beautifying medium of gratified affection.

John William Polidori
𝒯HE 𝒱AMPYRE

(1819)

The author: John William Polidori was born in London in 1795. His mother was English, while his father, Gaetano Polidori (1763-1853), was an Italian émigré who worked as a teacher and translator. He received a degree in medicine from the University of Edinburgh in 1815 and, one year later, he became Byron's personal physician. He kept a diary of his European trips. In June 1816, in a house rented by Byron on the bank of Lake Geneva, where they met Percy Bysshe Shelley and his future wife Mary, Byron suggested that they each write a ghost story. Both Byron's and Percy Bysshe Shelley's stories remained unfinished, but Mary's became *Frankenstein* and Polidori's became "The Vampyre." He travelled to Italy and returned to England, establishing a medical practice in Norwich in 1817. "The Vampyre," *Ernestus Berchtold* and *Ximenes, The Wreath, and Other Poems* all appeared in 1819. He was admitted to Lincoln's Inn in 1820 to study law. His last publications were *The Fall of the Angels: A Sacred Poem* and *Sketches Illustrative of the Manners and Costumes of France, Switzerland, and Italy* (with Richard Bridgens), both in 1821, the year of his death (he had gambling debts and may have committed suicide). Polidori's sister Frances married the Italian expatriate Gabriele Rossetti. All their children (Maria Francesca, Dante Gabriel, William Michael, and Christina Georgina) became authors.

The text: The circumstances in which the story was published are still (suitably) enigmatic and controversial. It first appeared in *The New Monthly Magazine*, Vol. XI, No. 63 (1 April 1819), 195-206, where it was preceded (under the headline "Original Communications") by an "Extract of a Letter from Geneva, with Anecdotes of Lord Byron, &c.," framed by a brief introduction and a footnote signed "Ed." (written by John Mitford). The story itself was subtitled "A Tale by Lord Byron" and was introduced by a long explanatory note on the belief in vampires, again signed "Ed."

Both the letter extract and the note (now titled "Introduction") preceded the text of the story in the volume form, in which the attribution to Byron had been discarded: *The Vampyre; A Tale* (London: Sherwood, Neely, and Jones, 1819). The volume ends with another "Extract of a Letter, Containing an Account of Lord Byron's Residence in the Island of Mitylene" (unsigned).

The excellent edition of *The Vampyre: A Tale; and Ernestus Berchtold; or, The Modern Œdipus*, by D. L. Macdonald and Kathleen Scherf (Toronto: University of Toronto Press, 1994; reprinted by Broadview in 2008) has emended the text according to manuscript suggestions left by Polidori himself in the margins of a copy of the book. In doing so, they have changed the name of the vampire from "Ruthven" to "Strongmore." However, Polidori did not live to supervise an edition of the "tale." The following is from the Sherwood, Neely, and Jones edition of 1819 (27-72).

Further reading: Simon Bainbridge. "Lord Ruthven's Power: Polidori's 'The Vampyre,' Doubles and the Byronic Imagination." *The Byron Journal* 34: 1 (June 2006), 21-34.

Gavin Budge. "'The Vampyre': Romantic Metaphysics and the Aristocratic Other." *The Gothic Other: Racial and Social Constructions in the Literary Imagination.* Eds. Ruth Bienstock Anolik and Douglas L. Howard. Jefferson, NC: McFarland & Co., 2004. 212-235.

Anne Stiles, Stanley Finger and John Bulevich. "Somnambulism and Trance States in the Works of John William Polidori, Author of *The Vampyre.*" *European Romantic Review* 21: 6 (December 2010), 789-807.

Henry R. Viets. "The London Editions of Polidori's *The Vampyre.*" *The Papers of the Bibliographical Society of America* 63: 2 (Spring 1969), 83-103.

It happened that in the midst of the dissipations attendant upon a London winter, there appeared at the various parties of the leaders of the *ton*[99] a nobleman, more remarkable for his singularities, than his rank. He gazed upon the mirth around him, as if he could not participate therein. Apparently, the light laughter of the fair only attracted his attention, that he might by a look quell it, and throw fear into those breasts where thoughtlessness reigned. Those who felt this sensation of awe, could not explain whence it arose: some attributed it to the dead grey eye, which, fixing upon the object's face, did not seem to penetrate, and at one glance to pierce through the inward workings of the heart; but fell upon the cheek with a leaden ray that weighed upon the skin it could not pass. His peculiarities caused him to be invited to every house; all wished to see him, and those who had been accustomed to violent

[99] The fashionable society.

The Vampyre

excitement, and now felt the weight of *ennui*, were pleased at having something in their presence capable of engaging their attention. In spite of the deadly hue of his face, which never gained a warmer tint, either from the blush of modesty, or from the strong emotion of passion, though its form and outline were beautiful, many of the female hunters after notoriety attempted to win his attentions, and gain, at least, some marks of what they might term affection: Lady Mercer, who had been the mockery of every monster shewn in drawing-rooms since her marriage, threw herself in his way, and did all but put on the dress of a mountebank,[100] to attract his notice:—though in vain:—when she stood before him, though his eyes were apparently fixed upon her's, still it seemed as if they were unperceived;—even her unappalled impudence was baffled, and she left the field. But though the common adultress could not influence even the guidance of his eyes, it was not that the female sex was indifferent to him: yet such was the apparent caution with which he spoke to the virtuous wife and innocent daughter, that few knew he ever addressed himself to females. He had, however, the reputation of a winning tongue; and whether it was that it even overcame the dread of his singular character, or that they were moved by his apparent hatred of vice, he was as often among those females who form the boast of their sex from their domestic virtues, as among those who sully it by their vices.

About the same time, there came to London a young gentleman of the name of Aubrey: he was an orphan left with an only sister in the possession of great wealth, by parents who died while he was yet in childhood. Left also to himself by guardians, who thought it their duty merely to take care of his fortune, while they relinquished the more important charge of his mind to the care of mercenary subalterns, he cultivated more his imagination than his judgment. He had, hence, that high romantic feeling of honour and candour, which daily ruins so many milliners' apprentices. He believed all to sympathise with virtue, and thought that vice was thrown in by Providence merely for the picturesque effect of the scene, as we see in romances: he thought that the misery of a cottage merely consisted in the vesting of clothes, which were as warm, but which were better adapted to the painter's eye by their irregular folds and various coloured patches. He thought, in fine, that the dreams of

[100] A mountebank was an itinerant quack physician who sold remedies and performed tooth extractions and various experiments on an assistant (named "zany," "jack-pudding," or "merry-andrew") dressed like a jester. The latter's gaudy, multi-coloured dress had become associated with the mountebank himself.

poets were the realities of life. He was handsome, frank, and rich: for these reasons, upon his entering into gay circles, many mothers surrounded him, striving which should describe with least truth their languishing or romping favourites; the daughters at the same time, by their brightening countenances when he approached, and by their sparkling eyes, when he opened his lips, soon led him into false notions of his talents and his merit. Attached as he was to the romance of his solitary hours, he was started at finding, that, except in the tallow and wax candles that flickered, not from the presence of a ghost, but from want of snuffing, there was no foundation in real life for any of that congeries of pleasing pictures and descriptions contained in those volumes, from which he had formed his study. Finding, however, some compensation in his gratified vanity, he was about to relinquish his dreams, when the extraordinary being we have above described, crossed him in his career.

He watched him; and the very impossibility of forming an idea of the character of a man entirely absorbed in himself, who gave few other signs of his observation of external objects, than the tacit assent to their existence, implied by the avoidance of their contact: allowing his imagination to picture every thing that flattered its propensity to extravagant ideas, he soon formed this object into the hero of a romance, and determined to observe the offspring of his fancy, rather than the person before him. He became acquainted with him, paid him attentions, and so far advanced upon his notice, that his presence was always recognised. He gradually learnt that Lord Ruthven's affairs were embarrassed, and soon found, from the notes of preparation in ——— Street, that he was about to travel. Desirous of gaining some information respecting this singular character, who, till now, had only whetted his curiosity, he hinted to his guardians, that it was time for him to perform the tour,[101] which for many generations has been thought necessary to enable the young to take some rapid steps in the career of vice towards putting themselves upon an equality with the aged, and not allowing them to appear as if fallen from the skies, whenever scandalous

---

[101] Often called the Grand Tour, it was a trip (and a rite of passage) undertaken by many young British men of good family who (accompanied by a chaperone) usually travelled through France, Switzerland, and Italy, returning home via Germany and the Netherlands. Seen as a must for most of the 18th century, it allowed the young man to discover the artistic and architectural riches of continental Europe, but also to revel in the liberality of mores far away from home. The practice was interrupted during the Napoleonic Wars (1796-1815), when some young men, like Byron, travelled to Greece and the Middle East instead, while others discovered the natural beauties of the British Isles; but it was resumed in the late 1810s, only to become out of fashion a few decades later, with the advent of the railways.

The Vampyre

intrigues are mentioned as the subjects of pleasantry or of praise, according to the degree of skill shewn in carrying them on. They consented: and Aubrey immediately mentioning his intentions to Lord Ruthven, was surprised to receive from him a proposal to join him. Flattered by such a mark of esteem from him, who, apparently, had nothing in common with other men, he gladly accepted it, and in a few days they had passed the circling waters.

Hitherto, Aubrey had had no opportunity of studying Lord Ruthven's character, and now he found, that, though many more of his actions were exposed to his view, the results offered different conclusions from the apparent motives to his conduct. His companion was profuse in his liberality;—the idle, the vagabond, and the beggar, received from his hand more than enough to relieve their immediate wants. But Aubrey could not avoid remarking, that it was not upon the virtuous, reduced to indigence by the misfortunes attendant even upon virtue, that he bestowed his alms;—these were sent from the door with hardly suppressed sneers; but when the profligate came to ask something, not to relieve his wants, but to allow him to wallow in his lust, or to sink him still deeper in his iniquity, he was sent away with rich charity. This was, however, attributed by him to the greater importunity of the vicious, which generally prevails over the retiring bashfulness of the virtuous indigent. There was one circumstance about the charity of his Lordship, which was still more impressed upon his mind: all those upon whom it was bestowed, inevitably found that there was a curse upon it, for they were all either led to the scaffold, or sunk to the lowest and the most abject misery. At Brussels and other towns through which they passed, Aubrey was surprized at the apparent eagerness with which his companion sought for the centres of all fashionable vice; there he entered into all the spirit of the faro table: he betted, and always gambled with success, except where the known sharper was his antagonist, and then he lost even more than he gained;[102] but it was always with the same unchanging face, with which he generally watched the society around: it was not, however, so when he encountered the rash youthful novice, or the luckless father of a numerous family; then his very wish seemed fortune's law—this apparent abstractedness of mind was laid aside, and his eyes sparkled with more fire than that of the cat whilst dallying with the half-dead mouse. In every town, he left the formerly affluent

---

[102] Faro (Pharaoh) was for a long time the most popular gambling card game, in which the players bet on the order in which certain cards come out of the pack. A sharper (today called a card sharp or card shark) is someone who has the skill to manipulate or to cheat in a game of cards.

youth, torn from the circle he adorned, cursing, in the solitude of a dungeon, the fate that had drawn him within the reach of this fiend; whilst many a father sat frantic, amidst the speaking looks of mute hungry children, without a single farthing of his late immense wealth, wherewith to buy even sufficient to satisfy their present craving. Yet he took no money from the gambling table; but immediately lost, to the ruiner of many, the last gilder[103] he had just snatched from the convulsive grasp of the innocent: this might but be the result of a certain degree of knowledge, which was not, however, capable of combating the cunning of the more experienced. Aubrey often wished to represent this to his friend, and beg him to resign that charity and pleasure which proved the ruin of all, and did not tend to his own profit;—but he delayed it—for each day he hoped his friend would give him some opportunity of speaking frankly and openly to him; however, this never occurred. Lord Ruthven in his carriage, and amidst the various wild and rich scenes of nature, was always the same: his eye spoke less than his lip; and though Aubrey was near the object of his curiosity, he obtained no greater gratification from it than the constant excitement of vainly wishing to break that mystery, which to his exalted imagination began to assume the appearance of something supernatural.

They soon arrived at Rome, and Aubrey for a time lost sight of his companion; he left him in daily attendance upon the morning circle of an Italian countess, whilst he went in search of the memorials of another almost deserted city. Whilst he was thus engaged, letters arrived from England, which he opened with eager impatience; the first was from his sister, breathing nothing but affection; the others were from his guardians, the latter astonished him; if it had before entered into his imagination that there was an evil power resident in his companion, these seemed to give him almost sufficient reason for the belief. His guardians insisted upon his immediately leaving his friend, and urged, that his character was dreadfully vicious, for that the possession of irresistible powers of seduction, rendered his licentious habits more dangerous to society. It had been discovered, that his contempt for the adultress had not originated in hatred of her character; but that he had required, to enhance his gratification, that his victim, the partner of his guilt,

---

[103] Also spelled "guilder" (Anglicisation of "gulden"), it was a Dutch coin worth at the time 1 shilling and 9 pence in British currency.

The Vampyre

should be hurled from the pinnacle of unsullied virtue, down to the lowest abyss of infamy and degradation: in fine, that all those females whom he had sought, apparently on account of their virtue, had, since his departure, thrown even the mask aside, and had not scrupled to expose the whole deformity of their vices to the public gaze.

Aubrey determined upon leaving one, whose character had not yet shown a single bright point on which to rest the eye. He resolved to invent some plausible pretext for abandoning him altogether, purposing, in the mean while, to watch him more closely, and to let no slight circumstance pass by unnoticed. He entered into the same circle, and soon perceived, that his Lordship was endeavouring to work upon the inexperience of the daughter of the lady whose house he chiefly frequented. In Italy, it is seldom that an unmarried female is met with in society; he was therefore obliged to carry on his plans in secret; but Aubrey's eye followed him in all his windings, and soon discovered that an assignation had been appointed, which would most likely end in the ruin of an innocent, though thoughtless girl. Losing no time, he entered the apartment of Lord Ruthven, and abruptly asked him his intentions with respect to the lady, informing him at the same time that he was aware of his being about to meet her that very night. Lord Ruthven answered, that his intentions were such as he supposed all would have upon such an occasion; and upon being pressed whether he intended to marry her, merely laughed. Aubrey retired; and, immediately writing a note, to say, that from that moment he must decline accompanying his Lordship in the remainder of their proposed tour, he ordered his servant to seek other apartments, and calling upon the mother of the lady, informed her of all he knew, not only with regard to her daughter, but also concerning the character of his Lordship. The assignation was prevented. Lord Ruthven next day merely sent his servant to notify his complete assent to a separation; but did not hint any suspicion of his plans having been foiled by Aubrey's interposition.

Having left Rome, Aubrey directed his steps towards Greece, and crossing the Peninsula, soon found himself at Athens.[104] He then fixed his residence in the house of a Greek; and soon occupied himself in tracing the faded records of ancient glory upon

---

[104] Although most of modern Greece is itself a peninsula, the Peloponnese, separated from the rest of the mainland by the Isthmus of Corinth, was sometimes called "the Peninsula." Athens, the capital of Greece, lies at the other end of the isthmus. At the time, Greece was still part of the Ottoman Empire.

monuments that apparently, ashamed of chronicling the deeds of freemen only before slaves,[105] had hidden themselves beneath the sheltering soil or many coloured lichen. Under the same roof as himself, existed a being, so beautiful and delicate, that she might have formed the model for a painter, wishing to pourtray on canvass the promised hope of the faithful in Mahomet's paradise, save that her eyes spoke too much mind for any one to think she could belong to those who had no souls.[106] As she danced upon the plain, or tripped along the mountain's side, one would have thought the gazelle a poor type of her beauties; for who would have exchanged her eye, apparently the eye of animated nature, for that sleepy luxurious look of the animal suited but to the taste of an epicure. The light step of Ianthe often accompanied Aubrey in his search after antiquities, and often would the unconscious girl, engaged in the pursuit of a Kashmere butterfly,[107] show the whole beauty of her form, floating as it were upon the wind, to the eager gaze of him, who forgot the letters he had just deciphered upon an almost effaced tablet, in the contemplation of her sylph-like figure. Often would her tresses falling, as she flitted around, exhibit in the sun's ray such delicately brilliant and swiftly fading hues, as might well excuse the forgetfulness of the antiquary, who let escape from his mind the very object he had before thought of vital importance to the proper interpretation of a passage in Pausanias.[108] But why attempt to describe charms which all feel, but none can appreciate?—It was innocence, youth, and beauty, unaffected by crowded drawing-rooms and stifling balls. Whilst he drew those remains of which he wished to preserve a memorial for his future hours, she would stand by, and watch the magic effects of his pencil, in tracing the scenes of her native place; she would then describe to him the circling dance upon the open plain, would paint to him in all the glowing colours of youthful memory, the marriage pomp she remembered viewing in her infancy; and then, turning to subjects that had evidently made a greater impression upon her

[105] Like Byron and other young Britons, Polidori was concerned about the fact that Greece, the cradle of European democracy, was reduced to the status of province in the Ottoman Empire. The Greek War of Independence began in 1821, less than two years after the publication of this story.

[106] According to a false notion, long perpetuated in Western Europe, women were considered soulless in Islam.

[107] Alludes to "the blue-winged butterfly of Kashmeer, the most rare and beautiful of the species" (as Byron describes this fictitious butterfly in a footnote in *The Giaour*).

[108] Pausanias was a 2nd-century Greek geographer, author of a *Description of Greece*.

The Vampyre

mind, would tell him all the supernatural tales of her nurse. Her earnestness and apparent belief of what she narrated, excited the interest even of Aubrey; and often as she told him the tale of the living vampyre, who had passed years amidst his friends, and dearest ties, forced every year, by feeding upon the life of a lovely female to prolong his existence for the ensuing months, his blood would run cold, whilst he attempted to laugh her out of such idle and horrible fantasies; but Ianthe cited to him the names of old men, who had at last detected one living among themselves, after several of their near relatives and children had been found marked with the stamp of the fiend's appetite; and when she found him so incredulous, she begged of him to believe her, for it had been remarked, that those who had dared to question their existence, always had some proof given, which obliged them, with grief and heartbreaking, to confess it was true. She detailed to him the traditional appearance of these monsters, and his horror was increased, by hearing a pretty accurate description of Lord Ruthven; he, however, still persisted in persuading her, that there could be no truth in her fears, though at the same time he wondered at the many coincidences which had all tended to excite a belief in the supernatural power of Lord Ruthven.

Aubrey began to attach himself more and more to Ianthe; her innocence, so contrasted with all the affected virtues of the women among whom he had sought for his vision of romance, won his heart; and while he ridiculed the idea of a young man of English habits, marrying an uneducated Greek girl, still he found himself more and more attached to the almost fairy form before him. He would tear himself at times from her, and, forming a plan for some antiquarian research, he would depart, determined not to return until his object was attained; but he always found it impossible to fix his attention upon the ruins around him, whilst in his mind he retained an image that seemed alone the rightful possessor of his thoughts. Ianthe was unconscious of his love, and was ever the same frank infantile being he had first known. She always seemed to part from him with reluctance; but it was because she had no longer any one with whom she could visit her favourite haunts, whilst her guardian was occupied in sketching or uncovering some fragment which had yet escaped the destructive hand of time. She had appealed to her parents on the subject of Vampyres, and they both, with several present, affirmed their existence, pale with horror at the very name. Soon after, Aubrey determined to proceed upon one of his excursions, which was to detain him for a few hours; when they heard the name of the place, they all at once begged of him not to return at night, as he must necessarily pass though a wood, where no Greek would ever remain, after the day had closed, upon any consideration. They described it as the resort of the vampyres in their nocturnal orgies, and denounced the most heavy evils as impending upon him who dared to cross their path. Aubrey made light of their representations, and tried to laugh them out of the idea; but when he saw them shudder at his daring thus to mock a superior, infernal power, the very name of which apparently made their blood freeze, he was silent.

Next morning Aubrey set off upon his excursion unattended; he was surprised to observe the melancholy face of his host, and was concerned to find that his words, mocking the belief of those horrible fiends, had inspired them with such terror. When he was about to depart, Ianthe came to the side of his horse, and earnestly begged of him to return, ere night allowed the power of these beings to be put in action;—he promised. He was, however, so occupied in his research, that he did not perceive that daylight would soon end, and that in the horizon there was one of those specks which, in the warmer climates, so rapidly gather into a tremendous mass, and pour all their rage upon the devoted country.—He at last, however, mounted his horse, determined to make up by speed for his delay: but it was too late. Twilight, in these southern climates, is almost unknown; immediately the sun sets, night begins: and ere he had advanced far, the power of the storm was above—its echoing thunders had scarcely an interval of rest— its thick heavy rain forced its way through the canopying foliage, whilst the blue forked lightning seemed to fall and radiate at his very feet. Suddenly his horse took fright, and he was carried with dreadful rapidity through the entangled forest. The animal at last, through fatigue, stopped, and he found, by the glare of lightning, that he was in the neighbourhood of a hovel that hardly lifted itself up from the masses of dead leaves and brushwood which surrounded it. Dismounting, he approached, hoping to find some one to guide him to the town, or at least trusting to obtain shelter from the pelting of the storm. As he approached, the thunders, for a moment silent, allowed him to hear the dreadful shrieks of a woman mingling with the stifled, exultant mockery of a laugh, continued in one almost unbroken sound;—he was startled: but, roused by the thunder which again rolled over his head, he, with a sudden effort, forced open the door of the hut. He found himself in utter darkness: the sound, however, guided him. He was apparently unperceived; for, though he called, still the sounds continued, and no notice was taken of him. He found himself in contact with some one, whom he immediately seized; when a voice

The Vampyre

cried, "Again baffled!" to which a loud laugh succeeded; and he felt himself grappled by one whose strength seemed superhuman: determined to sell his life as dearly as he could, he struggled; but it was in vain: he was lifted from his feet and hurled with enormous force against the ground:—his enemy threw himself upon him, and kneeling upon his breast, had placed his hands upon his throat—when the glare of many torches penetrating through the hole that gave light in the day, disturbed him;—he instantly rose, and, leaving his prey, rushed through the door, and in a moment the crashing of branches, as he broke through the wood, was no longer heard. The storm was now still; and Aubrey, incapable of moving, was soon heard by those without. They entered; the light of their torches fell upon the mud walls, and the thatch loaded on every individual straw with heavy flakes of soot. At the desire of Aubrey they searched for her who had attracted him by her cries; he was again left in darkness; but what was his horror, when the light of the torches once more burst upon him, to perceive the airy form of his fair conductress brought in a lifeless corse.[109] He shut his eyes, hoping that it was but a vision arising from his disturbed imagination; but he again saw the same form, when he unclosed them, stretched by his side. There was no colour upon her cheek, not even upon her lip; yet there was a stillness about her face that seemed almost as attaching as the life that once dwelt there:—upon her neck and breast was blood, and upon her throat were the marks of teeth having opened the vein:—to this the men pointed, crying, simultaneously struck with horror, "A Vampyre! a Vampyre!" A litter was quickly formed, and Aubrey was laid by the side of her who had lately been to him the object of so many bright and fairy visions, now fallen with the flower of life that had died within her. He knew not what his thoughts were—his mind was benumbed and seemed to shun reflection, and take refuge in vacancy—he held almost unconsciously in his hand a naked dagger of a particular construction, which had been found in the hut. They were soon met by different parties who had been engaged in the search of her whom a mother had missed. Their lamentable cries, as they approached the city, forewarned the parents of some dreadful catastrophe.—To describe their grief would be impossible; but when they ascertained the cause of their child's death, they looked at Aubrey, and pointed to the corse. They were inconsolable; both died broken-hearted.

Aubrey being put to bed was seized with a most violent fever, and was often delirious; in these intervals he would call upon Lord Ruthven and upon Ianthe—by some unaccountable combination

[109] Archaic variant of "corpse."

he seemed to beg of his former companion to spare the being he loved. At other times he would imprecate maledictions upon his head, and curse him as her destroyer. Lord Ruthven chanced at this time to arrive at Athens, and, from whatever motive, upon hearing of the state of Aubrey, immediately placed himself in the same house, and became his constant attendant. When the latter recovered from his delirium, he was horrified and startled at the sight of him whose image he had now combined with that of a Vampyre; but Lord Ruthven, by his kind words, implying almost repentance for the fault that had caused their separation, and still more by the attention, anxiety, and care which he showed, soon reconciled him to his presence. His lordship seemed quite changed; he no longer appeared that apathetic being who had so astonished Aubrey; but as soon as his convalescence began to be rapid, he again gradually retired into the same state of mind, and Aubrey perceived no difference from the former man, except that at times he was surprised to meet his gaze fixed intently upon him, with a smile of malicious exultation playing upon his lips: he knew not why, but this smile haunted him. During the last stage of the invalid's recovery, Lord Ruthven was apparently engaged in watching the tideless waves raise by the cooling breeze, or in marking the progress of those orbs, circling, like our world, the moveless sun;—indeed, he appeared to wish to avoid the eyes of all.

Aubrey's mind, by this shock, was much weakened, and that elasticity of spirit which had once so distinguished him now seemed to have fled for ever. He was now as much a lover of solitude and silence as Lord Ruthven; but as much as he wished for solitude, his mind could not find it in the neighbourhood of Athens; if he sought it amidst the ruins he had formerly frequented, Ianthe's form stood by his side—if he sought it in the woods, her light step would appear wandering amidst the underwood, in quest of the modest violet; then suddenly turning around, would show, to his wild imagination, her pale face and wounded throat, with a meek smile upon her lips. He determined to fly scenes, every feature of which created such bitter associations in his mind. He proposed to Lord Ruthven, to whom he held himself bound by the tender care he had taken of him during his illness, that they should visit those parts of Greece neither had yet seen. They travelled in every direction, and sought every spot to which a recollection could be attached: but though they thus hastened from place to place, yet they seemed not to heed what they gazed upon. They heard much of robbers, but they gradually began to slight these reports, which they imagined were only the invention of individuals, whose interest

The Vampyre

it was to excite the generosity of those whom they defended from pretended dangers. In consequence of thus neglecting the advice of the inhabitants, on one occasion they travelled with only a few guards, more to serve as guides than as a defence. Upon entering, however, a narrow defile, at the bottom of which was the bed of a torrent, with large masses of rock brought down from the neighbouring precipices, they had reason to repent their negligence; for scarcely were the whole of the party engaged in the narrow pass, when they were startled by the whistling of bullets close to their heads, and by the echoed report of several guns. In an instant their guards had left them, and, placing themselves behind rocks, had begun to fire in the direction whence the report came. Lord Ruthven and Aubrey, imitating their example, retired for a moment behind the sheltering turn of the defile: but ashamed of being thus detained by a foe, who with insulting shouts bade them advance, and being exposed to unresisting slaughter, if any of the robbers should climb above and take them in the rear, they determined at once to rush forward in search of the enemy. Hardly had they lost the shelter of the rock, when Lord Ruthven received a shot in the shoulder, which brought him to the ground. Aubrey hastened to his assistance; and, no longer heeding the contest or his own peril, was soon surprised by seeing the robbers' faces around him—his guards having, upon Lord Ruthven's being wounded, immediately thrown up their arms and surrendered.

By promises of great reward, Aubrey soon induced them to convey his wounded friend to a neighbouring cabin; and having agreed upon a ransom, he was no more disturbed by their presence—they being content merely to guard the entrance till their comrade should return with the promised sum, for which he had an order.[110] Lord Ruthven's strength rapidly decreased; in two days mortification ensued, and death seemed advancing with hasty steps. His conduct and appearance had not changed; he seemed as unconscious of pain as he had been of the objects about him: but towards the close of the last evening, his mind became apparently uneasy, and his eye often fixed upon Aubrey, who was induced to offer his assistance with more than usual earnestness—"Assist me! you may save me—you may do more than that—I mean not my life, I heed the death of my existence as little as that of the passing day; but you may save my honour, your friend's honour."—"How?

---

[110] The money-order office was founded as a private enterprise (Stow and Co.) in 1792, by three post office clerks. In 1838 it became a branch of the General Post Office.

127

tell me how? I would do any thing," replied Aubrey.—"I need but little—my life ebbs apace—I cannot explain the whole—but if you would conceal all you know of me, my honour were free from stain in the world's mouth—and if my death were unknown for some time in England—I—I—but life."—"It shall not be known."—"Swear!" cried the dying man, raising himself with exultant violence, "Swear by all your soul reveres, by all your nature fears, swear that for a year and a day you will not impart your knowledge of my crimes or death to any living being in any way, whatever may happen, or whatever you may see."—His eyes seemed bursting from their sockets: "I swear!" said Aubrey; he sunk laughing upon his pillow, and breathed no more.

Aubrey retired to rest, but did not sleep; the many circumstances attending his acquaintance with this man rose upon his mind, and he knew not why; when he remembered his oath a cold shivering came over him, as if from the presentiment of something horrible awaiting him. Rising early in the morning, he was about to enter the hovel in which he had left the corpse, when a robber met him, and informed him that it was no longer there, having been conveyed by himself and comrades, upon his retiring, to the pinnacle of a neighbouring mount, according to a promise they had given his lordship, that it should be exposed to the first cold ray of the moon that rose after his death. Aubrey astonished, and taking several of the men, determined to go and bury it upon the spot where it lay. But, when he had mounted to the summit he found no trace of either the corpse or the clothes, though the robbers swore they pointed out the identical rock on which they had laid the body. For a time his mind was bewildered in conjectures, but he at last returned, convinced that they had buried the corpse for the sake of the clothes.

Weary of a country in which he had met with such terrible misfortunes, and in which all apparently conspired to heighten that superstitious melancholy that had seized upon his mind, he resolved to leave it, and soon arrived at Smyrna.[111] While waiting for a vessel to convey him to Otranto, or to Naples, he occupied himself in arranging those effects he had with him belonging to Lord Ruthven. Amongst other things there was a case containing several weapons of offence, more or less adapted to ensure the death of the victim. There were several daggers and ataghans.[112] Whilst turning them over, and examining their curious forms, what was his surprise at

---

[111] Today Izmir, in western Turkey, a port on the Mediterranean.

[112] Yatagan, an Ottoman short sabre with a slightly curved blade.

The Vampyre

finding a sheath apparently ornamented in the same style as the dagger discovered in the fatal hut—he shuddered—hastening to gain further proof, he found the weapon, and his horror may be imagined when he discovered that it fitted, though peculiarly shaped, the sheath he held in his hand. His eyes seemed to need no further certainty—they seemed gazing to be bound to the dagger; yet still he wished to disbelieve; but the particular form, the same varying tints upon the haft[113] and sheath were alike in splendour on both, and left no room for doubt; there were also drops of blood on each.

He left Smyrna, and on his way home, at Rome, his first inquiries were concerning the lady he had attempted to snatch from Lord Ruthven's seductive arts. Her parents were in distress, their fortune ruined, and she had not been heard of since the departure of his lordship. Aubrey's mind became almost broken under so many repeated horrors; he was afraid that this lady had fallen a victim to the destroyer of Ianthe. He became morose and silent; and his only occupation consisted in urging the speed of the postilions, as if he were going to save the life of some one he held dear. He arrived at Calais; a breeze, which seemed obedient to his will, soon wafted him to the English shores; and he hastened to the mansion of his fathers, and there, for a moment, appeared to lose, in the embraces and caresses of his sister, all memory of the past. If she before, by her infantine caresses, had gained his affection, now that the woman began to appear, she was still more attaching as a companion.

Miss Aubrey had not that winning grace which gains the gaze and applause of the drawing-room assemblies. There was none of that light brilliancy which only exists in the heated atmosphere of a crowded apartment. Her blue eye was never lit up by the levity of the mind beneath. There was a melancholy charm about it which did not seem to arise from misfortune, but from some feeling within, that appeared to indicate a soul conscious of a brighter realm. Her step was not that light footing, which strays where'er a butterfly or a colour may attract—it was sedate and pensive. When alone, her face was never brightened by the smile of joy; but when her brother breathed to her his affection, and would in her presence forget those griefs she knew destroyed his rest, who would have exchanged her smile for that of the voluptuary? It seemed as if those eyes,—that face were then playing in the light of their own native sphere. She was yet only eighteen, and had not been presented to the world, it having been thought by her guardians more fit that her presentation

[113] Another name for the "hilt" (a sword's handle).

John William Polidori

should be delayed until her brother's return from the continent, when he might be her protector. It was now, therefore, resolved that the next drawing-room,[114] which was fast approaching, should be the epoch of her entry into the "busy scene." Aubrey would rather have remained in the mansion of his fathers, and fed upon the melancholy which overpowered him. He could not feel interest about the frivolities of fashionable strangers, when his mind had been so torn by the events he had witnessed; but he determined to sacrifice his own comfort to the protection of his sister. They soon arrived in town, and prepared for the next day, which had been announced as a drawing-room.

The crowd was excessive—a drawing-room had not been held for a long time, and all who were anxious to bask in the smile of royalty, hastened thither. Aubrey was there with his sister. While he was standing in a corner by himself, heedless of all around him, engaged in the remembrance that the first time he had seen Lord Ruthven was in that very place—he felt himself suddenly seized by the arm, and a voice he recognized too well, sounded in his ear—"Remember your oath." He had hardly courage to turn, fearful of seeing a spectre that would blast him, when he perceived, at a little distance, the same figure which had attracted his notice on this spot upon his first entry into society. He gazed till his limbs almost refusing to bear their weight, he was obliged to take the arm of a friend, and forcing a passage through a crowd, he threw himself into his carriage, and was driven home. He paced the room with hurried steps, as if he were afraid his thoughts were bursting from his brain. Lord Ruthven again before him—circumstances started up in dreadful array—the dagger—his oath.—He roused himself, he could not believe it possible—the dead rise again!—He thought his imagination had conjured up the image his mind was resting upon. It was impossible that it could be real—he determined, therefore, to go again into society; for though he attempted to ask concerning Lord Ruthven, the name hung upon his lips, and he could not succeed in gaining information. He went a few nights after with his sister to the assembly of a near relation. Leaving her under the protection of a matron, he retired into a recess,[115] and there gave himself up to his own devouring thoughts. Perceiving, at last, that many were leaving, he roused himself, and entering another room, found his sister surrounded by several, apparently in

---

[114] A formal reception held by the royal court at which young ladies were "presented," i.e., introduced into society.

[115] A secluded spot, a corner of the house.

The Vampyre

earnest conversation; he attempted to pass and get near her, when one, whom he requested to move, turned round, and revealed to him those features he most abhorred. He sprang forward, seized his sister's arm, and, with hurried step, forced her towards the street: at the door he found himself impeded by the crowd of servants who were waiting for their lords; and while he was engaged in passing them, he again heard that voice whisper close to him—"Remember your oath!"—He did not dare to turn, but, hurrying his sister, soon reached home.

Aubrey became almost distracted. If before his mind had been absorbed by one subject, how much more completely was it engrossed, now that the certainty of the monster's living again pressed upon his thoughts. His sister's attentions were now unheeded, and it was in vain that she intreated him to explain to her what had caused his abrupt conduct. He only uttered a few words, and those terrified her. The more he thought, the more he was bewildered. His oath startled him;—was he then to allow this monster to roam, bearing ruin upon his breath, amidst all he held dear, and not avert its progress? His very sister might have been touched by him. But even if he were to break his oath, and disclose his suspicions, who would believe him? He thought of employing his own hand to free the world from such a wretch; but death, he remembered, had been already mocked. For days he remained in this state; shut up in his room, he saw no one, and eat[116] only when his sister came, who, with eyes streaming with tears, besought him, for her sake, to support nature. At last, no longer capable of bearing stillness and solitude, he left his house, roamed from street to street, anxious to fly that image which haunted him. His dress became neglected, and he wandered, as often exposed to the noon-day sun as to the midnight damps. He was no longer to be recognized; at first he returned with the evening to the house; but at last he laid him down to rest wherever fatigue overtook him. His sister, anxious for his safety, employed people to follow him; but they were soon distanced by him who fled from a pursuer swifter than any—from thought. His conduct, however, suddenly changed. Struck with the idea that he left by his absence the whole of his friends, with a fiend amongst them, of whose presence they were unconscious, he determined to enter again into society, and watch him closely, anxious to forewarn, in spite of his oath, all whom Lord Ruthven approached with intimacy. But when he entered

[116] At least until the end of the 18th century, "eat" was the most common form of the past simple of the verb "to eat."

131

into a room, his haggard and suspicious looks were so striking, his inward shudderings so visible, that his sister was at last obliged to beg of him to abstain from seeking, for her sake, a society which affected him so strangely. When, however, remonstrance proved unavailing, the guardians thought proper to interpose, and, fearing that his mind was becoming alienated, they thought high time to resume again that trust which had been before imposed upon them by Aubrey's parents.

Desirous of saving him from the injuries and sufferings he had daily encountered in his wanderings, and of preventing him from exposing to the general eye those marks of what they considered folly, they engaged a physician to reside in the house, and take constant care of him. He hardly appeared to notice it, so completely was his mind absorbed by one terrible subject. His incoherence became at last so great, that he was confined to his chamber. There he would often lie for days, incapable of being roused. He had become emaciated, his eyes had attained a glassy lustre;—the only sign of affection and recollection remaining displayed itself upon the entry of his sister; then he would sometimes start, and, seizing her hands, with looks that severely afflicted her, he would desire her not to touch him. "Oh, do not touch him—if your love for me is aught, do not go near him!" When, however, she inquired to whom he referred, his only answer was, "True! true!" and again he sank into a state, whence not even she could rouse him. This lasted many months: gradually, however, as the year was passing, his incoherences became less frequent, and his mind threw off a portion of its gloom, whilst his guardians observed, that several times in the day he would count upon his fingers a definite number, and then smile.

The time had nearly elapsed, when, upon the last day of the year, one of his guardians entering his room, began to converse with his physician upon the melancholy circumstance of Aubrey's being in so awful a situation, when his sister was going next day to be married. Instantly Aubrey's attention was attracted; he asked anxiously to whom. Glad of this mark of returning intellect, of which they feared he had been deprived, they mentioned the name of the Earl of Marsden. Thinking this was a young Earl whom he had met with in society, Aubrey seemed pleased, and astonished them still more by his expressing his intention to be present at the nuptials, and desiring to see his sister. They answered not, but in a few minutes his sister was with him. He was apparently again capable of being affected by the influence of her lovely smile; for

The Vampyre

he pressed her to his breast, and kissed her cheek, wet with tears, flowing at the thought of her brother's being once more alive to the feelings of affection. He began to speak with all his wonted warmth, and to congratulate her upon her marriage with a person so distinguished for rank and every accomplishment; when he suddenly perceived a locket upon her breast; opening it, what was his surprise at beholding the features of the monster who had so long influenced his life. He seized the portrait in a paroxysm of rage, and trampled it under foot. Upon her asking him why he thus destroyed the resemblance of her future husband, he looked as if he did not understand her—then seizing her hands, and gazing on her with a frantic expression of countenance, he bade her swear that she would never wed this monster, for he—But he could not advance—it seemed as if that voice again bade him remember his oath—he turned suddenly round, thinking Lord Ruthven was near him but saw no one. In the meantime the guardians and physician, who had heard the whole, and thought this was but a return of his disorder, entered, and forcing him from Miss Aubrey, desired her to leave him. He fell upon his knees to them, he implored, he begged of them to delay but for one day. They, attributing this to the insanity they imagined had taken possession of his mind, endeavoured to pacify him, and retired.

Lord Ruthven had called the morning after the drawing-room, and had been refused with every one else. When he heard of Aubrey's ill health, he readily understood himself to be the cause of it; but when he learned that he was deemed insane, his exultation and pleasure could hardly be concealed from those among whom he had gained this information. He hastened to the house of his former companion, and, by constant attendance, and the pretence of great affection for the brother and interest in his fate, he gradually won the ear of Miss Aubrey. Who could resist his power? His tongue had dangers and toils to recount—could speak of himself as of an individual having no sympathy with any being on the crowded earth, save with her to whom he addressed himself;—could tell how, since he knew her, his existence had begun to seem worthy of preservation, if it were merely that he might listen to her soothing accents;—in fine, he knew so well how to use the serpent's art, or such was the will of fate, that he gained her affections. The title of the elder branch falling at length to him, he obtained an important embassy, which served as an excuse for hastening the marriage, (in spite of her brother's deranged state,) which was to take place the very day before his departure for the continent.

133

Aubrey, when he was left by the physician and his guardians, attempted to bribe the servants, but in vain. He asked for pen and paper; it was given him; he wrote a letter to his sister, conjuring her, as she valued her own happiness, her own honour, and the honour of those now in the grave, who once held her in their arms as their hope and the hope of their house, to delay but for a few hours that marriage, on which he denounced the most heavy curses. The servants promised they would deliver it; but giving it to the physician, he thought it better not to harass any more the mind of Miss Aubrey by, what he considered, the ravings of a maniac. Night passed on without rest to the busy inmates of the house; and Aubrey heard, with a horror that may more easily be conceived than described, the notes of busy preparation. Morning came, and the sound of carriages broke upon his ear. Aubrey grew almost frantic. The curiosity of the servants at last overcame their vigilance, they gradually stole away, leaving him in the custody of an helpless old woman. He seized the opportunity, with one bound was out of the room, and in a moment found himself in the apartment where all were nearly assembled. Lord Ruthven was the first to perceive him: he immediately approached, and, taking his arm by force, hurried him from the room, speechless with rage. When on the staircase, Lord Ruthven whispered in his ear—"Remember your oath, and know, if not my bride to day, your sister is dishonoured. Women are frail!" So saying, he pushed him towards his attendants, who, roused by the old woman, had come in search of him. Aubrey could no longer support himself; his rage not finding vent, had broken a blood-vessel, and he was conveyed to bed. This was not mentioned to his sister, who was not present when he entered, as the physician was afraid of agitating her. The marriage was solemnized, and the bride and bridegroom left London.

Aubrey's weakness increased; the effusion of blood produced symptoms of the near approach of death. He desired his sister's guardians might be called, and when the midnight hour had struck, he related composedly what the reader has perused—he died immediately after.

The guardians hastened to protect Miss Aubrey; but when they arrived, it was too late. Lord Ruthven had disappeared, and Aubrey's sister had glutted the thirst of a VAMPYRE!

Leigh Hunt

A TALE FOR A CHIMNEY CORNER

(1819)

The author: James Henry Leigh Hunt was born in Southgate (today in North London) on 19 October 1784. His parents were American Loyalists from Philadelphia, who had left the New World in 1777. He was educated at Christ's Hospital and began publishing poetry while he was working as a clerk for the War Office. In 1808, when his older brother John founded the influential newspaper *The Examiner*, Leigh Hunt began his long career as a journalist. From 1813 to 1815, he and his brother were imprisoned on charges of libel against the Prince Regent. He published poetry, translations, memoirs, anthologies, and essays. He collaborated with William Hazlitt (with whom he published *The Round Table*, two volumes of essays) and befriended the younger poets Shelley and Keats. His literary group, initially known as the "Hunt Circle," became synonymous with the Cockney School. He travelled to Italy to create a journal with Shelley and Byron, but Shelley died one week after his arrival. He lived in Genoa until 1825, when he returned to England. For most of his life, he found it difficult to make ends meet without help from friends. Finally, in the 1840s, he received an annuity from Mary Shelley and a pension from the Liberal government. He died in Putney (south London) on 28 August 1859.

The text: It was first published in *The Indicator* 10 (Wednesday 15 December 1819), 73-79. *The Indicator* was a weekly that Hunt edited from 1819 to 1821. The following is from Hunt's own edition of *The Indicator, and The Companion; A Miscellany for the Fields and the Fire-Side*. 2 vols. London: Henry Colburn, 1834, 99-112. Hunt took inspiration from a brief account that he had found in George Sandys's annotated edition of *Ovid's Metamorphosis Englished* (Oxford: John Lichfield, 1632), 354-355.

A man who does not contribute his quota of grim story now-a-days, seems hardly to be free of the republic of letters. He is bound to wear a death's head, as part of his insignia. If he does not frighten every body, he is nobody. If he does not shock the ladies, what can be expected of him?

We confess we think very cheaply of these stories in general. A story, merely horrible or even awful, which contains no sentiment elevating to the human heart and its hopes, is a mere appeal to the least judicious, least healthy, and least masculine of our passions,—fear. They whose attention can be gravely arrested by it, are in a fit state to receive any absurdity with respect; and this is the reason, why less talents are required to enforce it, than in any other species of composition. With this opinion of such things, we may be allowed to say, that we would undertake to write a dozen horrible stories in a day, all of which should make the common worshipper of power, who were not in the very healthiest condition, turn pale. We would tell of Haunting Old Women, and Knocking Ghosts, and Solitary Lean Hands, and Empusas on One Leg,[117] and Ladies growing Longer and Longer, and Horrid Eyes meeting us through Key-holes, and Plaintive Heads, and Shrieking Statues, and Shocking Anomalies of Shape, and Things which when seen drove people mad; and Indigestion knows what besides. But who would measure talents with a leg of veal, or a German sausage?

Mere grimness is as easy as grinning; but it requires something to put a handsome face on a story. Narratives become of suspicious merit in proportion as they lean to Newgate-like offences,[118] particularly of blood and wounds. A child has a reasonable respect for a Raw-head-and-bloody-bones,[119] because all images whatsoever of pain and terror are new and fearful to his inexperienced age: but sufferings merely physical (unless sublimated like those of Philoctetes)[120] are common-

---

[117] Empusa is a shapeshifting creature in Greek mythology, represented as a one-legged woman who can change her appearance into that of any beast.

[118] Newgate was a famous prison in London, until it was closed in 1902.

[119] Also known as Bloody Bones or (Tommy) Rawhead, this is a bogeyman in English folklore.

[120] Philoctetes was a Greek who went to war against the Trojans but, already wounded, he was initially left alone on an island. Sophocles wrote a play about his tribulations.

places to a grown man. Images, to become awful to him, must be removed from the grossness of the shambles. A death's head was a respectable thing in the hands of a poring monk, or of a nun compelled to avoid the idea of life and society, or of a hermit already buried in the desert. Holbein's Dance of Death,[121] in which every grinning skeleton leads along a man of rank, from the pope to the gentleman, is a good Memento Mori; but there the skeletons have an air of the ludicrous and satirical. If we were threatened with them in a grave way, as spectres, we should have a right to ask how they could walk about without muscles. Thus many of the tales written by such authors as the late Mr. Lewis,[122] who wanted sentiment to give him the heart of truth, are quite puerile. When his spectral nuns go about bleeding, we think they ought in decency to have applied to some ghost of a surgeon. His little Grey Men, who sit munching hearts, are of a piece with fellows that eat cats for a wager.

Stories that give mental pain to no purpose, or to very little purpose compared with the unpleasant ideas they excite of human nature, are as gross mistakes, in their way, as these, and twenty times as pernicious: for the latter become ludicrous to grown people. They originate also in the same extremes, of callousness, or of morbid want of excitement, as the others. But more of these hereafter. Our business at present is with things ghastly and ghostly.

A ghost story, to be a good one, should unite, as much as possible, objects such as they are in life, with a preternatural spirit. And to be a perfect one,—at least to add to the other utility of excitement a moral utility,—they should imply some great sentiment,—something that comes out of the next world to remind us of our duties in this; or something that helps to carry on the idea of our humanity into afterlife, even when we least think we shall take it with us. When "the buried majesty of Denmark" revisits earth to speak to his son Hamlet, he comes armed, as he used to be, in his complete steel. His visor is raised; and the same fine face is there; only, in spite of his punishing errand and his own sufferings, with

---

[121] *Dance of Death* is a famous series of woodcuts after designs by Hans Holbein the Younger (1497-1543), which he executed in the mid-1520s.

[122] Matthew Gregory Lewis (1775-1818) was a Gothic author, best known for his novel *The Monk* (1796).

137

> A countenance more in sorrow than in anger.[123]

When Donne the poet, in his thoughtful eagerness to reconcile life and death, had a figure of himself painted in a shroud, and laid by his bedside in a coffin, he did a higher thing than the monks and hermits with their skulls.[124] It was taking his humanity with him into the other world, not affecting to lower the sense of it by regarding it piecemeal or in the frame-work. Burns, in his *Tam O'Shanter*, shews the dead in their coffins after the same fashion. He does not lay bare to us their skeletons or refuse, things with which we can connect no sympathy or spiritual wonder. They still are flesh and body to retain the one; yet so look and behave, inconsistent in their very consistency, as to excite the other.

> Coffins stood round like open presses,
> Which shewed the dead in their last dresses:
> And by some devilish cantrip sleight,
> Each, in his cauld hand, held a light.[125]

Re-animation is perhaps the most ghastly of all ghastly things, uniting as it does an appearance of natural interdiction from the next world, with a supernatural experience of it. Our human consciousness is jarred out of its self-possession. The extremes of habit and newness, of common-place and astonishment, meet suddenly, without the kindly introduction of death and change; and the stranger appals us in proportion. When the account appeared the other day in the newspapers of the galvanized dead body, whose features as well as limbs underwent such contortions, that it seemed as if it were about to rise up, one almost expected to hear, for the first time, news of the other world. Perhaps the most appalling figure in Spenser is that of Maleger: (*Fairy Queen*, b. II. c. xi.)

---

[123] In Shakespeare's *Hamlet* (Act I, scene 2). Horatio is describing the ghost of Hamlet's father.

[124] Izaak Walton (1593-1683), in his biography of John Donne (1572-1631), relates how the poet, while still alive, posed in his burial shroud. An engraving of this painting was inserted in the posthumous edition of his last sermon, *Death's Duel* (1632).

[125] *Tam O'Shanter* (first published in 1791) is a narrative poem with fantastic elements by the Scottish poet Robert Burns (1759-1796).

A Tale for a Chimney Corner

> Upon a tygre swift and fierce he rode,
> That as the winde ran underneath his lode,
> While his long legs nigh raught unto the ground:
> Full large he was of limbe, and shoulders brode,
> But of such subtile substance and unsound,
> That like a ghost he seemed, whose grave-clothes were unbound.[126]

Mr. Coleridge, in that voyage of his to the brink of all unutterable things, the *Ancient Mariner* (which works out however a fine sentiment), does not set mere ghosts or hobgoblins to man the ship again, when its crew are dead; but re-animates, for awhile, the crew themselves.[127] There is a striking fiction of this sort in Sale's Notes upon the Koran. Solomon dies during the building of the temple, but his body remains leaning on a staff and overlooking the workmen, as if it were alive; till a worm gnawing through the prop, he falls down.[128]—The contrast of the appearance of humanity with something mortal or supernatural, is always the more terrible in proportion as it is complete. In the pictures of the temptations of saints and hermits, where the holy person is surrounded, teazed, and enticed, with devils and fantastic shapes, the most shocking phantasm is that of the beautiful woman. To return also to the poem above-mentioned. The most appalling personage in Mr. Coleridge's *Ancient Mariner* is the Spectre-woman, who is called Life-in-Death. He renders the most hideous abstraction more terrible than it could otherwise have been, by embodying it in its own reverse. "Death" not only "lives" in it; but the "unutterable" becomes uttered. To see such an unearthly passage end in such earthliness, seems to turn common-place itself into a sort of spectral doubt. The Mariner, after describing the horrible calm,

---

[126] Maleger is a character in Edmund Spenser's epic poem *Faerie Queene* (1590-1596). He commands twelve troops (representing the seven deadly sins and the temptations of the five senses). Despite his apparent undead nature, King Arthur manages to defeat and kill him.

[127] "The Rime of the Ancient Mariner" was first published in *Lyrical Ballads* (1798), Coleridge and Wordsworth's collective book. Although he admired his poetry and were often in the same society circles, Leigh Hunt knew Coleridge only slightly.

[128] George Sale (1697-1736) was an Orientalist who published a translation with notes of the Qur'an in 1734. This story about Solomon is told in the 34th chapter of the Qur'an, but Sale added in notes some opinions of Arab commentators.

and the rotting sea in which the ship was stuck, is speaking of a strange sail which he descried in the distance:

> The western wave was all a-flame,
> The day was well nigh done!
> Almost upon the western wave
> Rested the broad bright sun;
> When that strange ship drove suddenly
> Betwixt us and the sun.
> And straight the sun was flecked with bars,
> (Heaven's Mother send us grace!)
> As if through a dungeon-grate he peer'd,
> With broad and burning face.
> Alas! (thought I, and my heart beat loud)
> How fast she neers and neers!
> Are those *her* sails that glance in the sun
> Like restless gossameres?
> Are those *her* ribs, though which the sun
> Did peer as through a grate?
> And is that Woman all her crew?
> Is that a death? and are there two?
> Is Death that Woman's mate?
> Her lips were red, her looks were free,
> Her locks were yellow as gold,
> Her skin was as white as leprosy,
> The Night-Mare Life-in-Death was she,
> Who thicks man's blood with cold.

But we must come to Mr. Coleridge's story with our subtlest imaginations upon us. Now let us put our knees a little nearer the fire, and tell a homelier one about Life in Death. The groundwork of it is in Sandys' Commentary upon Ovid, and quoted from Sabinus.[129]

[129] Here, Hunt inserted the following note: "The Saxon Latin poet, we presume, professor of belles-lettres at Frankfort. We know nothing of him except from a biographical dictionary." Hunt is trying to suggest that George Sandys (1578-1644), who published an annotated translation (1632) of the *Metamorphoses* of Latin poet Ovid (43 BC – 17 AD) and who quotes a certain "Sabinus" as the source of a story (which Hunt expanded here) was not referring to Ovid's good friend Sabinus, but to a modern scholar. However, Hunt confuses Sandys's actual source (Angelo Sabino, a 15th-century Italian commentator of Ovid who also famously produced forgeries, pretending to have discovered literary works of the historical Sabinus) with the 16th-century German academic and poet Georg Sabinus.

A Tale for a Chimney Corner

A gentleman of Bavaria, of a noble family, was so afflicted at the death of his wife, that unable to bear the company of any other person, he gave himself up to a solitary way of living. This was the more remarkable in him, as he had been a man of jovial habits, fond of his wine and visitors, and impatient of having his numerous indulgences contradicted. But in the same temper perhaps might be found the cause of his sorrow; for though he would be impatient with his wife, as with others, yet his love for her was one of the gentlest wills he had; and the sweet and unaffected face which she always turned upon his anger, might have been a thing more easy for him to trespass upon, while living, than to forget, when dead and gone. His very anger towards her, compared with that towards others, was a relief to him. It was rather a wish to refresh himself in the balmy feeling of her patience, than to make her unhappy herself, or to punish her, as some would have done, for that virtuous contrast to his own vice.

But whether he bethought himself, after her death, that this was a very selfish mode of loving; or whether, as some thought, he had wearied out her life with habits so contrary to her own; or whether, as others reported, he had put it to a fatal risk by some lordly piece of self-will, in consequence of which she had caught a fever on the cold river during a night of festivity; he surprised even those who thought that he loved her, by the extreme bitterness of his grief. The very mention of festivity, though he was patient for the first day or two, afterwards threw him into a passion of rage; but by degrees even his rage followed his other old habits. He was gentle, but ever silent. He eat and drank but sufficient to keep him alive; and used to spend the greater part of the day in the spot where his wife was buried.

He was going there one evening, in a very melancholy manner, with his eyes turned towards the earth, and had just entered the rails of the burial-ground, when he was accosted by the mild voice of somebody coming to meet him. "It is a blessed evening, Sir," said the voice. The gentleman looked up. Nobody but himself was allowed to be in the place at that hour; and yet he saw, with astonishment, a young chorister approaching him. He was going to express some wonder, when, he said, the modest though assured look of the boy, and the extreme beauty of his countenance, which glowed in the setting sun before him, made an irresistible addition to the singular sweetness of his voice; and he asked him with an involuntary calmness, and a gesture of respect, not what he did there, but what he wished. "Only to wish you all good things," answered the stranger, who had now come up, "and to give you this letter." The gentleman took the letter, and saw upon it, with a beating yet scarcely bewildered heart, the handwriting of his wife. He raised his eyes again to speak to the boy, but he was gone. He cast them far and near round the place, but there were no traces of a passenger. He then opened the letter; and by the divine light of the setting sun, read these words:

"To my dear husband, who sorrows for his wife:

Otto, my husband, the soul you regret so is returned. You will know the truth of this, and be prepared with calmness to see it, by the divineness of the messenger, who has passed you. You will find me sitting in the public walk, praying for you; praying, that you may never more give way to those gusts of passion, and those curses against others, which divided us.

This, with a warm hand, from the living Bertha."

Otto (for such, it seems, was the gentleman's name) went instantly, calmly, quickly, yet with a sort of benumbed being, to the public walk. He felt, but with only a half-consciousness, as if he glided without a body. But all his spirit was awake, eager, intensely conscious. It seemed to him as if there had been but two things in the world—Life and Death; and that Death was dead. All else appeared to have been a dream. He had awaked from a waking state, and found himself all eye, and spirit, and locomotion. He said to himself, once, as he went: "This is not a dream. I will ask my great ancestors to-morrow to my new bridal feast, for they are alive." Otto had been calm at first, but something of old and triumphant feelings seemed again to come over him. Was he again too proud and confident? Did his earthly humours prevail again, when he thought them least upon him? We shall see.

The Bavarian arrived at the public walk. It was full of people with their wives and children, enjoying the beauty of the evening. Something like common fear came over him, as he went in and out among them, looking at the benches on each side. It happened that there was only one person, a lady, sitting upon them. She had her veil down; and his being underwent a fierce but short convulsion as he went near her. Something had a little baffled the calmer inspiration of the angel that had accosted him; for fear prevailed at the instant, and Otto passed on. He returned before he had reached the end of the walk, and approached the

A Tale for a Chimney Corner

lady again. She was still sitting in the same quiet posture, only he thought she looked at him. Again he passed her. On his second return, a grave and sweet courage came upon him, and in an under but firm tone of enquiry, he said "Bertha?"—"I thought you had forgotten me," said that well-known and mellow voice, which he had seemed as far from ever hearing again as earth is from heaven. He took her hand, which grasped his in turn; and they walked home in silence together, the arm, which was wound within his, giving warmth for warmth.

The neighbours seemed to have a miraculous want of wonder at the lady's re-appearance. Something was said about a mock-funeral, and her having withdrawn from his company for awhile: but visitors came as before, and his wife returned to her household affairs. It was only remarked that she always looked pale and pensive. But she was more kind to all, even than before; and her pensiveness seemed rather the result of some great internal thought, than of unhappiness.

For a year or two, the Bavarian retained the better temper which he acquired. His fortunes flourished beyond his earliest ambition; the most amiable as well as noble persons of the district were frequent visitors; and people said, that to be at Otto's house, must be the next thing to being in heaven. But by degrees his self-will returned with his prosperity. He never vented impatience on his wife; but he again began to shew, that the disquietude it gave her to see it vented on others, was a secondary thing, in his mind, to the indulgence of it. Whether it was, that his grief for her loss had been rather remorse than affection, and so he held himself secure if he treated her well; or whether he was at all times rather proud of her, than fond; or whatever was the cause which again set his antipathies above his sympathies, certain it was, that his old habits returned upon him; not so often indeed, but with greater violence and pride, when they did. These were the only times, at which his wife was observed to shew any ordinary symptoms of uneasiness.

At length, one day, some strong rebuff which he had received from an alienated neighbour threw him into such a transport of rage, that he gave way to the most bitter imprecations, crying with a loud voice—"This treatment to *me* too! To *me*! To me, who if the world knew all"—At these words, his wife, who had in vain laid her hand upon his, and looked him with dreary earnestness in the face, suddenly glided from the room. He, and two or three who were present, were struck with a dumb horror. They said, she did not walk out, nor vanish suddenly; but glided, as one who could dispense with the use of feet. After a moment's pause, the others proposed to him to follow her. He made a movement of despair; but they went. There was a short passage, which turned to the right into her favourite room. They knocked at the door twice or three times, and received no answer. At last, one of them gently opened it; and looking in, they saw her, as they thought, standing before a fire, which was the only light in the room. Yet she stood so far from it, as rather to be in the middle of the room; only the face was towards the fire, and she seemed looking upon it. They addressed her, but received no answer. They stepped gently towards her, and still received none. The figure stood dumb and unmoved. At last, one of them went round in front, and instantly fell on the floor. The figure was without body. A hollow hood was left instead of a face. The clothes were standing upright by themselves.

That room was blocked up for ever, for the clothes, if it might be so, to moulder away. It was called the Room of the Lady's Figure. The house, after the gentleman's death, was long uninhabited, and at length burnt by the peasants in an insurrection. As for himself, he died about nine months after, a gentle and child-like penitent. He had never stirred from the house since; and nobody would venture to go near him, but a man who had the reputation of being a reprobate. It was from this man that the particulars of the story came first. He would distribute the gentleman's alms in great abundance to any strange poor who would accept them; for most of the neighbours held them in horror. He tried all he could to get the parents among them to let some of their little children, or a single one of them, go to see his employer. They said he even asked it one day with tears in his eyes. But they shuddered to think of it; and the matter was not mended, when this profane person, in a fit of impatience, said one day, that he would have a child of his own on purpose. His employer, however, died in a day or two. They did not believe a word he told them of all the Bavarian's gentleness, looking upon the latter as a sort of ogre, and upon his agent as little better, though a good natured-looking earnest kind of person. It was said many years after, that this man had been a friend of the Bavarian's when young, and had been deserted by him. And the young believed it, whatever the old might do.

John Galt

𝒯HE 𝐵URIED 𝒜LIVE

(1821)

The author: Scottish author John Galt (1779-1839) was born in Irvine, in North Ayrshire. His father was a sea captain and was involved in the West Indian trade. He went to school in Greenock, on the coast of Scotland, where he joined the business of an uncle and served as junior justice clerk. He moved to London in 1804, studied law and economics and wrote essays on political and economic issues. During a European trip, he met Byron in Gibraltar and they travelled together in the Southern Mediterranean. He published travel memoirs in 1812 and 1813 and he began writing for *Blackwood's* in 1819. He next published a series of successful novels of Scottish country life, including *The Ayrshire Legatees* (1820-21), *Annals of the Parish* (1821), *Sir Andrew Wylie, of that Ilk* (1822). In 1824 he became secretary of the Canada Company and moved to Ontario, where he founded the town of Guelph. He was dismissed and returned to Great Britain in 1829, where he spent time in the debtors' prison. He published a *Life of Lord Byron* (1830) and then a series of political novels, including *The Radical* (1832), after which he retired and died in Greenock.

The text: It was first published in *Blackwood's* 10: 56 (October 1821), 262-264. One year later, Galt incorporated the story into the body of his novel *The Steam-Boat* (Edinburgh: William Blackwood; London: T. Cadell, 1822), 329-335, in which it is narrated by a "young man," at the beginning of the fifteenth chapter. The following is the original version from the magazine.

Further reading: Andrew Mangham. "Buried Alive: The Gothic Awakening of Taphephobia." *Journal of Literature and Science* 3: 1 (Summer 2010), 10-22.

I had been for some time ill of a low and lingering fever. My strength gradually wasted, but the sense of life seemed to become more and more acute as my corporeal powers became weaker. I could see by the looks of the doctor that he despaired of my recovery; and the soft and whispering sorrow of my friends, taught me that I had nothing to hope.

One day towards the evening, the crisis took place.—I was seized with a strange and indescribable quivering,—a rushing sound was in my ears,—I saw around my couch innumerable strange faces; they were bright and visionary, and without bodies. There was light, and solemnity, and I tried to move, but could not.—For a short time a terrible confusion overwhelmed me,—and when it passed off, all my recollection returned with the most perfect distinctness, but the power of motion had departed.—I heard the sound of weeping at my pillow—and the voice of the nurse say, "He is dead."—I cannot describe what I felt at these words.—I exerted my utmost power of volition to stir myself, but I could not move even an eyelid. After a short pause my friend drew near; and sobbing, and convulsed with grief, drew his hand over my face, and closed my eyes. The world was then darkened, but I could still hear, and feel, and suffer.

When my eyes were closed, I heard by the attendants that my friend had left the room, and I soon after found, the undertakers were preparing to habit me in the garments of the grave. Their thoughtlessness was more awful than the grief of my friends. They laughed at one another as they turned me from side to side, and treated what they believed a corpse, with the most appalling ribaldry.

When they had laid me out, these wretches retired, and the degrading formality of affected mourning commenced. For three days, a number of friends called to see me.—I heard them, in low accents, speak of what I was; and more than one touched me with his finger. On the third day, some of them talked of the smell of corruption in the room.

The coffin was procured—I was lifted and laid in—My friend placed my head on what was deemed its last pillow, and I felt his tears drop on my face.

When all who had any peculiar interest in me, had for a short time looked at me in the coffin, I heard them retire; and the undertaker's men placed the lid on the coffin, and screwed it down. There were two of them present—one had occasion to go away before the task was done. I heard the fellow who was left begin to whistle as he turned the screw-nails; but he checked himself, and completed the work in silence.

The Buried Alive

I was then left alone,—every one shunned the room.—I knew, however, that I was not yet buried; and though darkened and motionless, I had still hope;—but this was not permitted long. The day of interment arrived—I felt the coffin lifted and borne away—I heard and felt it placed in the hearse.—There was a crowd of people around; some of them spoke sorrowfully of me. The hearse began to move—I knew that it carried me to the grave. It halted, and the coffin was taken out—I felt myself carried on shoulders of men, by the inequality of the motion—A pause ensued—I heard the cords of the coffin moved—I felt it swing as dependent by them—It was lowered, and rested on the bottom of the grave—The cords were dropped upon the lid—I heard them fall.—Dreadful was the effort I then made to exert the power of action, but my whole frame was immoveable.

Soon after, a few handfuls of earth were thrown upon the coffin—Then there was another pause—after which the shovel was employed, and the sound of the rattling mould, as it covered me, was far more tremendous than thunder. But I could make no effort. The sound gradually became less and less, and by a surging reverberation in the coffin, I knew that the grave was filled up, and that the sexton was treading in the earth, slapping the grave with the flat of his spade. This too ceased, and then all was silent.

I had no means of knowing the lapse of time; and the silence continued. This is death, thought I, and I am doomed to remain in the earth till the resurrection. Presently the body will fall into corruption, and the epicurean worm, that is only satisfied with the flesh of man, will come to partake of the banquet that has been prepared for him with so much solicitude and care. In the contemplation of this hideous thought, I heard a low and under sound[130] in the earth over me, and I fancied that the worms and the reptiles of death were coming—that the mole and the rat of the grave would soon be upon me. The sound continued to grow louder and nearer. Can it be possible, I thought, that my friends suspect they have buried me too soon? The hope was truly like light bursting through the gloom of death.

The sound ceased, and presently I felt the hands of some dreadful being working about my throat. They dragged me out of the coffin by the head. I felt again the living air, but it was piercingly

---

[130] This appeared as "undersound" in *Blackwood's* (i.e., with the prefix "under" as part of the noun, thus meaning "muffled sound"), but we follow here subsequent editions which preferred to write "under sound" (with "under" as an adjective), which has a similar meaning and is consistent with the presence of the preceding conjunction "and."

cold; and I was carried swiftly away—I thought to judgment, perhaps perdition.

When borne to some distance, I was then thrown down like a clod—it was not upon the ground. A moment after I found myself on a carriage; and, by the interchange of two or three brief sentences, I discovered that I was in the hands of two of those robbers who live by plundering the grave, and selling the bodies of parents, and children, and friends. One of the men sung snatches and scraps of obscene songs, as the cart rattled over the pavement of the streets.

When it halted, I was lifted out, and I soon perceived, by the closeness of the air, and the change of temperature, that I was carried into a room; and, being rudely stripped of my shroud, was placed naked on a table. By the conversation of the two fellows with the servant who admitted them, I learnt that I was that night to be dissected.

My eyes were still shut, I saw nothing; but in a short time I heard, by the bustle in the room, that the students of anatomy were assembling. Some of them came round the table, and examined me minutely. They were pleased to find that so good a subject had been procured. The demonstrator himself at last came in.

Previous to beginning the dissection, he proposed to try on me some galvanic experiment—and an apparatus was arranged for that purpose. The first shock vibrated through all my nerves: they rung and jangled like the strings of a harp. The students expressed their admiration at the convulsive effect. The second shock threw my eyes open, and the first person I saw was the doctor who had attended me. But still I was as dead: I could, however, discover among the students the faces of many with whom I was familiar; and when my eyes were opened, I heard my name pronounced by several of the students, with an accent of awe and compassion, and a wish that it had been some other subject.

When they had satisfied themselves with the galvanic phenomena, the demonstrator took the knife, and pierced me on the bosom with the point. I felt a dreadful crackling, as it were, throughout my whole frame—a convulsive shuddering instantly followed, and a shriek of horror rose from all present. The ice of death was broken up—my trance ended. The utmost exertions were made to restore me, and in the course of an hour I was in the full possession of all my faculties.

Margaret Gardiner, Countess Blessington

THE AUCTION

(1822)

The author: Margaret (she later called herself Marguerite) Power was born in County Tipperary, Ireland, the daughter of a small landowner, on 1 September 1789. She became Margaret Farmer in 1805, when she was married to a well-off, but alcoholic, English captain whom she left after only three months. She lived with an aunt for a few years, and then a certain Captain Jenkins in Hampshire. That is where she met the recently widowed Earl of Blessington, whom she married in 1818 (Colonel Farmer had died in 1817). The Blessingtons set up a literary salon in London and Margaret began publishing her sketches. In 1822, they set out on a continental tour, during which they met Byron (in Genoa) several times. One of Margaret's stepdaughters married the French Count D'Orsay and they all moved to Paris, where the earl died in 1829. Margaret, the children, and the count returned to England, where she became the most sought after salonnière. When Count D'Orsay separated from his wife, he remained in London and lived with his mother-in-law. Margaret was the editor of several annuals and contributed to many periodicals. She also published popular travelogues and poems, but her most enduring contribution to English literature remains her *Conversations of Lord Byron with the Countess of Blessington* (1834). She died on 4 June 1849, in Paris.

The text: It appeared in Blessington's *The Magic Lantern; or, Sketches of Scenes in the Metropolis* (London: Longman, Hurst, Rees, Orme, and Brown, 1822), 3-17. The following is from the second edition (1823), 1-24 (in which either the author or the editor made a few corrections, signalled in 1822 only by an errata section). We have corrected here the spelling of some of the French words.

Further reading: Laura Engel. "The Countess of Blessington and Magic Lanterns." *Women, Performance and the Material of Memory. The Archival Tourist, 1780-1815*. London: Palgrave Macmillan, 2019. 81-106.

Passing, a few days ago, through one of the fashionable squares, I was attracted by seeing a bustling crowd around the door of one of the houses; and, on enquiry, I found that it was occasioned by an Auction.

Curiosity induced me to enter, and my mind soon became deeply engaged in the scene around me.

There are few occasions that, in a greater degree, furnish food for reflection, or indeed, more powerfully excite it, than an Auction; and, I am grieved to say, few that can show us our fellow beings in a less favourable point of view.

Each person is eager in the pursuit of some article that pleases his fancy, and seems to think of self alone.

The mansion that I was now in, had lately been the residence of a family of distinction, and bore evident marks of good taste. The furniture was rich and elegant, and chosen with a view to use as well as ornament: the pictures were the *chefs d'œuvres*[131] of the best masters; and a library of well-chosen books, with globes, fine maps, and all the apparatus for astronomical and geographical studies, marked the intellectual pursuits of the late possessors.

The morning room of the female part of the family next excited my attention: here were all the indications of female elegance and female usefulness,—the neat book shelves, stored with the best authors; the writing table, with all its appendages; the drawing table, on which the easel and pencils still rested, and the harp and piano-forte, with the music books still open, all spoke the refined taste and avocations of the owners of this room, and how sudden had been the ruin that had expelled them from it.

Some pictures, with their faces turned to the wall, were placed in a corner of the room, and curiosity induced me to examine them. I found them to be coloured drawings, admirably executed, and evidently portraits: on examining them more closely I discovered that some of the accompaniments were copies of parts of the furniture now before me: one of the drawings represented two very lovely girls performing on the harp and piano-forte, and never did I behold a sweeter personification of a duet, "Both warbling of

[131] French for "masterpieces."

one song, both in one key; as if their hands, their sides, voices, and minds had been incorporate."[132] Another represented a most animated, intelligent looking girl, reading to one who was drawing, and whose countenance, though pale and languid, was expressive of genius and sensibility. Here then, thought I, are the late actors in this domestic scene; and, as I gazed on the sweet faces before me, my interest became excited to a painful degree. Imagination pictured those delicate looking females driven from their home, stripped at once of all the elegancies of life, and sent to brave a world, the hardships of which they were now for the first time to learn. I saw them cling to each other in an agony of affection,—I saw the last looks of parting sorrow which they cast on this scene of happy hours for ever gone by; and I saw the efforts they made to compose their tearful countenances, and to regain some portion of fortitude, while with hurried steps, as if afraid to trust themselves with another parting glance, they left the apartment. My heart bled at the picture which my fancy had painted, and I hastened into the room where the sale was going on, to lose the poignancy of my emotions.—Here every thing presented a contrast to the quiet scene that I had quitted. Noise, bustle, and confusion on every side: here was a group of fashionables, male and female, whose bows of recognition, and smiles and whispers, betrayed that they were more occupied with each other than with the Auction. At another side was a set of elderly ladies, whose scrutinising glances, and airs of satisfied self-importance, were expressive of their conscious superiority. Next to these were some gentlemen, of a certain period in life, who had left their clubs to look in at the sale, and whose sapient looks and whispers declared them well accustomed to such scenes. The rest of the crowd was composed of brokers, and dealers in *bijouterie*,[133] who evidently wished the fashionables away.

Desirous of losing the painful impression left on my mind, I mingled with the crowd, and seeing a very beautiful fillagree box put up for sale, which I thought likely to attract the notice of the ladies, I sauntered round, and took a station close to a group of the youngest, who were chatting with some young men of fashion. The insipid countenances, starched neckcloths, and compressed waists of the latter bore evident symptoms of their belonging to the effeminate race which has, for the last few years, been known by the appellation of Dandy or Exquisite.

The box, as I anticipated, soon attracted their attention, and, "O dear, how pretty!" "How very elegant!" "How monstrous

[132] From Shakespeare's *A Midsummer Night's Dream* (Act III, scene 2), in which the possessive is "our."

[133] French for "jewelry."

charming!" with innumerable other ejaculations of admiration, were all uttered with great animation, and at nearly the same moment, by the ladies; while their attending beaux, between a languid smile and a suppressed yawn, merely said "Do you think so?" "Is it so very pretty?" or, "Do you wish to bid for it?" "O dear, no, I dare say it will go off horridly dear; and I have spent all my money at Jarman's,[134] where I bought the most exquisite piece of china that ever was seen. To be sure it was immensely dear, but it is such a love, that there was no resisting it: besides, I know Lady C—— will die with envy at my getting it, and I do so love to make people envious." This good natured sentiment extorted a smile of languid admiration from the beau, who rejoined, "If it gives you pleasure to excite envy, you must often enjoy that gratification, as all womankind must be ready to expire with envy whenever you appear." "Oh! you flattering creature, you don't really think so," was the lady's reply. I observed her female companions attentively listening to the dialogue, and regarding each other with significant nods and glances, not a little expressive of the passion which she had declared her wish to excite. Here, thought I, is the train laid for future scandal; and, perhaps, for future misconduct. This giddy young woman will go away with feelings of gratified vanity, at the compliments paid to her, and with complacency towards the individual who administers the adulation; and the gentleman, having seen the pleasing impression which his flatteries have made, will probably follow up his advantage by repeating them, when he meets her at some fashionable rout in the evening. Thus this silly flirtation, commenced in folly, and pursued through idleness, may end in the dishonour of this thoughtless woman, and entail misery and disgrace on an honourable family, and on innocent children.

From these ruminations I was disturbed by the lisping accents of another party of fashionables. "Do you go to Lady D——'s ball to night?" enquired a listless looking young man of an affected sickly looking young lady;—"I'm not quite sure," was the answer, "for Lady D——'s balls are, in general, so dull, that I don't much fancy going to them; I am to look in at Mrs. C——'s, and the Marchioness of L——'s, and if they offer nothing very tempting, I may go to Lady D——'s. By the bye, *apropos*, of balls—what very pleasant ones we have been at in this house; poor Mrs. B—— will give no more balls; for, I understand, they are quite ruined. Well, I declare, now that I think of it, I am very sorry; for there are so very few people that give pleasant balls."

[134] John Jarman had a fashionable shop on the Strand (later moved to St James's Street) that sold art, porcelains, furniture, and jewelry.

Here the conversation became general, each of the ladies, young and old, mingling their voices:—"Well, I must say, I always thought how it would end," says one; "What a very conceited woman Mrs. B—— was," cries another; "Yes, and what fuss people made about the beauty and accomplishments of the daughters;" observes a third. "I," said a pale sickly looking girl, "could never see any beauty in them; and I am sure they wore rouge and pearl powder." "They gave devilish good dinners though," said one of the beaux, "and I must do B—— justice to say, that he had one of the best cooks in London." "Yes, and he gave capital claret," rejoined another. "I thought his white hermitage[135] better than his claret," said a third; while another exclaimed, "Well, give me his hock[136] in preference to all his other wines, for that was *unique*." "I hope G—— will buy B——'s wines; as he gives such good feeds; his is the only house in town where you may rely on finding a perfect *suprême de volaille*; or where you get *côtelettes de pigeons à la champagne*."[137] "Oh! but," remarked the first speaker, "G——'s cellar is not nearly so cool or well arranged as B——'s, and the wine may get injured." "There won't be time enough for that, for G—— can't last long; he will be done up in a short time," was the reply. "I did hear some hint of that," said another. "It's a fact, I assure you, I had it from his lawyer," said the first speaker. "Well, G—— is a monstrous good fellow, and we must dine with him very often, that the wine mayn't be spoiled, before he is done up," said one of the Exquisites; which friendly intention they all expressed their willingness to carry into effect. "Have you any idea what is become of B——?" interrogated one of the party. "I did hear something, that he was in the bench;[138] or gone to France: but," yawning, "I really forget all about it." "I intend to bid for his curricle horses at Tattersal's."[139] "And I, said another, "will buy his Vandyke picture."[140] "What, do you like pictures?"

[135] White Hermitage is a French wine made from Marsanne grapes (more popular is the red Harmitage, made from Syrah). Claret is a (mostly British) term for Bordeaux wines.

[136] Hock is a (mostly British) term for German white wine, especially Riesling.

[137] Suprême de volaille (or chicken supreme) is a French dish made with chicken breast, vegetables, and a sauce based on chicken stock. Côtelettes de pigeons à la champagne are pigeon cutlets baked in a champagne sauce.

[138] That is, he is on trial.

[139] A curricle was a light, two-wheeled chariot. Founded in 1766, Tattersalls (as it is known today) is the main racehorse auctioneer in the UK.

[140] Anthony van Dyck (1599-1641) was a Flemish painter who lived and worked in London during the last and most prolific decade of his life. Titian, mentioned below, is a famous 16th-century Italian Renaissance painter.

said a third. "O, no; I have not the least fancy for them; indeed I don't know a Titian from a Vandyke: but one must have pictures, and I know that R——, who is a judge in things of that sort, wants to have this, and I am determined he sha'n't," was the reply of the intended purchaser of one of the *chefs d'œuvres* of Vandyke.

A young man of the party, who had hitherto been silent, and in whose countenance good nature and silliness strove for mastery, remarked that it was a pity that people who gave such good dinners were so soon ruined. "A pity!" replied another; "no, no; give me a short campaigne,[141] and brisk one; for let the dinners and wines be ever so good, one gets so tired of seeing always the same faces, and the same kind of dishes: if a dinner-giving man holds out many seasons, he gives so often the same sort of dinners, and the same set of men, that it at last becomes as tiresome as dining at the mess of the Guards. Believe me, there is nothing like a fresh start; and no man, at least no dinner-giving man, should last more than two seasons, unless he would change his cook every month, to prevent a repetition of the same dishes, and keep a regular *roster* of his invitation, with a mark to each name, to prevent people from meeting at his house twice in a season." "Would it not be better to cut his acquaintances every month, instead of his cook, particularly if he once got a perfect artist? Who is it that would not give up all his acquaintances, rather than part with such a cook as *Monsieur Ude*?"[142] All the party agreed in this sentiment, but the silent young man observed, that "Carrying it into practice might be attended with disagreeable consequences; for some men are so ridiculous, that if you take it into your head to cut them, they call you out, and nothing but a duel or an apology remains."

While this edifying conversation was going on, the elderly ladies were all haranguing on the follies, errors, and extravagancies of Mrs. B——; and the young ones were decrying the looks, accomplishments, and manners of the Misses B——. Each article of ornament or *virtu*[143] that was exhibited for sale elicited fresh sarcasms from the acquaintances of the unfortunate B—— family, who appeared to exult in the misfortunes of those for whom they once professed a regard.

[141] This French spelling of "campaign" was rare, but still in use at the time.

[142] Louis-Eustache Ude (c.1769-1846) was a French chef who popularised haute cuisine in England. He authored the influential *The French Cook* (1813). At the time Blessington was writing, Ude was in the service of Prince Frederick, Duke of York, the king's younger brother.

[143] A term (of Italian origin) both for fine taste in art and for exquisite objects of art.

I left this fashionable party, disgusted with their want of feeling, and took my stand near some elderly gentlemen, who were examining with attention a catalogue of the sale, and marking the articles for which they intended to bid.

One sapient looking gentleman observed, that "Mr. B——, though foolish and extravagant in some things, had considerable taste and judgment in others;—for instance, his books were all well chosen and well bought; he has two capital Wynkyn de Words, and three fine Caxtons; and those Elzevirs that he got last year were a great bargain: I think he gave only six-hundred for the set, and I would gladly give two hundred more. I have the Delphin edition of the Classics and the Variorum, and I am determined to have the Elzevirs."[144] "His busts too are very fine," exclaimed another, "and were bought for a sum much under their value. His Socrates is inimitable; I am determined no money shall keep it from me." "B—— had one merit," said the first speaker, "which was that of appreciating the talents of his countrymen, for while he transported to his residence the production of foreign geniuses, the admirable performances of his native land were also sure to find a place; and that exquisite sleeping child by Chantry,[145] as well as that splendid bust, do honour at once to the artist, the purchaser, and the country."

"For my part," said a third, "I like his statues better than all. What can be finer than his Venus by Canova, except it be the Nymph, by the same divine master?[146] That I will bid for." "Give me B——'s pictures," said a fourth, "for they are exquisite, and I shall not envy you the possession of all his other treasures. That portrait of a lady, by Hans Holbein, is charming; and I am convinced that picture of a young man is by Titian, though some

[144] Wynkyn de Worde (of German origin) first worked with William Caxton, who introduced the printing press in England in 1476. He later worked independently and even took over Caxton's business when the Englishman died c.1491. The Elzevirs were 17th-century Dutch printers, famous for their editions of Latin classics. The Delphin Classics (*Ad usum Delphini*) was a series of annotated editions of the Latin classics, published in France in the late 17th century. A variorum edition assembles all known variants of a text. Although they had been published in many countries, especially throughout the 17th century, bibliophiles often referred to all books marked *cum notis variorum* as "the Variorum collection."

[145] Actually, Francis Leggatt Chantrey (1781-1841), the leading English sculptor of the time.

[146] Antonio Canova (1757-1822) was arguably the world's most famous living sculptor (he was still alive when Blessington's story was first published). Copies of his most celebrated statues (usually produced by his studio) were regularly commissioned by the wealthy.

of our connoisseurs have doubted it; then his Snake in the Grass, by Sir Joshua Reynolds, is full of beauty and feeling; and that group, so exquisitely coloured, and so true to nature, could have been produced only by the inimitable pencil of a Lawrence. The two Claude Lorraines, and one of his Vandykes, I am determined on having."[147] "I am surprised," observed a fifth, "how you can look at the oil pictures, when those divine miniatures by Pettitot and Zink are present: they are indeed beautiful."[148] The first speaker now observed, that "had B—— confined himself to books, he would not have been blamable." "Or to busts," said the second, "for that is a rational taste." "I differ from you," said a third; "statues are the only things worth collecting." "No, no! pictures, pictures are alone worthy the attention of a man of true taste."—

Here all the voices became clamorous, each giving the preference to the objects of his own pursuit, and decrying those of the others, with no small degree of acrimony and ill-nature. I left them, with feelings very similar to those excited in my mind by the fashionables; and with more of anger than a Christian ought to feel, I exclaimed, "And this is an Auction! a scene so often the resort of the old and the young, the grave and the gay, where human beings go to triumph in the ruin and misery of their fellow creatures; and where those who have partaken of the hospitality of the once opulent owner of the mansion, now come to witness his downfal, regardless of his misfortunes, or else to exult in their own contrasted prosperity." Never were mankind so low in my estimation; and I was hurrying from this scene of heartless selfishness, when I perceived two females engaged in conversation, whose looks were expressive of the sympathy which they felt in it.

On approaching nearer, I heard the names of the Misses B—— pronounced in accents so full of pity and affection, that I paused to listen to the conversation. One of the females, whose appearance bespoke her to belong to the upper class of society, observed in reply to an enquiry of the other, that "The B—— family were all at her house, and perfectly reconciled to their misfortunes; that she hoped enough would remain, after paying the creditors, to enable the family to enjoy the comforts of life, in some retired country residence: that the Misses B—— only regretted their change of

[147] Joshua Reynolds (1723-1792) was the most celebrated 18th-century English painter and the first president of the Royal Academy of Arts. Thomas Lawrence (1769-1830) was the most popular portrait painter during the Regency (he had painted Margaret's portrait). Claude Lorrain (c.1600-1682) was a popular French landscape painter.

[148] Both the Swiss Jean Petitot (1607-1691) and the German Christian Friedrich Zincke (c.1683-1767) were miniature enamel painters.

fortune as dreading its effects on their parents, and as abridging their means of assisting their fellow creatures:" here the emotions of the other female became uncontrollable, and while the tears trickled down her cheeks, she exclaimed, with a fervency that displayed the sincerity of her feelings, "Oh! bless them, bless them! well I know their goodness: they found me out when oppressed by affliction and poverty; despair had nearly overwhelmed me, and I thought Pity and Benevolence had fled from the earth. They relieved my wants with a liberal hand; but, oh! what is of infinitely greater importance, they reconciled me to my fellow beings, and to my God. That I now live, and pursue a course of usefulness and industry, I owe entirely to their humanity; I shudder at reflecting on the fearful crisis to which poverty and despair had reduced me, when those amiable young ladies found me out. By their assistance I am now not only above want, but have a trifle to assist the unfortunate, and I came here to purchase some of the furniture of their own private apartments, which I know they valued from their childhood, in order to have it sent to their future habitation, as a trifling memorial of a gratitude that can end only with my life. But, alas! I am too late; for the auctioneer's clerk has told me that the furniture of their rooms, together with their clothes, books, and musical instruments, are all bought in by a friend; so that I am deprived of this opportunity of proving my gratitude. I have one more effort to make—they will want a domestic, and no where can they find a more attached one than myself. The life which they have preserved shall be devoted to their service."

The expression of the speaker's countenance became radiant with gratitude and benevolence, and the soul-beaming smile of approval with which the other regarded her, as by a gentle pressure of the hand, she marked her heartfelt sympathy, made its way to mine.

I longed to press both within my own; but this the usages of society forbade.

I enquired by a bystander the name of the lady, and on referring to the auctioneer, he disclosed to me in confidence, that she was the purchaser of the furniture, books, clothes, &c. &c &c of the Misses B———, and had given directions to have them all sent to a residence which she has presented to them.

My feelings glowed with delight at finding two such instances of benevolence; and I exclaimed with warmth, "Thank heaven, all goodness has not vanished from the earth! The virtues of those two amiable women have reconciled me to my species; and I find that even the selfish vortex of an AUCTION cannot ingulph true virtue."

157

William Harrison Ainsworth

𝒯HE 𝒲ANDERINGS OF AN 𝒥MMORTAL

(1822)

The author: Ainsworth was born in 1805 in Manchester, where he studied and prepared to become a lawyer. From an early age, however, he had started publishing poems, stories, and fragments of plays in *The Edinburgh Magazine*, *The European Magazine*, and *The London Magazine*. He moved to London and, in 1823, he collected his stories in *The December Tales*, but his father's death forced him to focus on his legal studies and he became a solicitor for the Court of King's Bench. He had his first novel, *Sir John Chiverton*, published in 1826, but only became a professional novelist after the success of *Rockwood* in 1834. This was followed by many other historical novels, including *Crichton* (1837), *Jack Sheppard* (1839), *The Tower of London* (1840), *Guy Fawkes* (1841), *Old St Paul's* (1841), *The Miser's Daughter* (1842), *The Lancashire Witches* (1848) and many others. He also edited for a while his own periodical, *Ainsworth's Magazine*. He continued to publish novels until his death on 3 January 1882.

The text: Submitted as "The Wanderings of an Immortal" to *Blackwood's*, it was rejected in February 1822. It was then accepted and published under the title "The Imperishable One" in the June issue of *The European Magazine and London Review* (510-515), in which he had already published two stories. It was signed "A." One year later, in his collection of *December Tales* (London: G. and W. B. Whittaker, 1823), he included it (125-148) with the original title and gave it two epigraphs. The first was from Barry Cornwall's "Werner" (from one of his *Dramatic Scenes* published in 1819, and included in 1822 in *The Poetical Works of Barry Cornwall* in two volumes; Barry Cornwall was the

The Wanderings of an Immortal

pseudonym of Bryan Procter [1787-1874]): "I/Was spurned and hated—but no more—I am/Immortal now—Hundreds of untold years,/That now lie sleeping in the gulf of time,/Shall rise and roll before me ere I die." The second epigraph is from William Godwin's 1799 novel *St. Leon*, whose main character, like Ainsworth's, finds immortality and is condemned to wander the world: "For me the laws of Nature are suspended: the eternal wheels of the Universe roll backwards: I am destined to be triumphant over Fate and Time. I shall take my distant posterity by the hand; I shall close the tomb over them." This is a fragmentary version of the epigraph Cornwall himself had used for his "Werner." The following is from the 1823 *December Tales*.

It was not a vain desire of life, or a fear of death, that made me long for immortality; nor was it the cupidity of wealth, or the love of splendour, or of pleasure, that made me spend years of anxious study to penetrate into the hidden recesses of Nature, and drag forth those secrets which she has involved in an almost impenetrable obscurity; but it was the desire of revenge, of deep-seated and implacable revenge, that urged me on, till by incredible exertion and minute investigation, I discovered that which it has by turns been the object of philosophy to obtain, and the aim of incredulity to ridicule—the philosopher's stone. And yet, I was naturally of a mild and compassionate disposition. I had a heart open to the tenderest and best emotions of our nature; injury heaped on injury,—received, too, from one whose highest aim ought to have been to manifest the gratitude which he owed to me, who, in the hour of danger and adversity, should have been the readiest to offer assistance,—has rendered me what I am.

It is useless to add to the instances of human depravity. I will not relate the miseries which I endured. I will not look back upon the prospects which have been blasted by the perfidy of him whom I thought a friend; suffice it, that they have been such as the soul shudders to contemplate; such as planted in my soul a thirst of vengeance, which I brooded over, till it became a part of my very existence.

I soon found, that by human means I had little chance of revenge. My enemy was powerful and cautious, and all my plans were anticipated and baffled. I determined to have recourse to darker agents. I had been accustomed to intense and mysterious study, and I knew that there are beings who exercise an influence over human affairs, and are, likewise, themselves in subjection to the wise and omnipotent Being, who is the mover of the first springs of the mighty machine of the universe. I knew, too, that it was possible to

159

exert a power over these beings; and henceforth, I applied the whole force of my mind to the acquisition of the knowledge, which would make me the possessor of this power. Ten long years I employed for this purpose, and my efforts were crowned with success. But though I could summon these spirits before me, and compel them to give an answer to my inquiries, that was all; I could not, I was sensible, subject them entirely to my will, without making, on my part, certain concessions, and to ascertain what these were, was the object of my first trial.

I fixed on a night for this my first essay, and it soon arrived. I repaired to the spot which I had selected. Its secrecy was well calculated for my purpose; it was a dark and lonely glen, but it was rich in romantic beauty. Rocks, whose brinks were covered with underwood and wild herbage, frowned on each side; a few stunted oaks threw out their roots clinging to the precipice, and an immense elm on one side spread its wide arms around. The bottom of the area was covered with dark luxuriant grass, interspersed with wild and fragrant flowers. At one end a narrow but deep river tumbled its waters over the precipice, and rushed down, sometimes almost concealed by jutting fragments of rocks covered with moss and plants, which clung to it as if for protection from the force of the cataract; then again spreading out and dashing its roaring waters along, till it finally vanished under ground in a cloud of mist and foam.

The moon was shining brightly, and I ascended an eminence which commanded an extensive prospect. On one side, wide and fertile plains extended themselves, spotted at a distance with straggling cottages and small hamlets, bounded with forests, whose dark and heavy masses contrasted finely with the light of the adjacent landscape. On the right, the river rolled its waves in calm windings, between banks of lively green, adorned with groves and clusters of trees, till it terminated in the waterfall, which dashed far beneath me with a softened murmur. It was a delightful scene. The sky was beautifully clear; fleecy clouds skimmed over it, lighted up with a silvery lustre that they caught from the moon-beams, which bursting from behind them as they passed, fell on the waters of the stream and the cataract, and trembled on them in liquid beauty. Waves, rocks, woods, plains, all glittered in the lovely rays, and all spoke of peace and harmony.

As I gazed on the beauties which Nature had here scattered with so profuse a hand, I heard the tinkling of a sheep-bell. What associations did this slight sound conjure up to me! All the loved and well-remembered scenes of childhood crowded on my mind. I thought of times and of persons that were fled; of those who were joined to me by kindred, who were united by friendship, or attached by a tender passion. Again, those short but blissful moments were present—perhaps more blissful, because so short—when I had strayed, at this same witching hour, with one whose remembrance will survive the eternity which I am doomed to undergo;—when we had gazed with all the rapture of admiration on the works which attest the power and mightiness of Providence—had listened to the note of the evening songster, and the sighs of the wind among the leaves; and with hearts unstained by one evil thought or passion, and feelings unmixed with aught unworthy, had breathed forth our pure and fervent vows to that Being, whose altar is the sincere bosom, and whose purest, most grateful offering, is a tear.

The night advanced. It was time for me to begin my terrible solemnities. I trembled at the thought of what I was about to do. I hesitated whether to proceed; but the hope of revenge still impelled me on, and I resolved to prosecute my design. It was soon done. The rites were begun; the flame of my lamp blazed clear and bright; I knew the moment was approaching when I should hold communion with beings of another world; perhaps with the prince of darkness himself. I grew faint, a heavy load weighed on my breast, my respiration grew thick and short, my eyes seemed to swell in their sockets, and a cold sweat burst from every pore of my body. The flame wavered—it decreased—it went out. The heavens were darkened: I gazed around, but the gloom was too great for me to see any thing. I looked towards the waterfall, and, amid the mist and obscurity which covered the place of its subterraneous outlet, a star shone with wild and brilliant lustre. It grew larger—it approached me—it stopped, and a brighter radiance was diffused around. The Evil One stood before me.

I gazed with wonder and astonishment on the being that stood before me in terrible beauty. His figure was tall and commanding, and his athletic and sinewy limbs were formed in the most exquisite proportions. His countenance was pale and majestic, but marked with the mingled passions of pride, malice, and regret, which, we conceive, form the character of the rebel angel; and his dark and terrible eyes gave a wilder expression to his features, as they beamed in troubled and preternatural brightness from beneath his awful forehead, shaded with the masses of his raven hair, that curled around his temples, and waved down his neck and shoulders; and amongst the jetty locks, a star, as a diadem, blazed clear and steadily. Never had I seen aught approaching to this grand and unearthly loveliness; I saw him debased by the grossness of sin, and suffering the punishment of his apostacy; yet he was beautiful beyond the sons of men. I saw him thus, and I thought what the spirit must have been before he fell.

Our conversation was brief: I wished not to prolong it, for I was sick at heart, and his voice thrilled through my whole frame. I rejected his offers, strong as was my thirst for vengeance. A small glimmering of cool reason, which I still retained, prevented me from sacrificing all my hopes of hereafter, to the gratification of any passion, however ardent. The demon perceived that I should escape his toils, and all the wild and ungoverned force of his fiendish nature burst forth; and overcome with fear and horror, I fell senseless on the ground. When I awoke, all was still; it was quite light. I felt the light breezes sweep over me, and I heard again the roar of the cataract. I arose and looked round, but there was nothing to indicate the late presence of the demon, with whom I had held unhallowed communion. I departed from the glen; the sun was just rising, and his rays shining on the summits of the lofty and distant hills. The air was sweet and refreshing, and the sky, rich in the glories of the opening morning, was painted with beautiful tints, which blend insensibly with each other, and present so lovely a feast to the eye of one, who loves to study the beauties which Nature offers on every hand, and in almost every prospect. The birds were singing in the trees; the flowers, which had drooped and hung their faded leaves the evening before, again raised up their heads, enamelled with dew; every thing was gentle, beautiful, and peaceful. The charm communicated itself naturally to my disturbed and agitated mind, and for a short time I was calm and serene; the headstrong current of my passions was checked, and the thought of revenge was forgotten. But I returned into the world; I found myself an object, by turns, of scorn and pity, and of hatred. Again, I cursed him who had wrought this wreck of my hopes; and again, was vengeance my only object.

I resolved to have no further communication with the beings of whom I have spoken. I determined, thenceforth, to depend on my own exertions. I again applied myself to study, and began to inquire after that secret which could bestow immortal life and wealth. I sought the assistance of none, but depended entirely on myself. I laboured long, and was long unsuccessful. I ransacked the most hidden cabinet of nature. In the bowels of the earth, in the corruption of the grave, in darkness and in solitude, I worked with unceasing toil. My body was emaciated, and I was worn almost to a skeleton; but the vehemence of my passions supported me. At last, I discovered the object of my search. It will prove how strongly my mind was riveted on one sole object, when I say, that when I beheld myself possessed of boundless riches, and, through their agency, of almost boundless power; when the pleasures and temptations of the world lay all within my grasp, I cast not a thought on them, or on any thing, save the one great object, on the furtherance of which I had bestowed such unremitting toil of body and mind.

The Wanderings of an Immortal

At this period, I learnt that the object of my hatred was going abroad, and I lost no time in preparing secretly to follow him. He shortly departed; and having disguised myself, I also commenced the journey. I was always on the watch for an opportunity when I could surprise my enemy alone; but I was still unsuccessful. We at last arrived at a sea-port town, and it was determined to proceed by water, and I entered as a passenger into the same vessel. I had never before been at sea, and the scene was new and astonishing to me, but I could not enjoy it; I saw every thing through a cloud. The ardent passion of revenge, which burnt within my breast, consumed and obliterated every gentle or pleasant feeling. At another time I should have enjoyed my situation; I should have beheld the seemingly boundless expanse of water around me, and have felt my soul expand at the view; but now I was altered, and my views of surrounding objects altered with me.

I had much trouble to keep concealed, for on board of a ship the risks of discovery were greater, because my absence from the deck, where the other passengers were accustomed to catch the fresh sea breeze, though for some time unnoticed, might at length cause me to be regarded as a misanthrope, who detested the society of his fellow creatures, which I wished to avoid equally with any other surmise which might make me an object of attention. I was standing one evening watching the gradual decline of the sun as he sunk into the heart of the ocean, which reflected his rays, and the lustre of the clouds around him. A sudden motion of the ship caused me to move from the spot on which I was gazing, when I observed some one looking steadily at me. My eye met his—our souls met in the glance—it was he whom I had followed with such relentless hatred. I sprung towards him. I uttered some incoherent words of rage. He smiled at me in scorn. "Madman," he exclaimed, "dost thou tempt my rage?—Be cautious ere it is too late—you are in my power—one word of mine can make you a prisoner; think you that I am ignorant of your proceedings against my life?—No—every plot, every machination is as well known to me as to yourself;—you confess it—your eye says it—seek not to deny it; for this time you are safe." He staid no longer, but retiring to his cabin, left me too astonished with what I had heard, to attempt to detain him. Could it be that he had spoken true? was he indeed so well acquainted with my actions? But if so, why had he not disclosed what he knew, when the civil power could at once have forfeited my life, and deprived him of an enraged foe? Was it that he hesitated to add to his guilt by the death of one whom he had driven to desperation by his treachery? or did some spark of awakening conscience operate on his mind? I was confused with my thoughts, for I knew not what to think; I passed the time in gloomy and painful meditation, and was glad when evening came, that I might retire to my place of repose.

I was awakened by the sound of men trampling over my head, the stretching and creaking of cordage, the dashing of waves, and the violent and repeated motions of the vessel. The wind, which had been remarkably still the preceding day, was blowing with the utmost violence, and roared amongst the sails and rigging of the ship as if it would split them to shivers. It would be useless to attempt to describe what has so often been described far better than I am able to do. I was filled with most dark and melancholy ideas—I paced the cabin in a state of feverish anxiety; but yet I knew not why I felt so. It was not the storm, for my existence was beyond the power of the ocean to destroy. The tempest raged with unabating fury during the whole night. At length a plank of the ship started, and she rapidly filled with water. The boats were got out, and the crew and passengers hastily endeavoured to get into them. The boats were not large enough to contain the whole number, and a dreadful struggle took place; but it was soon terminated by those in the boats cutting the ropes, fearful of perishing, if more were added to their numbers. Just as the boats were cut from the vessel, I saw my hated foe spring out of the ship; he was too late, and was whelmed in the ocean. I thought my hopes of vengeance would be entirely frustrated. I sprung after him. I fell so near him, that I caught hold of him. He grasped me by the throat, and we struggled a moment; but a wave dashed us against the ship's side, and we were parted by the violence of the shock. Daylight was breaking, and occasionally, when lifted up by a wave, I could discern bodies floating amongst casks, planks, and pieces of broken masts. In little more than a minute after we had left the ship, I saw her sink. Her descent made a wide chasm in the waves, and the rush of the parted waters was dreadful, as they closed over, and dashing up their white foam as they met, seemed to exult over their victim. I was dashed about in the water till I was exhausted: I could no longer take my breath, and began to sink; I struggled hard to keep up, but the tempest subsided, and I was no longer borne up by the force of the waves. I descended—they were the most horrible moments of my life. I gasped for breath, but my mouth and throat were instantly filled with water, and the passage totally obstructed; the air confined in my lungs endeavoured in vain to force an outlet; I felt a tightness at the inside of my ears; the external pressure of the water on all sides of my body was very painful, and my eyes felt as if a cord were tied tightly round my brows. At last, by a dreadful convulsion of my whole body, the air was expelled through my windpipe, and forced its way through the water with a gurgling sound:—again the same sensations recurred—and again the same convulsion. Then I cursed

The Wanderings of an Immortal

the hour when I had obtained the fatal possession which hindered me from perishing. Ardently did I long for death to free me from the sufferings which I endured. In a short time I was exhausted, the convulsions became more frequent but less powerful, and I gradually lost all sense and feeling.

How long I continued in this state, buried in the sea, I know not; but when I recovered my recollection, I found myself lying on a rock that jutted out into the ocean. I got up, but could scarcely stand, so great was my weakness; I soon, however, regained my faculties, and my first object was to ascertain where I was. I examined the spot—it was desolate and barren, but it seemed to be of considerable extent. I wandered about till hunger reminded me that I must look for food. A few shell-fish, which I picked up on the shore, satisfied for a time the cravings of my hunger. I then sought for a lodging, which might in some degree shelter me from the fury of the elements. There seemed not to be a tree on the whole surface of the place, nor were the slightest traces of a human habitation visible. At length I discovered a cave, into which I entered, and in which I passed the remainder of the day and the following night. I slept long and soundly, and was greeted, on awaking, by the hoarse and sullen murmurs of the waters breaking against the rock. I advanced to the shore, and strained my eyes over the sea; but nothing was discernible, save the uniform sheet of water, and the black clouds which seemed its only boundary. The day was gloomy, and hoarse sea-birds flew round, screaming and flapping their wings. The hours passed slowly on, and this day passed like the preceding one, except that I discovered a spring of water, which in my present situation was a treasure. At night I retired to my cave, where a little sea-weed, spread upon sand, was my only couch. The next day I determined thoroughly to examine the place on which my unhappy fortune had cast me, and I accordingly set forth, dropping sea-weed and pebbles at short intervals, to enable me to find my way back to the cave. I wandered as near as I could guess about two hours, without perceiving any difference in the scenes around me. I was about to return, when a sound struck my ear. I listened—I turned my head, and beheld at no great distance a human figure. I rushed towards it—it was my enemy! He saw me approach, and seemed astonished; but he did not move, nor attempt to avoid me. "At last," I said, "I have met thee on equal terms; now thou canst not escape me." "What seek you?" replied he; "but I need not ask. It is my life you wish to deprive me of—take it—in so doing, you will rob me of that which I wish not to preserve—a burden that I would gladly lose. You hesitate. Why do you delay now?—vengeance is in your power—do yourself justice—think of the wrongs that you have suffered from me—the miseries you have endured; and then can you remain long inactive?" I knew not what it was, but something restrained me from any deed of violence against him, whom I had followed so long, in hopes of vengeance; whom I had hated with unnatural hatred. While I looked at him he suddenly grew paler; he staggered, and fell down. I found he had fainted—I chafed his temples—I ran for some water, with which I sprinkled his face, and after some time he opened his eyes, but closed them again with a faint shudder. In a few minutes he recovered, but was unable to walk, the hardships he had undergone having weakened his frame, unsupported by the charm which gave strength and endurance to mine. I supported him towards the cave; but the slowness with which we proceeded was such, that it was near evening before we arrived at it. When we came to it, I placed him on my rude couch, and departed in search of food for him and myself. I had much difficulty in doing this, for even the wretched fare on which since being cast on the island I had subsisted, was scanty. When I returned, he was asleep, and I sat down to watch by him.

I have not an idea what it was that induced me at the time to concern myself about the welfare of one, whom I had such reason to detest as this man. It is one of those contradictions which so strongly marked all my actions, and which will ever characterize the proceedings of one of acute feelings and ungoverned passions.

For several days I continued to watch over him, with the attention of a brother; but he was sinking rapidly, and I saw that a very short period would put an end to his existence. During the whole time, he had never spoken; but on the day of his death he broke his silence. He asked why I had attended to his wants, and why I had not rather hastened to wreak my vengeance on him. I would not suffer him to talk long, for he was too feeble to bear the least exertion without injury. But the expression of his countenance spoke for him. His eyes rolled with a wild and frenzied gaze; his features were, by fits, twisted and convulsed with agony, and smothered and lengthened groans burst from him. The evening drew on, and the scene was still more dreadful, by the uncertain and fading light that prevailed. Suddenly he started; he gazed at me, and asked, in a voice which pierced me to the soul, "if I could forgive him?" I did forgive him; God is my witness how sincerely at that moment I forgave every injury, every offence which he had committed against me. He spoke not again. Two hours afterwards, he caught my hand—he pressed it fervently, and his dying look was such as I can never forget. Although I shall live till the last convulsion of the universe shall bury me in the ashes of the world, that look can never be effaced from my memory.

The Wanderings of an Immortal

It was night. I could not remove the body till morning, and the deep silence rendered my situation doubly horrible. The next morning I buried the remains of him, who, while living, had been my direst foe. But every thought of that nature had now departed; my injuries and my thoughts of revenge were alike forgotten. I shortly after left the island: I was taken up by a ship passing near to it, and conveyed again to inhabited countries. Such was the termination of my labours, my sufferings, my hopes, and my fears. When I reflect on the time which was consumed in this fruitless pursuit of revenge, it seems like one of those frightful dreams from which we start in terror, but even when awake feel horror at the thought. The inconsistencies of which I was guilty, more forcibly urge this idea;— while I spent years of loathsome and anxious labours in seeking for that gift, which, when obtained, is a curse to the possessor, I never thought of the probability, that the object of my hatred might die long before I had discovered the secret of which I was in quest. Such is the contradictory conduct of one, over whose actions reason no longer retains any controul.

I am now a lone and solitary being—isolated from the rest of my species, for the social tie which binds man to the world, and connects him with his fellow creatures, cannot long subsist without equality. I mean not the mere equality of birth or fortune. I have, as it were, acquired a nature different from the rest of mankind. The spring of my affections is dried up. Should I strive to acquire friends, to what purpose were it? I should see them drop silently and gradually into the grave, conscious that I was doomed to linger out an eternity. I care not for fame; wealth has no charms for me, for it is in my power to an unlimited extent. I must wander about, alike destitute of hope and of fear, of pleasure or of pain. I look on the past with disgust and inquietude; I regard the future with apathy and listlessness. It may seem egotism in me thus to intrude my personal feelings, but it is thus only that I can convey an idea of the misery, which attends the acquisition of powers, which nature has, for wise purposes, hidden from the grasp of mortals. Thus only can I hope to deter other rash and daring spirits from a like course, by showing the utter and abandoned solitariness, the exhaustion of mental and bodily faculties, and the dead and torpid desolation of spirit, which is the unceasing companion of the Wanderings of an Immortal.

Mary Russell Mitford

Cousin Mary

(1823)

The author: Mary Russell Mitford (1787-1855) was the only surviving child of a physician from Hampshire. She was educated in London and aspired to become a poet and playwright. She first published poetry: *Miscellaneous Poems* (1810), *Christina, the Maid of the South Seas* (1811), *Narrative Poems on the Female Character* (1813), while her plays were staged in 1823 (*Julian*), 1826 (*Foscari*), 1828 (*Rienzi*), and 1834 (*Charles the First*). In March 1821 she began writing short pieces for various publications, some of which were later gathered in the collection *Our Village* (5 volumes from 1824 to 1832), which established her fame. The villagers she wrote about were based on those of Three Mile Cross, a hamlet south of Reading, near London, where she lived most of her life.

The text: First published in 1823 in *The Lady's Magazine* (IV, 237-240) in the 31 May issue, then in the first volume of *Our Village: Sketches of Rural Character and Scenery. By Mary Russell Mitford, Author of Julian, A Tragedy* (London: G. and W. B. Whittaker, Ave-Maria-Lane, 1824). The following is from the fourth edition (London: Geo. B. Whittaker, 1828), in which a few minor changes occur (I, 91-99).

Further reading: J. C. Owen. "Utopia in Little: Mary Russell Mitford and *Our Village*." *Studies in Short Fiction* 5: 3 (Spring 1968), 245-256.

Franco Moretti. *Graphs, Maps, Trees*. London: Verso, 2005. 36-44.

Cousin Mary

About four years ago, passing a few days with the highly educated daughters of some friends in this neighbourhood, I found domesticated in the family a young lady, whom I shall call as they called her, Cousin Mary. She was about eighteen, not beautiful perhaps, but lovely certainly to the fullest extent of that loveliest word—as fresh as a rose; as fair as a lily; with lips like winter berries, dimpled, smiling lips; and eyes of which nobody could tell the colour, they danced so incessantly in their own gay light. Her figure was tall, round, and slender; exquisitely well proportioned it must have been, for in all attitudes, (and in her innocent gaiety, she was scarcely ever two minutes in the same) she was grace itself. She was, in short, the very picture of youth, health, and happiness. No one could see her without being prepossessed in her favour. I took a fancy to her the moment she entered the room; and it increased every hour in spite of, or rather perhaps for, certain deficiencies, which caused poor Cousin Mary to be held exceedingly cheap by her accomplished relatives.

She was the youngest daughter of an officer of rank, dead long ago; and his sickly widow having lost by death, or that other death, marriage, all her children but this, could not, from very fondness, resolve to part with her darling for the purpose of acquiring the commonest instruction. She talked of it, indeed, now and then, but she only talked; so that, in this age of universal education, Mary C. at eighteen exhibited the extraordinary phenomenon of a young woman of high family, whose acquirements were limited to reading, writing, needle-work, and the first rules of arithmetic. The effect of this let-alone system, combined with a careful seclusion from all improper society, and a perfect liberty in her country rambles, acting upon a mind of great power and activity, was the very reverse of what might have been predicted. It had produced not merely a delightful freshness and originality of manner and character, a piquant ignorance of those things of which one is tired to death, but knowledge, positive, accurate, and various knowledge. She was, to be sure, wholly unaccomplished; knew nothing of quadrilles, though her every motion was dancing; nor a note of music, though she used to warble like a bird sweet snatches of old songs, as she skipped up and down the house; nor of painting, except as her taste had been formed by a minute acquaintance with nature into

Mary Russell Mitford

an intense feeling of art. She had that real extra sense, an eye for colour, too, as well as an ear for music. Not one in twenty—not one in a hundred of our sketching and copying ladies could love and appreciate a picture where there was colour and mind, a picture by Claude, or by our English Claudes Wilson and Hoffland,[149] as she could—for she loved landscape best, because she understood it best—it was a portrait of which she knew the original. Then her needle was in her hands almost a pencil. I never knew such an embroidress—she would sit "printing her thoughts on lawn,"[150] till the delicate creation vied with the snowy tracery, the fantastic carving of hoar frost, the richness of Gothic architecture, or of that which so much resembles it, the luxuriant fancy of old point lace. That was her only accomplishment, and a rare artist she was—muslin and net were her canvas. She had no French either, not a word; no Italian; but then her English was racy, unhackneyed, proper to the thought to a degree that only original thinking could give. She had not much reading, except of the Bible and Shakspeare, and Richardson's novels, in which she was learned; but then her powers of observation were sharpened and quickened, in a very unusual degree, by the leisure and opportunity afforded for their development, at a time of life when they are most acute. She had nothing to distract her mind. Her attention was always awake and alive. She was an excellent and curious naturalist, merely because she had gone into the fields with her eyes open; and knew all the details of rural management, domestic or agricultural, as well as the peculiar habits and modes of thinking of the peasantry, simply because she had lived in the country, and made use of her ears. Then she was fanciful, recollective, new; drew her images from the real objects, not from their shadows in books. In short, to listen to her, and the young ladies her companions, who, accomplished to the height, had trodden the education-mill till they all moved in one step, had lost sense in sound, and ideas in words, was enough to make us turn masters and governesses out of doors, and leave

---

[149] Claude Lorrain (see note 147), also known simply as Claude in England, was a French painter whose name was synonymous with the art of landscape painting. Richard Wilson (1714-1782) was the most important landscape painter of 18th-century Britain. Thomas Christopher Hofland (1777-1843) was at the time a respected painter married to Barbara Hofland (1770-1844), children's author and short-story writer, a good friend of Mitford's.

[150] Paraphrase of a line from Beaumont and Fletcher's Jacobean play *Philaster*. "Lawn" is a fine linen fabric (originally from Laon, in France).

Cousin Mary

our daughters and grand-daughters to Mrs. C.'s system of non-instruction. I should have liked to meet with another specimen, just to ascertain whether the peculiar charm and advantage arose from the quick and active mind of this fair Ignorant, or was really the natural and inevitable result of the training; but, alas! to find more than one unaccomplished young lady, in this accomplished age, is not to be hoped for. So I admired and envied; and her fair kinswomen pitied and scorned, and tried to teach; and Mary, never made for a learner, and as full of animal spirits as a school-boy in the holidays, sang, and laughed, and skipped about from morning to night.[151]

It must be confessed, as a counter-balance to her other perfections, that the dear Cousin Mary was, as far as great natural modesty and an occasional touch of shyness would let her, the least in the world of romp! She loved to toss about children, to jump over stiles, to scramble through hedges, to climb trees; and some of her knowledge of plants and birds may certainly have arisen from her delight in these boyish amusements. And which of us has not found that the strongest, the healthiest, and most flourishing acquirement has arisen from pleasure or accident, has been in a manner self-sown, like an oak of the forest?—Oh she was a sad romp; as skittish as a wild colt, as uncertain as a butterfly, as uncatchable as a swallow! But her great personal beauty, the charm, grace, and lightness of her movements, and above all, her evident innocence of heart, were bribes to indulgence which no one could withstand. I never heard her blamed by any human being. The perfect unrestraint of her attitudes, and the exquisite symmetry of her form, would have rendered her an invaluable study for a painter. Her daily doings would have formed a series of pictures. I have seen her scudding through a shallow rivulet, with her petticoats caught up just a little above the ancle, like a young Diana, and a bounding, skimming, enjoying motion, as if native to the element, which might have become a Naiad. I have seen her on the topmost round of a ladder, with one foot on the roof of a house, flinging down the grapes that no one else had nerve enough to reach, laughing,

---

[151] The term "animal spirits" originates in Ancient Greece, but it was later made popular by René Descartes (1596-1650), who understood them as a fluid that transmits information from the mind to the body. It became obsolete once electrical impulses in the body and the role of neurons were better understood in the mid- and late 19th century. Early psychological studies believed some people had more and others less of the fluid.

and garlanded, and crowned with vine-leaves, like a Bacchante.[152] But the prettiest combination of circumstances under which I ever saw her, was driving a donkey cart up a hill one sunny windy day, in September. It was a gay party of young women, some walking, some in open carriages of different descriptions, bent to see a celebrated prospect from a hill called the Ridges. The ascent was by a steep narrow lane, cut deeply between sand-banks, crowned with high, feathery hedges. The road and its picturesque banks lay bathed in the golden sunshine, whilst the autumnal sky, intensely blue, appeared at the top as through an arch. The hill was so steep that we had all dismounted, and left our different vehicles in charge of the servants below; but Mary, to whom, as incomparably the best charioteer, the conduct of a certain non-descript machine, a sort of donkey curricle, had fallen, determined to drive a delicate little girl, who was afraid of the walk, to the top of the eminence. She jumped out for the purpose, and we followed, watching and admiring her as she won her way up the hill: now tugging at the donkeys in front with her bright face towards them and us, and springing along backwards—now pushing the chaise from behind—now running by the side of her steeds, patting and caressing them—now soothing the half-frightened child—now laughing, nodding, and shaking her little whip at us—darting about like some winged creature—till at last she stopped at the top of the ascent, and stood for a moment on the summit, her straw bonnet blown back, and held on only by the strings; her brown hair playing on the wind in long natural ringlets; her complexion becoming every moment more splendid from exertion, redder and whiter; her eyes and her smile brightening and dimpling; her figure in its simple white gown, strongly relieved by the deep blue sky, and her whole form seeming to dilate before our eyes. There she stood under the arch formed by two meeting elms, a Hebe, a Psyche, a perfect goddess of youth and joy.[153] The Ridges are very fine things altogether, especially the part to which we were bound, a turfy breezy spot, sinking down

---

[152] Diana (called Artemis in Ancient Greece) is the Roman goddess of the hunt, of childbirth and women, often represented in painting and sculpture as athletic and involved in hunting. A naiad, in Greek mythology, is a nymph protecting rivers and lakes. A bacchante (Roman version of a Greek maenad) is a female follower of Bacchus, the god of wine and ecstasy (Dionysus in Greek mythology), usually represented as full of frenzy and excitement.

[153] Hebe is the Greek goddess of youth. Psyche is the heroine of an Ancient Greek love story; after many tribulations, she marries Cupid, the god of erotic love. Her story is very old, but it is known especially in the version told by Apuleius in his late-1st-century novel *The Golden Ass*.

Cousin Mary

abruptly like a rock into a wild foreground of heath and forest, with a magnificent command of distant objects;—but we saw nothing that day like the figure on the top of the hill.

After this I lost sight of her for a long time. She was called suddenly home by the dangerous illness of her mother, who, after languishing for some months, died; and Mary went to live with a sister much older than herself, and richly married in a manufacturing town, where she languished in smoke, confinement, dependence, and display, (for her sister was a match-making lady, a manœuvrer,) for about a twelvemonth. She then left her house and went into Wales—as a governess! Imagine the astonishment caused by this intelligence amongst us all; for myself, though admiring the untaught damsel almost as much as I loved her, should certainly never have dreamed of her as a teacher. However, she remained in the rich baronet's family where she had commenced her vocation. They liked her apparently,—there she was; and again nothing was heard of her for many months, until, happening to call on the friends at whose house I had originally met her, I espied her fair blooming face, a rose amongst roses, at the drawing-room window,—and instantly with the speed of light was met and embraced by her at the hall-door.

There was not the slightest perceptible difference in her deportment. She still bounded like a fawn, and laughed and clapped her hands like an infant. She was not a day older, or graver, or wiser, since we parted. Her post of tutoress had at least done *her* no harm, whatever might have been the case with her pupils. The more I looked at her the more I wondered; and after our mutual expressions of pleasure had a little subsided, I could not resist the temptation of saying,—"So you are really a governess?"—"Yes."—"And you continue in the same family?"—"Yes."—"And you like your post!"—"O yes! yes!"—"But, my dear Mary, what could induce you to go?"—"Why, they wanted a governess, so I went."—"But what could induce them to keep you?" The perfect gravity and earnestness with which this question was put set her laughing, and the laugh was echoed back from a group at the end of the room, which I had not before noticed—an elegant man in the prime of life shewing a portfolio of rare prints to a fine girl of twelve, and a rosy boy of seven, evidently his children. "Why did they keep me? Ask them," replied Mary, turning towards them with an arch smile. "We kept her to teach her ourselves," said the young lady. "We kept her to play cricket with us," said her brother. "We kept her to marry," said the gentleman, advancing gaily to shake hands with me. "She

173

was a bad governess, perhaps; but she is an excellent wife—that is her true vocation." And so it is. She is, indeed, an excellent wife; and assuredly a most fortunate one. I never saw happiness so sparkling or so glowing; never saw such devotion to a bride, or such fondness for a step-mother, as Sir W. S. and his lovely children show to the sweet Cousin Mary.

Amelia Opie
A NEW TALE OF TEMPER

(1823)

The author: In 1820, Opie published *Tales of the Heart*, followed by two more novels, *The Only Child* (1821) and *Madeline: A Tale* (1822). In 1825, she joined the Society of Friends. Her father died the same year. She became more and more involved in the anti-slavery movement. She died in 1853, in Norwich.

The text: First published in *Friendship's Offering; or, The Annual Remembrancer. A Christmas Present, or, New Year's Gift for 1824* (London: Lupton Relfe, 1824 [1823]), 66-93. It was the only short story of the volume, which also included several poems by Opie. An abbreviated form appeared in *The Minerva* of 3 July 1824 (a New York magazine), I: 13, 193-199. The American text includes a few corrections, which have been taken into account here, although the following reproduces the original version from 1823.

"Well, my dear friend," said George Mowbray to Mrs. Sullivan, "I hope you will be satisfied now, for I have serious thoughts of marrying." "I shall not only be satisfied, but delighted," she replied, "if you make a choice worthy of you."

George Mowbray was an orphan who had inherited a large fortune from honourable ancestors, and in him, as he had neither brother nor sister, was centred all the accumulated wealth of his family. He had no vices; some virtues and talents; some learning; a great deal of taste; and a love for travelling and wandering about,

175

which had led him to remain single till nine and twenty, in spite of the earnest advice of Mrs. Sullivan, though her influence over Mowbray's mind was unquestionably great.

Mrs. Sullivan had been left a widow early in life, but had never formed a second connection; and had passed the greatest part of her time with Mowbray's widowed mother, till that lady died. She had therefore been very early interested in the fate of George Mowbray: and her sweetness of temper, her amusing talents, and the superiority of her understanding, made her society a constant source of benefit and pleasure to him, when, on Mrs. Mowbray's death, she took up her abode in the village adjoining Mowbray's estate.

Indeed, the tie was perfect which subsisted between them. Perhaps there is no friendship so entire, and so little likely to be injured by the usual accidents of life, as that which subsists between two persons of different sexes, where the difference of age, and other circumstances, make a tenderer attachment improbable, and marriage impossible. There can be no competition, no rivalship, between friends of different sexes. They can rejoice cordially in each other's welfare, and sincerely mourn over each other's adversity; and, with all its advantages, such was the friendship of Mrs. Sullivan and George Mowbray.

To her he imparted all his pleasures and his pains, his hopes and his fears; but hitherto they had not been those of a progressive attachment; now, however, to her great joy, there seemed a prospect of his having much to communicate; and she eagerly exclaimed, "Well, George, go on! is the wife found, or have you only resolved to look about for one?"

"She is found; and I verily believe I am now, for the first time in my life, really in love."—"I am glad of it; but who is the lady?"

"Do you not remember saying to me, as we were walking one evening at Tunbridge Wells,[154] Look, George! what a beautiful girl that is?" "I do," replied Mrs. Sullivan gravely. "So, then, it is Miss Apsley whom you have chosen for your wife." "It is that identical beauty, whom your good taste pointed out to me. While you were in London, her father, who has retired from business, hired that pretty house across the common which you admire so much."—"Indeed! Did you become acquainted with the family before he hired it?" "Yes, after you left the Wells, I was introduced to them; therefore, as soon as they came hither, I called on them." "No doubt." "And I soon found that I was almost in love." "Then it is still only *almost*

[154] Royal Tunbridge Wells, a town in Kent which became a fashionable resort in the mid-18th century.

A New Tale of Temper

in love?" "I am too old to love without some discretion, and I have taken care to be very *guarded* in my advances, as I wish to know something of the young lady's disposition and temper before I come forward as a lover."

"Very—wise but how are you to acquire this knowledge?" "I shall be observant and watchful myself, and you perhaps will assist me with your penetration." "But the real temper of man or woman can be found out entirely, only by living in the same house, or going a journey with the object of one's solicitude." "True—but, where there is a family, I think it can be discovered by tell-tale looks at each other, sudden sharpnesses of tone, and brusqueries of manner." "Perhaps so—and has Miss Apsley brothers and sisters?" "One brother, and two sisters." "Well, all I request is, that you will not let love throw prudence off her guard. We are agreed, that good temper is the most necessary quality in marriage—not for itself alone; but because it implies other good things in its possessor, namely, piety and good sense—as, without these, there can be no self-government, consequently, no good temper." "Yes—such is my opinion—and thence my projected caution."—"Which will be perhaps peculiarly necessary *here*." "Why that emphasis on here, my dear friend?"—"Because I once saw Miss Apsley in a milliner's shop with her mother, and when the latter contradicted her she had a suspicious nip of the brow, and answered in a sharp tone of voice."—"Impossible!—her brows are light—If they had been *black*, indeed! And as to her voice, her mother is so *deaf*, that she was forced to speak *loud*, and you mistook loudness for sharpness."— "But the *milliner* was not deaf—and she spoke to her in the same manner, till she saw me, and then her voice became soft and pleasing again."

"I am sorry," said Mowbray, rather pettishly, "that you are so prepossessed *against* Miss Apsley."—"Nay, there you are unjust—I know that a hasty judgement is likely to be an erroneous one, I have therefore no faith in mine."—"But will you call on the Apsleys?"— "Certainly, it is a duty which I owe you."—"It will be a benefit conferred on me, as I think highly of your penetration, you know; and as the day is fine, suppose we go now?"

They did go, but the family were out. The next day the call was returned—and so sweet was Miss Apsley's voice, so unruffled her brow, that Mrs. Sullivan was almost convinced she had judged her harshly. In the evening, Mowbray came to say, that, though she never went to evening parties, or any parties, he hoped she would accompany him the next day to tea at Mrs. Apsley's. "There will be (said he) no company—no cards—only a little family music,

177

which you, I know, will like."—"Oh yes,"—replied Mrs. Sullivan; "I will certainly go—as I am impatient to become acquainted with the fair Lavinia." Mowbray's park joined Mr. Apsley's garden; and, having borrowed the key of the garden door, he conducted Mrs. Sullivan that way to the house. As the evening was fine, and the French windows of the drawing room, which opened on the lawn, were thrown open, the senses of the visitors, as they drew near, were regaled by the perfumes from a conservatory into which the sitting room opened, and their ears by a glee sweetly sung by the young members of the family. While, ever and anon, the pauses in the singing were filled with expressions of admiration from the parents; and dear Mamma, dear Papa, darling John, dearest Julia, sweet Lavinia, words of affectionate import, met the ears of the involuntary, and, as *they believed*, unobserved listeners. "This is, indeed, *family harmony* in more senses than one," said Mrs. Sullivan as she entered the house, while George replied by a smile of sweet delight.

Every thing which Mrs. Sullivan saw, and heard during the evening, accorded with this favourable impression. Still, she could not help remembering that there are such things as company-looks, tones, and manners, as well as dress. Mrs. Apsley was deaf, as Mowbray had observed; and it seemed an habitual duty with Lavinia, to repeat to her dear Mamma all that was said which was worth notice. Her dear Papa was gouty and lame, and her arm was kindly offered to him on all occasions—while her eye was attentive to all his wants. Her tones to her brother and sisters were the essence of sweetness—and she seemed desirous of bringing forward into notice an ill-dressed, timid girl, with a pale cheek and downcast eye, whose name had been muttered, rather than pronounced, by Mrs. Apsley, when Mrs. Sullivan entered, and who was, she concluded, *a nobody*—a dependant on the family. It seemed therefore an amiable trait in Lavinia to notice her, and Mrs. Sullivan's kind heart made her eager to notice her herself. Nor could she help being much pleased with this nobody, whose name was Mary Medway; for the pale cheek could, she found, be crimsoned by sensibility, and the downcast eye could light up with intelligence. That eye had also an expression which is touching and interesting in a person of any age, but particularly so in the young, from the contrast it forms with youthful hopes. For either eye had an expression of *resignation*: it seemed to say, that the hopes of her youth had been prematurely

A New Tale of Temper

blighted; that she had suffered, still suffered, and was content to suffer. But Mrs. Sullivan came to admire Lavinia; she therefore tried to give *her* her undivided attention.

After tea, the brother and sister sung glees; then Lavinia sung alone, accompanying herself on the harp. While Mowbray hung over her enamoured, Mary Medway meanwhile took her work, and retired to a corner, as if unable to bear a part in the concert. "Do you not sing, Miss Medway?" said Mrs. Sullivan. "Oh, no, Madam," was the reply, "that is, I do not sing well enough to sing in company."—"No, no," cried Mr. Apsley, "Mary is no singer."—"Is she not?" replied John, with a tone of peculiar meaning; "but how do you know, sir? I am sure you never heard her." Mrs. Sullivan thought, as John said this, that Lavinia looked at her brother with that nip of the brow and flashing eye, which she had observed in the shop; but then it might be meant to reprove the disrespectful tone in which he addressed his father; and as she called him, soon after, "dearest John," and told him he should not make Mary blush by talking of her singing, she supposed she was unjust.

It was late before they took leave; and as they went home, she gladdened the heart of her friend, by telling him, that she really thought he might allow himself to love Lavinia, but that he need not be in a hurry to propose to her. "Why not? I have no doubt that she always is such as you now see her, gentle and affectionate to her parents, and the rest of the family, and that she will be such a wife!"—"Perhaps so; but becoming manners are sometimes put on with becoming dress—and—did you see the look she gave her brother, when he insinuated that Miss Medway could sing?"—"Yes."—"Was it not a vixenish look?"—"No, it was a justly reproving one; for it seemed as if he was laughing at the poor girl: she can't sing, and he ought not to laugh at a girl in her situation."

"A-propos—who is Miss Medway?"—"An orphan, and distant relation of the family, whom they have taken in on charity. She was born an heiress, but speculation ruined her father, and he died in a jail."—"Poor thing!" replied Mrs. Sullivan, adding, after a pause, "I hope they are kind to her!"—"Can you doubt it?" answered Mowbray rather pettishly; "but perhaps you do, as you could fancy Lavinia's look vixenish, and that she has a suspicious nip of the brow."—"I must own, spite of your frowns, that I see it still, and that doubts of her temper still cling to me."

"Surprising! light brows and eyes are commonly thought to give an impression of good humour; had she dark hair and eyes, like Miss Medway, then you might distrust her."—"Pardon me, but

179

had her eyes been like her cousin's, I should have had no distrust, for a milder, sweeter eye than Miss Medway's, I never parleyed with: I like that girl, she interests me excessively."—"What! that dowdy thing! you surprise me!"—"She is dowdily dressed, but no dowdy."—"May be so, but really I have scarcely looked at her, and I wonder you could, as you have such an eye for beauty and grace."—"I have an eye for expression also, and hers pleases me."—Mowbray was really piqued, and provoked, at this avowal; and as there is no one so apt to be unjust as a man in love, except it be a *woman* in the same situation, he suspected his dear friend was hurt at his having formed an attachment, and was averse, spite of her professed disinterestedness, at his being devoted to any other woman than herself; but the next moment he was ashamed of so unworthy a suspicion. However, he was glad that it was too late for him to continue the conversation, and he eagerly bade her good night. It was not long before the Apsleys were invited to return the visit, but Miss Medway did not come with them, though Mrs. Sullivan expressly invited her; but she had a head ache, they said, and could not come out. "What are you so loudly regretting?" said Mowbray to Mrs. Sullivan. "Miss Medway's absence, and her being too unwell to favour me with her company." On hearing this, Mowbray abruptly turned away, almost articulating, "Pshaw!" But Mrs. Sullivan did not observe him. She was taken up in reflecting on the peculiar expression with which John Apsley regarded Lavinia, while she was expressing her regrets. It was a look full of malicious meaning, and, she thought, of triumph also. There was a *dessein des cartes*[155] which she did not understand, and it made her thoughtful. But Mowbray had no eyes or ears for any thing but Lavinia; and when Mrs. Sullivan looked at her, and listened to her, she did not wonder at his infatuation.

During a whole month this visiting intercourse continued. The Apsleys knew that it was paying court to Mowbray, to shew great attention to his maternal friend, and Lavinia lost no opportunity of endeavouring to win her good opinion. But increased association with this family did not give rise to increased confidence in Mrs. Sullivan's mind; and, though she knew not exactly why, the pale, dowdy, dependant girl, and the abrupt John, were the only persons who seemed to her natural characters. She, therefore, exerted all

[155] A move in a card game that is supposed to be executed by two players from the same team (we correct here the French of the original, which reads "dessine des cartes").

her influence over Mowbray, to prevail on him to delay his offer awhile longer. To this he most reluctantly consented, and not without having fixed a day, at a fortnight's distance, for making his proposals: which day was rapidly approaching, when the Apsleys requested Mrs. Sullivan and Mowbray to dine with them, to partake of some fine moor-game.[156]

That day Lavinia was more than usually gay and beautiful, her mother more than usually deaf, her father more than usually lame, and her filial attentions more valued, and more marked. Mary Medway did not dine at home, but she returned in the evening, and in evident dejection. "Is she come?" said John, kindly, to her in a low voice—"Oh! yes, but she would not let me stay with her."—"I like her for that: I can't bear that you should run the risk of making yourself ill, Mary." Mrs. Sullivan's eye now turned on Mary with an expression of benevolent approbation, and she wished to hear more of the conversation; but Lavinia came between her and them, and, coaxing Mary's hair affectionately, and kissing her forehead, she called her "dear girl," with a degree of kind interest, which gave a favourable impression of her heart to Mrs. Sullivan, and made her ashamed of not loving her more than she did.

Mowbray now requested Lavinia to sing to the harp, and, while she was tuning her instrument, he stood lost in admiration of the beauty of her shoulders, and the back of her neck and head, as she bent over the strings.—At this moment John ran against the harp; and as Mary, who was passing, suddenly started back, to avoid John's treading on her foot, her work basket caught a part of Lavinia's dress of French work, and tore it. Lavinia's first impulse was evidently to give way to violent reproach against the carelessness of both; but she made an effort, and, forcing a laugh, cried "Careless brother! but I forgive you!" while her faultering tone, and the crimson which spread itself over her back, convinced Mrs. Sullivan that she was in a passion, though she could not see her face. "And mistress of herself, though her dress is torn!" cried Mowbray, rather *mal à-propos*, as his friend thought; but Lavinia smiled sweetly on him, and the flush of anger was mistaken by him for that of emotion at his praise. He might have been undeceived, however, if love had not blinded him; for as a pet dog jumped upon her, while she was preluding, Lavinia vented her concealed rage by giving it a blow, which sent it crying away. "Poor, little dear! I had no intention of hurting it," said she, alarmed at what she had done, "but that dog cries at a touch."—

---

[156] An old term for the red grouse, a common game bird in the British Isles.

"Any dog would cry out at such a touch as that," cried John, surlily. "You are always so cross to your sister, John," said the father. "She is always cross to him," said one of the younger girls, loud enough for her mother to hear. "How can you say so," said she, "but you always take John's part, Laura, and never do Lavinia justice."—"O yes, sometimes she does indeed, mamma," said Lavinia, "though I own I am jealous of her love for John. Come, thou cross darling! come, and sing a duet with me!" and Laura, in whose ear her mother whispered, smiled on her sister, returned her offered kiss, and sung as she was bidden. "How amiable, and how forbearing!" thought Mowbray, "was Lavinia's behaviour! and how I dislike that John's unkindness to her!" Mrs. Sullivan thought differently, and sighed when she recollected that, in a few hours more, perhaps, the offer would be made, and Mowbray's fate fixed.

As the evening was warm, and the moon shone very bright, Mrs. Sullivan and Mowbray walked home. "To what advantage Lavinia appeared this evening!" said Mowbray; "I hope you are convinced her temper is excellent now!"—"My dear George," she replied, "I never before was so convinced of the contrary!"—"Impossible! well, then, you are not the candid, kind creature that I once thought you." At this moment Mrs. Sullivan missed her bracelet, the gift of Mrs. Mowbray, and declared she must go back, for, no doubt, she had dropped it on the path, as she had, she believed, seen it on her wrist when she left the house. "Let me go back alone," said Mowbray; but she would not consent to it, as she could not be easy without seeking herself for a jewel so dear to her. Accordingly they slowly returned, searching for the bracelet at every step—but they had already reached Mr. Apsley's lawn without finding it, when they stopped at the sound of male and female voices in loud altercation. "What noise is that?" said Mrs. Sullivan. "I cannot tell," replied Mowbray hastily, "but you had better stop here, and I will go and look for the bracelet."—"No, I choose to go myself;" she replied, grasping his arm to prevent him from hastening on. By this means she ensured a continuance of their incognito, and thence she also hoped to ensure the detection of Lavinia's real disposition, for she was certain that she heard her voice the shrillest and loudest amongst them. She also heard epithets of an offensive nature applied by John to Lavinia, to which she replied in terms equally offensive, while the father tried to sooth, and the mother was sobbing hysterically.

"Surely we had better go back," said Mowbray, in a dejected tone, "we are stealing unhandsomely on their privacy."—"On, by all means," his friend replied, "for perhaps on this moment the happiness of your future life depends." So saying, she hastened forward; then, suddenly turning, she and her companion stood in front of the open French windows. There, what a scene presented itself! Mary Medway, with a countenance of mild distress, stood between John and Lavinia, trying to keep Lavinia from striking her brother, while the florid face of the former was pale, and every fine feature distorted with passion. "Hear me, Lavinia," sobbed out the mother.—"Rather hear *me*," she replied, stamping with anger, "for I know you can hear very well when you choose."—"Hold your taunting tongue, you abominable vixen!" cried the justly incensed father, seizing her arm as he hobbled forward; but with her elbow she pushed him from her, regardless of his lameness, and he nearly fell on the ground. At this instant the angry group turned, and beheld Mrs. Sullivan and Mowbray gazing on them in speechless and motionless surprise. In a moment the clamour was hushed— the lifted arm of Lavinia sunk by her side; and all, save the angry John and Mary Medway, fell back, consternated and ashamed.

"We beg pardon," said Mrs. Sullivan, coldly, "for intruding thus unexpectedly upon you, but I have dropped a most dear bracelet."— "I think, Mrs. Sullivan," said John, with a sarcastic smile, "that you complimented us when you first honoured us with a visit on our *family harmony*. Pray what do you think of it now? There's a vixen for you!" pointing to Lavinia. "The man who marries you, Miss Apsley, will have, as Benedict says, a predestinate scratched face.[157] I must wear a wig, for such pulls of the hair as you give are by no means pleasant."

Lavinia looked as if she had a mind to reiterate the said pulls, but she only burst into tears of rage and mortification, for she saw that Mowbray's eyes were averted from her, as if with disgust, and feared that she could never regain his good opinion. But her mother, by a white lie, tried to exculpate her in part. She said, that though Lavinia was rather hasty, she had a fine temper, and that John was monstrously provoking, always defending Mary Medway, and setting her up as a paragon. "And so she is," vociferated John, "when did you ever see her in a passion? and when taunted and tyrannized over, does she *ever* reply? When you made her give up

---

[157] Benedict, a character in Shakespeare's *Much Ado about Nothing*, addresses thus Beatrice (who confesses she is happy as long as she does not have to hear a man's declaration of love): "God keep your ladyship still in that mind! so some gentleman or other shall 'scape a predestinate scratched face" (Act I, Scene I).

going to Mrs. Sullivan's, because you wanted her to finish a gown for Lavinia, did she express one regret, though you know she had reckoned on going? Answer me that!" But his mother spoke not, for the unexpected truth filled her with consternation.—"And now," continued he, "when the poor thing has been acting a child's part by her dying nurse, and is tired to death, it was cruel in Lavinia to abuse her as she did for tearing her gown."—"I did not abuse, I only said she was awkward," replied Lavinia, sobbing. "And why did you say that, when you know that she offered to sit up all night to mend it?" "Dear John, pray say no more," said Mary, gently. "But I will speak, I will not sit tamely by and see you insulted, Mary—you, who never speak a harsh word yourself."—"You forget who are present," she answered, in a low voice. "No, I do not; I love the *truth*, and hate *disguise*; I should not like to be imposed upon myself!" he added, looking with great meaning at Mowbray.

"I have found the bracelet!" exclaimed Mrs. Sullivan, joyfully, who, with one of the younger girls, had been looking for it all this time, but listening carefully to every word that passed; then, with renewed apologies, she shook Mary kindly by the hand, slightly bowed to the rest, and taking the arm of the confused and bewildered Mowbray, led him in silence away.

In silence too he continued to walk, but deep-drawn sighs declared only too plainly the mortification and disappointment which he experienced. Mrs. Sullivan was too wise to make any comments. Had she made any severe remarks on Lavinia's conduct, she knew it would only provoke Mowbray to defend her, and for her to say any thing in palliation of it was impossible. "Will you not walk in?" said she to Mowbray, when they reached the door; but he refused, and went home to a sleepless and wretched pillow.

"Poor fellow!" thought Mrs. Sullivan. "He will not sleep tonight; but the wakeful misery of this night will, I trust, prevent that of many future ones; for happy, indeed, is that man, who, at whatever cost of present peace, escapes the wretchedness of a woman who possesses no control over her temper, and is that formidable person yclept a vixen!"

The next morning, but not early, Mowbray called on Mrs. Sullivan, who delicately forbore to speak to him concerning the event of the preceding evening, anxiously expecting, however, that he would name it to her. Nor was she disappointed. After making a considerable effort, he complimented her on her superior penetration into character, owned that he was now convinced Miss Apsley was not a woman with whom he could be happy, and thanked her heartily for having prevailed on him to defer his intended proposals. "Then you are resolved not to proceed in your addresses."—"To be sure; could you doubt what my resolve would be?"—"I could not tell, but I rejoice to find you so reasonable: but what will you do? gradually, or at *once* discontinue your visits?"—"I mean to go *abroad*. Vixen and actress as she is, (for I am sure you think as I now do, that her filial attentions are assumed) she is too handsome and too charming for me to trust myself near her as yet; therefore I mean to set off directly."—"A wise determination, indeed, and I shall be disinterested enough to rejoice in an absence which is so much for your good. Poor Mary Medway! what a life that sweet amiable girl must lead!"—"Pray, pray do not name her to me. She was the cause, you find, of all this misery."—"This happiness, you mean, ungrateful man! and you have reason to bless her."—"May be so; but my associations with her name are at present disagreeable ones. Farewell! my dear friend. When we meet again, I trust that I shall have come to my senses. Till then, all good be with you!"—"Shall you not call to take leave of the Apsleys?"—"Yes, for I saw them all drive out just now, so I shall, for form's sake, leave my card.—Once more, farewell!"

Like all men and women in love, Mowbray found that distance and absence from the object of attachment, does not at first weaken its power—and he was often on the point of coming back to England, in the hope that Lavinia returned his passion sufficiently to be induced to conquer her temper, now that she must be convinced the indulgence of it had lost her a lover whom she prized. But then he fortunately recollected, that the habit of giving way to it, was a habit of a much longer standing than that of caring for him; and that when he was her husband, the restraint would doubtless be again thrown off, even if it were ever assumed in reality—for was she not an actress? a being, who, for the purposes of pleasing, could assume the virtues which she had not?

The result of these cogitations was salutary—for it kept him abroad. In the mean while, Mrs. Sullivan had some difficulty in breaking off her intercourse with the Apsleys, whom she had made an acquaintance with only from necessity, and whom she now wished to drop from inclination. They were not willing to give up her society, though Lavinia evidently was never at ease in her presence, because they still hoped to receive Mowbray as a guest again; but as he did not return, and Mrs. Sullivan never accepted their invitations, they quitted their house when their short lease of it expired, and went to another part of the kingdom.

Mrs. Sullivan would fain have become more acquainted, had it been possible, with Mary Medway; but this she could not do without passing an obvious affront on the Apsleys; and when that family left the village, she regretted her inability to take a particular leave of her.

It was, therefore, an agreeable surprise to her to meet Miss Medway, not long after, in one of her evening walks. The poor thing was even worse dressed than usual, looked dejected, and had a vial of physic[158] in her hand.

She did not seem desirous of being known by Mrs. Sullivan; but that lady impulsively stopped her, and expressing her joyful surprise at seeing her, requested to know whether she had left Mr. Apsley's family.

She owned, with blushes and confusion, that she had done so, and was living at the cottage of her old nurse, who was, she feared, dying.—"But when she is dead, or better, you return to them, I conclude."—"No—never—I can never return to them," was the agitated answer. "I am going home; will you accompany me," said Mrs. Sullivan, kindly. "Not now; I must hasten back with this medicine."—"But may I accompany you?—I pique myself on my medical knowledge."—"But the cottage is such a poor place for you."—"Yet you inhabit it; and to enter it may be salutary to me."

Mary, seeing Mrs. Sullivan was determined, led the way. The cottage was, indeed, the abode of poverty, but of neatness almost approaching to comfort; and her visit to it was the means of great enjoyment to Mrs. Sullivan, for she saw there suffering and want, which she had the means of alleviating and removing; and she had the pleasure of hearing from the lips of the dying woman, such a character of her youthful nurse, such an account of the self-denial and self-sacrifice of her dear young lady, and child, as she called her, as more than justified the early impression which she had received in her favour.

To be brief, the poor woman died; and Mary Medway, as she threw herself into Mrs. Sullivan's arms when she came to her on hearing of her loss, exclaimed, in the bitterness of her heart, "Now then, I am indeed alone in the world!"—"And so am I nearly, as my adopted son is abroad!" was the kind reply: "therefore what can two lonely persons do better than live together, at least for a time?"

The heart of the poor orphan gave ready assent to this proposal—"but," she replied, "you do not yet know why I was forced to leave the Apsleys."—"Nor will I, till you are my guest, for I wish to convince you that I confide in you, and do not believe that you left them for any unworthy reason."

[158] Medicine; any medicinal substance.

A New Tale of Temper

Mary, however, insisted on being allowed to tell her story very soon after she became Mrs. Sullivan's companion. She informed her new friend, that, on finding John Apsley was seriously attached to her, and had offered her marriage, his parents had made her quit the house at a moment's warning; and that she had taken refuge at her nurse's. That she had vainly declared no power on earth would ever induce her to marry him—that they had disregarded her assurances, and had all of them, John excepted, sent her forth with great indignity.—"Have you seen John since?" said Mrs. Sullivan. "No—I refused to see him: I should have done so, I trust, on principle, even if I had returned his love."—"And did you not?" "No—I esteem him because he has good qualities, and was always kind to me—but I could not love him—and when I had an opportunity of contrasting him with other men—that is, I mean, with another man," she added, deeply blushing, "I felt I never could love him under any circumstances." "I own, my adopted son, if you mean him," said Mrs. Sullivan, "is very superior to John Apsley." "He is, indeed!" answered Mary, "and I pity poor Lavinia! but perhaps he may one day return, and marry her."—"Never—never!" was the energetic reply. "Oh! I am so glad," exclaimed the artless girl—"for his sake, I mean!"

Mary Medway had very little fortune remaining when her father's debts were paid, and the greater part of the income of it she had allowed to her bed-ridden nurse; what she retained of it, was just sufficient to keep her in clothes during her abode with the Apsleys:—she earned her board and lodging while there, by teaching the younger girls French, and flower-painting.

"You shall earn both with me also," said Mrs. Sullivan, on hearing those details. "I will not allow you to be idle. You shall spare my eyes by reading to me; you shall write my business letters, and keep my accounts. Do you consent to live with me on such terms?"—"Oh! most willingly," was the delighted answer.

This arrangement was productive of mutual comfort and benefit.

Mrs. Sullivan soon found that Mary united to unruffled sweetness of temper, and a total forgetfulness of self in little as well as in great things, considerable powers of mind, and feminine accomplishments.

She also discovered that her voice was not inferior to Miss Apsley's, but she had not been well taught; therefore, as Mrs.

Sullivan understood singing, though she had ceased to sing, she took great pleasure in instructing her; and was rewarded by her evident progress.

When the Apsleys heard where Mary now resided, they wrote most kindly to her, requesting her to return to them; informing her at the same time, that John was gone into business at Liverpool. But Mrs. Sullivan declared that she could not part with her; and Mary was very glad to stay where she was.

After a six months' absence, during which Mrs. Sullivan informed him that she had procured the most amiable and intellectual of companions, Mowbray returned, quite cured of his passion; and his friend welcomed him with the greatest joy.

Mrs. Sullivan was walking on the lawn before her house when he arrived; and, after taking two or three turns together, they went in. The door of the inner apartment was open; and Mary, unconscious that any one heard her, was singing in her best manner. Mowbray stopped, and listened in delightful surprise.—"Who is this charming singer?" whispered he, when she ceased.—"My companion—shall I introduce you?" "By all means"—and, to his astonishment, he beheld that "*dowdy girl,*" Mary Medway! But he could think her so no longer. Health bloomed on her round cheek, and her dark eye sparkled with happiness! And she could sing too, as well as Lavinia! Surely, then, it was jealousy that had led the Apsleys to conceal their knowledge of her musical powers! Another proof how fortunate he had been in escaping from Lavinia's chains. And Mary was the original cause of that escape.—Now, then, though not before, he felt that he could be "grateful to her;" and his "*associations with her name*" ceased to be "*disagreeable.*"

Mrs. Sullivan informed him, during the course of the day, while Mary was out of the room, that she had, though with some difficulty, drawn from her companion such accounts of Lavinia's bad temper, and of the daily domestic bickerings of the family, spite of their seeming affection before company, as had filled her with abundant thankfulness to heaven for his escape. "But I find that they are all spoiled children," she added; "therefore objects of the greatest pity. My dear George, remember, when you are a father, that the best lesson that a parent can inculcate in a child, is that of obedience; and that the best acquirement is a submitted will. It was according to this wise and pious plan, that Mary Medway was educated, and her conduct exemplifies its fruits. She was first taught submission to the will of her Creator, and next to that of her parents, as a duty enjoined by Him. Hence was she enabled to bear the loss of her fortune with cheerful resignation, and to endure the petty tyranny of the Apsleys with patient forbearance."

It was not long before Mowbray began to think, as Mrs. Sullivan hoped he might do, that a girl so educated must make a good wife. He also fancied it would be an advantage to marry this young and tender hearted being, who had none but distant relations; and who, if he could gain her heart, would love him not only ardently, but exclusively.

In short, with the entire approbation of his maternal friend, he wooed her interesting companion; and made her, after a short courtship, his wife.

"I wonder which of you will govern," said Mrs. Sullivan, smiling, while they were eating their wedding breakfast with her.

"Not I," said Mary, "for to obey will ever be my pleasure."

"Still," replied Mowbray, "I suspect that to govern would be your right, inasmuch as I doubt not but your will is a more submitted one than mine; and, (as our dear Mrs. Sullivan has often said) those only are fit to govern others, who have proved, on all occasions, that they are capable of governing themselves."

Walter Scott

Wandering Willie's Tale

(1824)

The author: Walter Scott was born on 15 August 1771 in Edinburgh, but grew up with his grandparents in the Scottish Borders, where he was recovering from polio (the disease left him lame for the rest of his life). He studied at the University of Edinburgh and practised the law, while collecting folk tales and translating poetry from German. His debut came in the form of a collection of folk ballads, *Minstrelsy of the Scottish Border* (1802). His friend James
Ballantyne had founded a printing press and a publishing house. He brought all of Scott's works to print: first the poetry (*The Lay of the Last Minstrel*, 1805; *Marmion*, 1808; *The Lady of the Lake*, 1810; *The Vision of Don Roderick*, 1811; *The Field of Waterloo*, 1815; etc.), then the historical novels (*Waverley*, 1814; *Guy Mannering*, 1815; *The Antiquary*, 1816; *Rob Roy*, 1817; *The Bride of Lammermoor*, 1819; *Ivanhoe*, 1820; *Kenilworth*, 1821; *Quentin Durward*, 1823; *Redgauntlet*, 1824; and others). He had become famous for his Romantic epic poems, but kept the identity of "the author of *Waverley*" a secret until 1827. His first attempts at short fiction consisted of brief satiric pieces in Edinburgh periodicals: "The Inferno of Altisidora" (in *The Edinburgh Annual Register for 1809*, published in 1811); "[Christopher Corduroy]" (in *The Sale-Room* 6, 8 February 1817); and "Alarming Increase of Depravity among Animals" (in *Blackwood's Edinburgh Magazine* of October 1817). His first supernatural short story, "Phantasmagoriana," appeared the following year in *Blackwood's* of May 1818.

The text: It first appeared in Scott's 1824 novel *Redgauntlet* (Edinburgh: Archibald Constable; London: Hurst, Robinson, and Co.), I, 225-261. The story has been published many times both in anthologies and as a standalone little volume. The following

Wandering Willie's Tale

is from the first edition, and not from the so-called "Magnum Edition" (1829-1832), supervised by Scott. We are in agreement with the editors of the Edinburgh Edition of the Waverley Novels (1993-2012), who also went back to the first editions of Scott's novels, in order to avoid both new mistakes and the historical and political notes. Some Scots words have been explained in footnotes in order to make things easier for the reader. Those that remain unexplained are similar to English equivalents.

Further reading: Daniel Cook. "Scott's Wandering Tales." *European Romantic Review* 34: 1, 47-65.

Ye maun have heard of Sir Robert Redgauntlet of that Ilk, who lived in these parts before the dear years.[159] The country will lang mind him; and our fathers used to draw breath thick if ever they heard him named. He was out wi' the Hielandmen in Montrose's time; and again he was in the hills wi' Glencairn in the saxteen hundred and fifty-twa;[160] and sae when King Charles the Second came in, wha was in sic favour as the Laird of Redgauntlet? He was knighted at Lonon court, wi' the king's ain sword; and being a redhot prelatist, he came down here, rampauging like a lion, with commissions of lieutenancy, and of lunacy, for what I ken, to put down a' the Whigs and Covenanters in the country. Wild wark they made of it; for the Whigs were as dour as the Cavaliers were fierce,[161] and it was which should first tire the other. Redgauntlet was aye for the stronghand; and his name is kenn'd as wide in the country as Claverhouse's or Tam Dalyell's.[162] Glen, nor dargle,[163] nor mountain, nor cave,

---

[159] The "dear years" were years of scarcity, when prices were high and wages were low. In Scotland, "the dear years" referred especially to the last years of the 17th century.

[160] Both James Graham, Marquess of Montrose (1612-1650) and William Cunningham, Earl of Glencairn (1610-1664) supported the Royalist cause in the British Civil Wars.

[161] The Cavaliers were the Royalists. The Scottish Covenanters wanted an independent Presbyterian Church and, although they had supported the royalist cause towards the end of the war, they were often persecuted after the Restoration of 1660, when Charles II became king.

[162] John Graham of Claverhouse (1648-1689) and Sir Tam Dalyell of the Binns (1615-1685) were both Scottish Royalists who subdued and persecuted the Covenanters.

[163] A Scottish term for a river valley.

191

could hide the puir hill-folk when Redgauntlet was out with bugle and bloodhound after them, as if they had been sae mony deer. And troth when they fand them, they didna mak muckle[164] mair ceremony than a Hielandman wi' a roebuck—It was just, "Will ye tak the test?"—if not, "Make ready—present—fire!"—and there lay the recusant.[165]

Far and wide was Sir Robert hated and feared. Men thought he had a direct compact with Satan—that he was proof against steel—and that bullets happed aff his buff-coat[166] like hailstanes from a hearth—that he had a mear that would turn a hare on the side of Carrifra-gawns[167]—and muckle to the same purpose, of whilk mair anon. The best blessing they wared on him was, 'Deil scowp wi' Redgauntlet!' He wasna a bad master to his ain folk though, and was weel aneugh liked by his tenants; and as for the lackies and troopers that raid out wi' him to the persecutions, as the Whigs caa'd those killing times, they wad hae drunken themsells blind to his health at ony time.

Now you are to ken that my gudesire lived on Redgauntlet's grund—they ca' the place Primrose-Knowe.[168] We had lived on the grund, and under the Redgauntlets, since the riding days,[169] and lang before. It was a pleasant bit; and I think the air is caller and fresher there than onywhere else in the country. It's a' deserted now; and I sat on the broken door-cheek three days since, and was glad I couldna see the plight the place was in; but that's a' wide o' the mark. There dwelt my gudesire, Steenie Steenson, a rambling, rattling chiel' he had been in his young days, and could play weel on the pipes; he was famous at "Hoopers and Girders"—a' Cumberland couldna touch him at "Jockie Lattin"[170]—and he had the finest finger for the back-lill[171] between Berwick and Carlisle. The like o' Steenie

---

[164] A (mostly) Scottish term for "much, a large amount."

[165] During the so-called "Killing Time" (roughly from 1679 to 1688), Covenanters were forced to take an oath (test) of abjuration, swearing to renounce the 1638 Covenant.

[166] A leather tunic worn mostly by officers in the 17th century.

[167] "Mear" is Scots for "mare." Carrigra-gawns is better known today as White Coomb. It is a hill in the Moffat range, in the Southern Uplands of Scotland. It is known for its western steep ridge facing Loch Skeen.

[168] Goodsire is an archaic term for grandfather. Primrose Knowe was actually the name of the estate of George Home, Earl of Dunbar (1556-1611).

[169] "Riding" times were times of war on the Scottish borders, especially in the two centuries before 1603.

[170] "Hoopers and Girders" and "Jockie Lattin" are traditional Scottish tunes.

[171] The lill is either one of the holes of a wind instrument or one of the pipes.

Wandering Willie's Tale

wasna the sort that they made Whigs o'. And so he became a Tory, as they ca' it, which we now ca' Jacobites, just out of a kind of needcessity, that he might belang to some side or other. He had nae ill-ill to the Whig bodies, and likedna to see the blude rin, though, being obliged to follow Sir Robert in hunting and hosting, watching and warding, he saw muckle mischief, and maybe did some, that he couldna avoid.

Now Steenie was a kind of favourite with his master, and kenn'd a' the folks about the castle, and was often sent for to play the pipes when they were at their merriment. Auld Dougal MacCallum, the butler, that had followed Sir Robert through gude and ill, thick and thin, pool and stream, was specially fond of the pipes, and aye gae my gudesire his gude word wi' the Laird; for Dougal could turn his master round his finger.

Weel, round came the Revolution, and it had like to have broken the hearts baith of Dougal and his master. But the change was not a'thegether sae great as they feared, and other folk thought for. The Whigs made an unca crawing[172] what they wad do with their auld enemies, and in special wi' Sir Robert Redgauntlet. But there were ower many great folks dipped in the same doings, to mak a spick and span new warld. So Parliament passed it a' ower easy; and Sir Robert, bating that he was held to hunting foxes instead of Covenanters, remained just the man he was. His revel was as loud, and his hall as weel lighted, as ever it had been, though maybe he lacked the fines of the non-conformists, that used to come to stock his larder and cellar; for it is certain he began to be keener about the rents than his tenants used to find him before, and they behoved to be prompt to the rent-day, or else the Laird wasna pleased. And he was sic an awsome body, that naebody cared to anger him; for the oaths he swore, and the rage that he used to get into, and the looks that he put on, made men sometimes think him a deevil incarnate.

Weel, my gudesire was nae manager—no that he was a very great misguider—but he hadna the saving gift, and he got twa terms' rent in arrear. He got the first brash at Whitsunday put ower wi' fair word and piping; but when Martinmas came,[173] there was a summons from the grund-officer to come wi' the rent on a day preceese, or else Steenie behoved to flitt.[174] Sair wark he had to get

---

[172] An odd boast.

[173] Whitsun or Whitsunday is the seventh Sunday after Easter. Martinmas or St. Martin's Day is celebrated on 11 November and used to be known as Old Halloween.

[174] Flit or flitt is Scots for removing or being removed from a place.

193

the siller;[175] but he was weel-freended, and at last he got the haill scraped thegether—a thousand merks[176]—the maist of it was from a neighbour they ca'd Laurie Lapraik—a sly tod. Laurie had walth o' gear—could hunt wi' the hound and rin wi' the hare—and be Whig or Tory, saunt or sinner, as the wind stood. He was a professor in this Revolution warld, but he liked an orra sound and a tune on the pipes weel aneugh at a bye-time; and abune a', he thought he had gude security for the siller he lent my gudesire ower the stocking at Primrose-Knowe.

Away trots my gudesire to Redgauntlet Castle wi' a heavy purse and a light heart, glad to be out of the Laird's danger. Weel, the first thing he learned at the Castle was, that Sir Robert had fretted himself into a fit of the gout, because he did not appear before twelve o'clock. It wasna a'-thegether for sake of the money, Dougal thought; but because he didna like to part wi' my gudesire aff the grund. Dougal was glad to see Steenie, and brought him into the great oak parlour, and there sat the Laird his leesome lane,[177] excepting that he had beside him a great, ill-favoured jackanape,[178] that was a special pet of his; a cankered beast it was, and mony an ill-natured trick it played—ill to please it was, and easily angered—ran about the haill castle, chattering and yowling, and pinching, and biting folk, specially before ill-weather, or disturbances in the state. Sir Robert caa'd it Major Weir, after the warlock that was burnt;[179] and few folk liked either the name or the conditions of the creature—they thought there was something in it by ordinar[180]—and my gudesire was not just easy in mind when the door shut on him, and he saw himself in the room wi' naebody but the Laird, Dougal MacCallum, and the Major, a thing that hadna chanced to him before.

Sir Robert sat, or, I should say, lay, in a great armed chair, wi' his grand velvet gown, and his feet on a cradle; for he had baith gout and gravel, and his face looked as gash and ghastly as Satan's.

---

[175] Hard work he had to do to get the money (the silver).

[176] The merk was an old Scottish coin worth two-thirds of a pound (or 13 shillings 4 pence).

[177] Completely alone.

[178] Today jackanapes is a term for a mischievous child or a conceited person, but at the time it meant a monkey or an ape.

[179] Major Thomas Weir (1599-1670), a former Covenanter soldier, and his sister, both of whom had presumably become insane in their later years, suddenly confessed to wizardry and other crimes and were promptly executed.

[180] Out of (or beyond) ordinary.

Wandering Willie's Tale

Major Weir sat opposite to him, in a red-laced coat, and the Laird's wig on his head; and aye as Sir Robert girned wi' pain, the jackanape girned too, like a sheep's-head between a pair of tangs—an ill-faur'd, fearsome couple they were. The Laird's buff-coat was hung on a pin behind him, and his broadsword and his pistols within reach; for he keepit up the auld fashion of having the weapons ready, and a horse saddled day and night, just as he used to do when he was able to loup on horseback, and away after ony of the hill-folk he could get speerings of. Some said it was for fear of the Whigs taking vengeance, but I judge it was just his auld custom—he wasna gien to fear onything. The rental-book, wi' its black cover and brass clasps, was lying beside him; and a book of sculduddry sangs[181] was put betwixt the leaves, to keep it open at the place where it bore evidence against the Goodman of Primrose-Knowe, as behind the hand with his mails and duties. Sir Robert gave my gudesire a look, as if he would have withered his heart in his bosom. Ye maun ken he had a way of bending his brows, that men saw the visible mark of a horse-shoe in his forehead, deep dinted, as if it had been stamped there.

"Are ye come light-handed, ye son of a toom[182] whistle?" said Sir Robert. "Zounds![183] if you are——"

My gudesire, with as gude a countenance as he could put on, made a leg,[184] and placed the bag of money on the table wi' a dash, like a man that does something clever. The Laird drew it to him hastily—"Is it all here, Steenie, man?"

"Your honour will find it right," said my gudesire.

"Here, Dougal," said the Laird, "gie Steenie a tass of brandy down stairs, till I count the siller and write the receipt."

But they werena weel out of the room, when Sir Robert gied a yelloch that garr'd the castle rock.[185] Back ran Dougal—in flew the livery-men—yell on yell gied the Laird, ilk ane mair awfu' than the ither. My gudesire knew not whether to stand or flee, but he ventured back into the parlour, where a' was gaun hirdy-girdie—naebody to say 'come in,' or 'gae out.' Terribly the Laird roared for cauld water to his feet, and wine to cool his throat; and, Hell, hell, hell, and its flames, was aye the word in his mouth. They brought

---

[181] Lewd songs.

[182] "Toom" or "tum" is an old Scots term meaning "empty" or "vain, futile."

[183] Old minced oath from "God's wounds!"

[184] To make a leg means to make a deep bow with the right leg drawn back.

[185] He gave a cry that made the castle rock.

him water, and when they plunged his swoln feet into the tub, he cried out it was burning; and folk say that it *did* bubble and sparkle like a seething cauldron. He flung the cup at Dougal's head, and said he had given him blood instead of burgundy; and, sure aneugh, the lass washed clottered blood aff the carpet the neist day. The jackanape they caa'd Major Weir, it jibbered and cried as if it was mocking its master; my gudesire's head was like to turn—he forgot baith siller and receipt, and down stairs he banged; but as he ran, the shrieks came faint and fainter; there was a deep-drawn shivering groan, and word gaed through the Castle, that the Laird was dead.

Weel, away came my gudesire, wi' his finger in his mouth, and his best hope was, that Dougal had seen the money-bag, and heard the Laird speak of writing the receipt. The young Laird, now Sir John, came from Edinburgh, to see things put to rights. Sir John and his father never gree'd weel—he had been bred an advocate, and afterwards sat in the last Scots Parliament and voted for the Union, having gotten, it was thought, a rug[186] of the compensations—if his father could have come out of his grave, he would have brained him for it on his awn hearth-stane. Some thought it was easier counting with the auld rough Knight than the fair-spoken young ane—but mair of that anon.

Dougal MacCallum, poor body, neither grat nor graned,[187] but gaed about the house looking like a corpse, but directing, as was his duty, a' the order of the grand funeral. Now, Dougal looked aye waur and waur when night was coming, and was aye the last to gang to his bed, whilk was in a little round just opposite the chamber of dais,[188] whilk his master occupied while he was living, and where he now lay in state as they caa'd it, well-a-day! The night before the funeral, Dougal could keep his awn counsel nae langer; he came doun with his proud spirit, and fairly asked auld Hutcheon to sit in his room with him for an hour. When they were in the round, Dougal took ae tass of brandy to himsel, and gave another to Hutcheon, and wished him all health and lang life, and said that, for himsel, he wasna lang for this world; for that, every night since Sir Robert's death, his silver call had sounded from the state chamber, just as it used to do at nights in his lifetime, to call Dougal to help to turn him in his bed. Dougal said, that being alone with the dead

---

[186] A good share.

[187] Neither wept nor groaned.

[188] The master bedroom. The "round" mentioned before is an alcove or a niche in the wall of a room (sometimes partitioned off the make a separate room). "Waur" means "worse."

Wandering Willie's Tale

on that floor of the tower, (for naebody cared to wake Sir Robert Redgauntlet like another corpse,) he had never daured to answer the call, but that now his conscience checked him for neglecting his duty; for, "though death breaks service," said MacCallum, "it shall never break my service to Sir Robert; and I will answer his next whistle, so be you will stand by me, Hutcheon."

Hutcheon had nae will to the wark, but he had stood by Dougal in battle and broil, and he wad not fail him at this pinch; so down the carles[189] sat ower a stoup of brandy, and Hutcheon, who was something of a clerk, would have read a chapter of the Bible; but Dougal would hear naething but a blaud of Davie Lindsay,[190] whilk was the waur preparation.

When midnight came, and the house was quiet as the grave, sure aneugh the silver whistle sounded as sharp and shrill as if Sir Robert was blowing it, and up got the twa auld serving-men, and tottered into the room where the dead man lay. Hutcheon saw aneugh at the first glance; for there were torches in the room, which shewed him the foul fiend, in his ain shape, sitting on the Laird's coffin! Ower he cowped as if he had been dead. He could not tell how lang he lay in a trance at the door, but when he gathered himself, he cried on his neighbour, and getting nae answer, raised the house, when Dougal was found lying dead within twa steps of the bed where his master's coffin was placed. As for the whistle, it was gaen anes and aye;[191] but mony a time was it heard at the top of the house in the bartizan, and amang the auld chimneys and turrets where the howlets have their nests.[192] Sir John hushed the matter up, and the funeral passed over without mair bogle-wark.[193]

But when a' was ower, and the Laird was beginning to settle his affairs, every tenant was called up for his arrears, and my gudesire for the full sum that stood against him in the rental-book. Weel, away he trots to the Castle, to tell his story, and there he is introduced to Sir John, sitting in his father's chair, in deep mourning, with weepers[194] and hanging cravat, and a small wallring rapier by his side, instead of the auld broadsword that had a hundred-weight of steel about it, what with blade, chape, and basket-hilt. I have heard

---

[189] "Carle" is a Scots term for a man, especially a commoner.

[190] David Lyndsay (c.1486-c1555) was a Scottish poet. "A blaud" means a bit or a fragment.

[191] Gone forever.

[192] A bartizan is an overhanging turret; "howlet" is a poetic term for an owl.

[193] Bogle is a Scots term for a ghost, a spectre, or a bogeyman.

[194] Here, something worn as a sign of mourning.

their communing so often tauld ower, that I almost think I was there mysell, though I couldna be born at the time.[195]

"I wuss ye joy, sir, of the head-seat, and the white loaf, and the braid lairdship. Your father was a kind man to friends and followers; muckle grace to you, Sir John, to fill his shoon—his boots, I suld say, for he seldom wore shoon, unless it were muils when he had the gout."

"Aye, Steenie," quoth the Laird, sighing deeply, and putting his napkin to his een, "his was a sudden call, and he will be missed in the country; no time to set his house in order—weel prepared Godward, no doubt, which is the root of the matter—but left us behind a tangled hesp to wind,[196] Steenie.—Hem! hem! We maun go to business, Steenie; much to do, and little time to do it in."

Here he opened the fatal volume; I have heard of a thing they call Doomsday-book—I am clear it has been a rental of backganging tenants.

"Stephen," said Sir John, still in the same soft, sleekit tone of voice—"Stephen Stevenson, or Steenson, ye are down here for a year's rent behind the hand—due at last term."

Stephen. "Please your honour, Sir John, I paid it to your father."

Sir John. "Ye took a receipt, then, doubtless, Stephen; and can produce it?"

Stephen. "Indeed I hadna time, an it like your honour; for nae sooner had I set doun the siller, and just as his honour, Sir Robert, that's gaen, drew it till him to count it, and write out the receipt, he was ta'en wi' the pains that removed him."

"That was unlucky," said Sir John, after a pause. "But ye maybe paid it in the presence of somebody. I want but a *talis qualis* evidence,[197] Stephen. I would go ower strictly to work with no poor man."

Stephen. "Troth, Sir John, there was naebody in the room but Dougal MacCallum the butler. But, as your honour kens, he has e'en followed his auld master."

"Very unlucky again, Stephen," said Sir John, without altering his voice a single note. "The man to whom ye paid the money is

---

[195] In *Redgauntlet*, Wandering Willie's Tale is retold by Darsie Latimer in a letter to his friend Alan Fairford. At this point in the letter, Darsie adds the following parenthesis: "In fact, Alan, my companion mimicked, with a good deal of humour, the flattering, conciliating tone of the tenant's address, and the hypocritical melancholy of the laird's reply. His grandfather, he said, had, while he spoke, his eye fixed on the rental-book, as if it were a mastiff-dog that he was afraid would spring up and bite him."

[196] A hesp is a length of yarn.

[197] Latin term for any kind of evidence, "such as it is."

Wandering Willie's Tale

dead—and the man who witnessed the payment is dead too—and the siller, which should have been to the fore, is neither seen nor heard tell of in the repositories. How am I to believe a' this?"

Stephen. "I dinna ken, your honour; but there is a bit memorandum note of the very coins; for, God help me! I had to borrow out of twenty purses; and I am sure that ilk man there set down will take his grit oath for what purpose I borrowed the money."

Sir John. "I have little doubt ye *borrowed* the money, Steenie. It is the *payment* that I want to have some proof of."

Stephen. "The siller maun be about the house, Sir John. And since your honour never got it, and his honour that was canna have taen it wi' him, maybe some of the family may have seen it."

Sir John. "We will examine the servants, Stephen; that is but reasonable."

But lackey and lass, and page and groom, all denied stoutly that they had ever seen such a bag of money as my gudesire described. What was waur, he had unluckily not mentioned to any living soul of them his purpose of paying his rent. Ae quean[198] had noticed something under his arm, but she took it for the pipes.

Sir John Redgauntlet ordered the servants out of the room, and then said to my gudesire, "Now, Steenie, ye see ye have fair play; and, as I have little doubt ye ken better where to find the siller than ony other body, I beg, in fair terms, and for your own sake, that you will end this fasherie; for, Stephen, ye maun pay or flitt."

"The Lord forgie your opinion," said Stephen, driven almost to his wit's end—"I am an honest man."

"So am I, Stephen," said his honour; "and so are all the folks in the house, I hope. But if there be a knave amongst us, it must be he that tells the story he cannot prove." He paused, and then added, mair sternly, "If I understand your trick, sir, you want to take advantage of some malicious reports concerning things in this family, and particularly respecting my father's sudden death, thereby to cheat me out of the money, and perhaps take away my character, by insinuating that I have received the rent I am demanding.—Where do you suppose this money to be?—I insist upon knowing."

My gudesire saw everything look so muckle against him, that he grew nearly desperate—however, he shifted from one foot to another, looked to every corner of the room, and made no answer.

"Speak out, sirrah," said the Laird, assuming a look of his father's, a very particular ane, which he had when he was angry—it seemed as if the wrinkles of his frown made that self-same fearful

---

[198] A woman, especially a young, unmarried one.

shape of a horse's shoe in the middle of his brow;—"Speak out, sir! I *will* know your thoughts;—do you suppose that I have this money?"

"Far be it frae me to say so," said Stephen.

"Do you charge any of my people with having taken it?"

"I wad be laith to charge them that may be innocent," said my gudesire; "and if there be any one that is guilty, I have nae proof."

"Somewhere the money must be, if there is a word of truth in your story," said Sir John; "I ask where you think it is—and demand a correct answer?"

"In hell, if you will have my thoughts of it," said my gudesire, driven to extremity,—"in hell! with your father and his silver whistle."

Down the stairs he ran, (for the parlour was nae place for him after such a word,) and he heard the Laird swearing blood and wounds behind him, as fast as ever did Sir Robert, and roaring for the bailie and the baron-officer.

Away rode my gudesire to his chief creditor, (him they ca'd Laurie Lapraik,) to try if he could make onything out of him; but when he tauld his story, he got but the warst word in his wame—thief, beggar, and dyvour, were the saftest terms;[199] and to the boot of these hard terms, Laurie brought up the auld story of his dipping his hand in the blood of God's saints, just as if a tenant could have helped riding with the Laird, and that a laird like Sir Robert Redgauntlet. My gudesire was, by this time, far beyond the bounds of patience, and, while he and Laurie were at de'il speed the liars, he was wanchancie aneugh to abuse Lapraik's doctrine as weel as the man, and said things that garr'd folks' flesh grue[200] that heard them;—he wasna just himsell, and he had lived wi' a wild set in his day.

At last they parted, and my gudesire was to ride hame through the wood of Pitmurkie, that is a' fou of black firs, as they say.—I ken the wood, but the firs may be black or white for what I can tell.—At the entry of the wood there is a wild common, and on the edge of the common, a little lonely change-house, that was keepit then by an ostler-wife, they suld hae ca'd her Tibbie Faw, and there puir Steenie cried for a mutchkin of brandy, for he had had no refreshment the haill day. Tibbie was earnest wi' him to take a bite

[199] Dyvour is a rogue; saft is mild.

[200] "Deil speed the liars" is an idiom for a quarrel; wanchancie is unsafe to meddle with; grue means shudder.

Wandering Willie's Tale

of meat, but he couldna think o't, nor would he take his foot out of the stirrup, and took off the brandy wholely at twa draughts, and named a toast at each:—the first was, the memory of Sir Robert Redgauntlet, and might he never lie quiet in his grave till he had righted his poor bond-tenant; and the second was, a health to Man's Enemy, if he would but get him back the pock of siller, or tell him what came o't, for he saw the haill world was like to regard him as a thief and a cheat, and he took that waur than even the ruin of his house and hauld.

On he rode, little caring where. It was a dark night turned, and the trees made it yet darker, and he let the beast take its ain road through the wood; when, all of a sudden, from tired and wearied that it was before, the nag began to spring, and flee, and stend, that my gudesire could hardly keep the saddle.—Upon the whilk, a horseman, suddenly riding up beside him, said, "That's a mettle beast of yours, freend; will you sell him?" So saying, he touched the horse's neck with his riding-wand, and it fell into its auld heigh-ho of a stumbling trot; "But his spunk's soon out of him, I think," continued the stranger, "and that is like mony a man's courage, that thinks he wad do great things till he come to the proof."

My gudesire scarce listened to this, but spurred his horse, with "Gude e'en to you, freend."

But it's like the stranger was ane that doesna lightly yield his point; for, ride as Steenie liked, he was aye beside him at the self-same pace. At last my gudesire, Steenie Steenson, grew half angry; and, to say the truth, half feared.

"What is it that ye want with me, freend?" he said. "If ye be a robber, I have nae money; if ye be a leal man, wanting company, I have nae heart to mirth or speaking; and if ye want to ken the road, I scarce ken it mysell."

"If you will tell me your grief," said the stranger, "I am one that, though I have been sair miscaa'd[201] in the world, am the only hand for helping my freends."

So my gudesire, to ease his ain heart, mair than from any hope of help, told him the story from beginning to end.

"It's a hard pinch," said the stranger; "but I think I can help you."

"If you could lend the money, sir, and take a lang day—I ken nae other help on earth," said my gudesire.

"But there may be some under the earth," said the stranger. "Come, I'll be frank wi' you; I could lend you the money on bond,

---

[201] I have been grievously ill spoken of.

but you would maybe scruple my terms. Now, I can tell you, that your auld Laird is disturbed in his grave by your curses, and the wailing of your family, and—if ye daur venture to go to see him, he will give you the receipt."

My gudesire's hair stood on end at this proposal, but he thought his companion might be some humoursome chield that was trying to frighten him, and might end with lending him the money. Besides, he was bauld wi' brandy, and desperate wi' distress; and he said, he had courage to go to the gate of hell, and a step farther, for that receipt.—The stranger laughed.

Weel, they rode on through the thickest of the wood, when, all of a sudden, the horse stopped at the door of a great house; and, but that he knew the place was ten miles off, my father would have thought he was at Redgauntlet Castle. They rode into the outer court-yard, through the muckle faulding yetts and aneath the auld portcullis; and the whole front of the house was lighted, and there were pipes and fiddles, and as much dancing and deray within as used to be at Sir Robert's house at Pace and Yule, and such high seasons. They lap off, and my gudesire, as seemed to him, fastened his horse to the very ring he had tied him to that morning, when he gaed to wait on the young Sir John.

"God!" said my gudesire, "if Sir Robert's death be but a dream!"

He knocked at the ha' door just as he was wont, and his auld acquaintance, Dougal MacCallum—just after his wont, too,—came to open the door, and said, "Piper Steenie, are ye there, lad? Sir Robert has been crying for you."

My gudesire was like a man in a dream—he looked for the stranger, but he was gane for the time. At last he just tried to say, "Ha! Dougal Driveower, are ye living? I thought ye had been dead."

"Never fash yoursell wi' me," said Dougal, "but look to yourself; and see ye tak naething frae onybody here, neither meat, drink, or siller, except just the receipt that is your ain."

So saying, he led the way out through halls and trances that were weel kenn'd to my gudesire, and into the auld oak parlour; and there was as much singing of profane sangs, and birling of red wine, and speaking blasphemy and sculduddry, as had ever been in Redgauntlet Castle when it was at the blythest.

But, Lord take us in keeping! what a set of ghastly revellers they were that sat around that table!—My gudesire kenn'd mony that had long before gane to their place. There was the fierce Middleton, and the dissolute Rothes, and the crafty Lauderdale; and Dalyell, with his bald head and a beard to his girdle; and Earlshall, with Cameron's

Wandering Willie's Tale

blude on his hand; and wild Bonshaw, that tied blessed Mr. Cargill's limbs till the blude sprung; and Dumbarton Douglas, the twice-turned traitor baith to country and king. There was the Bluidy Advocate MacKenyie, who, for his worldly wit and wisdom, had been to the rest as a god. And there was Claverhouse, as beautiful as when he lived, with his long, dark, curled locks, streaming down to his laced buff-coat, and his left hand always on his right spule-blade, to hide the wound that the silver bullet had made. He sat apart from them all, and looked at them with a melancholy, haughty countenance; while the rest hallooed, and sang, and laughed, that the room rang. But their smiles were fearfully contorted from time to time; and their laugh passed into such wild sounds as made my gudesire's very nails grow blue, and chilled the marrow in his banes.[202]

They that waited at the table were just the wicked serving-men and troopers, that had done their work and wicked bidding on earth. There was the Lang Lad of the Nethertown, that helped to take Argyle; and the Bishop's summoner, that they called the Deil's Rattle-bag; and the wicked guardsmen in their laced coats; and the savage Highland Amorites, that shed blood like water; and many a proud serving-man, haughty of heart and bloody of hand, cringing to the rich, and making them wickeder than they would be; grinding the poor to powder, when the rich had broken them to fragments. And mony, mony mair were coming and ganging, a' as busy in their vocation as if they had been alive.

Sir Robert Redgauntlet, in the midst of a' this fearful riot, cried, wi' a voice like thunder, on Steenie Piper to come to the board-head where he was sitting; his legs stretched out before him, and swathed up with flannel, with his holster pistols aside him, while the great broadsword rested against his chair, just as my gudesire had seen him the last time upon earth—the very cushion for the jackanape was close to him, but the creature itsell was not there—it wasna its hour, it's likely; for he heard them say as he came forward, "Is not the Major come yet?" And another answered, "The jackanape will be here betimes the morn." And when my gudesire came forward, Sir Robert, or his ghaist, or the deevil in his likeness, said, "Weel, piper, hae ye settled wi' my son for the year's rent?"

With much ado my father gat breath to say, that Sir John would not settle without his honour's receipt.

"Ye shall hae that for a tune of the pipes, Steenie," said the appearance of Sir Robert—"Play us up 'Weel hoddled, Luckie.'"

[202] The paragraph contains a long list of politicians and soldiers who persecuted the Covenanters after the Restoration.

Now this was a tune my gudesire learned frae a warlock, that heard it when they were worshipping Satan at their meetings, and my gudesire had sometimes played it at the ranting suppers in Redgauntlet Castle, but never very willingly; and now he grew cauld at the very name of it, and said, for excuse, he hadna his pipes wi' him.

"MacCallum, ye limb of Beelzebub," said the fearfu' Sir Robert, "bring Steenie the pipes that I am keeping for him!"

MacCallum brought a pair of pipes might have served the piper of Donald of the Isles.[203] But he gave my gudesire a nudge as he offered them; and looking secretly and closely, Steenie saw that the chanter was of steel, and heated to a white heat; so he had fair warning not to trust his fingers with it. So he excused himself again, and said, he was faint and frightened, and had not wind aneugh to fill the bag.

"Then ye maun eat and drink, Steenie," said the figure; "for we do little else here; and it's ill speaking between a fou man and a fasting."

Now these were the very words that the bloody Earl of Douglas said to keep the King's messenger in hand, while he cut the head off MacLellan of Bombie, at the Threave Castle;[204] and that put Steenie mair and mair on his guard. So he spoke up like a man, and said he came neither to eat, or drink or make minstrelsy; but simply for his ain—to ken what was come o' the money he had paid, and to get a discharge for it; and he was so stout-hearted by this time, that he charged Sir Robert for conscience-sake—(he had no power to say the holy name)—and as he hoped for peace and rest, to spread no snares for him, but just to give him his ain.

The appearance gnashed its teeth and laughed, but it took from a large pocket-book the receipt, and handed it to Steenie. "Here is your receipt, ye pitiful cur; and for the money, my dog-whelp of a son may go look for it in the Cat's Cradle."

My gudesire uttered mony thanks, and was about to retire when Sir Robert roared aloud, "Stop though, thou sack-doudling[205] son of a whore! I am not done with thee. HERE we do nothing for

---

[203] Donald of Islay, Lord of the Isles (died 1423), grandson of King Robert II of Scotland and chief of Clan Donald.

[204] This episode of Scottish history took place in 1452 and involved Patrick Maclellan of Bombie, head of Clan MacLellan, and William Douglas, Earl of Douglas. "Fou" means "full."

[205] To doudle is Scots for playing a musical instrument (especially the bagpipes).

Wandering Willie's Tale

nothing; and you must return on this very day twelvemonth, to pay your master the homage that you owe me for my protection."

My father's tongue was loosed of a suddenty, and he said aloud, "I refer mysell to God's pleasure, and not to yours."

He had no sooner uttered the word than all was dark around him; and he sank on the earth with such a sudden shock, that he lost both breath and sense.

How lang Steenie lay there, he could not tell; but when he came to himself, he was lying in the auld kirkyard of Redgauntlet parishine, just at the door of the family aisle, and the scutcheon of the auld knight, Sir Robert, hanging over his head. There was a deep morning fog on grass and gravestone around him, and his horse was feeding quietly beside the minister's twa cows. Steenie would have thought the whole was a dream, but he had the receipt in his hand, fairly written and signed by the auld Laird; only the last letters of his name were a little disorderly, written like one seized with sudden pain.

Sorely troubled in his mind, he left that dreary place, rode through the mist to Redgauntlet Castle, and with much ado he got speech of the Laird. "Well, you dyvour bankrupt," was the first word, "have you brought me my rent?"

"No," answered my gudesire, "I have not; but I have brought your honour Sir Robert's receipt for it."

"How, sirrah?—Sir Robert's receipt! You told me he had not given you one."

"Will your honour please to see if that bit line is right?"

Sir John looked at every line, and at every letter, with much attention; and at last, at the date, which my gudesire had not observed,—"*From my appointed place,*" he read, "*this twenty-fifth of November.*"—"What!—That is yesterday!—Villain, thou must have gone to hell for this!"

"I got it from your honour's father—whether he be in heaven or hell, I know not," said Steenie.

"I will delate you for a warlock to the Privy Council!" said Sir John. "I will send you to your master, the devil, with the help of a tar-barrel and a torch!"

"I intend to delate mysell to the Presbytery," said Steenie, "and tell them all I have seen last night, whilk are things fitter for them to judge of than a borrel man like me."

Sir John paused, composed himself, and desired to hear the full history; and my gudesire told it him from point to point, as I have told it you—word for word, neither more nor less.

205

Sir John was silent again for a long time, and at last he said, very composedly, "Steenie, this story of yours concerns the honour of many a noble family besides mine; and if it be a leasing-making, to keep yourself out of my danger, the least you can expect is to have a redhot iron driven through your tongue, and that will be as bad as scauding your fingers wi' a redhot chanter. But yet it may be true, Steenie; and if the money cast up, I shall not know what to think of it.—But where shall we find the Cat's Cradle? There are cats enough about the old house, but I think they kitten without the ceremony of bed or cradle."

"We were best ask Hutcheon," said my gudesire; "he kens a' the odd corners about as weel as—another serving-man that is now gane, and that I wad not like to name."

Aweel, Hutcheon, when he was asked, told them, that a ruinous turret, lang disused, next to the clock-house, only accessible by a ladder, for the opening was on the outside, and far above the battlements, was called of old the Cat's Cradle.

"There will I go immediately," said Sir John; and he took (with what purpose, Heaven kens,) one of his father's pistols from the hall-table, where they had lain since the night he died, and hastened to the battlements.

It was a dangerous place to climb, for the ladder was auld and frail, and wanted ane or twa rounds. However, up got Sir John, and entered at the turret door, where his body stopped the only little light that was in the bit turret. Something flees at him wi' a vengeance, maist dang him back ower—bang gaed the knight's pistol, and Hutcheon, that held the ladder, and my gudesire that stood beside him, hears a loud skelloch. A minute after, Sir John flings the body of the jackanape down to them, and cries that the siller is fund, and that they should come up and help him. And there was the bag of siller sure aneugh, and mony orra thing besides, that had been missing for mony a day. And Sir John, when he had riped the turret weel, led my gudesire into the dining-parlour, and took him by the hand, and spoke kindly to him, and said he was sorry he should have doubted his word, and that he would hereafter be a good master to him, to make amends.

"And now, Steenie," said Sir John, "although this vision of yours tends, on the whole, to my father's credit, as an honest man, that he should, even after his death, desire to see justice done to a poor man like you, yet you are sensible that ill-dispositioned men might make bad constructions upon it, concerning his soul's health. So, I think, we had better lay the haill dirdum on that ill-deedie creature,

Wandering Willie's Tale

Major Weir, and say naething about your dream in the wood of Pitmurkie. You had taken ower muckle brandy to be very certain about onything; and, Steenie, this receipt, (his hand shook while he held it out)—it's but a queer kind of document, and we will do best, I think, to put it quietly in the fire."

"Od, but for as queer as it is, it's a' the voucher I have for my rent," said my gudesire, who was afraid, it may be, of losing the benefit of Sir Robert's discharge.

"I will bear the contents to your credit in the rental-book, and give you a discharge under my own hand," said Sir John, "and that on the spot. And, Steenie, if you can hold your tongue about this matter, you shall sit, from this term downward, at an easier rent."

"Mony thanks to your honour," said Steenie, who saw easily in what corner the wind was; "doubtless I will be comfortable to all your honour's commands; only I would willingly speak wi' some powerful minister on the subject, for I do not like the sort of soumons of appointment whilk your honour's father——"

"Do not call the phantom my father!" said Sir John, interrupting him.

"Weel, then, the thing that was so like him,"—said my gudesire; "he spoke of my coming back to see him this time twelvemonth, and it's a weight on my conscience."

"Aweel, then," said Sir John, "if you be so much distressed in mind, you may speak to our minister of the parish; he is a douce man, regards the honour of our family, and the mair that he may look for some patronage from me."

Wi' that, my father readily agreed that the receipt should be burnt, and the Laird threw it into the chimney with his ain hand. Burn it would not for them, though; but away it flew up the lumm,[206] wi' a lang train of sparks at its tail, and a hissing noise like a squib.

My gudesire gaed down to the Manse, and the minister, when he had heard the story, said, it was his real opinion, that though my gudesire had gaen very far in tampering with dangerous matters, yet, as he had refused the devil's arles (for such was the offer of meat and drink) and had refused to do homage by piping at his bidding, he hoped, that if he held a circumspect walk hereafter, Satan could take little advantage by what was come and gane. And, indeed, my gudesire, of his ain accord, lang foreswore baith the pipes and the brandy—it was not even till the year was out, and the fatal day past, that he would so much as take the fiddle, or drink usquebaugh or tippeny.[207]

---

[206] Chimney.

[207] Weak ale.

Sir John made up his story about the jackanape as he liked himself; and some believe till this day there was no more in the matter than the filching nature of the brute. Indeed ye'll no hinder some to threap, that it was nane o' the Auld Enemy that Dougal and my gudesire saw in the Laird's room, but only that wanchancy creature, the Major, capering on the coffin; and that, as to the blawing on the Laird's whistle that was heard after he was dead, the filthy brute could do that as weel as the Laird himself, if no better. But Heaven kens the truth, whilk first came out by the minister's wife, after Sir John and her ain gudeman were baith in the moulds.[208] And then my gudesire, wha was failed in his limbs, but not in his judgment or memory—at least nothing to speak of—was obliged to tell the real narrative to his friends, for the credit of his gude name. He might else have been charged for a warlock.[209] Aye, but they had baith to sup the sauce o't sooner or later;—what was fristed[210] wasna forgiven. Sir John died before he was much over three-score; and it was just like of a moment's illness. And for my gudesire, though he departed in fullness of life, yet there was my father, a yauld[211] man of forty-five, fell down betwixt the stilts of his pleugh, and raise never again, and left nae bairn but me, a puir sightless, fatherless, motherless creature, could neither work nor want. Things gaed weel aneugh at first; for Sir Redwald Redgauntlet, the only son of Sir John, and the oye[212] of auld Sir Robert, and, waes me! the last of the honourable house, took the farm aff our hands, and brought me into his household to have care of me. He liked music, and I had the best teachers baith England and Scotland could gie me. Mony a merry year was I wi' him! but waes me! he gaed out with other pretty men in the forty-five—I'll say nae mair about it—My head never settled weel since I lost him; and if I say another word about it, de'il a bar will I have the heart to play the night.

---

[208] Soil, graveyard earth.

[209] Darsie Latimer's narrative intervention here has been removed, as well as the last sentence, which is addressed by Willie directly to Darsie.

[210] Delayed, postponed.

[211] Active, sprightly, vigorous.

[212] Grandchild.

Mary Russell Mitford

JACK HATCH

(1825)

The author: In the mid-1820s, Mitford continued to contribute stories, sketches, and poems to *The Lady's Magazine*. However, after the success of the first instalment of *Our Village* in 1825, she began contributing to annuals like *Forget Me Not*, *The Amulet*, *Literary Souvenir*, or *Friendship's Offering*, but most of her prose writings were sent to the *Monthly Magazine*. These were soon gathered into the second volume of her popular series.

The text: It first appeared as "A Village Sketch" in the annual *Forget Me Not; A Christmas and New Year's Present for 1826* (London: R. Ackermann, 1826 [1825]), 304-315. In the same year, it was also reproduced in the book review published in *The Literary Gazette, and Journal of Belles Lettres, Arts, Science, &c.* 459 (Saturday, 5 November 1825), 705-706. As "Jack Hatch," it was then included in *Our Village II* (London: Geo. B. Whittaker, 1826), 70-81, from where the following has been selected.

I pique myself on knowing by sight, and by name, almost every man and boy in our parish, from eight years old to eighty—I cannot say quite so much for the women. They—the elder of them at least,—are more within doors, more hidden. One does not meet them in the fields and highways; their duties are close housekeepers, and live under cover. The girls, to be sure, are often enough in sight, "true creatures of the element" basking in the sun,[213] racing in the wind, rolling in the dust, dabbling in the water,—hardier,

[213] A paraphrase of lines from Milton's *Comus*: "gay creatures of the element/ That in the colours of the rainbow live."

209

Mary Russell Mitford

dirtier, noisier, more sturdy defiers of heat, and cold, and wet, than boys themselves. One sees them quite often enough to know them; but then the little elves alter so much at every step of their approach to womanhood, that recognition becomes difficult, if not impossible. It is not merely growing, boys grow;—it is positive, perplexing and perpetual change: a butterfly hath not undergone more transmogrifications in its progress through this life, than a village belle in her arrival at the age of seventeen.

The first appearance of the little lass is something after the manner of a caterpillar, crawling and creeping upon the grass, set down to roll by some tired little nurse of an elder sister, or mother with her hands full. There it lies—a fat, boneless, rosy piece of health, inspiring to the accomplishments of walking and talking; stretching its chubby limbs; scrambling and sprawling; laughing and roaring; there it sits, in all the dignity of the baby, adorned in a pink-checked frock, a blue spotted pinafore and a little white cap, tolerably clean, and quite whole. One is forced to ask if it be boy or girl; for these hardy country rogues are all alike, open eyed, and weather-stained, and nothing fearing. There is no more mark of sex in the countenance than in the dress.

In the next stage, dirt-encrusted enough to pass for the chrysalis, if it were not so very unquiet, the gender remains equally uncertain. It is a fine, stout, curly-pated creature of three or four, playing and rolling about, amongst grass or mud all day long; shouting, jumping, screeching—the happiest compound of noise and idleness, rags and rebellion, that ever trod the earth.

Then comes a sun-burnt gipsy of six, beginning to grow tall and thin, and to find the cares of the world gathering about her; with a pitcher in one hand, a mop in the other, an old straw bonnet of ambiguous shape, half hiding her tangled hair; a tattered stuff petticoat, once green, hanging below an equally tattered cotton frock, once purple; her longing eyes fixed on a game of baseball at the corner of the green, till she reaches the cottage door, flings down the mop and pitcher, and darts off to her companions, quite regardless of the storm of scolding with which the mother follows her run-away steps.

So the world wags till ten; then the little damsel gets admission to the charity school and trips mincingly thither every morning, dressed in the old-fashioned blue gown, and white cap, and tippet, and bib and apron of that primitive institution, looking as demure as a Nun, and as tidy; her thoughts fixed on button-holes, and spelling-books—those ensigns of promotion; despising dirt and baseball, and all their joys.

210

Jack Hatch

Then at twelve, the little lass comes home again, uncapped, untippeted, unschooled; brown as a berry, wild as a colt, busy as a bee—working in the fields, digging in the garden, frying rashers, boiling potatoes, shelling beans, darning stockings, nursing children, feeding pigs;—all these employments varied by occasional fits of romping and flirting, and idle play, according as the nascent coquetry, or the lurking love of sport, happens to preponderate; merry, and pretty, and good with all her little faults. It would be well if a country girl could stand at thirteen. Then she is charming. But the clock will move forward, and at fourteen she gets a service in a neighbouring town; and her next appearance is in the perfection of the butterfly state, fluttering, glittering, inconstant, vain,—the gayest and gaudiest insect that ever skimmed over a village green. And this is the true progress of a rustic beauty, the average lot of our country girls; so they spring up, flourish, change and disappear. Some indeed marry and fix amongst us, and then ensues another set of changes, rather more gradual perhaps, but quite as sure, till gray hairs, wrinkles, and linsey-woolsey,[214] wind up the picture.

All this is beside the purpose. If woman be a mutable creature, man is not. The wearers of smock frocks, in spite of the sameness of the uniform, are almost as easily distinguished by an interested eye, as a flock of sheep by the shepherd, or a pack of hounds by the huntsman: or to come to less affronting similes, the members of the House of Commons by the Speaker, or the gentleman of the bar by the Lord Chief Justice. There is very little change in them from early boyhood. "The child is father to the man" in more senses than one.[215] There is a constancy about them; they keep the same faces however ugly; the same habits however strange; the same fashions however unfashionable; they are in nothing new fangled. Tom Coper, for instance, man and boy, is and has been addicted to posies,—from the first polyanthus to the last china rose, he has always a nosegay in his button hole; George Simmons may be known a mile off, by an eternal red waistcoat; Jem Tanner, summer and winter, by the smartest of all smart straw hats; and Joel Brent, from the day that he left off petticoats, has always, in every dress and every situation looked like a study for a painter—no mistaking him. Yes! I know every man and boy of note in the parish, with one exception—one most signal exception, which "haunts, and startles

---

[214] A coarse fabric made of a mixture of wool and cotton or wool and linen.

[215] More exactly, "The Child is Father of the Man," from a short poem by Wordsworth (known by its opening line as "My Heart Leaps Up when I Behold"), first published in *Poems, in Two Volumes* (1807).

Mary Russell Mitford

and waylays" me at every turn.[216] I do not know, and I begin to fear that I never shall know Jack Hatch.

The first time I had occasion to hear of this worthy was on a most melancholy occurrence. We have lost—I do not like to talk about it, but I cannot tell my story without—We have lost a cricket match, been beaten, and soundly too, by the men of Beech-hill, a neighbouring parish. How this accident happened, I cannot very well tell; the melancholy fact is sufficient. The men of Beech-hill, famous players, in whose families cricket is an hereditary accomplishment, challenged and beat us. After our defeat, we began to comfort ourselves by endeavouring to discover how this misfortune could possibly have befallen. Every one that has ever had a cold, must have experience the great consolation that is derived from puzzling out the particular act of imprudence from which it sprang, and we on the same principle, found our affliction somewhat mitigated by the endeavour to trace it to its source. One laid the catastrophe to the wind—a very common scape goat in the catarrhal calamity—which had, as it were, played us booty, carrying our adversary's balls right and ours wrong; another laid it to a certain catch missed by Tom Willis, by which means Farmer Thackum, the pride and glory of the Beech-hillers, had two innings; a third to the aforesaid Thackum's remarkable manner of bowling, which is circular, so to say, that is, after taking aim, he makes a sort of chassée on one side,[217] before he delivers his ball, which pantomimic motion had a great effect on the nerves of our eleven, unused to such quadrilling; a fourth imputed our defeat to the over civility of our umpire, George Gosseltine, a sleek, smooth, silky, soft-spoken person, who stood with his little wand under his arm, smiling through all our disasters—the very image of peace and good humour; whilst their umpire, Bob Coxe, a roystering, roaring, bullying blade,[218] bounced, and hectored, and blustered from his wicket, with the voice of a twelve-pounder; the fifth assented to this opinion, with some extension, asserting that the universal impudence of their side took advantage of the meekness and modesty of ours, (N.B. it never occurred to our modesty, that they might be the best players) which flattering persuasion appeared likely to prevail, in fault of a better,

[216] Paraphrase of a line from another untitled piece from Wordworth's *Poems, in Two Volumes*, known as "She was a Phantom of delight:" "A dancing Shape, an Image gay,/ To haunt, to startle, and way-lay."

[217] Chassé (as it is usually spelled) is a dance movement (a "slide"), in which both legs are first bent (here, sideways) after which they meet in the air straightened.

[218] A blade is a young man (especially a boisterous one); "royster" is an old spelling of "roister," i.e., bluster, swagger.

Jack Hatch

when all of a sudden, the true reason of our defeat seemed to burst at once from half a dozen voices, re-echoed like a chorus by all the others—"It was entirely owing to the want of Jack Hatch! How could we think of playing without Jack Hatch!"

This was the first I heard of him. My enquiries as to this great player were received with utter astonishment. "Who is Jack Hatch?" "Not know Jack Hatch!" There was no end to the wonder—"not to know him, argued myself unknown."[219] "Jack Hatch—the best cricketer in the parish, in the county, in the country! Jack Hatch, who had got seven notches at one hit! Jack Hatch, who had trolled, and caught out a whole eleven! Jack Hatch, who besides these marvellous gifts in cricket, was the best bowler and the best musician in the hundred,[220]—could dance a hornpipe and a minuet, sing a whole song-book, bark like a dog, mew like a cat, crow like a cock, and go through Punch from beginning to end![221] Not know Jack Hatch!"

Half ashamed of my non-acquaintance with this admirable Crichton of rural accomplishments,[222] I determined to find him out as soon as possible, and I have been looking for him more or less, ever since.

The cricket-ground and the bowling green were of course, the first places of search; but he was always just gone, or not come, or he was there yesterday, or he is expected to-morrow—a to-morrow, which as far as I am concerned never arrives;—the stars were against me. Then I directed my attention to his other acquirements; and once followed a ballad-singer half a mile who turned out to be a strapping woman in a man's great coat; and another time pierced a whole mob of urchins to get at a capital Punch—when behold it was the genuine man of puppets, the true squeakery, the "real Simon Pure,"[223] and Jack was as much to seek as ever.

---

[219] A common saying, suggesting one's lack of popularity if one doesn't know somebody really popular. It actually comes from Milton's *Paradise Lost*, in which Satan says, "Not to know me, argues yourself unknown,/ The lowest of your throng."

[220] A hundred was an administrative subdivision of a county, for military and judicial purposes.

[221] Mitford was an enthusiastic devotee of *Punch and Judy* puppet-shows. In a letter from 1816, she declared herself delighted at the prospect of a Punch show "which lasts three hours."

[222] James Crichton (1560-1582), known as "The Admirable Crichton," was a British Renaissance man, traditionally seen as the embodiment of all accomplishments.

[223] Slang term for "the genuine article, the real thing." The expression comes from a popular comedy (*A Bold Stroke for a Wife*) by Susanna Centlivre, first performed in 1718.

213

At last I thought that I had actually caught him, and on his own peculiar field, the cricket-ground. We abound in rustic fun, and good humour, and of course in nick-names. A certain senior of fifty, or thereabout, for instance, of very juvenile habits and inclinations, who plays at ball, and marbles, and cricket, with all the boys in the parish, and joins a kind merry buoyant heart to an aspect somewhat rough and care-worn, has no other appellation that ever I heard but "Uncle;" I don't think, if by any strange chance he were called by it, that he would know his own name. On the hand, a little stunted pragmatical urchin, son and heir of Dick Jones, and absolute old man cut shorter, so slow, and stiff, and sturdy, and wordy, passes universally by the title of "Grandfather"—I have not the least notion that he would answer to Dick. Also a slim, grim-looking, white-headed lad, whose hair is bleached, and his skin browned by the sun, 'till he is as hideous as an Indian idol, goes, good lack! by the pastoral misnomer of the "Gentle Shepherd." Oh manes of Allan Ramsay! the Gentle Shepherd![224]

Another youth, regular at cricket, but never seen except then, of unknown parish, and parentage, and singular uncouthness of person, dress, and demeanour, rough as a badger, ragged as a colt, and sour as verjuice, was known, far more appropriately, by the cognomen of "Oddity." Him, in my secret soul, I pitched on for Jack Hatch. In the first place, as I had in the one case a man without a name, and in the other a name without a man, to have found these component parts of individuality meet in the same person, to have made the man to fit the name, and the name fit the man, would have been as pretty a way of solving two enigmas at once, as hath been heard of since Œdipus his day. But besides the obvious convenience and suitability of this belief, I had divers other corroborating reasons. Oddity was young, so was Jack;—Oddity came up the hill from leaward, so must Jack;—Oddity was a capital cricketer, so was Jack;—Oddity did not play in our unlucky Beech-hill match, neither did Jack;—and, last of all, Oddity's name was Jack, a fact I was fortunate enough to ascertain from a pretty damsel who walked up with him to the ground one evening, and who on seeing him bowl out Tom Coper, could not help exclaiming in soliloquy, as she stood a few yards behind us, looking on with all her heart, "Well done, Jack!" That moment built up all my hopes; the next knocked them down. I thought I had clutched him, but willing to make assurance

---

[224] The best-known work of Scottish poet Allan Ramsay (1686-1758) is the pastoral comedy *The Gentle Shepherd* (1725). "Manes" is the spirit of someone dead (often used in invocations). A little before, "lack" is a minced oath replacing "Lord."

Jack Hatch

doubly sure, I turned to my pretty neighbour, (Jack Hatch too had a sweetheart) and said in a tone half affirmative, half interrogatory, "That young man who plays so well is Jack Hatch?"—"No, ma'am, Jack Bolton!" and Jack Hatch remained still a sound, a name, a mockery.

Well! at last I ceased to look for him, and might possibly have forgotten my curiosity, had not every week produced some circumstance to relumine that active female passion.

I seemed beset by his name, and his presence invisibly as it were. Will of the wisp is nothing to him; Puck, in that famous Midsummer Dream, was a quiet goblin compared to Jack Hatch. He haunts one in dark places. The fiddler, whose merry tones come ringing across the orchard in a winter's night from Farmer White's barn, setting the whole village a dancing, is Jack Hatch. The whistler, who trudges homeward at dusk up Kibe's lanes, out-piping the nightingale, in her own month of May, is Jack Hatch. And the indefatigable learner of the bassoon, whose drone, all last harvest, might be heard in the twilight, issuing from the sexton's dwelling on the Little Lea, "making night hideous,"[225] that iniquitous practiser is Jack Hatch.

The name meets me all manner of ways. I have seen it in the newspaper for a prize of pinks; and on the back of a warrant on the charge of poaching;—N.B. the constable had my luck, and could not find the culprit, otherwise I might have had some chance of seeing him on that occasion. Things the most remote and discrepant issue in Jack Hatch. He caught Dame Wheeler's squirrel; the Magpie at the Rose owes to him the half dozen phrases with which he astounds and delights the passers by; the very dog Tero,—an animal of singular habits, who sojourns occasionally at half the houses in the village, making each his home till he is affronted—Tero himself, best and ugliest of finders—a mongrel compounded of terrier, cur, and spaniel—Tero, most remarkable of ugly dogs, inasmuch as he constantly squints, and commonly goes on three legs, holding up first one, and then the other, out of a sort of quadrupedal economy to ease those useful members—Tero himself is said to belong of right and origin to Jack Hatch.

Every where that name meets me. 'Twas but a few weeks ago that I heard him asked in church, and a day or two afterwards I saw the tail of the wedding procession, the little lame clerk handing the bridesmaid, and a girl from the Rose running after them with pipes,

---

[225] From *Hamlet* (Act I, scene 4).

passing by our house.[226] Nay, this very morning, some one was speaking—Dead! what dead? Jack Hatch dead?—a name, a shadow, a Jack o' lantern! Can Jack Hatch die? Hath he the property of mortality? Can the bell toll for him? Yes! there is the coffin and the pall—all that I shall ever see of him is there!—There are his comrades following in decent sorrow—and the poor pretty bride, leaning on the little clerk—My search is over—Jack Hatch is dead!

---

[226] "The Rose" is the name of the tavern in Mitford's *Our Village*. "Bridemaid" is an obsolete variant.

Walter Scott

𝒯HE 𝒯WO 𝒟ROVERS

(1827)

The author: The Panic of 1825 brought about the collapse of James Ballantyne's printing business and Walter Scott, his partner, was financially ruined. In 1826 his wife Charlotte died and Scott was offered helped from many admirers, including the king. He refused and decided to write himself out of debt. On Friday, 23 February 1827, at the first Edinburgh Theatrical Fund dinner, he admitted publicly for the first time that he was the author of the Waverley novels.

The text: First published in *Chronicles of the Canongate*. 2 vols. Edinburgh: Cadell and Co.; London: Simpkin and Marshall, 1827. I, 293-351. The *Chronicles* appeared, as usual, as "By the Author of "Waverley," but it opened with an introduction signed "Walter Scott." The following is the original version of 1827 (the "Magnum edition" has been consulted for only a couple of misspellings).

Further reading: Seamus Cooney. "Scott and Cultural Relativism: 'The Drovers.'" *Studies in Short Fiction* 15: 1 (Winter 1978), 1-9.

W. J. Overton. "Scott, the Short Story and History: 'The Two Drovers.'" *Studies in Scottish Literature* 21: 1 (1986), 210-225.

It was the day after Doune Fair when my story commences.[227] It had been a brisk market, several dealers had attended from the northern and midland counties in England, and English money had flown so merrily about as to gladden the hearts of the Highland farmers. Many large droves were about to set off for England, under the protection of their owners, or of the topsmen whom

[227] Doune is a burgh in Perthshire, in the Scottish Highlands.

217

they employed in the tedious, laborious, and responsible office of driving the cattle for many hundred miles, from the market where they had been purchased to the fields or farm-yards where they were to be fattened for the shambles.

The Highlanders in particular are masters of this difficult trade of driving, which seems to suit them as well as the trade of war. It affords exercise for all their habits of patient endurance and active exertion. They are required to know perfectly the drove-roads, which lie over the wildest tracts of the country, and to avoid as much as possible the highways, which distress the feet of the bullocks, and the turnpikes, which annoy the spirit of the drover; whereas on the broad green or grey track, which leads across the pathless moor, the herd not only move at ease and without taxation, but, if they mind their business, may pick up a mouthful of food by the way. At night the drovers usually sleep along with their cattle, let the weather be what it will; and many of these hardy men do not once rest under a roof during a journey on foot from Lochaber to Lincolnshire.[228] They are paid very highly, for the trust reposed is of the last importance, as it depends on their prudence, vigilance, and honesty, whether the cattle reach the final market in good order, and afford a profit to the grazier. But as they maintain themselves at their own expense, they are especially economical in that particular. At the period we speak of, a Highland drover was victualled for his long and toilsome journey with a few handfulls of oatmeal and two or three onions, renewed from time to time, and a ram's horn filled with whisky, which he used regularly, but sparingly, every night and morning. His dirk, or *skene-dhu*, (*i.e.* black knife,) so worn as to be concealed beneath the arm, or by the folds of the plaid, was his only weapon, excepting the cudgel with which he directed the movements of the cattle. A Highlander was never so happy as on these occasions. There was a variety in the whole journey, which exercised the Celt's natural curiosity and love of motion; there were the constant change of place and scene, the petty adventures incidental to the traffic, and the intercourse with the various farmers, graziers, and traders, intermingled with occasional merry-makings, not the less acceptable to Donald[229] that they were void of expense;—and there was the consciousness of superior skill; for the Highlander, a child amongst flocks, is a prince amongst herds, and his natural habits induce him to disdain the shepherd's slothful

[228] A distance of about 650 km. Lochaber is far north in the Highlands, while Lincolnshire is a county in central England, on the North Sea coast.

[229] Here and elsewhere, Donald is used as a stereotypical appellation for a Scotsman.

The Two Drovers

life, so that he feels himself nowhere more at home than when following a gallant drove of his country cattle in the character of their guardian.

Of the number who left Doune in the morning, and with the purpose we have described, not a *Glunamie* of them all cocked his bonnet more briskly,[230] or gartered his tartan hose under knee over a pair of more promising *spiogs*, (legs), than did Robin Oig M'Combich, called familiarly Robin Oig, that is young, or the Lesser, Robin. Though small of stature, as the epithet Oig implies, and not very strongly limbed, he was as light and alert as one of the deer of his mountains. He had an elasticity of step, which, in the course of a long march, made many a stout fellow envy him; and the manner in which he busked his plaid and adjusted his bonnet, argued a consciousness that so smart a John Highlandman as himself would not pass unnoticed among the Lowland lasses. The ruddy cheek, red lips, and white teeth, set off a countenance which had gained by exposure to the weather a healthful and hardy rather than a rugged hue. If Robin Oig did not laugh, or even smile frequently, as indeed is not the practice among his countrymen, his bright eyes usually gleamed from under his bonnet with an expression of cheerfulness ready to be turned into mirth.

The departure of Robin Oig was an incident in the little town, in and near which he had many friends male and female. He was a topping person in his way, transacted considerable business on his own behalf, and was intrusted by the best farmers in the Highlands, in preference to any other drover in that district. He might have increased his business to any extent had he condescended to manage it by deputy; but except a lad or two, sister's sons of his own, Robin rejected the idea of assistance, conscious, perhaps, how much his reputation depended upon his attending in person to the practical discharge of his duty in every instance. He remained, therefore, contented with the highest premium given to persons of his description, and comforted himself with the hopes that a few journeys to England might enable him to conduct business on his own account, in a manner becoming his birth. For Robin Oig's father, Lachlan M'Combich (or, *son of my friend*, his actual clan-surname being M'Gregor,), had been so called by the celebrated Rob Roy, because of the particular friendship which had subsisted between the grandsire of Robin and that renowned cateran.[231] Some people even say, that Robin Oig derived his Christian name

---

[230] Glunamie or Glunimie is a Lowland term for a Highlander.

[231] Name given to a Highland brigand.

from a man, as renowned in the wilds of Lochlomond,[232] as ever was his namesake Robin Hood, in the precincts of merry Sherwood. "Of such ancestry," as James Boswell says,[233] "who would not be proud?" Robin Oig was proud accordingly; but his frequent visits to England and to the Lowlands had given him tact enough to know that pretensions, which still gave him a little right to distinction in his own lonely glen, might be both obnoxious and ridiculous if preferred elsewhere. The pride of birth, therefore, was like the miser's treasure, the secret subject of his contemplation, but never exhibited to strangers as a subject of boasting.

Many were the words of gratulation and good-luck which were bestowed on Robin Oig. The judges commended his drove, especially the best of them, which were Robin's own property. Some thrust out their snuff-mulls for the parting pinch—others tendered the *doch-an-dorrach*, or parting cup. All cried—"Good-luck travel out with you and come home with you.—Give you luck in the Saxon market—brave notes in the *leabhar-dhu*, (black pocket-book,) and plenty of English gold in the *sporran* (pouch of goatskin)."

The bonny lasses made their adieus more modestly, and more than one, it was said, would have given her best brooch to be certain that it was upon her that his eye last rested as he turned towards the road.

Robin Oig had just given the preliminary "*Hoo-hoo!*" to urge forward the loiterers of the drove, when there was a cry behind him.

"Stay, Robin—bide a blink. Here is Janet of Tomahourich—auld Janet, your father's sister."

"Plague on her, for an auld Highland witch and spaewife," said a farmer from the Carse of Stirling; "she'll cast some of her cantrips on the cattle."[234]

"She canna do that," said another sapient of the same profession—"Robin Oig is no the lad to leave any of them, without tying Saint Mungo's knot on their tails, and that will put to her speed the best witch that ever flew over Dimayet upon a broomstick."[235]

It may not be indifferent to the reader to know that the Highland cattle are peculiarly liable to be *taken*, or infected, by spells and witchcraft, which judicious people guard against by knitting knots of peculiar complexity on the tuft of hair which terminates the animal's tail.

[232] Loch Lomond, a large lake in the Highlands.

[233] James Boswell (1740-1795), the Scottish biographer and diarist, says this about his own ancestry, in *The Journal of a Tour to the Hebrides* (1785).

[234] A spaewife is a woman who foretells the future; a cantrip is a magic spell.

[235] Dumyat, a hill not far from the city of Stirling and from the historic Bannockburn battlefield.

The Two Drovers

But the old woman who was the object of the farmer's suspicion seemed only busied about the drover, without paying any attention to the flock. Robin, on the contrary, appeared rather impatient of her presence.

"What auld-world fancy," he said, "has brought you so early from the ingle-side[236] this morning, Muhme? I am sure I bid you good even, and had your God-speed, last night."

"And left me more siller than the useless old woman will use till you come back again, bird of my bosom," said the sibyl. "But it is little I would care for the food that nourishes me, or the fire that warms me, or for God's blessed sun itself, if aught but weel should happen to the grandson of my father. So let me walk the *deasil* round you,[237] that you may go safe out into the far foreign land, and come safe home."

Robin Oig stopped, half embarrassed, half laughing, and signing to those around that he only complied with the old woman to soothe her humour. In the meantime, she traced around him, with wavering steps, the propitiation, which some have thought has been derived from the Druidical mythology. It consists, as is well known, in the person who makes the *deasil*, walking three times round the person who is the object of the ceremony, taking care to move according to the course of the sun. At once, however, she stopped short, and exclaimed, in a voice of alarm and horror, "Grandson of my father, there is blood on your hand."

"Hush, for God's sake, aunt!" said Robin Oig; "you will bring more trouble on yourself with this *Taishataragh* (second sight) than you will be able to get out of for many a day."

The old woman only repeated, with a ghastly look, "There is blood on your hand, and it is English blood. The blood of the Gael is richer and redder. Let us see—let us—"

Ere Robin Oig could prevent her, which, indeed, could only have been by positive violence, so hasty and peremptory were her proceedings, she had drawn from his side the dirk which lodged in the folds of his plaid, and held it up, exclaiming, although the weapon gleamed clear and bright in the sun, "Blood, blood—Saxon blood again. Robin Oig M'Combich, go not this day to England!"

"Prutt, trutt," answered Robin Oig, "that will never do neither—it would be next thing to running the country. For shame, Muhme—give me the dirk. You cannot tell by the colour the

[236] The fireside.
[237] Deasil means sunwise (i.e., following the course of the sun) in Scots English. Scott refers here to the custom of walking sunwise around a person to induce good fortune.

221

difference betwixt the blood of a black bullock and a white one, and you speak of knowing Saxon from Gaelic blood. All men have their blood from Adam, Muhme. Give me my skene-dhu, and let me go on my road. I should have been half way to Stirling brig[238] by this time—Give me my dirk, and let me go."

"Never will I give it to you," said the old woman—"Never will I quit my hold on your plaid, unless you promise me not to wear that unhappy weapon."

The women around him urged him also, saying few of his aunt's words fell to the ground; and as the Lowland farmers continued to look moodily on the scene, Robin Oig determined to close it at any sacrifice.

"Well, then," said the young drover, giving the scabbard of the weapon to Hugh Morrison, "you Lowlanders care nothing for these freats.[239] Keep my dirk for me. I cannot give it you, because it was my father's; but your drove follows ours, and I am content it should be in your keeping, not in mine.—Will this do, Muhme?"

"It must," said the old woman—"that is, if the Lowlander is mad enough to carry the knife."

The strong westlandman laughed aloud.

"Goodwife," said he, "I am Hugh Morrison from Glenae, come of the Manly Morrisons of auld langsyne, that never took short weapon against a man in their lives. And neither needed they: They had their broadswords, and I have this bit supple (showing a formidable cudgel)—for dirking ower the board, I leave that to John Highlandman.—Ye needna snort, none of you Highlanders, and you in especial, Robin. I'll keep the bit knife, if you are feared for the auld spaewife's tale, and give it back to you whenever you want it."

Robin was not particularly pleased with some part of Hugh Morrison's speech; but he had learned in his travels more patience than belonged to his Highland constitution originally, and he accepted the service of the descendant of the Manly Morrisons, without finding fault with the rather depreciating manner in which it was offered.

"If he had not had his morning in his head, and been but a Dumfries-shire hog into the boot, he would have spoken more like a gentleman. But you cannot have more of a sow than a grumph.[240] It's shame my father's knife should ever slash a haggis for the like of him."

---

[238] Stirling Bridge, today known as Stirling Old Bridge.

[239] Scots term for superstitions.

[240] Grumph is Scots for grunt. The expression means that you cannot expect more from a hog or a sow than a grunt (you cannot expect people to behave in a way that does not fit their character).

The Two Drovers

Thus saying, (but saying it in Gaelic,) Robin drove on his cattle, and waved farewell to all behind him. He was in the greater haste, because he expected to join at Falkirk a comrade and brother in profession, with whom he proposed to travel in company.

Robin Oig's chosen friend was a young Englishman, Harry Wakefield by name, well known at every northern market, and in his way as much famed and honoured as our Highland driver of bullocks. He was nearly six feet high, gallantly formed to keep the rounds at Smithfield,[241] or maintain the ring at a wrestling match; and although he might have been overmatched, perhaps, among the regular professors of the Fancy,[242] yet, as a yokel or rustic, or a chance customer, he was able to give a bellyful to any amateur of the pugilistic art. Doncaster races saw him in his glory, betting his guinea, and generally successfully; nor was there a main fought in Yorkshire, the feeders being persons of celebrity,[243] at which he was not to be seen, if business permitted. But though a *sprack* lad,[244] and fond of pleasure and its haunts, Harry Wakefield was steady, and not the cautious Robin Oig M'Combich himself was more attentive to the main chance. His holidays were holidays indeed; but his days of work were dedicated to steady and persevering labour. In countenance and temper, Wakefield was the model of Old England's merry yeomen, whose clothyard shafts, in so many hundred battles, asserted her superiority over the nations, and whose good sabres, in our own time, are her cheapest and most assured defence. His mirth was readily excited; for, strong in limb and constitution, and fortunate in circumstances, he was disposed to be pleased with everything about him; and such difficulties as he might occasionally encounter, were, to a man of his energy, rather matter of amusement than serious annoyance. With all the merits of a sanguine temper, our young English drover was not without his defects. He was irascible, sometimes to the verge of being quarrelsome; and perhaps not the less inclined to bring his disputes to a pugilistic decision, because he found few antagonists able to stand up to him in the boxing ring.

It is difficult to say how Harry Wakefield and Robin Oig first became intimates; but it is certain a close acquaintance had taken place betwixt them, although they had apparently few common subjects of conversation or of interest, so soon as their talk ceased

[241] Smithfield Market is an old meat market in central London.

[242] The Fancy was a slang term for boxing.

[243] A "main" was a fight on which people bet, especially a cockfight. The feeders were the owners of the roosters.

[244] Sprack means lively.

to be of bullocks. Robin Oig, indeed, spoke the English language rather imperfectly upon any other topics but stots and kyloes,[245] and Harry Wakefield could never bring his broad Yorkshire tongue to utter a single word of Gaelic. It was in vain Robin spent a whole morning, during a walk over Minch-Moor, in attempting to teach his companion to utter, with true precision, the shibboleth *Llhu*, which is the Gaelic for a calf. From Traquair to Murder-cairn, the hill rung with the discordant attempts of the Saxon upon the unmanageable monosyllable, and the heartfelt laugh which followed every failure. They had, however, better modes of awakening the echoes; for Wakefield could sing many a ditty to the praise of Moll, Susan, and Cicely, and Robin Oig had a particular gift at whistling interminable pibrochs[246] through all their involutions, and what was more agreeable to his companion's southern ear, knew many of the northern airs, both lively and pathetic, to which Wakefield learned to pipe a bass. Thus, though Robin could hardly have comprehended his companion's stories about horse-racing, cock-fighting, or fox-hunting, and although his own legends of clan-fights and *creaghs*,[247] varied with talk of Highland goblins and fairy folk, would have been caviare to his companion, they contrived nevertheless to find a degree of pleasure in each other's company, which had for three years back induced them to join company and travel together, when the direction of their journey permitted. Each, indeed, found his advantage in this companionship; for where could the Englishman have found a guide through the Western Highlands like Robin Oig M'Combich? and when they were on what Harry called the *right* side of the Border, his patronage, which was extensive, and his purse, which was heavy, were at all times at the service of his Highland friend, and on many occasions his liberality did him genuine yeoman's service.[248]

>   Were ever two such loving friends!—
>   How could they disagree?
>   Oh, thus it was, he loved him dear,
>   And thought how to requite him,

[245] Stots are bullocks; kyloes are Highland cattle, small, with shaggy hair and long curving horns.

[246] Pibroch is the generic term for the music of the Highlands, usually associated with the bagpipes.

[247] A creagh is a plundering raid.

[248] Here, the 13th chapter of *Chronicles of the Canongate* ends and the 14th chapter begins (which explains the epigraph that follows).

The Two Drovers

>   And having no friend left but he,
>   He did resolve to fight him.
>   *Duke upon Duke.*[249]

The pair of friends had traversed with their usual cordiality the grassy wilds of Liddesdale, and crossed the opposite part of Cumberland, emphatically called The Waste. In these solitary regions, the cattle under the charge of our drovers derived subsisted themselves cheaply, by picking their food as they went along the drove-road, or sometimes by the tempting opportunity of a *start and owerloup*, or invasion of the neighbouring pasture, where an occasion presented itself. But now the scene changed before them; they were descending towards a fertile and enclosed country, where no such liberties could be taken with impunity, or without a previous arrangement and bargain with the possessors of the ground. This was more especially the case, as a great northern fair was upon the eve of taking place, where both the Scotch and English drover expected to dispose of a part of their cattle, which it was desirable to produce in the market, rested and in good order. Fields were therefore difficult to be obtained, and only upon high terms. This necessity occasioned a temporary separation betwixt the two friends, who went to bargain, each as he could, for the separate accommodation of his herd. Unhappily it chanced that both of them, unknown to each other, thought of bargaining for the ground they wanted on the property of a country gentleman of some fortune, whose estate lay in the neighbourhood. The English drover applied to the bailiff on the property, who was known to him. It chanced that the Cumbrian Squire, who had entertained some suspicions of his manager's honesty, was taking occasional measures to ascertain how far they were well founded, and had desired that any inquiries about his enclosures, with a view to occupy them for a temporary purpose, should be referred to himself. As, however, Mr. Ireby had gone the day before upon a journey of some miles' distance to the northward, the bailiff chose to consider the check upon his full powers as for the time removed, and concluded that he should best consult his master's interest, and perhaps his own, in making an agreement with Harry Wakefield. Meanwhile, ignorant of what his comrade was doing, Robin Oig, on his side, chanced to be overtaken by a well-looked smart little man upon a pony, most knowingly hogged and cropped, as was then the fashion, the rider wearing tight leather breeches, and long-necked bright spurs. This

[249] "Duke upon Duke" is a "play-house ballad" first published in 1720. It was definitively attributed to Alexander Pope in the 20th century.

cavalier asked one or two pertinent questions about markets and the price of stock. So Donald, seeing him a well-judging civil gentleman, took the freedom to ask him whether he could let him know if there was any grass-land to be let in that neighbourhood, for the temporary accommodation of his drove. He could not have put the question to more willing ears. The gentleman of the buckskins was the proprietor, with whose bailiff Harry Wakefield had dealt, or was in the act of dealing.

"Thou art in good luck, my canny Scot," said Mr. Ireby, "to have spoken to me, for I see thy cattle have done their day's work, and I have at my disposal the only field within three miles that is to be let in these parts."

"The drove can pe gang two, three, four miles very pratty weel indeed—" said the cautious Highlander; "put what would his honour pe axing for the peasts pe the head, if she was to tak the park for twa or three days?"

"We won't differ, Sawney,[250] if you let me have six stots for winterers, in the way of reason."

"And which peasts wad your honour pe for having?"

"Why—let me see—the two black—the dun one—yon doddy—him with the twisted horn—the brockit[251]—How much by the head?"

"Ah," said Robin, "your honour is a shudge—a real shudge—I couldna have set off the pest six peasts petter mysell, me that ken them as if they were my pairns, puir things."

"Well, how much per head, Sawney," continued Mr. Ireby.

"It was high markets at Doune and Falkirk," answered Robin.

And thus the conversation proceeded, until they had agreed on the *prix juste*[252] for the bullocks, the Squire throwing in the temporary accommodation of the enclosure for the cattle into the boot, and Robin making, as he thought, a very good bargain, providing the grass was but tolerable. The Squire walked his pony alongside of the drove, partly to show him the way, and see him put into possession of the field, and partly to learn the latest news of the northern markets.

They arrived at the field, and the pasture seemed excellent. But what was their surprise when they saw the bailiff quietly inducting the cattle of Harry Wakefield into the grassy Goshen[253] which had just

[250] A (rather derogatory) term for a Scotsman.

[251] Brockit means with black and white stripes or spots.

[252] French for the "right price."

[253] A place of comfort and plenty (so named after the biblical Land of Goshen in Genesis 45: 9-10, given to the Hebrews by the pharaoh).

The Two Drovers

been assigned to those of Robin Oig M'Combich by the proprietor himself. Squire Ireby set spurs to his horse, dashed up to his servant, and learning what had passed between the parties, briefly informed the English drover that his bailiff had let the ground without his authority, and that he might seek grass for his cattle wherever he would, since he was to get none there. At the same time he rebuked his servant severely for having transgressed his commands, and ordered him instantly to assist in ejecting the hungry and weary cattle of Harry Wakefield, which were just beginning to enjoy a meal of unusual plenty, and to introduce those of his comrade, whom the English drover now began to consider as a rival.

The feelings which arose in Wakefield's mind would have induced him to resist Mr. Ireby's decision; but every Englishman has a tolerably accurate sense of law and justice, and John Fleecebumpkin, the bailiff, having acknowledged that he had exceeded his commission, Wakefield saw nothing else for it than to collect his hungry and disappointed charge, and drive them on to seek quarters elsewhere. Robin Oig saw what had happened with regret, and hastened to offer to his English friend to share with him the disputed possession. But Wakefield's pride was severely hurt, and he answered disdainfully, "Take it all, man—take it all—never make two bites of a cherry—thou canst talk over the gentry, and blear a plain man's eye—Out upon you, man—I would not kiss any man's dirty latchets[254] for leave to bake in his oven."

Robin Oig, sorry but not surprised at his comrade's displeasure, hastened to entreat his friend to wait but an hour till he had gone to the Squire's house to receive payment for the cattle he had sold, and he would come back and help him to drive the cattle into some convenient place of rest, and explain to him the whole mistake they had both of them fallen into. But the Englishman continued indignant: "Thou hast been selling, hast thou? Ay, ay—thou is a cunning lad for kenning the hours of bargaining. Go to the devil with thyself, for I will ne'er see thy fause loon's visage[255] again—thou should be ashamed to look me in the face."

"I am ashamed to look no man in the face," said Robin Oig, something moved; "and, moreover, I will look you in the face this blessed day, if you will bide at the Clachan down yonder."[256]

"Mayhap you had as well keep away," said his comrade; and turning his back on his former friend, he collected his unwilling

[254] Leather straps used to fasten a shoe.

[255] A "fauce loon" is a sham rogue, someone who pretends to be your friend in order to use you.

[256] Clachan is Scots for a small village.

associates, assisted by the bailiff, who took some real and some affected interest in seeing Wakefield accommodated.

After spending some time in negotiating with more than one of the neighbouring farmers, who could not, or would not, afford the accommodation desired, Henry Wakefield at last, and in his necessity, accomplished his point by means of the landlord of the alehouse at which Robin Oig and he had agreed to pass the night, when they first separated from each other. Mine host was content to let him turn his cattle on a piece of barren moor, at a price little less than the bailiff had asked for the disputed inclosure; and the wretchedness of the pasture, as well as the price paid for it, were set down as exaggerations of the breach of faith and friendship of his Scottish crony. This turn of Wakefield's passions was encouraged by the bailiff, (who had his own reasons for being offended against poor Robin, as having been the unwitting cause of his falling into disgrace with his master,) as well as by the innkeeper, and two or three chance guests, who soothed the drover in his resentment against his quondam associate,—some from the ancient grudge against the Scots, which, when it exists anywhere, is to be found lurking in the Border counties, and some from the general love of mischief, which characterises mankind in all ranks of life, to the honour of Adam's children be it spoken. Good John Barleycorn also,[257] who always heightens and exaggerates the prevailing passions, be they angry or kindly, was not wanting in his offices on this occasion; and confusion to false friends and hard masters, was pledged in more than one tankard.

In the meanwhile Mr. Ireby found some amusement in detaining the northern drover at his ancient hall. He caused a cold round of beef to be placed before the Scot in the butler's pantry, together with a foaming tankard of home-brewed, and took pleasure in seeing the hearty appetite with which these unwonted edibles were discussed by Robin Oig M'Combich. The Squire himself lighting his pipe, compounded between his patrician dignity and his love of agricultural gossip, by walking up and down while he conversed with his guest.

"I passed another drove," said the Squire, "with one of your countrymen behind them—they were something less beasts than your drove, doddies most of them[258]—a big man was with them—none of your kilts though, but a decent pair of breeches—D'ye know who he may be?"

[257] John Barleycorn is a personification of liquor in British folklore.
[258] Doody is Scots for a hornless bull or cow.

The Two Drovers

"Hout ay—that might, could, and would be Hughie Morrison—I didna think he could hae peen sae weel up. He has made a day on us; but his Argyleshires will have wearied shanks. How far was he pehind?"

"I think about six or seven miles," answered the Squire, "for I passed them at the Christenbury Cragg, and I overtook you at the Hollan Bush. If his beasts be leg-weary, he will be maybe selling bargains."

"Na, na, Hughie Morrison is no the man for pargains—ye maun come to some Highland body like Robin Oig herself for the like of these—put I maun pe wishing you goot night, and twenty of them let alane ane, and I maun down to the Clachan to see if the lad Harry Waakfelt is out of his humdudgeons yet."

The party at the alehouse were still in full talk, and the treachery of Robin Oig still the theme of conversation, when the supposed culprit entered the apartment. His arrival, as usually happens in such a case, put an instant stop to the discussion of which he had furnished the subject, and he was received by the company assembled with that chilling silence, which, more than a thousand exclamations, tells an intruder that he is unwelcome. Surprised and offended, but not appalled by the reception which he experienced, Robin entered with an undaunted and even a haughty air, attempted no greeting as he saw he was received with none, and placed himself by the side of the fire, a little apart from a table, at which Harry Wakefield, the bailiff, and two or three other persons, were seated. The ample Cumbrian kitchen would have afforded plenty of room even for a larger separation.

Robin, thus seated, proceeded to light his pipe, and call for a pint of twopenny.

"We have no twopence ale," answered Ralph Heskett the landlord; "but as thou find'st thy own tobacco, it's like thou may'st find thy own liquor too—it's the wont of thy country, I wot."[259]

"Shame, goodman," said the landlady, a blithe bustling housewife, hastening herself to supply the guest with liquor— "Thou knowest well enow what the strange man wants, and it's thy trade to be civil, man. Thou shouldst know, that if the Scot likes a small pot, he pays a sure penny."

Without taking any notice of this nuptial dialogue, the Highlander took the flagon in his hand, and addressing the company generally, drank the interesting toast of "Good markets," to the party assembled.

[259] I wot, he/she/it wot are archaic forms of "I know, he/she/it knows." (The other persons use the form "wit.")

229

"The better that the wind blew fewer dealers from the north," said one of the farmers, "and fewer Highland runts to eat up the English meadows."

"Saul of my pody, put you are wrang there, my friend," answered Robin, with composure; "it is your fat Englishmen that eat up our Scots cattle, puir things."

"I wish there was a summat to eat up their drovers," said another; "a plain Englishman canna make bread within a kenning of them."

"Or an honest servant keep his master's favour, but they will come sliding in between him and the sunshine," said the bailiff.

"If these pe jokes," said Robin Oig, with the same composure, "there is ower mony jokes upon one man."

"It is no joke, but downright earnest," said the bailiff. "Harkye, Mr. Robin Ogg, or whatever is your name, it's right we should tell you that we are all of one opinion, and that is, that you, Mr. Robin Ogg, have behaved to our friend Mr. Harry Wakefield here, like a raff and a blackguard."

"Nae doubt, nae doubt," answered Robin, with great composure; "and you are a set of very feeling judges, for whose prains or pehaviour I wad not gie a pinch of sneeshing.[260] If Mr. Harry Waakfelt kens where he is wranged, he kens where he may be righted."

"He speaks truth," said Wakefield, who had listened to what passed, divided between the offence which he had taken at Robin's late behaviour, and the revival of his habitual habits of friendship.

He now rose, and went towards Robin, who got up from his seat as he approached, and held out his hand.

"That's right, Harry—go it—serve him out," resounded on all sides—"tip him the nailer—show him the mill."

"Hold your peace all of you, and be—," said Wakefield; and then addressing his comrade, he took him by the extended hand, with something alike of respect and defiance. "Robin," he said, "thou hast used me ill enough this day; but if you mean, like a frank fellow, to shake hands, and take a tussle for love on the sod, why I'll forgie thee, man, and we shall be better friends than ever."

"And would it not pe petter to pe cood friends without more of the matter?" said Robin; "we will be much petter friendships with our panes hale than proken."

Harry Wakefield dropped the hand of his friend, or rather threw it from him.

"I did not think I had been keeping company for three years with a coward."

[260] A pinch of snuff.

The Two Drovers

"Coward pelongs to none of my name," said Robin, whose eyes began to kindle, but keeping the command of his temper. "It was no coward's legs or hands, Harry Waakfelt, that drew you out of the fords of Frew, when you was drifting ower the plack rock, and every eel in the river expected his share of you."

"And that is true enough, too," said the Englishman, struck by the appeal.

"Adzooks!" exclaimed the bailiff—"sure Harry Wakefield, the nattiest lad at Whitson Tryste, Wooler Fair, Carlisle Sands, or Stagshaw Bank, is not going to show white feather? Ah, this comes of living so long with kilts and bonnets—men forget the use of their daddles."[261]

"I may teach you, Master Fleecebumpkin, that I have not lost the use of mine," said Wakefield, and then went on. "This will never do, Robin. We must have a turn-up, or we shall be the talk of the country side. I'll be d——d if I hurt thee—I'll put on the gloves gin thou like.[262] Come, stand forward like a man."

"To be peaten like a dog," said Robin; "is there any reason in that? If you think I have done you wrong, I'll go before your shudge, though I neither know his law nor his language."

A general cry of "No, no—no law, no lawyer! a bellyful and be friends," was echoed by the bystanders.

"But," continued Robin, "if I am to fight, I have no skill to fight like a jackanapes, with hands and nails."

"How would you fight then?" said his antagonist; "though I am thinking it would be hard to bring you to the scratch anyhow."

"I would fight with proadswords, and sink point on the first plood drawn—like a gentlemans."

A loud shout of laughter followed the proposal, which indeed had rather escaped from poor Robin's swelling heart, than been the dictate of his sober judgment.

"Gentleman, quotha!"[263] was echoed on all sides, with a shout of unextinguishable laughter; "a very pretty gentleman, God wot.—Canst get two swords for the gentleman to fight with, Ralph Heskett?"

"No, but I can send to the armoury at Carlisle, and lend them two forks, to be making shift with in the meantime."

"Tush, man," said another, "the bonny Scots come into the world with the blue bonnet on their heads, and dirk and pistol at their belt."

[261] Daddle was slang for "hand" or (in boxing slang) "fist."

[262] Gin (also geen of gien) is a (mostly Scottish) synonym for "if."

[263] Quotha (an alteration of "quoth he") was an expression of sarcasm.

231

"Best send post," said Mr. Fleecebumpkin, "to the Squire of Corby Castle, to come and stand second to the *gentleman*."

In the midst of this torrent of general ridicule, the Highlander instinctively griped beneath the folds of his plaid.

"But it's better not," he said in his own language. "A hundred curses on the swine-eaters, who know neither decency nor civility!"

"Make room, the pack of you," he said, advancing to the door.

But his former friend interposed his sturdy bulk, and opposed his leaving the house; and when Robin Oig attempted to make his way by force, he hit him down on the floor, with as much ease as a boy bowls down a nine-pin.

"A ring, a ring!" was now shouted, until the dark rafters, and the hams that hung on them, trembled again, and the very platters on the *bink* clattered against each other.[264] "Well done, Harry"—"Give it him home, Harry"—"Take care of him now—he sees his own blood!"

Such were the exclamations, while the Highlander, starting from the ground, all his coldness and caution lost in frantic rage, sprung at his antagonist with the fury, the activity, and the vindictive purpose, of an incensed tiger-cat. But when could rage encounter science and temper? Robin Oig again went down in the unequal contest; and as the blow was necessarily a severe one, he lay motionless on the floor of the kitchen. The landlady ran to offer some aid, but Mr. Fleecebumpkin would not permit her to approach.

"Let him alone," he said, "he will come to within time, and come up to the scratch again. He has not got half his broth yet."

"He has got all I mean to give him, though," said his antagonist, whose heart began to relent towards his old associate; "and I would rather by half give the rest to yourself, Mr. Fleecebumpkin, for you pretend to know a thing or two, and Robin had not art enough even to peel before setting to, but fought with his plaid dangling about him.—Stand up, Robin, my man! all friends now; and let me hear the man that will speak a word against you, or your country, for your sake."

Robin Oig was still under the dominion of his passion, and eager to renew the onset; but being withheld on the one side by the peace-making Dame Heskett, and on the other, aware that Wakefield no longer meant to renew the combat, his fury sunk into gloomy sullenness.

"Come, come, never grudge so much at it, man," said the brave-spirited Englishman, with the placability of his country, "shake hands, and we will be better friends than ever."

[264] Bink is a Scots term for a shelf.

The Two Drovers

"Friends!" exclaimed Robin Oig with strong emphasis—"friends!—Never. Look to yourself, Harry Waakfelt."

"Then the curse of Cromwell on your proud Scots stomach, as the man says in the play,[265] and you may do your worst, and be d——; for one man can say nothing more to another after a tussle, than that he is sorry for it."

On these terms the friends parted; Robin Oig drew out, in silence, a piece of money, threw it on the table, and then left the alehouse. But turning at the door, he shook his hand at Wakefield, pointing with his fore-finger upwards, in a manner which might imply either a threat or a caution. He then disappeared in the moonlight.

Some words passed after his departure, between the bailiff, who piqued himself on being a little of a bully, and Harry Wakefield, who, with generous inconsistency, was now not indisposed to begin a new combat in defence of Robin Oig's reputation, "although he could not use his daddles like an Englishman, as it did not come natural to him." But Dame Heskett prevented this second quarrel from coming to a head by her peremptory interference. "There should be no more fighting in her house," she said; "there had been too much already.—And you, Mr. Wakefield, may live to learn," she added, "what it is to make a deadly enemy out of a good friend."

"Pshaw, dame! Robin Oig is an honest fellow, and will never keep malice."

"Do not trust to that—you do not know the dour temper of the Scotch, though you have dealt with them so often. I have a right to know them, my mother being a Scot."

"And so is well seen on her daughter," said Ralph Heskett.

This nuptial sarcasm gave the discourse another turn; fresh customers entered the tap-room or kitchen, and others left it. The conversation turned on the expected markets, and the report of prices from different parts both of Scotland and England—treaties were commenced, and Harry Wakefield was lucky enough to find a chap for a part of his drove, and at a very considerable profit; an event of consequence more than sufficient to blot out all remembrances of the unpleasant scuffle in the earlier part of the day. But there remained one party from whose mind that recollection could not have been wiped away by the possession of every head of cattle betwixt Esk and Eden.[266]

[265] In *The Committee* (1665) by Robert Howard (1626-1698). The phrase is spoken by the Irishman Teague. It was long considered as the mightiest curse in Ireland. Yeats wrote a poem with the title "The Curse of Cromwell."

[266] One is a river in Scotland (Midlothian), the other in England (Cumbria).

233

This was Robin Oig M'Combich.—"That I should have had no weapon," he said, "and for the first time in my life!—Blighted be the tongue that bids the Highlander part with the dirk—the dirk—ha! the English blood!—My Muhme's word—when did her word fall to the ground?"

The recollection of the fatal prophecy confirmed the deadly intention which instantly sprang up in his mind.

"Ha! Morrison cannot be many miles behind; and if it were an hundred, what then!"

His impetuous spirit had now a fixed purpose and motive of action, and he turned the light foot of his country towards the wilds, through which he knew, by Mr. Ireby's report, that Morrison was advancing. His mind was wholly engrossed by the sense of injury—injury sustained from a friend; and by the desire of vengeance on one whom he now accounted his most bitter enemy. The treasured ideas of self-importance and self-opinion—of ideal birth and quality, had become more precious to him, (like the hoard to the miser,) because he could only enjoy them in secret. But that hoard was pillaged, the idols which he had secretly worshipped had been desecrated and profaned. Insulted, abused, and beaten, he was no longer worthy, in his own opinion, of the name he bore, or the lineage which he belonged to—nothing was left to him—nothing but revenge; and, as the reflection added a galling spur to every step, he determined it should be as sudden and signal as the offence.

When Robin Oig left the door of the alehouse, seven or eight English miles at least lay betwixt Morrison and him. The advance of the former was slow, limited by the sluggish pace of his cattle; the latter left behind him stubble-field and hedge-row, crag and dark heath, all glittering with frost-rime in the broad November moonlight, at the rate of six miles an hour. And now the distant lowing of Morrison's cattle is heard; and now they are seen creeping like moles in size and slowness of motion on the broad face of the moor; and now he meets them—passes them, and stops their conductor.

"May good betide us," said the Westlander—"Is this you, Robin M'Combich, or your wraith?"

"It is Robin Oig M'Combich," answered the Highlander, "and it is not.—But never mind that, put pe giving me the skene-dhu."

"What! you are for back to the Highlands!—The devil!—Have you selt all off before the fair? This beats all for quick markets!"

"I have not sold—I am not going north—May pe I will never go north again.—Give me pack my dirk, Hugh Morrison, or there will pe words petween us."

The Two Drovers

"Indeed, Robin, I'll be better advised before I gie it back to you—it is a wanchancy weapon in a Highlandman's hand, and I am thinking you will be about some barns-breaking."

"Prutt, trutt! let me have my weapon," said Robin Oig impatiently.

"Hooly and fairly," said his well-meaning friend. "I'll tell you what will do better than these dirking doings—Ye ken Highlander, and Lowlander, and Border-men are a' ae man's bairns when you are over the Scots dyke. See, the Eskdale callants,[267] and fighting Charlie of Liddesdale, and the Lockerby lads, and the four Dandies of Lustruther, and a wheen mair grey plaids, are coming up behind; and if you are wranged, there is the hand of a Manly Morrison, we'll see you righted, if Carlisle and Stanwix[268] baith took up the feud."

"To tell you the truth," said Robin Oig, desirous of eluding the suspicions of his friend, "I have enlisted with a party of the Black Watch,[269] and must march off to-morrow morning."

"Enlisted! Were you mad or drunk?—You must buy yourself off. I can lend you twenty notes, and twenty to that, if the drove sell."

"I thank you—thank ye, Hughie; but I go with good will the gate that I am going,—so the dirk—the dirk!"

"There it is for you then, since less wunna serve. But think on what I was saying.—Waes me, it will be sair news in the braes of Balquidder,[270] that Robin Oig M'Combich should have run an ill gate, and ta'en on."

"Ill news in Balquidder, indeed!" echoed poor Robin; "put Cot speed you, Hughie, and send you good marcats. Ye winna meet with Robin Oig again either at tryste[271] or fair."

So saying, he shook hastily the hand of his acquaintance, and set out in the direction from which he had advanced, with the spirit of his former pace.

"There is something wrang with the lad," muttered the Morrison to himself; "but we will maybe see better into it the morn's morning."

But long ere the morning dawned, the catastrophe of our tale had taken place. It was two hours after the affray had happened,

[267] Variant of "callan," which is Scots for young man, lad.

[268] Carlisle (also a major city) and Stanwix are districts of Cumbria.

[269] The Black Watch was the name for independent companies of the British Army raised in Scotland. It was recreated as a royal regiment of foot in 1881.

[270] Balquhidder is a village in Perthshire. Braes means uplands.

[271] Scots for a livestock market.

235

and it was totally forgotten by almost every one, when Robin Oig returned to Heskett's inn. The place was filled at once by various sorts of men, and with noises corresponding to their character. There were the grave, low sounds of men engaged in busy traffic, with the laugh, the song, and the riotous jest of those who had nothing to do but to enjoy themselves. Among the last was Harry Wakefield, who, amidst a grinning group of smock-frocks, hobnailed shoes, and jolly English physiognomies, was trolling forth the old ditty,

> "What though my name be Roger,
> Who drives the plough and cart—"[272]

when he was interrupted by a well-known voice saying in a high and stern voice, marked by the sharp Highland accent, "Harry Waakfelt—if you be a man stand up!"

"What is the matter?—what is it?" the guests demanded of each other.

"It is only a d——d Scotsman," said Fleecebumpkin, who was by this time very drunk, "whom Harry Wakefield helped to his broth to-day, who is now come to have *his cauld kail* het[273] again."

"Harry Waakfelt," repeated the same ominous summons, "stand up, if you be a man!"

There is something in the tone of deep and concentrated passion, which attracts attention and imposes awe, even by the very sound. The guests shrunk back on every side, and gazed at the Highlander, as he stood in the middle of them, his brows bent, and his features rigid with resolution.

"I will stand up with all my heart, Robin, my boy, but it shall be to shake hands with you, and drink down all unkindness. It is not the fault of your heart, man, that you don't know how to clench your hands."

By this time he stood opposite to his antagonist; his open and unsuspecting look strangely contrasted with the stern purpose, which gleamed wild, dark, and vindictive in the eyes of the Highlander.

"'Tis not thy fault, man, that, not having the luck to be an Englishman, thou canst not fight more than a school-girl."

"I *can* fight," answered Robin Oig sternly, but calmly, "and you shall know it. You, Harry Waakfelt, showed me to-day how the Saxon

---

[272] The song (known as "Hodge of the Mill and buxom Nell") was collected by Allan Ramsay (see note 224) in vol. IV of *The Tea-Table Miscellany: A Collection of Choice Songs Scots and English* (1723-1727).

[273] To have his cold kail (cabbage) heated again meant to have something done to you twice.

The Two Drovers

churls fight—I show you now how the Highland Dunniewassal[274] fights."

He seconded the word with the action, and plunged the dagger, which he suddenly displayed, into the broad breast of the English yeoman, with such fatal certainty and force, that the hilt made a hollow sound against the breast-bone, and the double-edged point split the very heart of his victim. Harry Wakefield fell, and expired with a single groan. His assassin next seized the bailiff by the collar, and offered the bloody poniard to his throat, whilst dread and surprise rendered the man incapable of defence.

"It were very just to lay you beside him," he said, "but the blood of a base pick-thank[275] shall never mix on my father's dirk, with that of a brave man."

As he spoke, he cast the man from him with so much force that he fell on the floor, while Robin, with his other hand, threw the fatal weapon into the blazing turf-fire.

"There," he said, "take me who likes—and let fire cleanse blood if it can."

The pause of astonishment still continuing, Robin Oig asked for a peace-officer, and a constable having stepped out, he surrendered himself to his custody.

"A bloody night's work you have made of it," said the constable.

"Your own fault," said the Highlander. "Had you kept his hands off me twa hours since, he would have been now as well and merry as he was twa minutes since."

"It must be sorely answered," said the peace-officer.

"Never you mind that—death pays all debts; it will pay that too."

The horror of the bystanders began now to give way to indignation; and the sight of a favourite companion murdered in the midst of them, the provocation being, in their opinion, so utterly inadequate to the excess of vengeance, might have induced them to kill the perpetrator of the deed even upon the very spot. The constable, however, did his duty on this occasion, and with the assistance of some of the more reasonable persons present, procured horses to guard the prisoner to Carlisle, to abide his doom at the next assizes. While the escort was preparing, the prisoner neither expressed the least interest, nor attempted the slightest reply. Only, before he was carried from the fatal apartment, he desired to look at the dead body, which, raised from the floor,

[274] A Highland gentleman, especially of secondary rank (from the cadet branch of a noble family).

[275] A sycophant, a flatterer.

had been deposited upon the large table, (at the head of which Harry Wakefield had presided but a few minutes before, full of life, vigour, and animation,) until the surgeons should examine the mortal wound. The face of the corpse was decently covered with a napkin. To the surprise and horror of the bystanders, which displayed itself in a general *Ah!* drawn through clenched teeth and half-shut lips, Robin Oig removed the cloth, and gazed with a mournful but steady eye on the lifeless visage, which had been so lately animated, that the smile of good humoured confidence in his own strength, of conciliation at once, and contempt towards his enemy, still curled his lip. While those present expected that the wound, which had so lately flooded the apartment with gore, would send forth fresh streams at the touch of the homicide, Robin Oig replaced the covering, with the brief exclamation—"He was a pretty man!"

My story is nearly ended. The unfortunate Highlander stood his trial at Carlisle. I was myself present, and as a young Scottish lawyer, or barrister at least, and reputed a man of some quality, the politeness of the Sheriff of Cumberland offered me a place on the bench. The facts of the case were proved in the manner I have related them; and whatever might be at first the prejudice of the audience against a crime so un-English as that of assassination from revenge, yet when the rooted national prejudices of the prisoner had been explained, which made him consider himself as stained with indelible dishonour, when subjected to personal violence; when his previous patience, moderation, and endurance, were considered, the generosity of the English audience was inclined to regard his crime as the wayward aberration of a false idea of honour rather than as flowing from a heart naturally savage, or perverted by habitual vice. I shall never forget the charge of the venerable Judge to the jury, although not at that time liable to be much affected either by that which was eloquent or pathetic.

"We have had," he said, "in the previous part of our duty, (alluding to some former trials,) to discuss crimes which infer disgust and abhorrence, while they call down the well-merited vengeance of the law. It is now our still more melancholy duty to apply its salutary though severe enactments to a case of a very singular character, in which the crime (for a crime it is, and a deep one) arose less out of the malevolence of the heart, than the error of the understanding—less from any idea of committing wrong, than from an unhappily perverted notion of that which is right. Here we have two men, highly esteemed, it has been stated, in their rank of life, and attached, it seems, to each other as friends, one of

The Two Drovers

whose lives has been already sacrificed to a punctilio, and the other is about to prove the vengeance of the offended laws; and yet both may claim our commiseration at least, as men acting in ignorance of each other's national prejudices, and unhappily misguided rather than voluntarily erring from the path of right conduct.

In the original cause of the misunderstanding, we must in justice give the right to the prisoner at the bar. He had acquired possession of the inclosure, which was the object of competition, by a legal contract with the proprietor Mr. Ireby; and yet, when accosted with reproaches undeserved in themselves, and galling doubtless to a temper at least sufficiently susceptible of passion, he offered notwithstanding to yield up half his acquisition, for the sake of peace and good neighbourhood, and his amicable proposal was rejected with scorn. Then follows the scene at Mr. Heskett the publican's, and you will observe how the stranger was treated by the deceased, and I am sorry to observe, by those around, who seem to have urged him in a manner which was aggravating in the highest degree. While he asked for peace and for composition, and offered submission to a magistrate, or to a mutual arbiter, the prisoner was insulted by a whole company, who seem on this occasion to have forgotten the national maxim of 'fair play;' and while attempting to escape from the place in peace, he was intercepted, struck down, and beaten to the effusion of his blood.

Gentlemen of the Jury, it was with some impatience that I heard my learned brother, who opened the case for the crown, give an unfavourable turn to the prisoner's conduct on this occasion. He said the prisoner was afraid to encounter his antagonist in fair fight, or to submit to the laws of the ring; and that therefore, like a cowardly Italian, he had recourse to his fatal stiletto, to murder the man whom he dared not meet in manly encounter. I observed the prisoner shrink from this part of the accusation with the abhorrence natural to a brave man; and as I would wish to make my words impressive, when I point his real crime, I must secure his opinion of my impartiality, by rebutting everything that seems to me a false accusation. There can be no doubt that the prisoner is a man of resolution—too much resolution—I wish to Heaven that he had less, or rather that he had had a better education to regulate it.

Gentlemen, as to the laws my brother talks of, they may be known in the Bull-ring, or the Bear-garden, or the Cockpit, but they are not known here. Or, if they should be so far admitted as furnishing a species of proof, that no malice was intended in this sort of combat, from which fatal accidents do sometimes arise, it can only be so admitted when both parties are *in pari casu*,[276] equally acquainted with, and equally willing to refer themselves to, that species of arbitrement. But will it be contended that a man of superior rank and education is to be subjected, or is obliged to subject himself, to this coarse and brutal strife, perhaps in opposition to a younger, stronger, or more skilful opponent? Certainly even the pugilistic code, if founded upon the fair play of Merry Old England, as my brother alleges it to be, can contain nothing so preposterous. And, gentlemen of the jury, if the laws would support an English gentleman, wearing, we will suppose, his sword, in defending himself by force against a violent personal aggression of the nature offered to this prisoner, they will not less protect a foreigner and a stranger, involved in the same unpleasing circumstances. If, therefore, gentlemen of the jury, when thus pressed by a *vis major*,[277] the object of obloquy to a whole company, and of direct violence from one at least, and as he might reasonably apprehend, from more, the panel had produced the weapon which his countrymen, as we are informed, generally carry about their persons, and the same unhappy circumstance had ensued which you have heard detailed in evidence, I could not in my conscience have asked from you a verdict of murder. The prisoner's personal defence might indeed, even in that case, have gone more or less beyond the boundary of *Moderamen inculpatae tutelae*,[278] spoken of by lawyers, but the punishment incurred would have been that of manslaughter, not of murder. I beg leave to add, that I should have thought this milder species of charge was demanded in the case supposed, notwithstanding the statute of James I. cap. 8, which takes the case of slaughter by stabbing with a short weapon, even without *malice prepense*,[279] out of the benefit of clergy.[280] For this statute of stabbing, as it is termed, arose out of a temporary cause; and as the real guilt is the same, whether the slaughter be committed by the dagger, or by sword or pistol, the benignity of the modern law places them all on the same, or nearly the same footing.

But, gentlemen of the jury, the pinch of the case lies in the interval of two hours interposed betwixt the reception of the injury

[276] Latin for "in a similar condition/situation."

[277] Latin for "superior/irresistible force" ("force majeure").

[278] Latin for "a controlled amount of blameless force."

[279] Premeditated injury (phrase of French origin).

[280] Benefit of clergy (abolished in 1827) afforded leniency to first-time offenders (mostly of lesser felonies). The name comes from the Middle Ages, when being a clergyman (afterwards, being literate) granted similar advantages.

and the fatal retaliation. In the heat of affray and *chaude mêlée*,[281] law, compassionating the infirmities of humanity, makes allowance for the passions which rule such a stormy moment—for the sense of present pain, for the apprehension of further injury, for the difficulty of ascertaining with due accuracy the precise degree of violence which is necessary to protect the person of the individual, without annoying or injuring the assailant more than is absolutely necessary. But the time necessary to walk twelve miles, however speedily performed, was an interval sufficient for the prisoner to have recollected himself; and the violence with which he carried his purpose into effect, with so many circumstances of deliberate determination, could neither be induced by the passion of anger, nor that of fear. It was the purpose and the act of predetermined revenge, for which law neither can, will, nor ought to have sympathy or allowance.

It is true, we may repeat to ourselves, in alleviation of this poor man's unhappy action, that his case is a very peculiar one. The country which he inhabits was, in the days of many now alive, inaccessible to the laws, not only of England, which have not even yet penetrated thither, but to those to which our neighbours of Scotland are subjected, and which must be supposed to be, and no doubt actually are, founded upon the general principles of justice and equity which pervade every civilized country. Amongst their mountains, as among the North American Indians, the various tribes were wont to make war upon each other, so that each man was obliged to go armed for his own protection, and for the offence of his neighbour. These men, from the ideas which they entertained of their own descent and of their own consequence, regarded themselves as so many cavaliers or men-at-arms, rather than as the peasantry of a peaceful country. Those laws of the ring, as my brother terms them, were unknown to the race of warlike mountaineers; that decision of quarrels by no other weapons than those which nature has given every man, must to them have seemed as vulgar and as preposterous as to the Noblesse of France. Revenge, on the other hand, must have been as familiar to their habits of society as to those of the Cherokees or Mohawks. It is, indeed, as described by Bacon, at bottom a kind of wild untutored justice; for the fear of retaliation must withhold the hands of the oppressor where there is no regular law to check daring violence. But though all this may be granted, and though we may allow that, such having been the case of the Highlands in the days of the prisoner's

[281] French for "chance medley," a legal term for murder without initial intent, an early version of "voluntary manslaughter."

fathers, many of the opinions and sentiments must still continue to influence the present generation, it cannot, and ought not, even in this most painful case, to alter the administration of the law, either in your hands, gentlemen of the jury, or in mine. The first object of civilisation is to place the general protection of the law, equally administered, in the room of that wild justice, which every man cut and carved for himself, according to the length of his sword and the strength of his arm. The law says to the subjects, with a voice only inferior to that of the Deity, 'Vengeance is mine.' The instant that there is time for passion to cool, and reason to interpose, an injured party must become aware, that the law assumes the exclusive cognizance of the right and wrong betwixt the parties, and opposes her inviolable buckler[282] to every attempt of the private party to right himself. I repeat, that this unhappy man ought personally to be the object rather of our pity than our abhorrence, for he failed in his ignorance, and from mistaken notions of honour. But his crime is not the less that of murder, gentlemen, and, in your high and important office, it is your duty so to find. Englishmen have their angry passions as well as Scots; and should this man's action remain unpunished, you may unsheath, under various pretences, a thousand daggers betwixt the Land's-End and the Orkneys."[283]

The venerable Judge thus ended what, to judge by his apparent emotion, and by the tears which filled his eyes, was really a painful task. The jury, according to his instructions, brought in a verdict of Guilty; and Robin Oig M'Combich, *alias* M'Gregor, was sentenced to death, and left for execution, which took place accordingly. He met his fate with great firmness, and acknowledged the justice of his sentence. But he repelled indignantly the observations of those who accused him of attacking an unarmed man. "I give a life for the life I took," he said, "and what can I do more?"

---

[282] A small round shield (and by extension any means of defence).

[283] That is, throughout Great Britain (Land's End is in the extreme southwest of England; the Orkney Isles are in the northeast of Scotland).

Mary Russell Mitford

𝒯he 𝒱illage Schoolmistress

(1827)

The author: All through the 1820s, Mitford published short stories that she later collected in her magnum opus *Our Village*. In 1835 she published a similar collection, set in an urban setting, *Belford Regis; or, Sketches of a Country Town* (3 volumes), followed by *Country Stories* in 1837. She was quite prolific (she also took various editing jobs), as she was trying to keep up with her father's gambling and spending habits. He died in 1842 and Mitford retired in a village in Berkshire. After a long break, she published *Recollections of a Literary Life* (1852) and *Atherton, and Other Tales* (1854), which included her longest fiction, the titular novella. During the last two decades of her life (she died in 1855), she frequently corresponded with her much younger friend Elizabeth Barrett Browning.

The text: First published in S. C. Hall's annual *The Amulet; or Christian and Literary Remembrancer* (London: W. Baynes & Son, 1828 [1827]), 53-68, as "The Village Schoolmistress. A Tale. By Miss Mitford." Republished as "The Village Schoolmistress" in Mitford's volume 3 of *Our Village: Country Stories, Scenes, Characters, &c. &c.* (London: Geo. B. Whittaker, 1828), 110-127. The following is from the third edition, published the same year.

Women, fortunately perhaps for their happiness and their virtue, have, as compared to men, so few opportunities of acquiring permanent distinction, that it is rare to find a female unconnected with literature or with history, whose name is remembered after her monument is defaced, and the brass on her coffin-lid corroded. Such, however, was the case with Dame Eleanor, the widow of Sir Richard Lacy, whose name, at the end of three centuries, continued to be as freshly and as frequently spoken, as "familiar," a "household word" in the little village of Aberleigh, as if she had flourished there yesterday. Her memory was embalmed by a deed of charity and of goodness. She had founded and endowed a girls' school for "the instruction" (to use the words of the deed) "of twenty poor children, and the maintenance of one discreet and godly matron;" and the school still continued to be called after its foundress, and the very spot on which the school-house stood, to be known by the name of Lady Lacy's Green.

It was a spot worthy of its destination,—a spot of remarkable cheerfulness and beauty. The Green was small, of irregular shape, and situate[284] at a confluence of shady lanes. Half the roads and paths of the parish met there, probably for the convenience of crossing, in that place by a stone bridge of one arch covered with ivy, the winding rivulet which intersected the whole village, and which, sweeping in a narrow channel round the school garden widened into a stream of some consequence, in the richly-wooded meadows beyond. The banks of the brook, as it wound its glittering course over the green, were set, here and there, with clumps of forest trees, chiefly bright green elms, and aspens with their quivering leaves and their pale shining bark; whilst a magnificent beech stood alone near the gate leading to the school, partly overshadowing the little court in which the house was placed. The building itself was a beautiful small structure, in the ornamented style of Elizabeth's day, with pointed roofs and pinnacles, and clustered chimneys, and casement windows; the whole house enwreathed and garlanded by a most luxuriant vine. The date of the erection, 1563, was cut in a stone inserted in the brick-work above the porch: but the foundress had, with an unostentatious modesty, withheld her name; leaving it,

[284] Archaic form of "situated."

The Village Schoolmistress

as she safely might, to the grateful recollection of the successive generations who profited by her benevolence. Altogether it was a most gratifying scene to the eye and to the heart. No one ever saw Lady Lacy's school-house without admiration, especially in the play-hour at noon, when the children, freed from "restraint that sweetens liberty,"[285] were clustered under the old beech-tree, revelling in their innocent freedom, running, jumping, shouting, and laughing with all their might; the only sort of riot which it is pleasant to witness. The painter and the philanthropist might contemplate that scene with equal delight.

The right of appointing both the mistress and the scholars had been originally vested in the Lacy family, to whom nearly the whole of the parish had at one time belonged. But the estates, the manor, the hall-house had long passed into other hands and other names, and this privilege of charity was now the only possession which the heirs of Lady Lacy retained in Aberleigh. Reserving to themselves the right of nominating the matron, her descendants had therefore delegated to the vicar and the parish officers the selection of the children, and the general regulation of the school—a sort of council of regency, which, for as simple and as peaceful as the government seems, a disputatious churchwarden or a sturdy overseer would sometimes contrive to render sufficiently stormy. I have known as much canvassing and almost as much ill-will in a contested election for one of Lady Lacy's scholarships, as for a scholarship in grander places, or even for an M.P.-ship in the next borough; and the great schism between the late Farmer Brookes and all his coadjutors, as to whether the original uniform of little green stuff gowns, with white bibs and aprons, tippets and mob,[286] should be commuted for modern cotton frocks and cottage bonnets, fairly set the parish by the ears. Owing to the good farmer's glorious obstinacy (which I suppose he called firmness), the green-gownians lost the day. O believe that, as a matter of calculation, the man might be right, and that his costume was cheaper and more convenient; but I am sure that I should have been against him, right or wrong: the other dress

---

[285] Paraphrase of a passage from Thomas Gray's "Ode on a Distant Prospect of Eton College" (1747): "some on earnest business bent/ Their murmuring labours ply/ 'Gainst graver hours, that bring constraint/ To sweeten liberty." "Constraint" in Gray's poem means "restraint" and this is how it is (mis)quoted by Edgeworth and by Mitford, here and elsewhere.

[286] When worn by women and girls, a tippet was a very short cape, covering mostly the shoulders (otherwise it is a ceremonial scarf worn by Anglican priests); the "mob" is the "mobcap" (see note 91).

was so pretty, so primitive, so neat, so becoming; the little lasses looked like rose buds in the midst of their leaves: besides, it was the old traditionary dress—the dress contrived and approved by Lady Lacy. Oh! it should never have been changed, never!

Since there was so much contention in the election of pupils, it was perhaps lucky for the vestry that the exercise of the more splendid piece of patronage, the appointment of a mistress, did not enter into its duties. Mr. Lacy, the representative of the foundress, a man of fortune in a distant county, generally bestowed the situation on some old dependant of his family. During the churchwardenship of Farmer Brookes, no less than three village gouvernantes arrived at Aberleigh—a quick succession! It made more than half the business of our zealous and bustling man of office, an amateur in such matters, to instruct and overlook them. The first importation was Dame Whitaker, a person of no small importance, who had presided as head nurse over two generations of the Lacys, and was now, on the dispersion of the last set of her nurslings to their different schools, and an unlucky quarrel with a favourite lady's maid, promoted and banished to this distant government. Nobody could well be more unfit for her new station, or better suited to her old. She was a nurse from top to toe. Round, portly, smiling, with a coaxing voice, and an indolent manner; much addicted to snuff and green tea, to sitting still, to telling long stories, and to humouring children. She spoiled every brat she came near, just as she had been used to spoil the little Master Edwards and Miss Julias of her ancient dominions. She could not have scolded if she would—the gift was not in her. Under her misrule the school grew into sad disorder; the girls not only learnt nothing, but unlearnt what they knew before; work was lost—even the new shifts of the Vicar's lady; books were torn; and, for the climax of evil, no sampler[287] was prepared to carry round at Christmas, from house to house—the first time such an omission had occurred within the memory of man. Farmer Brookes was at his wit's end. He visited the school six days in the week, to admonish and reprove; he even went nigh to threaten that he would work a sampler himself; and finally bestowed on the unfortunate ex-nurse, the nickname of Queen Log, a piece of disrespect, which, together with other grievances, proved so annoying to poor Dame Whitaker, that she found the air of Aberleigh disagree with her, patched up a peace with her old enemy, the lady's maid, abdicated that unruly and rebellious principality,

[287] A sampler is a needlework or quilting pattern, sometimes with a Christmas theme, used as a teaching tool for young girls.

The Village Schoolmistress

the school, and retired with great delight to her quiet home in the deserted nursery, where, as far as I know, she still remains.

The grief of the children on losing this most indulgent non-instructress, was not mitigated by the appearance or demeanour of her successor, who at first seemed a preceptress after Farmer Brookes's own heart, a perfect Queen Stork.[288] Dame Banks was the widow of Mr. Lacy's gamekeeper; a little thin woman, with a hooked nose, a sharp voice, and a prodigious activity of tongue. She scolded all day long; and, for the first week, passed for a great teacher. After that time it began to be discovered, that, in spite of her lessons, the children did not learn; notwithstanding her rating[289] they did not mind, and in the midst of a continual bustle nothing was ever done. Dame Banks was in fact a well-intentioned, worthy woman, with a restless irritable temper, a strong desire to do her duty, and a woeful ignorance how to set about it. She was rather too old to be taught either; at least she required a gentler instructor than the good churchwarden; and so much ill-will was springing up between them, that he had even been heard to regret the loss of Dame Whitaker's quietness, when very suddenly poor Dame Banks fell ill, and died. The sword had worn the scabbard; but she was better than she seemed; a thoroughly well-meaning woman—grateful, pious, and charitable; even our man of office admitted this.

The next in succession was one with whom my trifling pen, dearly as that light and fluttering instrument loves to dally and disport over the surfaces of things, must take no saucy freedom; one of whom we all felt it impossible to speak or to think without respect; one who made Farmer Brookes's office of adviser a sinecure, by putting the whole school, himself included, into its proper place, setting every body in order, and keeping them so. I don't know how she managed, unless by good sense and good humour, and that happy art of government, which seems no art at all, because it is so perfect; but the children were busy and happy, the vestry pleased, and the churchwarden contented. All went well under Mrs. Allen.

She was an elderly woman, nearer perhaps to seventy than to sixty, and of an exceedingly venerable and prepossessing appearance. Delicacy was her chief characteristic—a delicacy so complete that it pervaded her whole person, from her tall, slender figure, her fair, faded complexion, and her silver hair, to the exquisite nicety of

---

[288] Queen Log above and queen stork here are a reference to a fable by Aesop in which frogs ask for a monarch and are instead given first a log and then a stork.

[289] Archaic form of "berating."

247

dress by which, at all hours and seasons, from Sunday morning to Saturday night, she was invariably distinguished. The soil of the day was never seen on her apparel; dust would not cling to her snowy caps and handkerchiefs: such was the art magic of her neatness. Her very pins did their office in a different manner from those belonging to other people. Her manner was gentle, cheerful, and courteous, with a simplicity and propriety of expression that perplexed all listeners; it seemed so exactly what belongs to the highest birth and the highest breeding. She was humble, very humble; but her humility was evidently the result of a truly Christian spirit, and would equally have distinguished her in any station. The poor people, always nice judges of behaviour, felt, they did not know why, that she was their superior; the gentry of the neighbourhood suspected her to be their equal—some clergyman's or officer's widow, reduced in circumstances; and would have treated her as such, had she not, on discovering their mistake, eagerly undeceived them. She had been, she said, all her life a servant, the personal attendant of one dear mistress, on whose decease she had been recommended to Mr. Lacy; and to his kindness, under Providence, was indebted for a home and a provision for her helpless age, and the still more helpless youth of a poor orphan, far dearer to her than herself. This avowal, although it changed the character of the respect paid to Mrs. Allen, was certainly not calculated to diminish its amount; and the new mistress of Lady Lacy's school, and the beautiful order of her house and garden, continued to be the pride and admiration of Aberleigh.

The orphan of whom she spoke was a little girl about eleven years old, who lived with her, and whose black frock bespoke the recent death of some relative. She had lately, Mrs. Allen said, lost her grandmother—her only remaining parent, and had now no friend but herself on earth; but there was one above who was a Father to the fatherless, and he would protect poor Jane! And as she said this, there was a touch of emotion, a break of the voice, a tremor on the lip, very unlike the usual cheerfulness and self-command of her manner. The child was evidently very dear to her. Jane was, indeed, a most interesting creature: not pretty—a girl of that age seldom is; the beauty of childhood is outgrown, that of youth not come; and Jane could scarcely ever have had any other pretensions to prettiness, than the fine expression of her dark grey eyes, and the general sweetness of her countenance. She was pale, thin, and delicate; serious and thoughtful far beyond her years; averse from play, and shrinking from notice. Her fondness for Mrs. Allen, and

The Village Schoolmistress

her constant and unremitting attention to her health and comforts, very peculiarly remarkable. Every part of their small housewifery, that her height and strength and skill would enable her to perform, she insisted on doing, and many things far beyond her power she attempted. Never was so industrious or so handy a little maiden. Old Nelly Chun, the char-woman, who went once a week to the house, to wash and bake and scour, declared that Jane did more than herself; and to all who knew Nelly's opinion of her own doings, this praise appeared superlative.

In the school-room she was equally assiduous, not as a learner, but as a teacher. None so clever as Jane in superintending the different exercises of the needle, the spelling-book, and the slate. From the little work-woman's first attempt to insert thread into a pocket handkerchief, that digging and ploughing of cambric, miscalled hemming, up to the nice and delicate mysteries of stitching and button-holing; from the easy junction of *a b*, *ab*, and *b a*, *ba*, to that tremendous sesquipedalian word *irrefragibility*,[290] at which even I tremble as I write; from the Numeration Table to Practice,[291] nothing came amiss to her. In figures she was particularly quick. Generally speaking, her patience with the other children, however dull or tiresome or giddy they might be, was exemplary; but a false accomptant,[292] a stupid arithmetician, would put her out of humour. The only time I ever heard her sweet, gentle voice raised a note above its natural key, was in reprimanding Susan Wheeler, a sturdy, square-made, rosy-cheeked lass, as big again as herself, the dunce and beauty of the school, who had three times cast up a sum of three figures, and three times made the total wrong. Jane ought to have admired the ingenuity evinced by such a variety of error; but she did not; it fairly put her in a passion. She herself was not only clever in figures, but fond of them to an extraordinary degree—luxuriated in Long Division, and revelled in the Rule-of-Three. Had she been a boy, she would probably have been a great mathematician, and have won that fickle, fleeting, shadowy wreath,

---

[290] More commonly spelled irrefragability: the fact of being indisputable, incontestable. Sesquipedalian (literally, measuring "a foot and a half") is an adjective coined by Horace to describe long words.

[291] A numeration table was a learning tool used in mathematics in the 19th century to teach tens, hundreds, thousands, millions, etc. "Practice" refers to multiplication exercises.

[292] In the sense of someone who counts; "false" in the sense of incorrect.

that crown made of the rainbow, that vainest of all earthly pleasures, but which yet *is* a pleasure—Fame.

Happier, far happier was the good, the lowly, the pious child, in her humble duties! Grave and quiet as she seemed, she had many moments of intense and placid enjoyment, when the duties of the day were over, and she sate reading in the porch, by the side of Mrs. Allen, or walked with her in the meadows on a Sunday evening after church. Jane was certainly contented and happy; and yet every one that saw her, thought of her with that kind of interest which is akin to pity. There was a pale, fragile grace about her, such as we sometimes see in a rose which has blown in the shade; or rather, to change the simile, the drooping and delicate look of a tender plant removed from a hothouse to the open air. We could not help feeling sure (notwithstanding our mistake with regard to Mrs. Allen) that *this* was indeed a transplanted flower; and that the village school, however excellently her habits had become inured to her situation, was not her proper atmosphere.

Several circumstances corroborated our suspicions. My lively young friend Sophia Grey, standing with me one day at the gate of the school-house, where I had been talking with Mrs. Allen, remarked to me, in French, the sly, demure vanity, with which Susan Wheeler, whose beauty had attracted her attention, was observing and returning her glances. The playful manner in which Sophia described Susan's "regard furtif,"[293] made me smile; and looking accidentally at Jane, I saw that she was smiling too, clearly comprehending, and enjoying the full force of the pleasantry. She must understand French; and when questioned, she confessed she did, and thankfully accepted the loan of books in that language. Another time, being sent on a message to the vicarage, and left for some minutes alone in the parlour, with a piano standing open in the room, she could not resist the temptation of touching the keys, and was discovered playing an air of Mozart, with great taste and execution. At this detection she blushed, as if caught in a crime, and hurried away in tears and without her message. It was clear that she had once learnt music. But the surest proof that Jane's original station had been higher than that which she now filled, was the mixture of respect and fondness with which Mrs. Allen treated her, and the deep regret she sometimes testified at seeing her employed in any menial office.

At last, elicited by some warm praise of the charming child, our good schoolmistress disclosed her story. Jane Mowbray was

[293] A quick, stealthy glance (in French).

250

The Village Schoolmistress

the grand-daughter of the lady in whose service Mrs. Allen had passed her life. Her father had been a man of high family and splendid fortune; had married beneath himself, as it was called, a friendless orphan, with no portion but beauty and virtue; and, on her death, which followed shortly on the birth of her daughter, had plunged into every kind of vice and extravagance. What need to tell a tale of sin and suffering? Mr. Mowbray had ruined himself, had ruined all belonging to him, and finally had joined our armies abroad as a volunteer, and had fallen undistinguished in his first battle. The news of his death was fatal to his indulgent mother; and when she too died, Mrs. Allen blessed the Providence which, by throwing in her way a recommendation to Lady Lacy's school, had enabled her to support the dear object of her mistress's love and prayers. "Had Miss Mowbray no connexion?" was the natural question. "Yes; one very near,—an aunt, the sister of her father, richly married in India. But Sir William was a proud, and a stern man, upright in his own conduct, and implacable to error. Lady Ely was a sweet, gentle creature, and doubtless would be glad to extend a mother's protection to the orphan; but Sir William—Oh! he was so unrelenting! He had abjured Mr. Mowbray, and all connected with him. She had written to inform them where the dear child was, but had no expectation of any answer from India."

Time verified this prediction. The only tidings from India, at all interesting to Jane Mowbray, were contained in the paragraph of a newspaper which announced Lady Ely's death, and put an end to all hopes of protection in that quarter. Years passed on, and found her still with Mrs. Allen at Lady Lacy's Green, more and more beloved and respected from day to day. She had now attained almost to womanhood. Strangers, I believe, called her plain; we, who knew her, thought her pretty. Her figure was tall and straight as a cypress, pliant and flexible as a willow, full of gentle grace, whether in repose or in motion. She had a profusion of light brown hair, a pale complexion, dark grey eyes, a smile of which the character was rather sweet than gay, and such a countenance! no one could look at her without wishing her well, or without being sure that she deserved all good wishes. Her manners were modest and elegant, and she had much of the self-taught knowledge, which is, of all knowledge, the surest and the best, because acquired with most difficulty, and fixed in the memory by the repetition of effort. Every one had assisted her to the extent of his power, and of her willingness to accept assistance; for both she and Mrs. Allen had a pride—call it independence—which rendered it impossible, even to the friends who were most honoured by their good opinion,

251

to be as useful to them as they could have wished. To give Miss Mowbray time for improvement had, however, proved a powerful emollient to the pride of our dear schoolmistress; and that time had been so well employed, that her acquirements were considerable; whilst in mind and character she was truly admirable; mild, grateful, and affectionate, and imbued with a deep religious feeling, which influenced every action and pervaded every thought. So gifted, she was deemed by her constant friends, the vicar and his lady, perfectly competent to the care and education of children; it was agreed that she should enter a neighbouring family, as a successor to their then governess, early in the ensuing spring; and she, although sad at the prospect of leaving her aged protectress, acquiesced in their decision.

One fine Sunday in the October preceding this dreaded separation, as Miss Mowbray, with Mrs. Allen leaning on her arm, was slowly following the little train of Lady Lacy's scholars from church, an elderly gentleman, sickly-looking and emaciated, accosted a pretty young woman, who was loitering with some other girls at the church-yard gate, and asked her several questions respecting the school and its mistress. Susan Wheeler (for it happened to be our old acquaintance) was delighted to be singled out by so grand a gentleman, and being a kind-hearted creature in the main, spoke of the school-house and its inhabitants exactly as they deserved. "Mrs. Allen," she said, "was the best woman in the world—the very best, except just Miss Mowbray, who was better still,—only too particular about summing, which you know, Sir," added Susan, "people can't learn if they can't. She is going to be a governess in the spring," continued the loquacious damsel; "and it's to be hoped the little ladies will take kindly to their tables, or it will be a sad grievance to Miss Jane."—"A governess! Where can I make enquiries concerning Miss Mowbray?"—"At the vicarage, Sir," answered Susan, dropping her little courtesy, and turning away, well pleased with the gentleman's condescension, and with half-a-crown which he had given her in return for her intelligence. The stranger, meanwhile, walked straight to the vicarage: and in less than half an hour the vicar repaired with him to Lady Lacy's Green.

This stranger, so drooping, so sickly, so emaciated, was the proud Indian uncle, the stern Sir William Ely! Sickness and death had been busy with him and with his. He had lost his health, his wife, and his children; and, softened by affliction, was returned to England a new man, anxious to forgive and to be forgiven, and, above all, desirous to repair his neglect and injustice toward the only remaining relative of the wife whom he had so fondly loved

The Village Schoolmistress

and so tenderly lamented. In this frame of mind, such a niece as Jane Mowbray was welcomed with no common joy. His delight in her, and his gratitude toward her protectress, were unbounded. He wished them both to accompany him home, and reside with him constantly. Jane promised to do so; but Mrs. Allen, with her usual admirable feeling of propriety, clung to the spot which had been to her a "city of refuge," and refused to leave it in spite of all the entreaties of uncle and of niece. It was a happy decision for Aberleigh; for what could Aberleigh have done without its good schoolmistress?

She lives there still, its ornament and its pride; and every year Jane Mowbray comes for a long visit, and makes a holiday in the school and in the whole place. Jane Mowbray, did I say? No! not Jane Mowbray now. She has changed that dear name for the only name that could be dearer:—she is married—married to the eldest son of Mr. Lacy, the lineal representative of Dame Eleanor Lacy, the honoured foundress of the school. It was in a voice tremulous more from feeling than from age, that Mrs. Allen welcomed the young heir, when he brought his fair bride to Aberleigh; and it was with a yet stronger and deeper emotion that the bridegroom, with his own Jane in his hand, visited the asylum which she and her venerable guardian owed to the benevolence and the piety of his ancestress, whose good deeds had thus showered down blessings on her remote posterity.

Anna Brownell Jameson

HALLORAN THE PEDLAR

(1827)

The author: She was born in Dublin in 1794, but her father, a painter, took his wife and four daughters to London in 1798. The young Anna Brownell Murphy was hired as a governess by the powerful Marquess of Winchester; then by the Rowles family, with whom she toured the continent; finally by Edward Littleton, a prominent M.P. At the age of 27, she got engaged to Robert Jameson, but she broke off the engagement and went to Italy with one of her pupils. Upon her return in 1825, she accepted Jameson's proposal and she published *The Diary of an Ennuyée* (1826). Her husband became a colonial administrator first in Dominica, then in Canada, but Anna remained in Europe. In 1836, she finally travelled across the Atlantic to see her husband and the result was *Winter Studies and Summer Rambles in Canada*, published when she returned in 1838. In the 1840s and 1850s she emerged as one of the most important art critics in Britain: she wrote a series titled "Essays on the Lives of Remarkable Painters" in the *Penny Magazine* (1843-45) and published *Handbook to the Public Galleries of Art in and near London* (1842), *Companion to the Most Celebrated Private Galleries of Art in London* (1844), *Memoirs of the Early Italian Painters* (1845), *The House of Titian* (1847), *Sacred and Legendary Art* (1848) and others. She died in 1860 of influenza in London.

The text: First published in *The Bijou; or Annual of Literature and the Arts* (London: William Pickering, 1827 [dated 1828]), 205-239. The full title was "Halloran the Pedlar. An Irish Story" and it was signed "By the writer of the 'Diary of an Ennuyée.'" It was reproduced by several other publications and, seven years later, collected in Jameson's 4-volume *Visits and Sketches at Home and Abroad with Tales and Miscellanies Now First Collected and a New*

Edition of the Diary of an Ennuyée (London: Saunders and Otley, 1834), III, 75-117. The following is from Jameson's collection.

The title is accompanied by a footnote (inexistent in the magazine version): "This little tale was written in March, 1826, and in the hands of the publishers long before the appearance of Bainim's [sic] novel of 'The Nowlans,' which contains a similar incident, probably founded on the same fact." "The Nowlans" is a novel by John and Michael Banim, published in the first two volumes of the second series of their *Tales of the O'Hara Family* (1826).

Further reading: Shandi Lynne Wagner. "'Halloran the Pedlar' and the Heroic Wife." "Sowing Seeds of Subversion: Nineteenth-Century British Women Writers' Subversive Use of Fairy Tales and Folklore." Ph.D. Dissertation. Wayne State University, Detroit, 2015. 27-41.

"It grieves me," said an eminent poet once to me, "it grieves and humbles me to reflect how much our moral nature is in the power of circumstances. Our best faculties would remain unknown even to ourselves did not the influences of external excitement call them forth like animalculæ, which lie torpid till awakened into life by the transient sunbeam."

This is generally true. How many walk through the beaten paths of every-day life, who but for the novelist's page would never weep or wonder; and who would know nothing of the passions but as they are represented in some tragedy or stage piece? not that they are incapable of high resolve and energy; but because the finer qualities have never been called forth by imperious circumstances; for while the wheels of existence roll smoothly along, the soul will continue to slumber in her vehicle like a lazy traveller. But for the French revolution, how many hundreds—*thousands*—whose courage, fortitude, and devotedness have sanctified their names, would have frittered away a frivolous, useless, or vicious life in the saloons of Paris! We have heard of death in its most revolting forms braved by delicate females, who would have screamed at the sight of the most insignificant reptile or insect; and men cheerfully toiling at mechanic trades for bread, who had lounged away the best years of their lives at the toilettes of their mistresses. We know not of what we are capable till the trial comes;—till it comes, perhaps, in a form which makes the strong man quail, and turns the gentler woman into a heroine.

Anna Brownell Jameson

The power of outward circumstances suddenly to awaken dormant faculties—the extraordinary influence which the mere instinct of self-preservation can exert over the mind, and the triumph of *mind* thus excited over physical weakness, were never more truly exemplified than in the story of HALLORAN THE PEDLAR.

The real circumstances of this singular case, differing essentially from the garbled and incorrect account which appeared in the newspapers some years ago, came to my knowledge in the following simple manner. My cousin George C * * *, an Irish barrister of some standing, lately succeeded to his family estates by the death of a near relative; and no sooner did he find himself in possession of independence than, abjuring the bar, where, after twenty years of hard struggling, he was just beginning to make a figure, he set off on a tour through Italy and Greece, to forget the wrangling of courts, the contumely of attornies, and the impatience of clients. He left in my hands a mass of papers, to burn or not, as I might feel inclined: and truly the contents of his desk were no bad illustration of the character and pursuits of its owner. Here I found abstracts of cases, and on their backs copies of verses, sketches of scenery, and numerous caricatures of judges, jurymen, witnesses, and his brethren of the bar—a bundle of old briefs, and the beginnings of two tragedies; with a long list of Lord N———'s best jokes to serve his purposes as occasion might best offer.[294] Among these heterogeneous and confused articles were a number of scraps carefully pinned together, containing notes on a certain trial, the first in which he had been retained as counsel for the crown. The intense interest with which I perused these documents, suggested the plan of throwing the whole into a connected form, and here it is for the reader's benefit.

In a little village to the south of Clonmell[295] lived a poor peasant named Michael, or as it was there pronounced Mickle Reilly. He was a labourer renting a cabin and a plot of potatoe-ground; and, on the strength of these possessions, a robust frame which feared no fatigue, and a sanguine mind which dreaded no reverse, Reilly paid his addresses to Cathleen Bray, a young girl of his own parish, and they were married. Reilly was able, skilful, and industrious; Catherine was the best spinner in the county, and had

---

[294] Clearly a reference to Lord Norbury, also mentioned later (see note 303). Jests attributed to him were widely circulated at the time.

[295] Spelled "Clonmel" today, it is the largest town in county Tipperary, in southern Ireland.

256

constant sale for her work at Clonmell: they wanted nothing; and for the first year, as Cathleen said, "There wasn't upon the blessed earth two happier souls than themselves, for Mick was the best boy in the world, and hadn't a fault to *spake* of—barring he took a drop now and then; an' why wouldn't he?" But as it happened, poor Reilly's love of "*the drop*" was the beginning of all their misfortunes. In an evil hour he went to the Fair of Clonmell to sell a dozen hanks of yarn of his wife's spinning, and a fat pig, the produce of which was to pay half a year's rent, and add to their little comforts. Here he met with a jovial companion, who took him into a booth, and treated him to sundry potations of whiskey; and while in his company his pocket was picked of the money he had just received, and something more; in short, of all he possessed in the world. At that luckless moment, while maddened by his loss and heated with liquor, he fell into the company of a recruiting serjeant. The many-coloured and gaily fluttering cockade in the soldier's cap shone like a rainbow of hope and promise before the drunken eyes of Mickle Reilly, and ere morning he was enlisted into a regiment under orders for embarkation, and instantly sent off to Cork.[296]

Distracted by the ruin he had brought upon himself, and his wife, (whom he loved a thousand times better than himself,) poor Reilly sent a friend to inform Cathleen of his mischance, and to assure her that on a certain day, in a week from that time, a letter would await her at the Clonmell post-office: the same friend was commissioned to deliver her his silver watch, and a guinea out of his bounty-money. Poor Cathleen turned from the gold with horror, as the price of her husband's blood, and vowed that nothing on earth should induce her to touch it. She was not a good calculator of time and distance, and therefore rather surprised that so long a time must elapse before his letter arrived. On the appointed day she was too impatient to wait the arrival of the carrier, but set off to Clonmell herself, a distance of ten miles: there, at the post-office, she duly found the promised letter; but it was not till she had it in her possession that she remembered she could not read: she had therefore to hasten back to consult her friend Nancy, the schoolmaster's daughter, and the best scholar in the village. Reilly's letter, on being deciphered with some difficulty even by the learned Nancy, was found to contain much of sorrow, much of repentance, and yet more of affection: he assured her that he was far better off than he had expected or deserved; that the embarkation of the regiment to which he belonged was delayed for three weeks,

---

[296] The major port of Cork is southwest of Clonmel, in southern Ireland.

and entreated her, if she could forgive him, to follow him to Cork without delay, that they might "part in love and kindness, and then come what might, he would demane himself like a man, and die asy," which he assured her he could not do without embracing her once more.

Cathleen listened to her husband's letter with clasped hands and drawn breath, but quiet in her nature, she gave no other signs of emotion than a few large tears which trickled slowly down her cheeks. "And will I see him again?" she exclaimed; "poor fellow! poor boy! I knew the heart of him was sore for me! and who knows, Nancy dear, but they'll let me go out with him to the foreign parts? Oh! sure they wouldn't be so hard-hearted as to part man and wife that way!"

After a hurried consultation with her neighbours, who sympathised with her as only the poor sympathise with the poor, a letter was indited by Nancy and sent by the carrier that night, to inform her husband that she purposed setting off for Cork the next blessed morning, being Tuesday, and as the distance was about forty-eight miles English, she reckoned on reaching that city by Wednesday afternoon; for as she had walked to Clonmell and back (about twenty miles) that same day, without feeling fatigued at all, "*to signify*,"[297] Cathleen thought there would be no doubt that she could walk to Cork in less than two days. In this sanguine calculation she was, however, overruled by her more experienced neighbours, and by their advice appointed Thursday as the day on which her husband was to expect her, "God willing."

Cathleen spent the rest of the day in making preparations for her journey: she set her cabin in order, and made a small bundle of a few articles of clothing belonging to herself and her husband. The watch and the guinea she wrapped up together, and crammed into the toe of an old shoe, which she deposited in the said bundle, and the next morning, at "sparrow chirp," she arose, locked her cabin door, carefully hid the key in the thatch, and with a light expecting heart commenced her long journey.

It is worthy of remark, that this poor woman, who was called upon to play the heroine in such a strange tragedy, and under such appalling circumstances, had nothing heroic in her exterior: nothing that in the slightest degree indicated strength of nerve or superiority of intellect. Cathleen was twenty-three years of age, of a low stature, and in her form rather delicate than robust: she was of ordinary appearance; her eyes were mild and dove-like, and her

[297] To compare, by comparison (a sense that was already obsolete at the time).

Halloran the Pedlar

whole countenance, thought not absolutely deficient in intelligence, was more particularly expressive of simplicity, good temper, and kindness of heart.

It was summer, about the end of June: the days were long, the weather fine, and some gentle showers rendered travelling easy and pleasant. Cathleen walked on stoutly towards Cork, and by the evening she had accomplished, with occasional pauses of rest, nearly twenty-two miles. She lodged at a little inn by the road side, and the following day set forward again, but soon felt stiff with the travel of two previous days: the sun became hotter, the ways dustier; and she could not with all her endeavours get farther than Rathcormuck,[298] eighteen miles from Cork. The next day, unfortunately for poor Cathleen, proved hotter and more fatiguing than the preceding. The cross road lay over a wild country, consisting of low bogs and bare hills. About noon she turned aside to a rivulet bordered by a few trees, and sitting down in the shade, she bathed her swollen feet in the stream: then overcome by heat, weakness, and excessive weariness, she put her little bundle under her head for a pillow, and sank into a deep sleep.

On waking she perceived with dismay that the sun was declining: and on looking about, her fears were increased by the discovery that her bundle was gone. Her first thought was that the good people, (i.e. *the fairies*) had been there and stolen it away; but on examining farther she plainly perceived large foot-prints in the soft bank, and was convinced it was the work of no unearthly marauder. Bitterly reproaching herself for her carelessness, she again set forward; and still hoping to reach Cork that night, she toiled on and on with increasing difficulty and distress, till as the evening closed her spirits failed, she became faint, foot-sore and hungry, not having tasted any thing since the morning but a cold potatoe and a draught of buttermilk. She then looked round her in hopes of discovering some habitation, but there was none in sight except a lofty castle on a distant hill, which raising its proud turrets from amidst the plantations which surrounded it, glimmered faintly through the gathering gloom, and held out no temptation for the poor wanderer to turn in there and rest. In her despair she sat her down on a bank by the road side, and wept as she thought of her husband.

Several horsemen rode by, and one carriage and four[299] attended by servants, who took no farther notice of her than by

[298] Today spelled Rathcormac, a small town north of Cork.
[299] A carriage drawn by four horses (also known as a "coach-and-four").

Anna Brownell Jameson

a passing look; while they went on their way like the priest and the Levite in the parable,[300] poor Cathleen dropped her head despairingly on her bosom. A faintness and torpor seemed to be stealing like a dark cloud over her senses, when the fast approaching sound of footsteps roused her attention, and turning, she saw at her side a man whose figure, too singular to be easily forgotten, she recognized immediately: it was Halloran the Pedlar.

Halloran had been known for thirty years past in all the towns and villages between Waterford and Kerry.[301] He was very old, he himself did not know his own age; he only remembered that he was a "tall slip of a boy" when he was one of the ———— regiment of foot, and fought in America in 1778. His dress was strange, it consisted of a woollen cap, beneath which strayed a few white hairs, this was surmounted by an old military cocked hat, adorned with a few fragments of tarnished gold lace; a frieze[302] great coat with the sleeves dangling behind, was fastened at his throat, and served to protect his box of wares which was slung at his back; and he always carried a thick oak stick or *kippeen* in his hand. There was nothing of the infirmity of age in his appearance: his cheek, though wrinkled and weather-beaten, was still ruddy: his step still firm, his eyes still bright: his jovial disposition made him a welcome guest in every cottage, and his jokes, though not equal to my Lord Norbury's,[303] were repeated and applauded through the whole country. Halloran was returning from the fair of Kilkenny,[304] where apparently his commercial speculations had been attended with success, as his pack was considerably diminished in size. Though he did not appear to recollect Cathleen, he addressed her in Irish, and asked her what she did there: she related in a few words her miserable situation.

---

[300] In the parable of the good Samaritan (Luke 10: 30-37), Jesus tells the story of a man attacked and robbed by thieves, left half-dead on the side of the road. A priest and a Levite (assistant to the priest, from the Levi tribe) see him but go on their way, whereas a Samaritan (a member of a small religious community that had splintered off Judaism) shows mercy and helps the man.

[301] In other words, in the entire southern part of Ireland, from Waterford (a city in the southeast) to County Kerry, in the southwest.

[302] Coarse, shaggy woollen fabric.

[303] John Toler (1745-1831), known as The Lord Norbury after 1800, when he was raised to the Peerage of Ireland (he was then created earl in 1827). He was regarded as a very corrupt and bloodthirsty magistrate (nicknamed "the Hanging Judge"), but also as a buffoon, whose jokes and pranks were famous.

[304] City in the southeast of Ireland, north of Waterford.

Halloran the Pedlar

"In troth, then, my heart is sorry for ye, poor woman," he replied, compassionately; "and what will ye do?"

"An' what *can* I do?" replied Cathleen, disconsolately; "and how will I even find the ford and get across to Cork, when I don't know where I am this blessed moment?"

"Musha,[305] then, it's little ye'll get there this night," said the pedlar, shaking his head.

"Then I'll lie down here and die," said Cathleen, bursting into fresh tears.

"Die! ye wouldn't!" he exclaimed, approaching nearer; "is it to me, Peter Halloran, ye spake that word; and am I the man that would lave a faymale at this dark hour by the way-side, let alone one that has the face of a friend, though I cannot remember me of your name either, for the soul of me. But what matter for that?"

"Sure, I'm Katty Reilly, of Castle Conn."[306]

"Katty Reilly, sure enough! and so no more talk of dying; cheer up, and see, a mile farther on, isn't there Biddy Hogan's? *Was*, I mane, if the house and all isn't gone: and it's there we'll get a bite and a sup, and a bed, too, please God. So lean upon my arm, ma vourneen,[307] it's strong enough yet."

So saying, the old man, with an air of gallantry, half rustic, half military, assister her in rising; and supporting her on one arm, with the other he flourished his kippeen over his head, and they trudged on together, he singing Cruiskeen-lawn[308] at the top of his voice, "just," as he said, "to put the heart into her."

After about half an hour's walking, they came to two crossways, diverging from the high road: down one of these the pedlar turned, and in a few minutes they came in sight of a lonely house, situated at a little distance from the way-side. Above the door was a long stick projecting from the wall, at the end of which dangled a truss of straw, signifying that within there was entertainment (good or bad) for man and beast. By this time it was nearly dark, and the pedlar going up to the door, lifted the latch, expecting it to yield to his hand; but it was fastened within: he then knocked and called, but there was no answer. The building, which was many times larger than an ordinary cabin, had once been a manufactory, and afterwards a farm-house. One end of it was deserted, and nearly

---

[305] Irish interjection meaning "indeed," "well."

[306] Castlecoyne, a small townland (Irish geographical division) in County Tipperary.

[307] "My darling" in Irish English (a borrowing from Gaelic).

[308] Anglicised version of "crúiscín lán (an)," i.e., "my full little jug," the title of a traditional Irish drinking song.

261

in ruins; the other end bore signs of having been at least recently inhabited. But such a dull hollow echo rung through the edifice at every knock, that it seemed the whole place was now deserted.

Cathleen began to be alarmed, and crossed herself, ejaculating, "O God preserve us!" But the pedlar, who appeared well acquainted with the premises, led her round to the back part of the house, where there were some ruined out-buildings, and another low entrance. Here, raising his stout stick, he let fall such a heavy thump on the door that it cracked again; and a shrill voice from the other side demanded who was there? After a satisfactory answer, the door was slowly and cautiously opened, and the figure of a wrinkled, half-famished, and half-naked beldam[309] appeared, shading a rush candle[310] with one hand. Halloran, who was of a fiery and hasty temper, began angrily: "Why, then, in the name of the great devil himself, didn't you open to us?" But he stopped suddenly, as if struck with surprise at the miserable object before him.

"Is it Biddy Hogan herself, I see!" he exclaimed, snatching the candle from her hand, and throwing the light full on her face. A moment's scrutiny seemed enough, and too much; for, giving it back hastily, he supported Cathleen into the kitchen, the old woman leading the way, and placed her on an old settle, the first seat which presented itself. When she was sufficiently recovered to look about her, Cathleen could not help feeling some alarm at finding herself in so gloomy and dreary a place. It had once been a large kitchen, or hall: at one end was an ample chimney, such as are yet to be seen in some old country houses. The rafters were black with smoke or rottenness: the walls had been wainscoted with oak, but the greatest part had been torn down for firing. A table with three legs, a large stool, a bench in the chimney propped up with turf sods, and the seat Cathleen occupied, formed the only furniture. Every thing spoke utter misery, filth, and famine—the very "abomination of desolation."[311]

"And what have ye in the house, Biddy, honey?" was the pedlar's first question, as the old woman set down the light. "Little enough, I'm thinking."

"Little! It's nothing, then—no, not so much as a midge would eat have I in the house this blessed night, and nobody to send down to Balgowna."

[309] Old woman; often depreciative: a hag.

[310] Narrow candle made of the pith of a plant from the rush family dipped in tallow and carried inside a holder.

[311] A term from the Book of Daniel, which is repeated in the Gospels.

Halloran the Pedlar

"No need of that, as our good luck would have it," said Halloran, and pulling a wallet from under his loose coat, he drew from it a bone of cold meat, a piece of bacon, a lump of bread, and some cold potatoes. The old woman, roused by the sight of so much good cheer, began to blow up the dying embers on the hearth; put down among them the few potatoes to warm, and busied herself in making some little preparations to entertain her guests. Meantime the old pedlar, casting from time to time an anxious glance towards Cathleen, and now and then an encouraging word, sat down on the low stool, resting his arms on his knees.

"Times are sadly changed with ye, Biddy Hogan," said he at length, after a long silence.

"Troth, ye may say so," she replied, with a sort of groan. "Bitter bad luck have we had in this world, any how."

"And where's the man of the house? And where's the lad, Barny?"

"Where are they, is it? Where should they be? may be gone down to Ahnamoe."[312]

"But what's come of Barny? The boy was a stout workman, and a good son, though a devil-may-care fellow, too. I remember teaching him the soldier's exercise with this very blessed stick now in my hand; and by the same token, him doubling his fist at me when he wasn't bigger than the turf-kish[313] yonder; aye, and as long as Barny Hogan could turn a sod of turf on my lord's land, I thought his father and mother would never have wanted the bit and sup while the life was in him."

At the mention of her son, the old woman looked up a moment, but immediately hung her head again.

"Barny doesn't work for my lord now," said she.

"And what for, then?"

The old woman seemed reluctant to answer—she hesitated.

"Ye didn't hear, then, how he got into trouble with my lord; and how—myself doesn't know the rights of it—but Barny had always a bit of wild blood about him; and since that day he's taken to bad ways, and the ould man's ruled by him quite entirely; and the

[312] The ford of Ahnamoe, on the way to Cork, which, according to Thomas Crofton Croker (1798-1854), in his *Fairy Legends and Traditions of the South of Ireland* (1825), was "considered to be a favourite haunt of the fairies." A few pages above, where Cathleen wonders "how will I ever find the ford and get across to Cork," the version published in 1827 in *The Bijou* reads "the ford of Ahnamoe," but the name was removed in Jameson's 1834 collection.

[313] Irish term for a basket used mainly for carrying turf (understood here as peat, used as fuel).

one's glum and fierce like—and t'other's bothered; and, oh! bitter's the time I have 'twixt' em both!"

While the old woman was uttering these broken complaints, she placed the eatables on the table; and Cathleen, who was yet more faint from hunger than subdued by fatigue, was first helped by the good-natured pedlar to the best of what was there: but, just as she was about to taste the food set before her, she chanced to see the eyes of the old woman fixed upon the morsel in her hand with such an envious and famished look, that from a sudden impulse of benevolent feeling, she instantly held it out to her. The woman started, drew back her extended hand, and gazed at her wildly.

"What is it then ails ye?" said Cathleen, looking at her with wonder; then to herself, "hunger's turned the wits of her, poor soul! Take it—take it, mother," added she aloud: "eat, good mother; sure there's plenty for us all, and to spare," and she pressed it upon her with all the kindness of her nature. The old woman eagerly seized it.

"God reward ye," said she, grasping Cathleen's hand, convulsively, and retiring to a corner, she devoured the food with almost wolfish voracity.

While they were eating, the two Hogans, father and son, came in. They had been setting snares for rabbits and game on the neighbourhood hills; and evidently were both startled and displeased to find the house occupied; which, since Barny Hogan's disgrace with "my lord," had been entirely shunned by the people round about. The old man gave the pedlar a sulky welcome. The son, with a muttered curse, went and took his seat in the chimney, where, turning his back, he set himself to chop a billet of wood. The father was a lean stooping figure, "bony, and gaunt, and grim:"[314] he was either deaf, or affected deafness. The son was a short, brawny, thickset man, with features not naturally ugly, but rendered worse than ugly by an expression of louring ferocity disgustingly blended with a sort of stupid drunken leer, the effect of habitual intoxication.

Halloran stared at them awhile with visible astonishment and indignation, but pity and sorrow for a change so lamentable, smothered the old man's wrath; and as the eatables were by this time demolished, he took from his side pocket a tin flask of whiskey, calling to the old woman to boil some water "screeching hot," that he might make what he termed "a jug of stiff punch—enough to make a cat *spake*." He offered to share it with his hosts, who did not

---

[314] From James Thomson's 1726 poem "Winter," the first part of his *The Seasons*. Here, Thomson describes a pack of wolves.

Halloran the Pedlar

decline drinking; and the noggin went round to all but Cathleen, who, feverish with travelling, and, besides, disliking spirits, would not taste it. The old pedlar, reconciled to his old acquaintances by this show of good fellowship, began to grow merry under the influence of his whiskey-punch: he boasted of his late success in trade, showed with exultation his almost empty pack, and taking out the only handkerchiefs left in it, threw one to Cathleen, and the other to the old woman of the house; then slapping his pocket, in which a quantity of loose money was heard to jingle, he swore he would treat Cathleen to a good breakfast next morning; and threw a shilling on the table, desiring the old woman would provide "stirabout[315] for a dozen," and have it ready by the first light.

Cathleen listened to this rhodomontade in some alarm; she fancied she detected certain suspicious glances between the father and son, and began to feel an indescribable dread of her company. She arose from the table, urging the pedlar good-humouredly to retire to rest, as they intended to be up and away so early next morning: then concealing her apprehensions under an affectation of extreme fatigue and drowsiness, she desired to be shown where she was to sleep. The old woman lighted a lanthorn, and led the way up some broken steps into a sort of loft, where she showed her two beds standing close together; one of these she intimated was for the pedlar, and the other for herself. Now Cathleen had been born and bred in an Irish cabin, where the inmates are usually lodged after a very promiscuous fashion; our readers, therefore, will not wonder at the arrangement. Cathleen, however, required that, if possible, some kind of skreen should be placed between the beds. The old hag at first replied to this request with the most disgusting impudence; but Cathleen insisting, the beds were moved asunder, leaving a space of about two feet between them; and after a long search a piece of old frieze was dragged out from among some rubbish, and hung up to the low rafters, so as to form a curtain or partition half-way across the room. Having completed this arrangement, and wished her "a sweet sleep and a sound, and lucky dreams," the old woman put the lanthorn on the floor, for there was neither chair nor table, and left her guest to repose.

Cathleen said her prayers, only partly undressed herself, and lifting up the worn-out coverlet, lay down upon the bed. In a quarter of an hour afterwards the pedlar staggered into the room, and as he passed the foot of her bed, bid God bless her, in a low voice.

[315] Irish porridge made of oatmeal, wheatmeal or cornmeal, eaten with milk, butter, or honey.

He then threw himself down on his bed, and in a few minutes, as she judged by his hard and equal breathing, the old man was in a deep sleep.

All was now still in the house, but Cathleen could not sleep. She was feverish and restless: her limbs ached, her head throbbed and burned, undefinable fears beset her fancy; and whenever she tried to compose herself to slumber, the faces of the two men she had left below flitted and glared before her eyes. A sense of heat and suffocation, accompanied by a parching thirst, came over her, caused, perhaps, by the unusual closeness of the room. This feeling of oppression increased till the very walls and rafters seemed to approach nearer and close upon her all around. Unable any longer to endure this intolerable smothering sensation, she was just about to rise and open the door or window, when she heard the whispering of voices. She lay still and listened. The latch was raised cautiously,—the door opened, and the two Hogans entered: they trod so softly that, though she saw them move before her, she heard no foot-fall. They approached the bed of Halloran, and presently she heard a dull heavy blow, and then sounds—appalling sickening sounds—as of subdued struggles and smothered agony, which convinced her that they were murdering the unfortunate pedlar.

Cathleen listened, almost congealed with horror, but she did not swoon: her turn, she thought, must come next, though in the same instant she felt instinctively that her only chance of preservation was to counterfeit profound sleep. The murderers, having done their work on the poor Pedlar, approached her bed, and threw the gleam of their lanthorn full on her face; she lay quite still, breathing calmly and regularly. They brought the light to her eye-lids, but they did not wink or move;—there was a pause, a terrible pause, and then a whispering;—and presently Cathleen thought she could distinguish a third voice, as of expostulation, but all in so very low a tone that though the voices were close to her she could not hear a word that was uttered. After some moments, which appeared an age of agonising suspense, the wretches withdrew, and Cathleen was left alone, and in darkness. Then, indeed, she felt as one ready to die: to use her own affecting language, "the heart within me," said she, "melted away like water, but I was resolute not to swoon, and I *did not*. I knew that if I would preserve my life, I must keep the sense in me, and *I did.*"

Now and then she fancied she heard the murdered man move, and creep about in his bed, and this horrible conceit almost maddened her with terror: but she set herself to listen fixedly, and convinced her reason that all was still—that all was over.

Halloran the Pedlar

She then turned her thoughts to the possibility of escape. The window first suggested itself: the faint moon-light was just struggling through its dirty and cobwebbed panes: it was very small, and Cathleen reflected, that besides the difficulty, and, perhaps, impossibility of getting through, it must be some height from the ground: neither could she tell on which side of the house it was situated, nor in what direction to turn, supposing she reached the ground: and, above all, she was aware that the slightest noise must cause her instant destruction. She thus resolved upon remaining quiet.

It was most fortunate that Cathleen came to this determination, for without the slightest previous sound the door again opened, and in the faint light, to which her eyes were now accustomed, she saw the head of the old woman bent forward in a listening attitude: in a few minutes the door closed, and then followed a whispering outside. She could not at first distinguish a word until the woman's sharper tones broke out, though in suppressed vehemence, with "If ye touch her life, Barny, a mother's curse go with ye! enough's done."

"She'll live, then, to hang us all," said the miscreant son.

"Sooner than that, I'd draw this knife across her throat with my own hands; and I'd do it again and again, sooner than they should touch your life, Barny, jewel: but no fear, the creature's asleep or dead already, with the fright of it."

The son then said something which Cathleen could not hear; the old woman replied,

"Hisht! I tell ye, no,—no; the ship's now in the Cove of Cork that's to carry her over the salt seas far enough out of the way: and haven't we all she has in the world? and more, didn't she take the bit out of her own mouth to put into mine?"

The son again spoke inaudibly; and then the voices ceased, leaving Cathleen uncertain as to her fate.

Shortly after the door opened, and the father and son again entered, and carried out the body of the wretched pedlar. They seemed to have the art of treading without noise, for though Cathleen saw them move, she could not hear a sound of a footstep. The old woman was all this time standing by her bed, and every now and then casting the light full upon her eyes; but as she remained quite still, and apparently in a deep calm sleep, they left her undisturbed, and she neither saw nor heard any more of them that night.

It ended at length—that long, long night of horror. Cathleen lay quiet till she thought the morning sufficiently advanced. She then rose, and went down into the kitchen: the old woman was lifting a pot off the fire, and nearly let it fall as Cathleen suddenly addressed her, and with an appearance of surprise and concern, asked for her friend the pedlar, saying she had just looked into his bed, supposing he was still asleep, and to her great amazement had found it empty. The old woman replied, that he had set out at early daylight for Mallow,[316] having only just remembered that his business called him that way before he went to Cork. Cathleen affected great wonder and perplexity, and reminded the woman that he had promised to pay for her breakfast.

"An' so he did, sure enough," she replied, "and paid for it too; and by the same token didn't I go down to Balgowna myself for the milk and the *male*[317] before the sun was over the tree tops; and here it is for ye, ma colleen:"[318] so saying, she placed a bowl of stirabout and some milk before Cathleen, and then sat down on the stool opposite to her, watching her intently.

Poor Cathleen! she had but little inclination to eat, and felt as if every bit would choke her: yet she continued to force down her breakfast, and apparently with the utmost ease and appetite, even to the last morsel set before her. While eating, she inquired about the husband and son, and the old woman replied, that they had started at the first burst of light to cut turf in a bog, about five miles distant.

When Cathleen had finished her breakfast, she returned the old woman many thanks for her kind treatment, and then desired to know the nearest way to Cork. The woman Hogan informed her that the distance was about seven miles, and though the usual road was by the high-way from which they had turned the preceding evening, there was a much shorter way across some fields which she pointed out. Cathleen listened attentively to her directions, and then bidding farewell with many demonstrations of gratitude, she proceeded on her fearful journey. The cool morning air, the cheerful song of the early birds, the dewy freshness of the turf, were all unnoticed and unfelt: the sense of danger was paramount, while her faculties were all alive and awake to meet it, for a feverish and unnatural strength seemed to animate her limbs. She stepped on, shortly debating with herself whether to follow the directions given by the old woman. The high-road appeared the safest; on the other hand, she was aware that the slightest betrayal of mistrust would perhaps be followed by

---

[316] A town north of Cork, with about 5,000 inhabitants in the late 1820s.

[317] Irish pronunciation for "meal" used in cooking stirabout (see note 315).

[318] Anglo-Irish term for "my girl."

her destruction; and thus rendered brave even by the excess of her fears, she determined to take the cross path. Just as she had come to this resolution, she reached the gate which she had been directed to pass through; and without the slightest apparent hesitation, she turned in, and pursued the lonely way through the fields. Often did she fancy she heard footsteps stealthily following her, and never approached a hedge without expecting to see the murderers start up from behind it; yet she never once turned her head, nor quickened nor slackened her pace;

> Like one that on a lonesome road
> Doth walk in fear and dread,
> Because he knows a frightful fiend
> Doth close behind him tread.[319]

She had proceeded in this manner about three-quarters of a mile, and approached a thick and dark grove of underwood, when she beheld seated upon the opposite stile an old woman in a red cloak. The sight of a human being made her heart throb more quickly for a moment; but on approaching nearer, with all her faculties sharpened by the sense of danger, she perceived that it was no old woman, but the younger Hogan, the murderer of Halloran, who was thus disguised. His face was partly concealed by a blue handkerchief tied round his head and under his chin, but she knew him by the peculiar and hideous expression of his eyes: yet with amazing and almost incredible self-possession, she continued to advance without manifesting the least alarm, or sign of recognition; and walking up to the pretended old woman, said in a clear voice, "The blessing of the morning on ye, good mother! a fine day for travellers like you and me!"

"A fine day," he replied, coughing and mumbling in a feigned voice, "but ye see, hugh, ugh! ye see I've walked this morning from the Cove of Cork, jewel, and troth I'm almost spent, and I've a bad cowld, and a cough on me, as ye may hear," and he coughed vehemently. Cathleen made a motion to pass the stile, but the disguised old woman stretching out a great bony hand, seized her gown. Still Cathleen did not quail. "Musha, then, have ye nothing to give a poor ould woman?" said the monster, in a whining, snuffling tone.

"Nothing have I in this wide world," said Cathleen, quietly disengaging her gown, but without moving. "Sure it's only yesterday

---

[319] The first two and last two lines from a stanza in Coleridge's "Rime of the Ancient Mariner" (see note 127).

I was robbed of all I had but the little clothes on my back, and if I hadn't met with charity from others, I had starved by the way-side by this time."

"Och! and is there no place hereby where they would give a potatoe and a cup of cowld water to a poor old woman ready to drop on her road?"

Cathleen instantly pointed forward to the house she had just left, and recommended her to apply there. "Sure they're good, honest people, though poor enough, God help them," she continued, "and I wish ye, mother, no worse luck than myself had, and that's a good friend to treat you to a supper—aye, and a breakfast too; there it is, ye may just see the light smoke rising like a thread over the hill, just fornent[320] ye; and so God speed ye!"

Cathleen turned to descend the stile as she spoke, expecting to be again seized with a strong and murderous grasp; but her enemy, secure in his disguise, and never doubting her perfect unconsciousness, suffered her to pass unmolested.

Another half-mile brought her to the top of a rising ground, within sight of the high-road; she could see crowds of people on horseback and on foot, with cars and carriages passing along in one direction; for it was, though Cathleen did not then know it, the first day of the Cork Assizes.[321] As she gazed, she wished for the wings of a bird that she might in a moment flee over the space which intervened between her and safety; for though she could clearly see the high-road from the hill on which she stood, a valley of broken ground at its foot, and two wide fields still separated her from it; but with the same unfailing spirit, and at the same steady pace, she proceeded onwards: and now she had reached the middle of the last field, and a thrill of new-born hope was beginning to flutter at her heart, when suddenly two men burst through the fence at the farther side of the field, and advanced towards her. One of these she thought at the first glance resembled her husband, but that it *was* her husband himself was an idea which never entered her mind. Her imagination was possessed with one supreme idea of danger and death by murderous hands; she doubted not that these were the two Hogans in some new disguise, and silently recommending herself to God, she steeled her heart to meet this fresh trial of her fortitude; aware, that however it might end, it *must* be the last. At

---

[320] Opposite, in front of.

[321] The Assizes were the highest criminal courts in Ireland. The ones in Cork met twice a year, in spring and in summer.

Halloran the Pedlar

this moment one of the men throwing up his arms, ran forward, shouting her name, in a voice—a dear and well-known voice, in which she *could* not be deceived:—it was her husband!

The poor woman, who had hitherto supported her spirits and her self-possession, stood as if rooted to the ground, weak, motionless, and gasping for breath. A cold dew burst from every pore; her ears tingled, her heart fluttered as though it would burst from her bosoms. When she attempted to call out, and raise her hand in token of recognition, the sounds died away, rattling in her throat; her arm dropped powerless at her side; and when her husband came up, and she made a last effort to spring towards him, she sank down at his feet in strong convulsions.

Reilly, much shocked at what he supposed the effect of sudden surprise, knelt down and chafed his wife's temples; his comrade ran to a neighbouring spring for water, which they sprinkled plentifully over her: when, however, she returned to life, her intellects appeared to have fled for ever, and she uttered such wild shrieks and exclamations, and talked so incoherently, that the men became exceedingly terrified, and poor Reilly himself almost as distracted as his wife. After vainly attempting to soothe and recover her, they at length forcibly carried her down to the inn at Balgowna, a hamlet about a mile farther on, where she remained for several hours in a state of delirium, one fit succeeding another with little intermission.

Towards evening she became more composed, and was able to give some account of the horrible events of the preceding night. It happened, opportunely, that a gentleman of fortune in the neighbourhood, and a magistrate, was riding by late that evening on his return from the Assizes at Cork, and stopped at the inn to refresh his horse. Hearing that something unusual and frightful had occurred, he alighted, and examined the woman himself, in the presence of one or two persons. Her tale appeared to him so strange and wild from the manner in which she told it, and her account of her own courage and sufferings so exceedingly incredible, that he was at first inclined to disbelieve the whole, and suspected the poor woman either of imposture or insanity. He did not, however, think proper totally to neglect her testimony, but immediately sent off information of the murder to Cork. Constables with a warrant were despatched the same night to the house of the Hogans, which they found empty, and the inmates already fled: but after a long search, the body of the wretched Halloran, and part of his property, were found concealed in a stack of old chimneys among the ruins; and this proof of guilt was decisive. The country was instantly *up*;

the most active search after the murderers was made by the police, assisted by all the neighbouring peasantry; and before twelve o'clock the following night, the three Hogans, father, mother, and son, had been apprehended in different places of concealment, and placed in safe custody. Meantime the Coroner's inquest having sat on the body, brought in a verdict of wilful murder.

As the judges were then at Cork, the trial came on immediately; and from its extraordinary circumstances, excited the most intense and general interest. Among the property of poor Halloran discovered in the house, were a pair of shoes and a cap which Cathleen at once identified as belonging to herself, and Reilly's silver watch was found on the younger Hogan. When questioned how they came into his possession, he sullenly refused to answer. His mother eagerly, and as if to shield her son, confessed that she was the person who had robbed Cathleen in the former part of the day, that she had gone out on the Carrick road to beg, having been left by her husband and son for two days without the means of support; and finding Cathleen asleep, she had taken away the bundle, supposing it to contain food; and did not recognize her as the same person she had robbed, till Cathleen offered her part of her supper.

The surgeon, who had been called to examine the body of Halloran, deposed to the cause of his death;—that the old man had been first stunned by a heavy blow on the temple, and then strangled. Other witnesses deposed to the finding of the body; the previous character of the Hogans, and the circumstances attending their apprehension; but the principal witness was Cathleen. She appeared, leaning on her husband, her face was ashy pale, and her limbs too weak for support; yet she, however, was perfectly collected, and gave her testimony with that precision, simplicity, and modesty, peculiar to her character. When she had occasion to allude to her own feelings, it was with such natural and heart-felt eloquence that the whole court was affected; and when she described her rencontre at the stile, there was a general pressure and a breathless suspense: and then a loud murmur of astonishment and admiration fully participated by even the bench of magistrates. The evidence was clear and conclusive; and the jury, without retiring, gave their verdict, guilty—Death.

When the miserable wretches were asked, in the usual forms, if they had any thing to say why the awful sentence should not be passed upon them, the old man replied by a look of idiotic vacancy, and was mute—the younger Hogan answered sullenly, "Nothing:" the old woman, staring wildly on her son, tried to speak; her lips moved, but without a sound—and she fell forward on the bar in strong fits.

At this moment Cathleen rushed from the arms of her husband, and throwing herself on her knees, with clasped hands, and cheeks streaming with tears, begged for mercy for the old woman. "Mercy, my lord judge!" she exclaimed. "Gentlemen, your honours, have mercy on her. She had mercy on me! She only did *their* bidding. As for the bundle, and all in it, I give it to her with all my soul, so it's not robbery. The grip of hunger's hard to bear; and if she hadn't taken it then, where would I have been now? Sure they would have killed me for the sake of the watch, and I would have been a corpse before your honours this moment. O mercy! mercy for her! or never will I sleep asy on this side of the grave!"

The judge, though much affected, was obliged to have her forcibly carried from the court, and justice took its awful course. Sentence of death was pronounced on all the prisoners; but the woman was reprieved, and afterwards transported.[322] The two men were executed within forty-eight hours after their conviction, on the Gallows Green.[323] They made no public confession of their guilt, and met their fate with sullen indifference. The awful ceremony was for a moment interrupted by an incident which afterwards furnished ample matter for wonder and speculation among the superstitious populace. It was well known that the younger Hogan had been long employed on the estate of a nobleman in the neighbourhood; but having been concerned in the abduction of a young female, under circumstances of peculiar atrocity, which for want of legal evidence could not be brought home to him, he was dismissed; and, finding himself an object of general execration, he had since been skulking about the country, associating with housebreakers and other lawless and abandoned characters. At the moment the hangman was adjusting the rope round his neck, a shrill voice screamed from the midst of the crowd, "Barny Hogan! do ye mind Grace Power, and the last words ever she spoke to ye?" There was a general movement and confusion; no one could or would tell whence the voice proceeded. The wretched man was seen to change countenance for the first time, and raising himself on tiptoe, gazed wildly round upon the multitude: but he said nothing; and in a few minutes he was no more.

[322] Convicted criminals could be sentenced to penal transportation in North America (until 1776) and then Australia (after 1788).

[323] The place for public executions in Cork, on a strip of land out of the city, on the road to The Lough (today a suburb of Cork).

The reader may wish to know what has become of Cathleen, our *heroine*, in the true sense of the word. Her story, her sufferings, her extraordinary fortitude, and pure simplicity of character, made her an object of general curiosity and interest: a subscription was raised for her, which soon amounted to a liberal sum; they were enabled to procure Reilly's discharge from the army, and with a part of the money, Cathleen, who, among her other perfections, was exceedingly pious after the fashion of her creed and country, founded yearly masses for the soul of the poor pedlar; and vowed herself to make a pilgrimage of thanksgiving to St. Gobnate's well.[324] Mr. L., the magistrate who had first examined her in the little inn at Balgowna, made her a munificent present; and anxious, perhaps, to offer yet farther amends for his former doubts of her veracity, he invited Reilly, on very advantageous terms, to settle on his estate, where he rented a neat cabin, and a *handsome* plot of potatoe ground. There Reilly and his Cathleen were living ten years ago, with an increasing family, and in the enjoyment of much humble happiness; and there, for aught I know to the contrary, they may be living at this day.

---

[324] St Gobnait (also known as Debora, Deriola, or Abigail) is a saint of 5th- or 6th-century Ireland. She is venerated on 11 February and among places associated with her life are St Gobnait's Wood and St Gobnait's well (both in County Cork).

Walter Scott

The Tapestried Chamber

(1828)

The author: Scott continued writing during the last years of his life, hoping to get out of debt. He even premiered a play he had written in 1817, but it was a critical and commercial failure. He was more successful with his nonfictional books on the history of Scotland and with his short stories. He died on 21 September 1832. As his novels continued to sell, his debts were paid off only a short time after his death.

The text: "The Tapestried Chamber, or The Lady in the Sacque" appeared in *The Keepsake for 1829* (which came out in late 1828) together with two other pieces by Scott: "My Aunt Margaret's Mirror" and "Death of the Laird's Jock" (a historical tableau, of the same kind as his last story, "A Highland Anecdote," published in 1831 in *The Keepsake for 1832*). The following is from *The Keepsake for 1829*, edited by Frederic Mansel Reynolds (London: for the proprietor, [1828]), 123-142. It has been pointed out that a story with a very similar plot had appeared earlier in *Blackwood's* 3 (September 1818), 705-707, under the title "Story of an Apparition," signed "A. B." (probably Alexander Blair), who may also have heard it from Anna Seward.

Further reading: Fiona Robertson. "Historical Fiction and the Fractured Atlantic." *Rethinking British Romantic History, 1770-1845*. Eds. Porscha Fermanis and John Regan. Oxford: Oxford University Press, 2014. 246-270.

Walter Scott

The following narrative is given from the pen, so far as memory permits, in the same character in which it was presented to the author's ear; nor has he claim to further praise, or to be more deeply censured, than in proportion to the good or bad judgment which he has employed in selecting his materials, as he has studiously avoided any attempt at ornament which might interfere with the simplicity of the tale.

At the same time it must be admitted, that the particular class of stories which turns on the marvellous, possesses a stronger influence when told, than when committed to print. The volume taken up at noonday, though rehearsing the same incidents, conveys a much more feeble impression, than is achieved by the voice of the speaker on a circle of fire-side auditors, who hang upon the narrative as the narrator details the minute incidents which serve to give it authenticity, and lowers his voice with an affectation of mystery while he approaches the fearful and wonderful part. It was with such advantages that the present writer heard the following events related, more than twenty years since, by the celebrated Miss Seward, of Lichfield,[325] who, to her numerous accomplishments, added, in a remarkable degree, the power of narrative in private conversation. In its present form the tale must necessarily lose all the interest which was attached to it, by the flexible voice and intelligent features of the gifted narrator. Yet still, read aloud, to an undoubting audience by the doubtful light of the closing evening, or, in silence, by a decaying taper, and amidst the solitude of a half-lighted apartment, it may redeem its character as a good ghost-story. Miss Seward always affirmed that she had derived her information from an authentic source, although she suppressed the names of the two persons chiefly concerned. I will not avail myself of any particulars I may have since received concerning the localities of the detail, but suffer them to rest under the same general description in which they were first related to me: and, for the same reason, I will not add to, or diminish the narrative, by any circumstance, whether more or less material, but simply rehearse, as I heard it, a story of supernatural terror.

[325] Anna Seward (1742-1809), who lived all her life in Lichfield, was a widely praised poet in the late 18th century. Walter Scott began a correspondence with her in 1802 and in 1810 he edited her *Poetical Works*, in the preface to which he hailed her as a literary mentor.

The Tapestried Chamber

About the end of the American war, when the officers of Lord Cornwallis's army, which surrendered at Yorktown, and others, who had been made prisoners during the impolitic and ill-fated controversy,[326] were returning to their own country, to relate their adventures, and repose themselves, after their fatigues; there was amongst them a general officer, to whom Miss S. gave the name of Browne, but merely, as I understood, to save the inconvenience of introducing a nameless agent in the narrative. He was an officer of merit, as well as a gentleman of high consideration for family and attainments.

Some business had carried General Browne upon a tour through the western counties, when, in the conclusion of a morning stage, he found himself in the vicinity of a small country town, which presented a scene of uncommon beauty, and of a character peculiarly English.

The little town, with its stately old church, whose tower bore testimony to the devotion of ages long past, lay amidst pastures and corn-fields of small extent, but bounded and divided with hedge-row timber of great age and size. There were few marks of modern improvement. The environs of the place intimated neither the solitude of decay, nor the bustle of novelty; the houses were old, but in good repair; and the beautiful little river murmured freely on its way to the left of the town, neither restrained by a dam, nor bordered by a towing-path.[327]

Upon a gentle eminence, nearly a mile to the southward of the town, were seen, amongst many venerable oaks and tangled thickets, the turrets of a castle, as old as the wars of York and Lancaster, but which seemed to have received important alterations during the age of Elizabeth and her successor.[328] It had not been a place of great size; but whatever accommodation it formerly afforded, was, it must be supposed, still to be obtained within its walls; at least, such was the inference which General Browne drew from observing the smoke arise merrily from several of the ancient wreathed and carved chimney-stalks. The wall of the park ran alongside of the highway for two or three hundred yards; and through the different points by

[326] General Cornwallis surrendered after the Siege of Yorktown in 1781, forcing Great Britain to begin negotiations for peace. The controversy refers to George Washington's refusal to accept Cornwallis's request that loyalists be offered immunity. In the aftermath, many loyalists left the United States.

[327] A road on the bank of a river or canal, on which walked horses, mules or oxen towing boats (also called towpath).

[328] The Houses of York and Lancaster fought for the English crown between 1455 and 1487. Elizabeth (1558-1603) was succeeded by James I (1603-1625).

which the eye found glimpses into the woodland scenery, it seemed to be well stocked. Other points of view opened in succession; now a full one, of the front of the old castle, and now a side glimpse at its particular towers; the former rich in all the bizarrerie of the Elizabethan school, while the simple and solid strength of other parts of the building seemed to show that they had been raised more for defence than ostentation.

Delighted with the partial glimpses which he obtained of the castle through the woods and glades by which this ancient feudal fortress was surrounded, our military traveller was determined to inquire whether it might not deserve a nearer view, and whether it contained family pictures or other objects of curiosity worthy of a stranger's visit; when, leaving the vicinity of the park, he rolled through a clean and well-paved street, and stopped at the door of a well-frequented inn.

Before ordering horses to proceed on his journey, General Browne made inquiries concerning the proprietor of the chateau which had so attracted his admiration; and was equally surprised and pleased at hearing in reply a nobleman named, whom we shall call Lord Woodville. How fortunate! Much of Browne's early recollections both at school, and at college, had been connected with young Woodville, whom, by a few questions, he now ascertained to be the same with the owner of this fair domain. He had been raised to the peerage by the decease of his father a few months before, and, as the general learned from the landlord, the term of mourning being ended, was now taking possession of his paternal estate, in the jovial season of merry autumn, accompanied by a select party of friends to enjoy the sports of a country famous for game.

This was delightful news to our traveller. Frank Woodville had been Richard Browne's fag at Eton, and his chosen intimate at Christ Church;[329] their pleasures and tasks had been the same; and the honest soldier's heart warmed to find his early friend in possession of so delightful a residence, and of an estate, as the landlord assured him with a nod and a wink, fully adequate to maintain and add to his dignity. Nothing was more natural than that the traveller should suspend a journey, which there was nothing to render hurried, to pay a visit to an old friend under such agreeable circumstances.

[329] In British boarding schools, a "fag" was a younger student who performed chores for an older student in exchange for protection and mentorship. Christ Church is one of the colleges of the University of Oxford.

The Tapestried Chamber

The fresh horses, therefore, had only the brief task of conveying the general's travelling carriage to Woodville Castle. A porter admitted them at a modern gothic lodge, built in that style to correspond with the castle itself, and at the same time rang a bell to give warning of the approach of visitors. Apparently the sound of the bell had suspended the separation of the company, bent on the various amusements of the morning; for, on entering the court of the chateau, several young men were lounging about in their sporting dresses, looking at, and criticising, the dogs which the keepers held in readiness to attend their pastime. As General Browne alighted, the young lord came to the gate of the hall, and for an instant gazed, as at a stranger, upon the countenance of his friend, on which, war, with its fatigues and its wounds, had made a great alteration. But the uncertainty lasted no longer than till the visitor had spoken, and the hearty greeting which followed was such as can only be exchanged betwixt those, who have passed together the merry days of careless boyhood or early youth.

"If I could have formed a wish, my dear Browne," said Lord Woodville, "it would have been to have you here, of all men, upon this occasion, which my friends are good enough to hold as a sort of holiday. Do not think you have been unwatched during the years you have been absent from us. I have traced you through your dangers, your triumphs, your misfortunes, and was delighted to see that, whether in victory or defeat, the name of my old friend was always distinguished with applause."

The general made a suitable reply, and congratulated his friend on his new dignities, and the possession of a place and domain so beautiful.

"Nay, you have seen nothing of it as yet," said Lord Woodville, "and I trust you do not mean to leave us till you are better acquainted with it. It is true, I confess, that my present party is pretty large, and the old house, like other places of the kind, does not possess so much accommodation as the extent of the outward walls appears to promise. But we can give you a comfortable old-fashioned room, and I venture to suppose that your campaigns have taught you to be glad of worse quarters."

The general shrugged his shoulders, and laughed. "I presume," he said, "the worst apartment in your chateau is considerably superior to the old tobacco-cask, in which I was fain to take up my night's lodging when I was in the Bush, as the Virginians call it, with

279

the light corps. There I lay, like Diogenes himself,[330] so delighted with my covering from the element, that I made a vain attempt to have it rolled on to my next quarters; but my commander for the time would give way to no such luxurious provision, and I took farewell of my beloved cask with tears in my eyes."

"Well, then, since you do not fear your quarters," said Lord Woodville, "you will stay with me a week at least. Of guns, dogs, fishing-rods, flies, and means of sport by sea and land, we have enough and to spare: you cannot pitch on an amusement but we will find the means of pursuing it. But if you prefer the gun and pointers,[331] I will go with you myself, and see whether you have mended your shooting since you have been amongst the Indians of the back settlements."

The general gladly accepted his friendly host's proposal in all its points. After a morning of manly exercise, the company met at dinner, where it was the delight of Lord Woodville to conduce to the display of the high properties of his recovered friend, so as to recommend him to his guests, most of whom were persons of distinction. He led General Browne to speak of the scenes he had witnessed; and as every word marked alike the brave officer and the sensible man, who retained possession of his cool judgment under the most imminent dangers, the company looked upon the soldier with general respect, as on one who had proved himself possessed of an uncommon portion of personal courage; that attribute of all others, of which every body desires to be thought possessed.

The day at Woodville Castle ended as usual in such mansions. The hospitality stopped within the limits of good order: music, in which the young lord was a proficient, succeeded to the circulation of the bottle: cards and billiards, for those who preferred such amusements, were in readiness: but the exercise of the morning required early hours, and not long after eleven o'clock the guests began to retire to their several apartments.

The young lord himself conducted his friend, General Browne, to the chamber destined for him, which answered the description he had given of it, being comfortable, but old-fashioned. The bed was of the massive form used in the end of the seventeenth century, and the curtains of faded silk, heavily trimmed with tarnished

---

[330] Diogenes was a Greek philosopher of the 4th century BC. He made a vow of poverty and for a while lived in a large cask or barrel, accepting charity from passersby.

[331] Pointers are an English breed of dogs originally used in hunting. Whereas game was generally pursued in large numbers, to take one's "gun and pointers" indicated a more solitary activity.

The Tapestried Chamber

gold. But then the sheets, pillows, and blankets looked delightful to the campaigner, when he thought of his "mansion, the cask." There was an air of gloom in the tapestry hangings, which, with their worn-out graces, curtained the walls of the little chamber, and gently undulated as the autumnal breeze found its way through the ancient lattice-window, which pattered and whistled as the air gained entrance. The toilette, too, with its mirror, turbaned, after the manner of the beginning of the century, with a coiffure of murrey-coloured silk,[332] and its hundred strange-shaped boxes, providing for arrangements which had been obsolete for more than fifty years, had an antique, and in so far a melancholy, aspect. But nothing could blaze more brightly and cheerfully than the two large wax candles; or if aught could rival them, it was the flaming bickering faggots in the chimney, that sent at once their gleam and their warmth, through the snug apartment; which, notwithstanding the general antiquity of its appearance, was not wanting in the least convenience, that modern habits rendered either necessary or desirable.

"This is an old-fashioned sleeping apartment, general," said the young lord, "but I hope you find nothing that makes you envy your old tobacco-cask."

"I am not particular respecting my lodgings," replied the general; "yet were I to make any choice, I would prefer this chamber by many degrees, to the gayer and more modern rooms of your family mansion. Believe me, that when I unite its modern air of comfort with its venerable antiquity, and recollect that it is your lordship's property, I shall feel in better quarters here, than if I were in the best hotel London could afford."

"I trust—I have no doubt—that you will find yourself as comfortable as I wish you, my dear general," said the young nobleman; and once more bidding his guest good night, he shook him by the hand, and withdrew.

The general once more looked round him, and internally congratulating himself on his return to peaceful life, the comforts of which were endeared by the recollection of the hardships and dangers he had lately sustained, undressed himself, and prepared for a luxurious night's rest.

Here, contrary to the custom of this species of tale, we leave the general in possession of his apartment until the next morning.

The company assembled for breakfast at an early hour, but without the appearance of General Browne, who seemed the guest that Lord Woodville was desirous of honouring above all

[332] Murrey is a reddish purple colour, like that of the mulberry.

281

whom his hospitality had assembled around him. He more than once expressed surprise at the general's absence, and at length sent a servant to make inquiry after him. The man brought back information that General Browne had been walking abroad since an early hour of the morning, in defiance of the weather, which was misty and ungenial.

"The custom of a soldier,"—said the young nobleman to his friends; "many of them acquire habitual vigilance, and cannot sleep after the early hour at which their duty usually commands them to be alert."

Yet the explanation which Lord Woodville then offered to the company seemed hardly satisfactory to his own mind, and it was in a fit of silence and abstraction that he awaited the return of the general. It took place near an hour after the breakfast bell had rung. He looked fatigued and feverish. His hair, the powdering and arrangement of which was at this time one of the most important occupations of a man's whole day, and marked his fashion as much as, in the present time, the tying of a cravat, or the want of one, was dishevelled, uncurled, void of powder, and dank with dew. His clothes were huddled on with a careless negligence, remarkable in a military man, whose real or supposed duties are usually held to include some attention to the toilette; and his looks were haggered and ghastly in a peculiar degree.

"So you have stolen a march upon us this morning, my dear general," said Lord Woodville; "or you have not found your bed so much to your mind as I had hoped and you seemed to expect. How did you rest last night?"

"Oh, excellently well! remarkably well! never better in my life"—said General Browne rapidly, and yet with an air of embarrassment which was obvious to his friend. He then hastily swallowed a cup of tea, and, neglecting or refusing whatever else was offered, seemed to fall into a fit of abstraction.

"You will take the gun to-day, general?" said his friend and host, but had to repeat the question twice ere he received the abrupt answer, "No, my lord; I am sorry I cannot have the honour of spending another day with your lordship: my post horses are ordered, and will be here directly."

All who were present showed surprise, and Lord Woodville immediately replied, "Post horses, my good friend! what can you possibly want with them, when you promised to stay with me quietly for at least a week?"

"I believe," said the general, obviously much embarrassed, that I might, in the pleasure of my first meeting with your lordship, have

The Tapestried Chamber

said something about stopping here a few days; but I have since found it altogether impossible."

"That is very extraordinary," answered the young nobleman. "You seemed quite disengaged yesterday, and you cannot have had a summons to-day; for our post has not come up from the town, and therefore you cannot have received any letters."

General Browne, without giving any further explanation, muttered something of indispensable business, and insisted on the absolute necessity of his departure in a manner which silenced all opposition on the part of his host, who saw that his resolution was taken, and forbore all further importunity.

"At least, however," he said, "permit me, my dear Browne, since go you will or must, to show you the view from the terrace, which the mist, that is now rising, will soon display."

He threw open a sash-window, and stepped down upon the terrace as he spoke. The general followed him mechanically, but seemed little to attend to what his host was saying, as, looking across an extended and rich prospect, he pointed out the different objects worthy of observation. Thus they moved on till Lord Woodville had attained his purpose of drawing his guest entirely apart from the rest of the company, when, turning round upon him with an air of great solemnity, he addressed him thus:

"Richard Browne, my old and very dear friend, we are now alone. Let me conjure you to answer me upon the word of a friend, and the honour of a soldier. How did you in reality rest during last night?"

"Most wretchedly indeed, my lord," answered the general, in the same tone of solemnity;—"so miserably, that I would not run the risk of such a second night, not only for all the lands belonging to this castle, but for all the country which I see from this elevated point of view."

"This is most extraordinary," said the young lord, as if speaking to himself; "then there must be something in the reports concerning that apartment." Again turning to the general, he said, "For God's sake, my dear friend, be candid with me, and let me know the disagreeable particulars which have befallen you under a roof where, with consent of the owner, you should have met nothing save comfort."

The general seemed distressed by this appeal, and paused a moment before he replied. "My dear lord," he at length said, "what happened to me last night is of a nature so peculiar and so unpleasant, that I could hardly bring myself to detail it even to your lordship, were it not that, independent of my wish to gratify any

283

request of yours, I think that sincerity on my part may lead to some explanation about a circumstance equally painful and mysterious. To others, the communication I am about to make, might place me in the light of a weak-minded, superstitious fool, who suffered his own imagination to delude and bewilder him; but you have known me in childhood and youth, and will not suspect me of having adopted in manhood, the feelings and frailties from which my early years were free." Here he paused, and his friend replied:

"Do not doubt my perfect confidence in the truth of your communication, however strange it may be," replied Lord Woodville; "I know your firmness of disposition too well, to suspect you could be made the object of imposition, and am aware that your honour and your friendship will equally deter you from exaggerating whatever you may have witnessed."

"Well then," said the general, "I will proceed with my story as well as I can, relying upon your candour; and yet distinctly feeling that I would rather face a battery than recall to my mind the odious recollections of last night."

He paused a second time, and then perceiving that Lord Woodville remained silent and in an attitude of attention, he commenced, thought not without obvious reluctance, the history of his night adventures in the Tapestried Chamber.

"I undressed and went to bed, so soon as your lordship left me yesterday evening; but the wood in the chimney, which nearly fronted my bed, blazed brightly and cheerfully, and, aided by a hundred exciting recollections of my childhood and youth, which had been recalled by the unexpected pleasure of meeting your lordship, prevented me from falling immediately asleep. I ought, however, to say, that these reflections were all of a pleasant and agreeable kind, grounded on a sense of having for a time exchanged the labour, fatigues, and dangers of my profession, for the enjoyments of a peaceful life, and the reunion of those friendly and affectionate ties, which I had torn asunder at the rude summons of war.

"While such pleasing reflections were stealing over my mind, and gradually lulling me to slumber, I was suddenly aroused by a sound like that of the rustling of a silken gown, and the tapping of a pair of high-heeled shoes, as if a woman were walking in the apartment. Ere I could draw the curtain to see what the matter was, the figure of a little woman passed between the bed and the fire. The back of this form was turned to me, and I could observe, from the shoulders and neck, it was that of an old woman, whose dress was an old-fashioned gown, which, I think, ladies call a sacque; that is, a sort of robe completely loose in the body, but gathered into

The Tapestried Chamber

broad plaits upon the neck and shoulders, which fall down to the ground, and terminate in a species of train.[333]

"I thought the intrusion singular enough, but never harboured for a moment the idea that what I saw was any thing more than the mortal form of some old woman about the establishment, who had a fancy to dress like her grandmother, and who, having perhaps (as your lordship mentioned that you were rather straitened for room) been dislodged from her chamber for my accommodation, had forgotten the circumstance, and returned by twelve, to her old haunt. Under this persuasion I moved myself in bed and coughed a little, to make the intruder sensible of my being in possession of the premises.—She turned slowly round, but, gracious heaven! my lord, what a countenance did she display to me! There was no longer any question what she was, or any thought of her being a living being. Upon a face which wore the fixed features of a corpse were imprinted the traces of the vilest and most hideous passions which had animated her while she lived. The body of some atrocious criminal seemed to have been given up from the grave, and the soul restored from the penal fire, in order to form, for a space, an union with the ancient accomplice of its guilt. I started up in bed, and sat upright, supporting myself on my palms, as I gazed on this horrible spectre. The hag made, as it seemed, a single and swift stride to the bed where I lay, and squatted herself down upon it, in precisely the same attitude which I had assumed in the extremity of my horror, advancing her diabolical countenance within half a yard of mine, with a grin which seemed to intimate the malice and the derision of an incarnate fiend."

Here General Browne stopped, and wiped from his brow the cold perspiration with which the recollection of his horrible vision had covered it.

"My lord," he said, "I am no coward. I have been in all the mortal dangers incidental to my profession, and I may truly boast, that no man ever saw Richard Browne dishonour the sword he wears; but in these horrible circumstances, under the eyes, and, as it seemed, almost in the grasp of an incarnation of an evil spirit, all firmness forsook me, all manhood melted from me like wax in the furnace, and I felt my hair individually bristle. The current of my life-blood ceased to flow, and I sank back in a swoon, as very a victim to panic terror as ever was a village girl, or a child of ten years old. How long I lay in this condition I cannot pretend to guess.

[333] The sack or sacque had been fashionable in the 17th and 18th centuries. When first published, the story had the subtitle "The Lady in the Sacque."

285

"But I was roused by the castle clock striking one, so loud that it seemed as if it were in the very room. It was some time before I dared open my eyes, lest they should again encounter the horrible spectacle. When, however, I summoned courage to look up, she was no longer visible. My first idea was to pull my bell, wake the servants, and remove to a garret or a hay-loft, to be ensured against a second visitation. Nay, I will confess the truth, that my resolution was altered, not by the shame of exposing myself, but by the fear that, as the bell-cord hung by the chimney, I might, in making my way to it, be again crossed by the fiendish hag, who, I figured to myself, might be still lurking about some corner of the apartment.

"I will not pretend to describe what hot and cold fever-fits tormented me for the rest of the night, through broken sleep, weary vigils, and that dubious state which forms the neutral ground between them. An hundred terrible objects appeared to haunt me; but there was the great difference betwixt the vision which I have described, and those which followed, that I knew the last to be deceptions of my own fancy and over-excited nerves.

"Day at last appeared, and I rose from my bed ill in health, and humiliated in mind. I was ashamed of myself as a man and a soldier, and still more so, at feeling my own extreme desire to escape from the haunted apartment, which, however, conquered all other considerations; so that, huddling all my clothes with the most careless haste, I made my escape from your lordship's mansion, to seek in the open air some relief to my nervous system, shaken as it was by this horrible rencounter with a visitant, for such I must believe her, from the other world. Your lordship has now heard the cause of my discomposure, and of my sudden desire to leave your hospitable castle. In other places I trust we may often meet; but God protect me from ever spending a second night under that roof!"

Strange as the general's tale was, he spoke with such a deep air of conviction, that it cut short all the usual commentaries which are made on such stories. Lord Woodville never once asked him if he was sure he did not dream of the apparition, or suggested any of the possibilities by which it is fashionable to explain apparitions,—wild vagaries of the fancy, or deception of the optic nerves. On the contrary, he seemed deeply impressed with the truth and reality of what he had heard; and, after a considerable pause, regretted, with much appearance of sincerity, that his early friend should in his house have suffered so severely.

The Tapestried Chamber

"I am the more sorry for your pain, my dear Browne," he continued, "that it is the unhappy, though most unexpected, result of an experiment of my own. You must know, that for my father and grandfather's time, at least, the apartment which was assigned to you last night, had been shut on account of reports that it was disturbed by supernatural sights and noises. When I came, a few weeks since, into possession of the estate, I thought the accommodation, which the castle afforded for my friends, was not extensive enough to permit the inhabitants of the invisible world to retain possession of a comfortable sleeping apartment. I therefore caused the Tapestried Chamber, as we call it, to be opened; and, without destroying its air of antiquity, I had such new articles of furniture placed in it as became the more modern times. Yet as the opinion that the room was haunted very strongly prevailed among the domestics, and was also known in the neighbourhood and to many of my friends, I feared some prejudice might be entertained by the first occupant of the Tapestried Chamber, which might tend to revive the evil report which it had laboured under, and so disappoint my purpose of rendering it an useful part of the house. I must confess, my dear Browne, that your arrival yesterday, agreeable to me for a thousand reasons besides, seemed the most favourable opportunity of removing the unpleasant rumours which attached to the room, since your courage was indubitable, and your mind free of any pre-occupation on the subject. I could not, therefore, have chosen a more fitting subject for my experiment."

"Upon my life," said General Browne, somewhat hastily, "I am infinitely obliged to your lordship—very particularly indebted indeed. I am likely to remember for some time the consequences of the experiment, as your lordship is pleased to call it."

"Nay, now you are unjust, my dear friend," said Lord Woodville. "You have only to reflect for a single moment, in order to be convinced that I could not augur the possibility of the pain to which you have been so unhappily exposed. I was yesterday morning a complete sceptic on the subject of supernatural appearances. Nay, I am sure that had I told you what was said about that room, those very reports would have induced you, by your own choice, to select it for your accommodation. It was my misfortune, perhaps my error, but really cannot be termed my fault, that you have been afflicted so strangely."

"Strangely indeed!" said the general, resuming his good temper; "and I acknowledge that I have no right to be offended with your lordship for treating me like what I used to think myself—a man of some firmness and courage.—But I see my post horses are arrived, and I must not detain your lordship from your amusement."

"Nay, my old friend," said Lord Woodville, "since you cannot stay with us another day, which, indeed, I can no longer urge, give me at least half an hour more. You used to love pictures, and I have a gallery of portraits, some of them by Vandyke, representing ancestry to whom this property and castle formerly belonged.[334] I think that several of them will strike you as possessing merit."

General Browne accepted the invitation, though somewhat unwillingly. It was evident he was not to breathe freely or at ease, till he left Woodville Castle far behind him. He could not refuse his friend's invitation, however; and the less so, that he was a little ashamed of the peevishness which he had displayed towards his well-meaning entertainer.

The general, therefore, followed Lord Woodville through several rooms, into a long gallery hung with pictures, which the latter pointed out to his guest, telling the names, and giving some account of the personages whose portraits presented themselves in progression. General Browne was but little interested in the details which these accounts conveyed to him. They were, indeed, of the kind which are usually found in an old family gallery. Here, was a cavalier who had ruined the estate in the royal cause; there, a fine lady who had reinstated it by contracting a match with a wealthy round-head.[335] There, hung a gallant who had been in danger for corresponding with the exiled court at Saint Germain's; here, one who had taken arms for William at the revolution; and there, a third that had thrown his weight alternately into the scale of whig and tory.[336]

[334] Anthony Van Dyck (see also note 140) was a Flemish portrait painter who lived and worked mostly in England after 1630.

[335] Allusions to the British Civil War (1642-1651), in which the royalists (known as Cavaliers) were defeated by the Parliamentarians (or Roundheads).

[336] The portraits of Woodville's ancestors are arranged chronologically and Browne can follow the main events of the previous century and a half of English history. After the success of the Parliament in the Civil War, the family of the beheaded king Charles I lived in exile in France until the Restoration in 1660. William III came from the Netherlands in 1688 with the support of Parliament in what is known as the Glorious Revolution (the beginning of constitutional monarchy in England). The two political factions in Parliament (the Whigs and the Tories) fought for control of government until the Jacobite Rising of 1715, after which the Whigs held onto power for most of the period until the end of the American Revolution.

The Tapestried Chamber

While Lord Woodville was cramming these words into his guest's ear, "against the stomach of his sense,"[337] they gained the middle of the gallery, when he beheld General Browne suddenly start, and assume an attitude of the uttermost surprise, not unmixed with fear, as his eyes were caught and suddenly riveted by a portrait of an old lady in a sacque, the fashionable dress of the end of the seventeenth century.

"There she is!" he exclaimed, "there she is, in form and features, though inferior in demoniac expression to, the accursed hag who visited me last night."

"If that be the case," said the young nobleman, "there can remain no longer any doubt of the horrible reality of your apparition. That is the picture of a wretched ancestress of mine, of whose crimes a black and fearful catalogue is recorded in a family history in my charter-chest.[338] The recital of them would be too horrible: it is enough to say, that in yon fatal apartment incest, and unnatural murder, were committed. I will restore it to the solitude to which the better judgment of those who preceded me had consigned it; and never shall any one, so long as I can prevent it, be exposed to a repetition of the supernatural horrors which could shake such courage as yours."

Thus the friends, who had met with such glee, parted in a very different mood; Lord Woodville to command the tapestried chamber to be unmantled,[339] and the door built up; and General Browne to seek in some less beautiful country, and with some less dignified friend, forgetfulness of the painful night which he had passed in Woodville Castle.

---

[337] From Shakespeare's *The Tempest*, in which Alonso complains to Gonzalo: "You cram these words into mine ears, against/ The stomach of my sense" (Act II, Scene I).

[338] A chest containing all the documents of an aristocratic family.

[339] That is, dismantled, taken apart.

Anna Maria Hall

ᏨᎷASTER ᏨᏴEN

(1829)

The author: Anna Maria Hall (1800-1881) was born in Dublin, but moved to England with her mother in 1815. In 1824 she married Samuel Carter Hall and, for the rest of her life, she signed all her works "Mrs. S. C. Hall." Her debut came in 1826 with stories published in *The Amulet: A Christian and Literary Remembrancer.* She collected her stories in the three volumes of *Sketches of Irish Character* published in 1829 (a second series appeared two years later), followed by three volumes of essays and tales titled *Lights and Shadows of Irish Life* (1838). She published many other stories, as well as novels and plays. She launched *St James's Magazine* in 1861 and was a long-time editor of *Sharpe's London Magazine of Entertainment and Instruction.*

The text: First published in January 1829, in her husband's *Spirit and Manners of the Age: A Christian and Literary Miscellany* (New Series) (London: Frederick Westley and A. H. Davis), vol. 11, 35-41. The character of Master Ben is based on a real-life schoolmaster named Benjamin Radford. The story appeared the same year in her two-volume *Sketches of Irish Character* (London: Frederick Westley and A. H. Davis, 1829), II, 115-133. The *Sketches* were signed "Mrs. S. C. Hall" and were dedicated to Mary Russell Mitford. The following is from the third (illustrated) edition, revised by the author (London: How and Parsons, 1842, 267-274). An 1844 edition (London: M. A. Nattali) faithfully reproduces the one from 1842. The 1829 version was introduced by the epigraph "A village tutor!—say on, I pray you."

Master Ben

Tall, and gaunt, and stately, was "Master Ben;" with a thin sprinkling of white, mingled with the slightly-curling brown hair, that shaded a forehead, high, and somewhat narrow. With all my partiality for this very respectable personage, I must confess that his physiognomy was neither handsome nor interesting; yet there was a calm and gentle expression in his pale grey eyes, that told of much kind-heartedness—even to the meanest of God's creatures. His steps were strides; his voice shrill, like a boatswain's whistle; and his learning—prodigious!—the unrivalled dominie[340] of the country, for five miles round, was Master Ben.

Although the cabin of Master Ben was built of the blue shingle, so common along the eastern coast of Ireland, and was perched, like the nest of a pewet, on one of the highest crags in the neighbourhood of Bannow;[341] although the aforesaid Master Ben, or (as he was called by the gentry) "Mister Benjamin," had worn a long black coat for a period of fourteen years—in summer, as an open surtout,[342] which flapped heavily in the gay sea-breeze—and in winter, firmly secured, by a large wooden pin, round his throat—the dominie was a person of much consideration, and more loved than feared, even by the little urchins who often felt the effects of his "system of education." Do not, therefore, for a moment, imagine that his was one of the paltry hedge-schools, where all the brats contribute their "sod o' turf," or "their small trifle o' pratees," to the schoolmaster's fire or board.[343] No such thing;—though I confess that "Mister Benjamin" would, occasionally, accept "a hand of pork," a kreel, or even a kish of turf, or three or four hundred

---

[340] A dominie was a (mostly Scottish) term for a schoolmaster.

[341] The pewit or lapwing is a migratory bird, whose eggs were considered a delicacy in 19th-century Western Europe. Bannow is a parish in County Wexford, on the south-west coast of Ireland.

[342] A large overcoat worn especially by men (the term was also used for a hood worn by women).

[343] Hedge-schools (thus named because of the assumption that the teacher and the students congregated outside, along hedgerows) were for a long time illegal (though largely tolerated) in Ireland, as they offered education to Catholic children ("The Hedge School" is one of William Carleton's stories in his 1830 book *Traits and Stories of the Irish Peasantry*). They had a bad reputation, though Carleton insists that, at the very least, their existence proves that the Catholic Irish were interested in education. "Turf" here means a piece of peat used as fuel. "Pratee" or "pratie" is a mostly Irish and Scottish term for a potato.

of "white eyes," or "London ladies," if they were presented, in a proper manner, by the parents of his favourite pupils.[344]

In summer, indeed, he would, occasionally, lead his pupils into the open air, permitting the biggest of them to bring his chair of state; and while the fresh ocean breeze played around them, he would teach them all he knew—and that was not a little; but, usually, he considered his lessons more effectual, when they were learned under his roof: and it was, in truth, a pleasing sight to view his cottage assemblage, on a fresh summer morning;—such rosy, laughing, romping things! "The juniors," with their rich curly heads, red cheeks, and bright, dancing eyes, seated in tolerably straight lines—many on narrow strips of blackened deal—the remnants, probably, of some shipwrecked vessel—supported at either end by fragments of grey rock; others on portions of the rock itself, that "Master Ben" used to say, "though not very asy to sit upon for the gossoons,[345] were clane, and not much trouble." "The seniors," fine, clever-looking fellows, intent on their sums or copies—either standing at, or leaning on, the blotted "desks," that extended along two sides of the school-room, kitchen, or whatever you may please to call so purely Irish an apartment: the chimney admitted a large portion of storm or sunshine, as might chance; but the low wooden partition, which divided this useful room from the sleeping part of the cabin, at once told that Master Ben's dwelling was of a superior order.

At four, the dominie always dismissed his assembly, and heart-cheering was the joy that succeeded. On the long summer evenings, the merry groups would scramble down the cliffs—which, in many places, overhang the wide-spreading ocean—heedless of danger—

> "And jump, and laugh, and shout, and clap their hands
> In noisy merriment."[346]

The seniors then commenced lobster and crab-hunting, and often showed much dexterity in hooking the gentlemen out of their rocky nests, with a long, crooked stick of elder, which they

---

[344] A "kreel" or "creel" is a wicker basket, used mostly in fishing; the kish (see note 132) is bigger and was used mostly for carrying turf (see note 313). "White eyes" and "London ladies" were types of potatoes grown in Ireland.

[345] An Irish term for "boys."

[346] Just like the epigraph (see introductory note to the text), this seems to be Hall's, despite being presented as a quotation.

considered "lucky."[347] The younkers were generally content with shrimping, or knocking the limpits—or, as they call them, the "branyans," off the rocks;[348] while the wee-wee ones slyly watched the ascent of the razor-fish, whose deep den they easily discovered by its tiny mountain of sand.[349]

Even during their hours of amusement, Master Ben was anxious for their welfare; and, enthroned on a high pinnacle, that commanded a boundless view of the wide-spreading sea, with its numerous creeks and bays, he would patiently sit, hour after hour—one eye fixed on some dirty, wise, old book, while the other watched the various schemes and scampings of his quondam pupils[350]—until the fading rays of the setting sun, and the shrill screams of the sea-birds, warned master and scholar of the coming night.

Every one agreed that "Master Ben" was very learned—but how he became so, was what nobody could tell; some said (for there are scandal-mongers in every village) that, long ago, Master Ben's father was convicted of treasonable practices, and obliged to fly to "foreign parts" to save his life: his child was the companion of his wanderings, according to this statement. But there was another, far more probable;—that our dominie had been a poor scholar—a class of students, peculiar, I believe, to Ireland, who travel from province to province, with satchels on their backs, containing books, and whatever provisions are given them, and devote their time to study and begging. The poorest peasant will share his last potato with a wandering scholar, and there is always a couch of clean straw prepared for him in the warmest corner of an Irish cabin. Be these surmises true or false, everybody allowed that Master Ben was the most clever schoolmaster between Bannow and Dublin: he would correct even Father Sinnott, "on account o' the bog Latin[351] his

[347] The term "gentleman" was often used in various humorous phrases to refer to animals. The elder (or elderberry) is a small tree the branches of which contain a large amount of pith. The fact that elder branches are here considered "lucky" is a play on words easier to understand in early-19th-century Ireland and Scotland than today: "lucky" is an obsolete term for an elderly man or woman and was used for many family elders (e.g., "lucky-dad" meant grandfather).

[348] Younkers means youngsters. A limpit (or limpet) is a member of a large family of sea or freshwater snails. "Branyan" was an Irish slang term for a limpet.

[349] The razorfish here refers to the razor shell, which is a type of mollusc.

[350] They are, of course, quondam (i.e., former) pupils only inasmuch as this is happening after school hours.

[351] Name given in Ireland to bad, incorrect Latin, especially one learned in a hedge school (see note 343).

reverence used at the altar itself." "His reverence" always took this in good part, laughed at it, but never omitted adding, slyly, "the poor cratur!—he thinks he knows betther than me!" I must say, that the laugh which concluded this sentence was much more joyous than that at the commencement.

The dominie's life passed very smoothly, and with apparent comfort;—strange as it may sound to English ears—comfort. A mild, halfwitted sister, who might be called his shadow—so silently and calmly did she follow his steps, and do all that could be done, to make the only being she loved happy—shared his dwelling. The potatoes, she planted, dug, and picked, with her own hands; milked and tended "Nanny" and "Jenny," two pretty, merry goats, who devoured not only the wild heather and fragrant thyme, which literally cover the sand-banks and hills of Bannow, but made sundry trespasses on the flower-beds at the "great house,"[352] and defied pound, tether, and fetter, which the most roguish and provoking impudence. I had almost forgotten—but she small-plaited[353] in a superior and extraordinary manner; and—poor thing!—she was as vain of that qualification as any young lady who rumbles over the keys of a grand piano, and then triumphantly informs the audience that she has played "The Storm."[354]

"Changeful are all the scenes of life," says somebody or other;[355] and when I was about ten years old, "Master Ben" underwent two very severe trials—trials the poor man had never anticipated; one was teaching, or trying to teach, me the multiplication table—an act no mortal man (or woman either) ever could accomplish; the other was—falling in love. As "Master Ben" was the best arithmetician in the county, he was the person fixed on to instruct me in the most puzzling science—no small compliment I assure you—and he was obliged to arrange, so as to leave his pupils twice a week for two long hours. "Master Ben" rose in estimation surprisingly, when this was known; and, on the strength of it, got two-pence instead of three-halfpence a week

---

[352] Or "big house," the estate houses of the Anglo-Irish ascendancy.

[353] That is, she braided strands of fabric or ribbons into frills (ruffles).

[354] Beethoven's Piano Sonata No. 17, "Der Sturm" (known today in English as "The Tempest").

[355] There are, indeed, numerous versions of this maxim, in verse and prose; the most memorable at the time was probably in a poem by the famed satirist Charles Churchill (1732-1764): "Still as the scenes of life will shift away,/ The strong impressions of their art decay."

Master Ben

from his best scholars: he thought he should also gain credit by his new pupil's progress. How vain are man's imaginations! From the first intimation I received of the intended visits of my tutor, I felt a most lively anticipation of much fun and mischief.

"Now, Miss, dear, don't be full o' yer tricks," said pretty Peggy O'Dell, who had the especial care of my person. "Now, Miss, dear, stand asy—you won't?—well, then, I'll not tell ye the news—no, not a word! Oh, ye're asy now, are ye! Well, then—to-morrow, Frank tells me, Master Ben is come to tache you the figures; and good rason has Frank to know, for he druv the carriage to Master Ben's own house, and hard the mistress say all about it; and that was the rason ye were left at home, mavourneen, with your own Peggy; becase the ladies wished to keep it all secret like, till they'd tell ye their own selves. Oh, Miss, dear, asy—asy—till I tie yer sash!—there, now—now you may run off; but stay one little minit—take kindly to the figures. I know you can't abide them now, but I hear they are main useful; and take to it asy—*as quiet as you can*; Master Ben has fine larning, and expicts much credit for tacheing the likes of you. And why not?"

Poor Benjamin!—he certainly did strike to the manor, and into the study, next morning; and, in due time, I worked through, that is, I wrote out the questions, and copied the sums, with surprising dexterity, in "numeration," "addition of integers," "compound subtraction," and entered the "single rule of three direct," with much éclat. My book was shown, divested of its blots by my kind master's enduring knife;[356] and even my cousin (the only arithmetician in the family) was compelled to acknowledge that, if I did the sums myself, I was a very good girl indeed. That *if* destroyed my reputation. I had too much honour to tell a story.

What a passion, to be sure, the dominie got into the next day, when informed of my disgrace! I cannot bear to see a long, thin man in a passion, to this very hour; there is nothing on earth like it, except a Lombardy poplar[357] in a storm. However, if poor Master Ben was tormented in the study by me, he was more tormented in the servants' hall by pretty Peggy.

Peggy was exactly a lively Irish coquet: such merry, twinkling, black eyes; such white teeth, which were often exposed by the loud and joyous laugh, that extended her large but well-formed mouth;

---

[356] Ink blots were often removed at the time with an erasing knife.

[357] Also known as "black poplar," a tree that can easily reach 20-30 m in height.

and such a bounding, lissom figure, always (no small merit in an Irish lassie) neatly, if not tastefully, arrayed. She was an especial favourite with my dear grandmother, who had been her patron from early childhood; and Peggy fully and highly valued herself on this account. Then she could read and write in her own way; wore lace caps, with pink and blue bows; and, as curls were interdicted, braided her raven locks with much care and attention.

The smartest, prettiest girl, at wake or pattern,[358] for ten mile around, was certainly Peggy O'Dell; and many lovers had she; from Thomas Murphy of the Hill (the richest), who had a cow, six pigs, and all requisites to make a woman happy, according to his own account, to Wandering Will (the poorest), who, though not five-and-twenty, had been a jovial sailor, a brave soldier, a capital fiddler, a very excellent cobbler, a good practical surgeon (he had performed several very clever operations as a dentist and bone-setter, I assure you), and, at last, settled as universal assistant in the manor-house; cleaned the carriages and horses with Frank, waited at table with Dennis, helped Martha to carry home the milk, instructed Peter Kean how to train vines in the Portuguese fashion (which foreign treatment had so ill an effect on our poor Irish vines, that, to Wandering Will's eternal disgrace, they withered and died—a circumstance honest Peter never failed to remind him of, whenever he presumed to suggest any alteration in horticultural arrangements), had the exclusive care of the household brewing, and was even detected in assisting old Margaret hunting the round meadow for eggs, which the obstinate lady-fowl preferred hiding among brakes and bushes to depositing, in a proper manner, in the hen-house. Moreover, Will was "the jewil" of all the county during the hunting and shooting season—knew all the fox-earths, and defied the simple cunning of hare and partridge; made love to all the pretty girls in the village; and, as he was handsome, notwithstanding the loss of one of his beautiful eyes, everybody said that no one would refuse William, were he even as poor again as he was—an utter impossibility. The rumour spread, however, that his wandering affections were actually settled into a serious attachment for Peggy; but who Peggy was in love with was another matter. She jested with everybody, and laughed more at Master Ben than at any one else; she was always delighted when an opportunity occurred of playing off droll tricks to his disadvantage; and some of her jokes were so practical, that the housekeeper frequently threatened to inform her mistress of her pranks. Master Ben was always the first to prevent this; and his constant remonstrance—

[358] Pattern is the feast of a patron saint.

"Mistress Betty, let the innocent cratur alone, she manes no harm; she knows I don't mind her youthful fun—the cratur!" saved Peggy many a reproof.

One morning I had been more than ordinarily inattentive; and my tutor, perplexed, or, as he termed it, "fairly bothered," requested to speak to my grandmother; when she granted him audience. He stammered and blundered in such a manner, that it was quite impossible to ascertain what he wanted to speak about; at length out it came—"He had saved a good pinny o' money,[359] and thought it time to settle in life."

"Settle, Mister Benjamin!—why, I always thought you were a settled, sober man. What do you mean?" inquired my grandmother.

"To get married, ma'am;" rousing all his energies to pronounce the fatal sentence.

"Married!" repeated my grandmother; "married!—you, Benjamin Rattin, married at your time of life!—and to whom?"

"I was only eight-and-forty, madam," he replied (drawing himself up), "my last birthday; and, by your lave, I mane to marry Peggy O'Dell."

"Peggy!—you marry Peggy!" She found it impossible to maintain the sober demeanour necessary when such declarations are made. "Mister Benjamin, Peggy is not twenty, gay and giddy as a young fawn; and, I must confess, I should not like her to marry for four or five years. Now, as you certainly cannot wait all that time, I think you ought to think of some one else."

"Your pardon, madam; she is my first, and shall be my last, love. And I know," added the dominie, looking modestly on the carpet, "that she has a tinderness for me."

"What! Peggy a tenderness for you!—poor child!—quite impossible!" said my grandmother; "she never had the tenderness you mean for any living man, I'll answer for it:" and the bell was rung to summon Miss Peggy to the presence.

She entered—blushed and simpered at the first question put to her: at last my grandmother deliberately asked her, if she had given Mister Ben encouragement at any time—and this she most solemnly denied.

"Oh, you hard-hearted girl you!—did you ever cease laughing from the time I came in till I went out o' the house?—weren't you always smiling at me, and playing your pranks, and—"

[359] "A good penny of money," i.e., a goodly sum.

"Stop!" said Peggy, at once assuming a grave and serious manner:—"stop; may-be I laughed too much—but I shall cry more, if—(and she fell on her knees at my grandmother's feet)—if ye don't forgive me, mistress, dear—almost the first, sartainly the last, time I shall ever offend you."

"Child, you have not angered me;" replied my grandmother, who saw her emotion with astonishment.

"Oh, yes; but I know best—I have—I have—I know I have!—but I'll never do so more—never—never!"—and she burst into a flood of tears. Poor Master Ben stood aghast.

"Speak," said my grandmother, almost bewildered: "speak, and at once—what have you done?"

"Oh! he over-persuaded me, and said ye'd never consint till it was done; and so we were married, last night, at Judy Ryan's station."[360]

"Married! to whom, in the name of wonder?"

"Oh, Willy—Wandering Willy; but he'll never wander more: he'll be tame and steady, and, to the last day of his life, he'll sarve you and yours; and only forgive me, your poor Peggy, that ye saved from want, and that'll never do the like again—no, never!" The poor girl clasped her hands imploringly, but did not dare to look her mistress in the face. My grandmother rose, and left the room; she was much offended; nor could it be denied that Peggy's conduct was highly improper. The child of her bounty, she had acted with duplicity, and married a man whose unsteady habits promised little for her comfort.

Poor Master Ben!—lovers' sorrows furnish abundant themes for jest and jesters; but they are not the less serious, on that account, to those immediately concerned in *les affaires du cœur*.[361] When he heard the confession that she was truly married, he looked at her for a few minutes, and then quitted the house, determined never to enter it again. Peggy and her husband were dismissed; but a good situation was soon procured for Will, as commander of a small vessel, that traded from Waterford to Bannow, with corn, coal, timber, "and sundries." Contrary to all expectation, he made a kind and affectionate husband.

Winter had nearly passed, and Peggy almost ceased to dread the storms that scatter so many wrecks along our frowning coast.

[360] Station is (in Ireland) a visit by the parish priest on a weekday to a parishioner's house to say Mass and hear confessions.

[361] French for "the affairs of the heart."

Master Ben

Her little cabin was a neat, cheerful dwelling, in a sheltered nook; and often, during her husband's absence, did she go forth to look out upon the ocean-flood—

> "With not a sound beside, except when flew
> Aloft the lapwing, or the grey curlew;"[362]

and gaze, and watch for his sail on the blue waters. On the occasion to which I refer, he had been long expected home; and many of the rich farmers, who used coal instead of turf, went down to the pier to inquire if the "Pretty Peggy" (so Will called his boat) had come in. The wind was contrary, but, as the weather was fair, no one thought of danger. Soon, the little bark hove in sight, and soon was Peggy at the pier, watching for his figure on deck, or for the waving of hat or handkerchief, the beloved token of recognition: but no such token appeared. The dreadful tale was soon told. Peggy, about to become a mother, was already a widow.

Will had fallen overboard, in endeavouring to secure a rope that had slipped from the side of his vessel; the night was dark, and one deep, heavy splash alone knelled the departure of poor Wandering Willy.

Peggy, forlorn and desolate, suffered the bitter pains of childbirth; and, in a few hours, expired—her heart was broken.

About five years after this melancholy event, I was rambling amongst the tombs and ruins of the venerable church of Bannow. Every stone of that old pile is hallowed to my remembrance; its bleak situation, the barren sand-hills that surround it, and—

> "The measured chime, the thundering burst,"

of the boundless ocean, always rendered it, in my earliest days, a place of grand and overpowering interest. Even now—

> "I miss the voice of waves—the first
> That awoke my childhood's glee;"[363]

---

[362] From George Crabbe's *Tales of the Hall* (1819).

[363] Both these two lines and the one just above are from the same stanza in Felicia Hemans's "Where Is the Sea? Song of the Greek Islander in Exile," though the second passage is paraphrased: "I miss that voice of waves, which first/ Awoke my childhood's glee;/ The measured chime—the thundering burst—/ Where is my own blue sea?"

and often think of the rocks, and cliffs, and blue sea, that first led my thoughts "from nature up to nature's God!"[364]

I looked through the high-arched window into the churchyard, and observed an elderly man, kneeling on one knee, employed in pulling up the docks and nettles that overshadowed an humble grave, under the south wall. A pale, delicate, little girl quietly and silently watched all he did; and, when no offensive weed remained, carefully scattered over it a large nosegay of fresh flowers, and, instructed by the aged man, knelt on the mound, and lisped a simple prayer to the memory of her mother.

It was, indeed, my old friend, "Master Ben;" the pale child he had long called his—it was the orphan daughter of William and Peggy. His love was not the love of worldlings; despite his outward man,[365] it was pure and unsophisticated: it pleased God to give him the heart to be a father to the fatherless. The girl is now the blessing of his old age; and, as he has long since given up his school, he finds much amusement in instructing his adopted child, who, I understand, has already made great progress in his favourite science of numbers.

---

[364] The phrase, used thus in many sermons, comes actually from Pope's "Essay on Man": "Slave to no sect, who takes no private road,/ But looks through nature up to nature's God."

[365] From Martin Luther's distinction (elaborated in 1520 in *The Freedom of a Christian*) between the "inner man," "perfectly free lord of all, subject to none," and the "outward man," the man-in-the-world, "perfectly dutiful servant to all, subject to all."

William Mudford

The Iron Shroud

(1830)

The author: William Mudford (1782-1848) was born in London and studied at the University of Edinburgh. He published critical essays and translations, before getting some reputation as a novelist, especially with *Nubilia in Search of a Husband* (1809), written in response to a novel by Hannah More. He wrote the 21 numbers of his own weekly, *The Contemplatist* (1810), which included some short fiction. For a long time he worked as a journalist for the *Morning Chronicle*, edited by his good friend John Black, and then for the *Courier*, a leading Tory daily. After a spell in Canterbury (during which he became a contributor to *Blackwood's*, most notably with "First and Last," a short-fiction serial), as editor-owner of the *Kentish Observer*, he returned to London in 1841 as editor of the *John Bull Magazine*.

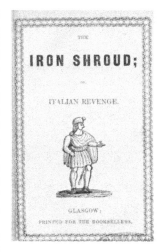

The text: First published in *Blackwood's Magazine* (Vol. 28, August 1830, 364-371). Many times reprinted by various periodicals in the following decades and selected by the editors of the posthumous collection *Tales and Trifles, from Blackwood's and other Popular Magazines. By the late William Mudford, Esq.* (London: William Tegg and Co., 1849, I, 281-301). The following is from the original version published in *Blackwood's*, where it was signed first as "by the author of 'First and Last'" (below the story's title) and then as "M." at the end of the text.

Further reading: Alison Milbank. "The Victorian Gothic in English Novels and Stories, 1830-1880." *The Cambridge Companion to Gothic Fiction*. Ed. Jerrold E. Hogle. Cambridge: Cambridge University Press, 2002. 150-152.

William Mudford

The castle of the Prince of Tolfi was built on the summit of the towering and precipitous rock of Scylla,[366] and commanded a magnificent view of Sicily in all its grandeur. Here, during the wars of the middle ages, when the fertile plains of Italy were devastated by hostile factions, those prisoners were confined, for whose ransom a costly price was demanded. Here, too, in a dungeon, excavated deep in the solid rock, the miserable victim was immured, whom revenge pursued,—the dark, fierce, and unpitying revenge of an Italian heart.

VIVENZIO—the noble and the generous, the fearless in battle, and the pride of Naples in her sunny hours of peace—the young, the brave, the proud, Vivenzio fell beneath this subtle and remorseless spirit. He was the prisoner of Tolfi, and he languished in that rock-encircled dungeon, which stood alone, and whose portals never opened twice upon a living captive.

It had the semblance of a vast cage, for the roof, and floor, and sides, were of iron, solidly wrought, and spaciously constructed. High above there ran a range of seven grated windows, guarded with massy bars of the same metal, which admitted light and air. Save these, and the tall folding doors beneath them, which occupied the centre, no chink, or chasm, or projection, broke the smooth black surface of the walls. An iron bedstead, littered with straw, stood in one corner: and beside it, a vessel with water, and a coarse dish filled with coarser food.

Even the intrepid soul of Vivenzio shrunk with dismay as he entered this abode, and heard the ponderous doors triple-locked by the silent ruffians who conducted him to it. Their silence seemed prophetic of his fate, of the living grave that had been prepared for him. His menaces and his entreaties, his indignant appeals for justice, and his impatient questioning of their intentions, were like vain. They listened, but spoke not. Fit ministers of a crime that should have no tongue!

[366] On the mainland side (i.e., in Calabria) of the Strait of Messina, which separates continental Italy from the island of Sicily. On both sides of the strait, according to Ancient Greek mythology, there was a monster (Scylla in Calabria and Charybdis in Sicily, which are the origin of the expression "between Scylla and Charybdis"). The town of Scilla, in Calabria, takes its name from that of the mythological creature. The promontory of Scilla is dominated by Castle Ruffo, an ancient fortification many times damaged and rebuilt over the centuries.

The Iron Shroud

How dismal was the sound of their retiring steps! And, as their faint echoes died along the winding passages, a fearful presage grew within him, that never more the face, or voice, or tread, of man, would greet his senses. He had seen human beings for the last time! And he had looked his last upon the bright sky, and upon the smiling earth, and upon a beautiful world he loved, and whose minion he had been! Here he was to end his life—a life he had just begun to revel in! And by what means? By secret poison? or by murderous assault? No—for then it had been needless to bring him thither. Famine perhaps—a thousand deaths in one! It was terrible to think of it—but it was yet more terrible to picture long, long years of captivity, in a solitude so appalling, a loneliness so dreary, that thought, for want of fellowship, would lose itself in madness, or stagnate into idiocy.

He could not hope to escape, unless he had the power, with his bare hands, of rending asunder the solid iron walls of his prison. He could not hope for liberty from the relenting mercies of his enemy. His instant death, under the form of refined cruelty, was not the object of Tolfi, for he might have inflicted it, and he had not. It was too evident, therefore, he was reserved for some premeditated scheme of subtle vengeance; and what vengeance could transcend in fiendish malice, either the slow death of famine, or the still slower one of solitary incarceration, till the last lingering spark of life expired, or till reason fled, and nothing should remain to perish but the brute functions of the body?

It was evening when Vivenzio entered his dungeon, and the approaching shades of night wrapped it in total darkness, as he paced up and down, revolving in his mind these horrible forebodings. No tolling bell from the castle, or from any neighbouring church or convent, struck upon his ear to tell how the hours passed. Frequently he would stop and listen for some sound that might betoken the vicinity of man; but the solitude of the desert, the silence of the tomb, are not so still and deep, as the oppressive desolation by which he was encompassed. His heart sunk within him, and he threw himself dejectedly upon his couch of straw. Here sleep gradually obliterated the consciousness of misery, and bland dreams wafted his delighted spirit to scenes which were once glowing realities for him, in whose ravishing illusions he soon lost the remembrance that he was Tolfi's prisoner.

303

When he awoke, it was daylight; but how long he had slept he knew not. It might be early morning, or it might be sultry noon, for he could measure time by no other note of its progress than light and darkness. He had been so happy in his sleep, amid friends who loved him, and the sweeter endearments of those who loved him as friends could not, that in the first moments of waking, his startled mind seemed to admit the knowledge of his situation, as if it had burst upon it for the first time, fresh in all its appalling horrors. He gazed round with an air of doubt and amazement, and took up a handful of the straw upon which he lay, as though he would ask himself what it meant. But memory, too faithful to her office, soon unveiled the melancholy past, while reason, shuddering at the task, flashed before his eyes the tremendous future. The contrast overpowered him. He remained for some time lamenting, like a truth, the bright visions that had vanished; and recoiling from the present, which clung to him as a poisoned garment.

When he grew more calm, he surveyed his gloomy dungeon. Alas! the stronger light of day only served to confirm what the gloomy indistinctness of the preceding evening had partially disclosed, the utter impossibility of escape. As, however, his eyes wandered round and round, and from place to place, he noticed two circumstances which excited his surprise and curiosity. The one, he thought, might be fancy; but the other, was positive. His pitcher of water, and the dish which contained his food, had been removed from his side while he slept, and now stood near the door. Were he even inclined to doubt this, he could not, for the pitcher now in his dungeon was neither of the same form nor colour as the other, while the food was changed for some other of better quality. He had been visited therefore during the night. But how had the person obtained entrance? Could he have slept so soundly, that the unlocking and opening of those pondering portals were effected without waking him? He would have said this was not possible, but that in doing so, he must admit a greater difficulty, an entrance by other means, of which he was convinced there existed none. It was not intended, then, that he should be left to perish from hunger. But the secret and mysterious mode of supplying him with food, seemed to indicate he was to have no opportunity of communicating with a human being.

The other circumstance which had attracted his notice, was the disappearance, as he believed, of one of the seven grated windows

The Iron Shroud

that ran along the top of his prison. He felt confident that he had observed and counted them; for he was rather surprised at their number, and there was something peculiar in their form, as well as in the manner of their arrangement, at unequal distances. It was so much easier, however, to suppose he was mistaken, than that a portion of the solid iron, which formed the walls, could have escaped from its position, that he soon dismissed the thought from his mind.

Vivenzio partook of the food that was before him, without apprehension. It might be poisoned; but if it were, he knew he could not escape death, should such be the design of Tolfi, and the quickest death would be the speediest release.

The day passed wearily and gloomily; though not without a faint hope that, by keeping watch at night, he might observe when the person came again to bring him food, which he supposed he would do in the same way as before. The mere thought of being approached by a living creature, and the opportunity it might present of learning the doom prepared, or preparing, for him, imparted some comfort. Besides, if he came alone, might he not in a furious onset overpower him? Or he might be accessible to pity, or the influence of such munificent rewards as he could bestow, if once more at liberty and master of himself. Say he were armed. The worst that could befall, if nor bribe, nor prayers, nor force prevailed, was a faithful blow, which, though dealt in a damned cause, might work a desired end. There was no chance so desperate, but it looked lovely in Vivenzio's eyes, compared with the idea of being totally abandoned.

The night came, and Vivenzio watched. Morning came, and Vivenzio was confounded! He must have slumbered without knowing it. Sleep must have stolen over him when exhausted by fatigue, and in that interval of feverish repose, he had been baffled; for there stood his replenished pitcher of water, and there his day's meal! Nor was this all. Casting his looks towards the windows of his dungeon, he counted but FIVE! *Here* was no deception; and he was now convinced there had been none the day before. But what did all this portend? Into what strange and mysterious den had he been cast? He gazed till his eyes ached; he could discover nothing to explain the mystery. That it was so, he knew. Why it was so, he racked his imagination in vain to conjecture. He examined the doors. A simple circumstance convinced him they had not been opened.

A wisp of straw, which he had carelessly thrown against them the preceding day, as he paced to and fro, remained where he had cast it, though it must have been displaced by the slightest motion of either of the doors. This was evidence that could not be disputed; and it followed there must be some secret machinery in the walls by which a person could enter. He inspected them closely. They appeared to him one solid and compact mass of iron; or joined, if joined they were, with such nice art, that no mark of division was perceptible. Again and again he surveyed them—and the floor—and the roof—and that range of visionary windows, as he was now almost tempted to consider them: he could discover nothing, absolutely nothing, to relieve his doubts or satisfy his curiosity. Sometimes he fancied that altogether the dungeon had a more contracted appearance—that it looked smaller; but this he ascribed to fancy, and the impression naturally produced upon his mind by the undeniable disappearance of two of the windows.

With intense anxiety, Vivenzio looked forward to the return of night; and as it approached, he resolved that no treacherous sleep should again betray him. Instead of seeking his bed of straw, he continued to walk up and down his dungeon till daylight, straining his eyes in every direction through the darkness, to watch for any appearances that might explain these mysteries. While thus engaged, and as nearly as he could judge, (by the time that afterwards elapsed before the morning came in,) about two o'clock, there was a slight tremulous motion of the floors. He stooped. The motion lasted nearly a minute; but it was so extremely gentle, that he almost doubted whether it was real, or only imaginary. He listened. Not a sound could be heard. Presently, however, he felt a rush of cold air blow upon him; and dashing towards the quarter whence it seemed to proceed, he stumbled over something which he judged to be the water ewer. The rush of cold air was no longer perceptible; and as Vivenzio stretched out his hands, he found himself close to the walls. He remained motionless for a considerable time; but nothing occurred during the remainder of the night to excite his attention, though he continued to watch with unabated vigilance.

The first approaches of the morning were visible through the grated windows, breaking, with faint divisions of light, the darkness that still pervaded every other part, long before Vivenzio was enabled to distinguish any object in his dungeon. Instinctively and fearfully he turned his eyes, hot and inflamed with watching,

The Iron Shroud

towards them. There were FOUR! He could *see* only four: but it might be that some intervening object prevented the fifth from becoming perceptible; and he waited impatiently to ascertain if it were so. As the light strengthened, however, and penetrated every corner of the cell, other objects of amazement struck his sight. On the ground lay the broken fragments of the pitcher he had used the day before, and at a small distance from them, nearer to the wall, stood the one he had noticed the first night. It was filled with water, and beside it was his food. He was now certain, that, by some mechanical contrivance, an opening was obtained through the iron wall, and that through this opening the current of air had found entrance. But how noiseless! For had a feather almost waved at the time, he must have heard it. Again he examined that part of the wall; but both to sight and touch it appeared one even and uniform surface, while to repeated and violent blows, there was no reverberating sound indicative of hollowness.

This perplexing mystery had for a time withdrawn his thoughts from the windows; but now, directing his eyes again towards them, he saw that the fifth had disappeared in the same manner as the preceding two, without the least distinguishable alteration of external appearances. The remaining four looked as the seven had originally looked; that is, occupying, at irregular distances, the top of the wall on that side of the dungeon. The tall folding door, too, still seemed to stand beneath, in the centre of these four, as it had at first stood in the centre of the seven. But he could no longer doubt, what, on the preceding day, he fancied might be the effect of visual deception. The dungeon *was* smaller. The roof had lowered—and the opposite ends had contracted the intermediate distance by a space equal, he thought, to that over which the three windows had extended. He was bewildered in vain imaginings to account for these things. Some frightful purpose—some devilish torture of mind or body—some unheard-of device for producing exquisite misery, lurked, he was sure, in what had taken place.

Oppressed with this belief, and distracted more by the dreadful uncertainty of whatever fate impended, than he could be dismayed, he thought, by the knowledge of the worst, he sat ruminating, hour after hour, yielding his fears in succession to every haggard fancy. At last a horrible suspicion flashed suddenly across his mind, and he started up with a frantic air. "Yes!" he exclaimed, looking wildly round his dungeon, and shuddering as he spoke—"Yes! it must be so! I see it!—I feel the maddening truth like scorching flames upon my brain! Eternal God!—support me! it must be so!—Yes, yes, *that* is to be my fate! Yon roof will descend!—these walls will hem me round!—and slowly, slowly, crush me in their iron arms! Lord God! look down upon me, and in mercy strike me with instant death! Oh, fiend—oh, devil—is this your revenge?"

He dashed himself upon the ground in agony;—tears burst from him, and the sweat stood in large drops upon his face—he sobbed aloud—he tore his hair—he rolled about like one suffering intolerable anguish of body, and would have bitten the iron floor beneath him; he breathed fearful curses upon Tolfi, and the next moment passionate prayers to heaven for immediate death. Then the violence of his grief became exhausted, and he lay still, weeping as a child would weep. The twilight of departing day shed its gloom around him ere he arose from that posture of utter and hopeless sorrow. He had taken no food. Not one drop of water had cooled the fever of his parched lips. Sleep had not visited his eyes for six and thirty hours. He was faint with hunger; weary with watching, and with the excess of his emotions. He tasted of his food; he drank with avidity of the water; and reeling like a drunken man to his straw, cast himself upon it to brood again over the appalling image that had fastened itself upon his almost frenzied thoughts.

He slept. But his slumbers were not tranquil. He resisted, as long as he could, their approach; and when, at last, enfeebled nature yielded to their influence, he found no oblivion from his cares. Terrible dreams haunted him—ghastly visions harrowed up his imagination—he shouted and screamed, as if he already felt the dungeon's ponderous roof descending on him—he breathed hard and thick, as though writhing between its iron walls. Then would he spring up—stare wildly about him—stretch forth his hands, to be sure he yet had space enough to live— and, muttering some incoherent words, sink down again, to pass through the same fierce vicissitudes of delirious sleep.

The morning of the fourth day dawned upon Vivenzio. But it was high noon before his mind shook off its stupor, or he awoke to a full consciousness of his situation. And what a fixed energy of despair sat upon his pale features, as he cast his eyes upwards, and gazed upon the THREE windows that now alone remained! The three!—there were no more!—and they seemed to number his own allotted days. Slowly and calmly he next surveyed the top and sides,

The Iron Shroud

and comprehended all the meaning of the diminished height of the former, as well as of the gradual approximation of the latter. The contracted dimensions of his mysterious prison were now too gross and palpable to be the juggle of his heated imagination. Still lost in wonder at the means, Vivenzio could put no cheat upon his reason, as to the end. By what horrible ingenuity it was contrived, that walls, and roof, and windows, should thus silently and imperceptibly, without noise, and without motion almost, fold, as it were, within each other, he knew not. He only knew they did so; and he vainly strove to persuade himself it was the intention of the contriver, to rack the miserable wretch who might be immured there, with anticipation, merely, of a fate, from which, in the very crisis of his agony, he was to be reprieved.

Gladly would he have clung even to this possibility, if his heart would have let him; but he felt a dreadful assurance of its fallacy. And what matchless inhumanity it was to doom the sufferer to such lingering torments—to lead him day by day to so appalling a death, unsupported by the consolations of religion, unvisited by any human being, abandoned to himself, deserted of all, and denied even the sad privilege of knowing that his cruel destiny would awaken pity! Alone he was to perish!—alone he was to wait a slow coming torture, whose most exquisite pangs would be inflicted by that very solitude and that tardy coming!

"It is not death I fear," he exclaimed, "but the death I must prepare for! Methinks, too, I could meet even that—all horrible and revolting as it is—if it might overtake me now. But where shall I find fortitude to tarry till it come? How can I outlive the three long days and nights I have to live? There is no power within me to bid the hideous spectre hence—none to make it familiar to my thoughts; or myself, patient of its errand. My thoughts, rather, will flee from me, and I grow mad in looking at it. Oh! for a deep sleep to fall upon me! That so, in death's likeness, I might embrace death itself, and drink no more of the cup that is presented to me, than my fainting spirit has already tasted!"

In the midst of these lamentations, Vivenzio noticed that his accustomed meal, with the pitcher of water, had been conveyed, as before, into his dungeon. But this circumstance no longer excited his surprise. His mind was overwhelmed with others of a far greater magnitude. It suggested, however, a feeble hope of deliverance; and there is no hope so feeble as not to yield some support to a heart bending under despair. He resolved to watch, during the ensuing night, for the signs he had before observed; and should he again feel the gentle, tremulous motion of the floor, or the current of air, to seize that moment for giving audible expression to his misery. Some person must be near him, and within reach of his voice, at the instant when his food was supplied; some one, perhaps, susceptible of pity. Or if not, to be told even that his apprehensions were just, and that his fate *was* to be what he foreboded, would be preferable to a suspense which hung upon the possibility of his worst fears being visionary.

The night came; and as the hour approached when Vivenzio imagined he might expect the signs, he stood fixed and silent as a statue. He feared to breathe, almost, lest he might lose any sound which would warn him of their coming. While thus listening, with every faculty of mind and body strained to an agony of attention, it occurred to him he should be more sensible of the motion, probably, if he stretched himself along the iron floor. He accordingly laid himself softly down, and had not been long in that position when—yes—he was certain of it—the floor moved under him! He sprang up, and in a voice suffocated nearly with emotion, called aloud. He paused—the motion ceased—he felt no stream of air—all was hushed—no voice answered to his—he burst into tears; and as he sunk to the ground, in renewed anguish, exclaimed,—"Oh, my God! my God! You alone have power to save me now, or strengthen me for the trial you permit."

Another morning dawned upon the wretched captive, and the fatal index of his doom met his eyes. Two windows!—and *two* days—and all would be over! Fresh food—fresh water! The mysterious visit had been paid, though he had implored it in vain. But how awfully was his prayer answered in what he now saw! The roof of the dungeon was within a foot of his head. The two ends were so near, that in six paces he trod the space between them. Vivenzio shuddered as he gazed, and as his steps traversed the narrowed area. But his feelings no longer vented themselves in frantic wailings. With folded arms, and clenched teeth, with eyes that were blood-shot from much watching, and fixed with a vacant glare upon the ground, with a hard quick breathing, and a hurried walk, he strode backwards and forwards in silent musing for several hours. What mind shall conceive, what tongue utter, or what pen describe the dark and terrible character of his thoughts? Like the

The Iron Shroud

fate that moulded them, they had no similitude in the wide range of this world's agony for man. Suddenly he stopped, and his eyes were riveted upon that part of the wall which was over his bed of straw. Words are inscribed there! A human language, traced by a human hand! He rushes towards them; but his blood freezes as he read:—

"I, Ludovico Sforza,[367] tempted by the gold of the Prince of Tolfi, spent three years in contriving and executing this accursed triumph of my art. When it was completed, the perfidious Tolfi, more devil than man, who conducted me hither one morning, to be witness, as he said, of its perfection, doomed *me* to be the first victim of my own pernicious skill; lest, as he declared, I should divulge the secret, or repeat the effort of my ingenuity. May God pardon him, as I hope he will me, that ministered to his unhallowed purpose! Miserable wretch, whoe'er thou art, that readest these lines, fall on thy knees, and invoke, as I have done, His sustaining mercy, who alone can nerve thee to meet the vengeance of Tolfi, armed with his tremendous engine which, in a few hours, must crush *you*, as it will the needy wretch who made it."

A deep groan burst from Vivenzio. He stood, like one transfixed, with dilated eyes, expanded nostrils, and quivering lips, gazing at this fatal inscription. It was as if a voice from the sepulchre had sounded in his ears, "Prepare!" Hope forsook him. There was his sentence, recorded in those dismal words. The future stood unveiled before him, ghastly and appalling. His brain already feels the descending horror,—his bones seem to crack and crumble in the mighty grasp of the iron walls! Unknowing what it is he does, he fumbles in his garment for some weapon of self-destruction. He clenches his throat in his convulsive gripe, as though he would strangle himself at once. He stares upon the walls, and his warring spirit demands, "Will they not anticipate their office if I dash my head against them?" An hysterical laugh chokes him as he exclaims, "Why should I? He was but a man who died first in their fierce embrace; and I should be less than man not to do as much!"

The evening sun was descending, and Vivenzio beheld its golden beams streaming through one of the windows. What a thrill of joy shot through his soul at the sight! It was a precious link, that

[367] Mudford clearly named his engineer after Lodovico Sforza (1452-1508), Duke of Milan and patron of Leonardo da Vinci. It is true that the real Sforza spent the last years of his life in captivity and the last months in a French dungeon.

united him, for the moment, with the world beyond. There was ecstasy in the thought. As he gazed, long and earnestly, it seemed as if the windows had lowered sufficiently for him to reach them. With one bound he was beneath them—with one wild spring he clung to the bars. Whether it was so contrived, purposely to madden with delight the wretch who looked, he knew not; but, as the extremity of a long vista, cut through the solid rocks, the ocean, the sky, the setting sun, olive groves, shady walks, and, in the farthest distance, delicious glimpses of magnificent Sicily, burst upon his sight. How exquisite was the cool breeze as it swept across his cheek, loaded with fragrance! He inhaled it as though it were the breath of continued life. And there was a freshness in the landscape, and in the rippling of the calm green sea, that fell upon his withering heart like dew upon the parched earth. How he gazed, and panted, and still clung to his hold! sometimes hanging by one hand, sometimes by the other, and then grasping the bars with both, as loath to quit the smiling paradise outstretched before him; till exhausted, and his hands swollen and benumbed, he dropped helpless down, and lay stunned for a considerable time by the fall.

When he recovered, the glorious vision had vanished. He was in darkness. He doubted whether it was not a dream that had passed before his sleeping fancy; but gradually his scattered thoughts returned, and with them came remembrance. Yes! he had looked once again upon the gorgeous splendour of nature! Once again his eyes had trembled beneath their veiled lids, at the sun's radiance, and sought repose in the soft verdure of the olive-tree, or the gentle swell of undulating waves. Oh, that he were a mariner, exposed upon those waves to the worst fury of storm and tempest; or a very wretch, loathsome with disease, plague-stricken, and his body one leprous contagion from crown to sole, hunted forth to gasp out the remnant of infectious life beneath those verdant trees, so he might shun the destiny upon whose edge he tottered!

Vain thoughts like these would steal over his mind from time to time, in spite of himself; but they scarcely moved it from that stupor into which it had sunk, and which kept him, during the whole night, like one who had been drugged with opium. He was equally insensible to the calls of hunger and of thirst, though the third day was now commencing since even a drop of water had passed his lips. He remained on the ground, sometimes sitting, sometimes lying; at intervals, sleeping heavily; and when not sleeping, silently

The Iron Shroud

brooding over what was to come, or talking aloud, in disordered speech, of his wrongs, of his friends, of his home, and of those he loved, with a confused mingling of all.

In this pitiable condition, the sixth and last morning dawned upon Vivenzio, if dawn it might be called—the dim, obscure light which faintly struggled through the ONE SOLITARY window of his dungeon. He could hardly be said to notice the melancholy token. And yet he did notice it; for as he raised his eyes and saw the portentous sign, there was a slight convulsive distortion of his countenance. But what did attract his notice, and at the sight of which his agitation was excessive, was the change his iron bed had undergone. It was a bed no longer. It stood before him, the visible semblance of a funeral couch or bier! When he beheld this, he started from the ground; and, in raising himself, suddenly struck his head against the roof, which was now so low that he could no longer stand upright. "God's will be done!" was all he said, as he crouched his body, and placed his hand upon the bier; for such it was. The iron bedstead had been so contrived, by the mechanical art of Ludovico Sforza, that as the advancing walls came in contact with its head and feet, a pressure was produced upon concealed springs, which, when made to play, set in motion a very simple though ingeniously contrived machinery, that effected the transformation. The object was, of course, to heighten, in the closing scene of this horrible drama, all the feelings of despair and anguish, which the preceding ones had aroused. For the same reason, the last window was so made as to admit only a shadowy kind of gloom rather than light, that the wretched captive might be surrounded, as it were, with every seeming preparation for approaching death.

Vivenzio seated himself on his bier. Then he knelt and prayed fervently; and sometimes tears would gush from him. The air seemed thick, and he breathed with difficulty; or it might be that he fancied it was so, from the hot and narrow limits of his dungeon, which were now so diminished that he could neither stand up nor lie down at his full length. But his wasted spirits and oppressed mind no longer struggled within him. He was past hope, and fear shook him no more. Happy if thus revenge had struck its final blow; for he would have fallen beneath it almost unconscious of a pang. But such a lethargy of the soul, after such an excitement of its fiercest passions, had entered into the diabolical calculations of Tolfi; and the fell artificer of his designs had imagined a counteracting device.

313

The tolling of an enormous bell struck upon the ears of Vivenzio! He started. It beat but once. The sound was so close and stunning, that it seemed to shatter his very brain, while it echoed through the rocky passages like reverberating peals of thunder. This was followed by a sudden crash of the roof and walls, as if they were about to fall upon and close around him at once. Vivenzio screamed, and instinctively spread forth his arms, as though he had a giant's strength to hold them back. They had moved nearer to him, and were now motionless. Vivenzio looked up, and saw the roof almost touching his head, even as he sat cowering beneath it; and he felt that a farther contraction of but a few inches only must commence the frightful operation. Roused as he had been, he now gasped for breath. His body shook violently—he was bent nearly double. His hands rested upon either wall, and his feet were drawn under him to avoid the pressure in front. Thus he remained for more than an hour, when that deafening bell beat again, and again there came the crash of horrid death. But the concussion was now so great that it struck Vivenzio down. As he lay gathered up in lessened bulk, the bell beat loud and frequent—crash succeeded crash—and on, and on, and on came the mysterious engine of death, till Vivenzio's smothered groans were heard no more! He was horribly crushed by the ponderous roof and collapsing sides—and the flattened bier was his *Iron Shroud*.

John Banim

𝒯HE CHURCH-𝒴ARD 𝒲ATCH

(1831)

The author: John Banim (1798-1841) was born and died in County Kilkenny, Ireland. He studied to become a painter but, together with his older brother Michael (1796-1874), he launched a career as a novelist and short-story writer. Together, they published the successful *Tales of the O'Hara Family* (two series in 1825 and 1826), followed by novels (mostly historical) and short stories, all set in Ireland.

The text: The story was first published in *Friendship's Offering: A Literary Album, and Christmas and New Year's Present, for 1832* (London: Smith, Elder, and Co., 1832 [1831], 305-320), where it was signed "by the author of 'Tales of the O'Hara Family.'" It was later collected in the brothers' *The Bit o' Writin' and Other Tales* (1838). In his preface to the 1865 edition of *The Bit o' Writin'* (Dublin: James Duffy), Michael Banim indicated that most of the texts (including "The Church-Yard Watch") had been written by his brother. The following is from *The Bit o' Writin' and Other Tales. By the O'Hara Family. In Three Volumes* (London: Saunders and Otley, 1838), III, 1-26.

Further reading: Julia M. Wright. "Domestic Terror and the Banims' 'Church-Yard Watch." *Representing the National Landscape in Irish Romanticism*. New York: Syracuse University Press, 2014. 146-158.

John Banim

The dead are watched lest the living should prey on them!—'Tis a strange alliance—of the living with DEATH—that His kingdom and sovereignty may remain untrenched upon. In different parts of England, we have seen watch-houses, almost entirely composed of glass, built in lonesome church-yards, of which generally the parish sexton, and perhaps his dog (ill-fated among men and dogs!) are the appointed nightly tenants; with liberty, ceded or taken, to leave their dull lamp in the watch-box, and roam, here and there, at their pleasure, among the graves, until day light. What stern necessities man forces upon man! There can scarce be a more comfortless lot, or, making allowance for the almost in-born shudderings of the human heart, a more appalling one, than that of the poor grave scooper or bell-puller who is thus doomed to spend his night, summer and winter. Habit, indeed, may eventually blunt the first keenness of his aversion, if not terror: he may serve a due apprenticeship to horrors, and learn his trade. After a thousand secret and unowned struggles to seem brave and indifferent, he may at last grow callously courageous. His flesh may cease to creep as he strides on, in his accustomed round, over the abodes of the silent and mouldering, and hears his own dull footstep echoed through the frequent dreary hollowness beneath. But what has he gained, now, beyond the facility of earning his wretched crust for himself and his crying infants!—We have seen and spoken with such an unhappy being, who seemed to have lost, in the struggle which conquered nature's especial antipathy, (nature in a breast and mind like his, at least,) most of the other sympathies of his kind. He had a heavy, ox-like expression of face; he would scarce speak to his neighbours (although *we* contrived to make him eloquent) when they passed him at his door, or in the village street; his own children feared or disliked him, and did not smile nor whisper in his presence. We have watched him into the church-yard, at his usual hour, after night-fall; and as he began to stalk about there, the ghastly sentinel of the dead, he appeared to be in closer fellowship with them, than with the fair existence which he scarce more than nominally shared. It was said, indeed, that, upon his initiation, at a tender age and under peculiar circumstances, into his profession

The Church-Yard Watch

of church-yard watchman, temporary delirium prepared him for its regular and steady pursuit ever since; and that, although he showed no symptoms of distinct insanity, when we knew him, the early visitation had left a gloom on his mind, and a thick, nerveless insensibility in his heart, which then, at forty-five, formed his character. In fact, we learned a good deal about him, for every one talked of him—and, as has been hinted, much of that good deal from himself, to say nothing of his wife, in his absence; and if he did not deliberately invent fables of his past trials, for the purpose of gratifying a little spirit of mockery of our undisguised interest, as mad as the maddest bedlamite he must have been upon the occasion alluded to: nay, to recount, with a grave face (as he did) the particulars of the delusions of his time of delirium, did not argue him a very sound-minded man at the moment he gave us his confidence. We are about to tell his story, at length, in our own way, however; that is, we shall try to model into our own language (particularly the raving parts) what his neighbours, his spouse, and his own slow-moving and heavy lips have, from time to time, supplied us with.

He was the only child of an affectionate and gentle-mannered father, who died when he was little more than a boy, leaving him sickly and pining. His mother wept a month, mourned three months more,—and was no longer a widow. Her second husband proved a surly fellow, who married her little fortune, rather than herself, as the means of keeping his quart pot filled, almost from morning to night, at the village Tap, where he played good-fellow and politician to the expressed admiration of all his companions. He had long been the parish sexton, and took up his post, night after night, in the church-yard. Little fear had he of what he might see there; or, he had out-grown his fears; or, if he thought or felt of the matter, the lonely debauch which he was known to make in that strange banquet-place, served to drug him into obliviousness. He deemed his duty—or he said and swore he did—only a tiresome and slavish one, and hated it just as he hated daily labour. And—as he declared and harangued at the Tap—he had long ago forsworn it, only that it paid him well; but, now that his marriage made his circumstances easier, he was determined to drink alone in the church-yard no longer: and he fed an idle, useless lad at home, who with his dog—as idle as he—roamed and loitered about, here and there, and had never yet done a single thing to earn their bread.

317

But it was full time that both were taught the blessings of industry; and he would teach them;—and—now that he thought of it—why should not Will take his place in the watchbox, and so keep the shillings in the family? His friends praised his views, one and all, and he grew thrice resolved.

Returned the next morning from his nocturnal charge, he reeled to bed in solemn, drunken determination. He arose, towards evening, only half reclaimed by sleep to ordinary sense, and set about his work of reformation. He ate his meal in silence, turned from the table to the fire without a word, looked at the blaze, grimly contemplative, then grumbling suddenly at his wife—"And where is that truant now?" he asked: "down by the marshes with his cur, I suppose; or gone a-nutting, or lying stretched in the sun, the two idlers together; what!—and must I work and work, and strive and strive,—I, I, for ever—and will he never lend me a hand?—go where he likes, do what he likes, and laugh and fatten on my labour?"

"Master Hunks," said the wife, "Will is sickly, and won't fatten on either your labour or mine—not to talk of his own;—you know 'tis a puny lad, and wants some favour yet a-while; with God's help, and ours, he may be stronger soon."

Will and his dog here came in. From what followed, this evening, it will be seen, that the ill-fated lad promised, in early youth, to be of an open, kindly, intelligent character, very different indeed from that in which we found him husked up, at five-and-forty.

He saluted his step-father, and sat down quietly near the fire. His poor dumb companion—friend of his boyhood, and his father's gift—coiled himself up before the blaze, and prepared to surrender his senses to happy sleep, interspersed with dreams of all the sports he had enjoyed with his master that day. Hunks, his eye glancing from one object of dislike to the other, kicked the harmless brute, who jumped up, yelping in pain and bitter lamentation, and ran for shelter under Will's chair. Will's pale cheek broke out into colour, his weak eye sparkled, his feeble voice arose shrilly, and he asked—"Why is my poor dog beaten?"

"The lazy cur!" said Hunks—"he was in my way, and only got paid for idleness."

"'Twas ill done," resumed Will—"he was my father's dog, and my father gave him to me; and if my father were alive and well,

The Church-Yard Watch

he would not hurt him, nor see him hurt!"—Tears interrupted his sudden fit of spirit.

"Cur, as much as he is!" retorted Hunks—"do you put upon me, here at my own fireside? *You* are the idler—you—and he only learns of you—and I hadn't ought to have served him out, and you so near me."

"It has been God's will," said the boy, "to keep my strength from me."

"Be silent and hear me!" roared Hunks—"this is your life, I say—playing truant for ever—and what is mine, and your own good mother's here?"

"Master Hunks," pleaded the wife—"God knows I don't grudge nothing I can do for my poor Will's sake."

"And you—not a word from you either, Missis!" grunted Hunks—"I am put upon by one and t'other of you—ye sleep in comfort every night, and leave me to go a-watching, out o' doors, there, in all weathers; but stop a bit, my man, it shan't be this way much longer; I'll have my natural rest in my bed, some time or other, and soon; and you must earn it for me."

"How, father? how can I earn it?" asked Will—"I would if I could—but how? I hav'n't learnt no trade, and you know as well as any one knows it, I am not able to work in the fields or on the roads, or get my living any one way."

"Then you can sit still and watch—that's light work," muttered Hunks.

"Watch!" cried mother and son together—"watch what? and where? or whom?"

"The dead folk in the church-yard."

"Heaven defend me from it!" cried poor Will, clasping his hands and falling back in his chair.

"Ay, and this very night," continued the despot—"this very night you shall mount guard in my place, and I shall have my lawful sleep, what the whole parish cries shame on me for not having months ago."

"Master Hunks, 'twill kill the boy!" cried the mother.

"Missis—don't you go for to cross me so often!"—remonstrated her husband, with a fixed look, which, short as they had been one flesh, she had reason to understand and shrink at.—"Come, my man, stir yourself; 'tis time you were at the gate; the church clock has struck; *they will expect us*"—he interrupted himself in a great rage, and with a great oath—"but here I keep talking and the cur never minds a word I say!—Come along!"

"Don't lay hands on him!" screamed the mother as he strode towards the boy—"what I have often told you, has come to pass, Master Hunks—you have killed him!"

Hunks scoffed at the notion, although, indeed, Will's hands had fallen helplessly at his side, and his chin rested on his breast, while his eyes were closed, and his lips apart. But he had only become insensible from sheer terror acting on a weak frame. Sighs and groans soon gave notice of returning animation. His mother then earnestly besought their tyrant to go on his night's duty, and, at least till the following night, leave her son to her care. Half in fear of having to answer for a murder, incredulously as he pretended to speak, Hunks turned out of the house, growling and threatening.

"Is he gone?" asked Will, when he regained his senses—"gone not to come back?"—and having heard his mother's gentle assurances, he let his head fall on her shoulder, weeping, while he continued:—

"Mother, mother, it would destroy the little life I have! I could not bear it for an hour! The dread I am in of it was born with me! When I was a child of four years, I had dreams of it, and I remember them to this day; they used to come in such crowds round my cradle! As I grew up, you saw and you know my weakness. I could never sit still in the dark, nor even in the daylight out of doors in lonesome places. Now in my youth—a lad—almost a man—I am ashamed to speak of my inward troubles. Mother, you do not know me—I do not know myself! I walk out sometimes down by the river, and, listening to the noise of the water over the rocks, where it is shallow, and to the rustling of the trees as they nod in the twilight, voices and shrieks come round me—sometimes they break in my years—and I have turned to see what thing it was that spoke, and thought some grey tree at my side had only just changed and become motionless, and seemed as if, a moment before, it had been something else, and had a tongue, and said the words that frightened me!—Oh, it was but yester evening I ran home from the banks of the river, and felt no heart within me till I had come in here to the fireside, and seen you moving near me!

"You know the lone house all in ruins upon the hill—I fear it, mother, more than my tongue can tell you! I have been taken through it, in my dreams, in terrible company, and here I could

The Church-Yard Watch

describe to you its bleak apartments, one by one—its vaults, pitch dark, and half-filled with stones and rubbish, and choked up with weeds—its winding, creeping staircases, and its flapping windows—I know them all, though my feet never yet crossed its threshold!—Never, mother—though I have gone near it, to enter it, and see if what I had dreamt of it was true—and I went in the first light of the morning; but when close by the old door-way, the rustle of the shrubs and weeds startled me, and I thought—but sure *that* was fancy—that some one called me in by name—and then I turned and raced down the hill, never looking back till I came to the meadow ground where cows and sheep are always grazing, and heard the dogs barking in the town, and voices of the children at play!"

"Will, my king," said his mother, soothingly, "this is all mere childishness at your years. God is above us and around us; and even if evil and strange things are allowed to be on earth, he will shield us from all harm. Arouse up like a man! for, indeed, your time of boyhood is passing—nay, it has passed with other lads not much older; only you have been poorly and weakly from your cradle, Will. Come, go to sleep; and before you lie down, pray for better health and strength to-morrow."

"To-morrow!" he repeated—"and did my step-father say anything of to-morrow?"

His mother answered him evasively, and he resumed,—"Oh, how I fear to-morrow!—oh, mother, you have loved me, and you do love me—for my weakness, my ill-health, and my dutifulness—and you loved my father—oh, for his sake as well as mine, mother, keep me from what I am threatened with!—keep me from it, if you would keep me alive another day?"

He went into his little sleeping-apartment, stricken to the very soul with supernatural fears.

After spending a miserable night, he stole out of the house next morning, and wandered about the private walks adjacent to the town, until he thought his step-father might have arisen and taken his usual walk to the Tap. But as the lad was about to re-enter the house, Hunks met him at the threshold. Will shrunk back; to his surprise and comfort, however, his fears now seemed ill-founded. The man bid him good morrow in as cheerful and kind a tone as he could command, shook his hand, tapped him on the head, and left the house. Delighted, though still agitated, Will sought his mother within doors, told her his good omens, and spent a happy day. At dinner, too, notwithstanding Hunks' presence, the mother and son enjoyed themselves, so amiable had the despot become, at least in appearance.

When their meal was over, Hunks, as if to attain the utmost civility, invited Will to go out with him for a walk by the river—"and let's have Barker (Will's dog) for company," continued Hunks; "he may show us sport with a rat, or such like, Will."

Accordingly, the three strolled out together, Will leading the way by many a well-known sedge or tuft of bushes, or undermined bank, the resorts of the water-rat, and sometimes of the outlaw otter; and Barker upheld his character, by starting, hunting down, and killing one of the first-mentioned animals. As twilight came on, they turned their faces towards the little town. They entered it. Its little hum of life was now hushed; its streets silent, and almost deserted; its doors and windows barred and bolted, and the sounds of the rushing river and the thumping mill were the only ones which filled the air. The clock pealed ten as they continued their way. Hunks had grown suddenly silent and reserved. They passed the old Gothic church, and now were passing the gate which led into its burial-ground. Hunks stopped short. His grey, bad eye fell on the lad—"Will," he said, "I be thinking we've walked enough for this time."

"Enough, indeed,—and thank you for your company—and good night, father," answered Will, trying to smile, though he began to tremble.

"Good night then, my man—and here be your watch-light"—and Hunks drew a dark lantern from his huge pocket.

"Nay, I want no light home," said Will; "I know the way so well; and 'tis not very dark; and you know you can't do without it on your post."

"My post!" Hunks laughed villainously—"your post you mean, Will; take it; I be thinking I shall sleep sound to-night without a dead-light—as if I were a corpse to need it. Come along."

"You cannot have the heart to ask me!" cried Will, stepping back.

"Pho, my man"—Hunks clutched him by the shoulder with one hand, with the other unlocked the gate and flung it open—"In with you; you'll like it so in a few nights, you'll wish no better post; the dead chaps be civil enough; only treat them well, and let them walk awhile, and they make very good company." He dragged Will closer to the gate.

The Church-Yard Watch

"Have mercy!" shrieked the wretched lad, trying to kneel, "or kill me first, father, to make me company for them, if that will please you."

"Get in!" roared the savage—"get in!—ay, hollo out, and twist about, so, and I'll pitch your shivering carcass half way across the church-yard!"—he forced him in from the gate—stop a bit, now—there be your lantern"—he set it down on a tomb-stone—"so, good night—yonder's your box—just another word—don't you be caught strolling too near the murderer's corner, over there, or you may trip and fall among the things that turn and twine on the ground, like roots of trees, to guard him."

With a new and piercing shriek, Will clung close to his fell tormentor. Hunks, partially carrying into effect a threat he had uttered, tore the lad's hands away, tossed him to some distance, strode out at the gate, locked it, and Will was alone with horror.

At first an anguish of fear kept him stupified and stationary. He had fallen on a freshly-piled grave, to which mechanically his fingers clung and his face joined, in avoidance of the scene around. But he soon recollected what clay it was he clung to, and at the thought, he started up, and, hushed as the sleepers around him, made some observations. High walls quite surrounded the churchyard, as if to part him from the habitable world. His lamp was burning upon the tombstone where Hunks had placed it—one dim red spot amid the thick darkness. The church clock now tolled eleven. It ceased; his ears ached in the resumed silence, and he listened and stared about him for what he feared. Whispers seemed to arise near him; he ran for his lamp, snatched it up, and instinctively hurried to the watch-box. Oh, he wished it made of solid rock!—it was chiefly framed of glass, useless as the common air to his terrors! He shut his eyes, and pressed his palms upon them—vain subterfuge! The fevered spirit within him brought before his mind's vision worse things than the church-yard could yawn up, were all that superstition has fancied of it true. He looked out from his watch-box in refuge from himself.

That evening a half-moon had risen early, and, at this moment, was sinking in gathering clouds behind distant hills. As he vaguely noticed the circumstance, he felt more and more desolate. Simultaneously with the disappearance of the planet, the near clock began again to strike—he knew what hour! Each stroke

323

smote his ear as if it would crack the nerve; at the last sound, he shrieked out delirious! He had a pause from agony, then a struggle for departing reason, and then he was at rest.

At day-break his step-father found him asleep. He led him home. Will sat down to breakfast, smiling, but did not speak a word. Often, during the day, his now brilliant eye turned to the west; but why, his mother could not tell; until, as the evening made up her couch of clouds there, drawing around her the twilight for drapery, he left the house with an unusually vigorous step, and stood at the gate of the churchyard. Again he took up his post. Again the hour of twelve pealed from the old church, but now he did not fear it. When it had fully sounded, he clapped his hands, laughed and shouted.

The imaginary whispers he had heard the previous night—small, cautious whispers—came round him again; first, from a distance, then, nearer and nearer. At last he shaped them into words—"Let us walk," they said—"though he watches us, he fears us." *He!*—'twas strange to hear the dim dead speak to a living man, of himself! the maniac laughed again at the fancy, and replied to them:—

"Ay, come! appear! I give leave for it. Ye are about in crowds, I know, not yet daring to take up your old bodies till I please; but up with them!—Graves, split on, and yield me my subjects! for am I not king of the church-yard? Obey me! ay, now your mouths gape—and what a yawning!—are ye musical, too?—a jubilee of groans! out with it, in the name of Death!—blast it about like giants carousing!

"Well blown!—and now a thousand heads popped up at once—their eyes fixed on mine, as if to ask my further leave for a resurrection; and they know I am good-humoured now, and grow upward, accordingly, like a grove of bare trees that have no sap in them. And now they move; passing along in rows, like trees, too, that glide by one on a bank, while one sails merrily down the river—and all is stark staring still: and others stand bolt upright against their own headstones to contemplate. I wonder what they think of! Move! move! young, old, boys, men, pale girls, and palsied grand-mothers—my church-yard can never hold 'em! And yet how they pass each other from corner to corner! I think they make way through one another's bodies, as they do in the grave. They'll dance anon. Minuets, at least. Why they begin already!—and what

The Church-Yard Watch

partners!—a tall, genteel young officer takes out our village witch-of-the-wield—she that died at Christmas—and our last rector smirks to a girl of fifteen—ha, ha! yon tattered little fellow is a radical, making a leg to the old duchess!—music! music!—Go, some of you that look on there, and toll the dead bell! Well done! they tie the murderer to the bell-rope by the neck, (though he was hanged before,) and the bell swings out merrily! but what face is here?"

It was the vision of a child's face, which he believed he caught staring at him through the glass of his watch-box—the face of an only brother who had died young. The wretch's laughter changed into tears and low wailings. By the time that his mother came to seek him, just at day-break, he was, however, again laughing; but in such a state as to frighten mirth from her heart and lips till the day she died. As has been said, symptoms of positive insanity did not long continue to appear in his words or actions; yet, when he recovered, there was still a change in him—a dark and disagreeable change, under the inveterate confirmation of which, the curious student of human nature may, at this moment, observe him in his native village.

1831

Letitia Elizabeth Landon

EXPERIMENTS:
OR, THE LOVER FROM ENNUI

(1832)

The author: Letitia Elizabeth Landon (1802-1838), also known as L. E. L., was born in London and published her first poem in 1820 in the *Literary Gazette*. The 1824 collection *The Improvisatrice* made her famous; this was followed by many other volumes of poetry, including *The Troubadour* (1825), *The Golden Violet, with its Tales of Romance and Chivalry, and other poems* (1827), *The Venetian Bracelet, The Lost Pleiad, A History of the Lyre and other poems* (1829), *The Vow of the Peacock and other poems* (1835). She published her first novel, *Romance and Reality* in 1831. In 1838 she married Captain George Maclean, who was in charge of the affairs of London merchants in the Gold Coast colony of West Africa, and whom she had met two years before. Soon after the wedding, they sailed to Africa, where L. E. L. died of poison, a few months later, with a bottle of prussic acid in her hand. It remains a mystery whether her death was accidental or she committed suicide.

The text: First published in *Heath's Book of Beauty 1833* (London: Longman, Rees, Orme, Brown, Green, and Longman; Paris: Rittner and Goupil; Frankfurt: C. Jügel, [1832], 222-244), from which the following has been selected. Rather than a collection from different authors, the annual was written entirely by L. E. Landon.

Experiments; or, The Lover from Ennui

Cecil Forrester was heir to many misfortunes, being handsome, rich, high-born, and clever. His father said it was a shame such a fine fellow should be coddled—took him out to hunt, and gave him port-wine after dinner: his mother said it was a pity such a sweet boy should be spoilt—heaped cushions on his favourite sofa, and perfumed for him a cambric handkerchief with *l'esprit de mille fleurs*.[368] His father died—his mother was inconsolable for six months, and then married again. Cecil was sent to Eton, where, instead of others indulging him, he indulged himself.

His education was finished by terms at college and seasons in London; and his twenty-second year found him without a pleasure, and without a guinea. The next spring he lived on *ennui* and credit. He disliked trouble, because he never took it; and he said things and people were tiresome and bores, till he firmly believed it. His feelings were never called forth, his talents never exercised; his natural superiority only served to make him discontented. He saw the waste of his life, but he lacked motive for change: his early habits were those of indolence; and being neither poor nor vain, he had no stimulus to alter them. He did a great many foolish things, regretted them, and did them over again.

One day, after driving in the Park, and wondering why so many people drove there, he turned homewards to dress for a late dinner at the Clarendon.[369] Giving his boy the reins, he resigned himself to meditation,—how unpleasant it was for the pedestrians of Piccadilly to hurry through the mud!—when he was interrupted by the boy's, "Sir, if you please," said in a tone of self-exertion, as if a great deal of mental energy had been collected for its utterance; then, in a deprecatory whisper, "you won't collar me and throw me out of the cab before I've said half, will you?"

"No, I will not," said Cecil.

---

[368] French for "the spirit of a thousand flowers." It was a perfume whose odour was supposed to be tonic; it was purchased as a powder or mixed with oils.

[369] The Clarendon Hotel, built between Albemarle Street and Bond Street, on land that had belonged to the Earl of Clarendon (1609-1674), Lord Chancellor to King Charles II. It was a popular venue among the upper classes.

To make our story shorter than the miniature groom's, he learnt that his own property in himself was in danger; and that, if the patriot's definition of liberty be true—"it is like the air we breathe, without it we die"[370]—his life was near its termination. A writ was issued against him; and, thanks to a douceur to his valet, two professional gentlemen, as he left his toilet, would deprive his friends at the Clarendon of his company.

"I wish I had spoken to my uncle sooner; but, hang it! it is so unpleasant speaking: I'll write."

Forrester was just now in that part of Piccadilly where the White Horse of our Saxon ancestors has degenerated from the banner of a sea-king to the sign of a cellar for taking places and parcels.[371] Still, even as of yore, it hangs over a most migratory multitude. "For Putney, ma'am?" "For Richmond, sir?" One coachman snatches up a child for Turnham Green, while another pops its mamma off to Camberwell.[372] One man blows a horn in your ear, and offers you the Standard; another exerts his lungs, and shews you the Courier.[373] Pencils are to be had for a penny; and penknives, with from three to six blades each, for eighteen pence a-dozen. A fellow with a trunk turns its corner on your temples; another deposits a box, with the grocery of a family—sugar, soap, candles, and all—on your toes. A gigantic gentleman nearly knocks you down in his hurry; and an elderly Jew slips past you so neatly, that you tumble over him before you are aware. Every body is always too late, and therefore every body is in a bustle. Two policemen keep the peace; and half-a-dozen individuals, whose notions on the law of property are at variance with established principles or prejudices, attend for the purpose of breaking it. Add to these

---

[370] This is in fact the definition, famous in Whig circles, of the freedom of the press, attributed either to John Horne Tooke or to the anonymous author of the *Letters of Junius*. It had been repurposed humorously as the definition of freedom in George Croly's 1824 comedy *Pride Shall Have a Fall* (Act II, Scene II).

[371] The White Horse Cellar, in Piccadilly, at the corner of Dover Street, was the starting place for coaches travelling westward, carrying passengers and packages. The heraldic white horse of Kent was associated with Horsa, one of the two legendary brothers (the other being Hengist) who had led the Angles, the Saxons and the Jutes to Britain in the 5th century.

[372] Putney, Richmond, Turnham Green and Camberwell are all parts of London today.

[373] The daily *Standard* was a leading Tory newspaper, while *The Courier*, originally Tory, had become Whig in 1830.

Experiments; or, The Lover from Ennui

some females with shawls and sharp elbows; and pattens,[374] whose iron rings are for the benefit of foot-passengers. Such is the White Horse Cellar, and the pavement from Dover Street to Albermarle Street.

Several coaches seemed to be just setting off.

"I will leave London at once," said Forrester. "Do you drive home—you know nothing about me. You are a fine little fellow; I shall not forget you."

So saying, he threw him two or three sovereigns, and got into the first coach. The boy took the money, drove the cabriolet to the stable, and ate and drank himself into a fever, out of which his mother had to nurse him.

Cecil opened his eyes on the grey sea-mist of a Brighton morning. Summer and Brighton!—the vicinity was dangerous. In all probability his tailor would be taking twopenny worth of pleasure on the pier; and if, like John Gilpin's wife, "though on pleasure he was bent," he should also "have a frugal mind,"[375] and keep an eye to business, that eye would inevitably fall on him. However, a temporary stay was necessary, for all the personal property he possessed was a handkerchief. Money supplies every want, and he had drawn his last from the banker's the day before. He did not mean to have stirred from his room, but seeing an acquaintance from the window, he resolved to ask him to dinner.

He knew Ravensdale was in love, therefore stupid; still, any company was better than his own. They dined together; and, as a companion is generally the straw that decides an idle man, he set out with him that evening for Hastings. There Mr. Ravensdale expected to meet "the beauteous arbiter who held his fate;" but some slight cause of delay had prevented, and would prevent for a short time, her family's arrival. Cecil quite envied the lover his disappointment—it so entirely occupied him.

A week passed away while he was making up his mind what he should say to his uncle, whose heir he was, and whose kindness he believed would be very likely to assist him; but long before the week was finished, he was quite convinced that Hastings was the most tiresome place on the whole sea-coast. *Oh, la peine*

---

[374] Pattens were wooden clogs with thick soles mounted on an oval iron ring, often worn over shoes to protect them against mud.

[375] From William Cowper's 1782 ballad "The Diverting History of John Gilpin": "O'erjoy'd was he to find/ That, though on pleasure she was bent,/ She had a frugal mind."

forte et dure[376] of idleness! Blessed is the banker's clerk, who on a November morning takes his nine-o'clock walk to business under a green umbrella, digesting the memory of his buttered roll and the anticipation of his desk! Blessed is the fag of fashions and fancies, who unrolls ribands from morn till night at Dyde's and Scribe's![377] Blessed is Mr. Martin, when, transgressing his own act, he urges along the heavy animal on which he perambulates in pursuit of an overladen donkey![378] Blessed were all these in comparison with Cecil Forrester, "lord of himself, that heritage of wo!"[379]

It was a wet morning, and he loitered at the breakfast-table, though he had long finished both meal and appetite. At length he rose, took two or three turns up and down the room, opened a book, then threw it aside:—(by the by, parents have a great deal to answer for who do not early give their children a taste for reading—novels.) He next approached the window, and proposed to his companion, who was letter-writing, to bet on the progress of two rain-drops. Not having been heard, he proceeded with his cane to trace his name on the damp glass; and at last, in desperation, exclaimed, "How devilish lucky you are, Ravensdale, to be in love! Nothing like love-letters for filling up a rainy morning. A mistress gives a man such an interest in himself! You cannot run your fingers through your hair, without a vision of the locket wherein one of your curls reposes on the fairest neck in the world. An east-wind only conjures up a host of 'sweet anxieties;' and if the worst comes to the worst, you can sit down and write sonnets to your inamorata's eyebrow. I have made up my mind—I will try and fall in love. Well, who is there here?"

"Lady de Morne, doing dolorous and disconsolate—only walks in her garden; to be sure, it overlooks the high-road."

[376] French for "hard and forceful punishment," a method of torture in which the bodies of defendants who refused to speak were slowly crushed by heavier and heavier stones until they spoke or died.

[377] Dyde's and Scribe's was a fashionable clothing store on Pall Mall. A "fag" is someone who toils tirelessly in a tedious job.

[378] Richard Martin (1754-1834) was an MP from Ireland and an early champion of animals' rights (the Cruel Treatment of Cattle Act of 1822, which he managed to get passed into law, was nicknamed "Dick Martin's Act"). He soon obtained the first prosecution for animal cruelty against one Bill Burns, whose abused donkey Martin brought into a courtroom (presumably after abandoning his own horse, as Landon ironically suggests). This turned him into the target of many jests in the press and on the stage and brought him the sobriquet "Jackass Martin."

[379] From Byron's 1814 poem *Lara* (I, ii).

Experiments; or, The Lover from Ennui

"What, a widow! warm or cold, which you will, from the kiss of a dead man! I should taste clay upon her lips!"

"Miss Acton, then, the heiress—*utile et dulce*."[380]

"No; she belongs to the romantic school, and expects you to rise in the morning to bring her violets with the dew on them; takes country rambles, which would spoil my complexion; and moonlight walks, which would give me cold. Charles Ellis told me that, in a fit of despair occasioned by a run of ill-luck at écarté,[381] he entered into her service for three weeks. He, however, soon found himself feverish—lost his appetite—had a hectic cough—and the fourth week retired on a consumption. I do not feel equal to the exertion."

"Mrs. Ellerby's two daughters."

"Yes, and never know which is which! I hate people cut out by a pattern. Besides, the only papers in the family are pedigrees; and I am not rich enough to keep a cook, a confectioner, and a wife. Moreover, Mrs. Ellerby, being what is called serious, would expect my attentions and intentions to be as serious as every thing else in the house. No; I want to find some unsophisticated being whose hair curls naturally."

"Now, in pity spare me the description of that never-to-be-discovered perfection, an ideal mistress! Be sure you will fall in love with the very opposite."

"I don't care, so long as I could fall in love. But the rain is over: you will not ride, will you?"

Cecil Forrester rode along the beach by himself. Most earnestly did he wish that some of the young ladies who were sketching "that beautiful effect of light on the grey rocks," would tumble into the water. He might have rushed to the rescue, and so lost his heart in the most approved fashion. Gradually he turned into the very road which he had taken every day, only because he had taken it first. There, as usual, he overtook the same respectable brown coat and horse, and their no less respectable proprietor, whom he regularly encountered. A sudden shower drove them simultaneously under an oak.

---

[380] Latin for "useful and agreeable," from a much quoted dictum by Horace ("Omne tulit punctum qui miscuit utile dulce," i.e., "He wins every vote, who combines the useful and the sweet") often used as recommendation for writers and artists.

[381] French card game similar to whist, very popular in the 19th century.

English people, as a foreign traveller mentions in his diary, never speak, excepting in cases of fire or murder, unless they are introduced. The old oak did this kind office for the riders.

"The country wanted rain, sir," observed the elderly gentleman.

Forrester felt that his companion had violated every rule of civilised society in thus addressing him; still, he was good-natured, and, moreover, was tired of himself. He therefore replied—"And we are likely to have enough now."

"Ay, ay; it never rains but it pours. I must say I have great faith in Moore's Almanac;[382] it said we should have rain a week ago."

It is needless to detail how acquaintance deepened into intimacy. Silence maketh many friends.[383] The old gentleman took quite a fancy to Cecil, pronounced him such a steady young man, and asked him to dinner.

Forrester went; his host had two daughters—one rather pretty and pensive, the other very pretty and lively.

The next week was quite endurable as to length: Cecil copied verses into the eldest Miss Temple's album, and held some green silk for the younger to wind.

The Saturday following his introduction it was a beautiful moonlight evening, and Miss Temple was walking up and down the lawn; she really looked very well, and Cecil was about to join her, when a light step, close behind him, announced her sister.[384]

"'The moon is bright on Helle's wave,
As on that night of stormy water,
When Love, who sent, forgot to save
The young, the beautiful, the brave.'

Even as Love forgot the lover, I have forgot the poet—not a line more can I remember; but I would wager the purse whose green silk I am knitting, and which you helped me to wind, against its weight in green grass, that those very lines are in Mary's head at this minute."

"Why those lines especially?"

[382] *Old Moore's Almanac* had been well-respected while Henry Andrews (1744-1820), who signed "Francis Moore, physician," had been its editor. Its reputation was in decline in the early 1830s.

[383] A paraphrase of a line from the Bible: "Wealth maketh many friends; but the poor is separated from his neighbour" (Proverbs 19: 4).

[384] The eldest sister in a family with two or several daughters was more commonly identified by her last name, e.g., "Miss Temple," whereas younger sisters were usually called by their first name, e.g., "Miss Elizabeth."

Experiments; or, The Lover from Ennui

"Oh, dear! now, cannot you guess?—why, every body knows!"

"But as I am not every body, I shall not know till you tell me."

"Oh, but really I shan't tell you!"

"Oh, but really you must!"

"To be sure, there is not a neighbour but is aware that she is engaged to such an interesting young man now in Greece.[385] But, dear, dear! you must have noticed how she coloured up when you talked about a turban's suiting her style of face. And did you observe my father's laugh at dinner, to-day, when he asked her if she liked Turkey?"

"And so Miss Temple has got a lover—and I need not ask if you have one also."

"Not I indeed—dear, if I had a lover one week, I should forget him the next!"

Somehow or other the dialogue ended in one or two pretty speeches—the last things in the world to particularise. And Forrester went home quite convinced that Elizabeth was far the prettiest of the two, and bound by promise to accompany them the next night to a fancy ball in the neighbourhood.

Now, a fancy ball is bad enough in London, where milliners are many, and where theatres have costumes that may be borrowed or copied; but in the country, where people are left to their own devices—truly to them may be applied the old poet's account of murderers, "their fancies are all frightful."[386] Miss Temple, we need scarcely observe, wore a turban, and looked as Oriental, at least as un-English, as possible. Elizabeth preferred going back upon the taste of her grandmothers; and when Cecil first saw her standing in the window, with the loose hanging sleeves of former days, and floating draperies of an antique striped silk—her pretty arms just bare to the elbow, and her fair hair in half-dishevelled curls,—he decided, that if you are very young and pretty, extravagance in costume carries its own excuse.

[385] The lines quoted above are the first lines from the second canto of Byron's 1813 poem *The Bride of Abydos*. Byron had died in Greece in 1824 after taking active part in the Greek War of Independence (1821-1829).

[386] There is no such old poetical account, but Landon, ever the ironist, might be referring here to a very recent (1831) poem by her friend Thomas Hood (1799-1845), "The Dream of Eugene Aram, the Murderer." In his preface to the poem, Hood speaks of "those unaccountable visions, which come upon us like frightful monsters." His antihero "told how murderers walk the earth/ Beneath the curse of Cain,—/ With crimson clouds before their eyes,/ And flames about their brain."

To the dance they went: the dancing was bad, the music worse, and instead of ice, sago was handed round to keep the young people from taking cold.[387] Yet Cecil had passed worse evenings. We talk of unsophisticated nature—I should like to know where it is to be found. Elizabeth Temple's hair did curl naturally—she made her own dresses—and for accomplishments, played on her grandmother's spinnet by ear, knitted purses, and took the housekeeping alternate weeks with her sister;—yet had she talents for flirtation at least equal to those of any young lady whose dress and accomplishments are the perfection of milliners and May Fair. Cecil was her partner the most of the evening; and, by a few ingenious and invidious parallels, implied not expressed, between him and the other cavaliers,—that preference of attention, the best of feminine flattery,—and a deference to his opinion, nicely blended with a self-consciousness of prettiness, Elizabeth contrived to keep him rather pleasantly awake. Mr. Temple's house lay in his way home; and though he had already ate supper enough for six months, his friends would make him go in for another. On his departure, Elizabeth gave him some trifling commission at Hastings; and while she was writing it down, Forrester, with that universal habit of the idle, took up whatever happened to be near, in the laudable intention of twisting it to pieces. It was the little green silk purse, and he looked on it with a remembrance of the slender fingers he had seen employed in its making. Could he be mistaken? no, he saw the letters distinctly, C. F. worked in light brown hair—his own initials; and he now recollected that Miss Temple had asked him the other morning what was his Christian name; on hearing which, she made the usual remark of young ladies in such cases, "Dear, what a beautiful name!"

Elizabeth, turning round at this minute, saw the purse in his hand, and also which of the stitches had fixed his attention. Blushing even deeper than the occasion required, she said in a low but hurried voice, "I really cannot have my work spoilt; give me the purse, Mr. Forrester."

"Never!" said Cecil, in what was for him a very energetic tone.

---

[387] Sago is the extract of a tropical plant, which is used in the United Kingdom especially in the preparation of the sago pudding, similar to the tapioca pudding. In the 19th century, however, it was often used in the preparation of a special kind of ice cream.

Experiments; or, The Lover from Ennui

"Oh, but I must and will have it!" making an attempt to snatch it from him—to which his only answer was to catch her hand and kiss it.

"Elizabeth, my dear, Mr. Forrester must be tired; do not detain him with your foolish commissions," said her father, who advanced, and himself accompanied his guest to the hall, taking leave of him with a mysterious look of mingled cordiality and compassion.

The young gentleman rode home, too tired for any thing but sleep; and when he arose the next morning, it was with a conviction that light brown hair was "an excellent thing in a woman." True, in a fit of absence, while debating whether or not he should write to his uncle before he rode out, he dropped the purse into the fire; nevertheless his vexation at the incident was sufficiently flattering to its maker. As soon as he had decided that he would put off writing till the next day, he ordered his horse and rode to Mr. Temple's. In the hall he caught a flying glance of Elizabeth, whose fair face was evidently much disfigured with recent crying. Lord Byron says,

"So sweet the tear in beauty's eye,
Love half regrets to kiss it dry."[388]

Now we, on the contrary, hold that a good fit of crying would, for the time, spoil any beauty in the world.

Cecil entered the parlour somewhat abruptly; Mrs. Temple was saying, "I do so pity the poor young man." On what account the "poor young man" was pitied, Forrester's entrance prevented his learning, for she instantly broke off her speech in great confusion.

Mr. Temple paced up and down the room, as if he thought exercise a great relief to anger. Both received their visitor with even more than their usual kindness, but with obvious and painful embarrassment. Husband and wife interchanged looks when the topic of the weather was exhausted, each seemingly expecting the other to speak. A few minutes passed in silence—at length Mr. Temple began.

"I am truly sorry—"

"My dear," interrupted his wife.

---

[388] Another quote from *The Bride of Abydos* (see note 385), although the first line should read "So bright the tear in beauty's eye."

"I am sure you will be very glad—"

"Nay," again rejoined the lady, "it is presuming too much on Mr. Forrester's kindness to suppose that he will take an interest in our affairs."

Mr. Forrester hastened to assure her he took the very warmest.

"My daughter Elizabeth," said the old gentleman.

"Good heavens!" thought Cecil, "he is not going to ask me what my intentions are! I am sure I can't tell him."

"My daughter Elizabeth,"—how the words were bolted out!—"is going to be married."

"My dear, how could you be so abrupt?" ejaculated the lady.

As if to give his visitor time to recover the shock, Mr. Temple went on rapidly, "To a son of a very old friend of mine—Charles Forsyth—you saw him last night—very fine young man; he made her an offer this very morning, before breakfast."

"My love, you need not be so particular."

Forrester, who, to tell the truth, had no stronger feeling on the subject than surprise—perhaps a little mortification—now offered his congratulations. Not being very desirous of encountering the fair fabricator of the deceiving initials, the betrothed of Mr. Charles Forsyth, he took the first opportunity of making his bow and his exit.

"Poor young man, how well he has behaved!" said the mother.

"I knew he wouldn't take it much to heart," answered the father.

As Cecil passed through the hall, he heard Elizabeth's voice tuned to rather a petulant key.

"In spite of all mamma says about feeling, and papa about principle, and you with your devoted affection to one object, I can't see the great harm of a little innocent flirtation—Mr. Forrester won't break his heart for passing an evening more pleasantly than he would otherwise have done; and if I had not flirted with him, Charles Forsyth, though he is the son of my father's old friend, would not have made his offer these six months—and one cannot wait for ever, you know."

"Very true," muttered Cecil Forrester, as the hall-door was closed after him. That evening he wrote to his uncle; and passed the intermediate time in cutting his name on the table, and wondering what would be the reply. He received an answer by return of post—angry and yet kind, requesting his immediate presence in town. He made a farewell call at Mr. Temple's—saw Elizabeth and Mr. Charles Forsyth in an arbour at the end of the garden, making love—thought they would soon be very tired—and bade the rest of the family good-bye, who thought he looked pale. Mrs. Temple for a fortnight afterwards read every article headed "Interesting Suicide," in the newspapers; and though they were all "interesting," they did not interest her. Cecil arrived at his uncle's, who commenced the conversation by declaring he would cut him off with a shilling, and ended by paying his debts and making him an allowance. The next week saw two different announcements in the Morning Post—one was the marriage of Elizabeth Temple to Charles Forsyth, Esq.; the other the departure of Mr. Cecil Forrester for Naples.

A friend had offered to take him thither in his yacht, and for that reason only he had gone. Of course he ascended Vesuvius—visited churches, pictures, statues, &c.; but, alas! these are tastes which require cultivation—and at present they appeared to Cecil in the light of duties. Not speaking the language of the country, he was excluded from all enjoyment of Italian society, and English he had entered an inward protest against. Two friends had refused to cash a draft for him: one because he could not, the other because he would not—one from inability, having no money to spare; the other from principle, as he made it a rule never to lend. A lady, with whom he had been quite *l'ami de famille*,[389] with four pretty daughters, had actually avoided seeing him in the Park before it was known that his uncle intended arranging his affairs. Cecil was therefore persuaded of the heartlessness of artificial society. Still, he had no innocent beliefs in rural unsophistication—Elizabeth Temple had cured him of any such vain fancies: he retained a predilection for the natural—only he decided that it was not to be discovered in any civilised country. He used to sit on the sea-shore, and spend the evening poring over some volumes of Lord Byron he had found by accident, and in throwing pebbles into the sea. A beautiful dream of a Circassian had been floating on his mind, when the arrival of the Dey of Algiers[390] with his harem at Naples changed his reverie to absolute reality.

[389] French for "friend of the family."

[390] The Dey of Algiers was the ruler of Algeria under the Ottoman Empire, that is, until 1830, when Algeria was conquered by the French. The last Dey, Hussein, went into exile in Naples. Circassian women (from North Caucasus, including Georgia) were famed for their beauty.

One fine morning, a whole array of palanquins, the forms within them shrouded from human eye, passed him on his ride—the next day the same—the third the curtains of one slightly moved, a sprig of jasmine was thrown out, and the day following one of myrtle. That night Cecil read Lord Byron—the Giaour and the Corsair were only interrupted by Lalla Rookh.[391] He went to bed, and dreamt of the maids

"Who blushed behind the gallery's silken shades."[392]

The next day he began to study Arabic, and to endeavour to find some means of conversing with this unknown Houri.[393] To be sure, there were curtains, bolts, bars, and cimeters;[394] still,

"Love will find its way
Through paths where wolves would fear to prey;
And if it dares enough, 'twere hard
If passion met not some reward;"[395]

and Cecil succeeded in establishing an intercourse with this Haidee[396] of his fancy, by means of a petty officer in the Dey's retinue, who contrived to bribe one of the slaves in immediate attendance on the harem, from whom he learnt that she was the last and loveliest purchase of his lord. The progress of love-affairs is usually very rapid, and this was no exception to the general rule. A plan of escape was soon organised; her especial guardian agreed to facilitate her remaining after dusk in the garden, which was bounded by a river; a few planks would form an easy communication with the water; a boat might be stationed there; and four good rowers would convey them in half an hour to a little villa, which Cecil, in a week's whim for solitude, had rented: once there, no trace would be left of their flight, and no fear remain

[391] *The Giaour* (1813) and *The Corsair* (1814) are Byron's epic poems. *Lalla Rookh* (1817) is an "Oriental romance" by Thomas Moore (1779-1852).

[392] From Moore's *Lalla Rookh* (see note 391).

[393] Houris are a kind of Islamic nymphs who are supposed to accompany the believers into paradise.

[394] Scimitars, Turkish sabres with curved blades.

[395] From Byron's *The Giaour* (see note 391).

[396] Haidee is Don Juan's Greek lover in Byron's epic poem *Don Juan*. She appears in Cantos II-IV (published between 1819 and 1821).

Experiments; or, The Lover from Ennui

of discovery. The night fixed on found them punctual to their appointment—so were the slave and the beautiful Georgian. The zeal of Sidi Mustapha, the first agent, was quite wonderful; he sprang up the boards to aid the lady's descent, and would scarcely allow Cecil to give himself any trouble in the matter, till it was evident she could not get down without help from both. After some effort, she and her drapery—the quantity of which seemed enormous—were deposited in the boat. They arrived in silence and safety at the villa: Sidi and Forrester supported their prize into the saloon, fear seeming to have deprived her of the power of motion; and the Algerine hastened to discharge the boatmen with all possible caution. Every thing had been prepared; the table was covered with the richest sweetmeats, the rarest perfumes, the most aromatic coffee. Cecil's impatience was now at its height.

"Gulnare!"—but she replied not:—"dear Gulnare!"[397]

Suddenly he recollected that she might perhaps not understand Arabic—at all events, his Arabic. Still, till his interpreter returned, it would be but civil to help her off with the large blue veil, or mantle, which entirely covered her. Politely proffering his assistance, he removed her veil, and flung it on a chair near.

The scream which followed this act astonished him far less than the discovery to which it led. The lovely Georgian was so fat, that it was with the greatest difficulty she could stand; and an exquisitely tattooed wreath of hyacinths, of a fine blue, began at her chin, meandered over her cheeks, and covered her forehead.

"Oh!" ejaculated Cecil, "if I had but profited by my reading! Why did I not sooner remember the traveller I studied in the days of my youth, who said that in the East a beauty was a load for a camel!"[398]

At this moment Mustapha re-entered the saloon.

"O Allah, how beautiful! By the head of the Prophet, she is a rose—a full moon!"

---

[397] The beautiful Gulnare is the slave that Conrad, the hero in Byron's *The Giaour* (see note 391), helps to escape and then takes home with him. Queen Gulnare is also a character in *Arabian Nights*. Byron explains in a footnote that the name means "pomegranate flower" in Arabic.

[398] From Mungo Park's popular *Travels in the Interior Districts of Africa* (1798), in which he wrote that "The Moors have singular ideas of feminine perfection. . . . With them corpulence and beauty appear to be terms nearly synonymous. A woman of even moderate pretensions must be one who cannot walk without a slave under each arm to support her; and a perfect beauty is a load for a camel."

Cecil sprang forward, with the true Englishman's impulse, to knock him down. Ill-timed admiration is enough to enrage a saint. The shrill cries of the lady, however, diverted his attention.

"Unless you wish me to be deafened outright, do learn the case of her horrible clamour."

"Your highness has taken off her veil."

"Which, for my own sake, I shall return as speedily as possible."

Without a moment's delay he restored the screen and quiet at the same time; and with the aid of Mustapha supported the fair slave to a pile of crimson satin cushions, which had been collected for her especial use.

"And now, in the name of the devil, what shall I do with her?"

Sidi seemed a little surprised at the question, and forthwith began a string of Arabic verses about this star of the morning, this pearl of the world, this rose of a hundred leaves, which the stranger was fortunate enough to possess. Well, to make the best of a bad bargain, and short of a long story, he married the Georgian to Sidi Mustapha.

After all, Englishmen *are* patriotic with partridges before their eyes; and this little adventure gave Cecil an excuse for returning to England before September. What is the reason that we find it so satisfactory to make excuses to ourselves—the only persons in the world to whom they must be altogether needless?

It was the last week in August when he reached the Abbey, his uncle's seat. How advantageously did the luxurious foliage of the thickly leaved woods, as yet untouched by one tint of autumn, and the bright green grass of the fields, contrast with the parched and sultry aspect of the southern summer he had left behind! It was long—in youth, every thing seems long—since he had felt a sensation of pleasure so keen as he experienced when the tall oaks of the avenue closed over his head. The rooks were gathering to their rest, as noisily as children; but the old and familiar are ever soothing sounds. In the distance he could see the slim and mottled deer sauntering lazily along in the full enjoyment of security; and the last red flush of evening was reflected in a large piece of water, which glittered through the dense branches.

At length he arrived in the court, where half-a-dozen gray-headed serving-men came out to meet "Master Cecil," as they persisted in calling him. It is very agreeable to have people glad to see you, even if there be no better reason for their joy than that

Experiments; or, The Lover from Ennui

they knew you as a child. A spaniel now put its nose into his hand: but the dog's memory was more faithful than that of its master; for the visitor had some difficulty in recognising, in the heavy and feeble creature that claimed his notice, the once slight and agile partner of his boyish amusements.

"My poor Dido! can this be you?"

"All my young mistress's care," said one of the servants.

At this moment the young mistress herself appeared, and Cecil found that he had forgotten her as much as his dog. He had left her a pale, sickly, even plain child: she had sprung up into a bright, blushing, and most lovely girl. Her flaxen hair had darkened into a rich chestnut; and the only trace of "little Edith" was in the large blue eyes, which remained the same. Cecil was quite surprised that she so instantly remembered him; but five years after twenty do not make the difference they do before that age.

Sir Hugh was as glad to see his nephew as a gentleman of the old school always is on the stage; and in half an hour the trio were comfortably situated in the library—some dinner ordered for Cecil—an extra bottle of port for the old gentleman—and Edith, seated on a low stool at her father's knee, was quite delighted when the conversation went back to their childish sports, and what a pet the poor little delicate child used to be of her cousin's.

The next month flew away imperceptibly. Cecil listened patiently to the politics of the Morning Post—for Edith read them aloud to her father. He also found that he could read at his young hostess's work-table; then he was so very useful in the flower-garden, which was especially hers; there were, besides, visits to the gold and silver pheasants, long rides over the heath, long walks through the forest, and long evenings, when Sir Hugh sat by the fire-side and slept, and Edith sung sweet old ballads to her harp. The result of all this was inevitable: had it been in a melodrame, the young people could not have fallen more desperately in love. Let others talk of the miseries of the tender passion, Cecil was eloquent on its comforts: he had never been so occupied or so amused before.

On the 1st of October, a bright clear morning, when the few flowers that still linger on sunny terrace or southern nook are in all that glow of gorgeous colouring which so peculiarly belongs to autumn, the young lady of the Abbey stept out on the balustrade to pluck the last buds of the Provence rose. A few late

341

geraniums and myrtles were yet beautiful and green; but suddenly Edith turned and gathered from a luxuriant plant its only cluster of orange flowers. They suited well her array, for Edith was that day garbed as a bride. The glossy brown hair—that golden brown which shines on the pheasant's wing—fell in large curls from her white wreath, half-hidden by the long veil; the white satin dress had no ornament—not a gem marred its rich simplicity. She leant pensively on a corner of the marble pilaster: for she stood now on the threshold of youth; she was about to put away childish things, to take upon her higher duties; and her destiny was given—how utterly!—into the hands of another. Already the shadow of love deepened the seriousness of that graceful brow. Still, she was only leaving the home of her childhood for a time, not as the young bride often leaves that home—for ever. To wed with Cecil was but giving Sir Hugh another child.

"Come, Edith mine!" said a sweet voice at her side; and the lover led her to her father.

In another half-hour the bells were ringing cheerfully on the air; and during the many years that the old Abbey was gladdened with their mutual happiness, Cecil never felt inclined to go to Hastings from *ennui*, or to Naples as an experiment; but found ample employment and content around his own home, and by his own hearth.

Milton Keynes UK
Ingram Content Group UK Ltd.
UKHW050329051023
R3427200001B/R34272PG429792UKX00001B/1